South of Jericho is a novel based on a true story that pulses with a storyline rooted more in fact than fiction, pointed details that only someone like "Ziki Barak" could know fill this book, from the attempted capture of 23 ex-Nazi scientists, planning for the terrorists a germ-biological attack on Israel that could spread throughout the world, to a car chase in the backstreets of Baghdad behind KGB agents involving a Swiss banker, an Arab nuclear plant, to a threatened to be stolen Russian super MiG fighter plane; The action is unrelenting and unmistakably...real."

**The Tel-Aviv Review and Haaretz English Edition**

"Absorbing and powerful—riveting, romance and the shadowy world of covert intrigue, terrorism, Israel's secret operatives, and the superpowers.
A glimpse of Mossad, and the unforeseeable future...You are in the heart of the action."

**Publishers Critic Review**

# SOUTH

## OF

# JERICHO

## MOSSAD–ISRAELI
## INTELLIGENCE AT WORK

## Jonathan Scharf

Library of Congress-Washington D.C.

# ©SOUTH OF JERICHO

*Based on a true story*

*This book is rooted in fact enhanced by fiction,
the reader must decide which is which.*

*The names have been changed for security reasons.
Most terrorist's names are real.*

*'Ziki Barak' is a code name.*

ISBN-0-9773239-0-0

Alef Publishing Company
Library of Congress-Washington D.C
Register of Copyrights, United States of America
TX 6-245-626

# SOUTH OF JERICHO
# ACKNOWLEDGEMENT

*Many generous friends in several countries, including Africa, the U.S., Europe and Israel gave their time, knowledge and counsel during the two years it took to write this book. Some cannot be named for security reasons. I offer them all my thanks for their skill and generosity.*

*Michelle LaFrance-Dept of English, University of Washington, Erin Carstens, General Ygal Alon IDF Ret., Isser Harrel IDF Ret., Shmuel Harrari, Moshe Zeitan, Eugene Fischer, Moshe Levi, Rafi Levi, Nathan Wilson, Brannon Laveder, Jon Virgin, Jon Wayland, Rabbi Mordechai Farkash, Rabbi Yitzhak Goldman, Ana Marshall, Lt.Rick Groenier Ret., Suzan Stone, Jordan Huang, 'Malkielly' and ' Halmi Pientz'*

# PROLOGUE

**"The Samson Option" Russians...**
**6AM—Geneva. A standard situation room—one year later**
**The lights were low and the air conditioning jacked high** to offset the heat of computer terminals and projection devices. A curl of smoke lazed in the center of the room above the polished conference table. US General Sam Armstrong flipped through a series of photographs, glancing up briefly when his aide returned with the man Armstrong sought to meet.

Armstrong rose to shake the man's hand. "I am told we're calling you back early from the Florida Keys, Colonel Sinclair."

Sinclair' grip was soft. The two men had met on previous occasions—state dinners, drinks following long evening planning sessions, a golf game once—but Sinclair generally moved in lesser circles.

"Family vacation, Sir. Yes."

"Your seat, Colonel." The aide who had escorted Sinclair through security gestured to a chair and Sinclair sat where indicated. He tugged down the jacket of his blues more tightly, preserving the line of his suit.

"Your first vacation in two years—a shame to ruin it. Perhaps your wife would approve of your early departure if she had had the Russian consulate on her phone for the last nine hours." Armstrong's aides loosed polite laughter. One of them lit a smoke with a flashing silver lighter.

"Nothing worse than a bunch of Russians with their panties in a bunch." The General smiled at his own levity. He extended a cigarette case toward Sinclair.

Sinclair grinned affably and declined the cigarette, but noted that they were French and expensive. The perks of being stationed in Geneva. And being General Armstrong, no doubt. "That, Sir, I could not guarantee."

Armstrong stretched his shoulders. "Well, we'll have to see that your next vacation is undisturbed."

"Greatly appreciated, Sir."

Armstrong rested one forearm on the smooth tabletop. "You were briefed on our situation in transit?"

"Yes, sir." Sinclair nodded, and with a breath he repeated the reports he'd committed to memory on his flight. "00:53 GMT yesterday, the Vela 6911 satellite system detected a 'double flash' over the South Atlantic—a position localized through later calculations at 47 deg. S, 40 deg. E—that is, just off the coast of South Africa's Prince Edward Island. The explosion was low kiloton—calculations approximate it at 3 kiloton. The signature of the hydro-acoustic signal indicates that the explosions were low altitude, most likely underwater. However, the distinctiveness of the light curve and the duration of the first, then the second flashes indicate with high probability that the event was nuclear in nature."

The General was pleased with Sinclair' recall. "And do you believe that South Africa is now among the nuclear contenders of the globe, Colonel?"

"No, Sir. I do not."

Sinclair slid his brief case onto the tabletop and flipped open its latches. He withdrew a fan of paper, deftly dealing a series of neatly stapled reports to the General and each of his aides as he began to explain:

"The information in front of you confirms intelligence commonly held since the late 60's. Operatives have been tracking the development of South African nuclear capabilities for the last ten years. Our data shows that South Africa has not previously been near to success in their nuclear research, nor could their facilities gain such capabilities in so short a time—more likely another country handed them the plans or is using South Africa as a front."

"In exchange for mining substances, Uranium….Yep—Uranium."

Sinclair nodded. "That would be the immediate conclusion—." He hesitated. "And if I may be so forward, Sir, the reason that you've asked me to step in here?"

The General inclined his head, considering Sinclair closely.

"I've asked you here because your record of service shows some foreign contacts. You have contacts that will be useful for a diffusion of our situation."

Sinclair' face showed a flash of understanding. "Israel."

The General nodded slowly. "We have reason to believe that Israel has been using South Africa and their Uranium mines for some time on the further development of a nuclear arsenal."

"The Israelis will neither confirm nor deny such allegations."

"We hadn't thought so."

"They are under no obligation to do so. They've signed none of the global nuclear test ban treaties—"

The General stopped Sinclair with a slow wave of his palm. "It is not in question whether the Israelis have nukes. We know they have nukes. Most recent Intel suggests their capabilities likely put them ahead of India and Pakistan, even the French and Germans. We visit their very secretive plant at Dimona in the Negev Desert each year and they allow us in to make it look good."

"That doesn't explain why you'd need me here, Sir."

"No," the General agreed. "It does not. Then let me say this. I have plenty of yes-men at my ready."

"Sir?" Sinclair frowned.

"You're well aware. . . " The General drew a breath and began again. "It has been in the best interest of the US to have an armed Israel, not to mention that ninety percent of our intelligence derived in the whole Middle East comes from them—from Mossad. But it is also in our interest to keep the Soviets' fears under control."

"Sir. The Soviets support Arab nations, provide jets, equipment and military training—"

"Yes," the General agreed.

"And, if I may speak plainly once more, Sir—"

"You will always speak plainly. I've no time for politicos at my table."

Sinclair took this in and set his shoulders to continue. "The Soviets know on which side of the tank their fuel reserves are filled: they've moved into the Middle East."

The General nodded again. "As do we. Which is why we will proceed cautiously."

"Sir?"

"The President is quite concerned. This is an international incident of radical proportions. Several nations within striking range are concerned, and the Israeli Jericho missiles have enough range to hit Moscow."

"Israel has its military build up because they find themselves in a constant state of war with the Arab countries that surround it, not to speak of the threat of direct Russian invasion, and of course the constant terrorism." He folded his arms across his chest.

"So if the Soviets have sweaty balls, I'm not sure how bothered we should be." Sinclair nodded in approval.

"Their right to build and test is not an issue," the General explained and shrugged. "We're selling them advanced A-4E Skyhawk tactical fighter jets that can carry nuclear payloads—what exactly else would they carry? At issue is the delegation of pissed off Russians arriving shortly on my doorstep."

"Not re-election?" General Scofield, sitting at the end of the conference table queried tactfully.

"Of course," the General agreed in amusement. "Re-election is always a concern when Israel is at the center of debate. Lost votes are on either side of the issue.

"Alienate Israeli lobby power, if the president calls necessary sanctions. Alienate the Arab oil countries and the oil money and supply, if he doesn't."

General Armstrong made a gesture of placation. "We'll leave that to politicians on the home front. For you and me, the Russians are three hours away and they want to know what we're doing about the 'pissy little country' that's crawling up their ass."

"Not so pissy with nukes and the sophistication of their armed forces," remarked General Scofield.

"They've heard talk of Gabriel and Jericho missiles and some on Israeli subs. Now this double nuclear explosion in the Indian Ocean. The Russians don't take kindly to that sort of sheer balls.  They don't even like their allies to get so cocky."

"The Israelis have always—"

"Yes, yes."  Armstrong lifted his hand again.  "The Israelis have their own ideas about international security.  But fourteen military brass, KGB no less, and a few 'civilian' engineers want to know if the Israelis can keep their dicks in their pants.  We need to convince them that for the moment our interests are their interest."

"An armed Israel is an insurance policy for Middle Eastern oil production, continued de-escalation of Cold War policies."  Sinclair seemed to be reciting.  "Oil, the Middle East and money."

"And not to mention that whether we like it or not, we all know—as you've said—that ninety percent of military intelligence that benefits us, America, comes directly from Israel's Mossad.  It saves American lives.  Without that intelligence we are walking around in the Middle East with blind folders."

"What else is there?"  The General waved one of his aides to action.

A shiny black folder was slid across the tabletop to Sinclair.

Another of the aides stood and switched on the slide projector.  A picture of Russian General Petrovsky—in full dress at the Opera—flashed upon the wall. "This is—"

Sinclair nodded.  "I've met the General."

The aide stiffened slightly.

Sinclair glanced at General Armstrong by way of explanation.  "We discussed Puchini.  Their big General Zhukov was also at the opera with Petrovsky."

"The fates shined on you, Colonel.  The General and I talked Wagner.  I despise Wagner."

The aide's delivery wavered a moment longer.  Then he continued.  "We'll ask you to escort General Petrovsky and his team when they arrive—"

"—Handle the General," Armstrong corrected.  "I want you to handle him. We'll wine them and dine them here in Geneva—remind them that the US is the true super power of the globe.  Flash cash and cars and jets at them until they bow to the mighty American dollar."

"And then what?" Sinclair asked.  "Bring up that stolen Mig?"

Armstrong's mouth made a thin line as he grew suddenly serious.  "We stall them until we can come up with enough conflicting evidence that our initial findings and any of theirs are turned inconclusive.

"That's where you come in, Colonel.  You and your Israeli buddy—Ziki Barak.  And it won't be easy—the Swiss couldn't produce enough vodka or hookers to keep this Rusky delegation happy.  For half the time they'll be digging around in our sphincters.  They'll be down the hall before you know it, sweeping the public areas of their hotel for bugs, and demanding that we wear Siberian bearskin before this thing goes public and tempers really start to fly. . ."

"Ziki Barak?" Sinclair echoed.  "We haven't spoken in months."

The General placed both elbows on the table.  "He'll be here in five hours. It's your job to have him help us keep those Russians confused and to keep them damn quiet."

**Au-Lac Airport-Geneva**

 **The man in question cut a charismatic picture,** trotting down the metal stairs of a jet liner onto a tarmac not yet lit by dawn's first rays. He was dressed in civilian attire, as usual, carrying a light jacket and a small satchel. But his characteristically slicked back hair and piercing green eyes were not at their best. His breath was white in the morning cold.

 "Shalom Jimmy-Ray!" He greeted his old friend.

 "Shalom to you, you look like hell." Sinclair offered a hand to Ziki Barak. They smiled warmly at each other, Sinclair clapping Ziki's shoulder as they shook.

 "Remember that night in Istanbul?" Ziki returned. "It's like that—. . . Only worse."

 "No—no—I don't remember a thing—that's my story and I'm sticking to it," Sinclair shook his head and laughed.

 Ziki laughed too. Who would have thought those Spanish girls could be so . . . well, what was the word for that sort of nubile flexibility?

 Sinclair turned him toward the car. "You didn't sleep on the plane?"

 Ziki cocked a brow. "Man of mystery. One eye always open. It was too cold, military cargo plane, I hitched a ride as soon as your General called us, across the Mediterranean—my legs fell asleep."

 Sinclair nodded in appreciation. "I'll order a carafe of coffee delivered to your room."

 "That would be a very good thing. Especially if something leggy and red headed delivered it."

 "Not today. Later, perhaps—once we've ironed the wrinkles out of some Russkie's."

 "Russians, without Iranians?" Ziki moaned humorously. "It's always the damn Russians pitching a fit."

 Sinclair led Ziki to the car that was waiting, its diplomatic flags twitching with the first hint of a breeze. The lights of the black car cut through the early morning dawn.

 "A black armored Cadillac?" Ziki remarked. "You're moving up in the world."

 "On loan from the General."

 "Armstrong or Petrovsky?"

 "So you know he's here," Sinclair surmised.

 "Unless his plane went down while I was in route?" Ziki ducked into the car and slid into a luxurious leather bucket seat. Sinclair had walked around the tail of the car, opened the door himself, and slid into the seat on the other side.

 A moment of silence while Sinclair settled himself, then Ziki continued— not entirely business like in his manner. "My sources reported a Russian delegation was scheduled to arrive several hours before me. I imagined I would be meeting with them later today. Who else, but that 'Comrade blow bag,' that is always around General Zhukov kissing his ass, would make the trip?"

 "At 1100 hours," Sinclair confirmed, he tapped the shaded glass behind the driver's head and gestured for the driver to go. "Just in time to spoil all of our lunches."

Ziki waved off the oncoming meeting with bravado. "1100—they'll be dead drunk by then. Enough vodka, you can get a Russian to look the other way long enough to—"

"Not this time, they look like they mean business."

"—Smuggle a Mig21 out of Iraq?" Sinclair met Ziki's gaze pointedly.

Ziki laughed outright and made an elaborate shrug. "What would I know about that? I'm only a simple soldier in the IDF."

Sinclair shifted in his seat as if he were feeling some unexpected heat. "Be prepared for questions about the Mig. Be prepared for Russia to throw its weight behind whatever cockamamie resolution they can offer that will let them save face. They're pissed, Ziki. And they aren't letting Israel off the hook this time. They think you've grown too big for your boots... Nukes for God's sake?"

Ziki's chin rose slightly. "Israel is prepared to protect itself—what nation isn't? The Russians should understand that better than anyone."

"It's politics. All politics. Generals screaming and waving and thumping chests. Heads of state losing their attack dogs. Shit—their UN consulate whipped his shoe across the general meeting room—winged a US aide in the temple. And this is just one more hot tamale they're trying to shit. Nobody likes the stink."

"This. . ?" Ziki pushed on Sinclair' vagueness.

"Two nuclear flashes in the Indian Ocean picked up by '*Vela*'—you know, our satellite system."

Ziki tucked his chin to his chest and smiled. His hand opened and closed twice in the shape of a flower... "Ba-boom."

"Exactly." Sinclair rested back in his seat watching his friend carefully. "When I heard they were sending you, I knew what your response was going to be. And I have to tell you, you're taking the hard road here. You won't win any friends with this route."

"Countries don't have friends—they have interests, well, except you guys and us. I think we are friends." Ziki replied flatly.

Sinclair swallowed slowly and released a long breath. "This is how it's going to be?"

"If you can think of a better response, by all means, enlighten us. But it seems awfully cozy on this side of the allies borders, friend. You should try spending more time in the gray areas."

Sinclair drew himself up, all business. "We've time for a short breakfast, you get one hour rest, but then we'll be meeting with General Sam Armstrong and his hoard. I'm sure you've got your wrap from Mossad down—right. Right? I know—'officially' you know nothing about an agency called Mossad. But, listen. General Armstrong is not going to roll out the 'welcome' mat for you. He recognizes the right of Israel to protect its own interests—so you're not dealing with an anti-Israel monger—but he's a patriot and one of the president's men. He'd rather this problem went away quickly and quietly, and he's willing to do just about anything to make that happen, including illegally detaining you for as long as necessary to procure your government's cooperation."

Ziki snorted at the likelihood, "The General isn't that stupid, besides it wouldn't do any good."

"No," Sinclair acquiesced, "but he is determined that an international crisis be avoided."

"Sort of like the Bay of Pigs?"

Sinclair fixed an unappreciative eye on his friend. "I can't help you if you don't let me."

"As of 24 hours ago—we made sure that we don't need anyone's help."

"If that's true, Ziki. What are you doing here?"

"My apologies, we are allies." Ziki hoisted his hands immediately, knowing that he was treading thinner ground than he would like. And Sinclair would try to help him and Israel, however misguided his definition of help.

"I'm tired. I flew all night—cargo plane and I'm just very, very tired."

Sinclair gave a perfunctory nod of his head. "Let's get you some breakfast and a shower. We have a long day ahead of us….both men paused.

"When you guys make a mess—you really make a mess."

"We learned from the masters of messes."

Sinclair' mouth turned in a wry grin. "I'm going to assume you're speaking of the French."

**Three hours later, Ziki was led to the conference room.** The Russians had not yet arrived, though their special communications men had swept the room three times for listening devices.

Even without the Russians, the pissing contest had begun.

Ziki held himself upright, trying to convey a cockiness that he didn't entirely feel. 0 % of success was simply showing up, he tried to remind himself. The other 20%. . . well, what the hell?—he knew what Malkielly and Pientz at Mossad wanted him to convey and anything else he'd just deal with it as he went along.

"General Sam Armstrong, NSA," the General was introduced by his aid, offering his hand now.

"Commander Ziki Barak."

"What kind of rank is Commander? Isn't that a navy term?"

"It is a non descript rank, we don't always advertise our rank."

Ziki took the General's hand and met his eye as they shook.

Neither man wished to look away first and they held the eye-lock until Sinclair interrupted. "Coffee? Tea? Water, Commander?"

Ziki shook his head and the General resumed his seat.

"No. Thank you. Nothing."

The General had lit a cigarette and surveyed Ziki with calm authority. "Do all Israelis have such a firm grip?"

Ziki returned his scrutiny, remembering that they were there to negotiate with him, not the other way around. "Only some General," he answered lightly.

The general blew out smoke with a half-smile of appreciation. "So. . .

You are Israeli Mossad. Special branch, Amaan, Shabak or Shin Bet?"

"I have no knowledge of such an organization, General. I am just a soldier with the IDF, Israel's Defense Army."

"Is it standard operating procedure for the IDF to test tactical nukes?" Armstrong nodded at his aide who slid a portfolio of information toward Ziki.

The folder made a whooshing noise as it glided across the tabletop.

Ziki slid the folder center in front of him and opened it by the edge of a corner. He knew what it contained, but would make a show of looking anyway. The photos were black and white, 'Vela' satellite surveillance. "Interesting photos. Is that Africa? And these flashes—. . . What are they?"

The General's smile widened but then went cold.

"Let's cut through all of this horse shit, Commander." He blew out a cloud of smoke. "We have all the evidence we need to prove that Israel was the primary interest involved in the detonation of two thermo nuclear devices in the Indian Ocean of the South African coast near Prince Edward Island, last evening..."He paused for effect.

"In twenty minutes you're going to have a pack of pissed off Russians in your face, not to mention their friends, the Iranians, chomping at the bit to get a few of those goodies, unless we handle them for you, it could get to be a real big problem. And later this afternoon more than a few concerned military brass from other nations will be eager to speak to you as well. And while I'm certain your briefings have prepared you well for these meetings. I'm going to propose that we actually make this much easier on you and your flyspeck of a nation—avoiding press, avoiding any inquest into UN-treaties, IAEA, International Atomic Energy Association avoiding a lot of unnecessary floss."

"And you're specifically proposing. . ?" Ziki lifted one brow.

"We determine a mutually beneficial course of action before these meetings so that we might provide a unified front."

"A unified front?"

"A deterrence to undue interest or concern."

Ziki considered this for a moment. "But, if I am not mistaken, neither you nor the Russians have any conclusive evidence that my country has taken actions that would warrant the sort of spin doctoring that you're proposing General."

"You deny that Israel has developed a nuclear arsenal."

"Your CIA men have been to our Dimona plant—we've allowed them in. Perhaps you should revisit their reports General, and General you may want to take a look at the thirty six underground locations were nukes are being cooked in friendly Iran."

The General considered Ziki shrewdly. A metallic gleam was in his eye. "Let me set it right here on the table where all of us can take a poke at it. Your country is on the edge of full-scale international—"

"General," Ziki spread his hands beneficently as he stared at the General.

"Israel has always had the highest of respect for your nation and your nation's leaders. Of course, we align our interests with the interests of the United

States. But our security comes first. We are one small country surrounded by a multitude of neighbors who would like little better than to see the whole of my country and all of its people whipped off the face of the globe, not to mention the Soviets... We are like a fish bone in the Russian's throat....If we weren't in their way there would be no one stopping them from taking over the whole Middle East. That would give them permanent military bases, access to warm water ports and control off the oil...It would change the balance of power in the world...We are the fly in their ointment."

An aide spoke up suddenly. "You won't withstand a full scale assault if the Soviets leave here determined to aide those neighbors of yours with their Red Army and manpower in their objectives. And I did not even mention Iran."

General Armstrong cast him a glance.

The aide fell immediately sullen.

Ziki reached into his own shirt pocket for his pack of cigarettes. He took his time pulling one out and lighting it. They were Swiss—custom made for Malkielly, one of his favorite brands. He savored them whenever he had the opportunity to taste them. Ziki continued...

"I heard an interesting statistic the other day. The US has 1/8 the world's population and yet it uses 1/3 of the world's crude oil supplies. It would make for an interesting cultural change should the fuel sources for the great car culture of North America be diverted into war in the Middle East."

The General frowned. "Are you threatening us, Commander?"

"I am simply offering you a sense of the Israeli perspective. We would like to think you see the same benefits of Israel's 'technical' innovations as we do... Plainly—a strong Israel keeps the Soviets puzzled and not letting them gain control, a relatively calm Middle East, even with the now and then flair upps, and that keeps your cars, trucks, power plants running....As long as they, and their Russky friends are afraid and respectful off our military strength..."

"What about terrorism?" Scofield at the other end of the table asked.

"Terrorism is a major issue, need I mention that they're getting biological-germ warheads, even portable nukes, and as of this moment we, mostly by ourselves are protecting everyone, including you."

"Compromise is the soul of friendship. . . " The General, lowering his piercing glance in concession said slowly.

"Indeed," Ziki nodded.

"However the US will continue to have concerns on the international front—what, for instance, does Israel suggest that we tell the IAEC? I have an urgent message in my phone log. The director would like to speak with me immediately."

"I would suggest that you tell the IAEC and the UN look over the official nuclear disclosures of China and France there are none not to mention North Korea...They do not admit having thermo nuclear devices."

One of the aides shifted in his chair uncomfortably.

The General smiled wryly. "I see." He rose swiftly, hurried now to be done with the whole matter. "Gentleman....

"Colonel Sinclair, our, the US official posture could be this; I'm afraid our

Intel has failed to provide sufficient and convincing evidence. To our knowledge Israel does not and has never had the capability to develop nuclear weapons—but you Commander have to tell me that you don't test any more of these *'Rosemarie's Babies'* without telling us first so we can cover our and your asses with the Russkies. And now, Commander Barak—"

"But that's not it, General." Ziki did not rise as would have been polite—instead he fixed Armstrong with a steady gaze. "If we are to be allies, we would presume that the US would honor the agreements it makes to Israel."

"Of course."

"And yet a year ago we paid for forty eight A4E Skyhawk tactical jet fighters."

"Big machines for a small nation," the General answered with amusement. The Skyhawk could carry a payload of eight thousand pounds, both men knew.

Ziki let the dig slide right by. "These were never delivered."

The General's gaze darkened.

Ziki pressed his advantage. "We'd like them delivered by the end of the month."

The General considered this. He gave the air of reluctance, but Ziki knew it was only for show. "Is that all, Commander?"

"No, sir." He leaned forward and tapped his cigarette on the rim of an ashtray. The smudge of his fingerprints appeared when he lifted his hand. "It has been two years since we paid for and were promised two hundred M-48 tanks from NATO stockpiles in Germany. We'd like to see those arrive within two weeks."

There was a shrewd gleam in the General's look. "Those are offensive weapons Commander, besides you manufacture your own tanks, Merkava's—I hear they're damn good. Who promised these to you?"

"As you know, Sir, your president did."

The General grunted in a sort of regard. "Sinclair. . . Your Israeli 'friend' drives a hard bargain."

"Not a bargain—simply delivery on old promises," Ziki reminded him. "Allies honor their word."

"And so they do." The General scratched his neck. "Your flyspeck will get your machines, Barak. Welcome to the big boys club…You have a deal Commander."

Ziki stood and put out his hand. "This time I won't squeeze as hard."

Armstrong left without shaking his hand.

With a look of anxiety, Sinclair nodded at Ziki and then followed the General.

**"Ahh, General Petrovsky, better late then never!"** Petrovsky was not amused.

Armstrong's voice was a far cry from his Texas drawl. Every word seemed to hang in mid air, chosen carefully and coldly with precise intonations to convey controlled anger…

"General I have some somber facts, it looks like the Israelis have real nuclear capability and we think they have some thirty, twenty kiloton devices." The Russian stared grimly into space.

"You promised a detailed briefing," he said with soft anger.

"Most of what I am about to tell you is conjecture, but it is what we think." He paused and ran his eyes around the room.

"As we all suspected their nuclear reactor is at a place called Dimona in the Negev desert, it has remote control missile defense systems that are impenetrable.... Plants and laboratories deep under ground and computer functioning centrifuges that are producing weapons grade plutonium."

One of the Russians blurted out *"Jesus Christos, yebutefoimath."*

"A weapons assembly plant in the north, outside the city of Haifa. All their facilities are mostly deep underground and are hooked up by computers and early warning electronic detection systems to missile batteries…No aircraft is permitted to over fly Dimona—even their own. With today's technology we have nothing that can touch any of their stuff and neither do you."

General Petrovsky lit a cigarette and drew in deep smoke, not caring if the Americans allowed smoking, no one was about to tell him not to.

General Armstrong avoided Petrovsky's eyes, fingering a Marlborough out of the soft shell of a pack to keep himself busy. He passed the pack to the Russian beside him once he'd drawn out his own cigarette. The Russians passed the pack around, savoring the American brand. The air quickly filled with smoke.

"All this is an educated guess and un-collaborated intelligence, but they did say one thing."

"What's that?"

"They call it **"The Samson Option"**

"What in hell is that?" Petrovsky growled.

"Ahh yes, I too forgot. You Comrades do not read the bible."

Petrovsky grunted in reply.

"According to the Bible Samson was a baaad boy, stronger then any mortal man. He was captured by his enemies after he was betrayed by Delilah he putt up and lost a bloody fight…. Samson's enemies were cruel. He was put on display to entertain them with his strength. His eyes were gauged out with hot pokers, but more importantly—his hair was cut short."

"The bible says that his strength was in the growth of his hair . . .he was not permitted to cut it, Delilah did—he prayed for deliverance, but none came. And finally, he asked God to give him back his strength just one last time."

General Armstrong noted that the faces of the Russians had slackened as they listened with intense interest… General Armstrong continued.

"Samson found his way to the two pillars that supported the whole roof of the great hall where he had been imprisoned."

The General paused for greater effect. "Samson pushed the two pillars apart, snapping the slabs of the roof and tumbling the stone amphitheatre to the ground unto his enemies that were gathered in the great hall. As the rocks and dust came down, Samson cried out:

*'I die but my enemies die with me!'"*

A brief silence lingered in the room. Then one Russian shifted in his seat and another—as if a spell had broken.

The General shrugged, "If the Israeli's view themselves as Samson did—I'd stay out of their way."

"What the hell does that mean? General? Petrovsky asks."

"I think what they're saying, Comrade General Petrovsky is; don't fuck with us."

# Chapter 1

## CHECKPOINT MEGIDDO

**Ali Hassan Salameh stood in line quietly...uneasy.** He tried to look unobtrusive and unnoticed, waiting his turn to pass through the roadblock ahead; his knees shook, but—as his training in Duma, just north of Damascus had taught him—he fought his trembling knees for control. The last thing he wanted to show was fear.

The sun began to set, night was getting ready to fall; scattered lights appeared in the distance.

This place is *Megiddo*, In Hebrew; Armageddon.

A flash of lightning in the clouds—an ill omen or a sign that Allah was watching.

Again lightning. Salameh raised his eyes to the darkening sky... The blaze burned his mentor's vision like a promise upon the terrain around him: *Megiddo...* *Megiddo* would become one of the dark places on earth. Allah's lightening would scorch the land and air, and the changing immensity of life would be known as just a flicker.

Darkness had come with him. His face twitched with strain, his hands moved with a slight tremble. He had already embraced the darkness.

Salameh had dark, watery eyes and a smooth, boyish face he shaved that morning for the first time in three years. He made himself as small as he was able, kept his eyes towards the dirt, and shuffled forward a few steps and a few steps again. Hunched shoulders and a bent neck made the unimposing frame he carried appear even smaller. He wanted to look bland, like a man of little conviction. Looks can be deceiving.

Despite his apparent ease, his knees would shake intermittently. He could be caught. He could disappoint his mentor, Zawahiri—and Allah.

Young Israeli soldiers stood ahead looking at the sea of faces, their Galil machine guns lax in their hands. They paid reluctant notice, one of them smoking casually. Another spat in the dust.

The young soldiers at the checkpoint might not be able to tell; but the border patrol sergeant that he saw, Salameh knew, could smell his fear.

The line crawled forward in silence; some of the men took the trouble to grunt. Pockets of them squatted here and there—others scratched and others talked in hushed tones back and forth.

The sky was the color of smoke—to his right a clump of olive trees made a shady spot, shelter from the setting sun. The path was steep and gave a clear view over the milieu that swallowed him. The rest of the world was gone, disappeared, nowhere; only whispers and shadows were left behind.  The ravine to the left was no more than a scar on the landscape.

Salameh held still when a dull detonation in the distance shook the ground. The men begun to chatter. Someone pointed: black smoke rising over the hill.

A bus… Salameh frowned. He knew that his nephew Iamael, from Gaza was waiting for a bus at that station. Dust clouds rose where the explosion had taken place. The shrill of a siren. There was the flux of confusion and agitation along the line.

The soldiers at the checkpoint were no longer casual—the noses of the guns had been raised toward the crowd. The sergeant was ordering the younger men to push the crowd back.

 The youth in their faces had hardened.

Salameh fell back with the crowd and fell in line once more as the line regrouped. The tensions knotted and slowly submerged, rolled into the process of waiting.

And so Salameh breathed and drew the energy from his legs into a cold fire of heart and prayed fervently behind lazily lidded eyes… *The end of the world, the beginning of everlasting life in the beneficent presence of Allah.*


Workers from Jenin and surrounding Arab villages were entering Israel from the West Bank.

Three young soldiers with youthful faces stood alongside a large jeep and checked identity cards with watchful eyes beneath the black berets that pulled low on their foreheads. Mounted below the barrels of the Galil machine guns were tear-gas launchers. That was a good sign: it meant that for the crowd control that was gathering, the young Israelis felt there was little danger and were willing to use tear gas instead of live ammunition.  Another good omen: An armored personnel carrier had a water cannon mounted on top.

The line showed several hundred Palestinians in this ancient place in the Valley of Jezreal checkpoint near Tanach, south of Megiddo.

 A bronze plaque just to the hillside of where Salameh stood bragged that Megiddo dates back to 3500 BC, as one of King Solomon's chariot cities; it sported a stable that sheltered 450 horses, and the prophet Josiah was killed here.  The plaque with a Biblical quote said: "*Megiddo will be the scene of a great battle between the forces of Good and Evil to be fought on the Great Day of Armageddon that this City is named for."*

Salameh mumbled to himself, *"Armageddon…Hmm—it is coming sooner than you may think."*

The soldiers at the checkpoint were checking identity cards and work permits, carefully. These men and women could earn seventeen to twenty times higher wages by working in Israel than working within the West Bank or Gaza where they lived.

The line crawled forward.

In the distance an army vehicle sped towards the bomb sight—a spew of dust and stone behind churning wheels. It moved at a higher speed than prudent, whirring a mysterious sound towards where the explosion occurred, grinding its wheels on the dirt road raising a cloud of choking gray dust. The rushing noise filled the stillness.

"You…" Salameh started. "Over here!" the officer checking documents called.

His pulse quickened. Me? He gestured to himself.

"You move, *yalla imshi*."

With dilated nostrils and eyes that narrowed and stared stonily into the distance with death like indifference, he moved forward and handed the soldier his identity card and work permit.

They were both well-made forgeries, from Damascus, Syria, by the same government office that made Syrian passports and identity cards. They did good work! He watched the soldier turn the pages in his papers.

The air was dusty and hot, but the scent of wild field flowers floated on the incoming breeze. A fat fly buzzed near Salameh's ear menacingly but did not sting.

"You're going to Sedot Yam near Caesarea?"

"Yes." Salameh kept his eyes fixed to the ground and spoke softly biting back the hatred.

"The crops are ripe and have been picked already in that region; what do they want with you?"

The weather had turned cold suddenly with a breeze from the west, but Salameh felt soaking sweat engulfing his body. "*Allah Almighty be merciful!*" he thought. "Could they know who I am?" He looked at the young soldier, immediately lowering his eyes to the ground and answered.

"I don't know for sure. They just said that they needed somebody to paint the trees white from bugs. That's all I know."

The officer scrutinized him once more, then handed him his papers back.

—"Well, you'd better hurry or you're going to be late."

Salameh put his documents carefully in his wallet, said "thank you," and went on his way to a waiting Egged bus on the other side, already half full with travelers.

As he approached the steps, the bus driver spoke in a calm cold voice— "Stop right there," the driver commanded, his tone clear and officious.

Salameh froze for a moment, his eyes, dark, almost black were exceptionally cold, his glance fell away from the driver as heavy as an axe.

The driver, a stocky middle-aged man with noticeably big hands, wore a short sleeve jacket of African safari style, khaki trousers and black unpolished boots, no hat. His hair parted to one side, thin strands hardly covering the bald side.

Half circles of sweat under his armpits and around his neck soaked the short sleeve shirt he was wearing; bushy eyebrows, with one quizzically raised marked a steely glare that betrayed years of experience. The man looked like he'd been driving that bus near this border region for years. He ran his eyes up and down over Salameh.

"Open your coat and leave your shirt out." He spoke in a tone that was not to be argued with. "Now—pull it up high where I can see the pants belt line."

"I am no *Shahid*," Salameh told him and hesitated. The driver's hand moved toward his right hip where a Jericho pistol was bulging out; "Aah…do it real slow. I want to drive this bus another 10 years."

"I have no…."

"Lift it up higher—"the driver mimed the movement. Salameh nodded tersely, his mouth was sour and dry "….No explosives belt. See?" He gave the driver a long look and spoke with confident arrogance.

The driver nodded. "Ok. Come on board."

Experienced with the passengers that would board his bus at this border town, he was looking for *Shahids,* suicide bombers with hidden explosives or arms. Even though Salameh had successfully passed through the checkpoint he relied on his own instincts…

Salameh glanced back at the checkpoint line and noticed that the young officer who had checked his papers kept his eyes fixed in the direction of the bus—a shiver ran through him.

Ahh…it's nothing, he assured himself as he climbed the stairs of the bus. The soldier catching Salameh's stare looked away.

Salameh took a seat and bowed his head. He was sweating, hot and thirsty.

*They suspect nothing.*

Ali Hasan Salameh had successfully passed through the Israeli checkpoint and was now on his way to Caesarea by the sea.

His eyes once more glued to the bus that Salameh had boarded, Lieutenant Ezra Sherer at the checkpoint moved casually toward his jeep and slid into the passenger seat, he dialed the secret number he had in the vehicle.

A calm deep voice from the other end answered. "Yes?"

"This is Ezra Sherer, at Checkpoint Megiddo. We've spotted one of the people that are on your list. He came through just now—headed for Caesarea. He boarded a bus. I can still see him."

"His name, Lieutenant?"

"Ali Hasan Salameh. Do you want me to grab him?"

"Oh, no. Do as you were told. Let him go. Did you harass him in any way?"

"Your instructions were to let him enter without difficulty."

"Good. Proceed as you were told. Let him go. Keep away from him. We'll take care of it from here—you got it?"

"Yes, Sir...." The young man wished there was conviction in his voice.

In his office just South of Tel Aviv in the Kirya, Mossad village, Ziki Barak sported a smile.  The first Islamic Jihad operative of this encounter had entered Israel and was on the move.

The indistinguishable gray Toyota pickup that carried a load of hay as its payload kept a discreet distance as it followed the bus...

## Chapter 2

**The American**

**Jimmy-Ray Sinclair, was CIA**. Ziki fished him out of a Syrian jail near Duma where he and Ziki had been.

Sinclair leaned back in his comfortable executive chair on the third floor of the American embassy in Tel Aviv, his office on Hayarkon Street  but a stone throw from Rotchild Boulevard where Ziki Barak had the use of a Mossad "Corporate" office.

His eyes closed, he almost dozed off; the warmth of a beautiful day seeped in through the open French doors. There was no need for the air conditioning system, it was off.

Ziki was about to visit Sinclair at the Embassy. He decided to bring the drink. He chose an aged Pernod, French, because he thought such a choice would leave the American thinking hard about where Ziki had been and why. In friendships with Americans it served well if they thought you had a cultural *savoir faire* that Yanks did not quite muster.

Sinclair' office of smooth pale wooden paneling and executive chairs, gleaming tables was high among towering green palms with an unfortunate layer of dust on their leaves.

Pernod in hand, Ziki waited to be announced. Through the glass door he could see Sinclair in his office—a desk that was obscenely big, photos of airplanes on the walls, and one of Sinclair in uniform, smiling with other men in uniform, and photos of the Pentagon and White House, and Jimmy Carter, all teeth, shaking Sinclair' hand in  a very official looking picture.

Sinclair' eyes were closed as if he were about to doze off.

The aid knocked loudly on the doorframe, startling Sinclair awake.

"Commander Barak, Sir."

Sinclair was bleary eyed and blinked rapidly.  "Well don't just stand there, show him in," he said in an imperious tone.

"Shalom—good to see you, thank you for coming—coffee?"

"Shalom—yes—coffee, cream and sugar—unless—"Ziki flourished the bottle and watched Sinclair' face peel back a smile.

The American took the bottle and held it in his paper smooth, pink fingers.

"Pernod," he mouthed. "Hemingway swore by the stuff. I've not had it myself, but there's no time like the present."

He waved Ziki to a chair, telling him to help himself to the Cubans in the black box to his left. Ziki did, and while Sinclair tinkered with glasses and ice and the foil and cork of the bottle, Ziki sliced his cigar and lit it with the enormous lion-shaped lighter next to the black box. A lion-shaped lighter. . . Ziki raised an eyebrow, inevitably a gift from Scotland Yard. Damn, but Sinclair got around.

Sinclair handed Ziki his drink and returned to his chair behind his desk. "How's that Cuban?"

Ziki drew a long inhale and another, the smoke escaping between the cigar and the sides of his mouth as he puffed. "Not bad. The Cubans may not know shit about what's good for them politically, but dammit, they do know their tobacco leaves."

Sinclair laughed. "Rumor has it the Bay of Pigs was all about Kennedy's craving."

"No shit?"

"I have it from the best of sources."

Ziki's mouth quirked in response. "Pretty damn good." He took the cigar from his mouth and blew out a long stream of purple smoke.

"Cheers," he said then, and clinked glasses across the desk with Sinclair.

Their glasses tilted upwards and they drank.

Sinclair' face showed his surprise at the depth of the anise flavored drink. "Surprisingly lighter than I thought it'd be."

"Really?"

"Well, Hemingway—you know."

"No," Ziki shook his head. "I read the whale story, Captain Ahab, and that, but he isn't really part of the canons."

"A real tough guy. You know. Ball player. Hunter. Chopped his own wood."

"Tough guys don't drink Pernod in America?"

Sinclair considered this a moment, apparently at a loss, and then twitched. "We've other things to discuss, my friend—" He turned from side to side in his chair.

"Yes," Ziki agreed.

Sinclair leveled his eyes toward the ceiling and scratched behind his ear straining to form a question.

"This. . . This *Arab*. . . you've got, Ali Salameh, belonged to El Fattah?"

"We assume so, yes. That's what our sources tell us," Ziki answered

"A big fish?"

"Midsize, fresh meat, rising—but with big information."

"Information? Oh, Yeah, like what?"

"Well—that—I can't. In good time—all in good time—security risks. Clearance. You understand."

"Of course." Sinclair answered, clearly disappointed. "The basics, then."

The need to know. He paused…C'mon Ziki, I thought we were becoming friends, what's the story with this Salameh, or whatever's his name that you boys got?"

Ziki stole a steely look at Sinclair, struck a match on his boot and lit a cigarette, slowly blew out the smoke. The man didn't know what he wished for. If Salameh's information was true—and Ziki found no reason to believe it was not— then it was extraordinary, it opened a door into unknown depths. He'd answered most questions and confirmed others half answered.

Ziki looked at his drink; it was good at first taste, now he pushed it away. Sinclair downed the delicate drink. "They're planning something."

"What?" Sinclair sat forward.

"I will tell you—in part —if you don't know something you cannot let it slip your lips. You Americans leak like a sieve."

"They're going to attack, big?"  He could see Sinclair staring at him and seeing a vision of apocalypse.

Ziki nodded.  "From what we can figure; we're still working on getting information from Salameh. Something about a hidden safe in an Islamic Jihad compound in the Be'eka Valley in Northern Lebanon."

"You think a no-warning attack? No warning?" Sinclair surmised.

"It always is–yes…it always is. Yes.  As usual.  There are some things you do need to know and where we're going to have to work fast."

Sinclair did not speak.  He simply cupped his chin, rubbing his fingers over his mouth.

Ziki rose and filled his own glass with more Pernod. He concealed a move of furious anger. "Okay—a few things I can tell you.  He was at the first Islamic Jihad, then moved on from there to El Fattah, he moved up—promoted."

"He was rewarded."

"That's right."

Sinclair' look turned pensive.  "We've been working for years on El Fattah—men lost, covers blown.  And we still don't know jack about any of them. Islamic Jihad, El Fattah, Hamas—any of these groups."

Ziki flickered an eyebrow at this.

Sinclair' eyes gleamed.  "But you Mossad boys know something.  . ." He spoke quietly; he knew that he owed Ziki Barak his life. When Golani, IDF commandos, had stormed into the medieval Turkish built prison at Duma in Syria to get Ziki and Melvin Finkle out, on Ziki's orders they took the American along for the helicopter ride to Tel Aviv and out of what the Israelis had dubbed 'Hotel Damascus.'

"We know now."

"Jesus," Sinclair breathed.  "That just makes this Salameh you got even more important.  Do you have him secure?"

Ziki ignored Sinclair' last question.

"You CIA boys need to know more about these groups, if you don't already. Eventually, you're going to have to deal with them."

"Oh, yeah? What about them?"

"A year ago, we acted on a tip from an informant in Amman Jordan."

Ali Hasan Salameh had been picked up over a year ago by the Jordanians—a few hours after the bombing of their consulate in Zurich—a bombing that they had officially attributed to the terrorist group Islamic Jihad.  Salameh had been armed, but convinced them that he had had nothing to do with the bombing; he had claimed that he was just visiting his cousin."

"They let him go?"

"They did."  Ziki drew on his cigarette and blew smoke.  "Our cameras poised at the Jordanian consulate shot a photo of him just before the blast.  We know it was him.  We know he's I. J.  When he was released from jail, he dropped out of sight."

"But now, you've picked him up.  C'mon Ziki, what can you tell us about this I. J.?"

"Islamic Jihad is one umbrella organization of many radical groups.  They follow the ideology of extreme Muslim fundamentalism; a rising star among them is an Egyptian named Aiman  Zawahiri."

"There's strong radical Islamic and Syrian fundamentalist presence in the Be'eka Valley in Lebanon."

Ziki couldn't keep back a caustic smile.  "You see, you do know something—they're led by fanatic clerics… Mullahs.  They use terror as their primary political means—kill anybody that's not Muslim."

"I guess they don't like us."

"Yeah, you can make book on that."  Ziki got up, walked over and looked out the window; the street below was bustling with people.  He downed his drink once more.  It was nice and cold, the ice having watered it slightly.

In the bright sun of the street, a little boy eating an ice cream cone and walking with his mother had caught his eyes….  "We need to know where and what they're going to hit."

"You've got my resources at your finger tips—whatever you need from the CIA—" Sinclair' eyes were shining with self importance.

Ziki nodded.  "I need to make a call; how 'bout the use of your phone?"

Frowning, Sinclair pushed it toward Ziki.  "Of course."

Ziki grinned.  "Here's your chance to listen in."

"We don't do that."

"Of course we don't," Ziki answered sarcastically

"Use the black one, it's a secure line," Sinclair protested.

"I believe you—" Ziki placated him as he raised the head set and waited for dial tone.

It came.  He dialed the secret number of an aide to General Malkielly.  The moment after the numbers had repeated their tones on the line to connect, he heard that extra faint click—"*We don't do that.*"  Of course they didn't listen in... not the CIA.

"Barak here," he said, slowly and clearly so that the man in headphones somewhere in the building could hear every word.

The aide told him that the General would be with him momentarily, and Ziki could not repress his smile as he heard a second faint click just before the General's voice boomed on the line—ahhh, the aide had informed his supervisor of the parties involved in the telephone call. And now, Ziki was certain the Americans would get what it was he needed them to get.

"Is this a secure line, Commander?" Malkielly demanded.

"Yes, sir." Ziki avoided a true answer.

"Just answer yes or no. Did they infiltrate the security codes of the American embassies?"

"Yes."

"What about Beirut—the American compound codes used by the Marines?"

"Yes."

"Ours?"

"No."

"That's all." Malkielly hung up abruptly.

Ziki grimaced and placed the receiver back in its cradle.

"What was that all about? What about our embassy codes?" Sinclair asked, frowning.

"I'm sure they'll brief you, I heard that extra click."

"No, no, that was a secure line."

"Yes, yes."

"Our embassies are in danger?"

"I would recommend that you not let that news get out."

Sinclair' face turned red. "What in God's name do the bastards want? How? How could Islamic Jihad or El Fattah get our security codes, enter our systems?"

"We don't know yet—. They're playing with us, building up their confidence. They want to show us that our technology is being outclassed."

Sinclair mumbled. "Mother fuckers."

"It's a warning—they want to make us sweat. Change your embassy codes, now. World-wide, I'd recommend. Pay special attention to the Marine barracks and compounds in Beirut."

Sinclair sat down slowly. "—Tell me about these sons of bitches, Ziki. I'd say we 'need to know' more than I could think possible."

Ziki bit off all the smart-assed responses that begged to fly from his tongue—. Instead he went to the bar and took the Pernod bottle in hand. A layer of cold condensation had gathered on the glass surface, soaking the label through. He poured three fingers worth into Sinclair' glass. Refilling his own glass, he was silent. He left the bottle on the desk and flopped back into his chair.

"It goes like this," he began. "Syria, Iran and others gathered a rag tag collection. They are headquartered in Ba'albek, in the Northern Be'eka valley in Lebanon and in Afganistan, with terrorist training camps spread out in Lebanon, Syria, Libya, Afghanistan, and Iran."

"Lebanon, we knew about—but—"

"It's time to get a sense of the world, especially this part of it," Ziki reminded him.

"Go on please."

"Their spiritual leader is Sheik Mohammed Fadlallah. He is their Chief *Mujtahid*, a judge of so-called Islamic law of all the Shiites in Lebanon. The brains and driving force is Aiman Zawahiri, as I've told you, an Egyptian. Their commander of operations is Abbas Musawi. What unites them—the same ideologies—the same war cry—Allah—the Koran—and no variance from ancient laws. Their principal goal is the establishment of an Islamic fundamentalist reign in the entire Mid East—ultimately to control the world's oil supply, direct its flow and cut it off when offended."

"The world's oil supply? The Middle East supplies most of the—"

"With sabotage, a little creative initiative, they could be the sole producers of oil."

"And distribution headed by religious Mullahs. . . "

"Yeah," Ziki nodded morosely. "They even have a name for their movement."

"They named themselves? What the hell is it?"

"Taliban and Al Qaieda."

"What is that—what does it mean?"

"Yes…It means that they are not your friends."

"I never heard of those names."

"Don't worry you will….Hmm...Yeah, just don't you worry, my American friend, I'm sure you will hear those names.

"Your bravado is a little disconcerting—."

"Bravado!" Ziki snorted. "It means they're calling you out—calling us out. You've walked around mostly blind in this part of the world. "We've long known . . . some things…" His response died on his lips. "If your CIA hasn't heard those names before, they will. Soon enough."

"What in God's name do they want?"

"They want to kill us all, that's what they want. They want the complete destruction of the State of Israel, with Islamic rule over Jerusalem as an expressed goal. They claim the destruction of Israel and the killing of all infidels, Jews, and Christians a 'religious obligation.'"

"The Iranians work with the Syrians and the Syrians with the Lebanese?"

"The Syrians have a strong military presence in Lebanon—30,000 men; they are not just offering camel rides to the tourists—. I'm sure your satellites picked this stuff up."

"Ziki—. . .I hate to admit it, you Mossad boys have a good grip in your back yard."

"Ok," he said, leaning forward and fixing Sinclair with a sharp eye. "These are not good guys. The Islamic Jihad, *Taliban*, *Hamas*, PLO-*El Fattah*—and a new one, well financed I hear: Al Qaieda—their acts of destruction, suicide bombings, are more thoroughly planned, more sophisticated, more deadly with each occurrence. Kill all the infidels—that's their motto and that's what you and I are."

"Infidels. Straight out of the Crusades."

"Yeah—that's right. Just like in the Crusades. Only instead of Kings—it's oil money that keeps it growing. Terrorism and opium grown in Afganistan and in the Be'eka Valley with you and us in their sights."

"Headquartered in Ba'albek Lebanon and Afghanistan?"

"That's what I said."

**Tel-Aviv's Dizengoff Street is peppered with sidewalk cafés, restaurants and bars**. In the evenings it is full of life. Two hours later, a few glasses of Greek wine, several Cubans, and a healthy dose of Russian Vodka later, Ziki and Sinclair sat at a bar named "Café Alhambra." The Americans from the Embassy liked to call it "Bar Water Hole."

Sinclair was nursing a tangier and tonic. "Damn crazy business, all of this. I was on vacation—wearing sandals, no socks—and toting around a camera everywhere. First vacation I'd had in two years."

Ziki laughed. "How'd your wife take it?" He took a long swig of the Ouzo he had before him. It was strong, licorice, good.

Sinclair shrugged. "What was she gonna do? Say you can't go save the world again? Naaaaaaaw."

"Is that what we do—save the world?"

"Probably not. But it sounds good."

"Makes my mother proud."

"That's right!" Sinclair clinked his glass into Ziki's.

"God, that shit stinks," Sinclair sniffed distastefully, indicating Ziki's glass of Greek Ouzo.

"Better than that sweet lady's drink," Ziki replied.

Sinclair laughed softly… "Lady? Speaking of ladies, I hear of your entanglement with one of ours, a Yank, what's her name? Oh yeah, Gavriella Ramon—I saw her once at Langley, she works with Kissinger and Walters, a knockout, but you better watch your buns my friend, I hear that she has leanings favoring the PLO. What's the matter, don't they have enough good looking women in Israel?" Ziki ignored his remark.

"How did this happen? How did we get here? I'm from half way around the world. You're from—" he waved his arm drunkenly in a huge gesture at something larger than the hotel "—over there somewhere. What are we doing here?"

"Drinking. . ." Ziki answered.

"Shut up," Sinclair knocked him on the arm. "I mean . . . tell me—how the hell did you get into this bastardly business?"

Ziki shrugged. He met Sinclair eye to eye.

Sinclair made a face that said, lay it on me.

"It was faith; I guess they thought—he can do it—."

"Hat racks—" Sinclair roared with appreciation.

"How did I get into this business…?"

An air of extravagant mystery appeared on Ziki's face. His mind wondered deep under the surface. His eyes were beyond reach and beyond Jimmy-Ray Sinclair' power of meddling.

Ziki drifted into his childhood when he was eight years old…

# Chapter 3

### Killing a Man

**Tanned and scruffy, with dusty feet shod in worn sandals,** dirty legs far too small in shorts far too big and loved-to-threads shirt hanging from skinny shoulder bones, eight-year-old Ziki Barak cut down the western slope of Mount Carmel.  Sent by his mother to pick oranges, he skipped the busy street of motorcars, buses, and bicycles, Rehov Mutanabi, and took the sun-bleached path lined by olive trees that led to his school.  The rocky soil crunched underfoot.  As he reached Rehov Abbas, the setting sun struck the colors from his sight.
It was the prime opportunity for two boys—one far bigger than Ziki, the other perhaps only a year or so older—silhouetted in the glare off the Mediterranean far below, to jump him.
Ziki recognized them; the two boys went to Ziki's school.  In a second, the big one had Ziki down on his knees, head locked between forearms.
"Let me go!  Let me go!"  Ziki struggled, but all he did was scrape his knees raw on the gravel.
"Tell us where you are going!"
"To pick some oranges," Ziki answered.
"Not our oranges?  Do you know the penalty for picking our oranges?"
"Not your oranges.  Wild ones!  The ones that grow in the *pardes* grove by the school."  He didn't want a bloody nose.
The smaller one put his face right down by Ziki's jaw.  His breath smelled of garlic and grape soda.  "Tell us your Daddy wears ladies' underwear and we'll let you go."
"No!"
"Your Daddy wears ladies' underwear!"
"Let me go.  Let me go!"  His shoulders burned against the solid hold.  He lurched against the bigger boy's arms and felt his weight give—aha!
"Your family eats dead dog."
"No!"  Ziki's toes dug in the dust and he leveraged his weight against the headlock.  The grip loosened, slipped, then broke—

Ziki was on his feet in a heartbeat, tearing down the path, the air stinging his knees, his sandals flopping on his feet. He heard the boys behind him—the big one huffing and puffing like an old sow.

Behind a tree and down on his belly behind a stack of orange filled crates waiting to be hauled off to market, Ziki weighed a fat orange in the palm of his hand, waited for the right moment. The boys had lost sight of him and stalled in their tracks—and blam!

An orange in the kisser took the big one off his feet. "Ow!"

The smaller boy sighted Ziki amid the crates and saw the second orange in Ziki's grasp. He froze.

The big one rolled on the ground and then sat up. Blood trickled from his nose to his chin and down his shirt.

"Hey, you—we were just having fun!" the smaller boy said.

"It wasn't so fun for me!" Ziki called back and he launched an orange, letting it fall short of the smaller one. It made a splatting noise at his feet.

"Stop! Our mom! The oranges—" the big one cried.

"You should have thought of that earlier." Ziki threw another orange, hitting the closest tree behind the big one. Several ripe oranges rained down. Both boys duck and covered, mincing until they were hugging tree trunks for cover.

"Wait! Wait! We'll tell you a secret!"

"Shut up, Iosi!"

"You shut up, Avi. If Mom finds out, I'm telling her you started it. Really, kid—it's the best secret we've ever had."

Ziki's next throw slowed. He held the orange above his shoulder. "Yeah?"

"Yeah."

Ziki put the orange back in the crate. "Curiosity killed the cat."

"You've heard of the gardens?" asked Iosi, a note of apprehension in his voice.

"What gardens?" Ziki's guard dropped ever so slightly.

Both boys looked nervous.

"The Persian Gardens," Avi said. He'd tipped his head back and was plugging his nose with his shirt to stop the blood.

The Baha'i, a Persian sect had built a temple there around the turn of the century, but as far as the boys knew, it had always been there, its solid-gold dome ensconced behind an impassable surrounding wall. Between wall and temple, grew lush and green, exotic flowers, exotic birds, with fountains, fruit trees, palms, vines, lawns.

"We know a way in."

"Liar," Ziki replied. Every kid in Haifa knew you couldn't go in there. Beyond the wall lay a labyrinth of hedgerows and then the temple itself, which according to stories, provided secret cover for religious rituals beyond the imagination of young Israeli boys. "No one goes in there."

"You wanna bet?" Avi grinned.

Iosi grinned, too. Their family resemblance became more plain in the expression. "We found a way in just last week, but we haven't tried it yet. You can't get over the wall—but it's not all wall. There's also a fence and there's a gap that you can slip under."

"You can have all the oranges you want from our grove if you bring back a white peacock feather," Avi dared.

"I'm not that stupid." Ziki played it cool. In actuality the thought of entering the gardens made him rigid with fear. The temple was off limits—trespassers in the garden would be sacrificed to the Baha'i gods, whoever they were. That's what everyone said.

And peacocks were the loudest and meanest birds.

"Scared?" Iosi taunted.

"Scaredy cat. Scaredy cat." Avi's eyes gleamed.

"I'm not scared," Ziki returned. "You're scared."

"Scaredy cat."

"Chicken!"

"You're the chicken!" And Ziki threw himself on Avi, taking him off guard. The bigger they are, the harder they—

Avi reeled backward only a step before he had gripped Ziki once more, trying to twist him into another headlock. Ziki kicked him in the shin and tried to slip away, but Avi's grip was too intense. "You little faggot. You won't get me this time."

"Let him go." Iosi interceded, wrenching at his arm. "I said, let him go."

At his brother's command, Avi released Ziki. "Little turd."

"Fuck head," Ziki shot back.

"Stop it." Iosi stepped between the two of them. His eyes studied Ziki's face intently for a long moment. "I've seen you at school, haven't I?"

Ziki nodded. "Yeah. I've seen you two."

"I'm Iosi," the smaller boy said, and then, jerking a thumb toward the other bigger boy; "That's Avi."

"I heard," Ziki answered.

And he meant for that to be that, but Iosi seemed to be offering a real peace. The announcement of their names didn't provide much comfort—Avi was still big and the boys were still glowering over him.

"You live up there?" Avi asked, motioning up the hill with his head.

"Yeah," said Ziki cautiously. "That house up there with the blue flower pots." Pot upon pot of lobelia were his mother's pride; passers-by would stop to admire and comment.

Iosi spoke up; "We live right there," and he pointed across the orange grove behind him. Across the street a wall surrounded a squat house. There were shade trees behind the walls—a court yard. Did they have a fountain inside?

"You guys are brothers?" They didn't look very much alike. Avi was almost a quarter again the size of Iosi and had nearly black hair and light-brown eyes—a real big kid. Iosi was Ziki's size—average for a nine-year-old—but with light blond hair and blue eyes. Still, Ziki wasn't going to argue.

"Avi's nine," nodded Iosi in explanation.

Avi still stood in the path, obdurate, with his arms folded across his chest, but it looked to Ziki like he was loosening up. "I guess we can let him pass," he said to Iosi, his eyes still on Ziki.

The three of them walked past the Abutbulls' house—that was the brothers' last name, Ziki was later to learn—cut south alongside a grove of fig trees and approached the Persian Gardens.

As the sun disappeared over the horizon, so went the glow of the temple's gold roof—it had turned a murky yellow. The boys crept more silently as they closed in on the gap in the fence that would allow their illegal access into this forbidden garden of adventures. Iosi motioned them to the right, skirting the perimeter of the garden wall. Ziki followed, with Avi behind him, looking out.

Sure enough, Iosi dodged and flattened himself against the mortar and white of the aged stone wall, a melodramatic display of courage and resolve. The stone wall gave way to a wrought iron fence. Overgrown bushes pushed between the rods of the fence. Iosi pulled back a bough, exposing a depression in the earth just below the fence.

"Probably made by animals," Iosi whispered.

Ziki nodded—it was just big enough to accommodate a boy. He cocked a brow at the older brother . . . though Avi might have a harder time than himself or Iosi.

"Who's first?" whispered Avi.

"I'll go," said Ziki, surprising himself. He had the sudden itch to impress these two.

"No," said Iosi, stretching his arm in front of Ziki's chest. "I found it. I'll go."

Ziki was secretly relieved that the kid had called his bluff. He stepped aside as Avi held back the bush and Iosi hesitated, his head cocked.

"Go. . . Go!" Avi urged, just a hint of challenge in his voice.

"What was that? Do you hear that?" Iosi's blue eyes were huge, his chin jutted just so as if to make his hearing more keen.

Ziki did. There came from under the fence just the faintest tinkling, faint and almost melodic.

"Bells?" asked Ziki.

"Only one way to find out," said Iosi, evidently having regained his bravado. He bent down and wriggled out of sight.

"Your turn," said Avi, still holding the bush.

There was no going back now.

Ziki fixed him with a steady gaze, as if to measure his mettle a final time, and then followed Iosi's lead.

It took Avi a few moments longer to squirm under the fence, his head popped from beneath the bushes and a few wriggles later his shoulders, his grimy hands and forearms, then chest and waist—he hoisted himself up as if doing a pushup. Iosi grabbed his brother under one armpit and hauled, helping Avi to his knees.

"I got it—I'm good." Avi pushed his brother away.

"Shhhhh. . . " Ziki hushed them.

They fell silent and the three boys looked around in wonder. It was darker and cooler inside the garden where the sun had been absent for hours, and the music was now clear in their ears though its meaning remained a mystery.

When their eyes adjusted they could see why it was so dark: solid hedgerows—easily three meters high—ensconced them. Like a hallway without a roof. They could only be seen by someone coming down the row.

"It's a maze!" breathed Ziki and he began, slowly, to walk toward a twist in the path.

"Me first. . . " Iosi led the way again, although none of the boys had any idea which direction they should be taking, nor what they'd find if they continued on the route ahead. Avi, seeming to understand that he was the muscle, the anchor, walked behind Ziki and cast periodic inspections over his shoulder.

There was no one.

Ahead lay a break in the hedge, where a bit of light shone through, and Iosi slowed. Ziki followed suit and Avi, who had been looking back, stepped on Ziki's foot, causing both boys to start.

"Shh," whispered Iosi. "Come look at this."

They crept around the opening in the hedges and looked. Where behind them stood row after row of tightly-knit, impenetrable hedges, in front of them hung streaming vines spangled with large white flowers. Despite the distance, the boys could smell the flowers—sweet, unlike any Ziki had ever smelled.

They looked to the left, then the right, and at Iosi's wave forward, the three moved into this inner circle of vines, still obscured from view by the thickness of the foliage.

The sound of the bells was stronger and clearer as they drew near the temple, and soon another fragrance hit their nostrils: a sweet, musky smoke. The scent was rich and mellow and good, but the unfamiliar scent quickened their fears of sacrifice and blood.

The hairs in Ziki's nose quivered.

Onward they crept until the vines, hanging thick from a wrought-iron trellis, opened into a courtyard. The temple loomed before them, maybe forty meters across a manicured lawn. Ziki could see candles glowing from within. He also noticed rose bushes, the thickest and tallest he had ever seen, with roses of every possible color: pinks, peaches, yellows, whites, and thorny bushes whose flowers were blood-red.

Avi poked a finger into Ziki's back, causing him to jump.

Ziki cast a glare at him and rubbed the spot.

Avi pointed: "Look."

As Ziki's eyes traveled down the soft path he wondered what Avi was pointing to. Iosi stifled a nervous laugh. "I think we've found your oranges."

Beyond the row of rosebushes, stood three of the most tidily manicured orange trees Ziki had ever seen. Each trunk dipped with the weight of a perfect mass—ripe, brightly colored fruit.

No. Ziki shook his head. There were plenty of other oranges outside the garden.

"You've got to do it!" said Avi.

"I dare you," whispered Iosi.

"No way!" Ziki protested.

"I told you he was chicken," Avi gloated.

Iosi tucked his thumbs under his arm pits and flapped his elbows, silently gawping, mouth open and closed.

Ziki stiffened. He was no chicken. "You guys keep look out. If anybody comes, whistle."

Avi and Iosi nodded vigorously and cackled silently to themselves as Ziki pushed by them.

He inched down the row of rosebushes, trying to stay in their shadows, and very nearly cried out when a large thorn tore at his shirt sleeve, pricking a line of tiny blood drops beneath the fabric. The cover of hedges and vines ended several feet from the orange trees. He would be picking the oranges—stealing them from a house of strange gods—in plain view of the temple. All it would take was someone walking outside and simply turning his way. . .

On the other hand, the oranges grew so close to the ground that all he would have to do would be to sprint to the nearest tree, pluck three fruits, and sprint back to cover.

He looked back at Iosi and Avi—they were holding their breath, beaming with barely contained glee. No time to back down now.

As he stole across the Baha'i courtyard, the bells resounded stranger than ever, mingled now with what sounded like a low chanting.

Creepy, Ziki thought.

The sweet incense stung in his nostrils and yet was somehow…inviting. It was as though, for a moment, he were being lured toward the orange tree, as though he were fooling no one.

Ziki did not hesitate. He reached the tree and had stuffed two oranges—beautiful oranges—down his shirt; his palm had cupped a third when he heard a faint whistle and the bells became much louder, followed by voices: one of the temple doors had opened and men were coming out.

Ziki froze.

They were a small group, bald, and wore saffron robes.

They hadn't seen him.

Ziki bolted to his right, seeking cover behind the nearest rose bush. For the moment, he was safe—though his heart had lodged below his Adam's apple and his mouth was as dry as the road. He peered around the bush, mindful of the thorns, and saw the men.

None seemed aware of his presence.

He sat back on his rump and caught his breath and tried to think.

Ok. . .

ok . . . ok. . . if he could get to the hedgerow—

Wait a minute! Where were Avi and Iosi?

He could no longer see them.

They'd called him chicken but at the first sign of trouble, they'd been the ones to turn tail and run.

*Hara*...crap.

Ziki was on his own.

Ok. . . ok.  ... He began to scheme in his head. How could he get out? If he took the open courtyard he'd be seen. If he sat there all night he might be caught. Would his mother thrash him more for being so late or for having trespassed in the garden?

There was—yes—the labyrinth! If he kept low . . . if he was fast . . . he might find a way to double back . . . he might be able to get out of sight.

He craned his neck for a last look at the temple doors. None of the men bothered to look his way.

Ok. Now.

GO!

—he launched himself into the darkness of the labyrinth, the hedges rising up around him on either side. He walked swiftly—seeking the end of the passage, hoping that he could veer back to the left, but no. He was forced to continue to the right—but left, left—he wanted to head back left!

Now he trotted, worried the passage he'd taken might let out directly in front of the temple doors. The night was growing quickly darker. The hedges seemed thicker and more menacing than ever. Vines clutched at him, took on a sinister edge, making the shapes of grotesque faces and malformed bodies. He continued right, looking for an opening, moving as fast as he quietly could, ignoring the knot of anxiety the bubbled up in his chest.

There was no way out!

A left turn—yes—finally.

No.

A dead end.

He breathed out in frustration.

He felt as if he'd gone kilometers.

He couldn't see over the maze's hedges.

He couldn't tell how far he'd gone from the place in the fence that would take him back to the street and then the slopes of Mount Carmel.

A hand shot out from the shadows and clamped down on his shoulder.

Ziki lurched away from it, nearly falling on top of himself before realizing it was Avi. Relief. Like cold water in his veins.

Iosi, grinning. "Hey, Mountain Kid! Where've you been?"

Ziki pulled the two oranges from his shirt.

Iosi clapped him on the back. "We get out of here alive, my mom will send a whole bag home with you."

Ziki scrambled after Iosi, barely noticing the vines and branches that whipped him in the face and arms.

Avi waited by the fence, rigid with nerves. "Come on. Come on!"

Iosi dug under the fence first and Ziki was right on his heels, so close that he tasted dirt dislodged by Iosi's toes. Avi came last, squirming through far faster than when they'd first set on their adventure raid.

The moment they were all clear they ran for the cover of the olive and orange groves and once hidden, bent double, laughing, panting and slapping each other on the back.

"You should have seen your face."

"My face? Yours was white as ghost!"

"And you were all 'Get me outta here!'"

"Yeah—who was it that disappeared?"

Their hysterics exhausted them until they stood looking at each other, almost sheepishly, wondering what to do next.

"I have to get these oranges to my mother," Ziki said.

"Take all you want from those boxes on the way home," Avi told him. "Our mom won't care if we tell her you're a friend."

Ziki nodded his thanks. His own mother might not mind how late he was, nor the dirtied state of his shirt and pants if he went home with arms full.

"I gotta go."

They stood back. Not much more to say.

Five steps toward home, Ziki heard Iosi calling after him. "Hey, Kid? Kid!"

"What?"

"What's your name? You never told."

Ziki smiled. "Ziki…Ziki Barak."

"See ya tomorrow?"

"Yeah, see ya tomorrow."

**Ziki, Iosi and Avi became friends, good friends.** They ate together, played together, slept over at one-another's houses.

They wrestled together in high school, where the coach, Mr. Thermopolous, a short tank of a man whose entire body was covered in coarse black hair and powerful runs of muscle, would make the boys jog down Mount Carmel and then back up it—backward. Avi, was the biggest member of the team and neither Iosi with his nimble mind nor Ziki with his strong arms could ever take him down.

They wooed the same girls—or, rather, Iosi and Ziki did. While Avi was gradually developing an Olympian's build, his wits were no match for Iosi's, whose words worked on the girls of Haifa like poetry.

Ziki liked Hanna, a green-eyed beauty from up the mountain, but she was interested in doing things with Iosi. So it went until Ziki and Iosi were 18 years old and fresh out of high school. The time had come for them to begin training for the military service that is the duty of every young man and girl in Israel.

The time had come for boot camp; the boys parted ways.

For a short time…

**Ziki moved around the heated embers of the dwindling fire with a long, rough stick.** In the background he could hear the high-pitched sounds of laughter filtering in and out of his ears. The waves of the Mediterranean lulled his thoughts into thoughts of repetition.

High school graduation was only a short time away and all he could think about was how a week after his 18th birthday, he would become a new man—. In the army. Inside, he wondered if he would still be Ziki. No longer a child.

Adulthood came early here, he would be a soldier in the IDF.

In a world that surrounded him with the unpredictability of the smoldering Middle East, war seemed constant, enemies plentiful... Supplies always needed to be replenished. He was the latest model: just like every new graduate before him and just like his friends would be in the following weeks, trickling new force into the military; as old bodies returned in caskets or worse, missing a leg or an arm, or blinded by a phosphorous missile, propelled grenade, or suicide bomber. The lucky ones were discharged whole having completed their tour of duty.

To be in the IDF was an honor, a duty to be filled and a certainty that was understood without contention.

Except that Ziki was afraid. Not of dying…he was afraid that he might have to kill someday.

Young, prideful and without context, he was numb and vulnerable to the ache of trepidation because he could not imagine its truth without experiencing it; and once tainted, such a distorted image was a heavy weight to bear.

He could not give this fear a name—he had no reference point except for the shivering and the knife that would cut at his heart each time he heard of someone else that had fallen: the way his body would freeze; the way his mind would slowly forget each death as laughter, schoolwork and survival would overtake the memory reserved for mourning. He might forget for a while. His life had him escaping into a reality that did not bleed from shrapnel… It bled in the mind and the heart.

Ziki closed his eyes and he could see his body stacked on top of the many others who had died on the Gaza Strip, the north valleys or some far off land.

One more mound of flesh that gave its once promised life for its country and earned an early death in return.

But he could not fathom how he could—if he had to—kill anyone. Anyone.

In this land, the dreams of young men and women hid inside them, their country first until their time was served; the fight for survival was growing up—whether it be in dreams or love or dark thoughts that fueled the mind.

It paled in the fight for survival and worked quickly at aging children into men.

His future was now moving fast-forward; restless nights where he could see ahead but did not know what. His mother's tears, the tears that could drown or comfort him in the darkness of night…

Leaving home, the sharp citrus smell of the orange groves of his childhood. It filled his days with sweaty anticipation, like a boy restless to play hide-and-go-seek in a field that he did not know… So expansive: he could be a hero and find everyone's secret hiding place or he could get so lost that home would never find him; paths carved by fighting; stagnant legs that mold into ashes. But neither one so certain as the heart that beat in patient rhythm inside his chest.

Ziki saw his role in the fight, war, a sword and a shield that continued to exist; this was his turn to count to ten and be counted—he loved this ancient land.

For Ziki, his future was entwined with this land. He would take things as they came; he knew his fate already… He had known it since he was a child and this day it had become real. This day he understood. It was to serve, stand up proud,—not die. He was just too innocent and young to fathom what death and killing meant for those who lived.

His mind seemed heavy on his shoulders, but tonight was not the time for such thoughts. Soon enough the weight would press and then, there would be some understanding. Until then, he tried to rally.

He looked around to see where his friends had scattered on the beach, when the sun had set in the west; he had stayed behind to build the fire. They had not walked far away, he could hear their sounds, but as he peered into the faded sky, they seemed like nothing more than shadows on the horizon. There were eight of his closest friends, most of whom he had known since grade school, Avi and Iosi were there, and Davidoff. They looked small next to the sky that blanketed them, but they all looked so vibrant.

Ziki straightened his legs that had cramped from being crooked for too long and heard the cracking of his joints. I'm getting old, he thought and smiled. In the pre-military the doctor had told him that he was "good to go."

A familiar voice shook him from his thoughts. It was Eli, his new friend that had moved to his school a time ago. Ziki's circle had long friendships, but Eli had found his way into Ziki's group. He was laid back and funny.

"Wake up, Ziki. What, you see naked girls on the back of your eyelids? "

"No. Just remembering last night with your mom. She does this thing with her tongue that just…" Ziki smiled at his joke. It was always good to get Eli at his own game.

"That is just wrong, big man," Eli laughed his jumpy laugh that seemed to scrape the roof of his mouth and never fall into his gut. "Listen, while you were dreaming about getting off with Hanna, we all decided that we needed to get this show started." He pulled out a white, unevenly plump joint from his buttoned pocket. "Figured you would need to cool down after the news today." Eli patted him on the back and stood up. His hands searched for matches. When he found them, he lit the rolled hash and inhaled deeply. He exhaled, sighed in satisfaction, and passed it to Ziki. Ziki rose laboriously and said, " No thanks—I'll have a beer."

"This is much better," Eli said, coughing lightly at the smoke enveloping his throat. "I hope one of the girls will give me a nice goodbye gift before I go in to basic."

"Not these girls, Eli, these are our friends. Go to the waterfront—find a hooker."

Hanna could make Ziki a boy again just by her presence. In all of Ziki's bolstering of manhood, Hanna knew him just as Ziki. He knew that Hanna was a virgin. They had been friends since they were little. She had blossomed into a dark-haired, olive skinned beauty with a voice that covered him in silk each time she said his name. He did not know what the feeling was, but he had liked her since third grade, when she had kicked '*Antiochus*' the bully in the shins after he'd made a joke about her. Hanna was not to be messed with and Ziki liked that too about her. Among all of the mess of the world, there was this one girl fighting for herself; she wanted to be a pilot. Tonight he knew that he wanted to be with her.

Ziki's thoughts had frozen him, wrapped him in thoughts of what's to come, excitement and the vast unknown. He knew that he was leaving for basic training camp right after graduation. Since he first held the notice in his hand, he had been consumed in thought. The notice, smelling of fresh paper and stale glue, said that everything he knew would change. Everything was always changing, but always within something he could understand... Not today. Today was the beginning of the countdown.

Tonight he was with his friends, Avi, Iosi, Davidoff...No one wants to die.

"Want" was such a trite word to express killing or dying...

# Chapter 4

**Negev Desert**

**Two strokes of good luck and two strokes of bad marked Ziki's last day as a free man.** **Stroke**: the driver for General David Elazar yelled to him across the dusty way. "Still want that ride to Nahal Oz?"

"Me?"

"You're headed for basic aren't you?" the driver asked.

"Yes, sir."

"Naw. Call the General 'Sir.' You just call me Danny."

"Ride with 'Daado'?" Ziki replied. He had told everyone who would listen that he was going to Nahal Oz—he wanted a night on the Kibbutz before his three months of basic training—but he hadn't expected to ride with the one General that every Israeli knew by name and reputation, nicknamed 'Daado.'

The driver looked Ziki up and down. He raised his eyebrows. "You might make it through alive okay." He motioned for Ziki to get in.

"I've a schedule to keep! Get your gear and get in or get on with it."

"Yes! Yes, sir. Thank you!" He scrambled into the oversized six-wheel drive Comandka jeep, his small pack of belongings tossed into the far back.

A jerk and a crunch of gears and the large jeep jolted off raising a tail of dust behind it. Ziki grabbed the brim of his hat, flattening it to his head against the gust of wind.

Eighteen years old and just out of high school, Ziki climbed into the jeep with a grin from ear to ear.

The jeep squealed to a stop for the General to climb in. He was older than Ziki would have thought—or he'd aged poorly in the last years. He wore no markings to tell of his rank or insignia. His eyes looked tired, his mouth was grim.

The driver and Ziki jumped out and saluted less as a matter of propriety than as an indicator of their respect, and as the General settled in, driver and Ziki returned to their seats. A jerk and a crunch and they veered away.

Ziki had fifty questions if not more for the General. Had he really met Daado on the first day?

Had Daado really started off as a private, just like Ziki?

Was it true that early in his career he'd routed out a nest of *mehablim* in Jerusalem?

Had he really defeated the Syrian T62 tank armada on the Golan combined with the Iraqis and Jordanian brigades? And now commander of the Northern IDF Armies.

But though Ziki turned in his seat to smile at the General, he felt the words dying on his tongue. He was a man now—not an eager little boy who gushed over personal and national heroes.

"Sir, a question, sir!" Danny called, watching the General with the corner of his eyes as he drove. He jerked the wheel to avoid a goat that had strayed from its fold on the country road. "My brother was on the Eilat. I'd like to know."

Ziki had heard. The whole country was buzzing: the Egyptians fired a new previously unknown Soviet missiles at an Israeli naval destroyer. There were many losses; officials were still counting and the casualty number was rising.

"When I know, you will know," was the General's only response.

After that, no one spoke on the otherwise bumpy and dusty drive.

**Stroke: The bleached hills near kibbutz Yad Mordechai** overlooking Gaza rolled and pitched and the road twisted through them. The sky was wide and open, a pale blue with a high glaze of cloud. They saw the dark vein of smoke rising to the sky long before they came upon the scene that awaited.

Ziki sat back in his seat, silently aware of the keen awareness of the other men as they approached. He saw the scorched tractor, its nose blasted black, and the tire that wobbled on its pivot as it still spun. He saw the drawn faces of the people who had gathered and heard the wail of the widow and her daughter, as they bent over a body. A funeral.

Ziki had seen the work of *mehablim*, terrorists before, but somehow, this time, the day before he entered the military and sharing Daado's jeep, it was all very different. A fist had formed in his gut, but he could not at first name what made it draw tighter.

He was not afraid…. He was not disgusted…. He only felt strangely simultaneously cold and hot…Anger.

He could taste salt and dust and smell the sharp stink of burnt oil and flesh. There was grit in his eye as they lurched to a stop near the small clan that milled about the body. They moved with intention, setting what could be set to rights. The body laid on the ground, covered with a plain white cotton cloth. He climbed out with the driver and General, and followed behind them as the mourners recognized Daado and pushed to his side.

Daado strode to the side of the widow and took her hands. "Shalom! My heart goes out to you for your loss."

"It must end, Daado!" the daughter said. Ziki thought her pride and defiance beautiful.

Daado took her hands and laid a hand on her brow. "—While I live, it will."

"We are farmers—you are Daado—can the IDF not protect us?" shouted a man.

"Will the border ever be secure?" another voice cried—this one belonging to a heavyset woman in an apron.

"When will the terrorists be stopped?" called another man.

"You do not know what we face—here by ourselves." The daughter of the dead man raised her chin and surveyed the General with a mixture of anger, grief, and defiance. "At night, our children have to sleep in the bomb-shelter. Is that a way to raise my children? And what will I tell them—their grandfather is dead, killed in his own field!"

The widow began to cry once more. She gripped the skirts of her daughter.

"I am moving to the city—I am done here!" shouted one of the men who had spoken earlier. "I am a mechanic—I can earn good wages in Tel Aviv and not worry that I cannot walk freely to the market."

A mumbling rose from the people. Agreement and dissent.

General David Elazar raised himself to his full height.

"Batya, I do not doubt you think of leaving. I know—I know, but you have to stay even when death is close to home." He paused…"I will tell you this. If people like you leave, if you take your family to the city and leave Yad Mordechai behind, we may as well disband the IDF. You see? Our enemies want you to tuck tail between your legs. They want to drive you out with fear and death. The land that we have worked so hard to hold, the land we have fought for, you have fought for—"

"We don't want speeches, Daado."

The General's voice hardened. "And that is what I too want. So believe me. We will make the terrorists pay. In Syria they will pay. In Lebanon they will pay. In Jordan, Hamas, El Fattah and the Islamic Jihad. Those who harbor terrorists will pay as you have paid. We are destroying their bases. We have sought them out and killed those who raised a hand against us. We won't stop until we have taken care of every last gang of murderers. This is my job and my pledge to you. We will have peace."

"Words—you are all talk—

"Is it true that the Gulf oil Arabs are rewarding the families of the *Shahids,* suicide bombers with twenty-five thousand American Dollars?"

"Yes, I'm afraid that's true." Then as if talking to himself Daado said in a soft voice, "*We will have peace when Arab mothers love their children more than they hate us.*"

"Yes!" he agreed. "Be strong. You must be strong! We are privileged and destined to live here; and for our enemies, I promise you, we will make enmity unbearable for them. That I swear to you. You are the strength… You must live here and endure."

Ziki found himself mesmerized and noted that others had fallen under the General's spell, as well. A few of the kibbutznicks wiped their eyes; others simply let tears gather and fall or be brushed away.

Ziki had rarely felt so proud to belong here, to be a part of building this land, to pioneer into history, to just be a part of this thing that was bigger than any one man or woman, a great ideal in this new and ancient land.

The crowd gathered about Daado, like a skirt, asking questions about the army, making it better, about the possibility of more patrols and alarm systems. There were questions as well about government subsidies which were always in arrears. The people in the cities did not know the difficulties of those who lived on the Israeli frontier. Bureaucrats dallied and dithered. Monies promised were slow in coming.

The General did his best to reassure them, but finally was led by a kibbutznick who took pity on his dusty path. Given a drink of cool water, the General raised it. He drained the glass and returned it into an open hand.

"Shalom," he said.

He strode to the jeep and his driver and Ziki followed.

They climbed in and sped away.

Danny stole glances at the General as he gunned the engine and swerved along the road. "A question, Sir."

"Ask it."

"Did you mean what you said to those farmers?"

"Every word." The general rested back in his seat. "We fight to exist. We will beat them back until they know that we will not die quietly. When there is peace it will be because we have shown them that we will not go anywhere."

Then his face hardened, his back straightened in his seat of the jeep; his jaw clenched tight, as he said in a low voice that would throw fear into most men, "Our people will never go quietly again….Never again."

**The next stroke: Up ahead in the distance a single soldier stood on the dirt road with thumb raised.**

It was a foolish thing to do this close to the Gaza border and against regulations. The sun was setting and the road swerved closer to the border than most men would stray alone in bright daylight. As they neared, they were dismayed to see it was not a man, but a girl, with her thumb raised. Though her cheeks were round with the remnants of baby fat, her uniform bagged. Her backpack was filled to bulging. An Uzi machine gun hung from her shoulder.

The General tapped his driver on the shoulder. "Stop and get her."

"Yes, Sir."

The wheels screeched throwing a cloud of dust around them. She ran to the Comandka and launched herself into the back with Ziki.

"Thanks for stopping. My boyfriend lives on that Kibbutz. She pointed… We had a fight."

"What is wrong with you?" Ziki said, his mouth close to her ear. They reared back as the jeep peeled away. "You could be brought up on charges."

The General looked her up and down from over his shoulder.

"Oh, yes," she replied, "and Daado himself is said to be coming this way. I should hide inside like a good girl."

"You must be talking of General Moshe Dayan," Daado himself said. His mouth was moved with a peculiar smile.

"I've heard he's a sex fiend. All officers are sex fiends. The more brass and the higher the rank, the worse they are."

"You're not afraid of terrorists, here near the border?"

"They're breaking through the borders at night. This road is not safe," Ziki told her.

Her hair smelled nice. Like sweat and perfume.

She met his eyes and smiled. "They're not going to influence when and where I go."

"That's right," the General said. "We will not live in fear."

"We just need to bloody their noses more often."

The General smiled and watched the road ahead.

No charges would be raised against this girl, Ziki knew.

She moved against him, settling her back into the seat and her side against his. She tucked her gun between her legs.

"Where are you going?"

"All the way to Nahal Oz," he replied.

"Wake me when we get there."

When she began to snore without a care, the General turned back to look at her once more.

Her head lolled and bounced on Ziki's shoulder with every bump in the road.

The General smiled.

**The final stroke: When they arrived at the kibbutz, t**he girl took her things and followed the General. Ziki watched her disappear with a strange sense of loss.

Bad luck all around….

Tomorrow he would take the bus to Tell Hashomer and spend three months in basic training. A little comfort would have made his last night as a civilian just a little less dark.

# Chapter 5

**His rear end was sore and his throat was dry with dust as they reached the base.** Flat and green-gray, the buildings were squat, with dark doorways and metal roves. The army must have made purposefully ugly the pale green paint that lathed the barracks, out buildings and offices of Tell Hashomer. No one in the real world would buy it. No one in the real world would find the color welcoming.

"Off the bus, Tel Aviv playboys!" The drill instructors were waiting the second the bus screeched to a halt. "From here on out you run. You understand? You don't walk, you only run!"

Ziki joined the line of hustling bodies. "Line up—run!"

He ran with the others from one pale-green room to the next pale-green room. The drill instructors yelled like hyenas if anyone slowed or thought of slowing. Even in place, in line, they ran, lifting their knees, their feet falling time and again in the same places.

First the uniforms. None of them fit. Too small. Too big. They couldn't plan it to be more awkward or taxing. The supply sergeant behind the desk would ask their size and hand them something else.

Then bedding. Dog tags. Identification records.

To the nurse for blood tests, at least she was pretty.

Running, running. Now holding a mountain of gear, none of which fit, they ran and sweated and wiped sweat from their eyes and slung the packs given to them on their backs and ran.

"What a disgrace—you worms! How will you make soldiers when you cannot even get the right size uniforms?"

Ziki was happy to be thin and in shape. The drill instructors were harassing the chubby guys.

"Put your gear on the ground. No—in a straight row. A straight row, I said! Get yourselves over there, girls. You're going to get your first proper IDF haircut. We're gone to try real hard to make men out of you."

Ziki thought of his beloved '*blorit*'—longish hair had become popular in Tel Aviv. The barbers only looked eager to inflict pain with their electric clippers, standing in the middle of piles of hair from the previous load of poor bastards.

"If one of them moves," the drill instructor shouted, "scalp them."

One by one the men fled the chairs, their heads shorn to stubble. They felt the roughness of their scalps and thrust on their hats as they stood in the sun. As soon as they were done, the drill instructor had them once more.

"Make a line! One behind the other!  Do not speak!  Did I give you permission to speak?"

Ziki stood where he had been appointed to stand. He tried to be still to avoid drawing attention to himself. He thought that might be the trick to survival for the next few weeks—avoiding any undue attention.

The big man who had driven them from task to task now stood before them, his hands behind his back and his feet planted. His uniform was perfectly fitted and pressed to sharp creases.

"I am Sergeant Major Kinsky. I am your instructor. These two gentlemen beside me are your drill instructors. This is Corporal Levi and this is Corporal Blum. You will address us as 'Sir' here at Tel Hashomer. When we speak to you, the first thing you will say is 'Sir.' You will not speak until you are spoken to, and then all I want to hear come from your lips is 'Sir, yes, Sir.' Do you Dizengoff, Tel Aviv hooligans understand that?"

Out of time and mumbled "Sir, yes, Sir," rose from the men.

The Sergent Major cocked his head. "I do not hear you!"

Again, the answer arose, slightly louder, but not in chorus.

"Say it like you got something between your legs, not chicken eggs! Let me hear you!"

"Sir, yes, Sir!"

The Sergeant froze. He looked the men over one by one. He spat twice—two big wads—and turned to his assistants shaking his head.

"There seems to be some mistake. We can't make soldiers out of this load of shit. This time they sent us a hopeless load of shit."

He stalked down the first line of men, observing them from a slitted, keen eye. "You little inferior lazy parasites. You little pieces of Tel Aviv dirt. Did you get that, girls?"

Nothing.

The sergeant major stopped and raised his head. "Did you get that, girls!"

"Sir, yes Sir."

One of the men whistled as if at a pretty girl on the street.

The recruits burst into laughter.

Sergeant Major Kinsky laughed sarcastically. "Ha. Ha. Ha." He measured his steps and walked slowly down the line of recruits, eye-to-eye. So close, Ziki knew the men in the first line could smell his breath.

"Who whistled?" the Sergeant Major asked.

When no one answered his eyes narrowed and he moved between the first and second rows of men. "You had the balls to whistle, have the balls to step forward."

Silence. And then Levi, a red headed *gingi* with kinky red hair and freckles, who looked like a kid stepped forward. "I did, Sir."

"What's your name, private?"

"Levi, Sir."

"Private Levi, you were told to say 'Sir' before you say anything else."

"Sir, I whistled at you, Sir."

"You whistled at me, do you like manly men like me, Private Levi?"

"Sir, no Sir."

"As you have *gingi* red curly hair, tell me; is it true that red headed women have the finest hair of all?

"Sir, I don't know, Sir"

"Well, I like your truthfulness Private Levi. But I have your number. I know who you are and I will not forget you. Have you ever cleaned a field toilet, Private Levi?"

"Sir, no Sir."

"Well you will become an expert: you'll be first in line this week, for a whole week, to clean the latrines."

The Sergeant stepped back and placed his hands on his hips. "When you worms leave this place, if you live through my training, you will become an awesome soldier; remember more sweat now, less blood later, your own that is.

"You will be soldiers. But until that day, you are less than human. You are less than nothing. You are the lowest form of life on this planet…"he paused and stared at them….

"Your mothers are not here and they cannot help or protect you. I will be your master and your torturer. You will sweat for me. You will bleed for me…. Do you ladies understand?"

"Sir, yes, Sir."

"All right. You worms have fifteen minutes to eat. Go through the line, gobble your food and get back here with your gear, you got that?"

"Sir, yes, Sir."

At the dining hall the drill instructor and his assistants stood over any man who had an extra pound on him and badgered him over every bite he took.

"You fat piece of shit. Do you think you'll make a soldier? You're a fat ass. Did your mother feed you all that chicken fat?"

Ziki ate as fast as he could and drank as much water as he could hold.

They made him and the others run the periphery of the camp with all of their gear held in front of them. There were pushups and sit-ups. The instructors yelled and cursed at them without stop until finally as the sun was setting they were confined to the barracks.

"One hell of a first day," Ziki's bunkmate breathed out as they lay down.

Some of the men were already asleep, stinking with the sweat of the day.

Ziki agreed with the man, whose rear end made that mattress sag above him, but as he fell asleep he realized he had forgotten to ask the man's name.

**4:30 AM. The slap of blaring light disturbed his dreams.** He rolled deeper into his pillow at the echoing boom of the drill instructor. As if from a distance he heard men shuffling and the booming of the instructors' voices again.

"Boker Tov! Good morning! Today, ladies, we will try again to make men of you."

Ziki groaned and thrust his head deeper into his pillow; the next thing he knew, the world swam off kilter, and the bunk was shifting out from under him, he was sliding, the bunk was falling, and—thud! He heard the impact of the floor in his hip and shoulder bones a moment before he heard the bunk crash to the cement. A second later the dull ache of impact swarmed from his hip and arm into his spine.

"Private Barak! Tonight you will assist Private Levi in the latrines; you will also become an expert in that field....Tomorrow you will awake and stand at attention with the other recruits; Levi has the latrines to himself for the rest of the week."

He turned away. "Ten minutes...." They scarfed breakfast and were told to run with the lump of cold eggs and bread in their stomachs. The sun was up and the day promised heat. They trudged along, their boots raising dust that clung to their sweat sheened skin. It pricked their throats closed.

Ziki was glad to be skinny, as once again, the drill instructors hovered like wolves at the heels of the guys who lagged behind. Some were flabby, but one—a kid named Nathan Zurinski—was outright fat. Zurinski huffed to another slowpoke, the only guy he was able to keep up with, that he had spent the last two years at the university until he couldn't put off his required service any longer. He was older than the others, Zurinski complained, he shouldn't be expected to keep up. When he ran his belly and thighs rolled. His face was bright red and he breathed as loud as a saw on wet wood.

The Sergeant barked into his ear. "You fat pig. Your tits sag down to your knees. You better haul your fat ass faster. Move, private. I said move, your fat ass."

Zurinski's steps became labored and his knees weakened. It was not long before he fell. Dust caked into his mouth and gravel bloodied his chin.

"Stand at attention, maggots," the sergeant called.

The ragged mess of panting men came to a grateful halt. Many bent over their knees and tried to catch their breaths before dragging their bodies upright with backs rigid and arms clamped to sides.

Zurinski lumbered to his feet, but fell almost immediately. His head rocked in the grit of the road and his eyes flickered white in their sockets. Heat sickness and overexertion turned him green.

Sergeant Kinsky stood in front of Zurinski and glowered over him. "I said get up, lard ass. At attention."

Zurinski propped himself on all fours and then pushed onto his feet. Slowly, he stood and righted himself, wobbling slightly in place, but his arms clapped firmly to his sides. A dark look flashed in his eyes before he could hide it.

"You don't like me, do you private?" Kinsky stepped toe to toe with the fat kid.

"Sir, no, Sir."

"No, you don't like me or no, I'm mistaken in thinking so, private?"

Zurinski considered his options quickly but carefully. "Sir, I meant that you were mistaken sir."

Kinsky's lips were a bare millimeter from Zurinski's cheek. "Then you're not only a lard ass, but you're a liar too. A fat fuck with chicken eggs, not balls."

Zurinski hadn't the self-control to keep his eyes free of emotion.

"Would you like to take a swing at me, private?" Kinsky asked.

"Sir, no Sir."

"Be honest fat ass. You'd like to pound one of your fat fists into my gut, wouldn't you?"

"Sir, yes, Sir."

Kinksy took half a step back. "Do it. You have my permission. I'll hold still and you hit me as hard as you can right here, he pointed his index finger at his stomach—in the gut."

An inaudible dismay moved through the men, registering most visibly on Zurinski's round cheeks and shiny pink lips. Still he hesitated, weighing his choices.

"What are you waiting for?" Kinsky taunted.

"Hit him, Nathan, and maybe we can go home," one of the new guys behind Ziki said.

"Hit him. Hit him," came other encouragements.

Ziki knew the fat kid was a goner either way; regardless of whether he showed himself gutless or stupidly-brave, his ass belonged to the Sergeant.

His left leg moved back and he twisted into the slug, aiming for the Sergeant's gut. The hit never struck. The Sergeant stepped into the punch to disarm the thrust and with a quick jab into the lower abdomen, folded the private neatly in half. The hit made an audible thump followed by a guttural burst of noise from the doubled man. Zurinski kept himself from falling on his face by throwing one hand in front of him, the other clamped to his belly as he sank to his knees.

He promptly vomited all over his trousers and the Sergeant's boots.

Ziki knew that couldn't be good.

The Sergeant looked down on the private. Contempt quirked the edge of his mouth upward. "Lard ass, you are too fat to bend over your belly and clean this shit from my boots. On your feet."

The private pulled himself up. He wiped a slick of vomit from his lower lip, but he made an attempt of another swing at the Sergeant, a mistake.

The Sergeant took him down.

Private Lard Ass wallowed in the dust.

"On your feet, fat ass."

This time Zurinski did not get up.

The Sergeant wiped his boots on Zurinski's chest. "You, will learn to run. You are a fat pig and you are going to become a non-fat pig. We will run you every morning, every afternoon, and every evening. We are going to make evolutionary history—we will make a man out of you. A man out of a pig! Do you understand me, fat boy?"

Zurinski raised his head and answered, but no one heard his whisper.

"I can't hear you."

"Sir, yes, Sir."

"On your feet, Pig Boy Fat Ass."

Zurinski climbed up.

The Sergeant eyed him a moment longer and then motioned to the group. "What are you looking at? Move out."

**The desert didn't take long to work on them.** The heat made their legs rubbery, but they ran as they were ordered. Many tripped and fell, but scrambled up before Kinsky and his jackals could snap at them. They ran over the hills and through the out buildings of the base, over the same hills again and through the same out buildings—nowhere near the women's barracks, no, nor near the officer's quarters, nor the eating hall. They did, however, run close enough to the chicken farm, called the Lull, on the hill to see the pile of chicken carcasses, freshly slaughtered, but not yet plucked. A pool of blood and chicken heads lay near the chopping block. A stink rose from the Lull and blood soaked dappled feathers.

Those men, who were not previously nauseous from the sun and the running, now joined those who had held their stomachs and spat bile from their mouths on the open road. Ziki, too, felt his stomach roll as if with too much grease. A moment before he'd been starving for lunch, but now he hoped there would be vegetables and cheese to fill him—he might never eat chicken again.

The instructors were still shouting and sniping as they stumbled to the open lot in front of their barracks.

A shower. A tall cool glass of water. A rest in the shade. Ziki panted and was grateful that for him it had not been as hard as for others.

"Fall in," Kinsky shouted and the men nearly fell into their places, coddling aching feet and scraped elbows and smarting backs. Others had puked or spat on themselves as they ran. Some had fallen and dirt marred the knees of their trousers. A few could scarcely hold themselves up right.

"I have never seen such a sorry lot of pussies," Kinsky growled. "Look at you the lot of you. You disgrace the IDF uniform. You are mama's boys. Little Coca Cola drinking Tel-Aviv play boys." As he spoke he stalked the length of the line, eyeing uniforms, plucking at soiled spots and loose shirttails or untied bootlaces.

The first man he came to that had a spot of vomit on his uniform was not Zurinski, but another soft-fleshed private. "Get that uniform off."

Kinsky turned on the lot of them. "All of you get those uniforms off. I want to see if they've sent me pussies or if you've hard balls in there between your legs. Move. Move. Move."

And the squadron moved—shirking out of sweat stained t-shirts and fumbling with their waistbands. They stood, baffled like sheep, hands over their crotches, not looking at one another. Kinsky stormed down the line, ordering the shy men to move their hands, examining with a vicious eye.

There was strength in numbers, Ziki had heard, but he could not remember ever feeling so unbelievably vulnerable. It was as if the Sergeant might pull a pair of scissors from his pocket and make short work of the men who felt short. He felt his parts seeking the solace of his body cavity, hiding from the scrutiny.

Kinsky stopped beside Zurinski. "You must be cold, private Fat Ass."

No one met anyone else's eyes.

"Or a woman. Which is it?"

Kinsky bent down and looked between Zurinski's legs. "The fat boy has balls under there. Not much to work with, but balls all the same. This sorry sack of shit will make a soldier if we work hard. And we will keep at you. You will have to lose all that weight. You know it. . . they know it. . . your Mama should have told you. In six weeks you will look like a soldier. I'm going to help you. It's going to get done. You are going to do it with me. Say 'yes' son."

"Sir, yes, Sir."

Kinsky moved away from Zurinski. "And that goes for the rest of you sad sacks, as well. Do you get me, ladies?"

"Sir, yes Sir!"

**Basic training made hell seem like heaven**. At 4:30 each day they were roused for a day of humiliation, brute exercise, and details. Work, work, work, until your muscles burned, then work your detail, practice arms, knives, hand to hand combat training, *Krav Maga* until dusk.

Bleach and scrub the toilets. Dish duty. Fold and align and make the corners just so. Polish boots. Clean rifles. Launder linen. Starch shirts and pants. March in the desert under a scorching sun on rationed one cup of water with cracked parched lips and shave clean out of that same ration. And when you thought you were finished and could not endure another hill carrying full battle gear, another hill would show itself like a mirage. All one could do is put one foot in front of the other without thinking any longer and just muster what strength was left to keep going, and going and going. Follow orders.

Dig a hole only to fill it again.

March through desert for six days with that cup of water to wet blistered lips.

Fifty sit-ups for falling in one minute late.

Fifty push-ups for a smile cracked at the wrong moment.

**Ziki's hands were cracked and his finger tips raw.** His mind was numbed from endless lectures on ethical conduct, how to avoid venereal disease from city hookers, first aid, morphine injections, the evils of Stalinism, Leninism, Marxism, and Communism. He had grown to hate the Sergeant during the *Krav Maga*, the hand to hand combat training where the Sergeant would set the men up only to bloody their noses with his bare hands and leave them sprawled on their backs.

Ziki hated the edge of his voice that drove into his head as loud as the live rounds on the shooting range. He hated the Sergeant as he crawled on his belly beneath barbed wire while live rounds were shot over his head. If he lifted his head, one neat red spot would appear on the crown of his helmet, and inside his helmet his brains would be made soupy by the tumbling bullet. The Sergeant reminded them that two percent was a "permissible loss." Worms could and would be replaced. It was the sergeant's face Ziki saw as he squeezed the trigger of his rifle and tagged a bull's-eye or when he cut a paper target to ribbons with his machine gun. He hoped against his better judgment that an accident might happen as they practiced night fire. Bullets strayed. In the dark it was impossible to really see or to see who had turned just inches the wrong direction. Moving shapes were moving shapes in the dark. The sergeant's constant motto—"The more you sweat now, the less blood later."

By the fifth week, Ziki's hatred had died from an ever present rushing of hot blood in his temples to a slow and chilly patience. But then something happened.

Ziki saw Zurinski in the shower one morning.

Private Fat Ass was far more trim and muscles bulged under the loose remnants of flab and sagging skin. The college boy had abs. Ziki glanced around the room.

All of the men . . . were more lean. More like men.

Funny he had not thought before . . . what a bunch of boys they had appeared, arriving from Tel Aviv.

**Graduation day. Polished boots and pressed uniforms.** Rifles cleaned and oiled. Ziki looked tanned, lean, and strong. He marched in step with his rifle at "port-arm," tall and proud. Zurinski carried the platoon's flag. They were tight, worked in unison.

Ziki didn't hear a word the General said as he sent them off with an inspirational speech. He barely heard Blum and Levine call roll, rather he answered out of habit.

Or instinct.

It was not so much that he had ceased to think, but rather, that the constant hum and press of worries and chatter in his brain had died.

Later Sergeant Major Kinsky approached the platoon, the list they had all been waiting for clasped in his hand. He began to read.

"Avi: Army paratroopers Golani."

They had not been given leave to pat or cheer, yet the thrill of final assignments ran through the crowd like electricity. Ziki smiled for Avi. A damn good man.

"Shmulik: Field Engineers—mine sweepers, fourth division."

Not great, but a good job, without as many casualties as most people would think.

"Davidoff: Army paratroopers, special forces, Golani."

Ahhh. . . so Avi and Davidoff would be buying each other beer and hookers for the next few years. Ziki hoped he would join them.

"Uri: Armored Division. Ze'evi: Army Special Forces Golani."

Very good placements. Yes. Yes.

"Manny: Special forces Givati."

Damn. Moshe and Ze'evi would argue over red heads.

"Ziki Barak. . ." The Sergeant read the list again, not so much as if he did not believe what he read, but rather, as if looking for some explanation. "Special Forces, additional training required following two weeks of patrol."

Ziki frowned. "Permission to speak, Sir! Where to, Sir?"

"Speak."

"Where to, Sir?"

"You have asked that already, Barak."

"My apologies, Sir."

"When the army is ready to tell you where you will be going, then you will know. May I continue, Barak?"

"Yes Sir."

"Iosi: Nahal. Report to kibutz Nahal Oz. Zurinski: Engineering—mine sweepers."

They couldn't complain.

The Sergeant lowered his list and nodded. "At ease, men."

The platoon relaxed.

Many smiled at their placements. One or two did not smile.

Ziki wasn't sure what direction his face should take.

But the Sergeant was not done with them just yet.

He looked over them and a trace of pride crept into his gaze.

He placed his hands behind his back. "Congratulations, men. Today you are no longer shit eating worms. Today you are soldiers of the Israeli Defense Forces. Until you die you will now be soldiers. Honor those that gave their lives before you. Honor your parents. Honor your country. Your land. Live with honor. Today you are men and you are IDF soldiers…. Good luck to each of you men."

## Chapter 6

**Mossad's Special Forces training camp**

**Outside of Beersheba... the desert, in the Negev, was a desolate hellhole.** They said they would teach him everything that he should need to know, they told him to forget everything he learned in basic. They trained him one-on-one now, his drill instructors as loud and as driven as Kinsky had been before only more intense. He learned to coexist with them. He kept his mouth shut.

He didn't expect anything any longer.

He belonged to the IDF.

He was tested and poked and prodded and watched and interviewed by men with clip boards and by men who never introduced themselves. Ziki could only think he had scored well on a test or two. He had always been quick to pick up new things. In Beersheba, he forgot what it meant to be tired and accepted exhaustion as his normal waking state.

He adapted. He forgot about life outside.

And then the order came.

"Patrol, Ziki Barack. Company Gimel."

"Yes, when?"

"Right now, Barak. Get your gear."

They told him no more.

# Chapter 7

**Patrol—**
**The first day—Gaza Strip**

**A transport helicopter took him deeper into the Negev Desert**.... The desert.... The desert. Hot and dry. At the ass end of the Gaza strip, hot and dry.... hot and dry, as his boots crunched gravel and raised a whiff of dust. Beth Shemesh... The desert was sure hot and dry.

He stopped at a brass plaque riveted to a stone at a road stop. Sweat collected above his eyebrows. He wiped it away and shaded his eyes.

". . . This site excavated to show the remains of a great city named for its king, Nebuchadnezzar. The city was destroyed in the 6th century B.C. Legend has it that the townspeople peered into the Ark of the Covenant and brought upon themselves *The wrath of God. . .*"

The heat was cooking Ziki's feet and brain and mouth and guts. Sweat trickled down his back and from under his arms.

**In the transport, close quarters**. The smell of men and sweat and gun oil. And dust. Always dust. Eight men on the road away from the heliport going into the Gaza Strip through ancient Ashkelon carried their helmets on their laps. Their guns rested between or against their thighs. Their knees swayed with the motion of the transport. A rutted road. Stones.

Ziki knew some of their names. Brolin—the Sergeant. Avner the tracker. Eli. He didn't know what they did. He thought they might be Southern Command Golanis, Special Forces—they had that look about them. Sharp eyes with that far away look of experience. Relaxed wrists.

Those other five . . . he didn't know . . . maybe Golanis, maybe the guys that go in first. The shortest one was trying to play off his anxiety as if he'd done it all before. The one that sat beside Ziki seemed . . . scouting, most likely—from his markings. The final two were new guys. Fresh faced, one of them, the other darkly tanned—small town kids, called up and come to learn the Special Forces way. They'd be all right.

Ziki didn't introduce himself, no one asked.

They were on their way to one of the most wretched pits of the world—the hell hole end of the Gaza Strip, the Palestinian refugee camp at Rafah-Khan Yunis, near the Philadelpi Strip at the Egyptian border and nearby Gaza City.

It would be hot and dry like the road, the buildings bleached, the sky bleached gray. . . damn he wanted a long drink of water. . . he wondered what his mother would make his father for dinner that evening—and realized that he had not thought of her or his father for a long, long time.

Then they were there and piling out of the transport into scattered cover, the Sergeant shouting at them to "move, move, and move—and for the love of Gawd, Joel, keep your head down and get out of sight like the others."

Ziki scanned the buildings, bombed out hovels, scrawled with graffiti.

*"All Jews and Christian Crusaders who enter here will die."*

He'd heard it described as a war zone by the men who'd been there previously. The descriptions were not lacking.

The patrol moved forward, wary and anxious.

Ziki's palm and fingertips began to sweat on the muzzle of his gun. He kept his line of sight moving, looking for the nose of a sniper rifle, his ears straining too for the telltale thunk and click of rounds loading. Avner stopped, his shoulders tense, and nodded at Ziki.

He whispered, "Head's up."

Ziki fumbled for his clips, sun heated, hot on his fingers.

Hand signals from the point man: Slow up; west man forward to the cover of a broken wall, center point to follow him, the others take cover as they could.

Ziki squatted in the shallow shade of rubble.

This was it. Just what drunks joked about and said over and over again— long stretches of boredom, punctuated by brief episodes of frenzy and fear.

The sweat on his spine had turned to ice water.

For a moment he closed his eyes and thought of his next leave. He would go home. Yes. Lobelia pots on the terrace and the breeze fresh from orange groves and Avi and Iosi and the cool, cool floor of his mother's kitchen. Ziki could smell the olive oil. Her bread baking. Tomatoes. His mouth watered. Water. A drink of cool, not cold, water. . .

The patrol moved slowly along deserted streets. The men hugged the walls behind them, spacing themselves ten meters apart. They skirted and dodged across dark doorways and blown-out windows, demolished rooftops.

Their gear swung in a rhythmic ringing.

The silence all around deepened in response to their noises. Boots on gravel. Gear. Breathing.

Quiet doorways, quiet windows, quiet road.

A flock of birds scattered.

Ziki's finger twitched, tightened on the trigger.

The backs of the others drew tight. They held their guns closer.

The others were pale.

They looked years younger than they had moments before.

"Hey, new guy…Yeah, you. Get up there!" The man behind Ziki gave him a shove. "Ten meters apart—if you step on a mine, I don't want to get it."

The rear guard slowed. "Point, you're paranoid. Nobody's here. They've pulled out."

"Keep moving," the other rear countered. "The sooner we're through the sooner we're home."

The 'point' man moved forward. His caution dissolved. He lowered his rifle. "There really doesn't seem to be anyone around."

A shot like a loud crack. A sniper rifle: maybe a Dragunov or just an AK.

Eli, second in line, doubled in a squat and fell. His left hip turned red and dark. Opened flesh. The rifle opened his hip right up—big bullet; it must be a Russian Dragunov.

Eli rolled to his belly. Blood in the dust.

He tried to crawl to cover in the shadows of the far walls.

A crack.

A dark line of blood jetted from the back of Eli's right thigh. A new flow of red, turning maroon so quickly.

"Fuck that," someone shouted.

Someone opened machine-gun fire.

Bullets raced around them. Ricochets. Little flowers of cement gravel flew toward the sky. Bricks chipped and shattered.

The point man fired the grenade launcher.

A wall in the distance burst and crumbled inward.

Ziki and others shouted and fired until over the roar he heard Brolin yell that there was nothing left to shoot at, they're gone.

Ziki lowered his gun.

He took his canteen from his belt and opened the cap.

He poured water on his face and into his mouth.

Eli was crawling face down in the dirt.

"Someone get over there—Chaim! Are you still the fucking medic, or what?"

"Yes, Sergeant."

Ziki drank his water until it was almost all gone.

Cool water in his belly.

The heat.

**Nobody was shooting back**. Maybe they had gotten him, the shooter.

Ziki didn't know.

What he did know was that it was barely dawn in Khan Yunis; he was not even an hour into his first day on patrol, just out of boot camp, and already there was blood.

The silence after a rally of gunfire was oddly thick. Dust swarmed and settled.

The alley and the air slowly stilled.

The men began to move.

Three of the men were loading the wounded Eli into the back of the first Comandka jeep when the radio crackled and Sergeant Brolin shouted to Ziki: "Barak! Let's go—you're coming with us!"

Always, it was shouting.

Ziki jumped into the vehicle, and had barely shut the door before they lurched down the pitted road and out of Khan Yunis. Steel reinforcement bars snaked jaggedly into the air from gaping, bombed-out walls. Those walls that still stood were pocked with bullet holes and mortar fire; the border with Egypt was right over there….

The early-morning sun glinted through the right hand window as they headed north. Ziki rubbed his eyes against the glare and leaned his head on his palm.

In the shade he could see—Eli's blood was on his boots.

"Sergeant," he called over the front seat, practically shouting himself now to be heard over the growl of the engine and the crunch of the tires, "Where are we going?"

" Kibutz Nahal Oz," said the sergeant, without turning his head.

Nahal Oz had peaches and oranges, but was known for its avocados. Ziki knew it better from the two summers he'd volunteered there during harvest time as a boy.

He and Iosi had kissed twin sisters after a double date—Ziki's first date—under the orange trees… Good memories. Ziki had stayed his last night before boot camp there—one last taste before those years slipped away.

But why were they going there? Not to eat peaches.

Ziki looked at the blood on his boots.

"Sir," he called over the front seat, "trouble, Sir?"

"You know as much as I do, Barak."

Ziki rested his head and stared out the window. The transport was warm and rocked him—but he did not sleep. The kibbutz appeared in the distance. Ziki hadn't realized how close they were.

Springing like an oasis just outside the southern end of the Gaza Strip, at this time held by Egypt, next week—who knew? Nahal Oz rose lush and verdant from the ground in an area where the horizon was otherwise brown and rocky for 360 degrees. Cultivated and cared for, Nahal Oz was a nexus of life.

They drew closer to a windbreak of eucalyptus trees.

It was early still, but kibbutznicks were early risers. They worked in the cool of early day. Yet, the orchards and groves were empty. Farm machinery stood mutely in the ploughed fields on either side of the road.

"What the hell?" the driver breathed.

"Slow up, soldier," the Sergeant said to the driver.

The Comandka slowed to a crawl.

Ziki craned his neck to see what had made them fall silent.

A dark mass in the road. Not a stone. Not an enormous bag of refuse—his eyes worked to focus and his mind to make some sense of it.

A chestnut stallion lay dead in an immense pool of blood in the ploughed field directly in front of them. The saddle had twisted onto the horse's side from its fall. Its leather was coated with a thick layer of dust and mud.

The Comandka lurched to a halt.

Slowly, the men got out, Ziki last.

"A damn waste," the Sergeant ground out. His eyes had turned hard.

Ziki approached the horse, his Uzi gripped with fists, the nose pointed at the ground.

A bullet had ripped the horse's round brown jaw and another had churned up a mess of blood and hair on the animal's neck that lay twisted all wrong. The horse's forelegs had been hacked off at the knee and lay in a pile near its groin. Flies crowded at the wounds and the horse's mouth and nose.

Ziki turned away, his jaw set tight against the queasy flow of saliva in his mouth. Who would do such a thing?

"Shit!" called one of the men—the curly-haired private. "Sergeant!" The young man stood beside a short outcropping of rock. He squatted.

"Sergeant! I think it's the guard!"

Sergeant Brolin wheeled on one foot and lurched toward the scene. A moment of hesitation felt as if it bent time into an untenable length, and then the rush of wanting to help—wanting to—Ziki and the others followed in one clumsy mass.

"Alive?" the Sergeant's voice was harsh.

"—Dunno, sir—"

"—Call a medic!—"

"—I don't think it's—"

"—Medic!—"

"—possible, sir."

"Medic!"

Ziki's chest impacted the back of the man in front of him, an abrupt halt. The man pushed back, without anger, setting Ziki back on his feet.

It was a body.

What Ziki saw first were sandals, dusty feet, long toenails with white half-moons at the cuticle, worn jeans, ankles, the skin bronzed beneath. A brown shirt… Twisted spine… Arms splayed like branches… Hair. Blood. A young man sprawled—as he had fallen from the saddle—on the ground of the freshly plowed field. Dark black and crisp fabric around the spray of tears in the fabric... Bullet holes: one in the chest and two in the stomach. The face turned away.

The Sergeant squatted. "Cancel medic," he intoned.

Ziki stepped more closely, giving the man he'd run into more elbowroom, not able to look away.

The Sergeant turned the boy onto his back. The body's head did not turn on its neck. The arms, stiff with rigor mortis, remained crooked, the wrists bent and fingers pointing toward the earth. The Sergeant and others emitted noises of dismay and disgust.

Dried black blood was caked across the dead boy's temple and matted like mud in the thick shock of blond hair. Still-blue, surprisingly blue, eyeballs lay drying in the sun on his cheeks, suspended from their empty sockets by heavy blue veins.

Ziki cocked his head. There was something. . .

The hair. . . The boy's face . . . mouth. . .

It was Iosi.

Ziki turned and vomited.

He was on his knees in his own puke when he came to himself again, reawakened to a fresh wave of hurt in his guts that made his voice far too large in his own throat.

He whipped off his helmet and wrenched at the neck of his shirt. The sound of denial became bigger and bigger, forging its way out of him as a push of breath, and finally a mewl. His head was in the dirt; he curled over it, digging fingers into the acrid till beneath himself as if holding onto the earth might help him birth the weight of his voice.

Ziki struck away the hands that sought to assist him, struck them away as they tried to stop him from lifting Iosi into his arms and rocking him. Ziki growled and threw dirt at the others when they tried to stop him from pushing the eyes back into place, he kicked and swam with pain, hauling Iosi with him when the others stepped away and let him have his darkness.

"He was alive," Ziki howled. "They—they—they—he was alive."

"The bastards took his eyes out when he was alive," someone uttered.

He surveyed the faces of the men around him looking for more than understanding, looking for outrage, looking for an unholy fire that might spark and kindle his own and stamp out the numb cold that had taken his ability to stand and breathe…

Dumb cows, they stood staring: looking down, looking anywhere but at him. All but Sergeant Brolin, whose hard eyes met his with something akin to emotionless empathy. Brolin knew loss himself.

And knew enough not to tolerate it. "On your feet soldier."

Ziki shook his head. "Sir—"

The Sergeant took a step toward Ziki. "The others will see to him."

A second IDF Comandka had pulled up. The men piling out of it seemed very far away, seemed to be running toward them so slowly.

"I knew him, sir. He was my friend," Ziki said. His voice was animalistic. His tears had seared tracks under his eyes. His eyes scratched as if with sand.

"Ziki Barak—"

"Let me take him to his mother."

The Sergeant shook his head. "That is not our task today, soldier."

"Let me—"

Sergeant Brolin studied Ziki for three seconds. "Ziki Barak."

Ziki held his gaze in return coming to slow understanding.

"Get in the Comandka, soldier."

Someone lifted Iosi from him—Ziki was not sure who. He clung to Iosi's shoulders for a moment and then realized the uselessness of the gesture and let him go. Still, Ziki did not move. Iosi's mother should know… Avi should know.

He would have to tell them.

Brolin ordered the other men to the Comandka transport. They responded with an air of reluctance, but went quickly—perhaps glad to have been spared Ziki's loss.

Only the two men that Ziki had known previously hesitated long enough for Ziki to search their faces. Their eyes glinted with a light of the thousand-meter stare that had come to resemble the light in Brolin's. Ziki realized that he was still breathing in deep gulps. He licked his lips and swallowed a bitter mouthful of bile and saliva.

Was this how men were made?

Brolin bent over him. "On your feet soldier." His palm was warm and firm on Ziki's shoulder… "The school was attacked."

Ziki did not look up at the Sergeant. "Murderers," he hissed. Medics from another Commandka were tending Iosi—laying his body on a black body bag. Forcing the body's arms to release their askew rictus.

Brolin stood and strode toward the transport. "Avner, assist Barak into the driver's wheel," Brolin ordered. "He was not the only one to lose a friend today."

Ziki was helped to his feet. His senses were clearing. His boots and legs were firm beneath him and his gut was burning with acid, but no longer turning over. He shrugged off the hands that had assisted him and tramped through the gutted field to the transport. "Murderers," he muttered once more.

Iosi's face burned bright in his mind.

The door of the transport yawned at Ziki and he slid in, finding determination once more in his fingers and motions.

The newest recruits seldom drove, and Ziki's senses were razed; but no one commented that he drove as if only half awake or somewhere else.

Ziki stamped the Comandka to a stop at the end of the drive, the gate to the kindergarten. Through the gate they could see a sweeping green lawn and the schoolhouse. Ziki sat behind the wheel as Sergeant Brolin and the others climbed out. He squared his shoulders and climbed out, falling in behind. Someone handed him his helmet.

The tread of boots on stone and a faint wind struck Ziki as incredibly overpowering—he pushed them from his mind—control. Control… He was a soldier now.

Through the gate—

More blood….Dead children… Flaky and dark blood on clothing. Running red in the green grass.

"You always know it happens. . ." someone said near to him.

"Survivors?"

One man had simply stopped in his tracks.

". . . But you never think it really. . . "

"Spread out," were Brolin's orders.

"Medic! Here—now."

Ziki picked through the patchwork carnage. He blinked slowly, noting that his thoughts were congealing into action only because there was nothing left to do. His eyes yet burned with tears and his lips were cracked.

A boy's severed head lay on its side next to a twisted tricycle. A little girl lay a few feet on, her eyes wide and staring in her pale, pale face. Her right foot rested upright a few meters away... Such a little white tennis shoe.

Ziki looked more closely at her dark pink lips, her tiny teeth. He started when her eyes focused on him and she blinked.

"Mama—. . . " her lips moved without sound.

Ziki moved to her side and dropped to his knees beside her in the grass, laying his gun down beside her. The rifle was as long as she was tall.

"Mama-. . . "She mouthed again.

"Mama," he said back to her. He meant to pick her up, but his hands seemed far too big and her body all wrong.

She looked into his eyes and her brow drew tight as if she were wondering who he was. Her lips moved. There was no sound. Her lips were now white chalk over blue. Her tongue extended purple.

"It's okay," he whispered. "It's—. . . "

Her gaze went lax.

He sat back on his boot heels. So quickly? So quickly a little thing could go. . . He closed his eyes, but lurched up when he heard transports pull up the drive behind him. There might be others living.

Rising, he felt a warm rise of unbidden giddiness and was forced to suppress the maniacal smile that took savage hold of his lips. His body would betray him with laughter—not now! Laughter or a howl. He forced the crushing in his diaphragm to release.

He lifted his boots over other small bodies, careful, careful to place them in the grass, careful to balance before each next step. Some had died of bullet wounds, he could tell. One boy had a small, neat hole in the center of his forehead. The back of his head was gone.

**Ziki found himself next to Sergeant Brolin, who was talking to a girl Ziki's age**, one of the kindergarten teachers. Ziki had not met her but he recognized her from the last night he had spent on the kibbutz. Her hazel eyes were spider-webbed with thin red veins. Her left arm had been blown off at the elbow; Brolin had wrapped it in a tourniquet.

Ziki could barely make out what she was saying: "...three of them... they told the children to throw them—grenades—they told the children they were balls—the children didn't know."

"Who did this?" asked Brolin.

She looked up at him with morphine glazed eyes: "I...don't know... PLO....Islamic Jihad, El Fattah, their *Kafias*, head gear I think was from Salameh's faction.— *Mehablim*, terrorists,— Kalashnikovs...They went west towards Egypt... into the Sinai. . ."

Anything else she said was blocked from hearing by the roar of helicopter rotors overhead—medical aid from Beer-Sheba. Behind the IDF transports, three medical evacuation vehicles were spilling aide from their doors. In a frenzy of organized activity, IDF men were now everywhere Ziki looked.

Brolin assisted the teacher to the stretcher laid out for her by the medics.

"Barak, we're going after them."

"Who?" asked Ziki. He could think of nothing else to say.

The sergeant spat on the ground, a big wad. "The men who did this."

"Murderers," said Ziki.

"Same thing—terrorists," said Brolin.

The Sergeant paced to the Comandka, summoning his men as he went: "Ze'evi! Avner!" One by one, men peeled away from the children they had been tending—to be replaced by medics—and they fell into line behind Brolin. Ziki walked beside the sergeant.

"West. . . " Brolin muttered and wiped his jaw. "Avner!"

"Yes, sir." A third man stepped into pace beside Sergeant Brolin.

"Can you track them? The Egyptian border is less than one kilometer. We might—"

"Russian jeep and Vladivostok tires."

"We will," Brolin responded.

**Ziki shifted into first gear**, hearing the engine choke and wretch as he forced the transport into motion. Avner hung out the window to read the road and direct their course. Brolin stewed in menacing darkness between them. Ziki glanced at the dead horse and past it to where he had last seen Iosi as they passed the field. Iosi's body was already gone. He remembered he had read somewhere:

*"Even Satan has not devised retribution for the blood of a child."*

The tracks led through Khan Yunis. Brolin estimated that they'd take the southernmost road out of the camp—

"Keep your eyes open and your safeties off."

Ziki nodded and readied his gun. He had swung his Uzi to the side in favor of the Heckler & Koch 308 long range rifle IDF had issued to the patrol... Ziki had completed his marksmanship trials.

Ziki had hoped that all his targets might be paper, but he did not hope that now.

Remarkably, Khan Yunis could look worse than it had earlier that morning. . . Shadows disappeared behind doorways; windows were shuttered as the IDF vehicle approached.

Perhaps word of what had happened at Nahal Oz had spread and the residents knew that the squad of young men rolling slow and taunting through their streets were in a mood not to be messed with. Joshua, a big young man, manned the M-60 machine gun mounted on a bipod on the roof; he would fix anyone that looked threatening and dared not disappear with a glare ravenous for slaughter.

They passed through Khan Yunis without confrontation.

The Sinai Desert loomed craggy before them. This was not a desert of sand, where one might see for miles without interruption. Rather, the Sinai was a landscape of rolling and at time jagged hills, capped and punctuated with rocky outcroppings and scraggly trees. Trees meant shadows and shadows meant potential cover for snipers.

Avner picked up the trail outside of Khan Yunis past Rafah at the Philadelphy Strip as Brolin had predicted. "It's them," he said, pointing to the rocky road.

It was a scant few kilometers before they found the Russian Povedka abandoned just off the dirt road—three figures on the horizon, scattering for cover. The dirt road dipped into a gulch—taking the fugitives temporarily out of sight; when the Comandka rose again they had vanished.

Ziki gunned the motor and all six wheels of the vehicle dug into the rocky ground, spitting grit and gravel.

"Where'd they go! Where the hell did they go?"

"Eleven o'clock," Avner returned.

"At two o'clock." He pointed.

Ziki saw two men on the left of the dirt road, scrambling for cover on a long, low, and bare hill.

"Give me the wheel!" Brolin shouted at Ziki. "Take the one on the right."

Ziki slid out as Brolin slid into his place and hit the ground at a run. His Uzi banged heavily at his back. He slowed to a stop, took one deep breath, raised the H&K to his shoulder in one motion, and pulled his elbow snug against the military sling, found the killer in his sights. Ziki had become a driving force of pain and rage.

*You point a loaded gun at a man's chest…You find out who you really are.*

"That's right . . . run," he breathed and squeezed the trigger.

Sharp crack of the rifle—the man's back arched and he spun violently to the ground, where he lay still.

Ziki's pulse came to life like thunder. He broke into a run toward the man. He hardly felt the pull of his muscles up the hill, hardly felt the weight of the man that he kicked onto his back in the dirt.

Blood and saliva welled between Ziki's lips.

The eyes of the man were wide open.

The bullet had caught him in the side of the chest; it had gone out of sight through a hideous gash... A pool of blood reflected a bizarre glow gleaming red, the eyes were wide open. Ziki made an effort to free his eyes from the dying man's gaze… He died without making another sound, without moving and not even twitching a muscle. In his last moments as if in surprise or fury he contorted his face in a grimace that engulfed his death with a menacing expression. Then his glance faded fast into vacant glassiness… He was dead.

"Murderer!" Ziki shouted down at the dead man. He threw the sniper rifle aside in fury and swung the Uzi around to his front, not needing to take aim as he laced into the already dead man at point-blank range with a full clip… First across the man's chest, then back across, then no pattern at all until the clip was empty. He cast it aside; a burst of justice served too late riddled the dead man's body.

"Barak." A voice sounded behind him and a strong arm pulled him gently away. It was Avner, the tracker, whom Ziki hadn't even realized had gotten out of the Comandka with him.

"That's enough," said Avner, turning Ziki away from the killer. "It's okay. You got him—we got them all."

**Ziki had a feeling like none he had ever experienced.** He felt sick, he felt like crying—he had been crying; he didn't know—.

He never thought he would kill, but here he had done it, with ease and even with hunger. He had willed the bullet into this man who had killed the children—killed Iosi. While he knew that not one of the slugs he had pumped into the man's lifeless body would bring back Iosi or anybody else, he whispered, 'Good God'... Ziki hoped that he was on the side of right in this battle.

Was Ziki a killer now too...? The difference between Ziki and the bloody pulp that lay at his feet that day in the Sinai Desert was Ziki would go on and this enemy would be no more... But not true: the man he killed this day would forever find a place in the woven shadows of Ziki's mind.

He had encountered evil; it embraced him now, howling sorrow seeking refuge in a dark place and taking the place of Ziki's young innocence...He had seen the flight of the last hope on earth...

He sniffled and smeared tears and grit from his eyes.

## Chapter 8

**LEBANON**

    **Young Iamael stood there and froze,** his goats scattered at the roar above him—demons! This was their time, the old woman had said.

    The sky was dark. It was many hours before dawn. What would his grandfather think? He had told Iamael to keep the goats close together, to keep his eye trained on the way the flock inched its way over the feeding ground so that he lost none in the *Jabal Lubnan* Mountains. What would his father think? He had told Grandfather that Iamael was big enough, strong enough to work.

    And now the demons roared overhead, the anger of their voices so strong it swallowed all other sound. It rent the air. It made Iamael want to fall to the earth and make himself as small as he could in the crook of a stone. If they didn't see him. . . if they passed over him. . . he would live.

    They must not see him, they must not—

    Something flashed overhead…reflection from the moon, a light so bright it lit the stones and trees around Iamael. He did hit the ground then and scrambled for cover, terrified—Oh, Father! I have lost Grandfather's goats and now I will die with no one to hear me as I scream and the demons tear me apart.

  The pads of his fingers began to sting where the stone had scraped them raw.

  Another flash…and another…and another. His knees were raw and scraped and hot—as if the skin were on fire.

    Iamael pressed his face to the cracked earth below him. The noise was now further away. . . He turned his head and peeked up at the sky. It was dark but for stars and the moon casting a dim silver shadow. In that almost light, he saw the nature of the demons—man-made, whirly birds, camouflage paint, the Israeli insignia on the belly.

    The dark shape of the IDF military flying machines cut a fast swatch through the sky. The noise moved further and further away and Iamael thought, "Someone else in these mountains will be punished tonight."

**The night incursion began in Northern Israel at *Metulla*:** Cobra helicopters hugging the curves of the *Histbani* River as it led a path into the *Jabal Lubnam.* They flew low, skimming the dirt almost, low enough at times to see the startled expressions of sheep and goat herders as they looked up into the dark. They held a tight formation: a sharp "V" as some birds flew to keep the air resistance down and conserve gas, to hide themselves in some degree, to keep the push of air from the blades from resounding for miles through the night. Heading north, crossing over at *Marj Uyun* and finding the *Litani* River, following its winding course, the choppers bobbed and reeled to keep themselves low through the night air, rising heavy and cool. And finally they crossed over into the the Shouff Mountains of Southern Lebanon and veered northward toward the Be'eka Valley.

Captain Davidoff sat forward next to the pilot in the lead helicopter. He was second in command. His legs had grown tired and needed a stretch. They would be there soon—he needed a cigarette and he needed to pee—might as well get both out of the way.

He slid from his seat with a gesture of his direction to the pilot and slipped into the cargo area, deftly stepping over the feet of some of the men. They were awake— they knew better than to let the drowsy nature of a long chopper ride blunt their senses.

The night air was heavy and cool— gripping a handhold, he leaned out of the mid-section's huge portside hatch and put his face into the wind to see across the machine gunner and out into the night. He knew more than he could actually see without night vision goggles. In past months he'd scoured this terrain many times and had come to feel he knew it like the valley where he and his friends had played when they were boys.

Davidoff was of medium height, just less than six feet. His face was rugged and leathery from the desert sun. His dark-brown hair was bleached to a peculiar shade of sandy blond as well by the sun. He'd just finished a stint in the southern *Negev* desert near the Gaza Strip. His drab green field uniform carried no rank on his shoulders; like other Israeli soldiers he went into combat without insignia or markings. The word on that tradition was that if—better said *when* for some posts—when captured, the enemy could not tell who or of what importance they were.

It followed suit in the IDF that soldiers rarely addressed one another by rank and title; rather, they were all kin of a sort, brothers in training, brothers at war, brothers.

On this mission, Davidoff's orders came only from Ziki Barak, their Commander.

He tugged at the rubber cover of his watch to check the time and buttoned his jacket over his chest. The night had grown colder. Davidoff looked lean, strong, and confident—someone you would not want to mess with. As Ziki teased him, he was someone you'd want on *your* side.

He looked towards the rear seat in the cobra, meeting the eyes of the creepy little clerk Melvin Finkle, registering the fear in the man's eyes, the roll of sweat despite the chilly mountain air. The clerk was a short stocky man—only about 5'7". He was in his mid-thirties and balding. He was equipped with full combat gear just like all the others, but he looked out of place among the heavily armed special-forces *Golani* who were the helicopter's other passengers. A pencil pusher, a white-skinned little rat of a man.

Nobody liked him.

The clerk was not armed. Ziki had taken the issue-desk Uzi that the clerk had held to his chest right out of Finkle's hands with a wry grin. "I don't think so," Ziki had said. He laid the Uzi on the board beside the grenade launcher and gas canisters and belts of shells. The other young men were sitting on their helmets and carried all of their gear with a casual ease born through training and practice. They were loaded to the gills with guns and ammo—a variety of machine guns: Uzis, Galils and a few M60's. They looked fit, strong and real sure of themselves. Melvin Finkle did not.

Davidoff didn't remember Melvin's name, nor did he care to. But he knew that the success of this mission depended largely on the little Mossad clerk. Why anyone would trust him was beyond Davidoff's powers of understanding. He looked as if he had been born into money. Born into a privilege that other men died for. . . He'd probably bought his way out of his mandatory tour of duty. Davidoff scrutinized the clerk and put his finger on the trigger of his Galil, a gesture that did not escape Melvin Finkle. If the man endangered the mission or any of Davidoff's men in any way, Davidoff's finger on the trigger of the gun would do the talking for him. Finkle had turned a shade of grey and looked away.

Davidoff gestured to the men over the noise of the turning rotors to again check their weapons and gear for the last time. He unbuckled himself and moved towards the pilots, looking over their shoulders at the instruments: a dozen dials in fluorescent green and red, the deep black of night swallowing the other details. The radar showed them clean and clear—not another formation or vehicle in sight.

Davidoff slipped his headgear on and connected to the intercom. "Do you think we've been tracked?"

"No, no chance. We're flying too low," the head pilot called back. Even though his voice was on intercom, clear as a bell, he turned his chin toward Davidoff as if to make himself more easily heard. "None of the instruments are showing a trace of interest—So far, we're in the clear."

Davidoff nodded, "Keep me posted."

The *Litani* River skirted the Mountains at *Aytanit* near the village of *Shaghbin;* twisting like a child's drawing of a snake, it made a moon-glinting highway all the way to *Ba'albek* at the north end of the *Be'eka* Valley.

The city was high in the mountains and would appear in the dark well before they were in range, flashing in the night like a treasure chest on the bottom of the sea.

The headwaters of the *Orontos* River and the *Litani* met near the rise upon which the city rested. *"City of the Sun"* Ba'albek was named in biblical times. The remains of imposing Roman temples now crumbled, remembered conquests of long ago and stories of men long dead—heroes never to return.

A clearing at the outskirts of Ba'albek, the Northwest slope, the landing zone. The pilot's voice blared through the earphones, "I have contact with Zero Coordinate Zone."

Davidoff nodded—Ziki was waiting for them there.

"Four minutes ready for landing."

The navigator co-pilot chimed in, "Coordinates on the screen now."

"Run through landing procedure—. . ."

The Cobra took a turn sharply.

"Fog—that can't be good," one of the men breathed. Davidoff realized it was the clerk from Mossad.

"This must be one of the foggiest places on earth," one of the men said.

"You've never been to London—"

"Ha! Try Paris—"

"Radio-silence, men," Davidoff reminded them. "Night-goggles on. . . now." Davidoff could see the clearing bellow. The pilot lowered the craft abruptly and put it down with a rough jar. Davidoff heard Finkle swear as his head bounced against the chopper's metal wall.

Davidoff jumped out first, gesturing the others to follow him, and they did. Three more helicopters landed within seconds, spread as far as the limited open terrain allowed. The men dispersed quickly out of the helicopters, falling into pre-designated formation.

A silhouette of a man appeared from brush at the edge of the clearing. His hands were extended slightly—Davidoff noted the machine gun hanging from one hand.

The man approached and called out, "Thunder."

The password.

"Barak," which meant lightning in Hebrew, was Davidoff's response. He took several steps toward the man.

*"Barak Shalom."* Peaceful lightning.

The two men met in the middle and shook hands.

"Good to see you, Commander," Davidoff said.

Ziki had parachuted into the location earlier with Avi. Their mission was to scout out the terrain for a secure landing zone.

"Anything around, Commander?"

"No, nothing. All's quiet. I have Avi posted just up the north hill at the edge of town. Get the men together, Captain. No radio chitchat of any kind until I say so. Am I clear?"

"Affirmative."

"Put two men alongside that clerk Finkle. And make damn sure Salameh is guarded. Get them out here!"

There was a hustle at the doors of Davidoff's chopper, the engines now silent.

"OK, gentlemen."

"Let's move it! We're on!"

"Right away—move out men," the Sergeant responded.

Ziki listened to the sounds of the night. It was a good quiet. No one was talking, no chatter on the radios, and no clattering or clanking of the equipment. Only the occasional snap of twigs beneath their feet.

Good…. Good… All very good… These were good men.

Ziki motioned Davidoff to follow him down the slope—below them was a creek, between them and it a hill of shale and twisted scrub. They needn't go all the way down, just far enough away to talk without being overheard.

"Yes, Commander," Davidoff breathed as he came to Ziki's side.

"This track we're on hasn't been used in a while."

Davidoff looked at his map. "It's the only stream in the area."

"Where did you get that map?"

"Intel—"

"Intel? *Aman*, hara, shit. What's the date on your map? Last year—the year before? The Syrians could have mined this whole fucking place."

"I'll check the map again—look for—"

"We're damn lucky we didn't land in Arafat's soup—"

"If there are mines around here they'll be close to the water—"

"Yeah, yeah—on the town side," Davidoff tried to reassure himself. "That's the direction we need to go."

"We will follow the creek on this side."

"Take it south; it flows through this valley north to south of the city."

"Very good, Captain—we'll have your unit lead—"

Davidoff's mouth was dry, but he met Ziki's gaze and slowly nodded. "Yes, we'll lead."

The line of Ziki's mouth had gone grim. "I'm with you every inch of the way, right behind you."

Davidoff straightened his back. "Right."

"You didn't think I'd leave you?" One of Ziki's eyebrows rose in a curve.

Davidoff shook his head. "I was just thinking that I should have taken a piss before I got off the chopper. I might stand less a chance of losing a leg."

Ziki nodded. "Let's get going."

Davidoff raised his arm and gestured for his men to fall in behind him.

Two hundred meters along the creek's bank, a soldier's boot touched ground felt and heard the metallic mechanics give beneath his weight.

Ze'evi froze in place.

Ziki and Davidoff heard the click and froze the moment after.

Melvin Finkle pushed forward, elbowing Ziki in the ribs and almost falling forward over himself. "What the hell was that?"

His helmet tumbled out of his hands and landed with a thud at Ziki's feet. "Lucky... son, the mine—it's a dud."

## Chapter 9

**In a minefield the first thing you wonder is what your legs will resemble if you're unlucky...** Will your guts be hanging out of your belly? Will you keep both of your arms or just one? Your eyes—so vulnerable to dirt and dust and grit and sweat and chemicals? You rail inside your head, I cannot go blind!

Then you think—will the pain be unbearable? Will you scream? Or will you be silent? Will you be afraid to look at your own body—afraid of the sight of your own flesh? Will bones be sticking out? You'll wonder if the medic brought enough morphine.

You know that you've wrestled with death but every man's number comes up at one time or another; you just hope it is not your time... You feel bad for the one that might get it. You know that your mother will weep...

For the moment you forget the enemy lurking below in the town.

Fear...The fear swells from your bowls and wedges in your throat—intense and hopeless despair. The next step could be the end; will it bring joy or horrible dismemberment? Maybe that foot will be a harbinger of joy: you are still in one piece. . . Or maybe that footfall is the cause of horrible pain, a moment in time where you step into the threshold of hell...

There really isn't much choice, one way or another. Your sweat means nothing. It drips down your brow, and from your armpits it rolls down your sides. Where do you step? On the grass or on the rock that looks green through the night vision goggles, or maybe that weed to its right? But you can't just stand there. You can't just stand there and hope. You've got to move. You've got to go forward...

And somehow you do.

Russian mines have earned nicknames. Each has its own mitts among the men. You know them—the names that is. "*Betty Kofetz,*" is a feared beast. It blows out of the dirt. Its explosive force throws fire and dirt a meter into the air; it causes maximum damage in a reliable and deadly and so clinical way. If you are very careful, and very lucky, and if that Betty has been in the ground a long time. And if it has rained once or twice since it was planted. IF... If you're careful and your fear hasn't made you half-mad or stupid or simply blind, you might notice three prongs sticking out of the dirt. The prongs are the Betty's firing device. Step on them and *boom.*

Then there is the antipersonnel mine, the "*M'fotzetz Etzbaot*," It usually just takes a chunk out of your foot. Most of the time a set of toes, but if you're just one of those guys who forgot to say his prayers, then…?

Who said that war was glorious?

Ziki turned to Davidoff. "Aren't you glad we brought a tracker?" he said with a smile.

Davidoff's face still had not regained its color. "Hell, yes."

The tracker's name was Avner; he'd pulled Ziki away from the dead man in the Sinai. Now he was in the midst of some calculations and a long stare at the map. He was usually a scout and a damn good one at that. "We're at the west edge of this mine field—if we veer left a short click, we're out of it, Commander."

"Let's make it happen," Ziki answered him. He waved Davidoff towards the small knot of dark bodies—their men, not moving an inch in any direction. "Tell the men."

A very long twenty minutes later, they were clear of the poisoned ground. They sighed collectively when Avner waved the all-clear sign. Melvin Finkle looked as if he'd lost five pounds of water weight.

**Ziki and Davidoff, flat on their bellies,** had wormed their way to the peak of the hill that overlooked Ba'albek. Scattered clouds allowed the dim light of the moon to sketch the outline of some of the houses and buildings. Much of the fog had lifted. They could see now without their night vision goggles.

The raiding force was nearing its target—some 200 kilometers deep over the border in Lebanon, the North end of the notorious *Be'eka* Valley, a stone's throw from Syria.

On signal the men stopped.

The silence was deafening.

Ziki signaled Davidoff and gave orders. "No night-vision goggles, unless we are in the dark, inside someplace. Pass that on."

Davidoff turned to the Lieutenant beside him and whispered Ziki's orders.

From the high ground vantage point Ziki ran his eyes over the valley before him. In this section of the township many streets merged into a main street. The side streets were unpaved, but the main street was paved with black asphalt broken here and there with potholes. Rows of houses and some shops with tall square windows were locked tight behind steel grates and heavy steel doorways as protection from thieves. Some of the houses had two stories, most did not. There was no pattern or design that he could distinguish. It seemed that the city planners hadn't bothered to lay down any rules of construction. Larger buildings showed their silhouettes on the horizon. The Roman and Cyclopean ancient relics were on the other side of town.

Ziki pulled out a small folding map showing this section of Ba'albek within the flat circle of his tiny hand-held light.

He checked his watch and whispered, "Captain?"

Davidoff simply nodded his awareness.

"Two and a half hours before daylight."

"We'll go with the existing plan?"

"So far, so good—except for the fucking mine field."

"Let's do it."

"Captain, have them bring out Salameh now. Gag him. And keep him near that Melvin Finkle."

"Got it."

Davidoff whispered Ziki's orders to the young Lieutenant behind him, who moments later emerged from the first helicopter with two men—between them, Salameh, dressed in dark Arab garb. He was brought in front of Ziki.

He was gagged as Ziki had ordered.

"*Atah mdaber Ivrit*? So, you speak Hebrew?" Ziki asked in Hebrew.

He shook his head—*no*.

Ali Hasan Salameh. Ziki would not be beguiled by the note of fear in the man's eyes—a master player, a brutal killer—.

Ziki, in Arabic now, his face close to the man's. "You will do what we agreed upon yesterday?"

Salameh nodded his head—Yes.

"*Taiyieb*…Good… Then we all will be happy," Ziki responded in Arabic once more. "Take him away," he told the two soldiers.

Looking at the young Lieutenant, Ziki asked, "How is he holding up, we still need him?"

Lieutenant Ze'evi was nervous. This was his first strike mission over an enemy border. But he tried to stay calm and appear confident. "Salameh is not happy, Sir. I'm afraid that my men are not the most subtle about their disgust." He forced out a smile; white teeth visible in the moonlight. "Commander, back home when I asked, they told me, 'on a need to know.' Now that we're here, I need to know. Is this whole mission to 'Paradise' based on the information we got from the Salameh interrogation?"

"Keep him close to you, Lieutenant. And watch him closely. Remember, he knows this place really well…. Yes it is"

Ze'evi nodded: "Yes, Sir. You can count on me."

"I know I can, or you wouldn't be here."

"Thank you."

"Don't thank me. Let's get the job done."

"OK then. Let's be on our way, move out men."

"Let's send them to hell."

"No—not hell; Paradise, let's send them to Paradise and their 72 virgins! Isn't that where they all want to go?"

The Lieutenant and his men took their places; they began to flow silently over the hill into the township. Without further orders, the columns knowing their tasks split into four sections, all going southward but spread out in the maze of alleys. They were stealthily out of sight within moments, invisible in the night.

Ziki turned to Davidoff. "What's the clerk's name, again?"

"Melvin Finkle."

"Yeah, Finkle. He understands that he has to handle Salameh in there?"

"Yes, he does."

"You think he's going to manage to do it?

"Well…he is one of ours.  I think you can make him do what you want him to do."

"All right.  If you think so, that's good, but keep him and the Arab on a short leash."

**"Paradise."  The target was a compound-like cluster of buildings joined** by a courtyard in the center. Its given code-name was "Paradise."

Pientz in Tel Aviv said, "Name the place 'Paradise.' If they want to go to Paradise so badly, who are we to stop them?"

This was a joined center of operations for Islamic Jihad and PLO's El Fattah also known as Black September.  They managed to keep the structure secret from Mossad thus far under the guise of Syrian ownership.

Back in Tel-Aviv at Mossad Melvin Finkle had been assigned to  interrogate  Ali Hasan Salameh.

Salameh's first mission had been foiled as Ziki's men shadowed Salameh from the moment he entered at Megiddo. Salameh planned to take shelter at the pre-arranged safe house at the home of *Gamal Abbas, an Israeli Arab* in the city of Haifa. He met up with him at *Sdot Yam,* a village just north of Caesaria. A recording device had been planted on Salameh at the checkpoint.

**"Allah be praised,** Sheik Yasmin sends you and your family Allah's blessings and gratitude which will not be forgotten for helping us the true children of Allah to kill the Jew infidels and their friends the Crusaders, the non-believers."

"Welcome my brother," answered Abbas; "did the Sheik send anything for me?"

"Sheik Zawahiri asked me to give you this package." Gamal stopped the Ford Tradesman van he was driving at the side of the road and tore the small package open; his face lit up with a grin showing yellow front teeth, as he counted the ten thousand American Dollars along with thirty-five thousand Swiss Franks.

"What's that in American Dollars?"

"About twenty five thousand Dollars; that was the arrangement, right?"

"Yes, yes." He tucked the money in his shirt.

"The Sheik asked me to tell you that there will be more each time we use your arrangements." He paused…  "You have a young son?"

"Yes, more than one," Gamal answered with hesitation. "So what?"

"We need blessed *Shahids*." Martyrs.

Gamal screeched the car to the side of the road and stopped in a cloud of dust. Gamal, a big burly man, turned in his seat towards Salameh and grabbed his shirt pulling him towards him.

"You stay the hell away from my son, you understand?"

Salameh's stare was cold. "It is you who doesn't understand, my brother. It is a great honor to be a *Shahid*.  How else can we ascend directly to Paradise and kill the Jew infidels and Christian crusaders?" Gamal let go of his shirt.

"…I don't hate the Jews. They are men like us. They sit at tables and drink coffee like us, and eat bread and meat like us. I have lived my whole life next to them; sometimes they are unreasonable, but no more than our people."

"Maybe the Sheik made a mistake in choosing you. The Jews must be slaughtered. They are Infidels, the same as their Christian friends and neither one of them prays to Allah. They are all the same, Christians and Jews. It makes no difference and by the will of Allah we will blow them into pieces and feed them to the dogs. That will be the day of glory for Islam.

"You may want to think about this, Gamal:  for each of your sons that become *Shahids,* you and your blessed family will receive twenty-five thousand American Dollars in cash."

"Twenty-five thousand?"

"Yes, American."

"Hmm… I'll think about it. Now get to the floor; we will be passing in front of the police station."

"I don't have to get to the floor; the dumb bastards let me pass through their checkpoint at Megiddo without any problems. I'm on their 'good list.' "

"Listen, this is my car so just get on the floor until we pass the station."

"All right."

Gamal drove from *Caesaria* on to the Tel-Aviv–Haifa highway, then south past *Atlit* towards the port of Haifa along the Mediterranean seashore before turning upwards and beginning to climb up Mount Carmel towards the *Carmel Tzarfati.* The suburb is called the "French Carmel" for some reason even though it has nothing to do with the French. Half way up the mountain, he turned on *Rehov Moutanabi* and drove towards his house, which was just below and to the north of the *Bahai Persian* Gardens.

The whole city lay beneath with breathtaking views. Haifa is a beautiful port city sprawling from the Mediterranean Sea upwards onto Mount Carmel. Further north on a clear day from Gamal's house you could see the ancient city of Ako and yet further on the horizon Lebanon was visible.

Gamal turned left into the driveway of his house. It was a structure built of stone blocks with arched brick enhancements. The stucco over the cement portions was painted a pale yellow with blue trim; it was two stories high with a large balcony surrounded by a waist high ledge on the flat roof.

Gamal's house was a large house on the side of the mountain with a view of the entire city. From the balcony you could see the blue lobelia flowers that Ziki's mother grew at Ziki's house just up the hill.

"This is your house?"

"Yes."

"A nice house like this? How come the Jews didn't take it from you?"

"They never took  houses of Palestinians who stayed and lived with them."

"I never heard that before."

In the morning, Salameh had left the Abbas house in the early hours before anyone was up. He had a meeting straight across from *Caesaria* at the border near

Jenin with four El Fattah *mehablim* coming over the border. Salameh was followed. The four got in a shoot-out with Ziki's men; Salameh had survived, but was taken. In return for a promise of his life, Salameh, at Finkle's interrogation gave away the Islamic Jihad headquarters in Ba'albek, and much other information about the Islamic Jihad compound in the Be'eka valley in Lebanon and El Fattah.

**Davidoff whispered....** "Lebanon has agreed not to hide them. They're all liars. There is not one promise that they haven't broken. I hope they understand the message they're about to get and know that it can happen to them at any time."

"What message?"

"What we're about to do here tonight."

"Davidoff, my friend, so far we haven't done anything, for one, and for two this is not a real good time for speeches—so shut up."

"Yes, Sir."

**In the Ba'albeck neighborhood around Paradise**, the strike force was working its way through alleys and the streets.

"Shit!"

"That's exactly what it is." The Captain stepped into the channel of sewage that ran twelve inches deep in the center of most alleys. Garbage was piled in heaps at the sides of the roads. The stench was suffocating.

The men were tense. Their own adrenaline spurted them on—ready with fingers on triggers. Less than a hundred meters to go, the men waited.

The radio crackled, Ze'evi said, "Sir, the Golani two squad is in position and ready."

Ze'evi passed that on to Davidoff.

Davidoff raised his thumb to Ziki. "Okay—done."

"Golani squads, one and three cover the West, North and East ends of town. Cut off any surprises. Cut off the road and take out all communication lines—and set up the jamming device for wireless communications."

"Just arriving now, Sir."

"Does he have that under control?"

"We'll know in exactly two minutes."

"Fine. Check in when it's done."

Ziki raised his fist signaling to stop. "Here it is. Paradise."

The radio corporal again whispered in the Lieutenant's ear, who in turn whispered to Davidoff. "The last squad is in place, covering the south end."

Out of habit, Ziki pulled the bolt lever on his Galil to make sure that there was a round in the chamber of the short barrel. He took a deep breath, looked to both sides—left and right down the street—and ordered. "Cut the electricity..."Night-goggles now."

There was a small rustle from the men as they put them on.

"Yes, sir."

" This is Red Falcon—North, South, and East—copy. Are you in place?"

A quick round of affirmatives. Each section checked in.

"Mark your watches on my order: three, two, one. . . *and mark*."

"We all enter simultaneously at 0400 hours."

"Yes, Sir."

He circled to the rear of the compound. Salameh and Finkle were brought along by their escorts. Avi was waiting at the rear and pointed to the back door.

"It's made out of thick steel set in a steel frame. No lock. No handle. It's like a fucking bank vault."

"*Pientz was wrong . . . This is hell not paradise.*" Ziki frowned in the dark.

Alex, the explosives expert, laid C-4 plastique around the perimeter of the steel enclosure. He flashed a look around himself—the Golani's looked eager, as if they couldn't wait to go through the opening.

"Hold—Hold!" Ziki ordered. "Blow it at exactly 0400 hours. Coordinate it now with your counterparts around the structure."

"Yes, Sir."

Alex placed the explosives, wired up the firing caps, and moved out of the way. He signaled to take cover. There was the dull sound of men falling behind what sturdy bulk heads that they could.

Alex staged whispered—"fire in the hole!" Then raised his arm, the detonator plunger switch clasped in his gloved hand, and threw the cover off his watch to count the seconds to 0400 hours.

Ziki lowered his face into the dirt, covering his head with both hands.

A muted explosion and the smell of chemical sulfur: the noise and stink followed by three other explosions from the other sides of the building. Boom! Boom! Boom! Boom! Like machine gunfire.

An ear numbing "clunk!" peeled through the sudden silence and the steel door tottered inwards, falling into the building. Bits of rock, shrapnel and debris from the blast rained down pelting helmets, guns and the cement beneath them.

"I hate explosions!" Ziki mouthed; he had felt the concussion lifting him off the ground. The smell of gunpowder and smoke hit his nostrils.

He jumped to his feet following the blast. The opening was still smoldering. Followed by his men, the assault inward began.

"It's no longer a secret that we're here."

The total darkness inside was overcome by the night-vision goggles—the marvels of technology—the building's interior was lit up as if with green daylight. A stairwell leading up and one leading down.

Every second now counted.

"Ze'evi! Have two men clear this area," he barked and ran up the stairs. The smoke filled air made his lungs cramp; forced to breathe shallowly, he coughed. For a second he feared that he should have ordered gas masks, but then rethought that fear—No, the smoke would dissipate.

At the top of the stairs, a doorway blocked the entrance.

It was locked. A gun burst of 9 mm rounds from Ziki's pistol frayed the wooden door frame and panels. He planted a solid foot into it. It collapsed beneath his kick.

The room had a portrait of Khomeini

Two men in long underwear—bare-chested, bare-shouldered, no shirts—shadowed the doorway carrying *Kalashnikovs.* They ran toward Ziki, firing a spray towards him, but without aim. A short burst had both on the floor in a widening pool of blood. The first had dropped face down.

Avi, behind Ziki burst into the room as the two were falling. "Nice shooting, Tex," he drawled in an unconvincing American Western accent.

Ziki kept his gun tight to his chest. "Check them—I'll cover you."

Avi moved forward and Ziki kept his back while he kicked and rolled the men over to make sure they were dead. The one face down had been shot in the throat and the bullet ricocheted downward and came out his right side—he was deader than dead.

Ziki pointed to the door in front of him.

"Remember, no full grenades. Concussion only—"

"Got it, boss." Avi tossed a concussion grenade through the opening. Again, the explosive burst that Ziki hated sent a shock wave through his bones. Gideon and Davidoff were running through the opening before the noise and smoke had cleared. Another Golani jumped over the dead men in the center.

The partner of the dead man lay twitching at the end of the corridor in his own pool of blood, his eyes wide open taking in the spectacle. - Last flickers of life. Not yet dead but unable to participate.

"Good God," Ziki groaned; he felt pity for his enemy. *"I wish this did not have to be so."* He sat there slumped without uttering a sound. His face twitched, his lips quivered, he could not move a limb. He met Ziki's gaze with flatness, a frankness that made Ziki's guts clench—and a lock with the man's eyes that would stay with Ziki forever. At the last moment of his life he tried to speak, whisper. He refused to accept the inevitable… Life faded … The death mask covered his face; he died with a menacing expression. The man's eyes became vacant, at last accepting the inevitable faith of this moment and at last glassy.

Ziki felt cut off from everything he had once known—someplace in another existence.

"Move on!" Ziki yelled out… "Don't stay too long in one place. Keep moving!"

The hallway in front of them was clear. It had two doorways, one along each wall. Another man, bearded, wearing a *Kafia* and long underwear, jumped out of a doorway—his AK47 firing wildly, without purpose. He had Ziki off guard, so close to where Ziki stood that Ziki could smell his sweat. Ziki backed peddled quickly and turned to fire at the new assailant—he knew instinctively that he hadn't a chance. That was it then—.

Damn.

He hadn't really thought he'd go out like this.

There was always a chance—but like this? Like this?

Machine-gun bursts came loud and clear over his shoulder and Davidoff charged forward with a cry of rage.

Ziki saw the orange flash of the muzzle, bullets spliced the man's chest—a spurt of blood streaming out of the fabric of his shirt. The man's eyes were wide open and a scream of surprise filled his face as he fell to the floor, dying... A flash, a horrible passing moment in the eternity of time. Silence driven away by the exploding noise....*they die so quick, is it unpardonable sin.*

Ziki jumped over the man as he saw two more coming out of the other doorway into the hallway. Again, a burst of machine-gun fire—this time his and Davidoff's simultaneously. The two men fell, the first almost bouncing off the door jam, the other one on top of the first, both barely out of the doorway. Blood spilled on the hallway floor and splattered the walls.

In the sudden silence Ziki blinked hard. "I owe you one—" he said to Davidoff.

"Who's counting?" Davidoff answered.

"All right then, let's just stay sharp," Ziki said. "I'm not going to talk to anybody's mother because we were stupid—got that?"

Grim nods. He needn't have said it.

Ziki ran up the hallway into the door at its end, Davidoff pushing right behind him. They scanned the room furtively—no one inside.

There were beds messily arranged and clothes strewn over the floor and a row of Russian AK 47 machine guns against the wall, one by each bed.

"Where are they?" Ziki muttered.

"Where are these fucking men?"

"According to intel they're supposed to be at the building next to the police station about 1500 meters away straight north."

"They'll be in check by Eli's third squad from coming back this way."

"This is insanity. They don't have their fire arms with them?"

"It could be a prayer meeting—?"

"Hey, without their guns—bring them on!"

Machine gun fire broke the silence. It could be heard in all corners of the compound... "I guess they're not all praying."

Ziki paused to reload. He clicked a thirty-round magazine into the Galil. It was hot and smoking; another gun would have jammed, but not a Galil. He remembered his gunsmith friend Iphtah complaining that he had calluses on his hands because they made him test new ones by firing 500 rounds at paper silhouettes. Only if the gun made it through the safety test was it considered reliable enough to give to a soldier. Men rely on their guns in the field; Ziki, Davidoff, and the men behind them were now checking the remaining rooms for unfriendlies. Smoke filled the hallways; the air was thick with the smell of gunpowder, sweat, blood and bile.

"You, there. Stay below the stairwell and keep your eye on it. Let no one come up through there!"

"Yes, Sir."

"How are the Golanis in Section two and Ze'evi's men doing?"

"I'll check. . . All areas of the building are secure. We have control of the compound—this arena is safe for now, Sir."

"Good."

"There is activity reported near the police station—but no hazard to us yet."

"—Yet?"

"Keep on your toes."

"All is right on schedule"

"Did we take any casualties?"

"No, two men lightly wounded."

"That's good."

"Right, then—start the next phase. Pick up anything that looks like documents that you can find in the entire structure. And you—"

"Who me?"

"Yes, you Sergeant, bring me Finkle—and the Arab Salameh—I want them over here—now."

"Right!"

"Let's go! Let's go! Time is against us. Let's move it!"

Davidoff rasped, "The whole building is in our hands now. We have complete control of the compound."

"Fine. . . Just fine. Have your men hurry up and move this thing."

In the distance, from the direction of the police station came the rattling sound of heavy machine gun fire once more.

"Ze'evi's section must be in business over there. Let me talk to him."

"Crows Nest Three—come in—this is Red Falcon-what's going on over there?"

Static... Then Ze'evi's voice clear and strong.

"Just a few stragglers. Some of the local police. We fired shots and they turned and ran."

Ze'evi's squad had M-60 teams perched on rooftops with an ammunition bearer. He didn't talk much, just cleaned and oiled his M-60. "We got this area secure for now; no one is coming your way from here."

"Okay, good work Lieutenant."

"But there's activity. They look like they might get reinforcements. We intercepted garbled radio communications; our radio jamming worked, but they must have had a back up. I estimate we have about—fifteen, maybe twenty minutes."

"Plenty of time. Let's get going here!"

Ziki knew, there was no time. Enemy reinforcements were coming and they would be here in less time than Ze'evi had estimated.

"We'll deal with them when they arrive."

Ze'evi knew what had to be done. Keep the police and any of the "praying" Jihad men out of the street complex that led to "Paradise." He would pin them in the police building and cover its exits.

Davidoff saw the crease of concern over Ziki's eyebrows. "You can count on Ze'evi and his men. They'll do what needs to be done. No one is going to get through his sector."

"I know that. We'll all be happier when we're on our way home, so let's stop the chatter and get on with business."

Escorted by two men, Salameh appeared with Finkle behind him. Ziki forced a friendly smile and said in Arabic, "*Yalla habibi. . . Come on, let's get going.* It's not that much longer. Let's do what we came here for."

Salameh hesitated, a strange look overtook his eyes.

Ziki turned to Melvin Finkle: Now in Hebrew. The Arab wouldn't understand them.

"*Ma zeh. . .? Zot ha-avoda shelcha?* What's this? This is your job. Get him to fucking talk. Get him to show us where the place is, where the lower safe is hidden. We came all this way for it, Finkle."

"I don't need you to tell me my job," Finkle replied. Sweat ran down his brow and his hand was shaking.

"Get a grip on yourself and talk to the man. He told you where it was. Do you know where it is without him?"

"No, I don't. But he'll tell me... He'll tell me, I'm sure of it. He promised he'll tell me."

"All right, you'd better be right—do your thing."

"Give me a minute alone with him."

"That's all you've got. A minute!"

Salameh was whimpering, his eyes fixed to the far corner of the room. He scurried over there, kneeling down to the man lying dead, a bullet shot through his forehead. Other bullets had torn his stomach.

Salameh knelt down and petted his hair. The blood was not yet dry—his other hand tried to stuff the man's guts back into his stomach. Salameh made a croon like a sick desert wolf.

"*Tayieb*—OK, Ali," Ziki said in Arabic. "Who is he? Who is this man?"

"He was my cousin. He is a Sheik He is the head of this section of the building. . . Here."

"I understand."

A look of defiance contorted Salameh's face. "I'm not going anywhere any more. I'm not doing anything. I'm staying right here." He crouched over the dead man.

"Your one minute is up, Finkle." Ziki put the barrel of the Galil to Salameh's head. "There's nothing you can do about the dead Sheik. So, I'll give you two choices: One—you can join him and die, or two—you can show me where that safe is. You have until the count of five."

Ziki began to count out loud in Arabic: *Hamsi, aarba, tlaat, shtain. . . oahad.* Five, four, three. . .

For the first count or two, Salameh appeared ready to keep the secret of the lower safe.

Ziki cocked the gun by wasting a round out and putting a new one in the chamber. It made a click and coked into place, so that Salameh would know that Ziki meant what he'd said.

Salameh jumped to his feet. "*Tayeb*—this way. Follow me."

He led the small group into a larger room at the end of the hallway, where Avi was now standing, securing the outer doorway at the far end of the room.

"Here," Salameh pointed at an enormous armoire filled with clothes. "Push it aside."

Behind it, two of the floor stones clicked sideways—he removed them. Beneath them lay what looked like a sewer cap. Salameh removed it revealing beneath the floor stones a small staircase that lead downwards into a tunnel.

Ziki followed Salameh cautiously, prodding him forward with the nose of his gun. No one was around. The silence was deafening in the chamber below as they crept forward into another room in the catacomb-like bowels of the compound. Salameh beckoned Ziki along after him and moved to the corner of a room where he removed yet another square stone in the floor. There it was: a Victroanoax Swiss floor safe.

"He knows the combination, right Finkle?"

"He said he did."

"Do you know it?"

"Yes—he gave it to me."

"Then open the fucking thing! Put those gloves on, no fingerprints. You do it, Finkle."

Davidoff pushed Salameh aside, told him to wait while the clerk was working the safe combination. Finkle was shaking, far too nervous, sweat poured like a dripping faucet from him.

Disgusted Ziki turned to the Arab. "*Tayieb,* Okay, Ali. You do it. You want to be good with me, right? You open the damn thing. *Yalla imshi.*"

Salameh, surprisingly calm compared to Finkle, nodded. His hands were still as stone as he reached for the combination dial. Not a flicker of tension or fear. This is a dangerous man, ran through Ziki's mind.

As he fell to his work, muted explosions resounded through the walls, loud enough to set everyone on edge—even this deep in the catacombs of the building.

"What's going on out there?" Ziki turned to the radioman.

The radio sergeant lifted the receiver to his ear and after a moment reported: "Two Lebanese police Armored Personnel Carriers tried our line. It's clear. Ze'evi took them out. Some are still shooting."

"The whole town must be awake by now," Ziki growled. "Let's move this thing."

"How's that combination coming, Ali Hasan?"

"*Illa shuwwaiye*—Almost. . . Almost. . . There—I have it. Should I pull it open?"

" *Laah*...No, don't touch it! Is the combination correct?"

"*Tayieb*…Yes, it should open now."

"Davidoff, get in there!"

Davidoff pulled the lid off the safe, and placed it on the ground. Ziki's men pulled Salameh away— "No need for him anymore"—as Davidoff pulled the lid open.

"Get him out of here, and give him that amnesia shot, 50 milligram Scopolamine and Zolpidem Tatrate, cocktail," Ziki ordered. "And get Finkle out of here, too! Sergeant—you're in charge of them both… Don't let them out of your sight."

The Sergeant, a big man with curly red hair and a face full of freckles, nodded vigorously. "Yes Sir, with that much stuff in him he will not remember this episode, maybe not even his own name."

"That's the idea sergeant."

Ziki gestured at the man who'd been sent along—a document expert. A young man with glasses that looked more like a scientist than a soldier.

"Take your photographs—photograph everything in there as quickly as you can—please."

The "please" had been an after thought.

"Yes, Sir."

The young man hunkered down onto his heels and removed stacks of boxes from the inside of the safe. Ziki watched as he copied the pages.

"They must be put back in the same order that they were before—no mistakes. Same order!"

"Yes, Sir, I know."

Davidoff smiled at Ziki. "Hey, this is what we came for—the risk—this is what we wanted, right?"

"I just hope there's something worthwhile in there."

In the safe were the names and locations of El Fattah operatives and cells within Israel, the West Bank and Gaza, Lebanon, Syria, Libya and Iraq as well as a good many of their plans for operation "*Paradise Fulfilled*" their largest operation planned in years, coordinated and backed by the Egyptians, Syrians and, the Lebanese.

"Commander—look at this one."

"Don't touch anything. It must go back in exactly the way it was. What is it?"

"Something about German scientists in Egypt and the 'ODESSA' organization… They're making rockets with—something…"

"Something what?"

"What the hell? I think with biological warheads."

"Bio-chemical warheads?"

"Yes."

"Dammit—we've hit the mother load."

"They are making biological loaded warheads on the edge of the Sahara in Egypt, let me see, near the Sudan border,—installed on rockets that can reach us."

"With what?"

"It's unspeakable stuff—straight from *gehenom*—hell."

"Are you going to tell us or what?"

"Yeah, I'll tell you. Bubonic plague—a mutated version—no known antidote or vaccine."

"The Black Death—that stuff spreads faster and deadlier than anyone can imagine—they'll wipe out…those crazy…."

"It would spread to other countries—"

"It could spread to anywhere on the planet."

Silence fell for a moment as the men looked at one another. "It is good that we're here."

This was the secret of Paradise—but now, Ziki muttered to himself, now we have the keys. He knew that if all worked as planned, they would never know that Ziki's raiders had found the lower safe.

Davidoff was already pressing the documents guy to close up shop and move on. "Careful—careful. They have to think we never found this safe."

Shooting and the sounds of explosions sounded again in the distance.

"Let's move it, gentlemen.

"How're we doing?" Ziki shouted at the radioman.

"We're okay, Sir. We still have time. They say we still have time. No one is getting through. They are not going to let anybody through."

"Fine—fine. That's good, but move it… We're running out of time."

The men knew that minutes were a factor in whether their lives would be long or short and desperately tragic; nobody wanted to choose between those extremes. Eventually the whole town—and maybe even the Syrians from just east of the border themselves—were going to get into the act.

"Sergeant Giora. Take six men and give the North squad a hand with some back-up out there. Make sure no one gets through the cauldron until we extract."

"Yes, sir. I'm on my way."

"Well, Davidoff, my friend. So far, so good. Now all we have to do is get the hell out of here—piece of cake—right?"

Davidoff's mouth curled grimly. "Right."

**"It's like walking through a fucking gauntlet;** every shack has a machine gun, RPGs or worse."

"We have to give consideration to the townspeople."

"What do you think?"

"What do I think?"

"I just hope they are more scared of us than we are of them."

"There'd be no problem if there weren't so many of the little bastards."

"If they all start shooting at once we're in deep shit."

"Well…I saw faces peering in the windows, but they quickly disappeared and got out of sight when they thought we saw them."

"They seem to be smart enough not want to tangle in a firefight with us."

"They've had so many in-fights with each other; do you think they even know who we are?"

"I'm going outside to take a look. You try to finish here as fast as you can. Tell the document guy to wrap it up now, and move out."

Ziki straightened the black strap on the night vision goggles and put them on; he went outside to work a glimpse around the corner of the sandstone structure. Several of the men in the section could be seen spread out on the east and west side of the street. The rest of the men were engaged in a full firefight.

It looked like some of the locals were involved.

The place was swarming with Islamic militias each with its own cause… Roaming the alleys, armed with a mixed variety of arms and machine guns, mostly AKs and some real nasty Russian RPGs and anti-tank shoulder rockets. Some of the Islamic fanatics would fight to their death.

They lived in a world that has no hope: shadows that had fallen in their final passage wrestling with life, welcoming death and ascension to "Paradise."

*"… Am I doing this thing right? What else did I not plan? I hope I don't lose any of these men."*

Davidoff smelled it first, the smell of baking bread… "Insanity, isn't it? In the midst of all this? Who in God's name is baking bread?" The wind carried the smell like a warning.

Gideon, the young Armory Sergeant, was crouching down. He looked left, then right, saw something and froze. He knew he was a dead man if there was anyone with bad intent and an AK at the other end of the narrow corridor leading to the alley: treacherous lurking death, cruel without courage, hidden evil.

His eyes caught flash movement. He had just enough time to gasp. The flash of the orange tongue from the machine gun's barrel sped toward him. *"No time to react; it's too fast."* The Kalashnikov's bullet came immediately behind the fiery orange glare; the explosion's noise was loud. The sound was familiar, he was used to it. The bullet whizzed with the noise of a jet engine as it passed a fraction beneath his ear: a weird sound, suggestive, almost appealing, it grazed the side of his Kevlar helmet; that took some getting used to.

He clawed the ground for cover, hugging it… He and the enemy—two shadows of unequal length…. The moment of truth—he was alone. Gideon feared neither G'd nor the devil; he would not surrender to this intrusion …. *"I will not be afraid."*

A second bullet found his leg just above the knee. He didn't see the second muzzle flash of the shooter but fired a short burst of rounds in the direction of the shots.

Davidoff on his belly hugging the earth crawled toward Gideon. A shattering explosion knocked him over, he screamed a yell. Intense pain in his ears, then silence—amazing, mysterious stillness–for a moment concealed reality. He was lifted of the ground by the blast, then dropped again. Getting straight up was foolish but he ran crouching into the menacing smoke and rising dust of the explosion.

There was a smell…. like gun powder and funeral dirt that had been disturbed….

Gun fire, both his and from the other side, sprayed the sides of the alley corridor. He grabbed Gideon by the back of his collar and dragged him to the side of the alley, away from the direct hail of gunfire.

Choking dust, gunpowder, and smoke again disturbed the momentary stillness.

Davidoff lay stunned, his head feeling as if it were going to explode. He opened his eyes. *"Oh good I can see."* He blurted out, he could see. His eyes burned like hell, they felt as if they were filled with sand—Avi hovering over him was suddenly talking to him.

He could see Avi's mouth moving, but he couldn't hear anything he was saying, big bells were ringing in there.

Avi yelled at the top of his voice. "Mediiiic! Where the hell are you?" He spotted him— "Over here, hurry."

The Medic was out of breath as he sat down beside Gideon. "I'm going to cut the pants so I can see, here hold onto this."

"Can you give me something for my ears, Doc?" Davidoff blurted out. The medic ignored him at first then turned his head towards him for a moment. "It'll go away on its own, leave it alone."

"Here tighten this tourniquet; yes just like that, not too tight, and one of you remember it has to be loosened in twenty minutes."

"Okay." A spray of bullets ricochet of the wall.

"You're on your own Doc," he yelled, "I have to take care of the shooter." Avi moved away like a cat, remarkable for a man his size; he was so much bigger than his brother Iosi.

He screamed back at them, "Put your fucking heads down, I have to shoot over your heads." Then came the roar of the Galil and from the other end of the alley the AK opened up… maybe more than one. Davidoff began just now to hear things around him; the ringing in his ears was almost gone, replaced by a humming noise. He realized that he must have passed out for just a few moments.

He ran his hands over his body to check that all his limbs were still there and to feel for blood if he'd been shot anywhere. All seemed okay. The medic caught up and sat on the ground in front of him. "How's your head, Captain?"

"I'm okay, but it's buzzing."

"Watch yourself, for a while longer, you passed out on me. You must have been just a little too close to the RPG they had rigged to blow us away."

"Yeah."

"Any closer, we'd be scraping you of that alley wall." Davidoff tried to talk but the  feel like too much 'Novocain' inside his mouth made it hard.

The medic picked up his aid bag and left.  "Avi, watch your step down that alley," he yelled.  "I think they took off, but they probably left a booby trap at the entrance to their hole.  He's halfway to Beirut by now thinking he blew you to kingdom come. I don't think he likes you; I think you nicked him."

Davidoff felt a shiver run up his back. His stomach was knotted in a ball and he broke into a sweat: "That Russian RPG does a real job."  He got up.

"….This area isn't safe," he mumbled.

"Hey, no place is safe, what's the matter with you? That grenade sure did a job on your head. . . .Safe? We're in the upper ass-end of the Be'eka Valley, hub terrorist center of the fucking world; you want safe? Stay with your mama!"

"That's enough, move on out behind me."

"Where did they go?   I don't see any…"

"Don't worry there'll be plenty."

"The first squad is heading out for the main street. Ruben said to tell you,

Captain, he's gone north to check out the other sniper's nest"

Avi broke away toward the main street. He took a peek around the wall down the alley and moved back. "I'll go, you cover me."

Davidoff clicked a fresh magazine into his UZI and kneeled down. "No, leave that son of a bitch he's mine."

"You sure? Is your head still messed up?"

Davidoff nodded and began moving down the alley hugging the stone wall, switching from side to side for cover behind Avi. The Sergeant who now joined them quickly motioned the two up and followed the men.

Davidoff stopped just short of where Gideon's helmet had been grazed and moving forward, peered into the side corridor where the shots had come from. There was a camouflaged covered hidden area. It was down. Slowly moving forward, Davidoff positioned himself behind Avi, just in case Avi were to fail. The line of fire was not visible when walking by, because of an obstructing structure, but crawling on the ground allowed a clear line of vision.

"They'd made themselves a cavern, like a small tunnel."

"Yeah…a rats' hole." The sniper's tactic was to let a couple of men pass by, then shoot the fourth or fifth man in the legs. The sniper would then wait until another man tried to help his buddy and shoot him, too, then finish them all off, once in clear view of the sniper, with head shots.

"I'm moving in closer," Avi whispered—sliding with the agility of a jungle cat. He had seen the enemy's eyes in that split second before the man panicked and jerked the trigger. Avi confused him, coming in as he did from the west, the sniper turned eastward for a moment; he was distracted by the explosion behind him where Davidoff had fired a grenade…

The man was his age, with a new haircut cropped on the sides—not the usual beard and long hair of the Islamic religious fanatics' style, yet he was hardcore Islamic Jihad from the glimpse at his *Kafia*. That meant that he had recently completed training, probably at Duma; the Russians demand short-cropped hair of this style. The sniper's eyes had been looking directly at the explosion, but without comprehension until they suddenly focused, showing fear just before jerking the trigger eastward. The war had been reduced to a battle between just these two men, just the way Avi wanted it now. The stronger man would survive, or maybe a force from above would intervene and help the man with the right cause; Avi hoped that was him. The enemy had his chance but had made an error. He'd lost his spirit to Avi. A split moment in time. Avi inched closer.

Davidoff wiped the beads of sweat running down his face as he kept the Galil pointed above Avi's head.

Avi, moving low to the ground, slowly, silently withdrew his knife. He moved forward, gun ready in his other hand. He began to quietly work the knife into the hairline crack of the camouflage cover. He felt the knife pierce through without resistance; he drove it deeper to get a better bite and froze for a moment listening. His sweat stung as it dripped into his eyes; he took in a deep breath then tightened his grip on the knife's handle. A lunge forward as he drove the blade deeper to cut a large slit in the canvas cover.

The man was startled; he looked up at Avi, their eyes met for an indefinite instant defining this moment of life and death. He instinctively turned towards him, let out a battle cry, raised his Kalashnikov and reached for the knife in his belt. It was too late. Avi plunged his knife into the man's ribs, his Galil squeezed off a short burst across the chest as Avi held him up with the plunged knife... He could smell the sweat and the man's breath. It was the enemy's last… The man was dead…

Ziki moved further down; he saw one of his men trying to bandage his own leg. Ziki quickly tied a tourniquet around his leg. "Come behind me, can you walk?"

"Yes, Sir, I can."

"Good. Then, come behind me, take cover inside. Stay with me. What's your name?"

"Élan Zavinsky."

"OK, Élan. You stay with me."

Uncommon valor was common that day.

Powering his intercom, he called, "Ze'evi, come over here, please. I'm at the South corner of the compound. Just turn your face. Am I in your vision now?"

"Yes, Sir, I can see you."

"Get over here.

"I want you and your men to go down to that main street….Yes this one right here."

"Whoa! Incoming!!" Face in the dirt….an unending moment of silence. Big caliber rounds ricochet off the stone wall. "It looks like more than AKs."

"These are 50's….All the way from the roof of the station up there at 12 o'clock, I think."

Whoosh…. the salvo stopped; both Ziki and Ze'evi kept talking.

"Go down that main street about one thousand meters and set your men up on both sides of the street and the adjoining side alleys on rooftops of buildings, here and here. If you have to pass the locals, just do it! I want M60s and Milans out there, oh yeah, those sharpshooters you have."

"What are we doing, Sir?"

"We are setting up a safety net and a trap."

"For whom? There is nobody there…."

"Insurance. You just do what you're told. They'll be there! I'll give you the order when you are to open fire; in the mean time get there and get your men to stay out of sight."

"OK, Sir."

"Do it right. Spread them out on both sides. Create a cauldron."

"You got it. You can count on it."

"I'd better."

"Sir, you want some of the heavy stuff in there, up at the head of the street and up on top of buildings?"

"Yes, I do. I want Tows and Milans and set charges scattered pattern below on the street.

"You want anti- personnel or anti-armor?"

"G'd damn it, did I said mines?....No, change that, mines are visible and we don't have time to work with the paved surface. I want Semtex 4 Plastique with remote detonation fuses controlled by you all over the place, am I clear?

"Yes, yes clear. Sir, still there's nobody there!"

"Don't worry about that. If no one comes you got off easy, OK? Let's move it, do it now."

"Yes, Sir."

Ze'evi and his men slid swiftly down the streets and the side alleys going to the location told, setting up their positions.

Inside 'Paradise.'

"How is he doing?"

"Who?"

"The safe document guy! What's his name?"

"Élan. Élan something...I don't know."

"OK, how's he doing?"

"I think he was getting near the bottom of the pile last I saw."

"Find out. Let me know, please."

"Right away."

"Élan Levine."

"What's that?"

"That's his name, Sir."

"I don't care about his name? How the hell is he doing?"

"He's finished, Sir."

"Oh, that's good news.... That's great! Did he make sure that he put everything back the way it was, and the closure, and the cover stones?"

"Sir, he did. I made sure of it, and he did. He was careful. He's professional."

"Fine..."Ziki paused thinking out loud. "It's really good news, and about time. All we have to do now is get rid of these damn Lebanese local police, get them off our backs. They don't seem to understand that they are in over their heads with us. I don't really want to have to kill them, but...."

"Sir, bad news from sector three. "

"What is it?"

"Two armored Syrian columns, APCs and motorized vehicles are advancing. We intercepted their communications. They're mobilizing some of their surrogates, the Lebanese army."

"Army not police? I expected that. Communicate with Ze'evi; let him know your position and get yourself and your men behind here; can you see on this map? Yes. Let them advance towards us."

"But Sir, you told me to hold them!"

"Your orders have just changed. Let them advance towards us now. Get your men in and regroup in this sector, north of Ze'evi's men. Communicate with him as to his exact location."

"Yes, Sir. Got it."

Ziki checked his gun and clicked in a new magazine.

"Sergeant, let Ze'evi know we're in position."

"Doing it Ziki, doing it right now." He took the cover of two Tow missile heads, gestured to the sergeant next to him to take one as he held onto the other.

"Corporal, you take the Milan? Over there, and make sure that we're plugged in with the missile-launcher guiding units."

He proceeded to set the reticule on his helmet into his field of vision choosing the Milan's ballistic engagement set up. He eased up to one knee. The missile launcher looked like a big, oblong, camouflaged tin can. Before firing he placed the hand grip close to his shoulder, the longitude angled down, making room with his head by turning. He set the site on top of the turret towards the far end of the street, now clearing a speck of dirt from his night-vision goggles. Down below in the street, Ze'evi's busy bees were setting explosives.

Ze'evi, on the roof of a two-story stone building whispered out orders in his microphone to his men; they scurried into position.

"There is no one around…. just as he said. I hope the Commander knows what the hell he's doing;  they could sure use us in section three instead of sitting here doing nothing."

Ze'evi was speaking to his second in command who was kneeling at the ledge next to him: Sergeant Major David Levy, a big man built like King Kong, his uniform pressed to perfection, even the camouflage paint on his face seemed to have symmetrical patterns, his Uzi oiled to perfection—not too much or too little oil. He was down on one knee. Without turning his head he asked Ze'evi.

"Have you been on a strike mission with Ziki Barak before?"

"No, this one's the first."

"He knows what he's doing.  Do as he says, trust him."

Ze'evi had time for a moment to think back…  A smile on his face, remembering that both his mother and two sisters were not happy with his decision to do a second three-year stint in the army; they were not happy about him volunteering for the Golani Special Forces branch of the Red Beret Paratroopers. Everyone knew that those were Special Forces; his mother knew that her son was a *good and kind boy.*' He told her that every mother doesn't want her child to go in harm's way, but if all the children listened to their mothers, no one would be left to go to war and some wars have to be fought." …*Mothers bear the burden of war…*

A rattle that seemed distant woke him up from his dreaming. His finger clenched the trigger of the device guiding the sight on the missile's initial look at a target in the distance. It was a Syrian armored personnel carrier moving slowly over the hill, coming down straight at them.

Ziki now ordered, "Squad one, begin withdrawing slowly southward down the main street… but do initiate sporadic fire against the pursuing Syrians and also fire at the Lebanese that are with them. Make them believe that they're chasing you down the street and that you're running away.  Don't move too fast! Let them see you and follow—I want them down here… You are bait."

"Got it."

"OK, then.  Good luck!"

"And to you, Sir."

"All the squads in position, Sir," Davidoff said quietly.  "There are no detected changes in the tactical strategy; all units are deployed and ready."

"How many Syrians do you think, judging from the first wave and their quantum of communication?"

"My best guess is 'quite a few,'" Davidoff answered with a blank expression.

"That's an accurate assessment, Captain."

"That's the best I can do."

"Get the photographer out of there. You take personal possession of the micro films."

"OK."

"Glue them, Salameh and Finkle' to the sergeant until we're back at the extraction point."

"Yes, Sir."

 "Yes, right there.  Stand for direct-linkage.  Ze'evi, you've set your men, right?"

"Yes, Sir.  I have them in sight.  Should we fire the missiles?"

"No, not yet.—Unit one, keep coming south! Lead your men down the street and lead them down here into the cauldron."

"They're coming all right.  They're right on my heels, Sir."

"Good."

"Not so good for me.   The sons of bitches are real close!"

"That is good, I said!"

"If you say so, it must be good, Commander."

"You'll see.  In the morning, we'll sit and we'll talk about it over coffee... Good luck."

"Yes, Sir!"

"Shem Tov, you're number two.  Move east northeast, stay half east half north to the flank and come up north behind them on my order. Stay on the flank till then out of our line of sight and fire. Got that?"

"Yes, Sir."

" Let us know your exact co-ordinance: we don't want to shoot you ourselves."

"Yes, Sir."

"Right." You haven't messed up bad enough for that yet, right?"

"No Sir, not yet."

"The Syrian armor is coming into range"

"Captain, deploy the robotic missile launching drones, now."

Davidoff ordered the drones out of the one Chinook. Straight ahead…

North, up that main street. Right up their throat.

The drones have tractor like tracks—about one meter in height, remote controlled:  small enough to escape counter missile fire but capable of launching rockets at two-second intervals. Their missiles are configured to zero in on any artillery fire profile, the guiding spin arching up and over the arm of the formation, then coming straight-nose down, hunting for the designated targets, seeking the heat of the diesel engines and the magnetic pulsation from the metal of the armored personnel carriers.

Infrared sensors at the tip of the anti-armored personnel rounds are programmed for scanning the specific geometric size and shape of the Soviet-made combat vehicles. Some of the drones carried anti-personnel multiple firing missiles that detonated while still in the air, causing a beehive warhead, spreading a swarm of razor-sharp shrapnel at speeds faster than the speed of sound.

They began work causing havoc to the Syrian APCs formation.  Explosions triggered fuel fires and their cache of ammunition created flames as the warheads exploded belching skyward fire and flesh.

Enough for now… Davidoff order the retrieval of the drones eastward and reloaded them.  The rest of the armored column that had made it through was now within Ze'evi's range. In the cauldron.

"Now, fire Ze'evi."

"Yeah.  Got it!"

"Hey ….we found you something to do."

"Right Sir, I see that."

"Go ahead and do it"

"I'm on it."

Ze'evi's first salvos were for exposed strays, Lebanese police hovering on foot around the APCs.

A Soviet OT 64-APC whipping off 30-mm rounds was coming directly at Ze'evi's position.  The artillery round hit dead center of the building that he was in, making a cloud of flying debris. The structure tremored, threatening to collapse.

"Hey, just look at that!   He missed me!"

"Well, eat this."

The Milan missile flared out of Ze'evi's tube within less than a second. The APC and its 30mm cannon went into history.

"Now is the time!  Order your men, Ze'evi. Unleash unrestricted fire! Fire! Don't wait!"

The new state-of-the-art anti-tank missiles that punched a small hole through armor of only the diameter of a pen seemed to work. Each puncture spewed a supersonic jet of flaming gas and melted metal into the confined space of the interior… A hatch opened, but out of the inferno  spewed a plume of smoke and flames.  Explosions could be seen near and far.  Some were echoing in the horizon. It seemed that the mechanized drones and their missiles hit their targets as well.

Ze'evi's unit should be able to clean out the majority of what's left. The skyline began to show the angry glow of an orangey-flaming color.  Ziki clicked the night-vision down a notch so as not to be blinded; light was streaming heavier from the flames. He turned to Davidoff,

"Get me a field report from all sides. How're we doing?"

Davidoff launched the missile he had in his hands, flying away at a curving trajectory. It dived down like a bird of prey on its pre-designated target and exploded with a spectacular burst right on the 30-mm shells turret mixing itself with flaming diesel.

"Whoa! Heads up! There are two something's in the distance, straight up at twelve o'clock… Two T54s tanks."

"Take care of it! Use the Milans."

"Yes! Yes! *Hamfake'd,* Commander Loading."

Davidoff and the two of the men next to him each slammed a missile into the smoking breech of the launchers.

"Round loaded. Clear behind."

The Milan let out a woof! And the missile took off up in the sky looking for the signature of its pre-designated target. It seemed to be stabilizing itself from wobbling when it found what it was looking for. The two "things" in the distance lifted off the ground on impact in a ball of flames; one's entire turret with its 30-mm went flying away.

"Do you have any more? Come on you bastards, bring them on. There is one more. There's one more T54! I told you it's like cockroaches: where there's one there's always more.

" Ze'evi! You're closest to that target. Do you see him? I see him. Take care of it!"

"I got him."

He locked the launcher into the red-fire mode, slammed into the ledge standing straight up and aiming it down from the building. He located  the target, programmed and squeezed the trigger. The driver of the tank, realizing that he'd been fired upon with all his warning instruments screaming and a fast-moving target would be harder to hit, slammed his tracks into gear and floored the accelerator; but he wasn't fast enough to escape the missile that had already honed in. The move did help him: it didn't destroy the entire tank. It just damaged the turret and bounced off, straying the missile aside, almost undamaged. The "thing" kept coming forward, its turret gun angrily spitting canon fire.

"Oh, shit! We're out of here!"

The T54 driver perched his vehicle into the hillside and gave the gunner the extra angle that he needed to fire a salvo of the 105-mm rounds right at them. Ears ringing, "Ze'evi, are you OK?"

"Yeah, I'm fine. What now?"

"We messed up. That tank is coming."

 Can you get him from here, Davidoff?"

"I'll try."

He took the Milan, loaded another missile into it. He programmed it and fired.

"Hello! And goodbye! He's gone!"

"OK Ze'evi. You can put your head up now."

"I had my head up before."

"Then pull it up from wherever you have it."

"He, he!" He spit a mouthful of dirt and grit. "There are still a few APCs down there, beyond the north ridge."

"… We'll be on the lookout, hold your position, and keep the cauldron position."

The Syrian APCs over the ridge were on the move.

"How many?"

"Six, I think. They are rolling towards us at about the speed of a fast paced walk. The advance may have some infantry walking alongside with them."

"Get that lead APC. And from up there, stay up there and take care of the infantry. Wait, there are a few more!"

"I expected that."

"Shem Tov, move now! You are on the flank right? Yes. Get in behind them."

"Yes, Sir. I've been waiting for your orders."

"Get in right behind them and clean it up."

"Got it."

"On my order, fire at will."

The surviving crews on the ground scattered. There was some crackle from a few AK47s and some 30-mm rounds, but mostly it was dying men scrambling for cover. Some of their fire now was with tracers. It was too late to try to intimidate us! We had to keep in mind that this was their home turf, not ours and we didn't know what they could pull out of the bag.

A stray round hit Davidoff in the right leg and took it out from under him. "I can't feel it. It's gone numb!"

"I'll put a tourniquet on it. You have that film? Let me have it!"

"Here it is."

"What's your name, soldier?"

"Ari Bellwin."

"Ari, you stay with Captain Davidoff from here on out and get him to the extraction zone. You hear me? All the way until he is on the chopper. That is an order not to be changed except by me. Understood?"

"Yes, Sir."

Ari was a big, burly young man: Ziki's friend was in good hands.

"Where's Melvin Finkle? Report to me. Where the hell is Finkle? The bald guy!"

"Who?"

"The bald guy! The clerk! And the Arab, Salameh. Where are they? Get on the radio. I want to know exactly where they are!"

The message came back: "The Arab, Sir?"

"Salameh?"

"The clerk decided to go his own way early—to the extraction zone. He ran down an alley away from us—I don't know where he is."

"What do you mean you don't know where he is?"

"He vanished—it's not my fault!"

"Did you see anything?"

"I chased him, but I had the Arab Salameh with me; it limited my movements. I followed him down the alley. All at once, two Syrian soldiers grabbed him; there were more Syrians. All I could do is get out of there alive... He's alive, but the Syrians got him."

"Oh, my God! You told me I could count on you, Sergeant!"

"He just took off, Sir! He just took off and ran in a side alley. There was nothing that I could do except shoot him!"

"Oh, maybe you should have just done that. Your orders were not to lose him…Shit—you've no idea what you've done."

"Commander, one more thing."

"What?"

"The Arab Salameh hit me on the back of the head when I was chasing Finkle and disappeared into the alley full of Syrians."

"You lost them both, Sergeant?"

"I did, Sir. It's a combat zone—things got hairy." Ziki was speechless for a moment…"I'll deal with you later… Move on with things… Head on out to the extraction point."

"How're you doing, Davidoff?"

"My leg. I can't feel it."

"Is it still attached?"

"Yeah, it's attached."

"You're going to be fine. It's just numb from the impact."

"Screw you, Zik! I know that! I don't need you to tell me that."

"I'm sorry. You are going to be fine."

"I'm always fine."

"Ari, start heading to the extraction zone with him now."

"Yes, Sir."

On the radio. "Pull back. It's time to withdraw to the extraction point! Core units, begin throwing smoke devices now.

From the east flank came chatter and shouting in Arabic.

The Syrians mingled with the local militias. They soon came within vision. Through the green images of the night-vision goggles, they appeared to be soldiers, not police.

They seemed to be running full steam right into the center of the cauldron.

"Open fire! At will! Everybody heads up! Ze'evi, time for those M60s to talk."

Ziki pulled the pin out of two grenades and threw them into the smoke-filled area. The men opened fire, spreading hundreds of rounds into the startled Syrian army and the *Jihadnicks*.

Hidden by the smoke, they yelled and screamed blood curdling screams, running aimlessly as they were hit by the hail of bullets… Most were cut down and fell within a minute or two. Those who survived the first salvo appeared to be confused by the dead all around them.     Even the sergeant operating the radio was firing full blast.

"Cease fire!" Ziki shouted into the radio.

There didn't seem to be any movement, and those who were still alive were playing dead hoping not to get shot.

"There are still live ones in there."

"That's all right, let them live.  I said, cease-fire.  Shoot only when shot at."

An eerie silence set in place, except for the explosions still thundering in the distance setting off yet unexploded munitions rounds that were inflamed by fire.

It was the silence of finality…

A look at Ziki's face would tell his thoughts:   pride at the mission's achievement thus far, but darkened with sadness and regret for the lives that had to be taken…

A bitter enemy, Ziki had respect for their lives; he thought… *That's what this* whole *thing is about—life!*

He peeled the cover off his watch.  "We should be hearing the helicopter's rotors arriving back at any moment now."

The helicopters arrived right on schedule, breaking the silence with thundering noise.

"Hey! It looks like we're going home." Avi shouted over the helicopter's noise. "Let's move it, men!"

"We're out of here!"

"If only I hadn't lost that son-of-a-bitch Melvin Finkle! He has information that could cost hundreds of lives. The fat little bastard has a photographic memory. When the Syrians interrogate him, and they will, he will spill his guts… Maybe I'm lucky… Maybe he is dead."

"More smoke canisters, "Ziki barked out over the noise.

"Execute the break away!"

"To the helicopters.  Count right on to zero."

"Yes, Sir. Loud and clear."

Multi-spectrum canisters spewing smoke were heaved out, hiding the ugliness and devastation below. The scars of combat all around them.  The men silently hurried into the damaged darkness of the night…

Dawn was beginning to fight its way through… Light was now winning over the darkness.  Hands on hips, Ziki watched his force getting ready for lift-off… Rotors turning, the helicopters were down at the southern area of the large clearing. On Ziki's orders, one chopper, downshifting, orbited in low spirals overhead standing guard.

The men were streaming from all directions into the helicopters.  The engines began sounding a high pitch. Dust was everywhere stirred by the turning blades that were kept running as the men were getting aboard… It looked like organized chaos… The men seemed calm.

*"What good men these men are!"*   The few wounded were loaded on swiftly but with care.

All was going according to plan. The sergeant next to Ziki was shouting, his voice loud enough to be heard over the helicopter rotors.

The Cobra above…began transmitting: "Desert Eagle to Red Falcon. I'm spotting Syrian troops and some stragglers one street north of your position, moving towards you. Permission to fire requested…Over."

Ziki looked up, the chopper had stopped spiraling and was moving downward and forward with its nose pointed towards the position of the enemy troops, awaiting Ziki's orders.

"Desert Eagle...This is Red Falcon…Static… Permission to fire granted… Static… Take them out!"

"Yes, Sir."

Ziki began walking towards the lead helicopter. Most of the men and all the wounded were aboard.

Young Ari carried Davidoff in his arms like a child. Ziki shouted. "How do you feel?"

"I still can't feel my leg."

"That might be a blessing."

"It doesn't hurt."

"Don't worry. You'll feel the pain soon enough… Get him aboard. And have the medic take another look."

"I got him… I got him, Sir!"

Ziki stopped in the open door to the chopper and bellowed an order. "Lieutenant tell section two to get going, lift off out of here."

His voice was accented by the sounds of heavy gunfire. He could see the tracer rounds from the gun ship's 30-mm cannons and M60 machine guns.

"More smoke! Heavy on the smoke!"

"Yes, Sir!"

Smoke grenades and canisters flared out around the extraction zone. There would be several minutes of clear and precious cover. The gunship above blasted again, they were not in the clear yet.

He stood calmly next to his helicopter and watched. Ze'evi and the men securing the area were just now climbing into the designated choppers. As they were getting aboard, he heard again the popping noise of machine-gun fire from above. The enemy was shooting blindly into the smoky area, hoping to hit something.

Ziki stood there motionless. As the last of the men scrambled on, Ziki looked over the arena. Davidoff was on board now. The last two men swung unto the step rail aboard together and hung on the rails as it lifted off out of the landing zone.

The gun ships were moving upward, clearing the smoke. Desert Eagle, the chopper that had circled, pulled up and joined the formation, gaining altitude but taking small arms, fire from the ground.

"You should have let us finish them off, Commander; they would not be firing at us now! Static…" Ziki ignored the outburst.

Ziki looked down. It was almost daylight.

Strewn bodies littered the alleys between "Paradise" the main street and the edge of town… The helicopters gained more altitude.

Suddenly movement on the ground caught Ziki's eye: rising dust from the north and from the west as well.

"Hand me those binoculars over there, please."

"Right here, Sir."

A line of Syrian mechanized armor, Soviet T-54 tanks and columns of armored vehicles numbering 50 or 60 were rushing straight for the square and the "Paradise" compound.

A smile worked its way on to Ziki's face.

"Hey, you're too late! Too late by just a few minutes."

Four Mirage jet fighters appeared; they joined the formation alongside the helicopters.

It was good to see the Israeli markings. Just in case Syrian MiGs were to arrive.

The helicopters climbed to 5,000 feet—no need to conceal their existence; the whole region knew that they were there. The altitude gave a nice ride, no bumps as it was when skimming the ground on the way in.

The Golanis were checking and unloading their weapons, dressing minor wounds, and already making up lies about their part in what had been a successful mission.

"Did we lose any men?"

"No, Sir. Not one casualty… We have five wounded, not seriously."

"Good! That's very good." He breathed a deep sigh of relief that felt as if he'd been holding his breath throughout the long night.

Ziki secured his own gun, took a round out of the chamber, made sure that he was comfortable in his seat, and lit a cigarette.

Some of the men were falling asleep…

# Chapter 10

## JERUSALEM

**Eight AM—the next day.**
Ziki had just enough time to wash off the dirt of Ba'albek, a hot shower—a few hours sleep, and on to Jerusalem. The Knesset itself.

The city appeared at peace. Jerusalem is always timeless. Quiet this day—on the surface:  new high-rise buildings—steel and glass, but the city still seems ancient. The bustling, modern governmental center of the 20th century contrasted with the old sandstone buildings and ancient structures of the city.

On a hill overlooking the city, stood the Knesset building; A sprawling Jerusalem sandstone structure embedded modally with glass, but maintaining the flavor of the ancient, surrounded by carefully manicured gardens.

Tens of bureaucrats powerful and not, occupied the building.  From these offices emerged a continuous stream of reports, regulations and directives.   A hurried look at the surface made it seem like they all were the same, somehow a uniform parade of clerks and bureaucrats.  Ministries and their various departments functioned with uncontested accuracy carrying out the policies … in the land.

The Security Council of the Knesset met in rooms well designed to defeat any attempts at electronic eavesdropping.  Windowless and buried deep inside the building complex, some twenty men with a designated charter of this country's policy apparatus, military services and security forces sat around a large oval table.

Ziki was ushered into this room.  Maps on computer screens and projected surfaces encircling the walls outlined Israel and its neighbors' most troublesome terrorist-infested regions and  townships.  Various colors designated degrees of danger and strengths. And then Israel's neighbors and concentrations of strength and weaknesses in an array of colors with an index chart as to their meaning which in most cases was not in use as no one wanted to admit that they did not know this stuff by heart. Ziki however had to use the index as some were staring at him for it. It was not because he didn't know it all by heart, he did perhaps more so than some in the room but Ziki was red - green color blind. He didn't bother to explain or make excuses for this handicap. The circles placed on the maps, surrounded by abstract symbols and in code, designated the numbers of thousands of active duty and reserve military awaiting orders generated from this room.

Near the end of the table sat Meir Amit, and at the opposite end sat Aharon Yariv; even the Shin Bet Director, Malkielly, and Halmi Pientz were present.

Ziki was ushered in by an aide who pointed to one of the chairs at the main table. He walked in and sat down. A dossier was placed in front of him. Embedded into the table a computer screen tilted slightly in front of each person. Ziki placed his right-hand index finger for identification personalized password to access the eyes-only screen.

General Amit continued the previously begun discussion, looking vigorous and pointing at the map on the large computer screen at the end of this room. "This plan is just what we need. Show them who is boss right from the beginning and save a lot of trouble later on, huh?"

"Yes, I agree. A major sweep through their infested camps and townships will flush out their worst and hopefully, some of their leaders. Once we have them we'll have an easier time for a while keeping order and slowing the infiltration into the country."

Amit abandoned his studying of the map, ran his eyes around the entire room. "Any further discussion on this particular subject?" Each shook his head from side to side indicating "No."

The Council knew the problems that the military was facing. General Amit's proposal was simple, straightforward and, unfortunately bloody. He continued.

Military teams, backed by special forces and Shin Bet Security forces in armored columns will descend on the most radical villages and townships in substantial numbers searching house-to-house for known terrorists. Anyone resisting would have to be dealt with. Any that shoot at us would have to be shot. This tough policy had to be enacted to protect the townships, cities and villages. 'Daado' was not present but Ziki could see his hand in this; he'd been trying to get them to approve tougher measures. Ziki remembered his ride with Daado to boot camp, the farmer's funeral and Nahal Oz. ...For if this was done here and now it would put a crimp in the terror acts, at least for a while.

"The plan to be approved. All in favor raise your hand. Two votes of no. So approved. Well this is the first leg. The Security Council has voted. Immediate action? No, we must have input and acceptance of the plan from Malkielly."

Peres watched the display before him with ill-disguised contempt. He represented the dovish Labor Party, every one in the room knew of his opposition to this plan that relied on the application of overwhelming power to root out the commingled terrorists from within the civilian Palestinian population. Even though he was in unison with the protection of civilians, he would have preferred a more surgical approach involving carefully selected areas. Peres would put his energy into intelligence gathering, specialized operations more delicate in nature.

Amit became conscious of Peres's scrutiny. "Let me bring you up-to-date on activities, which are designed to punish the nearest Arab states that are harboring terrorists and aiding them financially and militarily." Amit's aide unrolled another large-scale map of Israel and its Middle-Eastern neighbors. He stood up and walked to the end of the room to the large map. With a pointer tipped with a laser, he outlined the border of Syria and Lebanon in the north, southern Egypt in the south.

"I believe you are all familiar with our covert support in South Lebanon for the Falangists, the Christian militia." Most of the people in the room nodded their heads. "You all know they are involved with us in limited operation against Hezbollah in the north and any other terrorist that wander in their camps like PLO's El Fattah. Their movement is growing and becoming more dangerous. We must keep supplies and intelligence report flowing through the Falangist militias, and in return we'll expect stepped up patterns of attacks from them in the buffer zone from northern Israel through southern Lebanon."

Smiles and pleased faces grew through the room. "For a change, we have others to do some of the work for us—"

"Of course, with self-serving interests, as the Muslims hate the Christians as much if not more than they hate us. We are all infidels."

"So, those doing the fighting and dying would all be Arabs?"

Aharoni entered the conversation:

"What about the Soviet advisors in Syria now trickling into Lebanon? Can they, and will they interfere with the Falangists?"

"To hell with them. They are outsiders, and hopefully not entrenched here. Let the Americans worry about them. Let the two superpowers confront each other as they have been all along in the Cold War."

The door opened—the room fell silent. Malkielly with his barrel chest and big frame walked into the room escorted by an aide and his bodyguard who stayed by the door. Without acknowledging anyone in the room, he walked straight to the head of the table, where a large leather chair engulfed him. Even though the room had a sign "No Smoking," he puffed on the big Cuban cigar in his mouth… No one would say anything to him. He held his silence for a while longer; watching as tension built in the room. It may have served his purpose to have them all on edge. Their own inner alarms would give extra importance to what he had to say. He raised his eyes, glanced at Peres, and ran his eyes around the room.

"I'll come straight to the point;" he spoke in a low, deep, monotone voice. Malkielly kept his words clipped, signaling his authority and determination. "We've had some disasters. Many of our own Arabs, Israeli citizens, have among them packs of traitors and have shown themselves ready to sell us out. Any concessions that we give they interpret as a sign of weakness. The bestial nature of these fanatics is clear as the light of day—they want to kill us all; they don't want peace, they just want us all dead." As he looked straight at Shimon Peres, he said, "There is no further discussion. We must be prepared for immediate action. General Amit, my vote is with you, and I don't think that anyone here will question it," he said, staring fiercely at Peres, "I say we go ahead with your proposed action right away. That concludes this matter of business….Now…"

The men in the room lowered their eyes. No one was going to confront Malkielly, Ziki's boss, who now frowned, took a puff from his cigar and blew it in the direction of Ziki.

"Good work in Ba'albek, Commander Barak. I got your report and read it. But tell us about Melvin Finkle."

"Sir, the Syrians have him. I couldn't help it. He thought that he had a better way and ran off into the Ba'albek alleys by himself, I think towards the extraction zone. I had a reliable man guarding him and Salameh, but Finkle ran off into the night. The Syrians grabed him. It was not my man's fault. He is an experienced Sergeant. He got tricked by Finkle. That allowed Salameh to escape as well."

Aharoni addressed Ziki now, "Is it a fact that Finkle has a photographic memory?"

"Yes. He does."

"He has access to several hundred names of our operatives throughout the Middle East and Europe?"

"Yes, Sir. He had access to those intelligence records."

"God Almighty! How the hell could you lose him?"

Ziki moved back, holding back the anger, but knowing that Finkle's capture by the Syrians was bad.

"A battery of Syrians surprised my man. It couldn't be helped."

"That is straight bull! Answer me, Commander, Did you take Finkle with you into Lebanon?"

"Yes, I did."

"Did you have him with you over there?"

"Yes, I did."

"Do you have him with you now, here?"

"No, I don't."

"Then, without excuses, Commander Barak, you lost the son-of-a-bitch and put the lives of several hundred of our men and women, and uncounted operations and informants at risk. When tortured by the Syrians and then the Russians, Finkle is going to talk his head off.

What are you going to do about that?"

Malkielly now pounded the table with his fist… "This is my responsibility. I will send an operation into Syria to extract him or terminate him. Commander Barak, do you have someone in mind to take care of this thing?"

"I'll do it, Sir!" hoping for some hesitation from Malkielly. None came forth.

"Well Commander. I'm glad to see that you just '*volunteered*' for this mission."

# Chapter 11

### The Kirya, South of Tel-Aviv

The darkness of Malkielly's office matched Ziki's mood.

God and Country. . . Good and Evil. . . The line that defined the Mossad General's actions was always effusive—Malkielly moved it when it suited him. It was a condition of the work, Ziki supposed when he was afforded a moment of reflection. Ziki himself had found the difference between what was good and what was necessary became blurred. A blur, what to do, at times a blur what to think at moments when one would wish for the clarity of a defining line, of knowing what was right. Often when he found himself sitting across from the General—knowing that Malkielly would make the decision that was right—Ziki knew that eggs had to broken to make a cake.

He had thought Malkielly was one of the only people that could always tell the difference between what was right and what needed to be done. Now Ziki wasn't sure.

*Project fucking death trap—a dance with the devil...again. Is it worth it? I'm going to get my ass shot off this time for sure.*

In the gray blue smoke Ziki saw a figure move in the farthest corner of the room. He knew that no one else was in there. The figure lifted its head and showed the face of Satan. Ziki was dumbstruck, his eyes fixated on the image. He flashed a smile or a grin at Ziki. It moved, floating just slightly above the ground in the cigar smoke that was engulfing the room. He showed cloven feet to prove it was him—The Devil himself.

A stench of sulfur was in the air—ancient chariots and the smell of stale dirt—a cold wind. Ziki felt that something really bad was going to happen. *"Did Malkielly make a pact with 'Him'?"* He seemed so sure that nothing was going to happen to Ziki. What would be the price? Ziki felt the same, for that moment in time, invincible… Had some kind of a deal been made? Had Malkielly that day somehow sold Ziki's soul?

…Suddenly without warning a strange ray of light intruded into the room. It cut without effort through the grey-white smoke and darkness entering through the edge of one of the high shaded windows. Ziki felt protected, a feeling of good engulfed him. He thought, something good had come to his rescue….

Then the image of the figure in the far end corner of the room faded away into the darkness…

The man leaned forward.

Malkielly.

His usual cigar—a thick rolled Cuban that released a rich blue smoke—burned in an ashtray, dangling from between his fingers. The smell of it was already in Ziki's collar, acrid and stale.

"Commander Barak," Malkielly intoned with a tilt of his head that indicated as much concern as Ziki was likely to get out of him. "There is something on your mind."

Ziki met Makielly's eyes briefly and felt the black gaze chill his spine.

He broke his gaze away as Malkielly's secretary offered a welcome respite. With a clink of china and silver, she set the corner of her tray on the edge of the enormous mahogany desk and set a rattling empty cup on a saucer in front of Ziki. He let himself be occupied by her intercession.

He didn't want to say what he knew he had to say . . . didn't want the words burning a hole in his chest to be out there between himself and Malkielly.

Malkielly thought of himself as a father figure; several times that had played in Ziki's favor. Now he began:

". . . False intelligence was leaked to the Syrians. . ."

In 100 different ways Malkielly had opened doors to Ziki when he might have remained regular army. Malkielly found Ziki. Chose him. Trained him. Some said Ziki had gotten a ride from his mentor on coattails with buttons of gold. He was training Ziki to be his replacement.

*This is it. This is the mission that I'm not coming back from.*

Malkielly wasn't going to like what Ziki had to say. Ziki knew that already—"The objectives take precedence over your feelings, Commander Barak. One, you have to get Finkle out or kill him. As simple as that. You are the one that lost him to the Syrians."

No one could argue with that. Missiles were about to be shipped to the Arab countries. The Iraqis already had them. The Egyptians would cap them with the chemical stuff they had been cooking in labs near the Sudanese border. ….Terrorists could take them from the compound and fire before they could be stopped. A Russian directed base. If the threat wasn't handled, the Arabs would use any means to take out Tel Aviv. . or Haifa, and who knew how far that stuff would spread.

If there was another way to disable the threat, Mossad's intelligence hadn't come up with it. Ziki knew better. There were no easy ways out of this one. Finkle was maybe even more dangerous than the Iraqi missiles. In the back of his mind Ziki knew the lurking problem was Melvin Finkle, the clerk in Syrian hands. Any IDF Golani team could take care of the missiles.

Maybe, Ziki ruminated circumspectly; Malkielly already knew that Ziki was going to complain about this mission. Maybe Malkielly already had in mind the exact latrine that he would shackle Ziki to for the next five years in punishment for what he was about to say.

Better a latrine alive than dead face-down in the desert or Syria?

*. . . Dancing with the devil, the devil always gets to lead. . .*

Malkielly's secretary poured hot Turkish coffee into the cup. A drop splashed on Ziki's thumb as he held the saucer in place. He let the brief scalding prick his emotions into formation once more.

"Cream, Commander?" she asked.

She was pretty for her age. In her time, she'd been a looker, Ziki supposed. Her mouth—her eyes—nice calves and ankles—nice—. . .

He shook his head. "Black."

She nodded and drew back. Her fingernails were a deep, deadly red in the dim light of the office. Her fingers looked fragile in comparison to the thick white ceramic of the milk server. She was poised. Very poised. If she sensed the brewing confrontation, she gave no notice. The only noise in the room as she took her tray to the other side of the desk was of cups and spoons and the lid of the stainless steel pot jostled on the tray. She set down a cup primly and slowly served Malkielly coffee with a healthy helping of cream without asking what he wanted. A good secretary knew how a man like Malkielly liked his coffee.

Ziki rested his chin in his palm and watched the steam pour up from his cup and disperse into Malkielly's smoke-cloud. Steam and smoke hung in the air at shoulder height, undulating with the drafts of the room, briefly grey-white before disappearing into the dark.

"A special volunteer team has been assembled." He paused.

"Commander Barak, this one is yours. . ."

Ziki breathed in deeply, but tried not to show the expansion of his chest— as if Malkielly wouldn't already know that Ziki was furious—as if that wily old cat hadn't known from the tone of Ziki's voice on the phone or the set of his shoulders as he entered the room.

*Shit. How bad would it be to clean latrines?*

Malkielly was probably already five steps ahead of Ziki—their conversation was already over in Malkielly's mind and the man had moved on with set plans in place. That's how things worked in his office. Since Malkielly had picked Ziki out of the troops, it had always been like that.

The secretary returned the tray to the service station in the darkened corner and asked if there was anything else. Malkielly assured her there wasn't and she took her leave, formally; the hollow sound of her heels and her measured walk echoed in the stretch of quiet that occupied the office once she had shut the door. She had not hurried. Not once gave a slight acknowledgement that she'd made a temporary peace occur for purely practical reasons. Like when enemies stop shelling each other. . . Like when Kings needed to take a-break—*dammit—latrines. . .*

Still, Ziki thought he'd seen a flash of empathy in her eyes as she'd turned to shut the door.

But he'd most likely imagined it.

He picked up his coffee and took a sip. Hot and strong, it made his mouth feel dry and his tongue sticky. He turned the handle a little more away from himself as he set the cup down so that it would be easier to pick up next time.

Malkielly was waiting. He would not stammer again.

".   .   . False intelligence was leaked to the Syrians . . . confiding your group's activities in Iraq. The Syrians will hear about your group's incursion from the 'Iraqis'. . . We'll see to that.

".   .   . We want them to find you. We want you to be taken. . . Prisoner.

".   .   . Disable the mobile silos, cross the border and then intentionally let the Syrians capture you. . . They will not suspect your intentions. It will happen in the same region of the Duma jail where they are holding Finkle; they will take you there once you get captured in that region. That's what they always do with outsiders."

He would wait as long as necessary for Ziki to speak his piece.

So, he might as well— "Intentionally let myself be captured by the Syrians? Insanity! Insanity, General! You do it!"

"You are the one that lost Finkle in Lebanon, Commander not me."

"This is my last tour… Why don't you just shoot me here and now? It might be better than what the Syrians are going to do to me."

*Best to just come out with it.*

Malkielly nodded, that fat cigar going to his mouth for a long drag. He considered his smoke, rolling the Cuban between his fingers, taking his time.

"Is that what you came to tell me?" Smoke stuttered from between his lips as he spoke.

"That's it, Sir."

"Fine," Malkielly agreed. Without skipping a beat, he'd moved on. "One better. I'll message Pientz and we'll send security around to collect your effects in the next hour. Clean out your desk. You are relieved of duty, Commander."

Ziki felt as if he had been bracing himself against a wall that was no longer there. His lungs had suddenly been evacuated of air.

"Sir?"

Malkielly dragged a blank folder stuffed with reports toward himself as if to return to work. "That is all, Commander. You may go."

Ziki didn't move. He couldn't.

It didn't seem right…

He had to say something. "Those men—"

"Something else?" The cigar was held half way to Malkielly's mouth. Annoyance rimmed his eyes. Ziki was gratified when one thick eyebrow arched upwards on the older man's face.

"I am a busy man, Mr. Barak."

There was no phonetic stress upon Ziki's returned civilian status—which from Malkielly made an incidentally dropped title all the more sinister. The man didn't make mistakes—not over a single fucking little word. But it couldn't just be like that. No one left Mossad—Malkielly's service—just like that.

Ziki steeled himself. "I understand, Sir that your call for volunteers included a promise of an immediate retrieval team to be sent to Duma to get us out once the objective, getting Finkle out is accomplished."

"Oh, is that it?" Malkielly's look was one of amusement. He shifted back in his oversized chair and put the tip of the cigar in his mouth. All the while his eyes gleamed.

"Those men, 'volunteers' do not know that we're going to be captured, do they?"

"Shame to loose you, Barak... Really is."

Ziki blinked at this informal dismissal, but was yet determined to say his piece. "I have a friend on the retrieval team."

"And?"

"He warned me that you have placed the retrieval team on stand-by status. They are to launch rescue only at your orders. Is that true?"

"Is that what you've heard?"

"If I go or not—I need to know. Have you told them that they will be captured and you're not certain yet that you're going in after them?"

Malkielly squinted in assessment of Ziki's information. The cigar was held in his teeth and only his lips moved. "As a former member—."

"Will you tell me differently?" Ziki stood. "Tell me this isn't a suicide mission."

Malkielly was silent, but then shook his head shrewdly. "No.... No—I wouldn't dare. Your informant is correct."

Ziki dropped his gaze. "I want your word you'll send a retrieval team. Not—"

Malkielly snorted with mirth. "Assurances. I can't assure you that I'll be able to take a shit tomorrow—and you want a retrieval team dedicated to your team's retrieval?"

"I do, Sir."

"I could reassign you."

Ziki's mouth drew tight. "Hey, please do; send some other idiot, Sir.

. . . *Infiltrate Iraqi ground patrol . . . pick apart a Russian-built guidance system. . . Get yourself caught and go to jail, by the world's nasties, the fucking Syrians. . .*

"I don't think you will—"

"Don't you? I must say, I hadn't expected this from you, Commander."

"The request is not for me, sir. But—"

"For the widows you don't want to be made? Nobody likes widows, least of all me."

"I simply think—"

"Your men have their mission and you have yours. You will bring back Melvin Finkle and your men will assist you in disarming a threat to security since—"

"Sir, no, Sir. I won't knowingly lead men into a blind alley."

Malkielly's eyes narrowed. "Do you need me to say I chose you for this mission, Ziki? I chose you because I knew you could do this, not to mention that it was your screw-up that left that clerk Finkle in Syrian hands. I knew you'd make sure that as many men that could get out alive would." Malkielly blew a stream of dark smoke. "And I thought you'd be man enough to choke that look out of your eyes.

"The Syrians will hear about it from the 'Iraqis,' or they'll think its from the Iraqis, misinformation. They'll take your squad at their border. . .

"They will eventually place you in the same hole where they are holding Melvin Finkle."

Ziki sat rigidly, his eyes averted from Malkielly's. "I've no fear for myself."

"Get Finkle the hell out or kill him."

"Finkle cannot be left in the Syrians hands…"

"The measure of a soldier is what he does when he's got that feeling shriveling his balls into prunes."

"Yes, Sir."

". . . Two… Locate the guiding system of Russian missiles capable of carrying chemical and biological warheads. On the ground… Your area of concern will be this northern main supply route."

". . . Two nights ago the IAF was in the air ready to destroy these targets inside Iraq. But if Israel enters Iraq too forcefully the talks with the General Zhukov will crumble . . . giving the Arab league exactly what it wants. . . Later air strikes will take care of the fixed silos, later, after the Zhukov deal. That is your assignment as well. Nah…Don't ask any questions now.

"The mobile launchers are a different matter. They're almost impossible to locate. . ."

Ziki remembered the men growing uneasy in their briefing.

"The locale—it's like a billiard table."

"How the hell are we gonna find the needles in that haystack?"

"One in a thousand—best chance."

"The pin-point is not accurate . . . This whole thing is not how we usually do things." Ziki said nothing further as he stood erect, his shoulders straight, beneath Malkielly's gaze.

Malkielly began to laugh. He stubbed out his cigar. "You are a royal pain in my ass, Barak."

The old General reached for his cigar box and Ziki felt the tension break. He didn't know if he'd won any ground, or if he'd changed the score or if he'd even made a quarter of a difference. He was certain the men who'd volunteered still wouldn't know exactly what they were walking into. But there might be firm plans now for the retrieval team to sit on stand-by—a better chance for all of them.

As Malkielly clipped and lighted a new cigar, Ziki took out one of his own Marlboro Reds. He lit it and blew out smoke. "I'm asking for a guaranteed retrieval from Syria."

"Someone ought to beat your head in, Barak. The temper tantrums you throw."

"I learned from the best, Sir."

That drew a grudging smile from Malkielly. "All right. You got it. You have 48 hours. That's all. 48 hours to get your team in, take those missiles down, and get me Melvin Finkle."

Malkielly met Ziki's eye with a purposeful stare. "Does that get those panties unbunched, Commander?"

Ziki nodded. "For now."

"Now that we have that covered, you listen carefully to me." Malkielly placed both palms on his desk and slowly and deliberately leaned forward. "I didn't have you call up six other men because I'm a damn sadist. Do you think the Syrians would believe we sent a lone man in to disable those mobiles? No—I wouldn't think they'd be that stupid. It takes a crew of four or five or six—minimum. Explosives. Electronics. A.I. Detonator specialist. Not to consider long range fire and regular special forces grunts. I send you in alone—you're a dead man at the border, they'd just plain shoot you and no one believes your cover…. And then they have Finkle. You are a medic, Swiss, you can fake the accent well enough, and you are there to take care of oil company crews….They will get some gurbled misinformation to that effect from our people in Iraq." He paused to analyze Ziki's face. It was blank. I taught him well, Malkielly pondered.

"I send you in with a team; we don't have to explain to the international press—nobody knows what the hell we were up to. You got it?"

Ziki sucked on his cigarette. "You answer with tactics when I'm questioning your ethics."

"Ethics…. Do you know about ethics? You just carry out orders—I'll worry how ethical it is."

"If it were that easy—"

"By the way Ziki, not one word of this to that American girl you've been gallivanting all over Europe with, what's her name? Oh yeah, Gavriella Ramon."

"I don't plan on seeing her."

"Yeah—I hear that you are infatuated with her. Don't we have enough pretty girls in Israel?" Ziki didn't answer.

"Enough. . . All that philosophy weighs too heavy in a young man's head, " Malkielly mused. "You want to know what will happen to the men in the patrol. You wanna know why I'm okay with it? That son of a bitch Finkle knows too much, too many lives at risk, you have to do this, and so do these men. If I had your men extracted at the border before you cross into Syria your chances for survival go to hell. You're interrogated by the Syrians—they'll want to know where you've hidden your team. Why you're there without aide. When they don't find a team, they'll know we sent you there with more than one objective in Syria, not Iraq. They must believe that your business was in Iraq and you stumbled over their border by chance. They won't waste time asking about the mobiles—they'll try to find out what else is on our minds. They would get the Russians to do it. Believe me you don't want that. Got it? I called those men up for you, Ziki. For your life. And you'll need them; your mission will need them. The missiles are a bonus." He took a deep toke from his cigar and looked through the smoke at Ziki…

"And after this one, there's Egypt, the Sahara waiting for you to finish that nasty business…. You just go, take care of this one and you'll see everything will fall into place….I have it all planed and arranged."

"As decoys or as bait?"

"Perhaps both.  Perhaps neither."

"That's not much assurance."

"We're not in the business of assurances.  You want assurances, convert to Catholicism and you'll know you're going straight to hell.  The only assurance I will give you—in 48 hours, you get in there—and Davidoff with a team will come for you."

"We'll be ready.  And we'll all be alive."

"That's the spirit, Commander."  Malkielly grinned and stuck his cigar in his chops.  "That's the spirit."

He sat down and his voice lowered.  "Now get the hell out of my office and don't come back unless it's with that miserable Finkle… Ahh, and don't forget that you also lost the Arab, Salameh. I have a feeling that he is going to be trouble."

**Word of the raised voices in Malkielly's office** spread like an attack of smallpox through the Mossad building.  Avi, was waiting in Ziki's office when Ziki returned.

Avi's grin said it all.

Ziki slapped his legs off his desk with a laugh.  "Get out of my chair."

Avi shook his head.  "You know how to get your tits in a cinch, Ziki boy."

Ziki shrugged.  "A special talent."

"I'm surprised you can walk."

Ziki snorted.  "You underestimate me."

"Fucking superman."

"You got Intel for me, or are you just here to look pretty for the ladies?" Ziki made an exaggerated kissing motion and smacking noise in Avi's direction.

Avi lifted his middle finger in response.  "Some guy named Finkle. . . not a familiar name. . . ? Yeah, yeah, yeah. A mama's boy with a photographic memory. He is sure to crack if the Syrians applied any leverage at all."

"Never heard of him," Ziki answered.

"Oh yeah, what about that fucking Salameh?  You don't know anything about how Finkle lost his way in Ba'albek and landed in a Syrian jail?"

"Not a damn thing."

"Nothing about what the hell he was doing out of his office or all that sensitive information he keeps in his little pin head?" Avi was grinning widely again.  He cocked a brow.

Ziki shook his head at his friend.  "You were there. You tell me what I know."

Avi reached for one of Ziki's smokes—Ziki smacked his hand and snatched the pack away just a second before Avi's fingers curled around it.  He walked to the corner of his office and drew out a Marlboro and lit it.

When Avi's eyes turned round like a neglected puppy's, Ziki tossed him the pack.

"One of those things I'd do over if I could—that whole Ba'albek episode."

"Naaaah," Avi replied with a shake of his head. "That fucker deserved to be left right where he is. I hope he shat himself when he knew he was on his own, but that 'nasty,' fucking Salameh…I just know we're going to hear from him again. A shame to have lost him out there. "

"We got a lot of important information from that lower safe, didn't we?"

"Yes we did."

Ziki turned circumspect, remembering once more what was on the way. "Man, the Syrians will kick the hell out of him and then leave him to choke on his own spit. . .He'll talk." Finkle wasn't worth it, despite his photographic memory and all of his knowledge.

Ziki almost growled—"I should have left the little worm with a bullet in his head is what I should have done. His loss has the high brass p.o.ed. This*volunteer*' mission is all about penance. I'm supposed to get him back or kill him."

"Yeah, yeah, I know all that." He sniffed and mumbled, "volunteer my ass. Finkle's not worth dangling my dick in front of the Syrians to get him back."

"You're always dangling your dick somewhere, Avi. might as well be with me when you do. I might keep it from being shot off."

"Not like I've had much chance to use it lately."

"I'll make sure the Syrians hear that you'd like to get some exercise."

Avi crushed the now empty pack of Marlboros in his fist and winged it at Ziki. It glanced off Ziki's shoulder before he could bat it away. "Your reflexes are getting slow, friend."

Ziki held up his hands in supplication. "I've got a lot on my mind. What have you got from your sources?—let me have it."

Avi's natural talent at finding out things and his good nature had made valuable ins to the information behind the information. Funny what diesel helicopter mechanics could tell you just based on the task at hand: Helicopter pilots. Retrieval crews. Nurses. Medics. Errand boys. They could all give you a little extra edge if you knew how to ask the right questions and knew how to read between the lines.

Malkielly and team had taught Ziki more than just the usual.

Avi read from the back of the rap sheet that was given out for study after their briefing. Locations. Names. Panic spots. None of it of any real use—but the few words Avi had scrawled on the back of those notes were gold and might make a difference.

"We'll get in by helicopter, our drop off point being around 10K south of the target area; from there we move north and find a hideout. . . Once in position, we find the cable and place the charges on staggered timings, under three or four lengths. If we get in too deep, we call in the IAF and turn the spot into a parking lot… And then—"

"And then we make for Syria…. Yeah."

"One last thing."

"Hit me."

"Nobody else will know that you're intended to go into that jail alone."

Ziki grunted and nodded slowly. They don't even know yet that we'll have to make it to Syria. . .

"You got a retrieval team set up for us?"

"As much as we're likely to get, yes, Malkielly gave me his word."

"Is that all, Boss?"

"Yeah. That's it."

"A piece of cake—all we have to do is take on the Iraqi Republican guards—its okay, they can't shoot straight to save their mothers, and then the Syrians."

Ziki smiled broadly at his friend, demonstrating an assurance that he certainly didn't feel. "Couldn't hit a Goddamned Mosque," Avi mumbled.

## Chapter 12

### The Dutch Nurse

**Henny Waggenhoysen eyed the young security officers in Ben Gurion Airport** as they loosened up her taut backpack.  All her belongings were tightly rolled, folded, and forced where possible into the bag.  As they peeled out her belongings and placed them onto the search table, Henny wondered how she was ever going to make everything fit back again.  She ran a hand through her short brown hair and looked around at the passengers waiting for their early morning flights.  They were reading newspapers, bribing a baby to keep silent with promises of treats.

"Why did you come to Israel?" asked one of the security officers.  She couldn't help noticing a long scar running down the side of his face.

"I'm a nurse.  I'm here to assist in rehabilitating the soldiers and children in the clinics."  She watched the other guard intimately examining her bras and underwear and pulled them gently from his hands.  "I've been traveling in Europe for three weeks before this," she explained, "so my clothes aren't very clean."

She waited for the men to finish their laborious inspection process, which included checking the hems for smuggled in items, running metal detectors over every article of clothing, and opening film containers.  When they discovered her Karate outfit and Black Belt, both men burst into giggles.  The man with the scar asked, "Are you carrying any weapons?"

"No, of course not."

"So, why did you come to Israel?" He asked.  The other officer smirked and stuffed her Karate outfit back into the pack.

"I told you, I'm a nurse.  Besides that, I came to visit friends and plan on doing archaeological work near Jerusalem."

"Your passport shows that you were here last year." He held the passport up to her as if to accuse.

"Yes, I was."

"Why?"

"Same reason." Henny leaned over to her other foot, placing her hand on her waist. "I'm not here to hurt anybody."

"Very well, then. Welcome to Israel."

Her friend the American Gavriela Ramon that she befriended in Spain preferred Paris, Berlin, London, or even Dublin to the heat of the Mediterranean countries. It was hard to put into words just how the city moved her.

She thought of...her mission, why she was there, what the city reminded her of…. Her restful meditation would've been perfect if the teenagers in the apartment above the café were not playing Middle Eastern rock and roll full blast.

…Centuries of pilgrims and conquering armies—defeated armies.

There was something else about Jerusalem. Something in the air, the people, the water, the food, the heat. Henny loved the quick joking of strangers on city busses. Jew, Arab, Christian, Muslim—people mixed casually in the market and more reverently Jews by the Western Wall.

Jerusalem sang a song of convergence; religious tension, religious devotion, poverty, wealth, ancient stories, but also an awareness of the modern world at large.

'Jerusalem is the city of gold and copper and a strange light, Jerusalem is the city that stands alone all that visit it become its violin.' It was what it was. It made no excuses and no apologies.

It was Saturday morning and Henny was going to the Damascus gate. In the North of the old city wall, the Damascus gate was in old times one of the largest and most magnificent of the openings through which travelers entered and exited Jerusalem. For a small fee, tour guides would tell you its history; built by Ottoman ruler, 'Suliman the Magnificent' when the Turks invaded and occupied Israel, it defended the city from marauders. Archers could pick out horseman and standard bearers from slim apertures and trap doors were built to dump boiling oil onto assailants who might breach the heavy wooden gates.

In modern times, workers still passed through the gate each morning on their way to work. Black and white or red and white *kaffias* adorned the heads of those workers who came from Jordan. Others were bare headed, in sunglasses or colorless turbans. A stuttering flow of men and women and children from the West Bank.

Bedouin women hoisted boxes of figs and grapes and eggplant onto their heads, carrying them to the market. They would sit the rest of the day until their boxes were empty. The sun had baked them brown and creased their faces like leather.

Two boyish Israeli soldiers lounged high up on the wall above the gate. One smoked, flicking ashes behind him. Their Galil's hung from their shoulders—ready to fire if necessary. But so innocent and nice.

There was hope in each little child who ran the meandering passage ways. A swarm of schoolboys hurried through the crowd on their way to Saturday classes. They called to each other as they went.

Henny did not stop long at the Damascus gate. Just enough to feel the sun hot and hard on her cheeks. She held her hand to her brow to shield her eyes. Arab merchants called out to Henny. They called out to any pretty girl, tourist or native, who walked by.

"Come to my shop. It costs nothing to look."

*"Salaam aleicum,* welcome, welcome, eh?" That one had the look of a wolf about him.

"Are your eyes real? So blue? How could they be so blue?"

"No," Henny replied, laughing, but passing him by. She knew better than to stop to flirt. The bazaar merchants could be very persuasive. "They are not really mine. At night, I take them out."

Another merchant stepped right in her way, and before she knew it, he'd placed a silk scarf around her shoulders, stopping her from breezing by him.

"Where do you come from Lady? From England?" He was missing one of his front teeth and he smelled of lamb and garlic.

"No—no thank you!" She pushed against the scarf, refusing to make eye contact.

"New Zealand? Australia? South Africa?"

She pushed again and was free.

"Give me a smile, pretty lady."

"No smile for you, silk merchant." She was on her way again.

The incident was quickly from her head and she was once again lost to her inner thoughts. She talked to herself as if she were hosting a Public Broadcasting special.

Why did Henny Waggenhoysen come to Jerusalem?

Why would anyone?

Ask those who had been cast out. Ask those who had been invited inside. The Christians on Via de la Rosa following Jesus's path of the cross. Ask the people at the wall. What did Jerusalem mean to those who tucked their prayers on tiny scrolls into the cracks of the holy Western Wall of the temple of King Solomon? To those who left their shoes outside the Dome of the Rock. What was Jerusalem? . . Salvation. . . Forgiveness. . . The very city walls were the receptacles of memory and meaning, history and time.

"Watch out!"

The screech of a car's brakes ripped her from her inner space. It was huge and black and skidding toward her.

And suddenly she was on the ground, stars swimming in her eyes.

A sharp pain in her hip. Her back. Her other hip.

Her palms were raw and hot from the pavement.

Though she looked about her, and saw things as they had been a second before, the street, the sidewalk, passers by—an American couple in the most hideously gaudy matching shorts outfits, horrible—she couldn't quite think.

. . . How did she fall?

She heard a car door slam and the sound of running feet.

And then people were scrambling from all around.

"Is she hurt?"

She slowly propped herself up, realizing she had been hit by the shiny black car. It had government plates. Oh, crap—she moaned inwardly—with her luck it was the Prime Minister's cavalcade or a head of state who would now be late for an important meeting regarding foreign affairs. . . if only she had been watching where she was going—but perhaps she would be invited to dinner at the Knesset. Perhaps she would get to meet an ambassador. . .

Ohhhh. She drew pavement-and-car-exhaust hot breath into her lungs.

"Are you hurt?" A man with a deep tan had come from the car. His warm hand lay respectfully upon her shoulder. He was wearing loafers. Nice loafers. Comfortable, but stylish. And a suit. Armani. And a Rolex.

A throb in her hip. "I'm sorry. I wasn't looking," Henny blurted and she pulled her legs under herself. She groaned.

"No—no—don't move— to the driver, Nathan!—get an ambulance," he ordered. As if to support her weight, he put a hand at her back.

The sun was so hot that for a moment Henny could only blink and then look up into the stranger's face. "No ambulance," she protested.

"Don't move. You could be seriously hurt and not know it." The stranger knelt on one knee beside her. He examined her, his head bobbing up and down, looking for signs of injury. His fingers were gentle on her temples, holding her head still. "Is anything broken? Your back—is it okay? How is your neck? You didn't hit your head?"

"No ambulance." She said again and shook her head slightly, beginning to come to herself once more.

She stopped. She was a disheveled mess. Her legs were bare and dirty from the street. One sandal had fallen off and lay on its side next to the car's tire. There was a horrid little stone poking maniacally into the soft flesh of her thigh. Her hair. . .

Otherwise. . . she realized. . . she wasn't really hurt.

She was suddenly acutely embarrassed. People had gathered around, milling and watching from the sidewalk. Those Americans. Ugh. That color.

She flushed.

"I—. . . I'm okay." Her thigh was numb, her hip smarted, but there was no real damage. She shook her head with a little more life. "It just scared me, that's all."

She moved to stand and the stranger helped her up, with a reassuring grip on her elbow. "Easy now," he said.

Only her palms showed a bit of blood where the pavement had bit into her skin.

"Are you certain you're all right? We can have an ambulance here in no time."

"Really," she tried to assuage him, "it's just a bump and a scare."

"You can walk?"

"I can walk." Henny steadied herself on his strong arm.

The driver found his wits and rushed from the car to her side.

"My driver," the man said by way of introduction and perhaps explanation for the man's desperate state.

"Forgive me. Forgive me!" The driver begged. "I did not see you and then it was too late. I stomped the brake—"

"It's okay." Henny nodded and tried to soothe him. "I'm okay. I think it was my fault."

"You are okay?" The driver pressed. "I am completely responsible."

"We will take care of everything you need," the man in the suit confirmed.

"That won't be necessary." She felt so silly! "Really. I'm fine."

The driver in IDF uniform slung his machine gun towards his back in a non threatening manner, spread his hands and thanked her. "I'm so— . . . relieved. I thought—you were on the pavement and I thought—"

Henny waved her hands at him. "I should have been looking. I wasn't really looking."

A man on a moped wheeled himself slowly past the dark car, he had come from the line forming, when clear he flung them all a hateful look before speeding off. A yellow and a blue car were waiting behind the black car. Henny could see the drivers getting impatient. Heat waves rose from the hoods of their cars.

"The least we could do is give you a ride," the man in the suit said.

"Yes," the driver agreed, over enthusiastically. "I can take you anywhere."

"No, really—I was just walking. . ." Henny refused. He had very nice eyes, this stranger. Warm green eyes.

"Where can we take you?" His driver was now heading back to his car, beckoning her to follow.

She shook her head. "You really mustn't make a fuss over me."

One of the cars behind began to blare its horn.

The driver stopped to shout in the direction of the other cars before climbing in and slamming his door.

"My driver." The man in the suit said again, shrugging with chagrin. "I don't get to choose them. They're assigned to me with the car."

"No harm. We should just all forget about it."

"Truly," he said with the hint of a smile on his lips. "It would be my pleasure to take you wherever you want to go . . . Miss?"

"Henny," she answered and she couldn't help but smile herself.

"Ziki. Ziki Barak," he introduced himself. When the man smiled an array of soft creases appeared around his eyes… Very nice green eyes.        She felt warmth rising in her cheeks. "Thank you for checking on me, but I really do—"

"Nonsense," Ziki replied. "We will take you first to your hotel where you might wash up and then, to lunch. It is absolutely the least I can do. Considering."

Henny looked again at the waiting cars. Ziki's driver was behind the wheel, gripping it tightly. He looked relieved, but wary. Another blare of the horn.

"We can't stand here and argue all day, can we?" Ziki pressed her.

She shook her head and felt again the unexpected warmth spreading across her cheeks. "No."

"Then it's settled."

"Yes."

She let Ziki take her by the elbow and guide her to the passenger door of the car.  Sitting down, she was pleased to realize that she was hardly hurt at all.  Cuts and bruises, yes.  And, her back may be sore come morning.  All the same, she felt very little more than the heat of her cheeks sitting in the back of the big dark car.  Next to an olive skinned handsome stranger named Ziki.

"Hotel. . . ?"

"Hostel," she corrected.  "Markley Hostel.  On Ben Yehuda street.

Ziki thumped the seat in front of him.  "Markley Hostel for the crippled lady, Nathan.  And mind the tourists, will you.  We like to keep them alive."

## Chapter 13

**Syria Jail—Duma—Iraq**

**Later as he was approaching, Ziki listened in to the men while they packed their gear.** Their voices carried a distance—thin and hollow and young and damn stupid—in the empty helicopter hangar. The sun outside glared in through the wide open doors. The sky was washed out and hazy, a winter day.

Moshe: "What are you doing with that, David?"

David: "Getting rid of it."

Illan: "It's broken?"

"Nah, it's okay. I just don't want to carry all that shit."

"Pack it any way."

Gady perked up, butting in: "That's good stuff; the army says so."

Manny: "You don't even know what it does."

Now Gady left his packing and wanted to know: "What is it?"

"Green stuff. Some sort of instant crap for energy or something like that."

"Give it."

"No."

Avi came out of the latrine smoking one of Ziki's cigarettes and barked an order at the men. He called them "ladies" and that started a roll of replies that would have made the ears of Ziki's grandmother burn.

Ziki stayed where he was, slightly out of sight, slightly out of thought. He was lying low until the helicopter showed up to take them up into the air.

Voices.

He gave them half an ear.

"Cause you're the one that needs these—it's for wiggling your ass. This is a shiny thing, when I move it; I'll explain that one to you later."

"These are for what?"

"You got the choice of chocolate chip or raspberry cream."

"Take'm both."

"Fine, you carry them."

"Start packing, buddy."

"Nuts and bolts, shit. Weighs a ton."

"Why don't you put that big boulder in your pack?"

"Shove it, asshole."

"What about these here?"

Avi's voice inserted into the din, grinding out instructions like a truck driver at a car wash. "Take as much link ammo as you can carry—we'll want to feed the fuck out of the Mini-mighty. This is the first time that I am getting truly screwed with this kind of loser squadron—and my ass does not like the desert—you hear me, ladies."

"Hang yourself, grandma!" the reply.

"You call us ladies cause you like us?"

Ziki tossed his cigarette butt to the cement floor. He crushed it out with the toe of his boot. Time to get the show on the road.

"All right!" he shouted as he emerged from where he'd been sitting alone. "Get your stuff together. We're operational in fifteen minutes."

Avi echoed his command with a vague threat to get them moving more quickly. "This afternoon, Gentlemen."

The men scattered back to their tasks—packing and sorting and counting and keeping their heads suddenly low. "The Commander must be talking to me," Ziki heard Gady say to David.

"Oh yeah, why's that?"

"He said 'Gentlemen,' didn't he? He could not be addressing all of you."

"Funny guy—" Avi interceded as the soft laughter tossed between men dwindled. "You two—why don't you go see the supply sergeant. See if you can find 25 kilos of 'Clay' and a dozen RPGs."

"Do you want any Milans or TOWs?"

"Gimme some," came a reply.

"Me, too—but only if you are willing to carry them."

More laughter. Now nervous.

"Enough chatter," Avi silenced them. "We're airborne in twelve minutes. Time to take your last shit or forever hold it."

The last few minutes were a blur of activity: bodies in the way of bodies; packs cinched tightly closed; no spills, luckily, but Gady knocked his temple against David's helmet and complained.

They piled into the jeep that would take them to the airstrip, just thirty seconds under time. The drive to the waiting chopper was short. The air on Ziki's face dried the sweat under his eyes.

At the chopper the men scurried like beavers to fill a winter hoard. Boots on asphalt. The clinking of helmets, machine guns, ammo.

Sergeant Major Lipsky was shouting directions: "Unload this thing onto the chopper. Move it, you, or I'll have to have a word with you ladies about these war games."

Ziki and Avi let him shout himself hoarse.

"Hey David, see if you can get the other gear over there."

Manny bent over and picked up a folded piece of paper from beneath his boot. "You dropped this, David."

David lunged for it. "Don't unfold it…. Son of a bitch."

Manny danced back. "It was open."

"Don't read it."

"No?" Manny pushed back David's hand and began to read aloud.

"'Dearest Miriam. . . My dearest, dearest shiny thing. . .' "

"Hand it back," Ziki ordered, tossing down his cigarette. "We all got those letters. No need reminding us."

"'This is a letter I've never wanted to write or you to read, my love. . . . . . 'If you're reading this I'm dead. . .'"

A momentary silence fell over the squad.

Ziki's jaw was tight. Voluntary. . . volunteers. . . they all had those letters.

David had taken his letter and was tucking it into the breast pocket of his flack jacket. "How far we got on foot, Commander?"

"Enough," Ziki answered.

Avi was shouting: "That's it; we're in the air in three minutes—move it and bag it up. Squadron! You are what you carry. Everything goes in the chopper, except for the Map kit—"

"—Which we will carry in these 'designer sun bags.' Right, Moshe?"

"Anything we've forgotten…?"

"Only the obvious things."

"Listen up—" Avi's voice was far too big in the confines of the chopper. The blades squealed and then began to whoosh in wide arches over head. Everyone had tucked into his seat in the belly of the whirly-bird. "We're a search team looking for downed pilots of oil company crews."

Ground crew leaned his head in, his sunglasses like a bug's reflecting back suddenly pale faces. This was it. "All set?" the ground man asked.

Ziki nodded. The huge door, like a giant rib sliding into place, rolled closed.

The man ducked and scuttled away.

The chopper swayed, lifted, hovered, and rose.

This was it…

**The helicopter pilot had a freckled face that made him look like a kid.** The pilot gestured the men to gather around and yelled out. "Pay attention."

The rotary blades chopped the air in swift circular strokes. The whole craft echoed with the noise—pu-pupupupu-pu-pupupupu. They had to scream to be heard.

The pilot was shouting, "As of yesterday anti-aircraft missiles are on route, so we're going down a bit lower. . . To about 15 meters. . . Okay?"

"Let's go through those coordinates again. . . " Ziki said.

The pilot nodded and leaned his head back so that he could direct his shout toward Ziki—but his eyes remained straight ahead. "We'll brake and drop about 10k west. If attacked when you touch ground, call and I'll come back and give them a taste of our cannons.

"If we're met with force, I'll want plenty of covering fire from you on my approach, okay."

"Yeah, yeah," the pilot agreed. "If the shit hits the fan and my chopper goes down, whatever way you go we'll go the other—"

Moshe's smart mouth was a step ahead of his brain once more. "You're leaving us?"

"Nothing personal, son. To the Iraqis—us choppers, we're simply rescue air crew. But you guys are Godzilla."

Moshe sat back, apparently a little relieved. "We love you, too—air boys."

A few minutes later, Ziki was roused from his thoughts by a sense that the copter had descended yet again. The ground was close below them. In the darkness he could see features of the desert below: swaths of sand and barely discernable glimmers of reflected light pollution.

It was dark. Very dark.

He lit a smoke and realized that he'd forgotten to bring another pack.

No time like the present to quit. . .

Until he bought another pack, at least. And the Syrians weren't likely to hand a pack over.

Moshe was talking again. That boy had a big, big mouth.

"Chinook?" Moshe asked. It was the helicopter's model.

The pilot turned his mouth toward Moshe to answer, apparently not numbed yet to Moshe's many questions and ever-present and ill-timed sense of humor. "Is that a complaint about the American equipment?"

"Me—complain?"

"The bastards are great. Especially now that we modified them."

"Not—"

"Turn around to that heading—" The pilot pointed and his co-pilot flipped switches in response. To Moshe: "It's not your mother's Toyota."

Ziki leaned in. He knew they were close and he wanted unnecessary chatter to cease.

The pilot checked out the ground below them, nodding. "O.K. that's it. . . 90 knots. 25 meters. 90 knots. Point left 4k. Left. Left lights. . . Left lights on. Pay attention to the early warning systems."

"You see anything? Hostiles? Is anybody tracking us?" Ziki asked him.

The pilot shook his head. "Nothing to worry about—we come in here all the time. They really don't know how to work their radar systems. They almost never detect us."

"They do have those Russian Sams."

"Yeah, but they have to be able to read to use them. Pilot to crew—Commander, we are now over the border. We're over the Iraqi border."

Ziki stiffened. "Do not address me again as 'Commander' from here on out—that's an order."

Ziki was concerned. . . No recent satellite pics for their point of touch down, no decent details on the maps. And, of course, the plan in Iraq could be meant to fail... Malkielly.

You have to get on with what you got, the man said.

Their drop point was over the desert heights by the main supply route. . . . Finding a hide out in pitch black. . . Uncharted terrain. . . At first light you could find yourself in the middle of an Iraqi market. . .

The chopper swerved low, descended, and turned around its nose.

This was it.

The huge door slid open, and the men scooted to the lines. A clack-clack-clack of clips hooking onto the descent cables, and—

"Go!"

Moshe and David were first, sliding off the side of the chopper and cruising down the lines. Their hooks made a metallic sound—a whirring-scrape as the cables took their weight and bore them to the desert below.

"Next!" Avi shouted, and slapped the shoulders of Manny and Gady, who disappeared and slid down, down, disappearing into the night.

Ziki could already see Moshe and David with their guns dangling from slings. The next two men landed and joined them, unhooking themselves fast and spreading out, ready to deflect fire.

"Just you and me—" Avi grinned at Ziki. "Got a smoke?"

Ziki slapped his clip onto the line and grasped both clip and line tightly. "Smoke? Those things will stunt your growth." He fell out of the chopper, let the line snag and catch him, and then he was slipping down, and whomph, his feet hit ground, dust raised and gave under his boots.

Avi dropped to his side a half-second later.

The chopper circled above them, nose pointing downward. No gun fire . . . no lights . . . no noises—though Ziki's ears were still deadened from the popping air of the copter blades—nothing.

So far, so good.

The pilot rolled his copter upwards, hardly stopping to say good riddance, his face placid and focused on the distance. The black unmarked chopper lifted into the night sky and was gone as quickly, if not so quietly, as it came.

**Ziki ordered the men to knuckle down until daybreak.** They squatted on their packs, digging shallow beds in the ground to keep their heads and gear out of the line of sight.

Like graves. . . Ziki had always thought so of the man-sized hovels that it was customary to dig. Side by side so buds could pass nutri-packs or flasks or unlit smokes back and forth.

"In this mess you want to make the biggest hole possible to hide in." You'd take your spoon out and start digging if it'd help. But then the training takes over. You sit yourself up, straighten up your clothes and check your gear, your pocket grenades . . . check that your magazines are on tight and ready to go. "Digging in," as they called it, was the quickest and easiest way to stay out of trouble. Duck below the dirt. The wind skimmed right over you and in the dark a patrol could be virtually about to step into your ditch before they'd know you were there.

When dawn came, none of them had slept a wink despite the quiet calm all around them. The calm before the storm—they were all familiar with the expression. In the gray of first light, Avi cautiously stood and scanned the horizon, his binoculars to his eyes.

"There!" Avi pointed. Ziki hunkered down with the binoculars to look. On the white strip of sand . . . the missile junction boxes. They were not 10k off. It was right there in front of them.

Damn luck.

"David," Ziki ordered, "mark the land line."

The men were bustling around in their holes, packing up, stretching tight muscles. Moshe had ripped through another one of his meal packs and was pulling a face at the flavor. At the rate he was going through the mini-meals he wouldn't have a damn thing left if he had to walk home.

"Hey—" Ziki called to him. "Lay off those things a little."

"Right," Moshe responded, lowering the silver pack in a lax hand.

"Problem—Ziki." Avi nudged Ziki's shoulder.

Ziki turned to him. "Tell me."

"Three o'clock, Iraqi patrol on our doorstep."

"Shit."

The men jumped to. Binoculars pulled from packs, raised. . .

"Some damn luck," someone swore.

"They haven't seen us yet." David was watching the patrol as intently as Avi. "We can't stay here," he said. "We gotta move."

"Now?" Moshe's mouth was lined with chocolate.

"No." Ziki shook his head. "We wait. They haven't seen us. They may not. Locate and mark the land line."

David licked his lower lip nervously. "You don't think—"

"No," Ziki said, "you don't think. You follow orders."

David nodded hesitantly and went back to his figures.

Moshe brightened. "Maybe we can take one of their 'RVs' for all this stuff we're carrying. . . ?"

Gotta hand it to the kid, Ziki wryly observed, his mouth never stopped. Maybe like a snake, his mouth would keep on working after Moshe's head had been crushed with a rock. It was an ill thought and Ziki shook it off.

Avi leaned closer to Ziki. "Not trying to step on your toes, Ziki—"

Ziki lowered his gaze. "You think we should move."

"Yeah," he nodded. "I do."

Ziki leaned back against the dirt and took out a cigarette. He hadn't lit one since they landed so the flicker of his lighter wouldn't give their location away. Now with the sun up and Iraqis about to step on his toes, his whole body craved a smoke so badly he thought the hairs on his wrist might jump right out of their follicles.

"Ok. Where do we go?"

"We'll go for shelter—" Avi scanned the brightness, looking for caves, hollows, ravines, scrub—anything. "Right—over there."

He pointed to a dark line to the Southeast. "There. We go lay low in that brush, stay close to the ground."

"If it's not inhabited."

Avi nodded grimly. "I think it's far enough from the road—we'll be okay."

"I'd settle for a carton of cigarettes."

Avi laughed silently. "I'd willingly smoke your carton of cigarettes."

"Did I tell you that you're an asshole?"

"Not in the last fifteen minutes."

Ziki shook his head. "David—did I hear you say you marked the land line?"

"Yes, Sir," David replied. "I can radio in, Sir. Let air response know our position."

Ziki gave a cursory nod and sat in the dirt until David had the radio ready. *Shit. He should have let Malkielly make a civilian of him again.*

David handed him the mouthpiece. And he took it, letting his hands dangle limply between his knees for a long moment. Then he began the call. "This is Barak 2. We are on the ground. Call sign—over."

He could hear Moshe and Iosi behind him, "—carry equal ammo?"

"Fuck no."

He kept the mouthpiece close to his lips, and listened as David held the radio still.

The air waves were silent.

"This is Barak 2. We are on the ground—call sign—over."

Manny was shaking his head. "The transmitter took a bang on landing. I heard it hit the dirt."

"Without the radio we're in the shit, man."

Ziki let the transmitter hang limply on his knees.

"Quiet like a dead line . . . a dead line. . ."

*. . . Malkielly. . . When I'm back home you better*....Did Ziki know the full story—would he ever know the full story or only what Malkielly thought it useful for him to know?. . . He really wants that Melvin Finkle back. . . Or dead. What more does Finkle know? Only the names and locations of 200 or more covert agents in Arab countries and undercover assignments. . . How did a worm like that get so much sensitive information in his head?

Bad radio. . . a dead frequency? Meaning what?

Meaning we're not getting through. . . Meaning maybe Malkielly lied when he said he'd have retrieval at the ready. Meaning nothing, perhaps—dumbest of the dumb luck.

"So do we go for an 'RV' or what?" Moshe was eating another of his mini-packs. Strawberry; Ziki could smell the sickly sweet of it.

"Yeah," said Avi. "We'll go for the RV."

Ziki tuned them out. "Hello Zero, hello Zero. This is Barak2, radio check over."

Nothing. . .

"Hello Zero, hello Zero, this is Barak 2, radio check over."

"Hey… is there an apostrophe in 'we're in?'"

"In what?"

"As 'we're in the shit.'" There was no levity in Moshe's voice.

"Goddammit, Moshe. Keep your mouth shut just these five minutes."

"Oh, yes."

"Hello, Zero. Hello, Zero. This is Barak 2. Radio check over."

Not even the crackle of empty air.

Ziki tossed the transmitter into the dirt.

"Forget any help for now, the radio contact has gone south."

Avi tossed his cigarette butt into the ground. "In short, we're fucked."

"No," Ziki said, refusing to give into the rise of dread that had made the others pale. "Just keep us out of sight of that patrol and give me time to think."

"I think. . ."

"What are we doing, Commander?" David was showing strain around his eyes.

Ziki put his cigarette between his lips and looked off in the direction of the mobile missile launcher. "We're gonna do what we came here to do."

The look on Avi's face was more than priceless. The glare in his eyes suggested that Ziki had lost his mind.

Ziki took in each of the men as his gaze roamed over them and their equipment.

"We're gonna blow those mobiles sky high." He turned back toward the Iraqi patrol in the distance. "But first we're gonna get ourselves further out of their way."

Ziki motioned to Avi. "Lock and load, all of you."

They hurried through the harsh ground, crawling when necessary, stooping as low as they could while they moved. They passed info in harsh whispers.

"Phosphorous kit."

"Right. Got it."

"RPGs—I got mine. What about the shoulder thing?"

"Got it. . . come on. . . coming in."

"Which way?"

"Over there. Okay we—"

"If we were on the choppers now we wouldn't be sitting targets."

"That is ingenious of you."

Ziki was first to reach an outcropping of rock and hunch behind it. He motioned Avi and Iosi in. They squatted beside him.

Avi waved others toward them. "What's happening behind us, Moshe? I need to know. Talk to me."

"No one's behind us."

"We may as well have landed in the center of Baghdad."

"How many did you count?"

"Ten —maybe twelve if there are men inside that APC."

"That's just a couple a piece."

"They have an APC."

"We have the element of surprise; they don't expect us being here, they have not spotted us." Ziki said, noting the frowns all around him. "And we're going to use it."

"What? How?"

"We are going to attack before they know what hit them"

"He's gone nuts," someone whispered.

"It's the last thing they're expecting."

"It's the last thing I was expecting," Moshe returned.

The words were out before Ziki could stop them. "Well Moshe—you're dead anyway, so anything you do is a bonus. If you can accept the fact that you are already dead, then you will be fearless—invincible."

*Hell, no. Malkielly had taught him that.*

"But we need to be just that… A God forsaken place."

Moshe swore silently at the loss of the APC, he'd had his eye on the comfortable ride. They took the places Ziki assigned them.

The firefight was over, fast.

The surprise worked: the Iraqis didn't know what hit them; Ziki's grunts were well trained. The recoilless propelled shoulder rocket found its target, poof, the APC was gone in a plume of smoke.

Ziki had placed Avi and Manny in the rocks where they took aim, picking off what was left of the Iraqi patrol. David rushed to flank the patrol from the side and shot two more. He opened the way for Moshe to move in, close enough to pull the pin and roll the grenade under what remained of his much-coveted "RV."

From his spot, Ziki could see the regret on Moshe's face as the wagon bloomed outward in a smoke flower and then caught flame.

.

The remaining Iraqi followed him, tossing his gun aside as he went.

Another laid a round of fire toward Avi and Manny, firing wildly, his aim ineffective—he was watching where he was going, but shooting behind himself as he scrambled down into the desert. Thirty or forty paces he ditched his Kalashnikov and ran as fast as he could.

Ziki's men yelled out with triumphant joy.

Moshe loosed several shots into the air. "Hey, you bastards, we're still here—run, run!

The shots echoed across the empty expanse of sand and stone.

Ziki waved to Avi and Manny as they picked off the remaining couple from the higher ground.

"After all the smoke and noise we made, we need to get our asses in gear—those mobiles aren't gonna blow themselves up." Avi was already giving the orders. "Leave your packs—toss anything you don't need. Don't carry more than ten kilograms—water. But no mini-packs, and let's move it ladies."

Moshe was grumbling about the lost "RV" once more, but fell silent as they all fell silent when the march turned to a jog. They were at the mobiles in no time.

One cast a thin dark shadow, the missile's cone pointed toward the now almost blue sky.

"Goddamn missiles, Russian nasties," someone swore.

Ziki was unpacking the plastic clay and detonators. "Lay the explosives at that cable juncture and the cable by it."

"Yes, Sir. Pass it on."

"Shit. It's a green one; I hate these fucking green. Suppose to be nourishing things—taste like shit."

"Give it here, I'll have it."

"I'm gonna have a piece. We've still got the brown ones?"

"You gonna blow this thing or wait around eating nutri-caca—"Avi was muscling the slower ones to work. "The Iraqis will make housewives out of you. Move, move, move."

They had far more Plastique than was necessary. Each man kneaded a handful into place. Ziki set the caps and wires.

"When this is done, Commander, can we try to call in the cavalry?"

Manny laughed. "Hey, Moshe—see if you can raise David's mother on that radio? He wants to be rescued."

"Oh, yeah—I'll try; what's her number?"

"Assholes."

The last piece in place—Ziki waved them all clear from the launcher then flattened himself behind a rise of stone.

He connected wires and twisted them in the right order. Clutched the detonator in his right hand, making himself as small as possible behind the stones.

Three. . .

    Two. . .

        one. . .

The ground heaved once and gave a series of shudders. The mobile launchers splintered into twenty-dozen pieces and handfuls of flaming grit, flipping here and there across the sky.

Ziki caught his breath as sand and debris filtered down. *"I hate explosions."*

In the moment when all went still once more, he lurched up and ran to join his men, who were already heading back to their gear and the small amount of cover that they had made themselves.

They were suiting-up hurriedly as he approached, tightening belts and straps. Their faces were grimy with sweat and sand and dirt, their hands filthy.

"Move out; the whole Iraqi army knows we're here."

"Try again to call the choppers, David," Illan said. "We've blown the puppy—it's time to go home." Ziki knew that there would not be any choppers.

"The radio still isn't working," came David's reticent reply.

". . . That is a bad omen."

Avi stopped Ziki—"You're bleeding."

Blood? Ziki suddenly felt the flow of wetness that had soaked his socks and squinted with the recognition of suppressed pain. . . Air hitting a wound . . .

opened skin. . .

"We need the aid kit."

"Who's hit?"

"Nothing, just a scratch."

"Scratch—my ass."

Ziki sat in the sand and called to Manny. "Check our perimeters. Keep your eyes open… scan the horizon, stay alert."

"I'm watching! I'm watching!" The reply was terse.

"No one around? Good."

Avi used his knife to cut Ziki's pant leg to the knee. "You okay?"

"Yeah. I wasn't shot, if that's what you think."

"I was thinking shrapnel."

"Far less heroic—I 'm pretty sure I just gouged it on that hill."

"I better have a look at it." He paused. "You hear that?"

"Yeah. ."

It was the sound of explosions in the distance. Boom.

Boom.

Boom, boom, boom.

Moshe brightened. "Maybe we'll be getting some air support, maybe nothing to do with us. Maybe they're killing each other, they do that,—you know?"

"Try that radio again," Manny urged.

David scooped it up and handed the mouthpiece over to Ziki.

Ziki focused on the call he made—avoiding having to watch Avi clean his wound. "Come in anyone. This is Barak 2. We are at ground. Call sign, over. . . Hello, Zero. This is Barak 2. This is ground—call sign, over…" Nothing.

Dead air. Of course. The radio was never going to work. Malkielly…. It wasn't supposed to work. Of course, of course.

"Nothing. Shit." David's face showed the strain of the last hours; the terrain and elevation changed rapidly.

"Is it my imagination or is it getting cold?" Moshe hugged himself.

"We're higher up, the elevation, you know."

"This is Barak 2. We are ground. Call sign. Anyone up there? I'll have a fix for you, over. . . Hello? Any call sign. Any call sign? This is Barak 2. We are grounded. Call sign and need assistance, over."

Not a crackle.

"Give it up," Avi said looking at Ziki with a knowing look.

Ziki nodded. He tossed the mouthpiece down.

"What next, Commander?"

"A choice."

David called Manny and Havel in to listen. The men crouched around Ziki as he picked up a stick and drew what he remembered of the maps they'd all seen when they were briefed just hours before.

"Okay—the radio's out and we're just sitting here waiting to get caught or shot—not a choice any of us want. We have two options: one—we can go for the emergency extraction point and if we get there alive, we can sit and wait. They gave us 48 hours and we've spent—Avi how many since airlift?"

"16 hours, Sir."

"16 hours—okay that means 32 more hours out here in the cold. We can get to our pick-up point and dig in and hope the Iraqi patrols that come after us, now that they know we're here, are blind, deaf, and dumb."

"Or?"

Ziki straightened…Damn Malkielly. It was going just as he had planned, Ziki was sure. "Or . . . we head for the mountains—Syria; once past the border we steal some local clothes and blend in. Then make our way home."

"Syria? No fucking way."

"That's 15-20k at least—maybe more."

"Not even—we're closer than that."

"Listen up," said Avi, menacingly. "The Commander is talking."

The men fell silent, but they were not at ease.

Ziki nodded his thanks. "The first option means we cross away from the Iraqis' concentration. And that's just trouble now that they have wind we're around. Getting through to the Syrian border is the only choice."

"No kidding," Moshe sniffed.

A moment of silence felt interminable as the men seemed to sink into their bones and contemplation. David absently rubbed the spot on his jacket where he'd put the letter to his wife and kid.

"Exactly how far is the border?" Manny asked.

"Line of sight is about 15k," David said.

"That's a hell of a long way over mountains," someone scoffed.

"On the other hand . . . between us and the helicopter, there's a lot of pissed off Iraqis."

Another moment passed where no one said anything.

"So, it's the border?" Avi asked.

One by one, the men nodded. "The border."

"Syria."

"Shhheeeezzz, why not."

"Beats getting picked off by the Iraqis; personally I prefer the Syrians, they are dumber."

"Yeah…right."

Ziki stood. "We're decided then." Just as Malkielly planned it, son of a bitch.

"Let's not stand here checking each other out, ladies. Let's move!" Avi ordered, enforcing Ziki's orders.

Moments later, they had left the shallow cover and were cautiously picking their way out of the rocks and scrub.

Avi stayed at Ziki's side. "How's your leg?"

"It'll do. You go take point, then Illan and Manny, then the rest of you."

They did as he ordered.

"We're looking pretty good. . . We sort of have a plan."

"And no one's dead."

"Yet....Syria next!"

The thought went through Ziki's head like a sharp knife. . . Malkielly had it all planned in advance. . . he'd actually thought it through before Ziki had ever set foot in the chopper—perhaps even long before Ziki had set foot in his office—reducing the options so that the squad's only rational option was to head for Syria. He might not even have cared about the mobiles—or the threat they posed—convenient excuses, plausible deniability. Malkielly wanted Melvin Finkle out of there.

Yes, that's it. Ziki shook his head. It's all Malkielly.

The cold-brained, dead-hearted genius.

### The weather and terrain changed fast... Mountains.

"Holy crap—my fingers are frozen to this gun."

"Shut up, Moshe," someone growled. The others were growing tired of him, as well.

"Hey you're only as cold as your body wants you to think."

"How about dead. I want your body to think it's dead—maybe then you'll shut up." It was Manny. Manny who usually didn't say anything—Ziki sometimes even forgot that he was there, doing whatever it was Manny did, thinking whatever Manny thought in his quiet way. If Manny was loosing patience, God help the rest of them.

"Any chance we'll find some shelter?" David asked.

Ziki shook his head. He lit a cigarette to keep himself warmer.

"Those things will stunt your growth, you know," Avi said as he fell in at Ziki's side.

"At least it isn't snowing," David growled. His nose was bright red. His cheeks were pale. The others looked just as bad: down on sleep, tired from crossing kilometers at the half-lope that convinced them they were moving faster than if they were simply walking.

A scan of the horizon in all directions showed them no light, no buildings, not even a damn herd of goats.

"How far have we come?" Ziki asked.

Avi checked his pedometer. "6k over these mountains and a little over. We've got another hour or two, depending on the terrain."

"Right. It doesn't make sense to rest, does it? We should just keep moving."

"You're the boss."

Moshe was bartering for mini-meals with Ilann. "What is it? Vanilla or Chocolate?"

"Just take it. Whatever it is, it's warmer than my balls right now."

"Yeah, mine dropped off two k back."

"What the hell do you need balls for, Moshe?"

"Ask your sister—"

"That's enough," Ziki raised his voice.

The chatter dropped immediately.

A hushed question—the speaker was out of breath. "Are we gaining altitude?"

"Yeah—the wind is colder."

"These hills are killing me."

"Keep your eyes out for bogies," Avi hissed.

"I can't feel my toes."

"I can't feel my cheeks."

"Cut the chatter."

They trudged on, now in grudging and absolute silence, except for occasional grunts when someone missed a step or when Moshe belched loudly and brought a round of scattered, if tense, laughter.

Each step was closer to—home. . .Or hypothermia, if you wanted to be dark about it. It could happen so fast out here with no cover. Or death in a ditch? Or evisceration by a landmine. . . A fall down a rocky hill . . .

And the Syrians.

Each step only took them closer to Syria and Syrians. "At least they have a border with us—it's closer to home."

"Not the friendliest of friendly neighbors."

"Dammit."

They found what they thought was a dirt road—or a wash—they couldn't be sure and began to follow it without discussion, out of the certainty that roads and dried out irrigation ditches inevitably led to somewhere before they led to nowhere.

"Hey!" Manny was gesturing at the others. He was in the lead, temporarily. They'd started taking turns doing look-out, scouting slightly ahead of the others. "Hey! Heads up—there's some kind of vehicle coming up the road."

The men scattered and crouched at the side of the road, machine guns raised.

"Yeah, I see it."

"What is it?"

"An armored troop transport—"

"Nah. . . It's bright yellow. . . "

"Hand me those binoculars."

"What the hell—"

"It's a taxi!"

"A taxi—out here?"

"Good thing, too. I was about to convert to Islam."

Avi scrambled to the side of the road, pulling on jacket tails to get the attention of the others. "Clear out—off the road right now. Make yourselves invisible."

"Hey, Commander. Make sure it's got a heater and a radio!"

"Anything else?" Ziki laughed. "Maybe a bar?"

"Power steering, electric windows, ABS, tape player, and we really need a mobile phone."

"Zip it up—"

"Quiet—" Avi and Manny hushed Moshe at the same time.

The minutes felt like hours, before they heard the engine's steady thrumming as the car made its way along the road toward them. An old Mercedes taxi, painted putrid yellow, was coming slowly up the road.

On his sign, Ziki, Avi, and Manny jumped onto the road to block its way. Ziki pointed his machine gun at the driver—a middle-aged man with frizzy gray hair hanging from beneath his *Kafia* headdress. Manny and Ilan moved in behind the taxi as it came to a screeching and dusty stop.

"*Lah rimaya, lah rama*…..Don't shoot! Don't kill me," the driver yelled out. His hands in the air, palms white in his fear. "*La rimaya, lah rama*….Don't shoot! Don't kill me!"

Moshe pointing a handgun; he opened the driver's door.

"*Yalla imshi,*" Havel shouted. Move quickly! He grabbed the driver by his jacket and yanked him out to the side of the road.

"Havel—tie him and leave him there," Ziki said. "Make sure he can work his way out of his bonds and get himself home—or the desert will kill him."

Seven men with machine guns and gear in the taxi were outrageous, like a bad joke. Ziki had to stop Manny and Ilan from stuffing Moshe in the trunk.

Avi took the wheel. "Point me northwest. Geez this thing is a bastard to shift. How many ks to the border?"

"We lost ground on that ridge we couldn't cross." Had to backtrack and climb again. "Still about nine ks."

"Turn the heating onto high."

"Already did."

"You were dying of hypothermia an hour ago and now look at you," Manny snickered.

In the driver's seat, Avi flipped down the sun visor and laughed. "Ziki, look at this stuff."

Ziki laughed, too. He felt lightheaded now in this cab—although Manny was sitting on the tail of his jacket and he could hardly move.

A sign on the visor read, 'Kai'ima welcomes careful drivers.'"

"That leaves you out," Ziki muttered.

"Give me a goddamned smoke; this mission started me smoking again," Avi replied.

There was no one, the road was deserted. What would anyone seeing them have thought, seeing all those men crammed into a taxicab? And try as they might, there was no place to put all the guns and packs that didn't stick out like sore thumbs. No one felt comfortable with most of their fire power locked in the trunk. Avi was a keen enough driver to miss several pot holes that would have sunk the car. A broken axle or cracked radiator and they'd be back outside, in the cold, hauling to the Syrian border.

"What's that light up ahead?"

Avi slowed the taxi to a crawl. "David—how close to the border did you say we were?"

"3k. . .back there…. no. . . No—wait!"

Around a bend and down a hill—the border.

And half the Syrian army.

"That wouldn't be the border, would it, David?"

"No!" He shouted. "Moshe—your caca chocolate is all over my map."

"We've got trouble—" Avi shouted. "That's an Iraqi checkpoint straight ahead."

"Looks like Iraqi border police, not military."

"They'll still figure out who we are—"

"Bail out of the cab—"

"No," Ziki countered. "Stay put. Let me think this through. Avi—limp this thing into the waiting line. . . I need a minute to think."

"Commander—that's suicide!"

"We cannot stay."

Moshe was shouting. He tossed his pack out the window. "We're gonna go for that ridge at three o'clock."

"I said stay put, you fucking—" Ziki tried to grab him by the collar, but Moshe had opened the door and slipped out the side. The cab was moving so slowly he didn't even have to roll out.

"Dammit."

If one went, they all had to go. But maybe they still had some time.

Ziki turned to Avi. "As soon as that guard brings his face over here, take him out. Quietly. No gunfire."

"You're the boss, Boss."

Ziki spoke to the men still in the back seat, using the rearview mirror to make eye contact. "As soon as that guard falls, we all bail out. We have to now, they'll spot Moshe; there's no chance staying with the taxi…"

Right, came the unspoken reply. It was an idiotic plan and Ziki knew it. The men were low on ammo and sitting in the cab had allowed them to sink into tiredness and stiffness. What else could they do? Running gave the men a small chance. Ziki had no chance; he had to stay and be caught…Finkel!

Running to Syrians—a laughable comedy.

*Malkielly. . . I'm going to make you buy me a bottle of Château Briande 1953—one of the most expensive wines ever marketed. And, I'm going to make it fit in your rear end before I break it in there. . .*

"The Syrian border guards won't shoot you. They might mess you up, they want what's in your head too much to kill you outright." Ziki saw how pale this made David's face flush.

He nodded to David in reassurance.

The Iraqi guard was beside the car. Avi rolled down the window and the guard leaned in—frowning the moment he knew that something about this taxi full of men was not right. Damn idiot.

Avi was swift. An arm around the guard's neck and the knife through his windpipe. There was not even much blood.

All four doors of the cab flung open. Avi and Manny laid a line of fire from both sides, taking the checkpoint guards by surprise. The men behind the barricade fumbled for weapons and dodged for cover.

Ziki's men grabbed their guns from the trunk and ran.

Manny and David were separated, running in the wrong direction. Ziki didn't call for them; he had to trust they'd track back to the others. There was no time. Ziki drew his automatic pistol and gave fire so that Avi and Ilan could fall back from the cab. The others had lumbered over the hill and were making for inside the border.

Avi and Manny caught up with Ziki. The three of them fired as they followed the other men, over the hill and down a slight embankment that was all rocks and sand. It cascaded down around their ankles as they trudged through it.

And then there it was: the border.

They stumbled across the Syrian border.

The Syrians were waiting for them. Perhaps they'd heard about the mobile's destruction . . . or the hit on the Iraqi patrol . . . or had heard that seven idiot Israelis were bumbling around in the desert looking to get killed…Or Malkielly had a hand in it? In any case, an entire company of Syrian regular army was waiting at the border and in very little time had surrounded and disabled Ziki's overwhelmed men.

"Fuck… Fuck… Fuck."

*Malkielly…just as you planned.*

"We're fucked in Syrian hands."

It was of no use. To run was to be shot in the back.

Ziki put his hands up in the air to surrender.

A Syrian soldier came from behind him and cracked him in the back of the head with a rifle butt. A fleece of blackness blotted his sight for a moment, and Ziki fell to his knees. He could hear Moshe bartering mini-meals somewhere close at hand. The Syrian who'd cracked him with the rifle now stood in front of Ziki. He said something in Arabic, *Yahudi sharmuta,* Jew whore, then gestured with his gun.

*I'd be better off if they did shoot me.*

Ziki put his hands on his head. He looked up at the Syrian just in time to see the rifle coming down again. It connected just above his eyebrow with a dull throb that at first was not pain. Ziki fell forward, his open mouth tasting dirt.

*There's always time to die tomorrow.*

*So for now live and just take what's coming.*

A kick to the face woke him up. As he jolted awake the lingering feeling of a wet and hard boot sole made him wince. He groaned when the pain opened out from his cheek bone to his jaw and neck…

Damn.

He didn't have the wherewithal to fight back, but struck out blindly just the same, an instinct that was more limp than powerful. Then another boot kicked his ribs—a short, sharp shock, and the barrel of an AK-47 making an indention in his forehead.

Ziki rolled onto his back, his hands up and fingers curled limply.

A jeep screeched to a halt, spitting sand and stones, a Russian made Poveda, Ziki noted.

Out of it, a Syrian Captain, who shouted, "*Lah majnuns.* You idiots can kill him after I interrogate him. *Haalas....Haaji...* Enough…All right," he said.

The Captain approached Ziki and looked down on him. He spat in the sand just beside Ziki's face. "*Waqaaf Qaam…*Stand him up," he ordered.

Ziki was roughly hauled to his feet and stood upon wobbling legs and numb toes.

"*Darga? Mah  hadarga shelcha?* Rank? What is your rank?" The Syrian Captain asked. In Hebrew. The son of a bitch spoke Hebrew. Ziki raised his shoulders gesturing I don't understand… In English now. "What is your rank?"

"Sergeant."

"Your unit?  Your unit?  You are an Israeli  *Yahudi sharmutah,* a Jew whore."

"No," Ziki shook his head. "I'm Swiss  A medic."

The Captain's eyes narrowed. "A medic . . . ? With guns? And a squad?" He sneered. "We'll take him to Duma prison. Follow my vehicle." *Just as Malkielly had planned.*

Tossed in the back of the jeep, Ziki sat with his head falling onto his chest.

This was it.

It had only just begun.


**At Duma, the questions resumed on the same track.** "You are an Israeli, Jew *sharmuta...* You deny it? You take me for a fool? You tell me what you are doing here?"

"I'm a Swiss medic."

"You are an Israeli. Again—what is your name?"

"Jean Henry. I'd like some water. If I could—"

"Shut up. What kind of Swiss name is that—Jean Henry?"

"My father was French."

"Then you are not Swiss."

"I am a trained medic."

"Why does your uniform not have any markings or rank?"

"This is what they gave me."

"Your rank?"

"Sergeant. I told you."

"And your unit?"

"Under the Geneva Convention, I can't answer that question."

"We are not in Geneva, you Jew whore." The Captain leaned over him.

Ziki could smell garlic on his breath. "You think I'm stupid? You think we're all stupid? Tell me—what you are doing here?"

The Captain paced through the room clicking the heels of his boots together. "You like my English?"

"It's very good."

"Of course it is. You think we're all stupid."

"No," Ziki shook his head.

"I want you to tell me what Israel is doing here now?"

"I want to call the Swiss Consulate."

"Ahhhhh. . . if you were smart, you would decide to answer my questions."

"Please."

"What does Israel want in Syria?"

"I have gold. I can give you gold."

"What gold?"

"I have gold sovereigns. If you untie my hands."

"How much gold?"

"Enough. It would make you a very comfortable man. Loose my hands and I'll show you."

The Captain scrutinized him closely. Finally, he sniffed and nodded. He loosed one of Ziki's hands, keeping the other tied to the chair. "Show me."

"Here. You can have it all." Ziki tugged at the buckle of the belt of his pants. On the underside was a long, thin zipper. His fingers were firm as he pulled the tab, drawing open the pouch. Inside were gold coins—French Napoleons.

Always have an ace tucked away.

The Syrian's features showed a mixture of surprise and greed.

"Why you carry such wealth?"

"In case I need food and for occasions like these." Ziki handed the belt to him without reserve. "Take them. They're yours. And get the Swiss Consulate… There are more buried—in the desert—"

The door banged open and a Syrian regular army Major walked into the room.

"*Shu hadda?* What is that?" He grabbed the coin belt from the Captain.

Ziki tried to look horrified, knowing that even if the consulate had been called and the Swiss agreed to pull him out of this sinking hole, he still could not leave until he'd put a bullet in Finkle's head or got him out.

The Captain was pointing at Ziki. "You think you can bribe me?" His mock outrage was badly performed.

The Major snorted in disdain.

Ziki reached for the belt and then simply pointed as the Major's hand laid upon his pistol. "Look. The belt is hand-made. See, it says, 'Zurich.'"

The Major turned the belt in his manicured fingers.

"I told you. I'm Swiss."

The Major blinked slowly, considering the gold. "Your name is?"

"Jean Henry."

"Rank?"

"I've told you one hundred times—Sergeant. I don't understand why you can't call the Swiss Con—"

The Major struck Ziki across the mouth with a closed fist. He smiled as Ziki's head hung forward and a dribble of blood and mucous collected at the side of his mouth and streamed onto his pant leg. "Do you know who the '*White Socks*' are, Jean Henry?"

Ziki did not answer. He closed his eyes temporarily.

*Ohhh. . . he was going to kick Finkle's ass to China and back.*

The Major lifted Ziki's head by a handful of hair. "They are our Secret Police. And their methods are far more brutal than ours. I would suggest that you do much better talking to me. Why would an Israeli whore come to Syria?"

He jumped to attention as the door slammed open once more and raised his hand in a firm salute. Uniformed men stormed into the room. Behind them, dressed in a tailor-cut uniform to pompous perfection, came another man. The overcoat that hung from his shoulders bore the rank insignia of Colonel. Ziki also recognized the emblem of the 'White Socks'—the Syrian Secret Police, with the reputation of being one of the most vicious in this part of the world.

The Major had been right. Ziki would rather have dealt with the two who guarded a border crossing. But those two might never have gotten him to Melvin Finkle.

Ziki lurched forward in his chair, playing the earnest medic. "Thank God! Someone with some clout here. I'm a Swiss medic. I demand to see the Consul—"

The Colonel didn't strike Ziki himself. No… He snapped his fingers and one of his gorillas shut Ziki up with a swift punch to the face.

Ziki grunted. "Does everybody have to hit me?"

The Colonel considered him blandly for a long moment and then snapped, "*Akhaad hu, yalla imshi...* Take him, move, be quick—move."

**Duma prison…It was the shit hole that Ziki had always heard about.**

They took him to a large room with high ceilings. One wall had bleachers—like in a high school gymnasium. These went all the way to the ceiling.

It was dark. It was cold and damp.

It had probably once been a Turkish prison torture room, now under permanent ownership of the 'White Socks.' Ziki was tied to the gym-like steps. His shirt had been stripped off.

The stocky Colonel walked in accompanied by the same entourage as before.

"I am Colonel Salim El Farouk of the Syrian Secret police, *Mehke Arabie?* "Do you speak Arabic?" Ziki shrugged his shoulders… "Do you speak Arabic?"

"No."

"*Atah medaber Ivrit?* In Hebrew….Do you speak Hebrew?"

Ziki lifted his shoulders to signal I don't understand.

In not bad English. "What do your friends call you?"

"My friends call me Ziki." He answered with satisfaction in his voice.

"Perhaps you can help me, Ziki."

"I don't know anything important; I'm just a grunt sergeant."

"Of course. We have captured the other members of your group. But I need to know now, Ziki. Are you the same group that was discovered south of here in Iraq one day ago?"

"I am by myself; I don't know any group."

"I am trying to help you, Ziki."

"Thank you . . . but I just don't understand. The consulate can tell you."

"Now stop that. Tell me something—anything helpful and maybe we can become good friends, eh? Haven't I been nice to you?"

"I don't know jack shit. You've really got the wrong man."

"Have you eaten recently?"

"No."

The Colonel shouted an order over his shoulder. "Food and water." Most likely laced with truth serums or a slow acting who-knows-what that would have Ziki begging for anything in a matter of minutes.

"So, Ziki, what was your unit doing in this part of the world? Israeli, Swiss, it doesn't matter much to me, for now. However, both those countries would not send men who know "jack shit" into their enemy's territory. You are Special Forces—yes—Ziki?"

"Are the Swiss not neutral anymore Abdullah?" The gorilla nodded his head.

"No. I'm just a grunt medic. A sergeant for God's sake. I know nothing."

"I understand that you are still doing your duty and you must understand that I have to do mine."

Ziki shook his head. No.

"So what was your task, Ziki?"

"—Just to treat the injured. The Geneva convention Colonel, you must call the consulate."

"Yes, yes the Geneva convention, I have heard of it. But as you must understand, we are not in Geneva."

"Yes, so I've been told already."

The Colonel took out his pistol. It was a Soviet made Makarov. Some strangely removed part of Ziki's brain admired it. Sleek and black. A damn fine gun.

The Colonel's eyes narrowed. "Please don't insult me."

The gun came down—whack—across Ziki's nose.

Blood and spit and snot.

"I don't want to insult you." With each word, Ziki spat fluids.

"Very good," the Colonel smiled. "That is good."

Ziki forced a laugh. He couldn't stop thinking of Malkielly getting fat behind his great big desk, and the image in his mind made him laugh a tinge hysterically. "I know where I am. I know who you are."

The Colonel had lit a cigarette. He blew smoke Ziki's way.

"We found an empty pack of Marlboros in your shirt pocket. Do you smoke? The American brands are the best, I think. Don't you agree?"

"Believe me—I hate the army. If I knew a damn thing, I'd tell you. I'd draw you maps and give you secret codes—but I don't have any. They didn't tell me I would have to do things like this. I don't even know why we're here, I just stumbled across the border." Ziki shook his head as he talked far too fast and loudly.

The Colonel smoked—the picture of calm.

Finally, he stepped closer to Ziki and offered the cigarette. The two men eyed each other intently—though Ziki let his caution and fear intentionally reflect back at the man.

The Colonel gently placed the cigarette between Ziki's lips. "There now . . . that's it, take a drag. That's better, isn't it?"

Ziki nodded and looked away, the cigarette dangling now between his bloodied lips. It was actually good to have a drag. The taste and smell of nicotine were soothing and familiar, the little things survivors of this sort of mess had told him in the past. It's the little things that get you through.

But the Colonel's hand snatched the cigarette away—

The butt pressed to the skin just beside Ziki's left eye.

The smell of burning flesh and a sudden glaring pain.

Ziki heard himself scream. He pulled at the ropes and squirmed until the Colonel drew away and tossed the cigarette to the ground. There was a tiny piece of flesh hanging from the tip as it flew from his fingers.

Ziki felt his stomach roll.

Better skip that light lunch they were preparing for him.

"I will ask you again," the Colonel went on. "What is your unit and what were you doing in Syria?"

Ziki shook his head, though it made the burn sting with the movement of air.

*That's going to leave a huge scar. . . I'll have to explain it to my mother.*
. .

The Colonel was still talking, but Ziki wasn't really listening anymore. "If you answer me truthfully, I will see what I can do to have you protected. If you don't there is nothing more I can do to help you. And I do want to help you. I like you. . . Ziki."

The Colonel leaned closer to Ziki.

Ziki could smell the sweat on him and the bleach and starch in his uniform's shirt.

"I've told you what I know."

"You know I want to help you?"

"I wish--. . . " Ziki's voice failed. "I can't tell you anymore."

"What is your unit and what is your mission here?"

"We treat injured air crews for the oil companies."

"How very disappointing," the Colonel answered. "Well, no matter. My boys might like to be friendly with you, as well."

Colonel Farouk stepped away and signaled his men.  They were big and looked dark—who came eagerly closer.  Fists and boots.  The thud of landed blows.  Ziki felt the first pulling but little else once his face was pulped and massive.

There was still that little light of distance and reason in Ziki's skull: a voice that came to him with its reason and thoroughness of thought.  This is bad, it said . . . but they are still treating you like the grunt you claim to be . . . the methods of interrogation by Soviet experts are far more sophisticated and far, far worse.  Surely, they'd have him see one of their Soviet cutters or dentists if they truly thought him to know anything of value or be of high rank.

The 'gorillas' laid off at the Colonel's word.

Ziki shook his head, flinging blood and spit to the floor.

*Just pass out and stop the pain.*

*Just pass out and you'll be fine.*

*They haven't killed you already—you'll make it out of here.*

"You like all this?" the Colonel leaned close to ask him.  He had the cagey smirk of the interrogator.

What sort of idiot asked if someone liked being beaten to a bloody pulp?  "Ohh, yeah," Ziki answered, "my favorite vacation—ever."

This made the Colonel laugh in a childlike way.  "You will get much more, you know.  Yet . . . all you have to do to stop it is to tell us what you know.  Answer my questions and I will protect you, from them." He pointed at the gorillas.

"Just turn me loose in this room, you bastards, c'mon all of you and only me, I'll take you all apart.  "*Ibn El Sharmutah*" there's only one of me and a lot of you sons of bitches; c'mon let's see you  be real men."

"Are you sitting comfortably, Ziki?"

"Ahh yes, I've never been better; I told you, my favorite vacation." In his training Ziki remembered that he'd been told to act rough and insulting because then the worst he would get was a beating; but if they bought it that he was just a grunt and didn't know anything of value, they most likely would not bother to go to the trouble of a more complex and methodical interrogation.

"How are you feeling?"

"I think I need medical attention."

"Of course…. We are not animals.  But first you will tell us what you are doing in our country?"

"I'm trying to…"

"You are not helping us at all, Ziki.  Tell me the plans of the Israelis, Ziki."

"I have told you, I don't know any fucking Israelis.  I'm not Israeli."

"Untie him." A big hand grabbed him fiercely, then a Mack truck slammed into his face.  The blow could have broken something serious and knocked him out.

He tried to stay upright but could not; his legs jellified.  He went down to the floor.  It was cold, dirty and hard. A kick to the side from a gorilla's boot almost broke his right arm—but better a broken arm then a set of broken ribs. A clean shot at the ribs  would have broken one or more and could have collapsed a lung.

His arm almost separated from his body.  His side was on fire, lungs fought for air.  Maybe he was wrong—maybe the Colonel would let his thugs kick him slowly to death.  He curled himself into the fetal position.  Another kick from the gorilla's boot to the lower back; Ziki thought that he had been stabbed with a bayonet, the pain was so intense.

He knew he was running out of time. He rolled over from the fetal position just in time to meet the foot coming in for another kick.  He managed to grab it in full flight and instinctively used a *"Krav Maga"* move that twisted the gorilla's foot out of shape.  The gorilla let out a blood curdling yell, as if he was the one being tortured.

The big man can dish it out but can't take it. Ziki managed to work his way into a crouch so that he'd have a chance to defend himself. Hovelling on his good leg he spun 180 degrees.  The gorilla hurled another of those iron fisted artillery shots aimed at Ziki's face, but Ziki was ready for this one:   he went under the incoming punch with a solid foot to the solar plexus.  The gorilla let out another grunt in pain but came back towards him crouching. Stumbling forward when he came within reach, Ziki's foot to his genitals did some serious damage. He raised his head, a pair of beady eyes smoking with anger.

"I shouldn't have played with you *kus emak Yahud majnun,* your mothers genitals, you crazy Jew."  He reached for his holster, pulled out his Makarov.

*"Lah khalas.* That's enough, Abdullah."

The gorilla hesitated for a moment; he was in a frenzy and continued the hand motion of extracting his pistol. In a booming voice Colonel Farouk stepped in front of him.

*"Khalas!* I said that's enough—do you hear me?"

"Please, let me kill the Jew infidel, comrade Colonel."

"Give me your gun, Abdullah."

*"Shu?"*

"Give me your gun, now."

*"Quies."*  Okay.

Ziki thought, *I live another day.*

**There's nothing you can do about pain—you've just got to accept it.** Let it engulf you, go with the flow; when your body says that's enough, relief comes by way of unconsciousness.

"That is enough for today." The Colonel leaned a hair's breadth from Ziki's face. "Tomorrow I will start your day by taking out one of your eyes. Then, one by one, I'll personally cut off each of your toes.  And I'll have another interesting thing. Do you want to know what it is?"

Ziki shook his head from side to side indicating, No thanks.

"Okay, let that be a surprise for you.  Take him now to general quarters. *Yalla imshi.*  Hurry up move."

Only partially conscious, Ziki found himself falling.  His legs were jelly when they stood him up away from the wall. He ran his freed hands over his face:  it was like hamburger meat.  The two guards half carried him to a large communal jail that housed some three maybe four hundred men and shoved him in.

Ziki crawled to the wall and sat up, leaning on it. He liked having his back to a wall.

Arched passage ways. Rooms open to each other, maybe more than four hundred men.

He admired the architecture of this old structure built by the Turks in the Middle Ages during the grandeur and conquest of the Ottoman Empire. Some of the walls were three meters or more thick. He'd heard that the exterior walls were six meters thick, built of yellow stone.

Across the room, in the shadows, sitting on the ground—Ziki recognized Melvin Finkle. There he was—just like Malkielly said. He had not yet made Ziki. The blood and grime that covered Ziki's face disguised his features. Melvin was preoccupied and apparently did not care about the others…. Well, well he is here. Malkielly's plan at work.

*Wait a while and gather strength before dealing with Finkle.*

From the other room came a tall blondish man, not Arab looking. He moved toward Ziki… cautiously. Ziki tensed, but saw that he had a clean cloth in his hand and a small pot filled with water.

"I'm just going to clean your face some," the man said as he knelt. "Do you speak English?"

"Yes. I am Swiss." Ziki was still on his guard. Anyone in the cell could be one of Colonel Farouk's men.

"Here this may hurt a little." Ziki burst out laughing. "Unless you're going to do to me what they did out there—I think I can handle a little cleaning."

Both men were now laughing.

"I am Jimmy-Ray Sinclair. I'm American."

"Yeah, I can tell."

Jimmy-Ray raised his eyebrows, saying how?

"Your accent," Ziki told him.

"You can take the boy out of Seattle. . ." He began wiping the blood off Ziki's face. "Man—they really did a job on you."

"Yeah, they're trying to make me good looking."

"I guess. Were the Ruskies around working on you?"

"No. Just the locals. What brings you here?"

"They grabbed me in Beirut two weeks ago and put me up in this 'hotel.' Do you have any idea how long they keep people?"

"There's no rule, usually forever."

He finished cleaning Ziki's face. "That might stop an infection. All I have is water; here drink some, and you'll forgive me but you still look like shit." Both laughed again.

"Thank you. I won't forget it."

The American nodded.

Ziki closed his eyes for a short while opening one eye from time to time to keep Finkle in view. Later it seemed all went to sleep.

Ziki, feeling a little stronger, made his way across the room to Finkle's spot. Through the dim light coming through the jail bars, he could see that Finkle's eyes were closed. He was sleeping.

Ziki stooped down to the floor next to him, put the left hand firmly over his mouth and the right one grabbing the throat; holding him tightly now, aided by his knee planted in Finkle's chest, he pinned him to the wall. Finkle opened his eyes and tried to mumble something.

Ziki whispered, "It is me. Ziki Barak. If you make any noise, I'll kill you. Do you understand?"

"Mmmhh," he nodded his head in the affirmative with a bewildered look in his eyes.

"All right," Ziki hissed. "I'm going to take my hand off. Don't make any fucking noise, okay?"

"Mmmhh," an exaggerated nod.

Ziki released his hand from Finkle's mouth, but tightened the grip on the man's throat. Finkle let out a grunt.

"I said 'Quiet!' Did you hear me?"

"Yes," he let out in a whisper. "Don't kill me. I didn't run away—I just got lost. I swear it, Commander."

"Don't call me 'Commander'—you little worm—and don't make noise if you want to live…Am I clear?"

"Yes, Sir."

"I know you got lost,' Ziki lied to keep things calm—"I'm here to get you out and back home."

"I'm not escaping anywhere. The Syrians will kill us if we try; I'll just stay here and someday the war's going to be over."

"This is not up for discussion, you miserable fuck."

"Yes, and I'm sorry for what happened."

"You're Sorry?" The little clerk caused this whole catastrophe and now he's sorry.

"Just remember this, Melvin—I don't like you—I never have. If you give me any reason, I'll kill you."

"You're worse than the Syrians."

"And don't you forget it."

**"Now you will tell me huh, what is your mission and what else are the Swiss planning to do?"**

"I'm a, I'm a member of the Search & Rescue team."

"And what do you do, Ziki?"

"We rescue downed oil company crews, I told you. I'm a medic. A medic."

"And what was your mission on this occasion?"

"I don't know. The office operates on a—on a need-to-know basis. They don't tell us anything. They just tell us to get on the helicopter."

"Interesting. . . Would you like to eat? Why don't you. It smells good. Then we will talk some more."

"Thank you?"

"Yes, yes. First you will eat. How are your teeth? Are they giving you some problems? We have a dentist here. He worked in Berlin for years. One of the best. He just breaks a few teeth off. Now and then. Open wide please."

"Oww."

"Did you really think I was going to help you? You are irrelevant to us. You lied to us. You are the man from the south, aren't you? You are Israeli. You came from Iraq where you exploded things, valuable things.... You're stupid to lie to me. Stupid."

"I'll help you all I can. I'm just a medic."

"How many medics leave nine men dead? I'm speaking of the Iraqi patrol near Kai'ima. I know all about it. Tell me what your task was."

"I told you—I'm a medic...Oww."

"You are the senior ranking officer here, yes? No one knows you are alive or dead. We can let you die and no one would know. Your government—they do not care about you. To them you are just a tool to be used. If you're not going tell me who you are and what you were doing, we will simply let the others—yes we have all the others—die first.... Think about it, Ziki. ... How did you get in? Helicopter?"

**The next few hours were relatively quiet they left the men together,** they could talk to each other. "They're keeping Ziki in a separate place."

"Why did you join the IDF's Golani special forces?"

"To keep out of trouble."

"So you thought if you joined up there'd be no more trouble?"

"Best thing I ever did. Never been in trouble since."

"What the hell do you call this?"

**The booming noise overwhelmed the night's silence.** Bricks and sand filled the air, bursting through the thick walls behind the well placed rockets out of the four Cobra helicopters. The noise was a soothing sound to Ziki; he had expected the rescue raid. Davidoff and his men came in just before daylight.

"Get our man over there."

"Yes, Sir."

"You look terrible, Commander Barak, where is the one who did this? Do you know?"

"Ohh yeah, this one?"

"Yes, there's no time for this; let's get out of here. Take Finkle."

"Where is he?"

"Over there; if he refuses to move, shoot him."

"Finkle, move your ass now!"

"Take the American with us.... Yes that one" Ziki ordered. The American's eyes filled with tears of gratitude.

"Who did this to you, Commander? Do you know where he is?"

"That hatch, the big one."

Davidoff opened the hatch; Ziki's eyes locked and met for a split moment with Colonel Farouk's bellow. More than one of the men threw grenades down the hatch.

"They'll need a '*spachtel*' to scrape him off the walls," grinned Davidoff.

…The helicopter ride home seemed like riding on birds from heaven. They took Jimmy-Ray Sinclair, the American, along for the ride to Tel-Aviv.

## Chapter 14

**MIG 21**

**Ziki knew for certain that he was not incognito when his men teased him about his hair.** "Blondie!" his driver called. "They bleach your underarms, too?"

"No," Ziki replied. "That's your mother's job."

You got nice hair there Commander? Does it get the girls? Red heads or brunettes?"

"Naw. . .not really." Ziki grinned. "But your sister keeps me busy."

Ziki Barak was about to go to an Arab country. The odds were better to fit the European prototype that they would expect there. So if he carried a German passport than it is best to look it. He held a forged German passport its details were executed to perfection he was registered with the registrar of births and records as being born in Munich, it included his parents records it was more proper than any real German.

Papers that declared his employment with Rimmer Medical, a company headquartered in Hamburg that accommodated Mossad as a front for covert operations and would cover for him if they were called. He carried glossy catalogs from the supplier, samples of gloves, KY-jelly, tongue depressors, autoclaves and syringes, but also million dollar X-ray and MRI equipment catalogs, along with order forms printed in the upper right hand corner with the address of RMS head quarters, all printed with his name on them for the purpose of supporting his disguise. There was a phone number.

The line was answered by a young German woman who sounded pretty. She would take your message and deliver it as requested. She would take a message for Hans Breckenbauer who was currently out of the office. She would inform you that he had traveled to the Middle-East to meet with clients. Hans Breckenbauer. That was Ziki's name when he was using this German alias. Hans Breckenbauer could enter places that Ziki Barak could not.

In Zurich, in Syria, Iran, Iraq, Hans Breckenbauer had sandy blonde hair. It was best to be unseen. His languages served him well. German was his best after

Hebrew. Mossad drilled him to speak Duestch without a telltale accent, though he'd never been able to fend off the crisp residuals of Hebrew when speaking the softer Italian. He knew since playing with other boys in the streets of Mount Carmel in Haifa. And English. Of course English. Everyone spoke English, usually with a Swiss accent.

"Blondie" became Ziki's nickname when he gave his hair over to a barber to make the fiction of Breckenbauer more real. All of his hair—head, eyebrows, toes, legs, knuckles, arms, under arms, chest, and pubes—was touched up with bleaching cream and dye. He disliked the odor of ammonia and was certain he could smell traces of bleach, like chlorine from a pool, for days after his treatment. It exuded from his very fingers. It was a process far too undignified.

"So. . . I come to Zurich; you will show me the life?" The driver cocked one eyebrow in the rear-view mirror at Ziki. "We hunt the killers—the baby butchers."

"You'll get to Zurich," Ziki answered. "When I'm awarded the Nobel Peace Prize." ''Well, Commander I don't think that is a prize that they will give to you."

# Chapter 15

**Haifa—Tel-Aviv train**

**Crouched low in the brush and scattered rocks decorating the foothills of Mount Carmel.** Ali Hasan Salameh compared the browns and greens in his pants to those in the area's young trees and low bushes. Vegetation here made for mosaic bathas, but provided little in the way of protection and cover. He made his way back into the Carmel Mountains near Haifa after his escape with Finkle from Ziki and his men in Lebanon.

He licked his lips, bone-dry from the arid chill, and tried to ignore his hands. "Trembling in anticipation," he told himself.

Days of planning and preparation with comrades were finally approaching—sprinting towards—their climax. This 'job' was only one of many he had planed. These 'jobs' were still at the beginnings of his 'career', later he planed on bigger and 'better' things.

Salameh squeezed the cool aluminum of the launcher encasing his explosives, taking care to keep his fingers away from the trigger. He curled his lips under his teeth, wetting them again. The upper, sufficiently coated, slid back in place, but Ali held tight to the lower. He bit hard; his sharp incisors threatened to break through the warm flesh between them.

What was the matter with his friend, "Abdul? He wanted to be calm, motionless—like the men at his sides. But they had been here before. Abdul…was still new at this he had been plotting and strategizing, satiating himself with shock—images of success. Today those images would spool out of his head and before his eyes; his second in person execution. He faced it with equal parts honor and rabid fear. His best work was from a distance and with chemicals. Not this face to face stuff.

Abdul cocked his head until the poised bulk of Sabri I Banna now calling himself Abu Nidal appeared between the leaves of the stumpy brown bush giving him cover. Abu Nidal stood in a low squat, balanced on the worn heels of black military boots Abdul thought could probably each lace up the width of both of his own broomstick legs. He had heard legends of prisoners, wounded and lying on the ground, who had taken their own lives once their peripheral views showed those boots coming for them. One of Abu Nidal's hands held fast to an AK already loaded and ready to fire; the other perched atop a small radio communicator. Just minutes and Abu Nidal's bass whisper would crackle and Abdul would have the command he was waiting for.

Salameh's dark olive face, showed no emotion. Abdul lifted a hand to the soft fuzz—his best attempt at a beard—covering his chin and cheeks, wondering if his anxiety was as visible as his companion's eagerness.

Abdul shifted his attention past Abu Nidal to a patch of steel slats peeking through the layered branches of the olive trees populating the slope. If he stood, he would see the full tracks and their flanking power lines ramble through the basin below before gradually making the long climb up the foothills and around Mount Carmel. He would not see the molded fistfuls of C-4 interspersed beneath the overhangs of the tracks' parallel rails

A breeze picked up and wandered through the hills; Abdul breathed deeply, wanting to restore his calm and knowing that, soon enough, the air would not be so fresh. He closed his eyes and prayed; *Allah, I ask for strength only to do your work.* From somewhere invisible a soft clicking sound tickled his ears. Salameh's eyelids shot up.

Helicopter rudders.

Their intensity grew fast. When it hit, deafening Salameh thought he heard Abdul screaming at them—"Get lower! Don't move!"—but he couldn't help straightening a little to scan the horizon. It had to be close, but it was nowhere. It was…his pupils traced the sky behind the tracks; section by section…it was…there! Right there! An Israeli helicopter flying south and zigzagging, searching along the railroad tracks. For what it was worth, Salameh signaled to his cohorts, before flattening his own body on the ground.

The helicopter—part of a routine Israeli aerial sweep—was no surprise. Still, its rudders were too loud and much too close; the machine hovered just above the power lines.

Salameh flinched as the air stirred bits of debris into his eyes and up his nose. Through blurred vision, he could just make out the shadow of the helicopter flying towards him. A grip of needles shot through his nose; he badly needed to sneeze. *Sahrmuta, sharmuta.* Ali repeated the word until the sound of the chopper's engine was replaced by the hollow ringing of an ear-piercing noise gone silent.

The helicopter was gone. And the last threat of the Israeli patrol with it.

Salameh sat up but did not stand. Rushes of relief, joy, and purpose sloshed around his stomach. He would need a minute to recover.

"Get ready," Abu Nidal hissed through the static of the radio. "It's coming."

**It was true… In the distance—a blip of a train was now gliding along the tracks**. Abu Nidal curled his back and bent lower. The rustling sounds that had dotted the last fifteen minutes—men shifting and adjusting their positions—abruptly gave way to silence. From the train shot the wicked glare of windows reflecting the awkward angle of a day breaking sun. Abu Nidal pictured the faces behind those windows, smiling in remembrance of the ten straight mornings when his had been one of them while training in the Soviet vastness of Siberia, but now he was competing for glory with Salameh.

Though he could barely see it, Salameh knew that this train had two engines draped in red or orange paint. Strung between, sides covered with a navy-to-teal spectrum, were twenty passenger cars—a dining car for each, and a baggage carrier dividing them.

The train had left Tel-Aviv's Merkaz Station at 06:14. Three minutes later, it picked up the girls soccer team from the Nahman Bialik Junior High school before rolling out of the city and along the coast towards Herzliya, Bet Yehoshua, Netaniya, Hadera, Caesarea, Binyamina, and Atlit. A maximum four-minute layover in Binyamina and two minutes in Atlit allowed the train to compensate for time it gained or lost along the way. Having departed Atlit at 07:11, it was midway through its nine-minute journey to Haifa's Hof HaCarmel and, finally, Bat Galim station filled with people just going to work. As it pulled along the two stories of brick comprising Bat Galim, the black Roman numerals of the station's clock tower would make the imperceptible click to 07:27.

This day seemed no different than any other day, that was what the train's passengers thought.

Salameh hoped the bare-legged '*whore*' who had mocked a Muslim woman's covered head by wearing shorts beside her was lounging comfortably two hundred…a hundred ninety…a hundred eighty meters in front of him. And the three Israeli computer geeks, who wore light brown jackets with the Microsoft logo in Hebrew and used three extra seats in the Merkaz lounge. He hoped they were on board, drinking Coke's and complaining of the long morning ride, this morning too.

No longer inching towards them in the distance, the train was gaining ground fast. Still, Salameh's pulse had it beat… Sweat beaded and dripped from the blue-black hair caked to his forehead. A drop hit and rolled down his forearm. Several more muddied the dirt below. Another fell to the corner of a small black box clipped to his belt. Salameh eyed its control switch and checked to make sure the two bulbous lights on either side of the switch were sill a solid yellow.

*It is time.*

His radio bristled again.

"*HaDir*, Ready!" Abdul's voice huffed.

Salameh unhooked the box and slid out the safety blocking its detonator.

"*Ramah*, Fire!"

A yellow light began flashing. It meant that the box was transmitting and connecting with the remote detonating devices on the tracks. His focus was now on the tracks.

The train, now in plain view, almost right in front of them. Salameh waited until the engine passed, and then he flicked the second switch. One hundred kilograms of Semtex Plastique-C4 explosive that was shriveled along the railroad steel tracks exploded under the train, blowing some cars into the air in a cloud of orange-red flames and black smoke. Shrapnel and pieces of torn and twisted railroad track and machinery from the train flew high in the air, and bodies of people spilled out onto the side of the tracks. "*Ramah*, shoot at will." Salameh ordered… And then…"We are just about done here."

**In less time than it had taken the train to work its way** through the El Fattah men's line of vision, the ambush was complete. The train, having met it with little resistance, now lay woven between a scattered course of hollow flames and smoke, an abstract tangle of wrenched metal and shattered glass.

Salameh looked around him. Abdul stood, serene but on guard, a little to his left; most likely, he was counting to 300—the obligatory five minutes they needed to wait before advancing into the wreckage. Behind Abdul, Kamal Adwan, another Fattah recruit, crept forward to widen his view. Salameh was wary of Kamal—his darting eyes and frequent bouts of restlessness made Salameh nervous and, on this day, unsure if the young Iranian could hold himself together until they made it across the Syrian border. Three others—Sabri I Banna, Abdullah Mansour, and Abul Kassam—conflated inward until the six men stood in a loose clump admiring their work.

"That's five," Ali said as he reattached the detonator to his belt.

The men stiffened and readied their weapons. All were armed with Kalashnikov machine guns, Kamal and Abul with RPGs. Saib and Abdullah, since they had the same small, sturdy build, shared the ends of Russian machine guns. Creeping down the rugged slopes, the men moved towards the destruction. Limbs and shoes, chunks of luggage, melted flatware and fragments of china, all strewn across the side of the hill, met them three quarters of the way down. Salameh stepped over the top half of a young girl lying face up in a singed green jersey with a flat soccer ball on it. A few meters away was another one, bloody black, but in one piece. Salameh could make out that she was from the Junior High School: the emblem on her sweatshirt was charred but in one piece.

As he scanned the area for more, Kamal approached him and said, "Looks like the soccer team's gonna have to forfeit."

Salameh addressed the beads of sweat condensing on his forehead. "Just make sure they're all dead." Then, to the group: "Anything moves, kill it! A blanket flaps in the wind, open fire! We leave nothing behind—everything dead!"

Machine guns split the momentary silence; the AK-47s unleashed ammo that turned the remaining solid surfaces to mesh. Explosions followed—Saib and Abdullah unable to resist their new toy.

Salameh, lacking Abdul's gift of metronomic rhythm, set his watch to begin a second count, this one for seven minutes. At 07:31, Salameh held up his hand and stopped the fire. Surveying the scene, he breathed in the beauty of their effort. It would be El Fattah's defining moment. From now on, everyone would know their name and, more importantly, their capabilities. And once the Jews realized El Fattah had arrived, Salameh would waste no time in showing them that the destruction before him was only a small beginning.

Satisfied, Salameh shut his eyes and turned back toward the hills. He took his men up and into an adjoining valley to a dead end road encased in a clump of olive trees. Two hundred meters down, a Haifa truck driver would meet and transport them to near safety. The six wiggled down the road on their bellies, stopping periodically to check their alignment with the shadowy cover of the trees and underbrush.

Two hundred meters and fourteen minutes later Abbas and his truck were waiting. Blue block letters on the side of the metallic carrier read "Mobil," and, indeed, if one of the truck's top hatches were opened, the fumes of twenty-five barrels of prepared gasoline would assault the nose. But hidden beneath the carriage was an access door leading into a spacious hidden compartment replete with spare weaponry and additional ammunition.

Thirty meters from the truck, Salameh turned again to his watch, angling its glass face at a sun gathering momentum as it worked through a light haze to its peak in the sky. At about 30 degrees, a redirected ray bounced sharply off the truck's side mirror.

Signal received, the driver's door opened and, with slight hesitation, Abbas' round frame emerged. The road was empty, but Ali could tell by the way Abbas chewed on his thick, graying mustache and stole a glance down the road before moving from the shield of the door that the driver was worried someone had followed him. Still, Abbas approached his left rear tires and, feigning an examination of their lug nuts, flicked a latch that would give the onlookers access to their hideaway.

Abbas returned to the wheel, shut his door, and started the ignition.

"Now," Ali whispered, and the men, one by one, bolted for the truck, dove beneath its back bumper, and slid smoothly into the chamber awaiting them.

Abbas stuck to the speed limit and rolled north, through Nazareth, the foot of the Sea of Galilee Tivon, past Megiddo, on to Afula. The truck stopped along the city's outskirts and Abbas again swung open his heavy door, scanned the area and shuffled the length of the Mobil name.

Ali heard the pop of the latch, then the forced intimidation in Abbas' thin voice. "Get out of my truck. This is as far as I go for the money."

The men, still face to face with the collection of AKs, hand grenades, and over five hundred rounds of ammo, smiled at the menacing voice. Salameh was the first to emerge.

He took Abbas' rough and calloused hand and lowered his head in a gesture of appreciation he hoped would ease the driver's paranoia. "Thank you, Brother," he said. "You have served your people well."

Abbas relaxed his stiffened shoulders and pointed east. "Syria."

## The Kirya-Village

**He swung open the door to the dark sedan and slid out quickly,** the black bag that held his civilian clothes, a few books, and not much more in hand.

He stood for a moment facing the bare cement building that was this branch of Mossad. Above the entrance was the insignia of the intelligence organization that had awed the whole world for its proficiency: the Sword of Gideon, the Star of David, an olive branch. Men and women in green IDF uniforms and dark suits came and went from the front door like bees in and out of a hive. Straightening his shoulders, Ziki tucked his beret over his brow and strode toward the door.

Halmi Pientz's secretary met Ziki just beyond security screening.

The secretary was a kid with an acne problem and glasses that slid down his nose. Not more than 19, the secretary clutched his white pad under his arm and led Ziki through the sterile halls of Mossad through the security labyrinth directly to one of the conference rooms.

The committee had already begun to meet. A cloud of smoke hung above the table and the ashtray was already half-full. The secretary took a seat to Pientz's left and Ziki moved toward a chair on the far side of the table, alone. His closest companion was the recording device directly across from him.

General Halmi Pientz had aged. His temples were grayer than they were when Ziki had last sat in the same chair and agreed to lose his uniform two years earlier. The crags around his mouth and eyes were deeper, like the lines in the maps he had overlooked when conducting the campaigns he had won. The skin under his eyes was beginning to bag. However, the eyes themselves still contained the icy cold distance that always disturbed Ziki; those were "dead eyes," the kind that ordered a kill when the need arises without hesitation. They had the dead expressionless look of one of nature's most vicious predators, a great white shark.

No sense of humor. Since a sense of humor was what kept Ziki sane through all of this, he often wondered about Pientz.

Beside Pientz and his assistant ass-kisser sat the hawk-nosed Yosef Levitz, special liaison between Malkielly, chief of the Shin Bet, and Meir Amit, top dog of the Mossad division Aman, Military Intelligence itself. Levitz wore his Harvard education from head to toe. The fact that he was wearing the only suit in the room didn't seem to bother him. His face seemed pinched as if to affect the impression of a man who knew his business surrounded by men who knew theirs.

Beside Levitz were Lt. Colonels Avraham and Gould, both experts on the constantly evolving relationships between Russian and Mid-Eastern intelligence agencies. Avraham, in particular, was a specialist on Iraqi armaments. His father defected from Iraq in 1950, following a wave of thousands of other Jews. Avraham carried the drive of his father's flight across the deserts of Iraq to every meeting. His wiry frame would have leapt across the table to make every point, were it not for the steady stream of Lucky Strikes he smoked to contain his boundless energy.

Gould's penchant was for ciphers, codes, and communications. Ziki had slowly come to realize from previous interactions that no matter how distracted Gould might appear, how he shifted and fidgeted, his head was always completely in the game. His pair of glasses, without which he was legally blind, spent little time in front of his eyes. Instead, he wore them atop his head, placed the tips in his mouth, and dangled them from between his continually moving fingers. But, no, Gould never missed a beat. He was listening, thinking and listening, even when it appeared he was not. His massive frame seemed to threaten to send him tumbling from every chair he precipitously leaned back in. The only non-smoker in the room,

Gould scattered his table area with various wrapped candies and mints.

Avraham and Gould were a few years advanced of Ziki and had climbed the ranks as quickly. They were sharp, Ziki knew; good solid men to have on your side. In fact, the room was full of nothing but formidable men. But it was clear Pientz and Malkielly owned the room.

"Gentlemen," Ziki nodded and took his chair. He rested his palms on his knees.

"Commander," Pientz slid a glossy black and white photo across the table's shiny surface," do you know what this is?"

Ziki picked up the photo. The photographic paper had a good weight to it and smelled of chemicals.

"The Russian MiG-21," Ziki said. "Developed under intense secrecy. Fast. Small. Agile. Pilots call it the jet of jets—a pilot's plane. Supplied in the hundreds to friendlies—China, Czechoslovakia, Eastern Germany, Tanzania, Zimbabwe, Iraq, Eqypt, Syria, Libya, Pakistan," Ziki ticked the countries off on his fingers. "This super MiG out-maneuvers anything the Americans or we've got."

What Ziki didn't say was that the MiG posed a serious threat to Western air supremacy above the Pacific and certainly at Israel's borders where only minutes could allow enemies to reach its cities. It could allow its hostile neighbors to breach their air space for the first time. Even with all the wars and terrorist activities to this day no enemy plane had ever succeeded in entering Israeli airspace.

Every military machine in NATO wanted a look at it. The Americans were slobbering all over themselves for a peak. Not a single plot to uncover the jet's schematics proved successful. Israeli, Swiss, French, and US operatives had worked relentlessly to get a hold of one by any means and at just about any cost, without success. There were half-assed plans to hijack a plane at a transfer point or to shoot it out of the sky with a reconnaissance team standing by to sweep the remains across borders and into hiding. Each of these had been scrapped before they left conference.

Close calls, but no success; and any of these MiGs that were given or sold to the Arab countries by the Soviets had Russian security agents attached on the ground, in place to make sure that information did not leak out to the West or Israel.

**On the fashionable Rue De La Paix in Paris it was a quiet**. A non busy day at the Israeli Embassy or ambassador Rothman at his office on the second floor would not have taken this telephone call. Pientz pushed a black folder across the shiny tabletop at Ziki. "08:00 today. A man claiming the name of Solomon called the Israeli Embassy in Paris and offered to hijack a MiG from the Iraqis."

Ziki's first reaction was incredulous laughter.

"Impossible," Avraham contested with a snort.

"Out of the blue and into our laps?" Gould's glasses dropped over his eyes as he made a face at the acne-covered kid who also snickered.

Even Levitz smiled.

It was ridiculous, wasn't it? Unbelievable. But Pientz remained sober and

Ziki knew he wouldn't have been recalled if someone in Mossad had not thought there was a grain of truth in the call.

"Solomon's asking a million dollars," Pientz continued.

Another round of chuckles and curled mouths.

"Right, and I got a Cadillac I'd like to sell you for twenty dollars."

"The Americans would pay fifty times that."

"After hemorrhaging from envy."

Pientz clearing his throat brought the table to attention and cut short the laughter, but Avraham's and Gould's eyes still gleamed with humor as they watched Ziki take up the folder and flip it open. It contained a transcript of the call printed on Embassy letter head, signed and sealed by a variety of higher ups. The type was faintly purple from carbon paper:

". . . This is no joke. You tell Mossad. . ."

A series of other documents lay behind the transcript. A call log. The results of the trace. The call originated in Baghdad. That in itself was indicative of the stakes at hand or the lack of wits on the part of the caller. Iraq was at war with Israel. Mossad lost operatives to Arab nooses on a frequent enough basis. Whole families had been known to disappear into the night. The line might have been tapped. Prankster or no, the caller might now be facing interrogation at Iraqi hands.

Ziki's mouth curled downward as he closed the folder.

"I've included a transcript because a great deal of this is hard to understand," Pientz said as he motioned to his secretary. The kid up-tucked his yellow pad under his arm and went to turn on the reel-to-reel. A slither of tape on tape as the machine began to play.

Static. The voice was faint, hurried and frightened:

"This is Solomon. My name is Solomon."

Something unintelligible. Static. The operator's voice was on the line, some idiot kid who's family contacts had gotten him a position in Paris. His voice was indignant. He asked who was calling.

Solomon's voice: "I must be quick, so listen to me carefully. . . You tell Mossad. This is no joke."

As Ziki listened, he searched the faces around the table, trying to read each man. He found a mixture of amusement, disbelief, and . . . . surprisingly . . . hope on their faces.

"I know how to get a MiG. Yes, yes, that is it. I can acquire a MiG, I want a million dollars. A million dollars and the removal of my family from Iraq. . . But I will not speak to anyone in person. You can only contact me through Joseph… Yes, when you come to Baghdad. Static. Yes, when you come to Baghdad, you can contact me through Joseph. The call must come from inside Baghdad. Ask for Joseph. . ."

Again the operator: "Who is this? Who do you work for?"

Solomon hesitated. "You tell your superiors. A million dollars and my family is safe in Israel they get the plane…*Shma Israel Adonai Elohenu Adoni Ehad.*"

Gould's glasses fell into place. His head inclined toward the reel-to-reel.

"Wait, wait, wait—play that again. That last part."

The kid flipped a knob and the reels squealed backward. "A Moslem Arab would not say that."

"That's good. Good." Gould waved his glasses at the kid and sat back. You will tell them? Solomon asked the kid. You will tell them?

Sir, the operator said. Let me connect you to—

But the line was already dead.

For a brief moment after the tape finished, the men in the room remained silent. Gould popped a mint and rolled it between his teeth. Malkielly lit up another. Pientz's secretary scribbled fiercely on his bright yellow pad. The scratch of the pencil lead was audible.

Pientz leaned forward. "Traces confirmed the call's origin."

Levitz shifted as if to gather spare authority from his chair. "Baghdad."

What about this Levitz? Ziki wondered. A moment before Levitz was laughing with shrill intensity at the idea of an Iraqi simply flying a jet out from under Russian noses, now his small dark eyes mirrored the seriousness of Pientz. An act, Ziki thought. Ziki was good at reading men, and Levitz was generally good at putting up a face. Levitz had just a little too much poise and savvy. His nails were cleaned and perfectly pared. His mouth and eyes were soft at their edges. How was this guy a channel straight to the top? Family money. Yes, privilege. Ziki would bet Levitz had never spent a day in the field beyond boot camp and its required drills.

But sure. Pientz, Malkielly and the other big guns would want to keep themselves clear of this whole thing—in case it blew up or blew over embarrassingly. A mess or a colossal joke. What would it do to Pientz's standing with the IDF if word got out that he'd sent an operative chasing prank callers? Better to bring in Levitz. Levitz was here as the Amaan fall guy.

"Any idea who Solomon is?" Ziki asked Avraham. He pushed the folder toward him.

"None of my contacts know him. New. A fucking clean sheet," Avraham answered.

"A new operative? A hoaxer?" Ziki asked.

Malkielly shook his head. "I'd have feelers out already but—dead ends, this man has no prior history, but I think that he and Joseph are one and the same."

"—But we're keeping this as underground as possible," Levitz finally spoke up, leaning forward to mimic Pientz's posture.

"We don't want a single word to get out. Not a squeak about this to anyone—not even friendlies. The Americans would ride right over us if they caught a sniff of this thing."

"The Americans can't keep a secret for shit," Gould added, inflecting the point with a jab of the bow of his glasses. "The Americans hear about this and everyone on the globe will know, they leak like a sieve. We'll have Russkies up our asses more pissed off at us even than they already are and it could kill the Nazi scientists deal with General Zhukov."

"On this one our cards have to be played close to our vests."

"Yeah we have enough international trouble."

Ziki saw Malkielly slowly rise to a bristle and stare with something akin to horror at Gould. "You're—not—seriously—entertaining this?"

Gould's glasses went onto his nose. "And why shouldn't we?"

Malkielly belched smoke. "In six months I haven't found a single lead on the Soviets new MiG system, much less—"

Gould spread his hands. "—so despite the presence of a tape which suggests—"

Pientz simply lifted his hand. "Gould, let him continue. We need to hear all opinions."

Malkielly nodded, justified. "As I was saying." He drew a leisurely drag on his cigar and blew the smoke out in a long stream. "We've spent years developing contacts and no one has gotten us even close to a discussion about MiGs in Iraq. I know Iraq—no one in this room knows Iraq better than I do and I'm telling you, this is a set up. And you're willing to risk one of our operatives because someone calls up and says they have a jet—even their figure suggests they don't know what they're talking about. A million dollars? Any one in their right mind wouldn't even accept that as a good faith payment."

Having let Avraham have his say, Pientz sat back to let Gould go for him. Ironically, Gould and Avraham's arguments often produced the best results.

"And that's exactly why I believe it, exactly! A set up? Who would be so stupid as to contact the Mossad and speak with little to no knowledge about jets and ask for a low figure? Unless they truly believed that they had something to offer—"

"Because our contact is an imbecile he must be telling the truth?" Malkielly scoffed. "Only a sheep herder would think a million dollars could adequately—"

Pientz didn't need to intercede, Gould kept right on going. "And my friend," the bow of Gould's glasses was pointing at Avraham now. "You Might know Iraq, but you don't know language."

"I don't know—"

Gould waved him quiet. "Listen to the accent on the tape. The voice is scared, unsure, but most importantly, it is a voice that has an inflection of Hebrew in it. If you listen to the tape, you realize that he said "Shma Israel" and "Adonai Elohenu" You'd never hear an Iraqi Muslim say that, it would be against Alah. My instinct tells me that this Solomon or Joseph, whoever he is, does not only believe that he has access to a MiG, but that he is, in fact, an Iraqi Jew."

"So if he's one of us, why is he asking for so little money?" Ziki asked.

The laughter broke the tension in the room.

It gave Pientz the opportunity to collect attention and redirect. "Avraham, how hard would it be to check on the number of Jews still living in Iraq?"

"Not at all. We know where every single one of them is. Last count we knew of included the youngest."

A nod from Pientz. "If Gould is right and this Solomon is who he thinks he is, then he. . . And his family is in incredible danger. Which means wild goose chase or not, we need to act on this now, because the opportunity, if real, will be gone very soon."

"Timing is crucial," Levitz echoed.

The blonde hairs on the back of Ziki's neck stood on end. "So we are entertaining this?"

"I don't see as we have a choice" Levitz said. I believe Rav Seren Avraham has unintentionally made the case for it. If we have spent resources unsuccessfully making moves in Baghad, there is nothing to suggest that our ability to entice an Arab or Russian to defect is going to improve any time soon. "We need a MiG."

"Before they get them by the hundreds we have to try everything."

"Israel needs this MiG."

A restless silence settled in the room.

Had Levitz just insulted Malkielly's intelligence work?

Strangely enough, Pientz let Levitz keep talking, watching the man out of the corner of his eye. "What I can tell you from the offices which I represent, here, today," Levitz continued, like a politician—like a damn politician— "is that if you decide to act, you will have the full support of all the agencies that I speak for."

"I appreciate the support of your superiors if not their presence." The room relaxed as Pientz's underhanded thanks rectified Levitz's subtle insult of Avraham's efforts. Pientz would not allow the conversation or his control of it to be derailed.

"In the end, however, the decision rests in this room. I would like to hear your thoughts, Commander Barak."

Malkielly now moving the unlit but well chewed Cuban cigar from one side of his mouth to the other asserted himself as Ziki was his protégé; "go ahead Commander we all want to hear from you."

"Sir. I realize the . . . the potential for rewards are great" Ziki began. "I feel . . . that what Gould has had to say bears merit. But unlike Letvitz here, I do not believe what Avraham has said makes the reasons for going stronger. Let us suppose that Gould is correct. That these are frightened amateurs we are dealing with. As Avraham has pointed out, we lack contacts and a substantial intelligence infrastructure that we can afford to expose on a gamble like this one, when our people in there are involved in ongoing important other operations. Correct me if I'm wrong—I will essentially be on my own but for a contact or two. Couple this with the fact that I will be dealing with operatives that have no experience . . . and we're creating a recipe for disaster."

"Yes," Avraham agreed. "Let us say my friend, the teller of tales, is correct. And they are frightened Iraqi Jews reaching out to help and be helped. Who's to say they have not been merely allowed to do this and are not being used as bait in some sort of trap?" "They're not reaching out to help us, a million Dollars is still a million Dollars so they are helping themselves".

Gould snorted derisively. "Oh, I see. Makes all the sense in the world—I am wrong simply because I am right!"

"No, my friend," Avraham answered coolly. "You are seldom right."

"If that is the case, let us hope this mission breaks that particular tradition. You—"

Malkielly looked at Pientz and seemingly in accord with each other turned to Ziki. "You're on a plane via Rome in Twelve hours. Don't forget you have other business in Iraq—Osirak. So while you are there, check this thing out. "
It was decided.
Ziki nodded slowly. He'd known he was on his way somewhere the moment they'd called him with the order to report to Tel Aviv. "I will personally take time to arrange all the flight tickets." "It looks like you already have the right hair from your last mission Commander."
"Yeah I walk around with it knowing that you have it in for me for another one, just like this one coming up." The atmosphere became light again in the room with the laughter.

"We have prepared what you need," Levitz slid another folder across the table in front of Ziki. "Everything you need, including your itinerary, is contained in this file. We've already contacted all whom you'll need in Baghdad. They'll be waiting to assist you at your sign."

Avraham's eyebrows lifted ever so slightly in a surprise that he had the good sense to suppress. He let his eyes become hooded.

Ziki shot Pientz and Malkielly a look. "Everything is prepared. Had you decided before we convened this committee?"

"No," If he was lying, Pientz betrayed nothing. "But I decided that if we were going to do it we'd have to be ready the moment we did. Besides you're going that way anyway Commander. Remember the 'little bomb cooking problem' with the underground nuclear plant? Gentlemen."

Pientz stood and with a curt nod was gone from the room before the men could say anything.

Ziki sat back and released a breath that he didn't realize he'd been holding. It had to be Baghdad. The one place he really had hoped never to return to. He wondered if she . . . he put that from his mind.

Gould leaned over and put his hand on Ziki's arm, a welcome distraction. "If I am right, then you must be patient with this man, for I fear he has a lot to lose. Would you care for a breath mint—I bring them in the hopes that Avraham will use them, but he seems to think that cigarettes are an adequate substitute."

Ziki shook his head no as Gould rose from the table.

Avraham held the door for Gould and asked him "Is it your turn to by lunch?"

## Chapter 16

### IAMAEL

**Iamael Ibn Abu Wazerra went to the Israelis shortly after he witnessed the bombing**. He was sixteen and looking for work in the orchards—what a wonder, places that grew sweet fruit on sandy soil with water from the sea. But he had come at the lull in the season; there was no work, not for two, maybe three, more weeks.

The sky was clear and not quite blue. It was the heat of the day. Thirsty and foot-weary, Iamael stopped to rest in the shade of a station. Filling his canteen from the pump, he wet his lips. The dust rolled from his tongue. The flies were fat and slow over a trash can that smelled of rotting vegetables. A dog lay panting in the shade under a fruit stand. Dates and oranges and figs. The woman who ran the booth rested in the shady recess of a tent. She let her eyes slip half way closed. When the next bus arrived she would open one eye, then two, and squint at the travelers who looked over her precious commodities and hope for a few Shekels.

The bus rolled in with a squeal of brakes and rumble of engine, raising a cloud of dust. It was teeming with chattering men, women and children on the road to Beer Sheba. The driver opened the door and the people began to spill out, their feet dusty—the children screaming. One of them was crying.

Just off the bus, a little girl in pink woven sandals and a yellow dress stopped a few feet from Iamael. A little beauty. "Fruit look, Mama. Dog." She pointed at the stand and the dog, who had lifted his head and panted in the heat. The mother, tired and hot, took the girl by the hand… "Not today."

The girl's almond shaped brown eyes met Iamael's as she was pulled away by the elbow, fingers in her mouth.

A beautiful child. Iamael could not help it even if she was of the others. He smiled at her. She tagged along behind her mother, her little legs almost running to keep up, but she too smiled. Took her fingers from her mouth and showed him her scattered baby teeth.

Crank, crank, crank. The sound of the bus engine refusing to turn over drew Iamael's attention away. The Egged, (Israeli bus company) bus had filled up again with new passengers. It swayed under their weight.

A dark man, wearing sun glasses removed them, sat near the middle of the bus, looking out his open window. He wore Iamael's uncle Salameh's tribe, the Wahabi's head dress around his neck—Iamael recognized it. The man looked back at him… Deathly still.

Iamael felt the tingle of cold dread up his spine.

The bus. Iamael was on his feet. The bus! The driver cranked the ignition once more and the engine cranked—and the bus became a ball of flame.

The thunder of it and then a swell of heat knocked Iamael onto his back. His canteen fell from his hand and he heard water splash from it onto ground.

There was a moment of absolute quiet.

Then there were screams. The sound of debris falling. The crackle of flame.

For a second, two seconds, three seconds, Iamael could not think, could not move. He blinked. And the world was newly rushing around him in smoky and earsplitting chaos.

The children. The women. Bodies lay on the ground. Black and red and open and blown to shreds. A brighter red then he had ever seen. A satchel. A pair of glasses.   An arm with its bone sticking from oozing flesh. A yellow dress covered in blood… Pink sandals in the dirt. Oh, God. Where are you now? *Allah huu Akbar shu hadda? Great Allah what is this?*

**Hotel International – Baghdad**

**At the Hotel International no expense was spared to make foreign travelers feel as if they were staying in the best of European hotels**. Bouquets of fresh hothouse flowers decorated the front desk. Silken chaises and love seats gave tourists a place to sit as they awaited their tour guides. Dark mahogany paneling and mirrors gave the entry an air of a colonial presence that was echoed in the ornamental chandeliers and the gilded railing of the grand stairway.

The French style café opened onto the courtyard to let those tourists unused to the heat enjoy a breeze, cooled by mist from a fountain of Italian design. The spirits flowed liberally and the food was copious and delicious. Every tourist's dream oasis. Of course every room was bugged and all calls, in-coming or out-going, were monitored. What was more, Ziki wouldn't be surprised if the concierge and his assistants were not snitches for the Iraqi secret police.

A few more dollars to line the pocket of a humble desk clerk—who would say no to that?

Ziki strode through the bustling lobby, head high and shoulders wide. He wore a comfortable gray silk suit, the lapel pocket stuffed with a burgundy handkerchief. He walked with the presence of a man who owned those who worked for him. He surveyed the other guests like a man who knew that his net worth was over and above that of some small countries, smiled like a man who could make million dollar deals, returned the cool gaze of the concierge. Seated in the lobby were foreign women of all sorts. Ziki told the concierge that he'd left some clothes to be dry cleaned in his suite. Could they please be prepared for tomorrow morning?

He had an important meeting.

The concierge nodded. "Yes meiner Herr, I understand everyman wants to look his best."

It felt strangely good to be undercover again. The old jump of the blood was back.

The United Bank of Switzerland was a brief walk from the Hotel International. Ziki slid on shades as he walked through the doors. The door man bowed and offered a "Good Day" in perfectly Swiss English. Ziki returned a curt nod and answered the same, his English tempered with a German accent. Yes, it was good to be back.

The streets of Baghdad were hot and dusty as usual. Traffic filled the air with a cacophony of horns, and engines growled. The air smelled of diesel exhaust and cooking oil. Further on, smoke rose from the fingeans of the coffee vendors.

Ziki crossed a street, a square where a water fountain that—before running water—would have supplied travelers, cooks and servants in the area fresh, cool water for animals and washing. He passed the closed doors of a mosque, small shops and uncounted boots of all sorts. Butchers, bakers, a carpet weaver, basket weavers, metal and gold smiths. He passed and looked into, but did not enter, the Ali Baba bazaar on Fadaien Street that offered tourists all the little trinkets and knickknacks tourists like: cloth and embroidered bags and shoes, handmade dolls, handmade pottery, ribbons and clips for women's hair, necklaces, bracelets, anklets, earrings of gold and the cheapest silver.

Children were playing in a swarm with a dented tin can. The girls were screaming. Past the state buildings, the financial district awaited: banks and more banks, some state offices, title register offices for various property from homes and land to camels and donkeys, the business offices of refineries and shipping companies. And the UBS bank.

It was dim, cool and hushed inside the giant marble branch. Ziki's shoes sounded on the smooth stones of the lobby as he strode toward the bank manager's desk. A dark stained wooden gate swung silently and effortlessly on brass hinges as a clerk let Ziki pass.

The bank manager was not the same man who had greeted Ziki on his last trip to Baghdad. The bronze plaque on the man's desk read: Fahir Hoshel. Hoshel was tall and thin, with wire-rimmed glasses and slicked back hair. He stood and shook Ziki's hand as Ziki showed the key he held to a safety deposit box.

"*Kasse nummern* 369, *bitte*," Ziki said.

"Yes, yes, of course. Please sit down, Herr..." The bank manager, also one of the directors, like others in positions of authority and power in Baghdad, spoke English as if he had been taught by Swiss matrons. The carefully clipped sound of a man educated in Britain or perhaps Egypt in what remained of the educational institutions fostered by the Swiss Empire. Money. The man tried to appear as if he had more of it than he could possibly know what to do with, Ziki overlooked the veneer. He wore a large golden signet ring on the smallest finger of his left hand, and his suit and tie were of quality silk. But of course, every oil 'millionaire' had his Swiss holdings. This man would know many men's secrets: hidden accounts, accounts for mistresses, the purchase of houses hidden from the authorities, wives, children, in-laws. Hoshel's true skill was in knowing what men were really made of. Ziki thought, caution.

"Breckenbauer," Ziki replied, taking the chair indicated. He unbuttoned his suit jacket and crossed his legs as he sat back, arms resting leisurely upon the chair rests. "Hans Breckenbauer."

"Ahhhhh, yes. . . And is your trip to our fair city business or pleasure, Herr Breckenbauer?" The assistant bank manager to whom he'd been passed onto made a smile that was almost too wide for his face, and his eyes became like small black buttons.

Ziki didn't allow the wave of dislike that washed over him appear on his face, Hoshel was watching. Petty bureaucrats did not have the excuse of a meager salary to rationalize the bribes they accepted.

"It is always a pleasure to be in Baghdad," Ziki answered, though frankly he thought the question was out of line. Hoshel had asked no questions. Ziki answered and answered pleasantly because it wouldn't do to rile up the smarmy man. It was Ziki's plan not to catch anyone's eye. A wealthy businessman was a common thing in Baghdad where money could open almost any door, grease any wheel, or unstop any dam. "Even when I am here on business."

"You are West German?"

"I am. But my business sees no borders, you understand." Ziki reached into his pocket and pulled out a business card. The logo Rimmer Medical consisted of the staff and snakes common in many hospital signs, superimposed upon a glyph of the globe.

"Ahhhh, indeed. A doctor." The man's eyes gleamed as if with dollar signs.

"No. Medical supplies, dental supplies, machines."

"Ahhh." Did Ziki sense disappointment? "A salesman?"

"No, I am also a director and part owner of the company."

"A lucrative endeavor."

"Selling things necessary for saving lives. Some of our machines sell for more than a million American dollars and that helps the bottom line." He winked understandingly at Hoshel. "I would not be your client if it did not."

That seemed to sober Hoshel. He sat upright. "You will understand, Herr Breckenbauer, that we have security requirements." The manager drew a thick logbook from his desk. "Your passport please."

"Of course, of course," Ziki replied. "It is no problem." He dug the requested document from his suit jacket and handed it over. The key to the safety deposit box dangled from his fingertips, ringing faintly against the chair as it swung loose.

"Do you know the date of your last visit?" Hoshel opened the passport, examining it with sharp eyes.

The edges of the pages of Ziki's passport were frayed as if they had been handled everyday since their issue. The cover was aged and the forgers had stamped the pages over and again with the indications of border crossings. Not even an expert in forgery would be able to tell that the international document Hoshel held was a fake. The passport and identity were made to confirm access to the Mossad-held safe deposit box. Ziki looked the world traveler. He leaned his temple on his forefinger and let the slightest trace of a smile play his lips.

Ziki spread his hands. "Sadly it has been over a year."

"Ahhhh," came Hoshel's characteristic start. "And you have come from Rome?"

"Yes," Ziki replied. "It was hotter there than it is here today."

The lines about Hoshel's mouth released some their tension. "Good. You will sleep well here, then."

Hoshel flipped the log open. He ran his finger down the page, his eyes darting over text that Ziki could not see. "Number 369, yes. You will follow me."

With a nod Ziki rose.

The bank's lobby had been cool, but the air-conditioned vault was like ice. Ziki stayed at Hoshel's shoulder as the man unlocked a door and led him down a hallway. At the end of the hall, the vault yawned open, blocked only by a steel gate. Just to the right of this a gray haired man of small stature sat behind a glass window in a tiny security booth. Close-circuit television monitors flickered on the wall behind him.

The tightest security Ziki had seen in a bank, even Zurich. He wondered what had motivated the Swiss—a greater Russian presence in Baghdad? Or a new hotel down the street named "The Palestine," sure to attract every terrorist passing through Baghdad. Tighter security since Israel had refused to be wiped off the map? Had someone in Iraqi Secret Security Police been tipped off to the safety deposit box? It didn't matter. What Ziki was there to collect currently held no danger.

Hoshel tapped on the old man's window. "Deactivate vault room cameras."

"Yes, sir," the older man replied. He reached for his control board and there was a click and a whirr. One television screen went dead.

"Release security on vault gate," Hoshel ordered.

"Released," the old man replied. There was a whirr in the wall and a thunk! of metal on metal.

"Her Breckenbauer," Hoshel signaled Ziki forward.

Hoshel slid his key in the final lock and opened the gate. He locked the gate after Ziki. Safety boxes in assorted sizes lined the vault from floor to ceiling. The marble floor reflected their stainless steel faces and locks up at the two men. A dark metal table sat in the center of the vault.

Hoshel found 369 and inserted his key, turning it to the right. "And now you, Herr Breckenbauer."

Ziki stepped forward, inserted his own key, and turned it. Together the men drew out the box and placed it on the table. It was heavier than Ziki would have thought. He prepared himself mentally not to show surprise at the contents of the box.

"You will want privacy, I presume," Hoshel said.

Ziki shook his head. "Not necessary." The best hiding place was out in the open. Anything and everything in the box could have been seen by members of the Republican Guard themselves without giving Ziki or other Mossad operatives away.

Ziki flipped the safety box open and pulled out the smaller metal box nested inside. This he sat on the tabletop and opened as well. He noted the bank manger's attempt to restrain his obvious curiosity, but made no move to hide the contents; a wad of cash in a gold and diamond studded money clip. Gold chains. A Rolex. A velvet jewelry box marked "Cartier." Several ancient coins pressed in glass plates. A small silk bag that looked as if it would contain stones. Documents. Ziki collected the cash, the watch, the bag, tucking these into his pockets. He took the unmarked envelope on top of the other documents, sliding it into his breast pocket. It was quite thick between his fingers. He flipped the box closed.

"That is all."

"Very good, Sir." Hoshel stepped forward to place the box inside the other and to slide the lock box into its housing.

"We hope to see you again before you return to your home, Herr Breckenbauer," Hoshel said. His lips were shiny as he smiled that wide smile once more.

"I am glad to be in such competent hands," Ziki replied, and made a mental note to ask operatives in Baghdad about the man. There was something about him not quite right. Something more than a lust for rubles or dollars.

Ziki thanked the man with gentile grace and hurried outside to hail a taxi.

He was glad for the midday heat.

**It was only the envelope that Ziki wanted.** Inside were the address of a safe house and the information necessary to contact Joseph. He could make the call from the safe house on an untraceable phone and prep the local ops there to guard his back. They would have guns. Ziki would feel better meeting Joseph if he was armed. He missed the familiar weight of a mini Uzi at his side.

The taxi sped through Baghdad, taking Ziki through a suburban jungle of apartment buildings, storefronts, plazas and markets. His driver skidded to a halt at an intersection and laid on the horn as a boy with a small herd of goats crossed the street and disappeared down a curving alley. The driver swore in Farsi. What Ziki caught of the driver's oath did not bear well upon relatives from the country who did not leave their ways behind them.

## Chapter 17

### Safehouse—In Baghdad

**The safe-house was a two-story building of only four apartments with a b**land exterior. Several cars were parked beside it. Mossad would own the entire building through an untrackable chain of paper corporations and money transfers. Ziki saw a curtain draw back, showing the dimness behind the window and a face. The face watched him without expression for a long moment and then was gone. Ziki climbed the two stairs to the intercom and buzzed the first apartment. A dog barked from somewhere inside the building.

The click and static of the intercom. "Who is it?" a man's voice asked in Arabic. A young man. The intercom clicked.

"My name is Hans Breckenbauer.   We have business associates in common."

Click and static. "Breckenbauer, what is the name of your company?" Click. "Rimmer Medical Supply, and yours?" Click.

"Shalitco, and the name of your boss?"

"Armando."

Silence answered that.

And a final click.

Static.

"The first door to your left."

The door began to buzz as the lock released.

The heavily weighted door swung quickly closed as Ziki stepped inside. Fluorescent lamps lit the hallway. The one at the end of the hall flickered as if its life were to end at any moment. The air was close and humid with the smell of human sweat and dogs and baking bread. Spices. There were spices on the air too. The smell of bread made him simultaneously salivate and think of home.

He knocked on the door to his left as told.

It swung open to reveal the young man. He looked Arab with his dark curly hair and large dark eyes. His cheeks were smooth above the straggling hairs of what could never pass as a beard. The man wore a black shirt and jeans. His feet were bare. Behind him was a woman about his age, if not a year or two younger.

She had long hair that covered her shoulders and flowed. She was far too pale, leading Ziki to wonder if she veiled when she went about in public. She hid a gun behind her back, Ziki surmised—one arm held at an odd angle, her elbow sharply bent and hand at the small of her back. She was ready to shoot him.

"I am here looking for Joseph," Ziki told them.

The young man's eyes flickered with recognition. "As are others."

"And I have a delivery." Ziki reached into his jacket. The woman tensed, watching him, ready. She did not relax when he pulled out the envelope he'd taken from the safety deposit box.

"I believe it's for you." He held the envelope out to the girl. Beneath directions to the safe house and other important information had been a letter from home for her. Ziki hadn't read it.

The girl's face lit up a little, though she didn't like to show it.

"Search him." A third voice from a far doorway turned Ziki's head.

A large man, who also looked Arabic and dressed similarly to the others, entered the room from the right. His Uzi was trained on Ziki's mid-section. He had been around the corner, ready to wheel and fire if necessary. Ziki watched him move with confidence, holding the gun with one hand. He held a cigarette in the other.

The boss.

The young man stepped forward. "Hands up please," he said. Polite. Casual.

The search was a formality. Still no muzzles would be lowered until they were damn good and sure he was who they thought he was. The young man pulled out a small box with a display of lights on the end and swept this around Ziki's waist and chest as he patted Ziki's pockets. Jacket, waist, small of the back, arms, thighs, ankles.

"No bugs. He's unarmed. He's safe."

"It's from my mother. I've been waiting all week for it to arrive." The woman let her pistol come into sight, released the cocked hammer. In the next movement she shoved the pistol into the back of her waistband and simultaneously stepped toward Ziki to snatch the envelope from his hand.

Ziki hoped it was good news. He hoped it made her happy. She might be pretty if she cheered up a little.

"Mossad sent word this morning that you'd come to us. We've been preparing for you, Ziki," the boss said. He held out his hand and Ziki shook it.

"You know my name. Do I get to know yours?"

"You will know me by the name of Roshi Nitzan. I am known in Baghdad as Roshi."

"And your compatriots?"

"Yes. The front line of my team," the boss indicated the young man and young woman. "Hanna and Amit." They gave Ziki dark nods.

"Lunch will be ready in ten minutes," the woman, Hanna, said. And without another word, she returned to what Ziki presumed was the kitchen. Charming. Ziki wouldn't have wanted to be on the wrong side of her. Still, she was probably a hell of a cook—the smell of bread and garlic wafted about the room. He heard the sound of crinkling paper almost immediately.

"Come." Roshi gestured to Ziki to follow. Amit fell in behind him.

The toilet was at the end of the hall. Two other doors were closed on either side of its door. Roshi entered the one on the left.

The sun shone brightly through drapes that were pulled tight. The air smelled of gunpowder and motor oil. On a bench along a wall lay a collection of guns and paraphernalia—submachine guns and pistols, empty cartridges, shells, and two silencers.

"And what are your orders?" Ziki asked.

"My orders are to support you in any way you may need. You need guns. We have guns. Sweepers. We've got sweepers. You need contacts, background checks, tails on the bloody royal family, we provide. You need bugs placed; we've got the kit and the rats."

Rats. Ziki smiled. The best way to bug a building without hassle: loose a few rats that had been forced to swallow transceivers and explosive capsules the size of an aspirin. Let fifteen- twenty rats loose and in two days when they had set up shop about the building, the rats died. The whole building could be wired without anyone the wiser…We even do it to the Kremlin… Brilliant. Ziki knew but was silent.

"How much do you know about my mission?"

"I know you are to contact a man named Joseph. We are to tape all calls and to cover you when you meet. We stay out of the way unless you call us in."

"Good, that's good. You don't need to know more that that."

"Tell us what you need."

"I want a mini Uzi and about one hundred rounds for good measure. I'll want a 9 millimeter automatic pistol and silencer for close range."

"Knife?" Roshi asked. "We've got—"

Ziki laughed. "Arabs carry knives. I prefer something more long range."

"Browning high power—semi-automatic all right?" the young man asked.

"Yeah," Ziki answered. A 9 mm Browning or a Jericho, if you have one, and a mini Uzi would do the job," if he weren't stopped and searched by the Iraqi police. A German businessman would have a hard time explaining carrying those tools around. And if he were arrested, he'd never be seen again. "I need a safe phone line to call our contact—Joseph. I want the call traced, the address checked, and family history, everything on this man available before I meet him. And I want an oral disclosure of another operative center and maybe even Arab sleepers, so that I have some other place to go to if this thing turns to shit."

Roshi nodded. "We've got you."

"Yeah, but I only want one more contact than you guys, so that I don't involve anyone else."

"We've got you." Ziki hoped so.

He stayed at the "*safe house*" another few hours as they assembled his equipment—bug sweeper, explosive pellets, a lock picking set—and readied himself for the phone call he would have to make. But what would he say to Joseph? Let me write you a check for that MiG parked over there? The money was waiting; yes:

a quick transfer of funds, set the date, verify everything, get in, and get out.

Drinking coffees, Ziki waited on the sofa in the living room of the apartment as Amit finished the wiring for the call. Everything in the room appeared normal, as if a real Arab family lived there living their daily lives. The weapons cache and radios and other equipment were built into the walls with a system of a dumb waiter where they could be on the upper floor of the building if the lower were to be searched, and vice versa. So, like a normal person, Ziki switched on the TV and began to flip channels. News from Baghdad. A Turkish Soap Opera. A broadcast about the evils of Capitalism and virtues of Soviet Communism.

It was not long before Hanna, who had finished with the dishes came to join him. Ziki was surprised that she hadn't made Amit do them; it turned out that he had done the previous batch. She set a bowl of hummus, pita and lamb in front of him, a puddle of virgin olive oil collected with crushed herbs and paprika on the surface of the hummus. The bread was light brown and brushed with butter.

She flopped onto the sofa. "Thank you," she said.

"For what?" He sipped his tea.

"There was news of my sister's son in the letter. He has been sick. I worry."

Ziki watched the television. "Is everything okay?"

"I think it will be."

"Good."

She toyed with the fringe on a pillow and Ziki knew she was gearing up for something else. "How long have you done this?"

"Watch television?"

She smiled wryly at his stupid joke. Suddenly she was almost pretty. "No. Gone about like this. To places in the world. Hans."

He met her gaze with a blank stare.

"Hans," she said again. Her eyes flickered darkly.

Too long. Not long enough. He thought all the time about going home and staying there: a family, a small house, some flowers. And yet, he couldn't keep still long enough to think it would be possible or right. There wasn't much left to go home to. "Why do you want to know?"

"We know someone in common," Hanna said.

"Yeah?"

"Gavriella Ramon." Her fingers were busy with the fringe of the cushion. "Or that's the name she uses here anyway. An American—here."

A sleeper?

Ziki watched the television closely. He couldn't hear it any longer.

Gavriella wasn't a sleeper by any means. She was the primary connection for Americans working undercover in Iraq. She supplied them with guns, information, training, plans to go on missions. A very persuasive woman. "Yes, I know Gavriella."

Hanna smiled. "She said I'd know you if I met you."

"How?"

"The blonde hair; naaw, she said I'd just know. I think she really likes you."

"Does she?"

Amit came into the room. "Ziki—we're ready. You're on."

Ziki sat back, not looking at Hanna. "Let's do it."

The first phone call was nearly over before it started.

Ziki held the receiver to his ear, listening for the ring. His palm was damp against the plastic.

The ring sounded twice before it was picked up.

"Hello . . . ?"  The listener was a man—middle-aged. His voice was thinner than Ziki had expected. Was it the same man who had called Paris? Ziki couldn't be certain. Long distance and static had distorted that voice. This line was clear and secure.

"This call is for Joseph," Ziki said.

Silence in reply.

"Joseph. . .?" A hesitation. The muffled sound of the phone being shuffled on a shoulder. "Who would I tell him is calling?"

"A mutual friend in Paris suggested I contact him."

The voice betrayed anxiety. "Joseph cannot be reached at this number. Do not call here again."

"A friend interested in jet airplanes told me to call this number."

"Keep him on the line," Amit mouthed.

Ziki nodded, shifting the headset. "I was given this number by a friend in Paris. He told me I could reach Joseph here."  Don't lose your nerve, he silently prodded the caller.

"Joseph isn't here," the caller responded. "You can reach him at this number." The caller recited a series of digits. Ziki motioned at Amit who took down the number where Joseph could be reached. "Call tomorrow morning early. He'll be waiting."

The caller hung up quickly.

Ziki put the receiver back in its cradle and looked up to see Roshi and Hanna watching him intently. Roshi nodded as if to say, well done.

Amit clamped his headphone tightly to his ear, swiveling a dial on his equipment with the other hand. "Okay. . . Okay . . . your call was just long enough." Amit's head was bobbing up and down as he scratched random notes on a pad of paper.

Ziki found he was holding his breath.

Amit smiled. "Okay. I got a number. I got an address."

# Chapter 18

### GAZA – Iamael's Brother

**As a child of the Gaza Strip Iamael Ibn el Wazira grew up familiar with Jews, working for Jews**. He saw the Jew soldiers at the check points whenever he crossed into Israel. He heard his father and brother curse the Jews. The Jews were to blame for the poverty and containment of the Palestinian people. The Jews had to be destroyed if Palestine was to achieve glory…. Infidels.

Iamael was a sharp student. He studied hard in his school and earned top marks in reading and writing, math and science. But most of all, he loved to hear of the history of the world and to think of the great cities of the world where a man might travel. London. New York. Tokyo. He practiced his Hebrew until he spoke it as well as any man or woman he knew. He would leave Gaza and Khan Yunis and travel to places that were not dry as a bone and dusty as death.

Iamael's older brother told him he was wasting his time. There was no work for Palestinians outside Israel. The only good life was in service to Allah. A free Palestine needed young men eager to fight. In Paradise, 72 black eyed virgin brides would be the reward for killing Christian Crusaders and Jews. All the food you could eat and drink and all the virgin flesh a man could want awaited those who gave their lives for *Jihad* and were *Fadayeen and Shahids* for a free of the infidels' land.

He took Iamael to the corner on the slight rise of the arid ground that was the best spot to watch the Israeli soldiers lounge between patrolling and searching women and men. "How could men who were refused arms protect their young and old?" Iamael's brothers raged.

"Well we can get all the arms we want from every place like Egypt just across the Philadelphy over there, or Syria. You know that all you have to do is just ask the El Fattah on Sulemania Street, tell him that you want to kill Jews and he'll get you any Kalashnikov machine gun you'd want."

Iamael watched the Israeli soldiers, squinting in the sun and smoking as they leaned against a jeep, laughing. Iamael thought that his brother could not see how similar he and his friends were to the Israelis in uniform. Young Palestinian men also squinted in the sun, smoked cigarettes, and told jokes about girls. Young Palestinian men also talked about leaving behind the villages of their fathers for places where work was easy to find and jobs paid well.

It started as usual. A jibe or a taunt and suddenly it was boys with stones making young men with guns duck for cover. Iamael's brother hurled a rock hard. It bounced off the hood of a jeep, leaving a scratch and a dent.

Iamael felt a shove from behind. His brother pushed a rock into Iamael's hand. His brother's eyes said, time to be a man. Iamael weighted it and threw it, watching it arch in the sky. Iamael's rock took an Israeli by surprise. Before the soldier fell, Iamael saw red blood on the Israeli's temple.

"You hit him! Uncle Salameh will like what you did," his brother crowed. "Good shot!"

Iamael's brother and his brother's friends scattered.

Iamael watched for the young Israeli to rise.

An armored car roared forward. It shot water from a cannon at the boys. The boys ran and the cannon hit them with spray between the shoulder blades.

Iamael ran too, but he was far behind. The beating blow of water knocked him forward. His lips and teeth hit the earth hard. He tasted blood. He called for his brother. He called for help. Rough hands hauled him up by the ankles, dragged him a few feet and tossed him into the back of a van. It was dark inside and the windows were covered with grating.

He did not cry when the van began to move.

He did not cry when he was taken into the jail and made to shower naked in front of an old man with dark spots on his face. Nor when he was sprayed from head to toe with something that smelled funny, like chemicals, and stung his eyes and skin. He was given dry clothes and put in a white room with only a bed where he sat for what seemed like hours. But it was not dark when he was called from his cell and escorted to another white room where a man with a nice face sat.

The man sent a nurse in to put stinging antiseptic on his cuts and an ice pack on his mouth. Iamael was given a sandwich and a cool drink, a coke. He had heard of coke but never tasted it, sweet and smooth with a little tickle of fizz in his nose.

As he ate a man asked him questions, but what was more, he told Iamael all about himself: his performance in school, his mother and mother's brothers' names, all the names of his brother's children, where they worked. He said they would be watching him from now on, but more closely. He should be careful. It was easy to see things only one way. He also told him that, "The devil is not always as black as he is painted out to be, and if you look close he may not be the devil at all."

Iamael ate his sandwich slowly and drank all of his coke.

When he entered his neighborhood, he ripped off the bandages the nurse had applied and muddied his face again before turning onto his own street.

When asked, he told his brother he had run away and was not caught. He told his brother that he spent the day hiding in an onion cellar, afraid the Israelis would get him for what he'd done.

If he told the truth, he had feared his brother might have seen that there was no hatred for the Jews in his eyes.  Iamael could not find enough reasons to hate the Israelis.

But perhaps his brother had already known the rift in Iamael's heart.

"Liar—I saw them take you!  You sat with the fat man inside the jail and you ate and drank what he gave you."  Iamael's brother would not be soothed.

From that day it was different between them.

## Chapter 19

### Informants

**It was late; Iamael's friend in Gaza, Arjan, was scared**. With his older brother, Mahmoud, he led his small gray donkey carrying a wooden trailer down the streets of Khan Yunis. The wheels thumped along the dirt road. They could taste the stink of garbage and sewage that permeated the air. It dulled the senses and mingled with the dust, but the brothers were used to it.

The donkey stopped from time to time to sniff in the direction of darkened alleys. Windows with no glass and doorways with no doors gaped at them like open mouths. On the other side of town were many fancy houses, real fancy for a place like this. Rumor was that those were the ones in with the leadership of the El Fattah and all the others of their kind; the money came from the oil sheiks of Arabia. When the donkey stopped they prodded him along, the trailer being their only alibi for being in the city at this time of the evening.

There was no time to waste. The brothers knew it was well past an undeclared curfew in the town's center, and their presence would mean almost a certain beating at the hands of the 'Islam Leopards' or one of the other factions. Gangs of armed men roamed the streets all along and inside a four-block radius, their trigger fingers itchy. Never mind that the two brothers were blood, like thousands of others in the shack cities set up sporadically without a plan all over the Gaza Strip. Never mind that they shared the same religion and language as the militiamen: that they were related by blood, were Moslems and lived there. They would be beaten just as sure as the Jews would be killed. The gangs rarely showed mercy if young men didn't belong to them...

At only 17, Arjan did not fully understand what was happening, a little slow. Mahmoud, 19, didn't bother to explain.

"You will understand when you are older, Arjan, what we are doing here. It is complicated; perhaps something we can talk about when we leave this place," he had said in the darkness, his voice detached. They continued along the road with the donkey.

Leaving here. That tasted sweet in Arjan's mouth. He wondered what it would be like.

From time to time black and red hooded men carrying guns, members of the Islamic Jihad, made everybody they could bully along gather in the streets to listen to them talk of killing the Jews and becoming shahids. Riches that would only come once the Jews and the other Christian infidels were driven out of Palestine, all of it—not just Gaza. Out of the land that belonged to them, not the Jews. Killing them would be done with the blood of the shahids, who would wait in comfort in Paradise surrounded by their seventy black-eyed virgin wives, eating sweet fruit and adorned with untold riches.

"But why do they hate them this much, Mahmoud? Why will it come only from blood?" he had asked at the most recent Islamic Jihad rally, the shouts of the red turbaned speaker reverberating throughout the crowd, pumping them up to a chorus of shouts and weapons discharged in the air. "Why do we do this? Wasn't Grandfather Abdalah friends with the Jews?"

This was a question that normally would be directed at their father, Ahkmed. But he was dead. Strangled with barbed wire by a Jihad gang when he resisted them from dragging his daughter, Reenah, out to who knows where in the middle of the night. Ahkmed El Fawoud was murdered and they had taken Reenah anyway. The two had neither seen nor heard from her again.

"We do not do anything," his brother replied, pointing a crooked finger through where the crowd and towards the speaker. He lowered his voice so that only his brother, standing close, could hear him. "It is they. They are the ones that kill," moving his head in the direction of the group." Murder Father like a dog—drag our sister out of bed half naked by her hair kicking and screaming into the darkness to, to…" Mahmoud couldn't finish the sentence without his voice cracking, moisture appearing in the corner of his eye. Arjan lowered his eyes to his bare, dirty feet. Mahmoud continued, his emotions held in check.

"They would have everyone die for their cause. And what can we do? If we don't do what they say, they will kill us. Either way we have no choice. No hope. In times like these we must be strong, brother. We must never give up. Do you understand?" Arjan nodded slowly, understanding only half of what his brother had said. They had returned to their small shelter made of cinder cement blocks and a corrugated steel roof, the rear of wood lashed together with hemp rope, in silence.

It was two days later that a man had appeared out of the heat of the mid-afternoon sun. Arjan had pushed the curtain that served as a door to the side. The man was slim. He didn't look like an Arab. He was lighter and spoke Arabic with the hint of an accent. He wore nice clothes, in the Arab garb, with a white Kafia on his head that looked newly washed. Was he a Jew? The thought had struck Arjan as both fascinating and terrifying.

"I am looking for Mahmoud," the man had said. "Can I speak with him?"

"He is in the fields with our mother," Arjan had not joined them that day because he had been sick with food poisoning, too weak to be of much help. "They will be back later for bread and to pray." The man had nodded and thanked Arjan before leaving.

Later, Arjan had been sent to the well by his mother with an old bucket to get water, it was always the same, when he and Iamael went there. He had had to wait a long time, the older men forcing the younger to dip their buckets at the shallow end where the water was dirty and smelled bad.

An unusual day, the air was dark; a haze covered the horizon in vanishing flatness, brooding motionless in mournful gloom; a glow brought out the haze.

A Tanzim with a checkered headband and a machine gun had stood close by, making sure nobody got out of line.

When he had returned home, the man was back, he had green eyes and a straight back, talking to his brother in hushed tones. They had sat on the floor at the low table made of a piece of plywood that the family used to eat on. The man had talked with his hands. Mahmoud had nodded all the while. His mother had asked Arjan to go outside so as not to disturb the two. He had, and by the time he had returned the man was gone once again.

They stopped the donkey and trailer in front of a building, tying him to a beam with a short piece of brown rope. The building was bland; the paint all but stripped off completely from the relentlessly arid sun; the atmosphere became somber as if angered by the approaching sun. It was like most other buildings in Khan Yunis. Graffiti written on the side of the building boldly screamed: "Kill the Jews!" in Arabic. Other graffiti said, "Eat their flesh!" and "Shahids go to Paradise!" It was nothing new to either of them. Armed gangs rode around in small open vehicles painting up the walls, voices loud, weapons louder, making their presence and intentions known.

"Now what?" asked Arjan.

"Now we wait," his brother replied.

"Wait for what?"

"Don't worry. It's almost time, my brother, and we will have more money than king Hussein of Jordan." Arjan looked confused. He still didn't know what they were doing in a dangerous area of the city in the middle of the night. His brother never told him why, only that he had to come with him. He never told Arjan who the man that had been looking for him was or what they discussed, or that Iamael, his friend had described an Israeli that looked like Ziki. That was a week ago. He had noticed a change in his brother since then. He was happy. He smiled freely. He hadn't been like that since before their father died and their sister had vanished into the night air; but he told Arjan that Iamael, their friend, had seen the bus blow up near the checkpoint at Megiddo when he was up north helping his grandfather with the goats, and that Iamael did not like what he saw.

"You know where we are, right?" asked Mahmoud. Arjan looked around in the darkness. For now, nobody else was out on the street. That would change if they were there too long—if they were too loud. The little donkey paced back and forth on its short tether. He hoped nobody would come.

"Well," said Arjan, blinking his eyes rapidly, "I know we're at the city center. The Mahareesh Bazaar is right over there." He pointed to the empty shadowy skeletons of booths that merchants used to display their goods during the day.  At noon the ground they stood on was so thick with shoppers and lookers that it was easy to lose one's way in the swarm of humanity.

"You are correct, brother," said Mahmoud.  He pointed his thumb over his shoulder at the building they had tied their donkey to.  "So you must know what building this is, don't you?  You must, because we have been here before, Arjan.  We have been here many times before.  Do you remember?"  Arjan looked at the building, the memories forming in his mind's eye like phantoms.  The images panned out before his eyes in the darkness.

"It is the same square we were at that last rally.  The speaker with the red and white *Kafia*, turban."

"Precisely.  We were at this very spot listening to what that man had to say.  And now we are back.  This is where he and his men gather in the evening to gamble and smoke hashish.  I know.  I was in there before when they wanted me to join them."

Arjan gulped.  He looked at the faded green tattoo on his brother's exposed forearm.  Arabic writing declaring Mahmoud's loyalty to the Moslem Brotherhood.  His brother had had no choice:  either join or be an outcast, the same choice that every young man in Gaza would have to make at some point, when they came for you. It was accepted in silence; they lived in a flicker of time glaring at the darkness that came and was here to stay.

Arjan shuddered slightly, his arm trembling.  He didn't like the thought of being outside the house of a man like that.  A man like that had guns.  Lots of them.  That man had violence in his voice.  That man was dangerous, and with his other men roaming the city with their gang was terrifying.

"So what are we doing out here?  Mahmoud!  Why aren't we at home sleeping?"

"Lower your voice."  Mahmoud scowled at his younger brother.  Arjan nodded.  "Just please trust me and don't worry.  Remember, if anybody comes up to us we say that our mother had left this cart while she was in the market today.  We brought our donkey with us from home so that we could carry it back because we could not do it ourselves.  It is too heavy.  Can you remember that?  Arjan?  Can you remember that?  I'm counting on you."

"Yes, yes.  I know, I know.  But how long must we wait, brother?  What will happen to you?"

Mahmoud put up one finger as if to signify one moment.  He dug in the pocket of his simple brown pants and pulled out a little black box.  Even in the dark, Arjan could see that it was shiny because it reflected the moon.  A short stick was attached to it and it glowed with a small red light.  Mahmoud held it out before him with pride.  Arjan's eyes were wide with excitement and wonder.

"This is a radio—a transmitter, brother.  They will tell me when they are ready.  Until then we wait.  Don't worry about what happens to me.  All I want is for you and mother to be safe and have money, lots of money.  That is why we are here."

The scout Ziki had sent ahead to the high ground could see the two and their donkey through the green tint of his night vision goggles. Ze'evi was sprawled out chest down on the top of a building a half block away. It had been risky infiltrating the edge of the city alone at night with no one to back him up and to cover him. But it was crucial to the mission's success for them to accurately pinpoint the target buildings, to be certain what house Ali Hasan Salameh was in, and with some luck Abu Nidal as well.

He has risen into the higher echelons of the PLO after his escape from Ziki's grip in Ba'albek: the ringleader now of a litany of factions of terrorist organizations. There was a man constantly at Salameh's side known only as "*Abdul.*" He had an affiliation with the 'Oddessa' organization and with the Nazi scientists working in Egypt near the Sudan border on biological warheads. He ran a heroine processing plant, stuff grown in the Be'eka Valley and in Afganistan. The two were reported by an informant to be in Khan Yunis.

Ze'evi worked better alone. Less visibility. Davidoff had thought it a terrible plan, but Ze'evi had convinced him he could go it alone. He was capable, and the Captain could not find a reason to send in more than one man. He had given him his okay.

He reached over and silently grabbed his radio, turning the line to a secure frequency. He fumbled around in the Arab kafia that he wore, the fabric getting in the way of his hands so he bunched it up around his elbows. He hated wearing the garb, but it allowed him in. Anybody that had seen him earlier in the evening was indifferent, just what he wanted. He spoke quietly into the transmitter.

"Desert Eagle one, this is Scarecrow. We've got activity out on the street. Repeat, we have activity out on the street. Over." He waited for the reply and watched the two intensely through his goggles. They looked like kids... Where did they get these two?

"Roger that, Scarecrow. What have you got? Over," came the voice over the crackle of the radio in his ear.

"Two males. Arab. They have a donkey cart with them. The elder about 6'. Early twenties. The younger 5'8", 100 pounds. Teenager. Sound like anybody we know? Over."

"Roger that. The donkey should have a red ribbon attached to his neck... Scarecrow, does the donkey have a red ribbon attached to it? Over."

"Roger that Desert Eagle one. Two story building. Sun bleached white. Check out? Over." A pause.

"Roger that, Scarecrow. Target confirmed. Good job, Ze'evi. You sit tight for now. Sit back, keep your eyes open for us and watch the show. Over."

Ze'evi smiled. "Roger that, Desert Eagle one. Just don't take too long. I promised my girlfriend I would take her out tonight. Over." Laughter came over the receiver.

"We'll try, Scarecrow. We'll try. Desert Eagle one out."

Ziki reattached the receiver to his belt. The scout on the ground had the targets in sight. From the description and the camera view, it was identical to the one the other informant had described.

Ziki and a three thousand man force were in no position to be second-guessing the location of mission objectives. The Amman Intel reports seem to have been sound.

The two brothers were simple informants of opportunity. Unhappy with their lives in the camps a promise of pay off to them of two thousand American Dollars they became informants. They were like most in the region, poor, kicked around by leadership, victims of random violence. Little to lose, something to gain.

Ziki paid one thousand American dollars each to risk their lives. That amount was more than they would have likely made, combined, working Khan Yunis's barren fields. If they live, it would be enough for a long while. Maybe allow them to start life in another township. Allow them to have things they would otherwise never have a chance to possess. Or maybe they would stay. With a successful raid, Khan Yunis would by no means be an arid paradise. But maybe they would be able to breathe a little easier, for a while.

"Commander," said Ziki's friend Davidoff, lumbering up to Ziki's side, "all units are at ready. All present and accounted for, including the choppers. Looks like the politicians have started listening to us for a change."

"Let's just hope that holds up for a while longer," Ziki replied with a grin. "No good going in there with our pants at half mast."

"Exactly. What do you think about this mission, Ziki," Davidoff said, talking to him now as a friend and not a fellow officer. Ziki paused a second before responding, turning his gaze to meet that of his long time friend.

"Good. I feel good about it. Keep it simple. Go in. Catch them off guard. Secure the
 perimeter. Begin the clean-up. A nasty house to house search—locate the targets, snag and bag them and we're done. Shouldn't be more than a few hours. Civilian casualties minimal, I hope. You?"

"About the same. But my guts say not to think it so easy. Not to assume they'll go down so easily without a fight. I mean we're talking some real uglies here."

"Yes, there's always the damn unexpected. We must remember that they are fanatics, willing to fight to their death."

"We do have the element of surprise.
 We hope to make them fear us enough to be afraid to shoot at us. Take away their will to shoot. We do that and we take low casualties on both sides. Agreed?"

"Yeah, I guess so; the surprise. It will help a lot to reduce casualties."

"Surprise is the key to us getting as few casualties as possible"

"Not to mention nabbing the two 'big fish,' Salameh and that son of a bitch 'Nidal'."

"Yeah, let's hope that wind of this raid hasn't leaked out to them"

"From where, and by whom?"

"If it leaks the" fish" could swim away and lots of blood on both sides."

Davidoff folded his arms across his chest, kicking his boot into the hard ground of the command center. "You're right I think."

"Good," said Ziki, giving him a hearty thump on the back and leading him towards the awaiting briefing tent. "Now will you stop thinking about this so damn hard? You're giving me a headache."

**The command center was set up to the east of Khan Yunis towards Gaza** far enough that it would not play out the hand of the size of their presence.

## Chapter 20

**Gavriella—Langley Virginia**

**The men exited out into the early morning air.** Ziki stayed behind. He still had a matter to attend to. Something to do with how an ally, the Americans, would react to this raid. They had to be notified.

Ziki entered the tent that had been reserved for secured trans-Atlantic communications. He shut the curtain behind him and sat down at the folding metal desk that dominated the small space. A black phone with multiple buttons sat on the desk's surface. A secure phone line. He picked up the receiver and put it to his ear. It rang twice before a feminine voice answered on the other end.

"Hello, Ramon and Walters." The tone was efficient but cheery. It was her.

"Who is Walters, Gavriella?" He said, recognizing her voice.

"Ziki, how are you, or, more importantly, where are you? I miss you."

"Can't fool one another, hmm…Gavriella this is business, and I'm in a hurry." Ziki's blood turned icy. How he could have feelings and distrust this woman simultaneously was beyond his understanding. *I'll die and never understand women.*

"Enough. Look," he said, lowering his tone, "a military operation is currently underway."

"Okay…pause…thank you for informing us, it would have been nice had you told us before it began, don't you think?" He ignored her remark.

"It is a clean-up operation…"

"Our satellite surveillance has just now picked up troop movement in the southern Negev desert, is that where you are Zik? You boys are tricky with this stuff, I remember last May troop movement showing on satellite in the southern Negev desert as a diversion and your operation quietly ongoing under our noses in the north of the country. Is this one of those deals?"

"Gavriella, I am in the south."

"Where exactly is this raid of yours going to take place?"

"It is my duty as an ally of the U.S. to inform you of this, so here it is; we're going into Khan Yunis south of Gaza city to extract some terrorists and their leaders. If there are any of your people in that target area get them out, the fire works start in two hours, got it? Any and all American personnel should be evacuated quietly and with haste. It is currently 0300 local time."

Silence.

"Understood?" he said again into the receiver. He heard a sigh come through on the other side. Was she exhausted? It was possible. On the east coast of the United States it was evening.

"Understood. But I must ask, Ziki, if this mission has anything to do with…?"

"Don't ask. All other information pertaining to this mission is classified. I've told you all that I can, not to mention all that I want to."

"I see. So it does." He paused. Was he really that transparent?

"Just get any of your people out of there. Now. Tell whoever it is that you are answering to this information as well. I hope this message is not being leaked throughout your complex."

"No Zik, off course not!"

"Gavriella, I will hold you personally responsible for any and all misfortune that befalls an American from your lack of getting them out of there in time. But be sure it is only Americans that quietly get out of the way. No leaks. Am I clear? No leaks…Leaks to the enemy will cost lives." He surprised himself at the tone he had taken. Was it anger? Or something else?

"I see that you haven't changed your mind about me, you know that I wouldn't do anything to hurt you Zik."

"This is not a social call Gavriella."

"Ah, but you never could refuse me now, could you Ziki?"

"Get your people out of there. Shalom Gavriella."

"But don't you…"

Click. He abruptly hung up the phone. He was satisfied. He tipped a little back in his seat. Word travels fast when one has their ear to the ground. Her being a maverick CIA operative, Ziki was never surprised at what she was capable of, deep down he always suspected that under it all she was a Palestinian sympathizer, she'd shown tendencies in that direction. Maybe that's how the DDI (deputy director) of the CIA was using her talents.

He got up from the seat and pondered if she'd do anything against him, he hoped not, before joining the rest of the men outside. He turned to Davidoff. "Maybe I should have called that Jimmy-Ray Sinclair instead of Gavriella Ramon."

"Nah, he's small fry, besides I know you wanted to hear her voice."

**The sub cellar communications complex of the CIA.** A locked room was reserved for a unit of communication experts, seven men and two women, who worked in shifts around the clock. They were linguistic specialists and Arabic was prominent when tied in with business for the Middle East. This was the hub for absolute international telephone and radio traffic; all were ordered not to discuss their activities with anyone, even spouses.

A portly man not in the usual trim shape of CIA field agents, his gut hanging over his trousers belt that was to tight wheeled back his cushioned swivel chair and looked at the room that was now on the late shift, a woman and two other men; it was nearing morning, half their shift over.

"I've got something," he said to no one specifically.

"Where from."

"It's boring nothing too interesting going on."

"Just translate it up Virgil."

"Radio Damascus is putting me to sleep….boooring ."

"Go to Riyadh, see what the Saudis are doing not Damascus, or maybe Dubai, Damascus is real careful, the comrades trained them well."

"Yeah, but when we get something it's usually good." said Virgil.

"Uups, here's something from the oil Sheiks" Virgil looked up from his computer screen.

"That's just it, rich oil money. Our source in Dubai passed the word that two million, Swiss Francs had been transferred to a coded account in the Bahamas, to…."

"Two million?" interrupted the second man. "In this league that's chickenshit!"

"I haven't told you its destination or the method of transfer. The Bank of Dubai trough the Bahamas to Zurich's Union Bank of Switzerland in Baghdad-that is Fahid Hoshel territory."

"That's the Beirut routing that ends up in Gaza, its El Fattah, PLO money." Isn't that, that son of a bitch something Salameh, and Abu Nidal? They are still working together. I hear Nidal is splintering off. Virgil spoke with instant recognition.

"Destination?"

"Gaza, at Khan Yunis, ha, exactly what I said. The precise location unknown."

"Find it!"

"That's impossible."

"Okay, get it from Mossad."

"I hate being so fucking dependent for our intelligence on the Israelis and their fucking Mossad."

"If it can't be confirmed wire into them?" Two minutes go by. "We have a response from Tel Aviv."

"It's confirmed all right, they sure are quick, what does it say?"

"Its bad news, our informant was killed right after he contacted our man passing this information to us."

"The money, do they say where exactly the money is going?"

"Yep, Khan Yunis, to that 'rag head' Salameh."

"Gaza Strip, at Khan Yunis" said Virgil quietly. "The suicide bomber capital of the planet."

"Listen up, priority from the DDI."

"Gavriela Ramon is to immediately, repeat, immediately inform trough your section, Ali Hasan Salameh in Khan Yunis of the impending Israeli raid by secure line. Be sure the line is encrypted and absolutely secure so that the Israelis can not get a hold of it. Execute immediately. Signed V.W. DDI."

"Man oh man, we're screwing the Israelis here big time."

"Just follow the Deputy Director's orders Virgil." "I've heard that both the DDI and that Gavriela Ramon have pro PLO—Arab tendencies"

"You best mind your own business Virgil, you're stepping on hallowed ground"

"Yeah, you're probably right, but this stinks."

"Do we know who's in charge of this raid?"

"Yeah, it's that Commander Ziki Barak, he issued the warning to us, to get our people out of there before the raid starts. He, and the Israelis are doing the right thing by us."

"I don't know about this one Virgil, over there those Israelis have always been straight with me, and this is going to cost them lives, they best not find out about this leak. I've heard that this Ziki Barak has a reputation, and that he can be a nasty son of a bitch if fucked with."

"It's worst than that, I once intercepted an amorous conversation between our Gavriella and this Israeli Commander, I think they have a thing going, or did... And now she is really screwing him notifying that piece of garbage Salameh of the Israeli raid."

"Just do your job Virgil, do what the DDI director and this Gavriella Ramon ordered, just do your job."

**It was late in Langley.** Gavriella Ramon hung up the small phone that sat like a trophy on her polished desk. She ran a slender hand through her straight dark hair. She stretched her legs. Ziki had been right. There was no need for her to distribute his declaration. Every office concerned with Middle East foreign policy had by now received it she just had to push one intercom button to do that... The word would be spread. The consequence, however, would not be what Ziki had in mind.

There was a knock on the door. Once, twice, three times. Gavriella got up to answer it. She knew who it would be.

"Good evening, Director Walters," she said as she opened the door. The lanky frame of CIA Director Walters entered the room.

"Miss Ramon," he replied, nodding his head slightly in an old fashioned show of respect. He walked across the office floor to the comfortable chair directly across from Gavriella's desk. He slouched a bit, and put his feet up on the corner of her desk. He took out a cigar and lit it. Gavriella remained by the still open door, her arms folded across her chest. She stepped forward to break the silence.

"No doubt Kissinger sent you. No need for that confirmation. I take it you got the message."

"Yes I did," he replied, blowing a smoke ring out of his o shaped mouth. It continued on until it disintegrated against the surface of a window. "The question is how to respond to the message. How would you have it?"

She didn't like his tone. Walters had detailed intelligence on her private relationship with Ziki. Nothing was too sacred to be revealed.

"Does it matter how I would have it?"

"No, it doesn't. I just want to see where it is that your loyalty truly lies. That's all."

"I work for you now. The past is the past. No use resurrecting events that are buried."

"Just the answer I was looking for." There was an awkward pause. Gavriella, not sure of what answers the Director was looking for, she straightened out the front of her skirt with the flat part of her hand. She again ran a hand through her dark hair. She walked behind the desk and sat down. Walters never made eye contact. He just continued to sit, puffing at his cigar intermittently.

"Well," he said rhetorically.

"It's understood," she replied. She knew what she had to do. She knew why he still sat there. He wanted to see where her loyalty was. She would not disappoint.

She picked up the receiver. Her long fingers capped with bright red manicured nails wrapped around the black of the plastic. She pressed a button on the phone's base to get a line through to Khan Yunis. The phone rang seven times before a man answered in Arabic.

Gavriella's Arabic was near indistinguishable from a native speaker with only a hint of an Anglican lilt.

"Get me Ali Hasan Salameh," she said in the receiver, her accented words thick and rich. "I have something important to discuss with him."

## Chapter 21

**Khan Yunis—Gaza Strip**

**The shadows of men and machines cut through the night.** The air was filled with the smell of diesel fuel, the grind of metal on metal, the crunch of gravel under tracks. *Merkava* tanks paved the way for the ground troops, the APCs moving in sync between them. Then came the special forces of the Golani and the tactical units, complete with a full surgical unit just in case. Commandkas brought up the rear. A swarming military force moved through the arid outskirts of the Gaza Strip. Ziki's men at work. Fast. Efficient.

The column barreled head long due west. Soon it would be within Khan Yunis's line of sight. The choppers performing aerial coordination sweeps out of sight in the rear, they would move in on the township. The first phase would be underway.

From his Command car, flanked by Avi and Davidoff, Ziki used his transmitter. A trusted private named Rami alertly drove.

"Armor—Red Falcon, Ze'evi, come in. Repeat. Ze'evi, do you read me? Over."

"Ze'evi here, Sir."

"Spread out your units to begin target interception due north and east. Hold your middle units bearing due west. Do not engage the enemy unless fired upon. Repeat. Do not engage the enemy until after the air support has arrived; await my orders to engage. Over."

"Yes, Commander. Ze'evi out."

"It seems to be going according to plan: the encirclement is forming; we should have a perimeter in minutes to secure the whole area," said Davidoff.

"My gut is bothering me; the Americans always leak like a bucket with holes, never a good sign," added Avi, checking the lock on his standard issue Galil. "For all we know the whole place knows we're coming—they're lying in wait."

"Nah, stop worrying, the Americans are our friends; they wouldn't tip them off…" said Ziki.

"I just don't know; Walters likes them, the PLO."

**It was still dark outside, but the lair that contained Salameh and Nidal was well lit.** Tucked below the surface in a specially built shelter, each man sat in a chair, weighing the phone call that had just come through from Gavriella Ramon at Langley.

Salameh had grown a new beard. His beard looked like it had been splashed with whiskers, his eyes were red from lack of sleep. He mindlessly inspected a Russian-made RPG, admiring the fine piece of weaponry like it was a precious jewel. Armed militia lined the halls of the structure and the large box-shaped room, their guns gleaming in the candle and lamp light. One large man looked like a wrestler, two others looked like twins, small. Abdul inspected a box filled with electrical equipment, what looked like C4 Plastique, wires and fuses. Salameh spoke first.

"So, the Israelis think that they have us…..hmm, *ibn el sharmutas,"* he said in Arabic. One of the guards laughed openly. Salameh smiled at his interjection. "They are no match for us! They will never be a match for us, and so long as the infidels continue to occupy our land and claim it for themselves there will be no peace! Brothers, are you with me!?"

A loud chorus rose up from the men lining the walls, shouts of approval. Bloodcurdling bellows rose up in their throats. Salameh stood up to better address them and grabbed the long slender tube of his hookah. A young boy ran up with a lit match, igniting the bowl. Salameh pulled deeply on the copper mouthpiece, letting the smoke drift out of his nose slowly before blowing out smoke that shone blue.

"Brothers, the time has come to teach these dog Jews a lesson. By Allah we shall have our vengeance on the Jews, those that would take our lives and drive us from the land that belongs to us!" More cheers joined the loud voices, whipping the men into a frenzy. Small children banged on fired pots and pans, joining in on the chaos.

Nidal continued to examine the equipment, keeping quiet as he did. That was his way, stealth. A smaller man sat next to him, whispering to him from time to time, though the loud chorus of cheers drowned his voice out, making it impossible to hear what he spoke of.

"We must get ready, prepare for a fight, every house on the alert, pass the word around Abdalah; the camp has three hundred thousand of our people. They will not intimidate us. Come, brothers, the time has come!" Amidst screams and yells of approval, men started to slowly file up the narrow stairway to the surface level of the lair.

"Pass the word to be silent until the Israelis are in the camp. Let them think they are surprising us." Body after body, laden with arms and weaponry, made the pilgrimage upward toward the city streets. The growl of adult voices coupled with the squeaky voices of youths to awaken the sleeping city streets, and then all at once deadly silence.

As the underground room began to empty, Salameh sauntered over to where Nidal and the young man sat. Seeing that they paid no attention to him, he placed his hands on the box that Nidal so ardently examined. His eyes wide, the concentration of Nidal was finally broken. Salameh looked at him fiercely.

"The time has come. Right now we have no use for these machines. We have a people to awaken. Do you understand?" Nidal slowly nodded his head, moving his gaze back towards the thick hands of Salameh that were still positioned on his box of equipment. Noticing this, Salameh pulled his hands away and slapped the shoulder of the young man sitting there, holding his hand after making contact and shaking it excitedly. Nidal said calmly, "I'll rig this house to blow them up when they're in here.

"Ali," he said in a whisper, "what is that woman's name that called you from America?"

"Why do you ask? "

"I want to be grateful to her if my path should cross hers for the warning of the Israeli attack that's coming tonight; they will not surprise us now."

"Her name is Gavriella Ramon, an American."

"Hmm, interesting."

"Nephew, still here. Take this." Salameh reached over and grabbed the RPG that he had been coveting earlier, shoving it into the hand of his nephew.

Iamael took the large weapon hesitantly, propping it up against the side of his bare leg. Salameh's eyes grew narrow. His eyebrows arched.

"You are no longer a boy, Iamael, you are a man. And as a man, it is your duty to take on the armor of Allah and go to war against the Jews. Now is not the time to be afraid. Now is the time for action. Do you understand?"

"Yes uncle, I want to kill them," he said without meaning it. Iamael whispered weakly, his eyes fixed on the distance, his mind elsewhere. He noticed he was drawing too much attention from his uncle Salameh. He stood up and began to inspect the weapon, going through the motions of checking it to make sure it was ready to fire, just as he had been trained in Lebanon at the training camp. Salameh watched him with a pleased look on his face.

"That is right, Nephew. Always loyal. You just make sure and be brave out there. Show no mercy." Iamael nodded. Nidal continued to inspect his explosives. Salameh watched for a second before turning on his heel towards the narrow flight of steps and the waiting street above.

"I was just testing you, Nephew," he said to Iamael. "Put that weapon down and grab your Kalashnikov; you are coming with me and him," he pointed at Nidal. "We are crossing the border into Egypt and safety, the others will fight."

"When, Uncle?"

"Right now, before the Israelis get here. Move—Yalla imshi, Iamael."

## Chapter 22

### The Enemy

**She was shot twice. A young Arab woman**.
Things were quiet now in much of Gaza and at the Egyptian border, just a stone's throw away; in nearby Khan Yunis, most of the shooting had stopped.

They gawked but didn't know what to do. The bullet had gone through her garb into her chest between her ribs and out through her neck. She lay on her side, leaning against the building she probably lived in. The other bullet got the side of her stomach. Her eyes were open but squinty. She looked at them with far away eyes, from time to time she screamed. She groaned when she touched at her wounds. A slow, but steady stream of blood ran out of the holes, front and back.

She had her face resting on one outstretched arm; the rest of her lay in the street's dirt. Big and small flies were all over her… No relief from the flies. The morning sun began a hot day.

"Hey, medic…. Medic, over here."

"Give her morphine, what are you waiting for? She is in bad pain." The medic took her pulse. She opened her eyes wide for a short while, then she moaned.

"Give her some fucking morphine, will you please, don't you see…?"

" No, no morphine: it will kill her before the wounds do." The medic frantically worked to patch up the holes; she groaned and let out a blood curdling scream when he tried to plug one of them, her eyes wide open now. The medic cut her garb; one of her breasts became exposed covered in blood.

"She's a pretty woman, pretty for an Arab. You don't see many pretty Arab women in Gaza."

"That's damn sure."

"Well…. this neighborhood, it's Hamas country; they're always covered up."

"No, not here, they run around with their faces showing."

"Yeah, you're right this one's sure pretty."

"Fucking shame she's all shot up like this." Five or six IDF Golanis that came with the armor division and the medic hovered around her.

"She's going to die; what can I do to help her?"

"Whoa, just look at all that blood coming out; no one can fix up those bullet holes."

"She's gone."

"Yeah, I think you're right, she's gone."

"I want to help her… Can you help her live, medic?" The man who had shot her sat down in the street dirt beside her. "Didn't know she was a woman, she just looked like all the others."

"They hide in with the civilians."

"How was I to know? How do you tell them apart?"

"God, she must hurt. Get those shit flies off her." He tried to put his arm under her head. The medic yelled, "Don't do that."

"Well, can I put this under it?" He'd taken off his shirt. "I'm going to whether you like it or not." Gently he raised her head slightly, folded the shirt and put it under her head. She took her arm out from under her head and dug her fingers into the dirt; her eyes thanked the man who shot her for the small gift of the shirt.

He got close to her face. "Is she going to die? Can't I give her some water?" He pulled out his canteen, poured water into his hand and wet her lips; he waved his hands and swatted away flies from her face.

The young lieutenant standing near her called for a rescue helicopter.

The medic shook his head; there's nothing I can do. It seemed forever: they just stood around wanting to help but not knowing what to do. She was going to die.

"Where is that helicopter?"

Her black hair lay spread on the folded shirt.

"She is the enemy, isn't she? I just don't know any more."  The young man who had shot her patted her hair and looked like he was about to cry, but he did not. The other soldiers and the medic beside her swatted at the flies. Her garb soaked with blood now drying, changing color…dark. The wound hadn't clotted much; one of the men took out his personal bandage from his kit and put it on her wound trying to stop the blood. The man who had shot her held his canteen to her lips, she drank some water.

She just lay there waiting; they told her that the chopper was coming. She did not respond. The man who had shot her wet the corner of the shirt and put it to her forehead. She moaned again. The medic felt her pulse and said she was still going, just barely. She groaned now and then. She was not feeling any more pain now. Somebody said, "She is the enemy, isn't she?"

"Damn, she is so young and pretty. It's a fucking shame."

The chopper arrived and landed making a swirl of dust; she did not move. The men slid her unto a gurney and lifted her to the helicopter. The pilot secured the gurney in its place. The chopper sped up its still running rotors and in a fleeting moment lifted up and away. The pilot's voice came over the radio. "What do you think you're doing down there, making me risk my neck for the enemy?" The pilot continued. "It's weird: she is smiling as if she'd done something good; she seems happy."

"It is like a whiff from a corpse."

"Lieutenant, what did she leave in that bag in the dirt that was under her?"

"Where?"

"Over there, Sir, this one."

"Oh, shit, don't touch it….For a moment, a great silence around and above… The grenade in her bag blew up in a bowl of flames spewing shrapnel as blood splattered from the men around it.

The pilot looked back at her, she grinned a knowing smile at him—…. *like a whiff from a corpse*—then moved her arm pulling the cord. The rescue chopper exploded into a thousand fragments—it burst into a blinding satchel of flames. She was the enemy…

## Chapter 23

**Baghdad**

**It wasn't the waiting that killed him. . .** It was dwelling on all the other things he could be doing instead of waiting.

Ziki leaned on the railing watching the nearly empty street below his hotel room balcony. His behind had nearly worn the seat out of every chair in his suite. He'd smoked a pack of cigarettes between phone calls. He had lined up two car rentals, one extra just in case it was needed. That took no time at all. Room service had brought him a sandwich and a bottle of Vodka hours before. Both remained untouched on the tray where the busboy had left them. Ziki had given the kid a tip and then locked the door after him. He was considering going out, finding a place to drink alone amid company—other travelers. Journalists maybe.

But in truth he hated Baghdad.

There was a knock on his door.

Finally! Roshi had sent over what they'd found on the man who called himself Joseph.

He put the Uzi under his pillow and pushed the hand gun into the waistband of his trousers at the side of his hip, concealed with his shirt hanging out—within easy reach. He slid into his suit jacket and went to the door. Looking out the peephole, he saw dark hair. Long dark hair, a part in the middle… Hanna?

He unlatched the door and tugged it open to let her in—his lungs froze mid breath. The second long silence felt interminable. "Gavriella."

"Hello, Ziki."

Dressed in her standard black leather jacket, dark silk blouse and skirt, and knee-high boots, she stood on the threshold of his hotel room just as calm and cool as ever. She looked ready for the evening, as if she were a part of the night that had come to human form. Her lips were bright red and her eyes rimmed black with kohl. Her dark eyes flashed with an emotion he could not name. Her hair was as dark as cinders.

"You're not going to ask me in?"

He said nothing, but turned away from the door, leaving it ajar. She could come in if she wanted or she could go the hell away… He didn't care.

He went to the nightstand where his pack of cigarettes lay. He fished one out and lit it with his Zippo, closing the lighter with a loud snap. He heard her enter the room, shut and lock the door.

"I'll have one too, thanks," she said. She slipped out of her jacket and sat on the bed.

Ziki pulled out another cigarette, lit it, and handed it over to her without looking at her at all.

He went back to the sliding door that led to the balcony and leaned against the jamb. His jaw clenched as he watched the traffic on the street below. So soon? He thought she'd wait at least a while.

He heard her take a long drag and blow it out as if sighing. "You're going to tell me I shouldn't have come to see you."

He shook his head. "No. I'm not." He turned and he looked at her. "I'm not going to tell you shouldn't have come and I'm not going to ask for anything. I'm going to ask you to tell me what you've come to tell me and to get the hell out of here while you still can."

She drew in smoke. "You were never one to mince words, Zik." She pronounced it like Zeek. She was the only one who had ever felt it necessary to further truncate his already abbreviated nickname.

"You were never one to show sympathy for others," he replied.

It might have stung her if it had come out with the force he had intended but didn't quite muster. Still, he hoped it lodged somewhere like a dart to worry her later. If she ever worried, that was. He knew she'd never show any of her inner pain upon her cool painted face, but he hoped somewhere inside she was writhing with the consequences of her arrogance. He hoped she woke in a cold sweat at night unable to breathe.

"I'm glad you're mad," she said. "It means you still have feelings for me." She disregarded his stabbing glare… "There's hope."

"Three men," he suddenly raged. "Three men, my men, Gavriella. What did you, or your government care for three young Israelis? The hurt is deep—they were good men. They trusted me." He laughed at her motionless face, at her utter lack of heart. "I had to go home and face their mothers—"

"Oh, cut the melodramatic crap, Zik. We all knew what we were in for—besides it wasn't my call and it might have happened anyway—that fucking place, Khan Yunis, has three hundred thousand people, all of them your enemies...You might have lost three men no matter what? At those numbers it is, in military terms, an acceptable loss."

There was a fire in his temples. "Get out." Three strides to the bed and he grabbed her by the elbow, hauling her up. "Get the hell out of here before I send you to meet with them, although I doubt you'd be ascending in the same direction." His pulse throbbed in his ears.

She wrenched against his hold, "Let go! Stop acting like a thwarted teenager!" He was at the door, ready to throw her into the hallway. "Ziki! Zik—I have news. You need this. Don't be fucking stupid! Listen to me. I came because they know you are here."

He thrust her against the door, hearing the satisfying thud of her weight as her shoulder blades hit the heavy wood. He might have pushed her harder. He might have taken her by the arms and shaken her until her head snapped off her gorgeous, but treacherous little neck.

"Zik. The Russians know you're here."

His mouth was dry. "You get out and you never come back—"

"Listen to me," she shook her head. Her eyes were huge and dark and still deep enough to—he stopped that thought in its tracks, pushing the memory of three men once again to the forefront of his thoughts. "

His eyes hooded. "Why should I believe you?"

She hesitated and for the first time that he could remember he saw a ripple of what he might call doubt in her eyes. "Because I am sorry . . . I am really sorry."

That took the wind out of his sails. He released her arm... Damn. He stepped away from her and turned his back.

"Zik, it's my job. Like it's your job. None of us like it."

"You like it."

"I did what I was ordered to do, had to do—. . . Shit! My cigarette—your couch!"

Ziki smelled the acrid smoke of burning plastic. Turning, he saw the wide blackening hole her cigarette had eaten into the leather sofa. The smoke rising from it was thick and black. Shit was right. She must have dropped her cigarette when he'd man-handled her.

He hurried for the table and yanked the bouquet of expensive flowers out of the German crystal vase, throwing the dripping stems at her feet. The flowers scattered across the carpet. He hoped the roses still had thorns. Ziki dumped the vase over the smoldering hole. A loud hiss issued from the melted cushion and fabric. There was the stink of burning animal hair and leather. The damp warm smell of flower water wrapped itself into the stinging smell of smoke and chemicals.

She had the good grace not to laugh. She stooped and gathered the stems of the flowers. When he placed the vase back on its table, she stuck the stems in pell-mell. Blooms sagged and fell out onto the tabletop. Several landed on the floor once more, their petals crushed.

She wiped her hands together and waited for him to simmer a little lower. He paced to the nightstand, took out another cigarette and lit it, then saw his first cigarette in the ashtray beside the sliding door.

"I am sorry, Ziki," she said. "I have thought often of what was done... And you. I wonder if I had made another choice . . . if. . . "

So, she did have a conscience. He took a long deep drag on his smoke. Too little, too late.

"Tell me what you need to tell me," he commanded, "then please, just get the hell out."

"All right." She folded her arms. "One of my operatives intercepted an interesting message today. It seems there are rumors around that the Israelis have a line on some Russian and Iraqi intelligence. . . military intelligence. . . something big. When I heard you were in town, I just put two and two together."

That's all she had? Ziki suppressed a smile. "It seems that you've put two and two together to come up with zero. I'm in town to check in on some Arab sleepers that we've lost track of . . . no more."

He could tell by the tightening lines around her eyes that she didn't believe him.

"Is that so?"

He looked her in the eye and dared her to continue to push him. "But if you find out who's got that intelligence, you might begin to make up your debt to the families you've robbed."

A cool slight smile. "Well then, it seems I've broken our silence needlessly."

"Seems so."

She crossed her arms and the leather of her jacket rubbed upon itself softly. "Zik. . . You're not going to forgive me, are you?"

He returned her gaze with coldness.

She nodded with understanding and drew a breath. "Life will go on."

"For you I'm sure it will."

She gave a bitter little laugh and swore at him in a whisper, "Son of a bitch" under her breath. "Okay. Okay…I'm going."

She headed for the door. He followed, his hands balled into fists. In the back of his brain a soft and angry version of his own voice demanded that she get on her knees, that she cry, that she show some sign. He'd met only one or two other women who didn't cry—.

He opened the door and stood back to let her pass.

"All right," she said. "I guess this is goodbye."

"It is."

"It doesn't have to be like this."

"It does."

She stepped into the hall. "If you need me, your people know how to reach me."

"I don't need you. I won't."

"Okay, Zik. You win. Just promise me you'll be careful. If the Russians don't know— One more thing, Zik, pay close attention because it is more than even I want to know—"she paused…."The KGB knows that you took a side trip to Osirak."

Ziki stopped in his track and froze for a moment…."I don't know what the hell you are talking about."

"I'm trying to save your life here, Ziki, you know, Osirak, the Iraqi underground nuclear thing." She stood back on her heels; "Are you boys planning something for its future? Is that why you're here? Or are you just 'selling' medical equipment in Osirak? " she said sarcastically.

"Gavriella." He stepped back, his hand on the doorknob.

She met his gaze and held it steadily.

Fuck!  She was still more beautiful than any woman with such a cold heart deserved to be.

He slammed the door in her face.

## Chapter 24

**Joseph**

**The man that had called himself Joseph answered Ziki's telephone call the next morning.** Joseph directed him to go first to a café, where Ziki would find him by the book he carried: "Carry a small black covered book the size of a Sabbath prayer book." Ziki would then follow Joseph to the Iraq National Museum. They would talk in the main gallery as they circulated from work to work.

Despite the fact that Joseph had checked '*out*' according to Roshi, Ziki was both skeptical and anxious. About to be face to face with the mysterious Joseph, he couldn't stop thinking that nabbing a MiG so easily could only be a hoax or a trap.

The number traced by Roshi and Amit had left a confusing picture of what Ziki might expect. His name was Joseph Barashi, the father of three sons and four daughters. His wife was a schoolteacher, history and writing. His oldest sons and daughters were married and had children of their own. Joseph himself had served for twenty years as a servant for the same Arab Christian Maronite family.

The moment Ziki saw the man, he felt himself relax slightly. Smallish and brown, the man looked like a servant, stooped like a servant. His hands trembled slightly as he drank his tea with little guile, burning his tongue while Ziki watched. Ziki rose from his seat and approached him. The man nearly cowered in his seat as Ziki stood over him.

"Are you finished with your paper?" Ziki asked. "I'd like to read the financial section."

"Yes, you may read it," Joseph replied. "I am just on my way to the museum."

Ziki knew to follow. "Thank you, *Shukra*."

Ziki watched the middle-age man rise, but returned to his own seat and opened the paper as Joseph paid for his tea and shuffled toward the museum. Ziki opened the financial section and perused ads for accounting houses and banks in Baghdad, just long enough to make it look good. He folded the paper under one arm and left several coins on the tabletop.

The Baghdad museum was crowded, its front steps peopled with resting tourists who fanned themselves in the hot sun. Brown skinned children selling homemade candies and baklava ran up and down between the tourists, trying to wrangle pennies from their coin purses. Older ladies from the Northern European countries were the biggest marks. They'd been fighting the Babylon's Food Revenge from the grease and spoilage of the local food by the end of the afternoon.

Inside was cool and opened to early afternoon breezes. The halls echoed with the narrations of private and group tours. Students could make a good dollar or Swiss franc here and there by offering their knowledge of history and artistic advancements through the ages. Some tour guides were additionally quite charming and knew how to charm the crowd with wit and romance.

Joseph was nowhere to be seen in the main hall or in halls devoted to prehistoric art, the Samarians, the Acadians, Babylonians, or Kassites. Attempting to avoid visibility, Ziki tagged along with a group, then he finally strolled on his own through the lion-headed columns of Hall 10, into the collection of massive Assyrian sculptures. Had he missed the older man? Had something gone wrong?

He stopped below a rendering in stone.

"Nabu, the Assyrian God of knowledge and wisdom." Joseph stood by his side. "We must keep moving and we must not look as though we know each other."

"Of course."

As Joseph began to turn away, he met Ziki's eyes. "Who sent you?"

Ziki saw the edge of fear in Joseph's expression and heard it in the tone of his voice. He stayed a long moment where he was and then strolled to observe a statue so that his back would be to Joseph's.

"A business associate informed me that we have mutual interests in a MiG-21."

"You have come alone?"

"I will be your sole contact to negotiate this deal."

"You are a Jew?"

"I represent the interests of a business associate friendly to Israel."

Joseph moved to another sculpture and when Ziki moved to another, he positioned himself close enough that Ziki would see the slip of paper he dropped upon the floor. Ziki immediately put his foot over it so that no one would see it.

"Meet me here," Joseph said. "One hour. Be sure that you are not followed; be sure."

Joseph lived with his family in a modest house in a poor urban neighborhood within the limits of Baghdad. His wife met Ziki at the door. She looked like a member of her profession with her thick hair pulled back in a schoolteacher's bun and her glasses perched on her nose. Her clothes were gray as Joseph's had been. No frills. She introduced herself as Mala with a business-like manner. Her sharp eyes, trained from years of disciplining students, never left Ziki as she let him step inside the door.

With hardly a word, she led Ziki into the decrepit courtyard where a table for Shesh Besh had been set up. As he followed her, Ziki turned on the sweeping device Amit had lent him.

"Strong enough to pick up a signal from down the street," Amit had bragged as he showed Ziki how to use this model. If there were bugs the sweeper would vibrate silently in his pocket to alert him. Joseph and his wife need never know he'd conducted this search. If they were plants, if their house was bugged, all the better he got out without them knowing he was onto the trap they were setting.

The module lay still in his pocket. Nothing. The house was clean.

In a shady corner of the courtyard, Joseph sat on a cushion drinking tea and smoking a *Nargila,* hubbly-bubbly. From the scent of the smoke, he took his tobacco with a hint of hash as many Arabs did. Joseph removed the pipe stem from between his teeth and gestured for Ziki to sit down.

"You are in a dangerous line of work, Mr. Breckenbauer," Joseph said, "but you must like it, especially to come here. I must admit your Arabic is good.... . Me, I am not so fond of danger. And so I call the Israelis and offer a trade."

Ziki sat beside Joseph. "Tell me about the MiG." He surveyed the rooftops above, looking for anything out of the ordinary, half expecting to see a sniper or a guard. Nothing. Just the pale blue of sky behind white washed stone.

Joseph placed his pipe between his teeth and drew in smoke. "To tell one story, I must tell another."

Ziki nodded. He lit a cigarette and made his legs more comfortable.

Joseph drew another toke and began. "I have lived my whole life in Iraq. Me and my sister, Manu. We grew up here. In Baghdad. Me, my family, we are Iraqi Jews."

Get out of here, Ziki thought—Gould would be pleased. He had been right. He kept his chuckle to himself. "Go on."

"I have been a servant for a Maronite Christian family for twenty years. Twenty years I work for them, cook, clean, shine their shoes with my own spit. A couple of weeks ago they dismissed me. It is hard times for my family."

Joseph drew in a lungful of smoke and blew it out.

"I have no money, you understand. I have no money saved and it is not good for Jews in Iraq. We, my whole family, we want to leave Iraq. But we cannot just go, you know. This is not America where we can take our things and go where we want when we want. So I ask myself, Joseph, how do you get your family out of Iraq?"

Joseph smiled wryly. "And then it came to me. My sister—"

"—Manu?"

A nod from Joseph. "Manu. She has a son—a son-in-law. Munir. He is married to her daughter, and his father is Iraqi. . . Muslim. But his mother, she is a Jew. We are not very many left, Iraqi Jews."

"Your nephew-in-law is half-Jew?"

"Yes, but very pro-government. Very much with the military and with the Russians, you understand. The Russians took him to Moscow and trained him to pilot their fighter planes."

"He flies MiG-21s."

"Yes. MiG-21s. He flies those."

"You want your family out of Iraq."

"So they will be safe."

"You also want a million American dollars."

"Yes, that is what I want, out and one million American dollars. Half now, half when the plane is in Israeli hands."

Ziki sat back and took a long drag on his cigarette. "You have to understand how incredible . . . how unlikely . . . this seems to my business associates. A million dollars and your family out of Iraq, and you and a man who we also do not know will help us to steal one of the most heavily guarded military secrets of the Russians."

Joseph bowed his head. "My teacher who had been in the army always said that it is air supremacy that determines the balance of power worldwide. If the Israelis do not want this plane, perhaps others will, but I offered it to you first."

"I have not said we have no interest. But my business associates are cautious men. For everyone's interest, I must be cautious."

"You are a business man, too."

"Yes."

"You will profit from this venture."

Two statements, not questions. Was Joseph edgy? "I will," Ziki confirmed.

"Why should I not go straight to Mossad?"

"Do you think Mossad will deal with amateurs? Why do you think my contacts in Paris sent me? How much money will you make if they find out Joseph is an unemployed servant, begging for entry into a country? Besides I will deal with Mossad for you; my business associates and I have done business with them before—many times."

Joseph drew in smoke. "I wish to deal directly with Mossad."

"Of course. I understand." Ziki held up his hands. "But think this through. You have interests, I have interests. I promise you, both will be fully met. If you were to deal directly with Mossad—the world's most....Well, you know. To the world they don't even admit to exist. I'm already dealing with them for you. How would you know where and what?"

Joseph considered this a long moment. "A million dollars in a Swiss account in Geneva. Half up front. And my family gone from here... Or no deal."

"I will make inquiries. I think that all this can be arranged."

"I want to start that as soon as possible. It grows more dangerous here for us by the day. We haven't time to waste. I am in danger having just contacted you. You are Mossad, are you not? You must be?"

"Never mind about me; I am Hans Breckenbauer. When the deal is made things will move swiftly. Your family will be moved as efficiently as possible."

Joseph nodded. "I will have your word?"

"My word has been good my entire life; I don't give it easily or often but when I give it, it is never broken...... You have it."

"When I know the money is there. When I trust you will not abandon my wife or my children, I will take you to Manier."

"Fair enough. But you must know as well that the men I represent will need reassurance of your background."

"What do you want? My father's name, my mother's name, the name of my former employer—I give you it all freely."

"But how do we know you are not with the Iraqis meant to trick us out of a half million dollars?"

Joseph frowned. "I am a Jew!"

"I hope that's enough." Ziki thought that's not always the case; there is a big difference between being a Jew in the Diaspora and being an Israeli. The land has transformed us we are now a nation, not a religion.

Ziki raised his hands in supplication. "Just a few questions. . . Assurance, you see."

Joseph agreed.

Ziki started with an easy one. "Who in your household does the Shabbath blessing?"

"I do. I hold my son's head in my hands and recite the words over him."

"And who is standing at Shabbath?"

"All of us. We all stand."

"Your Hebrew—how is it?"

"I will read what you write."

"Good." Ziki pulled out a scrap of paper and pen and wrote Joseph's name on it. That was not enough to test a man's knowledge of the ancient language, so he wrote the first other thing that came to mind—a line from "Casablanca": "Play it again, Sam."

Joseph took the paper. "I always liked that film," he said, "Humphrey Bogart and Bacall."

Ziki nodded. "Good. Good. I will tell my associates. It looks as if we may have a MiG for the West and you, a rich man in a new home." Ziki stood up.

Joseph looked up at him. His eyes were bloodshot from hash smoke. A vile habit. Better to stick to cigarettes. At least they wouldn't kill you. "Ahh—Mr. Breckenbauer, just one more question."

"Okay."

"How come a man with a name like Hans Breckenbauer can read and write Hebrew? Now I can trust you, I know that you are Mossad."

"Nonsense; I am just a businessman." Ziki smiled. He is not as simple as he looks, Ziki thought.

"I will contact you when I return. It will not be long."

**Ziki was on a plane to Rome the same day after his meeting with Joseph.** He had stayed just long enough to delay suspicion. His order sheets were full from a standard round of meetings with a round of clients; amazing, they actually placed buy orders in substantial sums. From Rome, he hired a car to carry him south to the Mediterranean. Once in Naples he hopped an Israeli military transport to Tel Aviv and from the Tel Aviv airstrip took his parked car to Mossad's offices in the Kirya. He was met by Pientz's errand boy—the pizza face kid—at the security checkpoint and was led down a series of corridors to Pientz's office.

Pientz's office was cool, but smoke filled. The brightness of the afternoon sun bleached the streets outside the window, but the room itself was dim, without lights. Malkielly would not be joining them today, he was told. It would be Pientz and himself.

Pientz seemed satisfied as Ziki related  his meeting with Joseph. Ziki might even say that Pientz was pleased. "Cigar, Commander?"

Ziki took it and held it beneath his nose. Cuban. "Thank you." He clipped the tip with Pientz's  trimmer. The blades clicked together like a guillotine.

Pientz removed his own cigar and blew out blue smoke. "And Roshi's team checked out Joseph and his family?"

Ziki nodded. "They all check."

"100 percent."

"More like 90—95." A shrug. "Our loose canon is Munir Redfa."

Pientz sat back. "The damn pilot."

"Yes, Sir."

"As Joseph said on the tape, he is asking for a million and the removal of his family."

Pientz smiled with the cigar dangling from his teeth. Ziki could literally see the wheels in his brain turning. "Levitz and his bean counters will be pleased… Light?"

Ziki leaned forward to let Pientz fire up his cigar. He drew hard on the tip and took in thick flavored smoke. He held the toke in a good while, letting the lightness of nicotine swim up his spine.

Pientz laughed. "The first cigar I ever gave you. Do you remember?"

Ziki's raised his eyebrows. "Sick as a dog."

"You were as green as your uniform."

"I'm still sorry about your boots, Sir."

Pientz laughed. "I just exchanged them."

Ziki shook his head. "I was young. You corrupted me."

"We were all young, you are still young."

Both men fell silent and sucked on their stogies.

Ziki surveyed the wall behind Pientz, noting the pictures of Pientz with famous men:  Americans, Russians, an Italian and a Turk and a German—that must've been some summit or another.  There was Pientz with a woman—Golda. Golda Meir.

Then there were the pictures of Pientz's wife and children. It was obvious Pientz had married later in life than most military men.  His wife was pretty and slender with dark hair and sharp eyes.  In one picture Pientz held her close and smiled like Ziki had never seen him smile.  In another, the wife hugged two small boys and a baby girl close. There was a dog at their feet.

Ziki felt Pientz's eyes on him and didn't like it. The man was thinking far too much. "You still have reservations about the deal," Pientz surmised.

Ziki sat back and let smoke slowly curl out of his mouth. "It's my ass out there."

"That's why I'm asking, Commander."

"I'm not convinced Joseph won't bolt or that there isn't more to this than we know. A million, a half mill, is a lot of money to a man who is unemployed and has lived on nothing all his life."

Pientz agreed. "Scenario: we put the money in the account as he asks; he gets out of Iraq, makes a large withdrawal and disappears."

"Disappears," Ziki echoed a second after Pientz.

"In the actual scheme of things, Commander, half a mill—it's peanuts."

Ziki shrugged. "Then why am I getting so little; give me a raise already!"

"You and me, we are doing these things for God and country."

Pientz remained sober. "We've got that scenario covered. The money is in the account, but if Joseph or one of his sons leaves Iraq prematurely, the account evaporates as if it never existed."

"Poof, I didn't know that it could be done this way with the Swiss." Ziki said and a plume of smoke escaped his lips.

"'It' cannot, but we can… So what's bothering you, Commander?" Pientz's eyes narrowed. "Are you worried there's been a leak?"

That caught Ziki's attention. The man was good. Damn good. "There's an American agent in Baghdad. A woman. Gavriella Ramon."

"I know the name and I also know that you know it really well, Commander, don't you?"

"I've worked with her before. In Beirut. A joint operation, Washington/Tel Aviv."

"And she betrayed you . . .Khan Yunis… you lost men."

Ziki's eyes were temporarily sightless. "Three."

Silence.

"She made a choice; she is confused like many foreigners about their feelings of sympathy for the Palestinians," Ziki said. "And she or her boss—I'm not sure which yet—made the wrong choice… Someday that debt will have to be paid."

Pientz wasted no time on sentimentality. He had probably informed more widows and mothers of the coffins headed their way than any man Ziki had yet met.

"What do you think she knows? Do you think she sniffed anything about our interest in the Osirak Iraqi nuclear stuff? Speaking of that, make sure that Roshi and his people get you all you need on that. Tell them that it is a direct order from me."

"Nothing. Yet. But she'll keep at it until she knows something, or maybe Joseph is playing all ends against the middle and contacted them as well to cover all bases, and she already knows."

"Make sure that you explain to him the old Arab saying that he who rides on two camels usually falls in between them."

"Remember the Americans are after one of these MiGs, as much as we are."

"Take her out— and the Americans will know for certain that we're there for Osiraq and the MiG."

"My thoughts exactly. So will the Russians."

"Keep on her," Pientz said. "Have Roshi wake another sleeper and pin her to the ground if necessary. Keep her busy. Just keep on top of this."

"Right."

"I want you back in Baghdad no later than tomorrow night ready to tell Joseph he'll have his money and ready to get this deal going."

"He'll want to know about getting his family out."

"Yes. . . another matter all together."

"It may be our only key to keeping Joseph with us."

Pientz agreed and considered the surface of his desk while rolling the cigar between his fingers. "Does he have many children?"

"They're like rabbits," Ziki snorted. "His wife and her sisters. Three daughters married with a few kids each. His sons too are married. There are two of them. And children. An old aunt and an uncle. Joseph's father is long dead. So is his mother. But his wife's mother, she'll want to come, too. I don't know about cousins. That's . . . 30-35 in all. 40 if we want to remove extended family members as well."

"Options for removal? "

"Roshi says the western and southern borders are uncrossable. Iraqi babies, not to mention Iraqi baby Jews, would not receive the warmest of welcomes."

"And the Saudis are always wild cards," Pientz continued.

"They'd open up if the Americans had a stake in this," Ziki said.

"The Turks. . ?"

Ziki smiled. Pientz hadn't been in the field for years, but he knew the lay of the land better than most. "That's what I was thinking—the Kurds could be persuaded."

"It would mean cashing in a few chips."

"Roshi has already made connections with his informants."

"If the Kurds are with us?

"We might get a group of people out in two or three moves. It's risky, but the best plan."

Pientz leaned toward Ziki. "That's our plan; put it together, Commander."

Ziki sat back, his cigar hanging from his fingers over the arm of the chair. "May I ask to speak freely, Sir?"

A flash of dark in Pientz's eyes. "Speak."

"Will you retire once this and Osirak play themselves out, Sir?"

"A few medals and a pat on the back on the way out the door?" Pientz inclined his head. "Why? You want a desk job, Barak?"

"If I still got a rear end to plop into a chair, I might."

"I'm not dead yet and I still got a few moves in me, so don't put me out to pasture until I tell you to unlock the gate."

"Good to hear, Sir."

"Get out of here and don't come back without a MiG and the underground plan to send Osirak to hell, Commander; use whatever resources you need."

"Yes, Sir."

**Leaving Pientz's office, Ziki went to a phone.**

"Markley Hostel." He could be in Jerusalem in less than two hours.

"*Ken, (*yes). Henny Waggenhoysen, *bvakasha,* please," he asked the operator.

"I speak English, one moment, please," she replied.

Ziki lit a cigarette and leaned against the booth as he waited…

…Henny Waggenhoysen from Rotterdam, Holland… Beautiful. Smart. Carefree. She had been so bold, so brightly European sitting across from him at lunch in her sundress of deep blue gauze. She made him laugh like he hadn't laughed in a good while. She seemed pure and innocent compared to Gavriella. Maybe she could help get Gavriella Ramon out of his head.

"There was a moment there where I thought you were dead, too," Ziki confided about the accident. Now was the time to come clean. The aftermath of adrenaline had left them both a little slap-happy.

"No!" She shook her head, abashed. "I really should have been more careful. I practically had my head in a tour book. She laughed. With an audience of one, I'm not so sure."

Ziki sipped his coffee. "Who needs to be careful?"

She stalled, a half smile playing across her lips.

"Yes, I mean that," Ziki pressed. "If you had been more careful, I would not be having lunch here today with a beautiful woman."

Henny blushed three shades of red.

"It is a pity that my line of work takes me out of town tomorrow morning."

She blinked. "Are you on some sort of a 'secret mission'?"

"You watch too many movies." He reached into his pocket and pulled out his business card for medical sales. "Very top secret products. Stethoscopes. Sterile bandages, X-ray machines."

"You're giving me state secrets and I didn't even have to sleep with you?" Henny took his card, making it pop from his grip. She sat back and gave it a thorough inspection. "Rimmer and Shalitco, Medical and Dental Equipment? My father owns a sausage skin factory."

"Is that how you afford to travel to our part of the world?"

"No. I've taken a position with Hadassah: I'm a nurse for children with special problems."

"A good position," he approved.

She was still examining his card. "Zurich?" Her face fell slightly. "You're here on business?"

"I come as often as I can, but never stay long enough to get bored."

Some of the wind had gone from her sails. "But what sort of life is that for you? Where do you call yourself home?"

"Tel Aviv," he answered promptly. "When work does not take me away, my home is in Tel Aviv."

She recovered hope nicely. "That's good. I was just hoping . . . well, I'd like. . . Perhaps you'd show me some sights off the beaten track the next time you're back."

"I'd be delighted. But this leads me to assume that you'll be in the area awhile yourself?"

She smiled at him with eyes that sparkled mischievously. "I certainly hope so."

And Ziki was charmed.

**The voice of the Hostel operator came back on the line**. "I'm sorry; Ms. Waggenhoysen does not appear to be in currently. May we give her a message?"

Ziki took a drag on his cigarette and blew out smoke. "Tell her the medical equipment secret agent is back in town for another day. She has my number."

He placed the receiver back in its cradle not just a little disappointed.

Perhaps his next trip back to Tel Aviv would be more fortunate. He stopped at a corner flower shop and sent her a dozen roses.

## Chapter 25

### Iamael

**"Whore sons born of dogs!" Iamael's brother said each day he came home from Israeli territory.** Iamael's brother smoked the hubbly-bubbly in the front room of their small cement house with his father and their friends, and sometimes Iamael smoked with them.

When Iamael could avoid these meetings, however, he studied. The men in the front room filled the house with clouds of dark smoke and the smell of spiced tea and sweet goat's milk. They complained and planned and told their stories: whose son had been shot, where the Israelis had stolen land, what someone ought to do, someone else. And Iamael went to the kitchen where his mother patted flat bread between her calloused palms and cooked pots of lentils and yellow peas. He bent over his books and memorized everything he could. He worked on his English. He worked on his Hebrew. The Koran was left on the shelf.

"A woman's language best learned in the woman's kitchen!" Iamael's brother laughed.

And Iamael laughed for now, too. But none of them would laugh when he made his way out of Gaza and Khan Yunis forever. Nor would they laugh when he sent money from America.

"You are my hope," his mother would say when the others were not in earshot. "You keep to your books and let trouble pass you by. My son... my favorite son."

Iamael was 16 when his brother joined the El-Fattah, 'Black September' branch of the PLO and just turned 17 when his brother brought home the making of the bomb that would be his end.

Iamael's brother was shaking with fervor when he spoke of his mission to his father and his father's friends. A holy man had promised him paradise for his self-sacrifice. 72 virgin wives awaited him if he killed just one Israeli.

"Will you get 144 Virgins if you kill two Israelis?"

Iamael asked, because he knew there was no reckoning with his brother. He had never told him the story of the bus near the checkpoint at Megiddo. His brother would not be haunted by almond shaped brown eyes nor pink and yellow dresses. Iamael's brother would never wake at night having dreamed the sound of the blast and the splatter of limbs and blood once more.

"You would not know what to do with one virgin, let alone my 72," Iamael's brother scorned him. "You with your books. What will you find outside Gaza that could equal the rewards of heavenly ascension?"

"Will there be peace or more Israelis to kill in Paradise?"

The other men looked at him as if he were the enemy.

"You are one of us but you understand nothing," his brother answered, and if they had not been in their house he would have spat on Iamael's shoes.

Iamael's brother hid the plastic explosives and wires in the root cellar and covered the trap door to the root cellar with a rug. Iamael wondered if his brother really thought the Israelis would be so stupid as to pass by such an easy hiding place. Not that they would come to Iamael's family home. The Israelis had no reason to suspect them yet, and Iamael's brother exploited this at every turn. The Islamic Mullahs, religious leaders, had warned Iamael's brother to lay low for several weeks before he was called to his "duty."

"And, you. Coward," his brother warned, "remember whose son you are… Remember where you come from."

The unspoken threat: *"We have our eyes on you."*

Iamael tried to forget what lay at the summit of the path his brother had chosen. The explosives lay beneath the floorboards and at night Iamael could almost hear them ticking like a time bomb. Deep in the middle of the night he would climb from his matt and stand above them, feeling the slight give of the trap door beneath his weight   and thinking. Sometimes he would put his ear to the floor, his cheek to the rug, to listen to their silence.

He remembered whose son he was and where he came from. He did nothing to give his brother away.

**The day came…** There would be no body to collect for burial the day it was done. There were reports from neighbors—Iamael's brother had taken 23 lives and wounded scores more in a café in Jerusalem next door to Markley Hostel on Ben Yehuda street where Henny Waggenhoysen roomed. The Israelis swept the neighborhood shortly after. Their search proved fruitless. What they wanted was already gone.

A sizable 'anonymous' donation came almost immediately.

"Look, school girl," Iamael's father held up colored bills in a foreign denomination. "Enough for you to study in London. Enough for you to go to America. In his death your brother honors us."

Iamael sat in the front room and smoked the hubbly-bubbly with the men who came to thank Iamael's father for the gift of his son's life. He said prayers with the Mullah's holy men who came to escort Iamael's brother through the wilderness of the afterlife to Paradise and his virgins.

Iamael sat with his mother in the kitchen and watched her bake flat pita bread. She did not speak to him, but her eyes were dark and the tucks from her nose to her mouth had deepened.

It was two weeks of mourning until she spoke to him. "Iamael. My son. Keep away from uncle Salameh, I will not lose two sons."

She had rolled some bills into a wad with his other pair of jeans, his change of under-drawers, and a shirt.

"I know you cannot stay."

"Mama," he said.

"May Allah bless you and all you do."

He swore when he got to New York he would send for her, but he did not say this. He merely took the duffle bag she had stuffed with his things and two days worth of bread and walked from her kitchen. It was two days arduous walking to Beer-Sheba; if he got there safely then he could get a bus to Tel Aviv. Once out of Gaza, he never dreamed of the bus or the little girl again.

## Chapter 26

**Brainwashing**

**The right tools, environment, patience and an experienced trained interrogator** made it possible to brainwash a man—it took lots of patience and the right handler to mold the brain of another man.

And no man ever believed he had been brainwashed—but he had.

Ziki was always amazed. It worked with most. Even those men he thought for sure would hold out eventually came to see the world as he was trained to mold them to see it. Those same men would swear to their mothers and best of friends that they had simply been shown the light.

Of course training someone to see the world the way you wished them to was difficult; you had to show them how passionately you yourself believed that which you wanted them to believe. Long sessions took much out of the interrogator as he poured out his soul onto the target and merged with it in dreamlike sessions that created a confused mixture of thoughts. Then he was subjected to the unique techniques perfected by the experts and operatives of the Mossad.

Mossad was far too savvy to use torture and starvation as tools.

Sleep deprivation and confusion was a tool. The rules had to be skirted at times when necessary. The greatest impact was not made by beating a man until he came around… No… Rather, the man was given a friend. A confidant. A confessor and a master all in one.

A man's beliefs had to be cultivated slowly… Slowly. A man's beliefs must be allowed to ripen… He must be allowed to listen to silence and to the voices in his own head and then believe that those thoughts were his and never think that someone else put those thoughts in there, it had to be planted deep in the mind. That was the art. He must be encouraged to think of his own heartbeat. To rest, to think, to absorb like a sponge the handlers wishes.

The interrogator had helpers; those would some of the time use mild beatings and force of various kinds as the situation demanded. All of it was played and directed carefully like fine violinists or performers of marionettes until the m danced to Ziki's music.

Iamael was given his meals at regular intervals. He was given water and a soft comfortable bed and a window that he could open and close. He could see a broad expanse of open land outside of it and in the near distance, a fence.

His toilet worked and the water in the sink ran hot and cold. He was given clean clothes and a hot shower every other day. He was given a radio that tuned in the news of the world. And wonder of wonders, he was given a television that offered Tel Aviv channels, all with controlled content but without him knowing that. It was the first time he had ever had such a pleasure. He was taken to a courtyard each afternoon for exercise. Here he would run in formation with other men, sometimes Israeli soldiers in training. Practice, he was told, for when he himself would go into training.

Thump-thump-thump. The boots of men drummed the dust.

When he was not running, Iamael was left alone.

He was told he had to wait until the man who would travel the journey with him returned to the country. He was told he would be made comfortable while he was to wait, but that only meager quarters would be available. He was told the whole country, Jew and Arab, thanked him for being a good human being and wanting to stop the bloody explosions—murders of women and children and old men—and for his willingness to consider service in their behalf.

His mind once more drifted and so images of the yellow dress of the little girl on the bus and the pink sandals in the desert dirt. He was told he was a hero of sorts. Honorable.

At night Iamael would lie in his bed and close his eyes. His handlers hoped that he'd dream of his own heart beating. . . Like the boots of men on the courtyard. Like the strange whir when his radio was turned on. His television flickered at the same tempo. And they were pleased when he took to leaving the television on at night; there was no turn-off knob: the subliminal messages were continuous, sinking deep into the subconscious without a shadow of suspicion that it was going on. Late at night, when the programming had ended for the day, Iamael lay and watched the flicker of blue light it cast dancing upon the flat white wall.

When asked how he was, he said he could not remember when he had ever felt so peaceful. Good, it seems to be working; the carefully designed program was getting his mind molded for its maker and ready for Ziki to take it to the next step.

**"He was picked up at the Gaza border last week**. Apparently we've been watching him for a while . . . Arjan, one of our young Arab informants in Khan Yunis, is his friend and told us about him.

Pientz and Ziki watched Iamael on a television monitor. Iamael lay, eyes half closed, on his mattress. The man was awake. Every so often his lashes flicked Iamael blinked... "He wants to go to school. We had hoped to pay him to ʼn."

"A scholar?"

ʼHe wants to be a teacher."

ı noted the now faint tinge of a bruise around one of Iamael's eyes. "He ʼd again while I slept, by Eli?"

"Yes, he gave up nothing new, all as you directed; here is the transcript. He claims to know nothing of the bombing in Jerusalem."

"It's only been a week; we can't be sure of that yet."

"How long has he been subjected to the ELFS?" Pientz asked. The acronym stood for the process of applying Electromagnetic waves. Combined with a mild hallucinogenic drug and at low frequencies, they threw most men into a trance state. Men in a trance were easily confused. His sleep would be fitful and he would think and speak slowly.

The technician checked his log. "Six days. . . "

"And the pulse?" That meant the use of sound waves. Set to mimic a man's heart beat, they would subliminally emanate from the very walls at a level not heard by the human ear, but felt by every hair and every cell.

"Six days. He no longer sleeps. He daydreams."

"Good."

"He is almost ready for intervention."

Pientz got tired of watching Iamael on the monitor; he yawned and stretched his arms as far as they could go then cracked his knuckles. That small sound awoke Ziki from his short nap on the couch in Pientz's office.

"You watch him for a while: he is, after all, your piece of work; I sure hope you're right about this one, you're planning to put him in a very sensitive spot."

"I know, I think he has some good blood in him."

"Aha, don't forget who his brother was, that murdering son of a bitch. I'd like to kill the little bastard all over, and don't forget who his uncle is,' ' Pientz lamented with anger and whispered to himself, "Ali Hassan Salameh, you do know that he runs around with the Egyptian, Aiman Zawahiri? Ahh, not to mention that Abu Nidal."

"You have a point, General, they're all on my wanted list; but my nose is usually right and we may be able to use his family ties, especially his uncle Salameh."

"We'll see Commander, we'll see. For now I'll yield to your judgment."

**Ziki knew that the blue flickering on the TV and the unheard subliminal sounds** coming in special frequencies from more than one source into his room, combined with the "friendship" now developing with Ziki and his men at never ending talks at irregular set intervals around the clock, were doing their job and Iamael was now in a trance, half awake and half asleep. Pientz's monitor showed him sitting on the floor with his legs crossed under him as if meditating. He spoke to himself in a soft whispery voice…

**…I am Iamael. I was born in Khan Yunis outside of Raffa south of Gaza City in the Gaza Strip during the riots**. Since many things in here took place before my birth, "How could Iamael, me, know of them?" Take the case of my father, Mustaffa, becoming the Muktar of Rafah.

In the Arab world the repetition of stories is a way of life; it is how we keep our history. Everyone eventually knows all of the tales of the past. Many things happened here when I was not present. Aha! How could I know of these? Our tales come from one to another from the old men with the *Nargilahs* to the young; the women listen in from the shadows of the huts and tents and then gossip while they hold their children; and from the sun and the moon and the stars above and from ancestors on the other side, I know them, the tales, with the help of Allah and our special magic…

I was lucky to be a male child: I was entitled to my mother's breasts for milk and have as much as I wanted for as long as I demanded them and was not weaned until my sixth birthday. I was small and still able to hide among the women. My mother, Fatmah, was a heavy set woman with great breasts. They were filled with milk; they gave me a place where I could find comfort. I did hide from the world of men until I was nine years of age.

One day my father, Mustafa, sent my mother away. It was a few days after my grandmother died that my mother was sent away.

I had gone to the village well with my mother every day. Now she was gone. I was

greeted with taunts. The women all cackled and laughed at me. The rumor was that my father was going to take a second wife. That was why my father had sent her out of the village, not to have to deal with her anger. The kids in the village joined in the chorus of taunts and some spat at my shoes.

I saw my father taking his morning stroll to the small coffee house, which was owned by him and my Uncle Abaas and which was where he spent most of his day sitting with the men, most smoking Nargillas, hubbly bubblys, drinking Turkish coffee and playing Shesh Besh with the dice. Sometimes my other uncle Salameh would join them. I hid when he came; his black eyes had a look in them that scared me and I could see that it also scared my father.

My other uncle Abaas was from Haifa, the *Carmel Tzarfati,* called for some unknown reason the French Carmel. He lived just bellow Muttanabi Street and everybody knew that he was friends with the Jews' family Barak and their son Ziki who spent a good deal of his time while he grew up at their house. He, Ziki, even helped the Arab women at olive harvest season to crack the green olives and put them in big wood vats, now Ziki was here with me.

I ran up to my father and cried, telling him what was happening. He brushed me aside harshly, walking on. I ran after him and tugged at his coat. My father grabbed me by the arm and shook me so violently I thought I would faint. Then he tossed me aside like garbage. I landed in the open sewer channel where the women pour their pots of urine at night, and *hara*, feces, in the middle of the dirt street that runs down from the top of the village to…? I don't know where; what happens to all that sewage?

I smelled bad, shrieking at the top of my lungs… I was screaming to an unhearing Allah.

I could feel salt from my tears and snot from my nose dripping into my mouth. I yelled in desperation, for even at that age I realized there was nothing I could do about my situation. There was no way to rebel or protest—that is our way—even though we male children had more rights than women.

Allah, the merciful, the compassionate, be praised, even donkeys and camels have more rights than women… I am sure lucky to be born male…

Our Village of Rafah was in the Negev Desert, bordering the Great Sinai Desert on the road to Ber-Sheeba, just next door to Khan Yunis.

My family was of the Soukori tribe, which had once belonged to the Wahhabi Bedouin tribe. The Wahhabis were great warriors who came from the Arabian Peninsula about one hundred years ago and purified the region for Islam. They killed all the Jews and Christian priests and monks they could find through sword and fire; they bravely took their land and houses and even the animals. The Muchktar of the region declared it their lands and beasts.  They did not care that others called them thieves and squatters; theirs was a noble task for Islam and the purity of Allah untainted by infidels.

Eventually the power of the Wahhabi was broken by invading Egyptian armies. Many of the tribes split off from the main tribe, and some migrated to what the English, when they came, now called *Palestine*. Our branch of the tribe roamed an area between Gaza and Beer-Sheba, crossing back and forth from the Negev to the Egyptian Sinai Deserts, as nomads.  Some of the tribe numbering over two hundred and fifty families moved north and settled on the land as squatters. However, we still retained very close ties with the Wahhabi through marriage, the ties becoming bonded, again reinforced, at weddings and funerals.

The Egyptian great village of Tabah had in its sites the smaller villages of former Wahhabi Bedouins in the area, and my other uncle Ali Hasan Salameh controlled those.  Salameh's power came from the fact that he and his father Hassan ran the Islamic Jihad's Mullahs and police apparatus and was endowed to verify the documents that spelled out the property of the villagers.  Also some of the goons that called themselves police were on his baksheesh payroll and people were scared of him.

At first he was known as Ali Hasan el Wahhabi, to denote his tribe, but Arab names change with the birth of male children.  The women at the village well whispered behind his back that he was *'Abu Banat,'* A Father of Daughters, a most terrible insult.

My father who had daughters threatened to get rid of my mother, who had brought this humiliation upon him.  By Allah's will their third child was a son, my oldest brother, Wazeera. After his birth my father could then assume the honorable title of *Mustafa Abu el Wazeera,* which means "Mustafa father of Wazeera."  Two more sons followed Wazeera and my father basked in glory. But alas, three more daughters came before my own birth. It was usual for a family of ten to lose three or more children in our village, but my father felt particularly blessed to have four sons who survived.

When Uncle Salameh went to Cairo in Egypt, no one in our family was invited. When he came back he talked more than I had ever heard him talk before about his meeting with this Egyptian that wanted to come and live here, Yasser Arafat, and the other Egyptian, Aiman Zawahiri. Uncle Salameh said that they had become fast friends. My uncle even met there some important Saudis from the Bin Ladin family. His eyes were very black… I hid from him once again.

My two oldest sisters were eventually contracted into marriage. They married in the Wahhabi tribe but to men from distant villages.

My father ran his beads through his hands, recited the Koran under his breath, and generally reinforced his small position. Most of the day he held court at the cafe, smoking his *Nargila,* greeting and listening to complaints of the villagers. Mostly, he and the other men repeated stories from the past: they talked of this Yasser Arafat and the Muchktar who hated the Jews and wanted to kill them all.

"Father do you think that Uncle Salameh also hates the Jews and wants to kill them?"

"Be quiet boy, you don't know anything—this is men talk."

"But why does he hate the Jews?"

"I will not tell you again; be quiet."

When my father came home each night, my mother washed his feet and he sat on his large pillow on the floor. Before we ate, my brothers came into the room, knelt and kissed his hand. Some male cousins or neighbors were sometimes invited to sit with us for the meal, which was eaten sitting on the floor;  all ate with their fingers from a common plate of humus and lamb shashlik, which was for the men. Later, my mother and I ate in the kitchen from the leftovers.

My father had an Arabian horse, a faint reminder of our Wahhabi and desert dwellers Bedouin past, I wondered why we came here and took the land from the Jews.  Didn't we have enough land in Arabia?

**Iamael's brother climbed the hill in the wadi to get a better look.**
There overlooking the new *Kibutz* …."*Kibutz* is a farm, isn't it?"

"No one can farm that land over there."  Lowly Jews…. men would leave the cafe every day and watch the Jews, busy little bees hmm….it added fuel to the day's conversation.  Iamael's brother brooded as it sunk in that the Jews were going to make a go of it.

"I know that place that they are working now, "said Mahsud, a fat round-faced man with a huge mustache, coffee shop regular, as he rolled the *Shesh Besh* dice and took a sip of his Turkish coffee. Beads of sweat rolled down his brow and face onto his shirt that was soaked with big wet sweat pools under his arm pits.

"So what, what's there to know?" somebody said.

"Well… I found ancient Jew coins there in the ground just below the surface and old oil lamps buried that I sold for a good price at the *Shuk* market, in Ber Sheba; some had pictures of their queen of Sheba."

"So what does that mean?"

"Don't you see, you idiot, that it means that they…. Who?  The Jews have been here always; they were here a long, long time ago, maybe thousands of years, long before our Arab Wahabis came here from the Sinai and Arabia."

"So, what does that mean?"

"It means that this land was theirs long before we came to these parts; they even say that God gave it to them."

"Allah gave them nothing; they are infidels."

"Allah wasn't around then.  This happened a long time ago even before Allah and Mohamed the Prophet came here."

" Well it's ours now and they are all going to die."

"Yeah, yeah, by the will of Allah the great and the merciful, his name be praised, we'll kill them just like we killed the others that were here."

"Send them all to the sword. They're all infidels and no infidel belongs here—our land or not."

He watched the Jews through the Turkish field glasses as they went about draining the swamp. Within the week, stone walls had been erected as a new perimeter and these were surrounded by high watchtowers with guns. A diesel generator not only lit bright floodlights to allow them to work through the night but made a future attack on them all but impossible.

The sound of their building never stopped. The tent city gave way to buildings of stone. There was a hospital tent; sometimes half of them were down from the heat and fever at the same time. It did not stop them.

The Jewish land across the wadi was mainly a few thousand dunams of swamp and marshlands, and rocks, lots of rocks: a vicious place inhabited by snakes, mosquitoes, and other slimy creatures. Iamael wondered how anyone could make anything grow there.

The other section of the Jews' lands was flat land, ancient ruins of the kind that the Jews of old had build thousands of years before. It looked like those of Biblical fame all over Judea; they, the Jews called it Israel or Judea. They didn't like the new name the English gave this place; *Palestine,* they kept saying there's no such place. "Who are the English to come here from…..Where do they come from?"

"I don't know, what difference does it make?"

Stones were many and scattered in the fields. The Jews collected and carried them by tractor to the base of the valley. From there they were taken by hand. The Jews brought in from afar and planted strange trees,

"What do they think they can do with those trees?" Iamael's brother muttered, "drink up the swamp?"

"That is what the men are talking about happened in the swamps of Achulla and in the Samaria valley," Iamael answered.

"They cannot change what Allah has willed. It can never work. They are idiots," said Iamael's brother.

"I heard in the market, that the trees have come all the way from Kenya and they are always thirsty."

"Kenya? Don't they have savages in Kenya?"

"I don't know."

"Where is it?"

"Someplace past India, as far south as the earth goes east before it turns into being west."

"Do they really believe those trees will drink up the swamp and grow here? Look around, Iamael do you see any trees around here?"

A few months after the Jews did to the land whatever they did, an amazing event occurred. The Jews pushed aside the earthen dams that divided the canals from the swamp. Iamael could not believe his eyes: they opened up the connecting ditches and sent the putrid waters of the swamp oozing into the canals. Soon the canals were bulging and began running downhill, and before his very eyes the level of swamp began to drop. It only took days and he could see the Kenyan trees grow fat with the waters of the swamp. As the swamp drained and then dried under the hot valley sun, black, rich topsoil appeared. A good amount of it was carried up to the rises, the rest was reditched and turned over to drain off every last remnant of the swamp.

The canals had emptied into a lower level.

"Why did they not let the foul waters run down to the sea? It is all down hill."

"It is some kind of madness."

"They are leaving it as a resting place for migrating birds. Why would any one do something like that? It is a waste—the birds can go some place else."

It enraged Iamael's brother that the Jews sang and danced in the evenings. It enraged him that they were able to sing and dance after the energy they had put into their work by day. When he compared it with the slow way of life and lethargy of his people the Wahabi Arabs, he realized that two strange worlds were heading into a conflict.

What the Jews had done had greatly discouraged the villagers. "We will never get vengeance," Wazzera whimpered one day.

"We shall get our vengeance," Iamael's brother retorted angrily. "The Jews can perform all their tricks. They shall learn the code of Islam. Wait . . . patience moves mountains."

What the men at the coffee shop brooded about most was the frightening pattern of land sales. At first the eroded fields were being dumped on the Jews as they came from the cities—Haifa, Jaffa, Tel Aviv and even Jerusalem—and bought all that was for sale. That was all right in the beginning because he and every *Sheik, Mukhtar, and Fellah* did not believe the Jews' soil was tillable. Sooner or later the Jews would give up and leave… It did not happen.

Even the English gave titles to land that were never theirs. Deeds changed hands with bribes to low level clerks. The Jews had been disinherited over the centuries by the various conquerors; now they were buying from the Arab land owners. The land was sold to the Jews at outrageous prices. A land boom was on because an unexpected vein of gold had been discovered by greedy men. It took no mental giant to figure out that a dunam of land sold to the Jews would bring more profit than if it were sharecropped for twenty years by the Arab *fellahin*.

"For some reason our lands had been spared. Why?" Iamael wondered. Their fields were the richest in the valley and would certainly bring a king's ransom; maybe because the Egyptian army was in control of the Gaza strip, and that made some kind of a border.

**In Raffa, Khan Yunis and Gaza with open sewers in the streets** and uncollected hills of rotting garbage the flies were big. The stink was overpowering. Idleness—young men hanging out at the street corners not working or really doing anything, ripe for the picking—and the constant prodding of the old men, holding out to be Islamic Mullahs pretending to instill in them a pride and courage they never really owned, combined with the gift of guns that were abundant—coming in, Iamael heard from Egypt, Syria, Iraq and many of the Arab countries—to give birth to the Shahid, suicide bomber.

Iamael's brother was a leader among these roving gangs. They wore no uniforms; hatred was their heritage. They identified themselves with headbands of bright orange and black cloth. Soon they became El Fattah and the PLO, and many sub names: Black September, Moslem Brotherhood, Islamic Jihad, Leopards…..
At the Khan Yunis camp, the gang was the Liberating Sharks. At the Bedouin camp farther up they were the Desert Wolves, and at the small Falangeas camp farther on the gang was named there Black Death. All of the gangs were prodded on by elders and by Egyptians of the Islamic Jihad Brotherhood.

Fear grew in Raffah and Khan Yunis over the Moslem Brotherhood and the Islamic Jihad. They stalked about looking for boys like Iamael to recruit: join them or take a bad thrashing. They roamed the alleys with clubs and guns. Iamael was able to stay clear—his brother embraced it.

Killing Jews was now an obsession, and the Shahids' families started to get lots of money for their sons' suicides and the killing of Jews, any Jews: it does not matter; they are all Infidels after all.

At night the gangs would gather in the Wadi, where they conducted initiation rituals on new recruits, including bloodletting. They had secret signs and swore an oath of allegiance to the Moslem Brotherhood and one of vengeance filled with promises of dismemberment and skull crushing and hot pokers in the eyes of the Jews. Old men they called Mullahs of the Egyptian Brotherhood would come each night and hold prayers and make a promise to each of them of direct ascension to Paradise when killing Jews: a good life and seventy-two black eyed virgin brides when they got there.

"Death to the Jews, death to the Christian crusaders, death to the Infidels!" Their calls came humming down the mountain on the leaden night air. They tested each other's courage with running over hot coals, jumping from high ledges, running past a line of stone throwers, leaping over fires, biting off the heads of live chickens and snakes, and strangling cats and small dogs barehanded. That fed their illusions of bravery and manhood; those were performed all day, every day. They became roving gangs with guns and clubs roaming and beginning to control their villages.

Some of the elders and the other old-time mukhtars and sheiks saw these gangs as a growing threat to their own rule, but they had to tread lightly in curbing them, for they offered no alternative: no schools or organized games, no movies, no police, no work; they did whatever they wanted. The only lectures they heard were from the Brotherhood, glorifications of martyrdom and death.

"You are the Moslem Brotherhood, and El Fattah, you are the great young soldiers of the Prophet and Allah, preparing to become shahids, martyrs!"

"Kill the Infidel, " they heard in Gaza.

"Kill," they heard in the cafes of the camps. "Shahid, kill," they heard in their homes. They grew ugly. None of them worked or tried to look for work; they were enticed by small gifts and meals and speeches, even during harvest-time when field hands were needed by the *Fellahin*. Their mothers and sisters, the women did that labor. They began to hire themselves out to "*protect"* the farmers' fields.

If a man in the camp had a run-in with a Brotherhood gang member, he could expect his home to be broken into and looted and his son to be beaten up. The Moslem Brotherhood and the El Fattah were out in numbers. Arab merchant's trucks had to watch their wares. If a driver dozed off or left his truck, the gangs would quickly empty its contents. Sheik Yasin arrived and now lived in Gaza; his wheel chair did not slow down his fervor.

The Hamas group was born.

The gangs became a major factor in the raging black market. With little curb on their activities, they prowled around Gaza and blackmailed merchants who had been fingered for them. They raided and robbed Red Cross supply depots. Things began to come to Iamael's brother—a battery-operated radio, a wristwatch, new shoes, trinkets to give to the girls, hashish, and two guns—a Russian Makarov pistol and an AK 47…. Father did not question him.

Iamael accepted in silence what his brother had become—a gangster and a thief. Father even seemed to bask in the manhood of it; his brother became different. He had a gun in his belt, money in his pockets, and father was happy about the gifts.

**"He was ready the day he came in."**

"Don't be so hasty—how do we know he is not a plant?"

"We don't," replied Pientz.

"But soon enough, we will," Ziki finished.

"We have to kill him with kindness," Ziki said.

"Since we can't just kill him," Pientz answered.

It was in this way, through the process, Ziki and Iamael came to know one another.

Ziki was polite most of the time, he did not use force. At this point he was cool and distant.

He circled Iamael, looking menacing examining him from every possible angle.

"No. . ." Ziki said. "No. . .I don't know about you…. "He shook his head. He put one boot on a chair and drew a pack of cigarettes from his pocket. "Smoke?"

Iamael shook his head. "I don't smoke."

"You don't smoke? What are you, a woman?"

Iamael's gaze dropped to the tabletop. "I hate the smell of tobacco; that's all the men do in Gaza."

Ziki laughed. "Then you are in the wrong place, my friend; we smoke here also." He struck a match on the sole of his boot and set the flame to the tip of his smoke. "You won't mind if I smoke?"

"Suit yourself."

Ziki smiled. "Suit myself? Do yourself a favor. Don't develop a big mouth."

Again he circled Iamael, took a deep drag from his cigarette and blew the smoke at Iamael. He kept circling without saying anything; he looked menacing. The young man was disturbed, but he did not cower. Ziki couldn't decide if this was a good sign or a bad sign.

Ziki frowned at him. "…You don't look like a killer."

"I am not a killer."

"Aren't you?" A wry smile. "Scenario: 2 PM Monday afternoon, April 24. Café Bistro at 239 Ben Yehuda Street, next to Markley Hostel, Jerusalem. Ever hear of it?"

"No."

But Ziki could see the quaver of recognition in his eyes. What else was in there, waiting to come out? Given a push . . . what would he find? flashed through his mind… A lull in the day, what else is in there?

Iamael's hands were clasped between his thighs, a posture of subordination: perhaps guilt, perhaps grief…. Waiting.

"I knew nothing of my brother's plans," he burst out. "He knew I would not kill with the Jihadis or the El Fattah."

"Ahh, so you have heard of the Café Bistro, you know the one next to the Hostel in Jerusalem." Iamael lowered his eyes to the floor…. Silence for a short while.

"You expect me to believe you simply walked away from your family?" Ziki asked Iamael.

"My mother—"

"You left her to grow old without your support."

"I want to study—"

"You left your books, your school, your friends?"

"I--. . ." Iamael slowly blinked, like a child in an unexpected trap. "I can tell you no other truth but the one I have lived."

Good. Let him be confused. "You come into this country from Gaza, from Khan Yunis with killers in your family and expect us to embrace you as one of our own?"

"I am not a killer; I want to go to America or stay in Israel. I want to study."

"Well, then go ahead, be on your way, I'll let you leave; but don't you think you'll need money to do that?"

"Probably."

"Yeah….All you did is throw a stone at a young soldier at the border, about your age; it hit him in the back of the head just below his helmet."

"I'm sorry."

"Oh, yeah, so is he; he lost sight of his right eye. Would you like to meet him? I wonder what he would want to do to you. Ahh, America? New York?

Hollywood? You are looking to become a movie star?" Ziki surveyed him a long moment…. "Well, if you want to go there, this is where you'll get money, right here; from me, that is if I want to give it. Do you understand me?"

Iamael swallowed. Under other circumstances, Ziki would have offered him water. "I want to be a teacher."

"Teach what, the Koran, or how to kill children?"

"No, I want to teach history"

"History, well here's some; your brother butchered innocent women and children.　　　"You want to get out of Gaza, you want to study, it looks to me that you don't want to die a shahid, martyr, and maybe you don't want to blow up and kill old men, women and children on buses and in cafés. I said maybe. Is that right? Is that what you want?"

"Yes."

"And why should I believe you, or help you?"

"….I can give you names. . . "

Ziki grinned. "Ahhhhh, okay, now maybe we're talking."

Iamael said nothing to this. "I know the truth. I know—"

"Yes, yes," Ziki snapped. "And we have our truth as well."

Ziki moved his face close to Iamael's; each could feel Ziki's anger and Iamael's fear exuding from the pores of their skins… sweat. Ziki's eyes, piercing with intensity, showed disgust… Iamael lowered his.

"Look at me, you little fuck?"

He opened a folder that had lain unnoticed on the table and drew out a stack of photos. He watched Iamael's mouth become thinner with dread. He threw one photo onto the table in front of Iamael. It made a noise like a slap.

The photo was of two dead girls: about sixteen, one with honey blonde hair, another with dark hair—their faces were pitted and bloodied from flying glass—their cheeks were singed and smudged with soot.

Their mouths were open as if they had tried to scream…

"Miriam and Anna Metz. DOA, did you hear me? Dead on arrival!" Ziki said.

He watched Iamael look at the pictures. Iamael's face was flat, but his eyes widened ever so slightly.

Another photo. Shlap!

This one of a young couple: their faces had been close when the blast occurred. The young man had a moment to throw his arm up—as if protecting her face. His jacket was eviscerated and blackened. Shreds of blue nylon were soaked black with blood and ash. Her face was hidden. His face was burned and smashed so that it no longer looked human. "Wilma and Yavin Feld. Married five weeks… She had just started art school. He was in residency at the Hadassah Hospital… DOA."

Shlap! Shiny photo paper slid on the table making a hissssss.

An Arab servant lay in a pool of his own blood next to a large poodle whose neck was twisted all wrong. "Aiman Shahir and Curly. They just happened to be on the wrong corner at the wrong time. He's from Gaza. Near you… Look familiar? No? DOA."

Shlap! A mother and her son blown face down into the street by the blast. "Malcha and Friedric Stein... DOA."

Shlap! An older woman and a younger woman. "Anna and Vida Gould. DOA."

Shlap! Two young men who looked like off-duty fireman.

Shlap! A business man with his brief case.

"—Stop!" Iamael jerked forward. His eyes were wide with horror and disgust.

Ziki's hand stopped mid-air. The stack he held was still quite thick.

"Stop?"

"Please. . ." Iamael said. "I despise this... I am no killer."

"And why should we show you mercy? This is your brother's work, right there in your family."

"I can give you names. . . I can get into places, my uncle is Ali Hassan Salameh. . ."

Ziki laughed softly. Pientz had been right. He had come ready to be molded. Ziki spread the photos out so that each was visible. "Do you recognize any of them?"

"No. None."

"Did your brother know any of them?"

My brother? Iamael mouthed. "These. . ?" he squeezed his eyes narrow and took up the photo nearest him. He held it up, searching it as if for fingerprints or a token that he recognized.

"What sort of man kills people he has never met?" Ziki leaned closer to Iamael and held up the one picture he knew would stay with Iamael if none else did... "Innocents?"

He heard Iamael's sharp breath and the tremor of emotion in him as he recognized from the picture of a finger with a ring on it, what little was left of his brother. He knew the ring, it was his fathers; it was given to Iamael's brother when he decided to become a suicide bomber, a *Shahid*.

"Are you like him? A murderer and a butcher?"

"No I am not; I don't want to kill and I want all this killing of innocents to stop."

Iamael's eyes did not waver from the photo.

"You came to us because of this, but we think to ourselves that the apple does not fall too far from the tree."

Iamael's face had a green tinge to it. "I could not live there any more."

"So you would exile yourself, but will you help me to stop these murders?"

"Yes I will, I want to help you, I want to be your friend."

"Yes, and I want to be your friend, Iamael."

"Yes, I am your friend and I know that you love the Wahhabi Arabs."

"Oh yeah, and what makes you think that?"

"I know things, I'm not stupid. But I'm not suppose to talk about it because it can get you in trouble with the Israelis and your boss,."

"Really, and what might that be?"

"I don't want to talk about it."

"Well, you're going to have to; I thought you said that you are becoming my friend.  It's just the two of us, no one can hear us, you can tell me."

Iamael looked around the room as if to see that no one else was around. "I know that you are life long friends with my uncle's family on uncle Salameh's side of the family, the Abaas family in Haifa near the Bahai gardens, where you lived."

"You're right, I know them; thank you for not talking about it." Ziki turned and winked into the monitor at Pientz."

"We'll see if you are truly with us… What if I wanted you to go to your uncle Salameh and tell him that you are ready to join the 'El Fattah,' his group?"

"Nahh, I never would. I don't want to be like them."

"You don't understand. What if I wanted you to join them so that you can save lives, tell us ahead of time about their plans?"

"Ahh."

"We will train you first secretly and then let them train you to become a shahid…This is how you could help the most."

Iamael's face lit up with recognition. "Yes, I will do what you tell me to do."

"And Iamael, remember we know where your mother lives, remember—we know where your father lives and the rest of your family…. Don't ever fuck me, Iamael, remember this well; I can be your friend or I can be your enemy"…he drew his face again close to Iamael…".and you don't want me as your enemy."

"No, I never will."

"Just remember one more thing….."

"What's—that?"

"That is…" he pulled Iamael's face close to him again; "never, never betray me.  If you do, no matter where you go, no matter where you hide, I will find you, I will hunt you down and I will kill you. Do you understand me?"

"Yes, I never will. And yes, I will do it."

"….Well then, welcome to Israel."

# Chapter 27

## Baghdad

**Ziki could usually tell when he was being followed.** The little hairs on the back of his neck tingled. Davidoff called this his sixth sense. And with an innate sense he could track men—and women—without being detected. Did he cover himself with sand? Did he turn himself into scrub grass and desert flowers? He would never tell. Watching people without being seen to be watching them was another story. At night, it was not as simple as letting the darkness shroud him from view. He had to avoid watching people straight on, instead trailing their every move from the corners of the eyes—people could feel eyes on them if watched too long. In the night, he wore dark to let the shadows cling to his heels.

In the daytime if stationary, it was best to find a terrace or a rooftop, for most people rarely looked up. Conversely, an underground sewer's wide mouth sometimes afforded a good view of the face of a building, provided no cars pulled in front of the curb. An additional plus was the dry location a sewer offered to set up camera equipment, if it was off the main line. In the day, it was best to blend, looking like a tourist who had lost his way and was resting his feet.

Dusk was the best time to stalk someone. As the light dimmed while the sun set, colors dimmed and shadows drew closer. Most people had a difficult time seeing—car accidents occurred more frequently near the hour of sunset simply because of the murky quality of the light. A hat, with a brim wide enough to shade Ziki's face from the last rays of the sun, made his features nearly inscrutable as the light waned.

And so dusk was the time that Ziki planned to meet Joseph and whoever Might be with him once more. A meeting to seal the deal…

Later to meet the other about Osirak.

Joseph was waiting at the entrance to the outdoor market, *Shuk El Jaball*, where, adjoining it, would be a large garden where they might walk, as planned. He looked out of place on the sandstone steps—a regular sore thumb—looking all around himself as if he were waiting for the angel Gabriel to arrive in a fiery chariot, though the man did have the sense to wear a red and white Kafia, head dress, to blend more fully.

The street was busy enough, near to the downtown area with a few commercial buildings and several cafes. The rumble of buses and the occasional zooom! of a motor bike punctuated the evening. It was warm—far warmer than anyone preferred; because of this Ziki would like to have left his coat in the waiting van with Amit and Hanna, but the guns….had to be covered.

Vendors and people returning from work walked the street, and a newspaper seller did a brisk trade from his booth near where Joseph stood.

Ziki hesitated on the corner, watching the people, scanning the customers of a bistro with sidewalk seating and a café next to that. No one noticed him and that suited him just fine. Not even Joseph, nearly turning circles in his place as he sought a familiar face among the crowds, saw him. But Ziki did not go to meet him.

There was something . . . wrong . . . he felt the familiar creeping sense of eyes on him as he surveyed the little Iraqi. Had he been followed from the car? Was this a set up? Was Joseph being watched?

He watched Joseph and slowly considered his options: cancel and arrange another meeting, take his chances in directing Joseph into a café where they might make casual conversation and Ziki could drop hints, try to flush his stalker out. Ziki knew neither of them could wait much longer without calling attention to themselves—or in Joseph's case, more notice than anyone wished to attract. Ziki's skin tingled as the sensation of being observed intensified.

When the light changed Ziki made his decision. Not half a second later, he was crossing the street. Without making eye contact he passed him by, knowing they would have to wait before rescheduling, just to dampen the spirits of their audience.

Who could it be? Gavriella? Someone from Iraqi Secret Police or Intelligence? His arm tightened against the mini Uzi. Ziki wasn't sure.

Yet.

In his worst case scenario he never imagined how badly the little man could blow it.

"Herr Breckenbauer!" he called as Ziki passed him.

Damn.

Ziki went rigid. If whoever was watching did not already know the little man was waiting for Ziki, they did now…. For a moment, Ziki could only stand with his back to Joseph.

Civilians. He sent a sideways look over his shoulder.

Joseph took an eager step toward him like a lost puppy.

"Well, come on then," Ziki said.

Joseph fell into step with him and Ziki quickly took him by the arm. "We're being watched."

Joseph's neck craned to look over his shoulder. "I don't see—"

"Don't look," Ziki seethed. He jerked Joseph's arm and dragged him along. He hated working with amateurs. "Stay with me. Be ready—"

"I knew this wasn't safe."

"Keep your head down and your mouth shut and keep up. I've a car waiting."

Joseph nodded and hurried at Ziki's side. Rounding the corner, Ziki took the opportunity to scan rooftops and the street behind. He saw—

No one?

That didn't set him at ease.

Hanna and Amit waited at the car. When they saw him bringing Joseph, Amit slipped inside and started the engine. Hanna opened the passenger door.

"I was followed," Ziki told them as he pushed Joseph into the car and took a seat after him.

"Did you see who it was?" Amit asked.

Joseph turned around, shoving his nose almost to the back glass. "I still don't see—"

"Sit down," Ziki said and tugged him back into his seat by the belt of his pants.

"That's a problem," Amit said. And Ziki wasn't certain if Amit was referring to their being observed or Joseph's utter lack of ability to be calm.

"No kidding," he answered, not caring which it was Amit had referred to. He pulled his mini Uzi from its shoulder holster. Hanna had uncovered the Uzi across her lap and deftly inserted two clips that she had pulled from the glove compartment. They slid into place with a reassuring clap.

"Just in case," she said.

Amit had his gun out too, and flicked off the safety. It lay between the two of them on the front seat. "Let's hope the Iraqi police are too busy to pull over anyone speeding," he joked, but it was nothing to make light of.

"Drive at the speed limit, that's an order," Ziki said briskly.

Caught with guns, the next logical step was to uncover their true identities. They'd all be shot as spies. Amit instantly slowed the car.

"Guns. . ." Joseph murmured, "spies. . . This is what we've come to." He seemed to have shrunk into himself, his neck into his shoulders, his spine slinking down the seat. His head was almost below the seat, out of sight.

Ziki was disgusted with the man. "If you get down on the floor, you'll be safer," he told Joseph. Though he doubted it would be necessary. A quick look over his shoulder confirmed for him that the van had not been followed. He recognized none of the cars behind them, saw no motor cycles—a tag's vehicle of choice—and no delivery trucks that would have disguised expensive eavesdropping equipment.

He leaned forward and tapped Amit's shoulder. In Hebrew, "I think we're safe. Go to the drop-off point as previously arranged. We don't want Joseph anywhere near the safe house."

Amit nodded.

As Ziki leaned back, he caught a flicker of intrigue moving through Hanna's gaze. She caught his look and held it a moment, but then turned to look out the window. Her grip was too loose on the Uzi. Ziki sensed something off.

"When was the last time you saw Gavriella?" Ziki asked Hanna. If Gavriella had been tipped off, she wouldn't need to follow Ziki. She would know exactly where to find him.

Hanna turned toward him and had the good sense to look surprised. "It's been months."

His mouth curled wryly. "When was the last time you spoke to her?"

Hanna's mouth twitched into a smile that matched his. "Are you afraid she isn't getting updates on your hair color?"

"I'm afraid someone on our team may not stay out of American's beds."

The glare she shot at him could have stripped paint from wood. "You can go to hell."

"Did Gavriella know I was meeting someone today?"

Hanna's features turned sour. She turned her face toward the window.

"Did she follow us?" he pressed.

Hanna's features turned surly. "If she did, I have nothing to do with it."

"I hope so."

Amit pulled the car into an alleyway and flipped off the car's lights.

Joseph looked out on the alleyway with something akin to horror or revulsion.

Ziki knew how vulnerable the little man must feel and tried to lay his annoyance to rest. It wouldn't do for professionalism to slip. He laid his hand on Joseph's forearm. "Stay down," he said in Arabic; Joseph did not understand Hebrew.

Hanna got out and with a final glare at Ziki strode down the alley, checking it. She motioned to Amit that it was all clear and Amit turned back to Ziki. "It's clear."

Behind a row of trashcans a Ducati street bike waited for Hanna. She pulled it out and climbed on it putting on her helmet and snapping the visor into place. Ziki watched her roar away.

Amit climbed out of the van leaving Joseph and Ziki alone in the back seat so they might talk freely. Vigilant and still hyped on adrenaline from their scare, the young man waited outside Joseph's door, his jacket pulled back just enough to reveal the Uzi in his shoulder holster. Apparently he didn't trust Joseph either.

Ziki placed his briefcase on his lap. "My business associates would like to accept your offer. They agree—one million American dollars is the price and they will see your family to safety in Israel."

"A Swiss bank account. . ." Joseph insisted.

"You will have it." Ziki flicked up both latches on the briefcase and opened it. He pulled out and thrust a large manila envelope at Joseph.

"This has all the information you need—a bank account has been set up as you requested. Our people are in the process of confirming the names and locations of your family members so that we may make arrangements for their removal as soon as we are satisfied that you will complete our transaction."

"My wife, her mother, and my children—"

"Of course—we are seeking anyone with strong enough ties to you to provide any possible leverage should our plans fail to meet expectations." A look of confidence now came onto Joseph's face; he was inspired by the efficient handling of things.

"Tell me what to do next."

"You will arrange for Munir to take the MiG. When the time comes I will give you exact directives and make sure that he is firmly on board. And you yourself must prepare to leave your home. But I will warn you. The money will not be released to you if you attempt to withdraw it from inside Iraq. The account becomes accessible only if you make your first withdrawal from Tel Aviv."

He watched this sink in and saw no sign of frustration or duplicity on Joseph's face. He might be a little weasel, but he seamed to be an honest little weasel.

Joseph nodded with resolve. There was a far away look in his eyes and the remnants of fear. "My family will be safe," he intoned.

"Yes."

"That's what I want most."

"Then serve us well." Ziki thrust the envelope at Joseph. "Put that under your shirt so no one can see it. Ahh yes, there are five thousand Iraqi Dinars in the envelope to tide you over."

A gleam appeared in Joseph's eyes. "Thank you."

"There is a bus stop two blocks west. You will take your usual bus home and tell everyone you have been to the city looking for work. You walked to the bazaar section of the city and got lost in the winding streets."

"Yes... Yes, I will." Joseph moved to pull up his tunic, tucking the envelope into his belt and against his emaciated chest. "How can I contact you?"

"You don't. We'll be in touch as soon as the arrangements are made."

Ziki leaned across Joseph's lap and tapped on the window.

Amit opened the door.

Joseph nodded and climbed out of the van, careful not to touch Amit or disturb the jacket that hid Amit's gun from view.

"Don't look back," Ziki told him. "Makes you look like a mark and a mark is an easy target."

Ziki saw Joseph's eyes widen just before Amit slammed the van door closed.

When Amit climbed into the driver's seat he turned to look at Ziki. "I'll tell Roshi to put Hanna on a tighter rein."

"Do it. I want her watched 24-7."

## Chapter 28

### A 'Tourist couple'

Ziki had only been seated a few moments when Gavriella made an appearance in the dining room of his hotel. He was not surprised. He might have set his watch to her arrival. Even her performance was predictable; she pretended that she didn't know he was there. The maître d' escorted her to her table and as soon as she saw him she made an artificial high noise, as if in surprise and delight.

"Herr Breckenbauer," she crooned and held out her hand to him.

"Ms. Ramon." He took her hand and kissed the pale back of it, noting that she no longer wore the ring she once refused to remove.

Ziki sat back and surveyed her coolly. "I don't know why I shouldn't have expected you. You'd like to join me, I suppose?"

With every inch of public space in the hotel undoubtedly bugged, she knew she had him. He would have to keep up appearances—a sort of slow torture she would very much enjoy.

"This table will be fine, thank you," Gavriella told the maitre d' and let him pull her chair out for her at Ziki's table.

The maitre d' was trying to complete his duties while at the same time avidly appearing to mind his own business. "Shall... I will bring a place setting promptly."

Ziki rose as Gavriella sat.

He nodded to the maitre d'. "The lady likes to drink Chateau Neuf de Pape. Your oldest bottle please."

"Hans. . . you've always had such a memory. . ." She laughed like a private escort laughs at all of her consorts' jokes.

"Immediately, sir. Enjoy your meal." The maitre d' snapped his heels together, made a swift bow and was gone.

Gavriella was doing her best imitation of a starry eyed tourist. "Such a lovely dining room, isn't it? Like Paris or—"

"What do you want, Gavriella?" Ziki leaned in close. He couldn't keep the strain of contempt out of his voice.

"I'm in the market for a supply of dental drills, Hans. . ." she reached for his hand.

He snatched it away. "Cut to the chase."

She smiled and sat back coolly. The slit of her skirt opened to reveal pale and shapely legs. Noting where his gaze fell, she crossed them slowly, like a cat who thinks itself queen of the forest. As if that wasn't enough, she let the top leg bob to draw his eye once more. "Don't be sore. . . "

"You were watching me today."

"You. . . " she confirmed, "and a little Arab of very poor means. I'm wondering what he might have to do with the rumors I'm hearing."

"Yes, those rumors."

"He wouldn't have anything to do with—"

Ziki knew to choose his words wisely. "The servant of a business associate," he explained.

"I hardly believe—"

"Believe it."

"Indeed? He seemed a little more frightened than I would think a servant—"

"He was recently terminated for accruing several unseemly debts."

Her eyelids were heavy and her smile never wavered. "Debts?"

She didn't believe him.

He spread his hands. "What can I say—I am a generous man."

She snorted. "You're unbelievable."

The waiter returned to the table with Gavriella's wine. There was a temporary ceasefire as the waiter opened the bottle with a silver corkscrew. He offered Ziki the cork, but he declined.

"It is the lady who considers herself a gourmand," he said.

"Hans!" Gavriella mockingly scolded. "You will spoil me."

She smelled the cork and tasted the wine, swirling the dark richness in her glass before sipping it. "Delicious. You'll just love it."

"Of course." Ziki accepted the glass that the waiter poured and sipped it. It was, as she said, delicious. If only she were as easy on the palate as a fine wine.

"So you're not going to give me a clue?" Gavriella asked as the waiter left them.

"There is nothing to clue; it's not important, petty stuff."

"You know I'll find out."

"If that's what you like to tell yourself."

"Must you always do things the hard way?"

"If you continue to travel a road that is obviously a dead end, yes. That was a long time ago and before…" he paused leaned over the table and hissed in her ear, "Khan Yunis at Gaza, you double crossing bitch."

She whispered back. "It wasn't my call."

"Can't we simply have a nice dinner without the battle of wills?"

He looked at her through cold eyes.

"Remember," she said, returning his indifference with a warmth that did nothing to move him, "Paris. You and me, that little hotel near Le Tour Eiffel on Rue De La Paix. Or better, the night we skied the Swiss Alps at Ementhaler… The lodge lighted below us and all the stars above."

He looked away from the table. The bar was busy with foreign travelers, business men and their wives. Anyone who saw them would think that of them a business man or a tourist and his willful beautiful wife.

He was suddenly tired of fighting.

"I see them too," she said.

He met her gaze, but it dropped immediately to her wine glass.

"Your men," she said.

"Another topic, please."

She leaned forward and placed her hand on his wrist. The shadow of her cleavage was bared as her dress fell open. "Listen, Hans," she stopped and mouthed Ziki, her eyes lingering now on his. "I have seen them so many times. . . I've sent people into the field and wondered if I would have to tell their families they weren't coming back."

"Not here—" he said.

"No. I must say this now. I should have said it. A year ago, I should have."

He stood, fingers pressing the edge of the table. "A pleasure to see you again." He wiped his mouth with his napkin and threw it down. "I remembered a telephone call that I must make to a client in Tokyo."

Gavriella sat back.

For a moment he stood looking down on her, not certain if he should believe her or not. Her eyes were huge and full of sadness, but she was a consummate actress and a consummate liar. She had played him before.

"Please. . . " she said, "I need you to forgive me."

And somehow that struck a chord in him.

"If you leave now, you'll never see me again," she said. "I'll leave Baghdad. I'll leave the Middle East. I'll leave Europe."

He sat slowly. But that was what he wanted, wasn't it? To never see her again?

The waiter was at his side. "Is there a problem with the wine, sir?"

Ziki placed his napkin on his lap once more and slid himself closer to the table. "No, no problem," he said.

And he hoped he wouldn't regret it. He already regretted it, but….

Aside from the ins and outs of his profession, Ziki knew few things better than Gavriella's body. And yet, naked, spread before him, she seemed a strange country. He tossed the crumpled bed sheet into a corner of the room while watching her stretch across the queen size mattress playfully, offering herself in an exotic dance form.

He would discover her all over again. The darkness of her tan was thrown into relief by the almost glowing bed spread. It took his eyes a minute to adjust but soon he began to recognize the body that he had known. It was the same with its seductive shape. He would not be able to understand her through his gaze, so he descended between her legs; as if somehow by not kissing her, he could keep his thoughts straight.

Her smells seemed to reacquaint him almost immediately. Her deep sigh acknowledged he had not forgotten her way. He wondered how she responded to the cosmetic changes in his body. Was she able to remember him in the same way despite the blonde hair? His passion mixed with amusement, not love. He could sense feelings in Gavriella as she gave direction to his affections. She possessed full knowledge at how he would respond to her every physical offering. So much was mixed into this hotel room tryst: the physical reconciliation of lovers, the memories of that which once had been, and the undercurrent of doubt.

Ziki knew that the further he threw himself into her world, the more dangerous it would be. It could also prove useful. Any lie he had told her at dinner would now have the ring of truth, because Graviella might assume that he spoke to her in earnest with the hopes of being exactly where he was at this moment. No, that is not possible he thought, she knows I may be lying and may simply believe this lovemaking to be a form of it.

Gavreilla laughed. Ziki could not place her giggle. Was it simply pleasure or did she know something that he did not? Did she know his thoughts and was merely laughing at him for being so simple in his complexity? Or was it a giggle because she felt the same way and instinctively knew they shared the same doubts? Or did she just simply giggle? She reached down to touch his head and slowly guided his way up her torso until their lips locked and Ziki joined with her in a place of forgetfulness…

The steam of the shower filled the bathroom; Ziki heard the television set in the room go on. It could only mean Gavriella wanted to talk. The bathroom door opened.

"Forgive me, Father, for I have sinned," Gavriella giggled. It was the same giggle. She closed the door.

"What's that? Again with your Catholic stuff?" He had hoped for the privacy of the shower to clear his thoughts in the aftermath of their encounter. She was pursuant.

"'Forgive me, Father, for I have sinned.' Isn't that what the Catholics say in the confessional?" He could make out her silhouette on the other side of the frosted glass. And then immediately understood her reference to the confessional.

"I was never an expert in your religion. What made you say that? Have you something to confess?" It was obvious that she was over by the mirror now and looking at herself.

"We both do, Ziki."

"And how is that?"

"We each have something the other wants."

"I thought we'd already given it, Gavriella."

He thought about shampooing his hair but was afraid he would miss some subtlety in what she had to say. Instead, he let the steaming water relax his body while he listened.

"That was between us… Ziki and Gavriella. What I speak of is—

"Between two countries. I understood your meaning. I understand what it is that you want from me."

"And that is?"

"What you want is an unnecessary discussion unless you can explain to me what it is I want from you."

"Must you be so difficult? You might make me believe what just happened in the bedroom was to stiffen your resolve against my persuasions."

"It was, Gavriella. Partly. But it doesn't take away from the fact that I made love to you out of desire rather than my believing you have anything to offer me…. You, on the other hand—"

Ziki could see her body slump into a posture of pouting. "What a terrible thing to say, Ziki. First of all, I am not foolish enough to believe that sex could ever persuade you to do anything. Second, I do not need sex to convince you to negotiate with me. I have a great deal to offer you. After all, I know what the most difficult charge of your mission is."

"And that would be?"

"How do you plan to exit this place? And don't you think you need powerful allies after whatever it is you plan to do at Osirak?"

He caught her meaning, but he would not make it easy. "You still have not given me an answer to what it is you have to offer me."

Gavriella was enjoying the exchange more than Ziki. "My answer is the question I have asked of you."

"My exit plan is simple, Gavriella. I come and go as I please—"

"It is not your exit that concerns you, your abilities at sneaking yourself from place to place…. On the other hand, larger things—

"I see."

"Do you?"

"You are not offering me an exit plan… your offer is an exit plan for my mission."

"Exactly. Now, that you understand what it is I am offering, let me tell you what it is I understand. You wish safety not only for your contact and but also that which he must acquire."

"I hope you are not threatening his well being?" He thought she was not but wanted to know if he was right.

"I would only threaten his well being if my desire was blackmail. I do not desire money."

"You desire my mission."

"In a way. But not in a way that would threaten you. You may have what you desire. I simply wish to share in it."

"So, my contact is to do all the work; I am to take all the risk; and you are to share in the benefits?"

"No, Ziki, I am to provide a service. I will ask you again. What is your exit plan?"

"You seem to know the answer."

"Because you are surrounded by enemies. How do you plan to smuggle a MiG out of this country when they don't allow more than fifty kilometers' worth of fuel and there is no friendly landing space?"

She had finally come out and said it. What did she have? "Do you know of such a space?"

"Turkey."

"Turkey? While they have the semblance of democracy, they are still a Muslim state."

"With close ties to the Americans. And close ties in particular to Kissinger."

Kissinger. That name should have been the first thing Gavriella uttered. It would have made their conversation more economical. It would have explained who she was working for and what she wanted.

Ziki thought about the Americans. After all, in the end, the Americans had friends when and where it was convenient; when it was not, they had interests. Recently, it seemed the Americans were occupied with protecting their interests. No one embodied this policy more than Kissinger.

Many in Israel's corridors of power perceived him to be the second greatest threat to the nation's security right after the Kremlin and the Arabs. When it came to foreign affairs, no one had Nixon's ear more than Kissinger. It was a frightening combination for Israel: Kissinger whispering into the ear of a president who did not like Israel. They would only come to Ziki's country's side if it meant maintaining the balance of power against the Soviets, a nuclear threat and oil…nukes and oil were the big thing. Anything that might tip that balance, they would move to block.

Ziki sat down in the shower. He would stay in it as long as he could in order to avoid having to look at Gavriella. He was angry that she was working part time for the Americans and who knows whom else? Ziki did not yet know all the details about her call to Salameh at Khan Yunis. He took solace in the fact that Kissinger must have been pulling that thick Austrian hair out at the dilemma that Ziki's mission presented him. Kissinger and Nixon's primary focus of energy was the Soviets, and access to their cold war enemies' state of the art MiG 21 fighter jet was tantamount. Osirak and the nukes there should have worried them more.

However, Israeli possession of the MiG meant an advantage for Ziki's country against its Arab neighbors, since the Israelis would figure out better uses of the technology than their adversaries had and more important—combat countermeasures.

Now, because of Gavriella, Ziki found himself in the same dilemma that Kissinger did. He would have to make a deal that left a bad taste in order to serve what he believed to be the greater good. But with the MiG—with nothing to lose, Ziki would share it with the Americans any way, deal or no deal.

"Secretary Kissinger can offer me Turkish landing fields and refueling?"

"It depends on what you can offer Secretary Kissinger."

"I suppose he would want access to the technology."

"And probably immediately."

"I don't think we're going to allow your government to have first glance before handing it over."

"The Turks, if they have any sense, are also going to insist on seeing the technology. Why does that matter to you? The Americans have airfields in Turkey. That is probably what the Americans are going to trade with the Turks to make your mission happen."

"Then it seems like I must deal directly with Secretary Kissinger, Gavriella."

"That is not possible." Her shadow moved towards the curtain. He had finally caught her off balance.

"Then we are to have no deal." He cut the shower off for effect. It was clear she was not going anywhere until she had achieved her goals. Besides, his fingers were beginning to prune.

He pulled the curtain back with an abrupt jerk. He was face to face with her. Reaching out in front of her, Ziki snapped up a towel from one of the racks.

"Ziki, you insist on a face to face meeting with Secretary Kissinger?"

"Have you met with Secretary Kissinger?" He was beginning to towel off his backside. His casual mannerisms were a ruse to keep her off balance. He had to. If she insisted that the meeting would not take place, he would have no other options than to work through his government.

"Yes, but—"

"But nothing, Gavriella. It should not be that hard to set up."

"You risk being cut out of the loop of your own mission."

She had made an error with the suggestion that Ziki might be removed from his mission. He went on the attack, "Do not threaten me again."

"Ziki, I was not threatening you—"

He dried his chest while maintaining eye contact with her, "Yes you were. It is bad enough…" he paused. "I might suspect that you are working with people who would be content with our removal—no, my removal from the map."

"That is not true." She seemed genuinely hurt. Then again, when had she ever faked anything that had not seemed genuine?

He moved the towel rapidly against his scalp playing the tension between them nonchalantly. "I have heard both Kissinger and Nixon on tape, and I will not waste my time discussing their merits. I am not sure how I feel about having slept with someone who has been in bed with Kissinger, even if only in a political manner. But I do not have to endure threats."

Nearly dry, he stepped into her space. His sunburned body leaned in, "You want access to the technology that I have. You will offer safe passage for the technology into Turkey through your friends. For this passage I will share the technology with the Americans who in turn can share it with whomever they want. But this bargain cannot be struck unless I am able to look Secretary Kissinger in the eyes and make the deal with him. Besides, your people need to know more about Osirak, and frankly you are not to be trusted right now after your stunt at Khan Yunis… So it's Kissinger or nothing."

They stood there a moment. Ziki knew Gavriella was sizing up the seriousness of his demand. Before she could answer, she stiffened. What had she noticed?

The volume of the television set had increased. Ziki signaled Gavriella with his hand to continue speaking as if they hadn't noticed anything.

"Do you have the time to go to Washington and return before your plans are in motion?"

The two of them slowly stepped into the bathtub as Ziki continued. "My plans are already in motion. As you have said, my ability to move back and forth out of Baghdad is not in question. I would be back in enough time to make sure the plane touches down in Turkish territory." He had grabbed the pole of the towel wrack in the shower and had pulled it out of the wall. He placed Gavriella behind him and eased her down into a crouched position.

"I would need at least a day to make this happen. It would then be at least one day's journey followed by one day's meeting. Then for the trip back we are talking about over half a week before you return to Baghdad."

He had noticed through the slight crack in the door a maid's cart. Could it possibly be just a maid? Hardly likely, unless it was a blind maid who ignored the "do not disturb" sign.

"Then we must make it happen." A shadow fell across the cart as the door began to slowly open.

The first bullet exploded the toilet seat.

Porcelain flew into the shower. Ziki felt a fragment strike his cheek bone as the door was kicked in.

Three quick pops of the distinctive sound a silencer makes. The first two struck the wall over the shower head. The final shot blew the shower head itself clear off the wall. It turned the bathroom into a lake with a geyser.

Ziki leapt from the tub while swinging the bar in one motion. He was not sure what he struck other than it made a groan. The hardware that the assailant was carrying was professional; the practitioner was not. Ziki lifted his arm to strike again and struck the shower curtain rod behind him. The force of the impact knocked the bar from his hand.

"Ziki! Ziki! The gun! The gun!"

Gavriella was leaning out of the tub attempting to reach the Walter PPK pistol. PPK—silencer? That was British intelligence, but this could not have not been English… He did not have time to figure out the nature of his attacker. His blow to the assassin's face had broken his nose. His nose? Ziki could not be too sure; since the attacker who fled was dressed in a now blood covered hotel aid's outfit.

Ziki scooped the gun and ran to the door. He spun through the doorway and managed to pull off three more shots at his assailant before the stairwell door at the end of the hall closed shut. There was blood on the sill, but it was impossible to tell whether it was the result of the towel bar or the bullets.

Either way, Ziki was now going to insist on meeting the American .

## Chapter 29

### The American Secretary

**Kissinger removed his glasses and rubbed his eyes.** Ziki had always heard Kissinger described as a thick presence. Thick hair, thick glasses, thick accent.

It only took a few moments of conversation to slightly, but crucially, change that assessment. Thick suggested plodding. That was far off the mark. Instead, Ziki, who stood next to Gavriella in the Secretary's office, was impressed less with a sense of thickness and more with Kissinger's density, his gravitas. Any slowness of the Secretary's part was less a matter of plodding and more a case of being methodical. Every motion, every utterance was deliberate and considered. Ziki felt himself in front of the Bobby Fisher of international relations.

"Has someone looked at your face, Mr. Ziki?"

Gavriella was quick to pipe in. "Of course not, Mr. Secretary. He wanted to get here as soon as possible."

"You may want to consider having your injury looked at Bethesda Naval Hospital. I could have that arranged."

Kissinger's feigned concerned did not warm his original assessment of the Secretary. It only put Ziki further on guard.

Kissinger put his glasses back on and thumbed through the dossier on his desk. He moved quickly through the pages in the folder and occasionally uttered a portentous sound as if to suggest something had caught his interest. It was obvious that he had read the document and his movement through it was more performance rather than a quick study. His positioning of the document on the edge of his desk convinced Ziki it was an intimidation tactic. After all, the dossier on Kissinger's desk was Ziki's, or so Kissinger thought, everyone at Mossad had a duplicate dossier one sometimes made available for convenience to allies or foes depending on the circumstances. He could never see the real files that were contained at Mossad's archives. Nice double message Ziki thought let me see that they know who I am and let them think that they have access to my dossier.

Even the secretary's smile seemed a plan, "Ziki, may I call you Ziki Commander?" He did not wait for an answer. It is odd that a man of your reputation is not more a part of the corridors of power. You dossier would suggest that you are further up the chain of command, then again, you are very young." Obviously this

European, now American Jew did not understand the rougher leather neck Israelis. "It is a choice. " He could not quite glean Kissinger's motivations. Was he genuinely curious as to Ziki. As the file the Americans had showed or was he prepping Ziki for what? Or was he just measuring who could piss further?

Was this how they played Gavriella? After all she had been ambitious, hadn't she?

"A choice?" Ziki was not going to give the secretary anything. The closer Ziki played it to the vest, he hoped, the easier it would be to see the secretary's motivations.

Graviella's voice came out nervously, she spoke out in a giggle, "Ziki's skills would be wasted behind a desk. Or in an executive meeting." She was obviously swaying in tentativeness. Ziki wondered if she was worried as to what he might say in the presence of the Secretary.

Ziki spoke to Kissinger as if he was the one who had made Gravriella's comment, "I like what I do." He could feel his former lover's energy slump when she became aware he did not consider her part of the conversation.

Kissinger acknowledged Gavriella's comment in such a way as to make her feel part of the negotiation, and he then turned back to Ziki, "feel as if you have more to offer your country in such a service?"

*Why the small talk? He thinks he knows all there is to know about me. Maybe he is one those men who feels he has to get a personal sense. I think he's just curious about real Israelis. Naah, there's more to this than the MiG. I'm sure Osirak is in the backdrop.* Ziki resolved to give him nothing he did not already have, *just play along, and see where it goes.* "Maybe so."

Ziki could see Kissinger was looking at a particularly heinous job that he had worked on, and used it to continue his line of thought, "Still, your work in the field suggests an exceptional mind that could do even more valuable work directing numerous operations simultaneously. So, you are or not where a man of your skills should be?" How this Kissinger relished talking in carefully constructed riddles.

Ziki brought him back to the point. "I am here."

"And yet you are negotiating with the American Secretary of State." He did not resent Kissinger putting him in place. "So, I guess you are where you should be."

Ziki could not stop from smiling at the word game Kissinger was playing with him, and played back, "As we both are, Mr. Secretary."

"You must tell me how you like this end of the job once we have finished our business. Perhaps as you get older you will take more of liking to it. We would like closer ties with you." Did Kissinger have something particular in mind that Ziki might take more of a liking to?

If that was the case, Ziki let him know how much he relished the idea of working with him: "I can tell you right now how—I like it."

Kissinger obviously saw Ziki's comment as a scored point rather than a personal insult and slid nicely into his next transition, "Your friend here tells me that you believe me to be an antagonist to your country."

Gavriella stared nervously at Ziki. She seemed more ill at ease than she had in the bathroom of the Baghdad hotel.

Ziki reminded himself that Gavriella was not the issue; Kissinger's deal for the MiG and Osirak was and whatever else he had in mind. "I can only believe what I see and hear, Mr. Secretary."

"And what is that, Mr. Ziki?"

"A willingness to trade us for oil. A willingness to sell out your only ally in the region if it means a momentary strategic advantage over the Soviets."

Kissinger dispassionately nodded and in his clipped Austrian shot back, "Now I know why it is you are not behind a desk."

"And why is that?"

"A lack of diplomacy."

"If your diplomacy doesn't include Israel on the map, I am not interested in it, 'Mr. Henry.'"

Kissinger scoffed but gave another look at the Henry comment. "Your country takes everything so personally, as do you, Commander. Of course, the big picture includes your country. Why would we want to rid the region of a democracy? Information flows more easily in your state. It is also easier to get our people out of the Middle East through such a place... You must get past your dislike of me, Commander, and begin to see the larger geopolitical map if we are to help each other."

"And you, Mr. Secretary, should try getting out of your office and work in the field a few times; it might give you a new perspective, or is that too dangerous?"

"Immediacy?"

"Something all who work in the field have. Must have if they are to survive: the ability to see the next move."

"And why is that so important?"

It was hard to read Kissinger. It seemed more than a game to him, but at the same time, it seemed too inhuman. "Because the next move might mean death, Mr. Secretary."

"Very true. From sources other than the misleading file that Mossad let us steal I hear that you, Ziki, are a player."

"Don't forget who makes the first move, Mr. Kissinger."

"And you are a player, correct?"

"Mr. Secretary, I've had no sleep in the last 36 hours; I am tired and I have things to take care of, let's cut the bullshit please... What do you want—Sir?"

"How is that?" Kissinger kept calm.

Gavriella blurted out. "You're still thinking about the assassin at the hotel."

Of course I am, Gavriella, Ziki thought, we both are. I like knowing who tried to kill me and if it had anything to do with this office."

Instead of sharing his thoughts, Ziki merely cut her off. "Thank you, Gavriella."

Kissinger pursed his lips. It was the only time he was curt in the conversation, "She is correct. You have been distracted, not focused on the task at hand, which is arranging for the escape of the technology; because you are still trying to figure out who it was that tried to assassinate you both."

"Who says they were trying to kill us both?" He actually had not thought of the possibility of two birds with one stone until this very moment. He had played out all the possible reasons for the assassinations of both Gavriella and himself but not who might want them both dead in the same mission.

"You cannot honestly believe that they weren't?" It was obvious that it was the only option Kissinger had considered. He seemed very sure.

"It could have been meant only for one of us."

"And which one would you suppose it was?"

"If I knew that, I might be more interested in this conversation."

This comment was met with a dismissive wave from Kissinger. "You must move past it. We have important subjects to discuss."

"That assassin is important: what does he or she know about this mission, and more important who informed them? Did it come from here? You Americans need to tighten up, you leak like a sieve. I'm able to shake off the thought that someone is trying to kill me, there's always someone. Whoever that is, is still at large."

"Will you allow me to speculate?"

"Speculate or confirm, Mr. Secretary?"

"I can promise you that it is not confirmation. Our agents had nothing to do with what happened in that Baghdad hotel room. If they had, there would be no meeting now. They are still checking into it, but I have a distinct idea as to what has happened."

"Then speculate."

"With this condition, you accept my speculation, for the time, as the truth and allow our conversation to focus on the big picture, as I believe that your country's existence is more impacted by our mutual interest in MiG flight technology and the Osirak nuclear reactor project than a botched KGB assassination contract. It also might have something to do with your dealings with that rebel Soviet General Zhukov."

Ziki was silent; Kissinger's mention of Osirak and Zhukov took him off guard for a moment... Damn, where are these leaks coming from?

"It was the KGB?"

"What sort of gun was used for the contract?"

"A Silverballer Walter PPK."

"And who uses those, Mr. Ziki?"

"Why would the British be trying to kill us?"

"Wrong question. Right question: why would an assassin be carrying the weapon of a British agent?"

"Because he had killed a British agent to get it."

"Exactly. Which means that you were being tailed by an MI6."

"How did you come to that conclusion?"

"I didn't. It came to me. Our friends in Britain had been tailing you."

"And they informed you of this?"

"Yes. They had to when they informed us of his disappearance and asked for our help. It is here that I must speculate. I can only assume, the KGB has become aware of your efforts to acquire their technology and let's hope not Osirak."

"I don't know anything about that place, what did you call it?"

"Osirak."

"How is that possible?" This sent a chill into Ziki. What Secretary Kissinger said immediately confirmed Ziki's fears.

"Someone in those corridors of power has made them aware."

"And why would the  KGB kill the MI6 agent?"

"Perhaps, Commander, because he had become aware of who it was in your own government that had tipped them off to your mission. If that is why he was eliminated, then it is really quite elegant, when you think about it. Let's go through this slowly." Ziki laughed when he thought about Kissinger taking anything quickly.

He built his scenario from the ground up. His pleasure with his story grew in its momentum. "A British agent is tailing you. Possibly to intercept any MiG 21, or more likely your interest in the Osirak project and the Egyptian deal in the Sahara that Zhukov is sniffing at, or other information you may have acquired… Who knows, maybe those nuclear-tipped Jerichos you've got?"

"It seems you are a busy man, Commander." He paused again… "The KGB, who is already aware of your efforts, becomes aware. The British agent is eliminated. With his elimination is the elimination of the knowledge of the mole within your government's agency. His weapon will then be used to execute you. And the gun will be left with your corpse to indict the MI6 which in actuality indicts my government."

"Ahh… this is why this whole twisted conversation is taking place."

Gavriella thought aloud, "Because after all, anything the English are doing must be backed by the United States."

"Quite elegant. Elegant except in the way your execution was botched. One can only assume that they didn't send their best man. Puzzling because they should have known they were dealing with you." Kissinger seemed genuinely pleased with his little story. He sat back in his chair and placed his hands together, "And here you are, Mr. Ziki."

"Here I am Mr. Secretary. "

"Good. Then we can move above the clouds to look at the big picture. "

"There are some things I think you know that you left out. The British agent was part of a joint operation, was he not?"

"I don't know what you mean."

"Even if you don't, for the sake of plausible deniability, than I am sure Ms. Gavriella does."

More giggles from Gavriella. "Ziki, what are you talking about?"

"I am talking about a joint op. How did the British find out what I am up to? You told them.  Gavriella was the public face and this MI6 op did the tailing. You hoped that my field work would give you a way to sneak the MiG out on your own without my help. Gavriella was a distraction while he looked for a way that could cut us out."

"My nation has a history in dealing with big thinkers. "So, you will forgive me, Mr. Secretary, if I fail to see the big picture or trust that there is a place for my people in whatever big thoughts that you have."

"Everyone who dreams of world stability, Commander, does not necessarily set sites on the elimination of Israel from the earth."

"When that organization arrives, Mr. Secretary, let me know."

"It is in this very office. And I find your comments offensive."

"Do you?"

Ziki suddenly was aware of what Malkielly meant when he referred to the American power as the '*jaws the jackal*.' He realized he had best come to the business at hand. " Back to simple things, Mr. Secretary. You understand what it is I need from you?"

"Airspace in which to move the technology and keep the Ruskies calm when you do whatever it is you plan to do with  Osirak. And What about those nuclear tipped Jericho's, Commander?"

"All I need for now is Turkish airspace—are you willing to provide it?"

"Your flight will be escorted by two Turkish planes."

"Unacceptable."

"The problem?"

"I do not trust the Turks. It must be American planes."

"Why don't we split the difference? The insignia on the planes does not matter, does it?"

Ziki understood the compromise immediately. "American pilots in Turkish planes?" It was acceptable before Kissinger explained.

"They're just American planes with Turkish insignia. That way you feel secure and there is no apparent American involvement. It prevents an international incident."

"Do you think your president will approve of this?"

"He just did. Now, the least of your problems have been solved."

"The least?"

"Once the plane is in the air, there is no one in the region who can compete with the skills of any of the pilots who will be executing the mission. You've a great deal more to worry about on the ground. You need to finalize your finances and figure out a way to get the bird in the air. "

"Have you read my file, Mr. Kissinger?"

"Of course."

"Then you know I will put the bird in the air."

"I have no doubts. Thank you, Commander."

"For what?"

"Most of my dealings are so concerned with the big picture that I rarely get the enjoyment of such minutae."

Ziki did not feel that comment merited a response. He moved to leave the office. As he approached the door, Ziki heard Kissinger clear his throat, "However, you do realize the problems you will have in getting the MiG in the air are now secondary."

"Secondary to what?"

"Someone in Mossad or close to the Mossad is not what he seems to be, and we hear rumors about your behind-the-curtains dealings with General Gheorghy Zhukov without the Kremlin's knowledge; those are dangerous waters, Commander.

"By the way, I want to personally thank you for fishing our Major Jimmy-Ray Sinclair out of the Duma Jail in Syria"

"Major?  I thought he was Colonel Sinclair."

"He got promoted to Colonel because of his connection with you, Commander."

"I didn't know your office paid this much attention to me and my doings. I'll have to be more careful."

A wry smile spread on Kissinger's face… "Ahh, yes, you are a busy boy, Commander Barak."

He began counting on his fingers…. "A Soviet MiG, The Osirak nuclear plant in Iraq…The Russian General Zhukov, thermo nuclear tipped Jericho missiles? Shall I go on, Ziki?" Without waiting for a reply he continued as Ziki's face contorted ever so slightly.

"By the way did you get that El Fatah terrorist, what's his name…Salameh and his cohorts?"

"Not yet." Ziki gritted his teeth. "I had him at Khan Yunis but for some interference…" He turned and gave a frozen look in Gavriella's direction.

"Where was I?  Ahh yes, General Zhukov and the Egyptian biological plant in the Sahara, and I must not forget the preemptive assassination teams in Zurich and East Germany, Halle and Jena…Am I leaving anything out, Commander?"

"And I hear of great ambitions in Africa, especially Kenya, Nigeria with their oil and last but not least South Africa with those real rich Uranium mines."

"I have no idea what you are talking about, Mr. Secretary."

"You need not worry all this stays in this office. You seem surprised Ziki, but you need not worry. We are allies Ziki my friend and we will assist you with all these things. You can trust me. And the MiG from Iraq, consider our help in Turkish air space a done thing. You just go get the damn thing and let us have a little peek."

"Hmm… They shook hands and locked eyes. "Goodbye for now Commander Ziki…"

"Goodbye Mr. Secretary."

# Chapter 30

**Hadasah hospital, Henny**

**"The field of medical equipment is a little more dangerous than you led me to believe."**

It was Henny Wagenhoysen that Ziki wanted to see when he returned to Tel- Aviv—a breath of fresh air. He'd gone to Hadasah, her hospital the moment he could.

It wasn't as if he didn't have reasons. The cut on his temple hadn't healed. A touch, a pat on the head—hell, a swift wrinkle of the eyebrow—and it would open up again.

She gently touched the healing cut on the side of his face. He felt sad that he did trust her bedside manner but was analyzing her actions as he had analyzed the actions of strangers.

"And you're all cut up, too. You look like you got shelled."

"By a toilet bowl. How long have I been out?"

Ziki struggled to sit up in his hospital bed, only to be engulfed in a rising tide of nausea. Henny quickly moved to restrain him.

"Don't move! You could have done yourself some real damage, you know, letting a concussion go like that."

He smiled wryly.

"Lucky I have you to take care of me."

"Just returning a favor. If it weren't for you, I'd be seeing the sights as a hood ornament on that car."

"So that's why you've taken me in? To return a favor?"

Henny grinned.

"That, and my strict sense of professional ethics."

"Oh, of course. Speaking of professional ethics…"

"Yes?"

"You do look good in that uniform."

She smoothed down the front of her starched white blouse and giggled girlishly; turning so he could get a full view of her body and the backs of her long, well-tanned thighs.

"You like it? All the nurses are wearing them."

Ziki strained not to ogle her. "Not as well as you are."

"Thank you. And what about medical equipment secret agents? What are they wearing these days? Besides bandages, of course."

"It's a very relaxed work environment. No uniform required."

She smiled at his joke, but it did not reach her blue eyes, which were narrowed with concern. "It's a very dangerous one too, it would seem. What were you doing when you got these injuries? Selling tongue depressors to foreign powers?"

"I was doing some home repair, actually."

"Really? In your backyard minefield?"

"No, I was," Ziki hesitated momentarily, thinking back to the events in the Baghdad Hotel. Briefly, he remembered the feel of Gavriella's smooth skin beneath his fingers, and shook his head, instantly regretting both the memory and the surge of pain the sudden movement caused. "I was remodeling the bathroom."

"Ah. The most dangerous room in the house, they say."

"Do they say that? I hadn't heard it before." They don't know the half of it, he thought, his mind reeling back to the hail of bullets that sent porcelain shards flying through the still air like knives. And for the sake of women like this one, I hope they never do. He noticed her still-narrowed eyes.

"You don't believe me, do you?"

She sighed.

"I believe whatever happened, happened in the bathroom. You've managed to stick close enough to the truth to make it impossible to tell where your stories begin. But you forget the sights I've seen, Ziki. It's not only soldiers and assassins that are wounded in wars, it's children too. Some of the little ones who come in here…they're shell-shocked, Ziki, they've seen sights I can't even imagine. Things I've never even dreamed of seeing. They have scars sometimes… Scars like ones you're going to have." Ziki noticed she was still competently doing her job all throughout this conversation. It was almost a pattern: professional behavior, coupled with conversation, and finished off with a moment of affectionate concern. *Damn it, Ziki he told himself, stop reading everybody.*

But no sooner than he had chided himself then she followed the pattern right on schedule. Once again, she ran her cool hand caressingly over his face.

"I don't know what's happened to you, and it frightens me. I'm scared of where you've been."

He caught her small hand in his, and pressed it reassuringly. "There's nothing about me that should frighten you, Henny. I'm really a very ordinary man."

She pulled her hand and wrung it against her chest.

"Everything is so violent here, Ziki. So very different from Holand. Strange men, like you, coming in from the desert with faraway eyes and wounds they won't explain. Sometimes, I miss Holland… I miss my simple life."

"Nothing is ever simple, Henny. Even in your Holland, men were doing things they could not explain, things that kept you and your family safe from harm."

He smiled ruefully. This was hardly the romantic reunion he had daydreamed about. It could still be saved, though. Ignoring her gasp of disapproval and the rushing wave of vertigo, he sat up in bed and pulled Henny towards him by her nervously clasping hands.

"But enough of this. It's been too long since I've seen you smile, Dutch girl. Did you get the roses I sent you?" It seemed strange even to mention the roses, since it was the only thing approaching normal he'd done in the last few days. It played in his head like someone else had done it.

Ziki got the smile he wanted as her face lit up. It suddenly made the purchase of the flowers seem like something he was responsible for.

"Oh yes! They were lovely. But you shouldn't have!" and she said it such a way as if to let him know that he should have.

"Really? And why not? What better way is there to spend a man of mystery's salary than roses for beautiful women?"

She struggled to keep her face composed, but a smile kept playing with the corners of her mouth. Throughout it all she continued her physical check of his well being.

"There you go again. Using that word."

"What word?"

"'Beautiful.' Never, Ziki-Medical-Equipment-Secret-Agent, have I had a man tell me how beautiful I was as many times in one meeting as you have today. It must be your concussion that's making you act this way."

He grinned.

"I'm sure that's it. It couldn't actually be how beautiful you are."

Just as she had at the restaurant in Jerusalem, Henny blushed bright red. "Stop that. I can't have my patients seeing me like this."

"Well, I can think of a way to fix that."

She twirled a lock of hair about one well-manicured finger and cocked her head to one side.

"And what would that be?"

"Let me up out of this hospital bed and I'll take you out to dinner. No one but tourists and waiters to see your blushes."

"No."

"No?"

Ziki was shocked. He had been so certain Henny liked him, so certain that she was as interested in him as he was in her. He wondered if she sensed that he was only using her to get the real heart throb, Gavriella out of his head… Had she just been leading him on?

"No, because you need to spend at least another day here in the hospital for observation. Concussions don't just go away by wishing, you know."

Carefully checking to see if anyone was passing by the open door, she leaned over and pressed her soft, full lips against Ziki's cheek, sending a rush of warm happiness over his tired body.

"After that, though, I'm up for just about anything. Now, get some sleep."

"Okay, I'll stay overnight until morning, but I have to leave first thing."

Looking back over her shoulder to wink at him, Henny sashayed from the room, leaving Ziki alone with the darkness and his thoughts, which were no longer as dark as they had been before. Perhaps I'll enjoy this mission after all, he thought, and resolved to dream of Henny's lips against his skin instead of the blood and bullets that had haunted his sleep since the loss of his men at Khan Yunis.

# Chapter 31

### Hoshel - UBS

Ziki removed his pack of cigarettes and slid them across the table to Hoshel. The haughtiness of the man across the table had been replaced by the nervous shaking of a hand wrestling to light the cigarette pursed in his lips.

The waiter brought the tea and baklava. It was obvious stress had passed between the two men at the table. But the waiter, as all waiters in this part of the world, pretended not to notice any change in the relation of the table.

Ziki paid the waiter to prevent Hoshel from reaching for anything.

"Sip your tea while I think this through, Hoshel."

The cigarette smoke poured out of Hoshel's mouth and blew the steam away from the glass mug he tried to bring to his dry lips. He worked his tongue against his lips to separate them from the dryness caused by panic and fear.

*Let me play with him a bit here. . .*Ziki curled his lips into a smile. "You might want to squeeze your lemon or I will think that you lie not only to me but also to this waiter who has done nothing but serve you your tea."

The lemon squirted across the table and sent its pulp onto Ziki's shirt. Hoshel's eyes went wide with fear.

"If I did not kill you for what you've done, I am not going to end your life for a little lemon juice, but be careful with your answers: the wrong one and I might kill you."

The clink of the spoon on the inside of the glass seemed to focus Ziki's thoughts. He smiled. He understood.

"You are not working for the KGB, are you?"

"No."

"But they think you are."

"Yes."

"And you are not so much betraying a country but enriching yourself?"

" Yes. Precisely."

Now Ziki decided to take a calculated risk. Get him at ease and this might not cost anything.

"Tell me, Hoshel. You helped the KGB figure out who my contact was on both issues?"

"Correct."

"And gave them my location at the hotel."

"No… No, no, no. You must not believe that. It was not I. You gave them your location."

"I am not that sloppy."

"Your contact is. They followed him to you."

"I would've seen them. I would have been aware of their presence at the hotel."

"Your contact was not just followed once. It wasn't just one time, Ziki. They followed him often. It was only after a time—"

Ziki shook his head with a sudden dawning of thought. "That they began to notice my presence was repeating itself."

"And don't forget that you spent time with the American woman—Gavriella Ramon. Your casualness was less in your movements than in your associations."

'I am looking at one example in particular. Do they know why I am here?"

"They will if they interrogate your contact."

"They haven't interrogated him yet?"

"They don't know we have him yet."

He had to hand it to Hoshel, the little man had played this well.

Ziki would now see if he could break his streak of perfection. *Get him at ease, Ziki, and you can end this in the café...* "They don't know? So, you have him in a safe location?"

"Yes."

"And your partner is better at kidnapping than the contract to kill me?"

"I am better at it."

"Be careful with your answers. How did you do it?"

"I told your man that there had been a problem and that you needed to see him."

"Did the KGB ask you about me?"

"Yes."

"And what did you tell them?"

"Nothing, except that it would be a mistake to send only one man against you. Except someone expendable." Ziki Ignored the back sided compliment.

"Who is now my partner."

"How did you manage to turn him?"

"He thought he had turned me. He had been working on me for sometime. I did not know how I was going to turn him to my advantage. That is where you provided the help. Your were quick enough to prevent him from killing you—"

"But not quick enough to kill him?" Ziki nodded as he tallied his thoughts. "I have a feeling if you had not had to deal with Gavriella, you would have made short work of him. But that is incidental. Once you both missed each other, I was able to put my plan into effect. After the disaster that almost befell him in his ham-handed attempt at your removal, it was quite easy to turn him against the KGB operatives that put him up to it. They did nothing to make it clear the level of threat they were putting him against. It was very easy to turn him against them. Revenge and a pay-off was his big plan." Hoshel was growing with pride. He seemed actually proud of what he did.

Ziki pushed him for further explanation. Ziki rubbed his mouth thoughtfully. "But you had bigger plans."

"Actually, smaller plans. I am not interested in the balance of power. I think the balance of power takes care of itself, don't you? There will always be people like yourself who will take care of the balance on our—your side—and people on their side who will make sure that you merely maintain the balance rather than tip it. It all seems futile to me. It has seemed futile for quite sometime."

There was no disillusionment in Hoshel's voice. It did not seem a decision he had reached in any sense of sadness or regret. It was all just practical. This world was simply too much for him to handle. It was time for a new career.

Hoshel sipped his tea as if he just moved some money into a new account.

In a way, Ziki thought, he actually had.

"You know, if enough people thought as you did, our enemies would drive us into the sea."

"Ziki, there will always be believers."

"So, Hoshel, you thought you would just get out?"

"Get out and go where I would never be found."

"Being found is easy. You just hoped that no one would come looking."

"Hence the fact that no one is dead. Or will die."

"Except your partner. And the reasonable price?"

Hoshel was gaining his confidence back. The banker squared his shoulders ever so slightly and continued, "Precisely. You'll have your contact back. You'll eliminate the fool who tried to assassinate you. And the KGB will once again be at loose ends."

"Just because you might avoid the Mossad's wrath doesn't mean the KGB won't come looking for its pound of flesh."

"They always do when it comes to our kind. That's where you are going to help me."

"I am?"

"You're going to kill me." There was a quelling in his eyes that was beginning to annoy Ziki.

"I am to both pay you for your efforts and make arrangements to manufacture the illusion of your death. I believe that can be arranged. But why create illusion when the reality can be achieved much easier."

Hoshel stared up from his tea… Alarmed.

Good. Put him off. He's back to quivering. I still might be able to do this the easy way.

Having kept Hoshel dangling long enough, Ziki slipped him deftly off the hook, "For God's sake man?"

Hoshel nervously laughed.

His hands were lily white.

Ziki continued to reassure him. "Your demands are not exorbitant and you actually would be helping me send a message to those who moved against us."

"How so?"

"Both your partner's elimination and your manufactured death will tell the Russians that I am not to be fucked with—not today, anyway."

"Ziki, I don't believe they have ever perceived you that way."

"You are probably right, but it never hurts to make a statement."

"Unless one is part of that statement."

Ziki shared Hoshel's laugh. Okay, now try. " Now be precise, where would I be making this statement on your partner?"

"It is not to far from here, it is only—"

Hoshel cut short.

Panic.

His eyes scrambled across the words he had just uttered to make sure that he had not given away the location. He realized he had not and his eyes went from panic to relief to anger in the blink of the realization.

Damn. Now I will have to pay him. And probably more.

"Ziki, you will give me one hundred thousand dollars."

"It is a small price to pay for the prize."

"You tried to cost me my life."

"I tried to enrich myself. It is not the same. We will meet here tomorrow. You will have a briefcase with nothing but folders detailing frivolous matters. Three folders. There will be numbers written on each folder. On the middle folder will be the location to a locker. In that locker will be my money. On the third folder will be that locker's combination written backwards."

"And on the first folder?"

"Nothing. I just like the power of three."

The waiter had come alongside to ask if Hoshel wanted more tea. Hoshel raised his glass to hand it to the man.

The glass evaporated in a puff of red dust.

The waiter began to drop slowly to his knees.

His chest was a spreading crimson.

Ziki felt the slight slivers of glass near the corners of his eyes. He made eye contact with a stricken Hoshel who seemed to know what was coming next.

Ziki reached under the round table, flipped it, and had it airborne just as Hoshel's head for all intents and purposes exploded. He landed on his knees hard, the table coming down with him. He ducked behind the thick wood, drew his legs in tight.

The headless corpse slipped off its seat, falling heavily next to the body that only a moment earlier was pouring tea.

Ziki removed his pistol from his hip, took a deep breath, and brought it above the table he had converted into a shield.

Nothing. No one.

Broken glass.

Scattered trash.

The sidewalk was empty.

But he saw a car squealing away from the restaurant just as the realization of what had happened hit the café like an airplane suddenly depressurized.

There were screams from the kitchen, a flood of heated Arabic, the sound of broken dishes.

Pursue the car or search Hoshel's body? There was only a moment to decide. Would Hoshel be that foolish? Would he have any information on his person to lead me to…?

No.

Ziki was on his feet and running toward the street…

# Chapter 32

## ASSASSINS

**I'm looking for a Hugo?**

Of course, an Eastern European piece of junk for a couple of Eastern European assassins.

After figuring out what the car he was tailing was, two thoughts occurred to Ziki as he jimmied the lock to the BMW in front of the café... First, they had never intended to kill Ziki, but Hoshel had almost given him to the KGB assassins.

The efficiency of their work was that of the KGB, a double bonus. They had eliminated the man who stood in the way of their preventing the loss of the MiG and the dark work deep underground in the Iraqi nuclear plant, almost killed the man who stood to steal the MiG. The only way the KGB could have gotten that close to Ziki was if someone had led them there, again.

Unintentionally, because an intentional tail would have been detected... No, Ziki's discovery had to have been Hoshel's sloppiness. He could imagine the delight at seeing Ziki there with their prey, followed by their disappointment when they failed to kill them both.

The car was having trouble turning over. It chugged and wheezed. A sputter.

"Damn!"

Ziki could only imagine what sort of engine was underneath the shell he was trying to start. Whatever it was... it was not a BMW but a clone... Goddamn Third World. The engine came to life just as Ziki heard the shouts of a voice he believed belonged to the rightful owner.

The second thought occurred only a split second after the first and was what prompted Ziki to steal this car that he was now screeching into traffic: the KGB would never have tried to kill Hoshel if they did not know the whereabouts of Joseph. . .

Ziki could only hope that the hit men were also the same people who were going to retrieve Joseph. If they were, this car chase would lead him to the whereabouts of his missing contact or at least prevent them from picking Joseph up. If they were not, then he would have to run them off the road and get any information he could out of them.

Great. Just fucking great...

They are probably part of a larger team and have no idea of where Joseph is. But let's say I'm not on a wild goose chase after two dangerous men. Let's say they do know where he is. I'm not chasing some hack job amateurs—no, these two could probably place in the Indianapolis 500—and even if I do catch them, they're trained to withstand interrogation, that means that I can hope there is information in their car that will lead me to Joseph.

And if Hoshel was smart enough not to have that information on him——fuck, fuck, fuck!

The rage is what caused the other car to slam into his. It was all he could do to stay behind the wheel. From the corner of his eye he saw the car that had struck him careening into a fish stand. The collision had happened simultaneously with Ziki spotting the car of his prey.

The Hugo accelerated.

Damn, a supped-up Yugo! Well, now they know I'm here.

Okay, here's hoping the car has distinctive plates. Lots of Yugos on the streets.

No plates! Great—did you really think there would be? Okay, okay. Memorize features. Pick something on the car that makes it stand out. All right, I have it. There is a big distinctive crack in the rear window. It moves across from the bottom right hand corner into the middle of the window. It looks like the lifeline of a palm.

He had also noticed there were three men in the car. That did not make sense. What would be the use of a third? They only had one target; so, more than one gun would not be necessary. It was not a long-range shot; so, there was no need for a sniper.

Possibly, someone to communicate with a home base once the job was done?

No, that would be easy enough for the driver…

Never mind that Ziki, two or three, what does it matter? Focus on the crack in the back windshield.

Only one strategy seemed to make sense. He would have to give chase and then let them somehow believe that they had lost him. Once they believed him off their tail, Ziki would then pick up the scent and follow them back to wherever their rendezvous point was and hope he would discover Joseph's location, that was the strategy—but he'd play it as it came.

The wreck had obviously tipped the Hugo off to the fact it was being tailed. The third man was no longer in view.

Had he slipped down away from the window.

The crack of three bullets into Ziki's windshield confirmed the thought that had begun to form in his head before the bullets made it difficult to see. He may not have liked German cars, but they made a hell of a car exterior. It had saved him.

The placement of the shots was perfect.

That's right, Ziki, if they had been aiming for you in the café, you would be dead now.

You may be dead yet.

The window had not shattered…Not bulletproof glass—or maybe it is; third world countries! Not bad…

He punched the accelerator and swerved past the cars that were quickly making it easier to close in on his prey—able to see the front seat shooter holding down the man in the backseat and shouting at him while trying to take aim at Ziki.

He thought that was odd as he slammed into the rear of the Hugo. The small car fishtailed, but quickly regained its bearings and swung around a corner into another street of dense traffic.

Ziki would not blow the horn or swerve his way in and out until the clueless drivers understood what was going on. In a moment, he was on the sidewalk where he found the pedestrians without the benefit of a car to shield them got the idea to move more rapidly than their driving counterparts. Bags and produce flew into the air but no bystanders, as of yet, had gone airborne.

Thank God, law enforcement in a police state like Iraq was so bad. Instead, the response to this was large groups of shouting people who were either cursing and gesticulating this game's two participants or enjoying the spectacle.

Ziki caught sight of the cracked windshield as he flew by a gang of young boys who decided to hurl rocks at his car. What is it with kids and rocks in the country? He felt the thuds against his door as he moved his car onto the road and directly behind the pursued. The front seat shooter was holding his pistol towards the head of the man who was in the back seat.

Now, why would he be doing that—? It was at that moment that Ziki understood why the Russians had a trio in the car.

…The third one was Joseph.

Ziki, you are the luckiest son of bitch in the world. The British Secret Service were the most polite; the CIA were the least emotional, or at least liked to appear that way; but the KGB, The KGB, they prided themselves on being ruthless monsters who loved to teach people lessons. They wanted to teach Joseph a lesson; they wanted to show him what happens to people who cross their path; they wanted Joseph to fill his pants so that he might tell them how he planned to get the MiG out.

They didn't need to do it; Joseph would have told them in a heartbeat. No, they just liked being vicious. It was their way. Just like when they cut the testicles off Chechnyans, stuffed them in their mouths, taped their mouths shut, tied their hands behind their backs and dropped them off in the middle of their hometown marketplace… all while they were still alive. It was their way.

Well, this made it possible; Ziki had a chance to get back his contact. This fact had changed his strategy. He had to drive these KGBs off the road and kill both of them.

His gun out. He moved the wheel quickly to the left in order to draw the Hugo with him, and when the other car began to break that way, he slid the BMW in the opposite direction and increased his speed.

It worked.

In a moment, he was alongside the Hugo and unloading the clip of his Jericho through the passenger window. He shot his way down. The shooter had lowered his window before deciding to shoot from the back of the car and not bothered to roll it back up.

Thank heaven for little favors. Bye-bye.

He watched the shooter slump in the front seat as blood splattered on the driver and the windshield. Ziki kept firing into the car until his shots reached the front right tire. It exploded and sent the car directly into the BMW. Ziki had been braced for that and took the blow with only a slight struggle for recovery.

The Hugo was not so lucky. It moved past the BMW and straight into a light pole. Joseph was on the floor in the back of the car. He should survive the impact.

The driver, a slender bald man, flew through the front windshield and head first into the same pole he had hit.

It was only then that Ziki had become aware of the sirens.

He swung the car around while continuing to accelerate. Ziki's car came to an easy rest alongside the smoking ruin of the Hugo. Ziki got out and walked to the car.

He opened the door and saw Joseph on the floor. Blood was streaming from his head. Hey... Blood – it looks like just a skin break. He checked closer to make sure Joseph would not die in the car. Ziki took his arm and led him out of the back seat. "It's okay... you'll be all right now...I got you."
They were gone as the Baghdad police arrived.

Joseph's injury made it impossible for them to dump the car and go it on foot. He would stick out. Stealing another car might be the only option. Ziki decided that he had to ditch the BMW and figure out what to do next.

"Joseph, are you injured anywhere besides your head?"

"I don't think so." The little man held Ziki's jacket against his scalp. The blood kept coming. If it did not stop soon, Ziki's place of destination would have to include a doctor.

"Well, you better check. The way our luck is going today, it would be in perfect order for you to die from hemorrhaging." Finding a safe place would be hard enough; finding a doctor would be a nightmare. Just add it to the list.

Joseph shook his head sadly and almost laughed. "Glad to see you care, Mr. Breckenbauer."

Ziki was in no mood to be placating. "Not a luxury of our situation. This has speeded up our timetable. I am not going to tell you that I am going to do different when this is all over, or that we'll laugh about this over drinks someday. As a matter of fact, if I never see you again .... I know you think likewise."

I need to find a car; an alley might be good, a swap. One car for another outside of the sight of passersby. His palms were beginning to sweat. Was it nerves or had his hands just not gotten a sufficient enough break from holding the wheel? He was beginning to become cognizant of each car that appeared in his rearview. He was sure the first one he would not be aware of would be the end of this mission.

Joseph broke the uneasy silence in Ziki's head, "What do you mean 'speeded up our timetable?'"

"Did you tell the Russians about your son-in-law Munir the pilot?"

"Not one word, there was no time to ask me anything, it all happened so fast and then you came."

Good.  Keep talking.

"I am going to have to talk to my people and get them to open airspace for your son-in-law in the next couple of days, I have some other business here that needs my attention."  It was amazing how far away only a few days seemed.

"The whole operation could already be in jeopardy.  Depending on who Hoshel talked to and whether or not those he did, talked to their contacts, the KGB already know who you are and maybe who your son-in-law is. . .  If that is the case... However, I am hoping that they didn't have time to interrogate  Hoshel, or, and this would be better, he wouldn't tell them what or who he had in order to insure his own safety and the agents who picked you up were the only ones who were aware of your identity."

"I believe they were, they talked to no one except each other." Joseph's matter-of-fact delivery gave Ziki hope.

It did not seem he was answering Ziki's inquiry in the hopes of pleasing but instead as a simple statement of the reality.

Still no combination of alley with car appeared.  Plenty of both, just not together.

Just as he thought it would happen, once he was not looking, a car appeared in his rearview as if right on schedule.  He could not see the driver, but it had been with him since this random route had begun.  He had a bad feeling.

Ziki decided it would be better to keep this to himself. "Now, Joseph, although I think I know, tell me how you came to be in a car with the Russians."

"It wasn't the first time I've been kidnapped in the last day."

"I know.  Hoshel, the banker was your first."

"The Russian agents brought me with them because. . .  I was taken along, in their own words, 'to show the range of their power.' They knew Hoshel was going to double-cross them and sell me back to you."

"How did they know?"

"Hoshel's partner, the young Arab man, told them in Arabic."

Poor Hoshel, so smart, so stupid.  Were you counting on his stupidity? He forgot that stupidity and cunning are not mutually exclusive.

I know this is an obvious question, but I have to ask, "Did they let the Arab live, Joseph?"

"Right up until they picked up Hoshel's tail.  I'm getting ahead of myself." The little man minced.  "Yesterday, Hoshel approached me as I was approaching my home.  He told me he was working for you.  And that you needed to see me."

"And you believed him?"

"Of course not.  I may not know much about you, but I know that you would never have sent someone for me without letting me know personally they were in your employ. So, I said I would be happy to accompany him once I had spoken to you. He said that you had been called back to Israel at the last minute and the action would take place sooner than we had anticipated."

Ziki thought it ironic that Hoshel's actions had made his statement a reality. "So, how did he get you?"

"The back and forth went on for awhile. I thought it might make him impatient and that he'll slip up and give his intentions away. But he remained impeccably polite and even entertained contacting you. While I was trying to get away from him, his Arab partner came up from behind me and placed a pistol in my rib cage."

# Chapter 33

**The Tail**

**Ziki thought that the car that was on his tail was doing an excellent job.** It had disappeared twice only to reemerge each time Ziki believed he had lost it. It was obviously neither Iraqi nor KGB. Neither would have been so subtle: the Russians because they had no reason to be subtle, the Iraqis because they had no ability to be subtle.

"Did they tell you anything once they had you?"

"While I was being led to their car, I was told not to worry. They said I would get what I wanted and that I was safe. They explained that they had promised the KGB I would be handed over, but that your people would be willing to pay more for me."

"Did his partner give any reason for betraying him?"

"Once Hoshel had left to meet you, the Arab spit in my face and told me I would not live to see the day's end. He knew that you might let Hoshel live, but once you knew that he was the other partner, you would certainly kill him. He asked the KGB to double their price."

"And they picked you up."

"Picked us up. Told the Arab they would take him to the money once he had led them to Hoshel who they knew would be with you. He seemed leery about getting into the car—"

"You mean they didn't arrive with a briefcase?"

"I knew he was dead. But the Arab didn't see it. He jabbered for the entire ride. About anything that came into his mind. I am almost ashamed to say this, but it was almost a relief when they shut his mouth permanently."

"Don't be. He tried to kill me."

"They turned into an alley right after they saw Hoshel walk into the café to meet you. Took him around to the back of the car under the pretence of giving him his money—"

"And that's where they killed him?"

"Good riddance, and he surely will not talk to anyone ."

Still, Ziki felt a pang of regret for not having paid back Hoshel's associate in person. It was disappointing that the KGB decided they could be bothered to get more creative with his disposal.

"Someone should find him in the trunk of the Hugo—big trunk for a small car."

"Actually, the local police will find him. They are probably there already. Which is why our timetable has speeded up. Did either of those men make a phone call or contact anyone after they saw you?"

"No, I told you, I was never out of their sight."

"Did anyone else come into contact with you while you were in Hoshel's possession?"

"No, but there was a voice."

"A voice?"

"It was woman."

Gavriella? No. Not possible. If she's working for anyone, it's the American State Department. If she knew they had him, she would have killed them both. Certainly the Arab. After all, he had tried to kill her. She didn't take well to that sort of thing. Who could it be?

"A woman? And you didn't see her?"

"No. Just a voice. Last night, there was knock on the door. It was definitely a woman's voice. I heard her talking with Hoshel. She insisted on seeing me. Hoshel would not let her. Said he wouldn't give his prize away that easily. She became combative and insisted. Talked about wanting to make sure that I was okay."

"Did she give a reason?"

"Wanted to make sure that I would be in condition to be interrogated. Hoshel, as calm as he was when he abducted me, said that while he understood she was uniquely qualified to make that determination, she would just have to take his word for it."

"Uniquely qualified?" Use your head, man. Think. There is a clue to her identity in there…

"He wouldn't let her in. When she persisted, it was obvious Hoshel and his associate produced guns. She said she wouldn't forget this."

"And you didn't get a name?'

"That I would have told you."

"You did well Joseph, thank you."

Ziki was almost relieved that Joseph did not produce a name. It allowed him to hold out hope that he did not know the identity of the woman. Although he knew in his gut that it was only a matter of time before his fears were confirmed.

That feeling in his gut is what distracted him from the fact that his tail was now right behind him.

The driver was signaling him to pull over.

The driver was a woman. The driver was Gavriella.

"How long have you had him?" She was moving rapidly toward the car as she asked the question.

Ziki slowly raised the gun. He had a clean shot at her. She, on the other hand, would have to shoot through the car or pull off a perfect headshot to get him.

"Gavriella, given the way this day has gone, you're going to have to forgive me if I tell you that if you step an inch closer to this car before answering some questions, I am going to kill you where you stand."

Given his own appearance, Joseph's head wound and bleeding skull, and the mangled wreckage that was the two KGB bodies, Ziki resented her pristine appearance.

He laughed at the thought that he was angry at her because there was no blood on her dress.

His chuckle seemed to break the tension for her. "You don't think I had anything to do with the Wild West show you just perpetuated in the streets?"

Wild West Show? Americans.

"Of course not. There wasn't a moment of what just happened that wasn't improvised. You were always a stickler for planning."

"That's right. Anything I did that was meant to kill you might not have succeeded, but it would not have been so poorly executed. So, why are you pointing that gun at me?"

He adjusted his grip for both comfort and effect. "Because I want you to clear up a few things before you and I talk further."

Gavriella assumed a casual position to show she wasn't frightened. "We're already partners."

She really is amazing. I know a dozen men who try to fake not being scared, but I can smell it on them. She is perfect; which means I can't trust her.

"No, I am partners with the American State Department—Kissinger. This offer is exclusively to you, a little something extra. I'm going to get you money."

"Money? Hmm, interesting."

"After all, you're working for the Americans, maybe, and that, after all, is what Americans seem most interested in: money."

"You know what? You can insult me in the car." She began to walk back to her car.

He raised the pistol and pulled the hammer back. "That's far enough, Gavriella. You are still working for Kissinger, right?"

She turned back, giving him a nonchalant eye. "Right."

He could see she was going for the back door. Could she have a heavier piece of artillery back there? You could kill her before she even drew aim.

Ziki realized the unintended consequence of the conversation was his body; it was finally clearing itself of all the adrenaline that had pumped through it. It helped him think better, but it also made him exhausted. The pistol felt like a hundred-pound weight in his hand. His breathing slowed.

"How long have they had you on this one?"

"Since the beginning," she said. "I was recruited simultaneously when Joseph's phone call came to your Paris Consulate."

"There wasn't a turning point? You betrayed everyone from the get go?"

"I don't see it that way. I never saw the two countries as competing interests. Let's face it, Ziki, you need my help—"

He knew he did not have time for anger. She managed to seem as if she was lurching into his face without moving a muscle. "Ziki! Why are we having a geopolitical conversation in an alley with the Iraqi police and the KGB looking for the car you are leaning on? Wouldn't this situation be better served in my car? A car they will not be on the look out for?"

He shook his head. Blew out a long breath. He put his hands down, made fists, and raised them again.

Dammit.

"Ok. I'm going to trust you for now. And since I can't trust, I have at least got to understand what the hell you're doing. So I am not getting in that car until I understand who I am dealing with, and I don't buy your Israel-America-not-mutually-exclusive bullshit."

"Then hang onto everything. That might ease your doubts. Now please Ziki, get in the car, we need to get out of here—or shoot me!"

"Is Kissinger going to play it straight once it is in Turkish airspace? Or am I going to be left holding my genitals?"

"I think so? You're just going to have to get that thing airborne and find out."

He almost slumped, but knew better. "How the hell did you find me?"

"I just drove towards the sound of the screeching tires and the guns."

"Nice try. You were on my tail before a shot was fired—"

"Don't flatter yourself, sexy. I was on Hoshel's tail."

'You watched that entire incident go down and didn't do a—?"

"Oh give me a break, Ziki! What would you have done? Okay, we knew Hoshel grabbed your contact. We knew that he might lead us to him—"

"And you were going to cut me out of the loop?"

"Just as you were probably still going over scenarios that might extricate yourself from Kissinger. This is how the cards fell, Ziki. We missed. The KGB missed. You've got your guy. But I've got a car that can get us out of here."

"I can find other cars."

"Your friend in the front seat needs a doctor. I could provide him one here in Baghdad."

"And you think that I can't?"

"There is nothing that I believe you not capable of, but I offer an immediate ride. That gets you to the doctor faster and allows you to speed up your timetable as I know you want to."

"I have other options."

"And yet here you stand, gun in hand, trying to determine whether or not you can trust me."

"You do present the simplest option."

"The simplest option is shooting me and taking my car." There was almost a lilt of humor in her voice.

Smart. She is making me think through it. Now, I can't do it as a rash act.

He shook his head no, not this time… "No thank you. We wouldn't do anything as sloppy as the KGB sideshow we just witnessed… Don't you want to hear my offer?"

'It's money, right?"

"Do you think it is for the pleasure of your company? With money on the horizon I can trust you for the moment."

"I was sort of hoping…"

"I am not going to give you one hundred thousand dollars for a ride through the streets of Baghdad to a safe house and a doctor. That is as much in your interest as it is in mine."

"One hundred thousand dollars? Where are you going to get that kind of money on this short notice?"

"Hoshel continues to do us both favors from the grave. He asked for nearly as much to return Joseph. I had to do something quickly. I was able to put such a sum together for him before the KGB provided him with an early exit. It is as easy to secure that sum for you. And you'll be providing me protection from a potential NSA-Kissinger report. I think protection is fifty thousand."

"You said one hundred."

"I did. We'll discuss the other half on the way."

"So, I guess you're getting in the car."

"I am driving."

"Shall we go to the doctor first?"

"No. We have something to take care before it takes care of us."

'What's that?"

"Getting you to earn the other fifty thousand."

"What do we have to do?"

"I think I know who the mole's helper is. You're going to help me kill her."

**Ziki's announcement of his knowledge of the mole created a silence in car.** The fact that he said "she" meant that Gavriella did not have to ask the next question. She knew too. She knew it was devastating for Ziki. She knew he was asking for help, because he would need it. He would not be able to do this alone.

It was clear it was Henny.

Henny, who had been a smiling angel in Ziki's life. Henny, who had given Ziki care in a time of pain and tried to fill the void in his heart that had been broken by Gavriella's betrayal at Khan Yunis. It would be sad if the heartbreak was not so etched into Ziki's face.

Amazing, Gavriella thought, that Henny's romanticism—for what else could it be?—would have swerved Ziki's feelings about her… No. I will get Ziki's heart back, somehow… I can't think about this right now. There is too much going on to let this distract me, but I can feel it every moment that I am in the car with this man.

Gavriella could only speculate, but she guessed that Henny was not working for the KGB but the Palestinians, a sympathetic convert. It was the question that caused her to break the silence.

Ziki sounded mournful in his confirmation of Gavriella's suspicions: "She must believe they are denied justice. She must have come to see things their way. It is the worst kind of turning. Other forms of turning need not end with death. Greed can be corrected. One simply ups the ante. If an agent turns because he feels betrayed then that can be corrected through rectification. But when they turn because they think they see the rightness of the other cause, then they are a '*true believer.*' True believers are the most dangerous of adversaries."

Gavriella knew most of what Ziki was saying. But she also knew Ziki was not so much saying it for her benefit as he was trying to make sense of a betrayal that cut him to the quick.

He shook his head and sighed. "True believers. They see the world in three ways: those who are with the cause, those who would be with the cause if they only saw the truth, and those who must be eliminated because they will never see the cause."

"It is why we must kill her; I have instructions from Langley… I don't know why I am telling you this, because I think you know. But I am worried, Ziki, you seem clouded."

"I know. Don't you think I know?" He nearly hung his head. "We would never be able to make her see the error of her ways—"

"It doesn't matter, Ziki, if we could. She isn't important enough to us to try and save even if we could."

Ziki stiffened. Even the most merciful of executions would be horrific. To simply drive by and shoot her? To blow up a car? But that was not a luxury they could afford right now. This might be painful for everyone.

Gavriella could see Ziki at work in his head. His mind was racing. He was not trying to save her. He was trying to figure out a way he could kill her quickly and then forgive her…

Gavriella could not allow it. She spoke as if responding to his thoughts, "Ziki, we have got to get her comfortable so we can find out what has been jeopardized. She almost cost us both our lives, and we must find out what she knows, if anything, about Osirak. She has been feeding the KGB information. It may not have been for their benefit, but it has been. Even worse, Russia could care less if Israel makes it, but the PLO, whom we have to assume she is working for, are out to eliminate your state. It is an unforgivable— " Ziki realized that it was Henny's voice that Joseph had heard speaking earlier to Hoshell.

"As opposed to playing America off Israel? That, on the other hand, is forgivable? Is that what you say? And you, notifying Salameh of my coming in at Khan Yunis?"

"I'm not going to let you do this! You cannot compare my actions to hers. I never gave the KGB information that almost twice resulted in your death. I took you to see Kissinger and softened the terrain for you. I am helping you—and I am going to help you as you get deeper into things here, including that real shady business at Osirak, and I'm not even mentioning the stuff across the border, over that way." She pointed in the direction of Iran."

"For a 'peek.'"

"Something she would never do. And it might not make me a better person, but it certainly makes me more reliable. She is a paragon. She cannot be bought. It is all almost admirable. It is all noble—she thinks. It would be perfect if it were not for the fact it is all in the service of Jihad and the PLO. For all I know she sleeps with Yasser Arafat. Now there is an imprint for your mind."

"That's enough. Let Joseph sleep. He is not equipped to deal with any of this. Let him rest and let me rest my mind." Ziki envied Joseph's position. He was lying on the back seat. The bleeding had subsided—he needed stitches.

Gavriella resumed her words in a raised whisper, "You're not resting. Your mind is racing in a million different directions. But I will tell you this. You will get the information that we need, and you will terminate her. Or I will do it."

"You will do it. I prefer not to do it."

"How do you want to do this?"

"I don't. But we must. So, we have to find out where she is. That shouldn't be a problem. Mossad will know. They put her into the field."

"Mossad? I thought you said she was PLO?"

"Use your head, woman. She would be of no use to the PLO if she were just a citizen. If that were the case, she might be good for a bit of information here and there—"

"How do you know this?"

"I don't. But if she was simply a nurse then turning her would be no big thing. This makes sense. No. I think I understand what has happened. She works for both sides. She was probably a street operative of sorts sent on very selective missions to infiltrate the PLO. I can't believe I didn't see this. I can only surmise that the closer she got to the PLO, the more her romanticism overcame her common sense."

"If that is the case, then her elimination won't be a simple affair."

"No. And the worst part for me is that the only way I can get to her is by appealing to her romanticism."

"For you?"

"Yes. Joseph is the bait. We will slowly reveal everything. We must watch her carefully to see how much of the information we give her appears new. If she doesn't already know it, she will want to discover Joseph's identity as she tried to do the other night from Hoshel. She will treat his wounds, then she will attempt again to give the KGB his identity. They won't even have to come for him. They will simply take either his name or his description and will trace him back to his son-in-law. And that would be that."

"And that is what she is to believe is going to happen? So, what are you hoping to get from her?"

"We are trying to discover whether she already knows his identity and that of Munir, and—if she has any wind of Osirak."

"Well, doesn't it go to follow if she knows him already, she won't come?"

"No. It would be out of character. It would set off suspicions. The character that she plays will do anything, and if I suddenly have an emergency that she won't help with, it might tip me off."

"You will have to explain why you know she is in Baghdad."

"I will tell half the truth. I will say the Malkielly disclosed to me her name and put me in touch with her."

"Which means you have to pretend to be surprised to see her."

"That won't be a problem."

"You also have to pretend to be angry with her once the 'surprise' of seeing her has worn off—"

"I am angry with her—"

"No, I mean angry with her for not telling you she was 'working' for Mossad—"

"I am enraged, Gavriella, not clouded. I understand full well what I need to do."

"Well, assure me, and explain to me how this is all going to play out."

"It is a matter of using my anger at her betrayal to appear as if I am simply angry at her for not telling me that we were working not only on the same side but also in the same field. I will be tense and curt and accuse her of lying. I will also say that I could have been of help to her if she had only let me in on the secret. Instead she played the innocent and allowed me to think there was a part of my life that was separate from all this. By appearing unreasonable I will not arouse her suspicions, and I hope she will open up and talk."

Gavriella gave Ziki an uncharacteristic soft look. She looked in the back; Joseph had fallen asleep. Ziki was going to say something but she put her hand gently over his mouth… It smelled nice.

"Ziki, I want you to know something. I have seen your country now; I understand and I was wrong, very wrong. I beg you to believe me… I am with you now. The more I am with you the stronger this feeling is… I am in love with you and I will never again do anything to hurt you…I will love you forever… And I will do anything you ask me to do…." He believed her.

"You do mean that?"

"With all my heart. I want to help and make up for Khan Yunis…I know that I must gain your trust again."

"Then, you are going to 'volunteer' and join the PLO's El Fattah, Salameh's faction. They will trust you because of Khan Yunis… What do you say?"

"I say yes, I'll do it." He picked up her hand and kissed it. "Now, I believe it would be better if Joseph were not in the car. We will take him back to the safe house and maybe a doctor. We don't want that woman anywhere near him."

Ziki winced at hearing Henny called 'That woman'…

Exactly how Ziki explained how he would behave is exactly how he behaved when he picked Henny up from the market near the safe house. She sat in the back. Putting Gavriella in the passenger side was a risky move especially if 'this woman' was as dangerous as he now believed. But to have picked up Henny and insisted on sitting her in the front seat with a known operative sitting behind her might have set off her suspicions.

She tried to smile, but it came off as more than a bit forced, "I know you are disappointed with me."

"I am disappointed in myself. To not have seen through the bullshit you have been feeding me. That was my fault. I am simply angry with you. Angry with you for not being who you said you were. By the way, nice work, the 'car accident.'"

"I am that person. Who I am in this car is not far removed from the person you spent time with."

Gavriella could not resist, "Except for the fact you're probably an expert in small arms and covert tactics."

Ziki could see the comment, "I do not wish to be rude, but I am trying to talk to my friend."

"You can do that once this thing is done. Right now you will have to forgive us both for being a little too distracted to hear your life story."

"I think Ziki wants to hear it."

"So do I, but there isn't time. I would rather have him focus on the road. Since you are no longer perceived as innocent, I should not have to explain to you that three people in this car could each have separate tails. He has to be extraordinarily careful, and the last thing that he or I need is you distracting him with your silly explanations."

"Then maybe you should drive."

"I am also looking for outside danger, as you should be. Like I said, the potential for tails is endless given the combination of our passengers."

"So, shall we sit in silence?"

"No, we will discuss the affair you are walking into. Gavriella will brief you."

"I understand?"

"That is correct."

"Is he an agent?"

"No. He is a contact. Nothing more."

"And the nature of this contact." God everything she says now seems so loaded. So double edged. It was killing Ziki. Gavriella could see this.

She tried to fill his terse silences. "He has access, through associates, to a piece of technology the entire world, with the exception of the Soviets would like to get their hands on."

Don't talk in clever riddles, Gavriella, she may feel she is being toyed with. Don't give us away.

"I understand. I understand."

Understand that you shouldn't know? Or understand in that you get what we are talking about? He just wanted to ask her why she had done this. He was angry at himself for feeling this way. He had let someone in and of course she had betrayed him. Not that he had given her any secrets. He had given her something more precious… But not really. And she knew he had done it. How did that make her feel?

"He has family in the region?"

Where was she going with this? "I don't know."

"Will they be there? And if not, is there a way to bring them in?"

That's it, Ziki thought, she doesn't know who he is.

If she did, her question would have been if arrangements had been made. Still it is not enough. But this is a good place to begin. If she continues to probe for background information on this man, she will give away everything. Then Gavriella can finish this day with Henny.

She flashed him that smile he had come to rely on. He did not want to but he caught himself smiling back.

"Possibly..."

Gavriella did what Ziki had asked her to do ...

## Chapter 34

**—Northern Lebanon.**

### Terrorist training camp.

The head *Shahid* stopped where she sat winding together two thin black wires and lifted her hand. "Very good." His voice, bland and monotonous—like all the voices that spoke to her here—eked through a thick, wiry beard.

"Thank you," she said, tugging lightly at the hand he still held.

Raiid Ibn Mohammed's grip tightened as he lowered the smallish hand, palm down. Before them, a dusty gravelly field fanning a hundred feet in front of and behind them and about half that to each side. The split cuticles and dry, cracked knuckles filled with a paste of sweat and dust were a nice complement to the ashen brittle bits of ground and chunks of glass and AK shells surrounding them.

Gavriella couldn't help but squirm to adjust to this new level of life. She'd 'volunteered' after some training by Mossad she 'joined' Salameh's faction of the El Fatah as Ziki had asked her.

Raiid's response—and who knew whether to attribute it to instinct or that fact that he was an evil, self-important man—was to eject a six-inch steel blade from his right hip that, unfortunately for Gavriella and her pinned limb, was another perfect match for the gray-brown color scheme and ominous mood just established.

Winding the *Shabaria*'s tip between her fingers to the *crrch, crrch* tune of the disturbed silt below, he told her. "Do not stop. You must be prepared to fulfill your duty. No matter what you lose. Things happen. You may not always have the use of both legs…both eyes…both hands…no mistakes, you hear, no mistakes… they are punished by the rules of Islam, and you are just a woman."

Gavriella struggled to maneuver the wires into their proper sockets; the blade was burning her skin and the training putty they were using in place of C4 was oozing between the fingers of her free hand in the hundred-degree heat. When she—aiming for the 9-volt battery's positive charge—poked a wire's exposed copper end deep into the putty, the instructor coughed in disgust and mumbled. "Stupid American *sharmuta*."

The wire emerged dragging strings of putty; Gavriella cleared her throat and, concentrating hard on the thumbnail she was using to scrape it off, said to Raiid, "I'm sorry, I'm still perfecting my Arab tenses. I caught the 'American cunt' part, but did you say you are one or you have one?"

For a moment, Raiid was silent, still; and peripheral vision showed her no more of him than a scuffed brown boot toe and a small chunk of beard curls. She did notice that the pressure with which he pushed on her hand remained strong and constant.

A full minute—or maybe it was just a few seconds—passed before a quick, controlled upward stroke flew by the corner of her eye. A jerk of her head and the full picture—Raiid with his *Shabaria* blade centered high above her hand—came into view.

Gavriella inhaled sharply and, trying to spit the breath back out, felt her throat constrict around her windpipe. She had never not been able to scream before. Sensing the knife in motion, she closed her eyes and reassured herself, "It's just a hand, it's just a hand, it's just a—

"Forty-one! Twenty-nine! *Bwa, bwa!* Twenty-two! Sixty-two! Forty-eight! *Ee, ee, ee, ee, ee,*! *Oahad*! *shtaiin*! *tlaat*! *aarba*! One! two! three! four!"

Gavriella—surely with someone else's voice—was screeching, two-digit numbers and interspersing them with random, rabid howls. She had never done this out loud before. Cocking her head, now almost as curious as she was scared, she scanned Raiid's face. He had not flinched and his expression had not changed. But his grip on her pinned hand had loosened just enough for her to jerk it back as his heavy *Shabaria* blade thunked into the dirt.

Slowly, Gavriella rolled her eyes downward. Raiid's followed. Below them, two pools of blood infiltrated the rock and threatened to merge. The pools reminded Gavriella of her middle school science units on cell meiosis.

"Whoa," Gavriella said out loud, "are we spinning?" She took a deep breath to calm herself and puked up her meal of humus and shish-kebab—that, at long last, got Raiid to let go of her hand.

Gavriella lifted it and stared hard. She saw fingers, but couldn't quite make out how many. She tapped against the areas spouting blood. They were not yet causing her much physical pain, but coming face to face with her blood making a mad dash for her exterior delivered a severe blow to her long-held contention that she could handle herself in any situation. The effect was paralyzing.

From somewhere inside, she screeched again. *Snap out of it! Stop the bleeding, you dumb woman!*

The command inspired her to jam the bloody mess between her knees and squeeze. *Apply pressure to stop the flow at the source.*

Raiid took in the scene, but made no effort to stop the blood flow or help her. "Interesting," he said as he wiped the drops of blood that clung to his knife on the fatigued print covering his legs. His voice was soft now.

Gavriella lifted her head and stared languidly at the spot in front of his mouth.

"Your act may have saved you four finger joints."

So she had at least four knuckles.

"Or," he continued, pausing, without smiling to return the clean knife to its tattered holster, "it did cost you two fingertips."

# Chapter 35

**Shuff Mountains.**

### SALAMEH'S DEN

**The man turned and faced her,** his oceanic black eyes flickering in the light with an oily iridescence.

"How fitting," she blurted out in an Arab accent so flawless the eyes dilated in surprise.

"I'm going to have to disagree," he returned. "Few non-natives make the effort to master our language."

His voice tickled her ears, its soothing deepness rushing over and through her arms and eyelids as if ignoring the physical presence in front of it and heading straight for her subconscious. And Gavriella, perpetually on edge and exhausted, would have given herself to the hypnotic coo were its own physical presence not so strikingly discordant and equally deserving of her attention.

The smooth caramel of his skin ran invisibly between boyish cheeks and a chin that glistened naked in the light. It seemed puberty had gotten so caught up in perfecting his vocal cords that it had forgotten to teach his face how to sprout much hair. Then again, the oversight could have been deliberate—a beard, after all, would have covered his delicate jaw line and distorted the perfect cabernet heart that wound itself around his lips.

"Please." He gave a nondescript wave. "Make yourself at home."

Gavriella forced herself away from the voice and vision that seemed to be surrounding her and focused on the interior of what was actually surrounding her.

"Home" was a deep cave surrounded by bulbous walls and covered with a low and jagged ceiling. Piled high against the back wall were white bricks each wrapped in clear plastic—not bricks, heroine she realized. Probably from poppies grown in the Be'eka valley. The effect was engulfing—somewhere between comforting and confining. Sections of it had been hastily partitioned with burlap screens whose must penetrated even the thick woodiness of the incense filling the area. More inviting were the rich brown wool tapestries covering some of the quarters' rocky walls.

"What," Gavriella inquired, fingering the fringe on a piece hanging nearby, "no introductions?"

The mouth puckered, then relaxed. "It's Moroccan," he said, focusing on the rug. "A member of the *Ait Ouaouzguite* tribe—Berbers—wove it in the late nineteenth century. They live in the Siroua Mountains where the climate is arid and inhospitable to crops." He ran his own hand down the side of the rug before turning to face her. "They breed their sheep to survive in the harsh, dry conditions, and to produce a wool that is finer, lighter than most. And they weave and trade…and survive." *Pause.* "And I know who you are, Ms. Ramon. That's all that matters."

"W-well," she stuttered, unprepared for their abrupt departure from the Sirouas.

Ali Hassan Salameh walked past her to a collapsible table and picked up a crusty iron kettle. "Coffee?"

Gavriella flicked away her disconcertion and ignored his offer. "Of course I know who you are too." She didn't dare say his name. "In fact, I think I know you pretty well. I just thought we'd make it official."

She gave him a brief opening to jump in or become intrigued or grow angry, but Salameh, who had been showing nothing but polite interest to this point, took it, turned away from her and fiddled with his own coffee.

"Because I'm actually a little surprised," Gavriella, undeterred, continued. "You don't look anything like your picture."

Salameh took his time pouring a stream of the thick liquid into a squat earthen cup and, facing her again, took a sip. "I did not know that anyone had a picture of me. Then I am doing well."

"No," she pressed, unsure why she wanted to rile him, "I mean, you almost look more like—"

"An Israeli than an Arab?"

The genuine curiosity inflecting his words threw Gavriella from her intended path.

"Oh. Well, no." She thought about it. "I mean, well…well, yes, actually. But I was going to say—" Gavriella's past experiences with Arab male temperament spoke to her. " –more like a spoiled Saudi prince than a cave dweller." *That should do it*, she thought, flashing a playful smile.

Salameh made no response. However, the force with which he scooped up one of the half dozen oil lamps sprinkled throughout the cave was enough to send chills down to her missing skin on her fingertips.

Salameh moved close to her and raised the lamp to eye level. "But you forget, Ms. Ramon," he whispered," this is a very flattering light."

Salameh lifted Gavriella's bandaged hand and, unwrapping the gauze, said, "I heard about this…accident."

She nodded. All things considered, the fracas had left her with minimal damage. Still, she mourned the sixteenth-inch chunks of skin on her pointer and middle fingers Raiid ibn Mohamed laid to rest in the dismal muck of the training field.

"And I presume," he continued, discarding the covering, "that we have made no apologies for it."

She nodded. "No."

The two, at Gavriella's suggestion, were now seated, cross-legged and face-to-face, on a multi-colored woven rug. She had hoped sitting on her smart ass might help to shut it up. Plus, she was fast discovering that if she had to bump knees with a master terrorist, Salameh—in the strictest of physical senses, of course—was a not a bad choice.

Salameh tasked and lifted the exposed spread of raw, gooey skin. He brushed it lightly across his lips. Gavriella cursed the goosebumps that sprung up the length of her spine. *Don't forget who this man is Gavriella...*

"Then let me say that I am very sorry. I don't believe in destroying beautiful things." He returned her hand, which she let fall loosely to her side. "Unfortunately, there are many people helping me who do not share in my beliefs, they will distrust you because you are a woman and American, maybe even CIA."

"I helped you—probably saved your life!"

Salameh fell silent but Gavriella, content floating in his eyes, forewent her turn to say something.

He scratched his missing beard and cleared his throat. "I also heard, Miss Ramon, about your tactics in making your encounter with Raiid...significantly less severe. Tell me, what were those numbers you mumbled?"

Gavriella emerged, momentarily disenchanted, from Salameh's eyes.

The numbers? That was what this was about?

"They were just...numbers. The first ones that came to my head."

It wasn't entirely true, but didn't matter. The numbers were from her brother's funeral. A few of them were, anyway—the funeral went on a lot longer than the thrust of Raiid's knife. But they were nothing. Just—what would Freud call it? A defense mechanism? They were her weird, personal defense mechanism.

Salameh's narrow shoulders sloped inward as he crossed his arms. "They meant nothing to you then."

Gavriella was eight when John died and hadn't wanted to cry at his funeral because John had always told her crying was for sissies.

She reached down and picked her crumpled gauze up from the floor. "Nothing important. Not some—"she scoffed at the cliché, "—secret code if that's what you're insinuating."

By the time Gavriella was old enough to know things, her father had already been involved with the CIA for over twenty years and John was working on making the transition from Eagle Scout to Army Ranger. So the one thing Gavriella knew for sure was that the wisest men in the world all had big collections of badges, uniforms, and awards.

Sitting in her father's lap, fighting back tears, Gavriella looked up to see John's naval Captain, fully decorated, entering the funeral home. She broke away from her father's helpless embrace and approached the man's smattering of medals in desperation.

"Young lady," he told her, "it's a terrible thing to lose a young life. It's especially terrible when that young life was one led as admirably as this soldier's, err, your brother's."

The Captain seemed huge at that moment. His Adam's apple danced as he spoke and he smelled like the round racks of suits Gavriella wandered through with her father in the JC Penny men's department.

Gavriella gave a solemn nod and waited for him to continue.

Instead, he patted her on the head and said, "I can tell you're a brave little girl."

Twenty minutes later, Captain Arnold stood at a podium next to John's casket and told a crowd of two hundred: "It's a terrible thing to lose a young life." *Dramatic pause.* It's especially terrible when that young life was one led as admirably as this soldier's." *Name check.* But I ask John Ramon's family to think, in this terrible time, of the countless terrible times this great country has faced. I ask them to think of these times and know that they will plough through. That *they* will persevere as *we* always have…"

It was then—when the captain had asked her to think of the countless terrible times her great country had faced—that  the numbers came. Starting in 1776, Gavriella worked her way through the years, singling out every worst day of America's life and pitting them against this worst day of her own.

She always won.


"A secret code?"  Salameh's teeth, sinister in the low glow of the lamp, made their first appearance. A discordantly jolly chuckle followed. "No, Ms Ramon, I don't think the fear of harm prompted you to betray a secret code. I asked because I was curious. You are…unique in your choices."

His casual condescension brought out her indignation; Gavriella stood. Flipping him a cold smile, she said, "Curiosity is all? Well, in that case, I think you should mind your own damn business.

"*Tsk, tsk, tsk*, Salameh clicked, rising to her side. "I see your encounter with Raiid has left you on constant guard."

"Ha! Raiid had nothing to do with that."

Salameh shrugged. "Okay. The point is, I don't want you to feel like that with me.." He took the limp gauze back into his hands and re-wrapped her fingers. "Remember, Gavriella, I do remember what you did for us at Khan Yunis—we are on the same side."

# Chapter 36

**Zurich, Switzerland.**

**Gavriella wiggled a semi-attached handrail leading upstairs and wondered what was so safe about this house**. The furniture was cheap—was that balsa wood pretending to be a coffee table?—the floors' constant creaks and pops suggested they were one wrong step from retirement, the formerly beige damask drapes had de-threaded to near translucence, and…oh…oh…maybe that was what kept the infidels away.

Gagging, she cupped a hand over her mouth and nose.

"What is the matter?" Salameh came in behind her, closing and bolting the heavy steel front door.

"What is that smell?"

Salameh sniffed the air. "Iamael, my nephew, he is with us now—he will be a good fighter. His brother is a martyr, he is in paradise now. He left us dinner."

"So it's Iamael or dinner?"

Salameh had already started up the stairs and didn't answer. Instead he told her, "Stay there. I'll be back."

"Okay, but I'm not hungry," she called through her fingers behind him.

Now alone in the vestibule, Gavriella slowly extracted her hand and peered deeper into the adjacent living area. "Ugh," she thought, catching her second full whiff of the air, sweaty curry. Must be his nephew from Gaza, Iamael and dinner. *Didn't he have something to do with Ziki?*

Balsa table and faded canary divan aside, the room was pretty sparse. She aimed for a door leading through it to the next when something in one of its far corners caught her eye. Draping her trench coat and hideous orange—it had to be orange—scarf on the scooped arm of the divan, she strolled over to the tarnished horn of an old phonograph.

A lone 45, green label worn beyond legibility, sat on the machine's turntable, itself sitting atop a dinged and scratched wooden box. A metal disk pronouncing the thing a "Columbia Player" lay on the hard wood floor below. Gavriella scratched at a ring of white on the box's face—remnants of the disk's glue that had, apparently, grown only half tired of its adhesive. She glanced behind her and called out quietly for Salameh. No response. She moved from the leftover glue to a silver switch and flicked it on. The turntable spun lazily.

"I wonder," she said, lifting the arm and placing the needle on the edge of the record, "what in the world you people are listening to."

*"I know a ditty nutty as a fruitcake…"*

Gavriella burst out laughing.

"What is so funny?"

"Oh!" She spun around, still coughing up chuckles. "Ali, God, you scared me." Then, in all seriousness: "Ali, God. 'Mairzy Doats?'"

He glanced at the phonograph, seemingly noticing it for the first time. The concerned frown he had carried down the stairs with him eased. He nodded. "'Mairzy Doats,' yes that's it. What is so funny?"

"Nothing. I mean…the song."

"This song is funny?"

"No, it's not funny—"

"A kiddledy divey too, wouldn't you?"

"No, it is funny—fun. It is meant to be fun and funny."

Gavriella took a deep breath; another chortle sneaked through as she let it out. "Yes, but really, it's really stupid. Meaningless. And that's just it. It's meaningless. It doesn't belong in a place that's—that's—" she gestured for him to take in what she saw, "so full of meaning."  Not to mention one that's been kissed by the armpit of hell.

"What does this house mean?"

The notions about the house she had carried as far as its doorstep flashed through Gavriella's mind. It was supposed to be an invisible refuge, craftily stashed amidst the animosity of the world it was hiding from. Its interior would be lush, spectacular—but draped in the same unassuming façade as all the other quaint homes unknowingly sharing its neighborhood.

To say she was disappointed would have been an understatement.

Still, Gavriella knew this house was different. Having knuckled them earlier, she knew the walls surrounding her were not plaster. She would not have to go through the operator to make a phone call. And, taking a second look at the crooked banister, the thought occurred to her that its looseness reflected the number of times it had been lifted and replaced for ease of access to the weapons she sensed were hidden in the hollow stairs below.

"This house," Gavriella concluded, "is volatile."

Salameh nodded in agreement, but had obviously not yet made a similar connection.

She tried again. "On the one hand, it's your haven from danger, but on the other, it's your stepping stone into it. It's where you go to prepare for something important, then where you come to stay safe afterward.  I don't know, Ali.  It's just something other than mares and oats."

Salameh moved deeper into the room and extended a hand. "Why must the song mirror the house?"

"It doesn't have to, I just expected it to. And when things aren't what I expect, I am very surprised." Gavriella panned from Salameh's face, out to his hand, and back. "What's with the pose?"

"Ah, of course, I beg your pardon." Now standing at attention, he lowered and crossed his right hand in front of his body and his left behind him. His body creased in a bow.

"You want me to dance with you?" Suspicion nudged the amusement from her face. "But you don't dance."

By "You don't dance," Gavriella meant, "No Muslim man dances with a woman, especially not a Western woman and especially not using Western steps and Western music." "And, speaking of Western music, it's sacrilege—why are you letting us listen to it? Why is it even in this house?"

"I do dance," Salameh insisted. "Now you have a second surprise." Once again, he extended his hand.

The reservation with which Gavriella acted out her role in her "relationship" with Ali Hassan Salameh peaked and troughed in sync with their respective levels of paranoia. Her paranoia wrestled with her own exposure, subsequent torture and death; both of their exposure - to one of the half dozen other than Israeli groups that wanted Salameh dead, subsequent torture and death; and, during especially low troughs, the possibility that she was maybe starting to believe—what? His paranoia wrestled with: anyone's guess these days. Being targeted, trailed, watched. Feeling "the barrel of an Uzi searing down her spine from above" when he was in a basement two stories underground. For the past week—since they had arrived in Switzerland—he had been ordering one of his men to preface all of his bathroom activity with five flushes of the most suspect designated toilet.

Gavriella looked at the hand with heightened reserve, wary of what was behind or under it. Or in the other hand. At last, she took it.

And Salameh cha-cha'd her around a small open space between the protruding sheet of glass covering the balsa wood and a row of slatted chairs folded shut against the blank, unpapered wall.

Gavriella, having attended her twenty-seventh political gala only a week before her latest trip to the Middle East, had had many occasions to cha-cha. And the smoothness and grace with which Salameh's feet responded to the music was… "Yet another surprise. A playboy of El Fatah? Nah."

"Hmm?"

"You're good. I had no idea."

"I thought," Salameh said, sending her into an effortless spin, "when we first met, you said you knew me, Gavriella…

Gavriella laughed. "I said I knew you? When we first met? Hmm, I said a lot of things that day."

The skin surrounding his mouth rippled as Ali allowed himself a brief smile. "Yes. You did. And that much has not changed." His expression fell back to its neutral, brooding state as he considered the likelihood of a day passing without this woman saying a lot of things.

Staring past her now, Salameh shook his head. "For all you have worked to learn about our language and our culture and our mission, and how to be a freedom fighter—maybe even a *Shahid,* Gavriella, you have yet to put an ounce of effort into learning how to be a woman."

Her words were flippant. "A woman? You mean a Muslim woman. I know exactly how to be one of those. But *hijabs, burkas* and reticence aren't for me. I choose not to go down that road." Her actions included sliding her slender fingers from his shoulder to his back, working her way downward—. She wanted him to be attracted to her, then he might confide more in her, talk, just as Ziki  planned; she just hoped that his attraction to her did not go beyond talk.

Unnestling a stiff navy blue tail of his freshly starched Oxford and the white undershirt below it from a pair of gray slacks, she lightly ran her nails into the warm skin underneath.  "Plus, we both like me better this way."

Salameh's body, in a vain attempt to restore balance, met her inward pressure with one pushing outward. On any other day—who knows—there would have been no need to dis-embed her claws and push away. The way she manipulated her body, he realized she was trying to manipulate him; it disgusted and angered him. Islam's powers took over. "How easily you confuse 'we' with 'you.' Perhaps Raiid was right to define you... 'You stupid *sharmuta.*'"

Gavriella's lips parted and fell from a seductive pout to a gaping "O."

Salameh felt his disgust elevating fast, racing toward hatred. He blurted in third person at her;

"This woman is no different from other infidel women. Hair blown full and straight, sprayed stiff in place. Faces smothered in colors insulting to nature. Blouses unbuttoned down the neck; skirts exposing knees and the fleshy stockings clinging to them. All topped by a false sense of empowerment. I knew them well." He paused.

"An infidel woman—American—is bored with her life. She leaves the ski slopes in the Alps and safari in Kenya when she wanders into our Palestine. She has heard the area is "troubled,"  and her morbid sensibilities convince her that breezing through a war torn world will result in personal growth. First, she sees the Israelis—drives through their cities and roads and businesses built on greed—and she feels at home. And is soon bored again. So she keeps going. And maybe she gets lost. Or maybe she doesn't know any better..." He continues.

"Now she's in Gaza. She sees the Palestinian refugees and feels both disgusted and sorry for them, forced off of the land and living like stray dogs in their camps. Perhaps one in particular—a wide-eyed, child in rags—draws special pity. Enough to, in that moment, convince her that these people and their cause are what will bring meaning to her life. That if she fights for the Palestinians, they will need her as much as she needs them."

Salameh had released himself from Gavriella's clutch and now stood at arm's length as he spoke. The typical smoothness permeating his voice hardened to a hiss.

"Talk to me about choice? The one choice you had to make—to join my fight or mind your own business—is over. Now your whore's painted face and dress, your speech and shameful actions—those are my bad choices. They exist because I chose for you to blend in with us, but you are like all the other filthy whores walking the streets of corrupt America. You were here on my orders and only to benefit our cause. And now you are no longer of use—thh... You stupid *sharmuta*.."

His saliva hit the bridge of her nose, paused, and then started down her face.

Be calm, Gavriella, she thought. *He has not discovered the homing device Ziki implanted in the heel of my shoe...*

**Gavriella spent a full week gnashing her teeth** and stepping over the sleeping bodies of fifteen-year-olds hugging AK-47s to pace the brittle floors of their haven in Lebanon. Finally in Zurich as Salame's latest bout of paranoia subsided he allowed her an afternoon away from his world, alone.

Her heart raced, she sat in a taxi heading for a downtown destination she had not yet specified. She could not yet tell if he had sent someone to follow her, if he had, the United Bank of Switzerland should not be her initial stop. But what if she spent the whole day touring the city and acting normal and wasn't allowed back in tomorrow? Or the next day? What if this was her only chance to report to Ziki where she was and what she knew?

Some information had come from the Shuff mountains training camp; rigid dogmas, various schemes, weaponry production—guerilla strategies and mindsets, but the Mossad no doubt already knew. Things had progressed rapidly since the scene change to Zurich. Salame had "meetings" most days and "appointments" most evenings. Gavriella translated his words to "attack plotting" and "strip clubs", repulsed by the tinge of jealousy she felt imagining him with a Swiss whore at the latter. Ahh, stupid, you are stupid, Gavriella!

And aside from a few names and phone numbers and a string of profanities she had overheard Salame butcher over the phone late the night before, Zurich had not validated her attempts at espionage either. Still, it would feel good to make contact with Israel. Make sure they were still there. And by "Israel" and "they", she meant "Ziki Barak."

After their initial encounters and her...'conversion'...Gavriella had twisted and turned for three nights in three different hotel rooms trying not to fall in love with him. And it should have been easy—there hadn't even been great love making in the third—well, but the first and second? He'd gotten called to Berlin from their cozy little pillbox on Paris's rue du Champs de Mars just as his fingers slid the hooks from the eyes of her bra. But her memories of him stomped around inside her head...and everything below it... louder than any ever had—ever.

"How about the most expensive hotel in the city? Can you take me there?" Gavriella, an idea fast forming, asked the sparse brown wisps of hair covering the back of her driver's head.

"Yah, of course." His accent was inflected with thick consonants of German, but had the congenial mark of the Swiss. "Baur au Lac."

"Baur au Lac. Perfect... Driver, please turn left here, yes, and now right trough that alley—good, and now right again. "

The luxury spread of the lakeside hotel bordered Zurich's Banhofstrasse shopping and, more importantly, the banking district. As the taxi headed downtown, Gavriella threw a couple of quick glances behind her, pausing for three seconds before blinking snapshots of every vehicle within fifty feet of her own. It was a surveillance skill she knew well. Both Ziki and Salame had taught it to her. No one was following.

Zurich was luxurious by anyone's standards; to Gavriella, it was a glimpse of Shangri-La. The barrenness and decrepitude she had become accustomed to during her Lebanese training was still fresh enough in her mind that the mere sight of life—swishing leaves on dogwood trees, water shifting in the winds brushing Zurich Lake, cheeks the color of ripening apples being kissed hello—was enough to send her reeling over the precariousness of her own.

The driver deposited her in front of the Baur au Lac's revolving glass doors and, after fiddling with her francs long enough to do another quick scan of the area; Gavriella thanked him and calmly entered the lobby in search of her new destination; the ladies' room.

Working for  Mossad was a dangerous privilege on many levels. When she accepted this assignment, Gavriella understood that most in Mossad were only acknowledged as such within the agency's iron-clad walls. Outside, on missions, in the hands of the enemy, they were nameless faces to the government. They had no contacts waiting for their status reports, no trailers ensuring their safety, no one to call if things went wrong. From her first rendezvous with Salameh's men in Khan Yunis to her tense encounters with the man himself, Gavriella comforted herself with the fact that she was a foreigner, an American, not that it would help her, and a recent recruit. Gavriella was merely a Mossad informant, which meant her assignments always came with what Ziki used to chide her were "Mommy Amenities".

Before she left Tel-Aviv, she had memorized addresses, phone numbers, pickup points, safe deposit boxes in banks and hotels with communication devices, or jamming ones, with —an array of people to contact and places to go if she found herself in the soup. She used to recite the information every night as she lay away awake perspiring through the musty straw mat bedding in her cavernous quarters in Lebanon. The information in her head was as precious as her life. Literally.

Gavriella had been schooled on a series of communication techniques she was to use in passing to Ziki when abroad. First, she had to establish her presence.

Wandering through the lobby, mouth slightly ajar, she ran her fingers along the leather of stately cabernet couches and sleek oak side tables in mock awe, replicating what she imagined a twenty-five-year-old fresh out of Ohio would be doing and feeling if she weren't helping to orchestrate the extermination of an important El Fatah terrorist.

"Oh, excuse me," she gushed, reaching out for the dense maroon sleeve of a passing bellboy, "do you speak English?"

"Yah, of course." His face—or what was visible of it from beneath the brim of his oversized hat—was young and expectant, his mind obviously still on where his body was headed before she stopped it.

Gavriella couldn't see his eyes, but batted hers a few times to let him know the interruption wouldn't be too painful. "Why, I was just wondering if you might have a ladies' room on this level."

"Yah, yah, it is right—maybe you would like to follow me there?"

On their slow walk to the restroom, Gavriella entertained the bellboy with her idle chatter  in between grilling him on some flourish—an elaborate rug here, a miniature chandelier there—In every corner of the lobby to give herself the opportunity to mentally record the people with whom they were sharing it.

"It is here, Madamoiselle, or…how do you say?"

"'Miss', but I prefer 'Mademoiselle.'" She held out her hand. "Thank you very much for the escort…"

"Jürgen."

"Jürgen. I'm Cindy, Jürgen. Cindy Lyons. Oh, and Jürgen, could I possibly bother you with one more question?"

"Yes, please bother me."

"There are pictures of a big, beautiful bank in all of my travel books and I read that it gives tours. I think it's called the National Swiss…something?"

"The Swiss National Bank, Mademoiselle?"

"Yes! That's it! Do you know when these tours are?"

"They are all the time. How do you say—once on each hour?"

"Every hour? Perfect. Well, thank you so much again, Jürgen. So long!"

Gavriella turned and pushed through the heavy "Femme" labeled door to the restroom. Not to be outdone by the lobby it dripped with extravagance. Mirrors framed in hearty wood, stained, and elaborately carved. Chaise lounges clothed in rich fabrics and topped off with creamy silk pillows. More merlot, more fancy fixtures gleaming crystalline in the soft light—all needless ornamentation intended to convince potential hotel guests that they and their Swiss francs would feel right at home at the Baur au Lac. But as it were, she had time to inspect only one more element of the contrived décor: the pearly white, gold rimmed courtesy phone in this particular ladies room and no one else in the room.

"Okay, 'Mommy Amenities', here we go." She picked up the receiver.

"Operator. How may I direct your call?"

Gavriella recited the ten numbers in the operator's German.

"Thank you. Hold for your connection."

Three rings. Three short beeps. Go. The direct connection-it worked.

"Daddy? Hi daddy, it's Cindy! I can't talk long—I'm standing in the bathroom—no—the ladies' lounge—of the swankiest hotel in the city, but I just had to tell someone so I'd stop pinching myself to know it's true—I'm in Zurich! Can you believe it?  Oh I'm having a ball. Staying in this little gray stucco house on Vindegaard lane—number 25 just like me! Who am I staying with? You know the friend I telephoned from America when I wasn't supposed to, yeah, the call that really upset you. The house is fantastically safe; in fact the doors are solid steel. Ohh, don't worry I will leave you a key at the bank here in Zurich. Yes, lots of people—really interesting people, you would find them very interesting. People who have traveled the whole world and done things. They're really super protective of me. In fact, this is my fourth day here, but it's really the first time I've ventured out. What's that? Money? Oh no, don't be ridiculous, I don't need any money. I'll just stop at the bank in a few—they have a beautiful one right in the middle of downtown, the United Bank of Switzerland—and cash in some travelers' checks. Oh Daddy, I wish you could be here. And I wish I could tell you more, but I've really gotta go—literally, ha ha! Can't wait to see you, love you Daddy! Bye bye!"

## Chapter 37

**Safehouse in Zurich-**

A scarlet dawn lay in wait behind cotton ball clouds. As it nudged their edges, impatient for its cue to strike, five men emerged from a large white Volkswagen van bearing the words Privat Polizei along either side. Erik, the driver, had parked on the street in a small residential area of forgetful, but tidy homes in a neighborhood approximately 12 minutes from downtown Zurich. Most of the homes were attached, their large façades forming one massive über-house, much like those in London and the eastern United States. Across from the van sat numbers 4 and 6 Vindegaard Lane, beige, fenced with waist-high wrought iron, and comfortably distanced from the men's final destination. Twenty-two Vindegaard Lane, backed by Iranian oil money and filled with an unspecified number of Fatah members, awaited at the near top of a shallow hill.

The gray exterior and white trim of the safe house broke the domestic continuum that began at the men's van. But aside from standing alone, the building itself was distinguishable only by the streaks of moss growth that had not been cleaned off of its stucco siding. Still, the men knew they stood before doors fortified with steel and blast-resistant locks, and that, behind those doors, men armed with Kalashnikovs and who-knew-what-else awaited them. Dark curtains covered windows made of bullet proof glass and number 22's walls, modified to contain any and all communications those inside received and transmitted, were likely a foot deeper than others on the street and lined with lead.

Erik puffed on an imported cigarette, his cheek pouches expanding like a chipmunk's with each inhale. Plumes of bluish smoke took their time dissipating in the disappearing night's breeze with each release.

"Put that out," Ziki ordered without turning his head.

A few people had emerged from their homes, pressed to get out of the neighborhood before navigating through downtown Zurich became troublesome; they took no notice of the five men dressed in black pants and brown work shirts red embroidered with names across the fronts of their breast pockets.

Ziki squinted as the dim remains of moonlight scraped across his cornea.

With Erik's cigarette stamped out, he imagined he could smell the men he came to "collect" less than a hundred meters away.

"How about we take them out with explosives…just like those sons of bitches did in Tel-Aviv?"

Perhaps, Ziki thought, he should have let Erik keep the cigarette—it would have given his mouth something to do instead of its usual, rampant chattering.

The Tel-Aviv incident he referred to was a recent attack on one of the city's teenage nightclubs. Saturday night, loud music, dancing. At first, no one noticed when the ground shook. Not until the trembles became too fierce to be the blaring speakers. Then their bodies were cut, open. They could see little through the flames and fear and hear nothing through the screaming. People fell to a floor, now a nasty cocktail of dust and blood.

"Take the whole damn building down in a ball of flames, that's what I say," Erik continued, his bitter gaze steadied on the house before him as if the sheer intensity of the stare would set the building afire.

A light shone through the main window but there was no movement within. That was expected. Those outside knew they were there.

"We've gone over this. Catch the big fish, Salame, alive for interrogation. All the others, less our two inside, are expendable. Though we are—" he paused to clear his throat before continuing. "Strongly urged to take prisoners instead of leaving bodies."

The men nodded in unison.

He continued, "two groups. Three in front, two to the back." He looked to the bulky, typically level head of his second-in-command, "you and Alex will come with me we'll take the front. Erik, you and Yaakov will go around the back to seal off the area. Nowhere for the rats to scurry off to. As always, we move to leave no evidence we were ever here. Stay alert, stay alive."

Amit popped the trunk and lifted the panel the spare tire they had replaced with five snub-nosed Uzis that Ziki had collected from the Swiss National Bank vault the previous morning. Each man carried a personal sidearm, the Uzis, in preparation for a close range fire fight. Each Uzi came with a bloated mesh sack that attached to the side of the weapon where the shell casings were expelled. The group was to move in and out as quickly as possible, leaving no traces of who they were or what they were doing there. That meant no straggling shell casings.

The explosives were nestled next to the guns in a separate compartment along with the electrical devices and remotes needed to control their detonation. Finishing off the assembled arsenal were some smoke grenades and enough gas masks for each man, plus the only two people currently inside number 22 that Ziki would risk every ounce of his being to get out alive. Amit passed an Uzi to all in turn, with none but Alex checking to make sure that the lock and chamber were operational.

"What, you don't trust my driving? You think that the bumpy ride did something to the guns…?" asked Erik.

"I don't trust anything. Trust gets people shot." Alex's response was cold, emotionless. His steely blue eyes stared straight ahead. Alex's demeanor was one

Ziki had hoped all of his men would adopt. Of course, from Alex, there was no adoption. The icy removal of himself from his work was bred into him.

Alex rarely spoke, though his words came out as aphorisms filled eerily with the wisdom of one who knew too much. Now he circled around Amit to the open trunk and pulled out the remote detonator for the explosive charges, a thin black device resembling a television remote control re-wired by a very disturbed viewer. Though the other men had the basic skills and training necessary to use them, explosives were Alex's specialty.

Ziki watched him tuck the detonator safely into a pouch at his waist, giving Ziki his sole reassurance about the mission at hand: the building would not blow up unless he gave the order.

"That's good advice, Alex. Yaakov, are you listening? Trust gets people shot." Ziki shot at the fresh-faced rookie. It was only his second assignment and his first, a fairly tame recon mission, had done little to wipe away the machismo that dripped from his creaseless brow.

Ziki doled out a few more instructions and reminder while looking over the building's blueprints one more time. Layout was simple: two doors, one in front, and one in back. No alternate way out. No heads up from Langley. No escape this time.

"What do you think, you think you can take the pressure?"

Yaakov's authority gave him only one choice: grin and bear it. Eyes open, mouth shut: the rookie mantra. Yaakov, cocky beyond his status, did manage to mutter,"Yes, Grandpa."

"Here," Ziki said, placing a smoke grenade and a key in Erik's outstretched right hand, "take this. I have the key to the front door, the American, Gavriella." Grins all around.

"How nice of them to provide us with the keys," Erik cut in. "Heaven knows that walking right in the front door with grins on our faces is the safest way to take them out…."

"At exactly 0545 we begin the raid…at exactly 0545, you, Erik, will follow up by opening the back door and discharging this grenade—make sure your watches are set, all of you. Use the confusion that ensues to your advantage—remember, you know exactly what's going on and you have a plan. They don't. I don't want this to take long—15 minutes max and we're off. Clear?"

"Clear."

The men broke into their cluster groups, fanning around the haphazardly clipped shrubbery bordering the house. Ziki's squad crouched down in the lawn only a few meters from the door. Seconds ticked by. Ziki felt his heart pulse. Erik and Yaakov inched silently through the alleyway between 22 and 24 to cover the back door.

All five men donned their masks. Ziki crept closer to the door, chest on the doorstep, until his arm was near enough to slide the key into the lock. While turning slowly with the raised arm, he maneuvered the stun grenade attached to the strap he wore across his chest into his free hand and pulled the pin.

0545.

"Now."

A soft click and the door disengaged from the lock. Its heavy steel studs forced Ziki to nudge it with the butt of the grenade to separate it from the frame before he hurled the weapon, already hissing and rumbling with gas, inside. He had only to blink twice before the initial stream of white-gray smoke asphyxiated the room.

Frantic shouts in Arabic, orders, emanated from deep within the house. By now, the gas was billowing out of the crack of the front door and snaking lazily across the lawn. The three at the door moved quickly.

Crack, crack! A burst of machine gunfire responded to his calls, followed by more shouting from voices gripped with hysteria. Ziki searched the voices for one in particular. The gun fire continued, two more gunmen now joining in. He squinted, eyes struggling to focus on the chaos unfolding before him, and sought out her long dark hair and delicate outline. Shells hit a cheap particle-board table and splintered it, sending shards flying in every direction and adding to the difficulty of pinpointing men who knew the inside of the house far better than those who had let themselves into it. Ziki had warned her about this; he had told her to stay off the main floor, to hide until one of them found her.

The men ducked behind the few pieces of furniture the room contained, Ziki and Alex shielded by a big sofa, Amit a turned table. Seconds passed. An orange flash—the product of more discharged weapons split the smoke, clearing a temporary hole in the otherwise darkness. Then the footsteps, like lead against the weak floorboards supporting them, rushing through the second story.

"Ziki, that sounds—" Alex began.

"Like more than we bargained for."

Ziki swore under his breath. The smoke had begun to clear, but visibility was still bad. If not for the gas masks, he wouldn't be able to tell their men from his own. But he knew the gunfire had come from the immediate right, at waist height.

Alex heard the same and trained his Uzi in that direction, aiming low, hoping for a leg wound. He unloaded a burst until he heard the unmistakable whelp and subsequent Arabic curses of a hit target.

"Yahudi ibn el sharmuta!"

One hit, maybe two.

As the hit party's outburst subsided into low moans, Erik's stun grenade came barreling through the house's back door.

0548.

On the other side, Erik and Yaakov stood against the house's shingles on either side of the back door, waiting to spring the trap. They had heard the gunfire coming from within, and held their positions, just as planned.

"Can you—," began Yaakov tentatively, his school boy conceit subdued by a sudden rush of fear and adrenaline. Erik cut him off before he could finish the thought.

"No, I can't see a damn thing. The smoke spread the moment we entered, and I can't tell who's doing the shooting, Ok? Now shut the fuck up and pay attention!"

Yaakov did as he was told.

A smoke grenade—things were bad for someone in there and if it was his team, all he had contributed to the fight was a little smoke. Erik wanted badly to burst through the door.

As if hearing his plea, justice, Erik would later claim, flung two figures from the smoke. One wore no shirt and a pair of loose-fitting brown pants with scuffed brown commando boots laced to the calf. A loosely wrapped bright white and orange turban imprisoned his head, his long hair, shooting out from underneath it. The other, a slightly shorter and stockier version of the first man, was dressed in the dark green, brown, and black of camouflage. With clenched fists and arms flailing, both chugged their legs relentlessly to freedom. The men were at the edge of the square patch of browning lawn, almost to the fence that separated this property from the next, before the two posted by the door felt their reflexes kick in.

Erik jerked his weapon forward, finger on the trigger. "Stop where you are or I will take you down!" he boomed in Arabic.

Deaf to his warning, the men continued towards the fence, hands grasping upward for what would be a trying passage over. Erik pulled the trigger to open fire.

Tick! Nothing. He squeezed harder. Still nothing. Something had happened to his gun. It was…jammed. But Uzi's never jammed. It couldn't be the gun. It…

"Yaakov, I can't fire! Shit!" It wasn't the gun. It was the ammo. Unmarked, specially made, non-traceable rounds of ammunition that couldn't quite make the transition from cartridge to barrel. Helluva time to figure out something they needed to work on. The few words Alex had spoken that day rung through his ears. Sometimes he hated that guy.

Erik fingered the bolt, struggling to pull it back into place. It didn't budge.

"Christ, Yaakov, they're getting out of range!" The men had reached the fence and each had an arm flung over the top. "What are you waiting for?! Shoot, Boy!"

Yaakov, frozen, felt a warm trickle of sweat roll slowly down the back of his neck and down his spine. Erik's command blended with the sounds of the morning—chirps of rising birds, the passing breeze, light early-morning traffic less than 50 meters behind him. He watched himself lift his weapon and pulled the trigger. The first round pierced the first man, hitting him twice in the shoulder, one in the neck; he died instantly. Rivulets of blood clawed the air, seemingly suspended in the same vortex Yaakov found himself occupying. But the blood stayed only a moment before leaving him behind to saturate the thirsty grass.

His weapon still engaged, Yaakov made a half turn to the left. Another clip popped quickly into the chamber of his Uzi, and unloaded on the camouflaged man.  Strike one in the hip rendered his climbing attempts futile, but he still clung to the fence's wooden top edge.  Strike two—in between the ribs at the small of his back—dismantled the grip and, as he fell, perfectly erect, towards the ground, strike three drove into the thigh of his left leg, shredding the material of his pants and birthing a deep black wound.  This man still breathed.

Yaakov slowly let out the breath he had been holding, releasing with it the unmistakable feeling that he was about to be ill.

0550.

The smoke nearly dispersed, Ziki and his men took in the details of their surroundings through the condensation accumulated on the insides of their gas masks.  Clumps of it hung on to the thick plastic visors, forming drops that worked themselves** into the eyes, down the neck.

Alex crawled over to the area where he had unloaded his clip.  As it was, only one man had been wounded, and he laid face up, one leg unhinged and contorted to the side.  The Uzi's 9-millimeter rounds had riddled the man's thigh, leaving it to expel blood freely into a pool on the thick carpet, which likely accounted for his unconcern with the corresponding leg's positioning.  If he were speaking honestly, Alex would say that he would be perfectly content for the man before him to be dead, as long as it was not at his own hand, and as long as he did not have to watch him die.  Though Alex believed in his country and its defense of itself, and though the thirst for revenge struck his gut just as often as it did Erik's and Amit's, he did not like inflicting pain or looking into the face of the dying.

Explosives was the closest he could get to emotional distance in the army. The bombs he made and, often, detonated took lives; but he was usually able to stay far way.  Raids like these were rare for him, and left him even more sullen and removed than his typical state of "sullen and removed."  But Ziki Barak had requested him specifically for this mission and his respect for the Commander's ability to envision a scene and map out the cleanest way to storm it had persuaded him not to object.

Hunched above the injured man, Alex acted quickly, not knowing if he was the primary target or not.  Yet another reason not to let him die—it was imperative that Salame be apprehended alive.  Alex ripped a chunk of material from the man's shirt and hastily made a tourniquet, tightening it just below the joint of the hip. It would stop the bleeding some, enough for the man to survive, and keep him conscious long enough to interrogate him.

"Mayy."  He wanted water.    And he was shaking uncontrollably, convulsing—the onset of shock from the loss of blood.

"What you need is blood," Alex mumbled, wiping his soiled hands on a patch of carpet.  "Help me," was his next request, his steely gaze communicating the immeasurable fear of death.

Alex took out a long measure of electrical cord he had kept wrapped around his belt. He hastily tied the man's legs and arms together, making sure that he would not be a variable as the team moved deeper into the house.

"You help me first," Alex said to the man. "How many more of you are in here?"

Ziki lunged in the fog, reaching for a dark object that cut a silhouette of a man, grabbing it around the waist and thrusting the barrel of his Uzi into its ribs. They were plastic. A mannequin. A diversion.

"Secure the perimeter!" he hollered. "Amit, to the rear, secure the door and see that Erik and Yaakov are holding their own. Alex, back over here—that man is as good as he will ever be."

Ziki wove cautiously through the vicinity, confirming his suspicion that whoever had been on the first story had either fled through the back door or been hit. Or fled to the safety of the story above them. Ziki glanced up. The floorboards had stopped creaking. He moved towards the stairwell, his chest turned towards the room's center, unwilling to turn his back, and craned his neck upward.

"The only way out is up, Commander," Alex's voice whispered from behind. "Intel said there were six people here and I got one, so there are at least--"

"Five more upstairs," Ziki finished. Plus, possibly, his protégé, Iamael. Plus, probably, his…what was she at this point anyway? "And two of us. Just cover me."

"Yes sir."

0552. Erik had grabbed the man still breathing by the lapel of his shirt, bringing the blood-soaked face towards his own.

"Who are you?! What is your name?! Speak or so help me I'll let you bleed to death right here you murdering son of a bitch!"

A blood clot shot from the man's nose onto Erik's Privat Polizei uniform as he tried to articulate his speech. Mere gurgles and guttural incoherencies were all he could manage.

"What in the hell are you doing? Let that man go this instant, he's dying!" Amit had appeared at the entrance of the back door.

The mission was to take these men alive and interrogate them, not to plug them full of lead and let them bleed to death before asking the questions!"

Yaakov kept his distance as Erik and Amit hovered over the man, one trying to choke him, the other trying to resurrect him.

Erik pulled out a six-inch commando knife that had been hidden in the trunk of his boot and placed it against the man's mess of a neck, his eyes sinister. "Now talk, damn you! What is your name? Where is Salameh? Where are your superiors?"

"Dammit Erik, stop! You slit this man's throat and he won't be able to say a damned word!"

"Don't turn your back on me! You were to take these men alive, not kill them in cold blood. You're no better than these terrorists?"Erik called over his shoulder.

"This blood doesn't belong on my hands—just ask golden boy over there. If anybody should be down giving that bastard mouth to mouth it should be Yaakov.

As he disappeared through the mouth of the door, Amit turned his gaze on Yaakov, who was now looking at the lifeless body of the main lain across the lawn.

"Yaakov, tell me, you did this?"

"Yes sir." He gulped, unsure of himself, looking down at the ground and trying not to meet the intensity of Amit's gaze.

"Hell," Amit muttered.

Gavriella Ramon had assumed the earthquake position—ducked and covered—in a tiny dank space filled with dirty towels, empty hangers, and what felt, under her drawn knees, like a small door in the floor. The sound of gunfire and smell of smoke slowing making its way into her space and filled her with a combination of relief and sheer joy.

"Efficient, that Mossad," she thought through the vibrations of another round from below. They had gotten her messages, planned a raid, and dispatched a team in less than a day. And by "they" she meant…

"Get out! Get out! Use the roof to the adjoining buildings!" The Arabic voices were frantic, young—probably some of the teenage "recruits" who had been scattered throughout the rooms and halls the past few nights. Impoverished kids from the dregs of the Gaza Strip and The West Bank who had consumed the passion and promises of a man named Ali Hasan Salameh and his sometime companion Abu Nidal, as if they were the rich meals they themselves would never enjoy. Now bound to him, Gavriella watched the loyal subjects handle guns and curse the "enemy" with a violent anger that could only be a mask for the awkwardness and trepidation no adolescent—Arab, Israeli, or American—can avert.

"No, the front! They're in the back too, the pigs! Look outside—stay low!"

The footsteps entered the room.

"Where is he?" one whispered.

He—Ali—was gone. Gavriella took a moment to regret that Ziki had chosen a morning that one of Ali's "Russian dinner parties" had extended through the night to make their move, and then quickly returned to thinking exclusively about getting out of Zurich alive.

"I see one!" Gavriella detected a slight squeak in the voice. "Jew bastard—I bet we could shoot him from here."

Both seemed to consider this option, with neither wanting to ask the obvious "What if we miss?"

Finally, one concluded, "He's not out far enough from the door. The angle's—Allah no!"

More shots, followed by more footsteps, the latter belonging to the boys, who ran from the room, presumably in search of a better window from which to plan their attack or escape.

The gunshots, replaced by muffled shouts, stopped for a while, and though the sweetish smell of smoke grew stronger, Gavriella began to wonder if she shouldn't move from her hideout to the window and flag down Ziki's man the kids had spoken of.

"Gavriella, listen to me—are you listening?" His words pestered her ears. "If we are successful, that means that there will be a lot of firing, a lot of gas, and, possibly, some explosives. When these things begin, you find somewhere small and covered, and you hide, you understand?"

"But Ziki, won't they wonder—"

"Once they realize they are under attack, they won't wonder anything but how they are going to save their own asses, find a hiding spot and stay put. You will become invisible to them."

And she had. Men pushed by, shoved her aside, gave her not a second look once the "Raid!" warning had been given. Even Raiid, the head instructor from Lebanon, whose contemptuous looks and hisses had become an addendum to their every passing, would have passed right through her in his mad dash for the staircase had she not been a solid mass. Instead, he had simply ordered, "Move!" and spun her behind him.

She understood perfectly now. And so she continued to sit, in her small, covered space. Waiting.

0558. Ziki and Alex were halfway up the narrow flight of stairs, hidden behind a small chunk of the once-coffee table, when gunshots fired from above. Instinct sent them low, turned sideways between stairs as bullets whirred past them. The smoke, as much protection as it was hindrance on the first floor, had not yet had enough time to infiltrate the second.

Two more shots—these from handguns. The men, still grasping the flimsy table piece with their left hands, raised their Uzis in their right, as they made their way on to the landing at the top of the stair case. To their right, a door way led into a room devoid of furniture, a small, burned out light bulb dangling from its socket in the middle of the ceiling. With his back to Ziki's, Alex moved alongside the near wall until the tip of his Uzi passed over the door's threshold and could be swept across the interior.

A shuffling from inside and then, boom! Alex opened fire into a dark corner obscured by the arc of the door. Ziki, who had began to creep past the doorway, spun around backwards, bumping backs with Alex once again. The shuffling stopped. Alex slowly poked his head around the edge of the door, in line with the barrel of his gun. A big black rat lay dead before them.

Alex exhaled in relief. "Dead rat. Not a problem for me."

Ziki allowed himself to breathe as well. "Always calm in a crisis, that's why I like you Alex."

"Crisis isn't over yet, Commander. Those gun shots didn't come from that rat. You got the lead into the next room?"

"Let's move."

Directly behind them and to the left of the small clearing at the top of the stairs was another room, this one's door closed. The two moved along either side of the walls towards it, their hands squeezing their weapons tighter. Ziki looked at Alex and nodded, before moving in front of the door.

Ziki took a two step start before lurching forward and impacting a forceful kick just to the side of the doorknob. Snap! The door was open.

"Ugh!" Alex groaned, covering his mouth as the scene spanned before them and the stifling scent of blood mixed with perspiration and mildew reached their nostrils.

Two bodies lay limp, inglorious, in the middle of the floor, both hemorrhaging from the forehead. The wounds had already blackened from an entry powerful enough to shatter the brain pan and what rusty blood that hadn't splattered on the dirty, chipped walls congregated in the center of the room. Behind the bodies, a smaller, doorless entry way suggested the makings of a small bathroom.

Taking no chances, Ziki and Alex kept their weapons trained on the two men until they were close enough to check their pulses. Ziki bent down to check the larger man, a squat, oafish character with self-inflicted scars and symbolic tattoos ornamenting his forearms. "Dead."

"Him too," Alex said of the slighter, equally decorated man.

Both still clutched their weapons in one hand, the larger man holding fast to a velvet and gold-plated copy of the Koran in the other.

Ziki stood motionless; his back to the small bathroom and his head down to observe the carnage sprawled before him. "A double suicide. Don't see that everyday."

"Not unless they take someone else out with them."

"Must've known just a little too much. Couldn't risk being taken alive. Probably following a direct order. Whatever these two were up to in here must have been one helluva a secret to cause such a—"

A sharp pain in the side of his leg stopped Ziki short. He looked down to see the hand of a boy, no older than 12, wrapped around the handle of a blade that was now a good four inches inside his thigh.

Gavriella didn't know how long she had been in this space. An hour? A year? There had been a flurry of activity several minutes ago. Shots, then more, then…nothing. The silence worried her more than the shooting. The people she shared the house with were trying to escape and the people who had broken into it were trying to rescue her. If her people had fired the shots and the others hadn't escaped, there would be no quiet. There would be footsteps, Ziki's men checking the rest of the place. Calling her name. Looking for her. If her people had not fired the shots—

Before she could refuse to complete the thought, the small door swung open and a man in a gas mask bearing an Uzi loomed above her.

Gavriella screamed.

Off came the gas mask and an arm, attached to the face of Ziki Barak, reached down, and pulled her to her feet. "Shushh, Gavriella! You wanna get us both killed?"

"Oh my…" was her answer. She collapsed into him, spreading her arms and hands across his chest the same way she used to spread them across the oven door when her mother was baking Christmas cookies. The familiar smell, the cozy warmth, the knowledge that her laborious would be over soon and the good things behind that door would be hers….

"Shhh! I'm here," Ziki whispered. He had curled his arms around her and now stood slowly rocking them both back and forth. "It's okay. We're leaving now. It's over. It's almost over."

"Oh Ziki," she said, suddenly returning to Vindegaard Lane, "he's not here. Salameh isn't here."

A grim nod: "I know."

"I didn't know you would come so soon. I thought—I don't know why I thought it—but I thought I would know beforehand. I was…so stupid. I'm so sorry."

Ziki shrugged. "This part here, this house, this is over. That part," he nodded toward the window the two Arab boys had studied not fifteen minutes before, "it's not over. We'll get him."

"I'm just so thankful—"

**"I knew it! You evil bitch!** American *sharmuta,* whore! I told him you were not ours—so many times but he would not listen! I should have cut your whore heart out when  I had the chance!"

Raiid Hassan Mohammed stood, despite his contentions otherwise, dumbfounded, three paces outside her space. Gavriella knew he was dumbfounded because his weapon, on him, now lay limply in his hands awaiting a new cartridge load.

Ziki noticed this too but, having swung aside his own weapon to embrace Gavriella, reacted by lunging at Raiid.

Raiid's weapon—an AK—flew from his hands and scuttled into the passageway behind him. The two men fell to the floor rolling, each grabbing first for the loose weapon, then for the other's. Ziki, momentarily on top of the flailing Raiid, arched his back high and grabbed for his enemy's neck, but Raiid thwarted the attempt and spun Ziki over to regain control.

"Backup!" Ziki yelled.

"Back up where?" Gavriella cried, stepping away all the same. She searched the room for a weapon.

Raiid, maintained his upside stronghold,

A choking Raiid had managed to clutch one hand to the one around his neck. Gavriella watched the grooves of Ziki's calloused knuckles glisten with blood as Raiid employed long, jagged fingernails to loosen his assailant's grip. He used his other hand not to fend off the ambush from above, but to reach blindly, seemingly searching for something at Ziki's side.

Gavriella spat and wiped the acidic remains of the vomit covering her chin. "Arghh!"

The cry was long, drawn out…and from Ziki. Gavriella followed Raiid's wandering hand to a spot on Ziki's leg that she had not noticed was soaked with blood. He was injured. And Raiid's fingers digging into his injury inflicted pain enough to loosen Ziki's grip on the Shahid's jugular.

Raiid jerked his neck back and swatted Ziki's arm to the floor before heaving forward to return the  favor.

Ziki groaned, his body flailing more in reaction to the pain in his leg than in a bona fide attempt to fend his enemy off.

Gavriella made a second move towards the them, this time stopping short at Raiid's right pant leg. Beneath it, she could see the outline of the *shabaria*, the same *shabaria* that he had used on her fingertips in Lebanon.

Raiid was laughing aloud now; delighting in the power awarded him as he held his Ziki's life between his fingers. Gavriella was invisible—or, at least, inconsequential—to him. As such, it took her only a single motion to slide her hand beneath his baggy fatigues and pull the *shabaria,* knife, free.

The man's cackle slowed, recognizing what its vanity had allowed. Raiid let go of Ziki's throat and turned his attention to the woman whose arm now gripped his knife and aimed its steely tip high.

"Ba'albek!" she screeched.

And drove the long blade upward into the soft flesh of his neck.

"Commander!"

Alex had appeared in the doorway.

"It's alright, Alex. Everything's alright."

Once Raiid had fallen dead before him, and Gavriella stood safe—albeit covered in his blood and her own vomit, and refusing to loosen her fierce grip on the *shabaria* she had used to kill him—Ziki's adrenaline rush subsided and he began to feel the muscles in his right leg constrict, the slow, deep throb of his wound setting in.

Alex said nothing, but reached for Ziki's leg.

"Salameh's missing, and everyone else is either with us, gone, or dead. We're done here."

"Did anyone find Iamael?"

"Iamael, he's with Salameh, he takes him everywhere with him." Gavriella said, his food stinks."

"Get her in the van—and try to help her get cleaned up."

Amit shifted his severe brow to Alex's other side, furrowing it deeper when he saw that one of the brown pant legs of Ziki's Privat Polizei uniform had been sliced open and wrapped tightly, tourniquet-style, around his thigh.

"Boss, you're still bleeding."

"I'll be fine, Sergeant. But," he continued, scanning the small collection of men they had bound with additional cord and positioned against the fence in the back yard, "where's the little prick that did this to me?"

"Prickette, you mean," Erik replied, motioning towards his feet.

Barely visible behind the leather and rubber of Erik's boots sat a creature so frail the sinews of its arms threatened to burst through its yellowed skin.

"Time to face your accuser, kiddo," Erik said, crouching down and gently coaxing the girl into the open.

In the light—it was now well past 6 a.m., well past the time they should have been gone—the young boy was more obviously a young girl. Her large, wide set eyes and narrow tulip-like mouth drooped low, reminding Ziki of a marionette his cousin Rachel once had whose face could transform from delight to sorrow with the soft tug of a string. Taking in the ribs jutting sharply from beneath her tattered t-shirt, Ziki imagined the sorrow in this girl's face was not affected so easily.

Still using Alex as a crutch, Ziki bent as low as he could and, in Arabic, asked, "What is your name?"

"She can't—"Erik began, but stopped when the girl opened her mouth and pronounced a garbled syllable of nothing.

Staring her full in the face, Ziki saw what Erik had started to warn him of; a blackened stump rolling around in the cavity where her tongue should have been.

His face tightened and his stomach churned, fatigue being the only thing keeping him from getting sick. "That monster," he said, "what in the name of G'd has he done to you?" Then, to his men: "Get her in the van. And give the rest of them a shot of morphine and bring them too. Amit," he reached out to the Sergeant, "I'll need a hand."

**The man upstairs spat.**

"That's what I thought. You're a real hard ass. Don't move. Don't you realize that there is no getting away for you, that you are at the end of the line? The only thing that will save you is you telling me everything that I want to know? Will you do that? Will you talk? Will you talk!?" Meekly, imperceptibly and defeated, the man nodded his head in the affirmative. "Okay then."

"Where is Ali Hassan Salameh?"

"He left last night, as you were coming in the morning," he mumbled.

"And the one they call 'Abdul?'"

"He left with Salameh."

"Where did they go? Do you know?" They left through the tunnel that led out to the sewers. He hesitated… "Do you know?"

He nodded his head—"They went to Halle…they went to Halle and then to Jenna…in East Germany."

"Do you know the exact location?"

"In the papers upstairs behind the fireplace."

"Who are they seeing there? Talk?"

"Okay, okay—Two old Germans, rich ones, members of the 'Odessa,' you know?….Nazis, something, scientists…That's all I know."

"You are going to be okay, we'll take care of you now. Patch him up." He had given out all they wanted to hear. At that Ziki plunged the needle into the man's neck, morphine for the pain causing his body to instantly relax. With any luck he would remain that way, docile, until they could get him to the rendezvous point where he would be shipped to Israel through Piraeus in Greece. No such interrogation was needed for the other man, the man that Alex had in the back. The last thing he had said before fainting was the Arabic equivalent to: "I'll do anything you want, just don't kill me. I beg you, anything but death… I'll tell you anything you want to know." He now lay in a heap on the floor, his head propped up at an awkward angle against the leg of a blown-out sofa seat.

…There was no telling what the mounds of papers were, which ones held future plans, which ones held the key to saving lives… A no-warning strike.

"It won't stop them but it will slow them down."

Amit came up to Ziki, a spiral bound notebook cracked at the seam and draped across his forearm. "It looks like a training manual…something that has to do with rockets and chemicals. Take a look at it, my German's not as good as yours."

"German not Arabic? That's interesting." Amit was correct, it was a manual including painstaking details of the inner workings of specific biological agents. Bubonic plague of a mutated strand and some drawings of ballistic missiles.

"This confirms what we found in the safe in Ba'albek," a find that didn't really surprise Ziki. Mossad had already known that the Odessa organization, had ties to Salameh's and Abu Nidal's networks. Nidal had splintered from the PLO and formed his own group.

"Gather as much of this paper work as you can," Ziki ordered. "Be thorough going through the cabinets, and be doubly sure to get all those papers that they tried to burn in the fireplace, no matter what condition you find them in. And search well behind the fireplace."

"There is something more behind there, something …dates, locations of several planned strikes, and look here…The Jenna and Halle details."

"I will say, gentlemen, aside from the big mess that you made, this throbbing pain in the back of my leg and that we missed Salameh and 'Abdul' once more… This is good work." The other men agreed in unison, sharing warm smiles, except for Yaakov. To anyone's knowledge, he hadn't muttered a word since gunning that man down seven minutes ago. Knowing this and reading his body language, Ziki came up to him and put his hand on his shoulder.

"Yaakov, I know what you're thinking. We all felt the same way that you do at one time or another. It happens. Just remember that by the actions you took today—that all of us took today, we have made the world just that much safer from the clutches of madmen. Surely that's something to be proud of, don't you think?" Yaakov nodded his head, a little bit of zest beginning to again shine from his eyes.

"That's right, so wipe that look off of your face and pick your head up. Once we're done here I'll buy you a beer—just you and me. How does that sound?"

"Yes, Sir."

"That's much better."

"Let's move; we have to get out of here." Ziki looked at his watch. "The schedule says now." By the time they had finished searching the house for information they could glean and ferreted it in the recesses of their security van, Alex had strategically laced the building's supporting walls and foundation with enough explosives to sink a small island. The explosives were meticulously laid out to ensure that the building would collapse on itself and not spread a fire to any adjoining buildings. It was a routine; one that Alex was renowned for. No evidence, not even the bodies of the dead.

0609. Halle and Jena addresses in hand, along with the medicated captives, the group was ready to move. Packing themselves into the van as if they were just there on a tour de jour, they headed off into what was turning out to be a clear and warm day in Zurich. Cruising along at the speed limit, the van pulled around the edge of the street.

"Now, Alex, blow this shithole down." Said Ziki. Alex pushed the button of his device; it was done. Just beyond their vision, large flames shot out the windows of the two-story house, the broken glass belching black smoke out into the air in a great ball. The temperature within the house would be immense. The explosives had been laid to vaporize everything, no evidence except for the fire. The morning carried the sound of wood shattering and splintering as the house collapsed on itself, holding still for an instant before the top floor slipped off its hinges and the walls came tumbling down. Nothing left but ruble.

"Fitting end," muttered Erik.

"Anybody up for breakfast?" asked Amit.

"Sounds like a plan," said Ziki. "We need all the strength we can get if we are to make it to East Germany today."

"Germany?" asked a confused Erik. "What's in Germany?"

"Two words," Ziki replied, "Jenna and Halle."

## Chapter 39

**Ziki removed the cover** from the outgoing end of the room's telephone receiver and nestled a small, fine-toothed chip inside. A thin black wire ran from one end of the chip to a thick, gray metal box with its own receiver and 12-key pad. Ziki cradled the latter receiver between his right ear and shoulder.

"Hey Gabby," he called. Gavriella sat on a cushioned window bench fiddling with the knobs and antenna of a finicky radio. "Can you do me a favor?"

"What's that?"

"I'm about to get on with the big dogs here, so do you think you can keep your hands off me for a few minutes? I know I'll be hard to resist sitting here shirtless and all, but I really need to concentrate, so, just for a few minutes okay?"

"Oh, Zik," she mock pouted, tossing aside the radio and pawing her way across the bed behind him, "that's a lot to ask."

Her hands crawled up the small of his back, sending him into an involuntary shiver. "Cold?" she asked.

"Amongst other things." He grinned. "I think I'd like my shirt back."

"What," she asked, fingering the collar, "this shirt?"

"Yeah, that shirt," he said and, reaching for the strategically placed middle buttons, continued, "Here, let me help you get it off."

She dodged his lurch and jumped to her feet. Sliding it effortlessly over her head and tossing it onto his, she balked, "Make your phone call. I'll put on my own clothes and go get some ice."

Ziki ran his eyes down the curve of spine and rear end following her to the room's bureau. Gavriella Ramon was a perfect woman, and without doubt she had an ass like a peach. It always reminded him of one of the first love lessons his father taught him. He was eight years old, the day after he'd met Iosi and Avi at the Bahai Persian gardens on Mount Carmel in Haifa. Sitting at the kitchen table cutting bright red hearts out of construction paper. Taking the seat beside him, his dad picked up his own piece of paper and meticulously wove his scissors around it.

"It's perfect!" his young self had exclaimed.

"Of course it is perfect. It is love. Love is perfect." His Dad then turned the heart upside down, laid it on top of another, uncut piece of paper, and drew two legs protruding from the edges of its curves. Wryly, he added, "This is perfect too.

But it is not love. It is lust!"

"Be back in a minute, I want some ice," Gavriella called as her contour disappeared behind the door. Ziki smiled at his father's words. None truer had ever been spoken.

Now alone, Ziki's attention, once again, returned to the receiver, which now laid unattended on his pillow. He reclaimed it and gave the keypad its requisite numbers.

The voice came after the first ring.

"So, Barak, the time has come to pay an old bill—remember Khan Yunis—you left three dead behind, Salameh and Nidal escaped, and then there's this girl—. The girl you trusted—then you go off to have a party."

"Sir, that is not how it happened."

"I know exactly how it happened," Malkielly hissed. "I know how everything happens. And you would be wise to never forget that, Commander."

"Yes, Sir."

"The American girl. Is she with you?"

*You know everything, asshole, you tell me.* "Yes, Sir."

"Get rid of her. She's finished."

"I'm sorry, Sir?"

"Get rid of her. Make it an accident or an accidental shooting in one of your favorite regions, maybe Gaza."

Ziki felt his heart stop. His throat contracted hard, leaving him gasping for air.

"Is there a problem, Commander?"

His voice was weak, pinched, but he forced himself to recover. "A problem, yes. Sir, I know that Zurich did not go exactly as planned, but we haven't lost everything and that 'safehouse' was destroyed. We are one stroke away from him and his entourage, like Abu Nidal—'The Chemist, and she is the key."

"Gavriella Ramon—who, not too long ago, sold out you and endangered 3000 of our men—is still the key you say to our obtainment of Salameh?"

Ziki didn't know if Malkielly was challenging or mocking him. "She is the key." He had regained his balance and his voice, he hoped, was resolute.

"And it's a mere coincidence that this key has long legs and nice tits and your every move wrapped around her little finger?"

"Sir, that is not the case. She has changed. You saw her change. You—we changed her. She is in this for us. She led us to him in Zurich." No doubt Malkielly and his omniscience would know that that last statement was partly true.

"Fine. Then let her prove it for now, but after that she is finished. Do you understand me Barak—that is an order. I hope, Commander, that the head you are using to make this judgment call does not forget what we have at stake here. Their successful termination is crucial."

"I Understand. I'll be in touch, Sir."

"Fine. And call downstairs to get the latest brief. Our friends seem to have felt it was time for a vacation."

"**Geez, the city hits seventy-two degrees** and all of the cold blooded German tourists start camping out at the ice machines." Gabby kicked the door shut with a slippered foot and held up two beige plastic buckets brimming with square cubes of ice. "I figured I should horde what I could before one of them dives in and taints the supply."

"Yeah, yeah that's a good idea," Ziki nodded, his mind still conversing with Malkielly.

"Hey," she said, plopping down next to him, "what's wrong?" She moved her head along the curves of his hunched neck and shoulders down to the receiver that still lay in his hands. "Did someone call?"

He thought a moment too long.

"Oh God, Ziki, what? What happened? Should I pack?"

She jumped up, kicking one of the buckets she had set down on the floor beside them. Ice tumbled silently across the carpet. A piece caught the artificial glow of a brass desk lamp and flickered in Ziki's eye.

"No!" He reached out to stop her and, grabbing the white fluff of her bathrobe, drew her back to the spot beside him on the bed. "Everything's fine. I just got word on Salameh's status."

"What? Where is he?"

"After his little business in Halle, East Germany, then on his way to the U.S. with Arafat—he knows we can't touch him on American soil he and Arafat are under DDI and CIA protection—. Your friend Walters, some kind of a deal with Arafat and the PLO—. They don't hurt you and you leave them alone. Hard to believe but true. And you guys," he nudged a bare knee that had broken through the robes' closure, "aren't going to hand him over to us. So—"

"That sonofabitch!" Gavriella broke in.

"Yeah, but a slick one. He—"

"He split into the sewers in Zurich and I am lucky he just left me behind! Well.

Ziki gawked, frozen in positions "dazed" and "dumb".

"Oh, close your mouth, Cave Man, I did not sleep with him, I just led him on" she snapped. "If you sacrificed two weeks and two fingerprints for some evil twisted…

Her lips turned down into a chin jutting with indignance. Ziki wondered if he was actually going to have to reassure the woman he loved that his sworn enemy and her self-absorbed terrorist faux associate didn't mean to desert her after she helped set him up.

"Okay, Gavriella, I am very sorry that this evil spawn of Satan proved not to be loyal. But you're going to have to fume about it later. I need you to play nice for now," he handed her the phone, "and give him a call. See if you can convince him to  meet you in Beirut."

## Chapter 40

**EAST GERMANY**

**JENNA—HALLE**
**The black hull of the late model Land Rover sped along the road in the dim moonlit night**. Flashes of the countryside flew by for those interested enough to watch through the windows. Road signs. Cows. Even people here and there, early risers—probably farmers, wrapped up in bundles of clothing looking more like stuffed dolls loosely sewn together at the seams than real living entities. Kilometer after kilometer of fences in symmetrical patterns, making one wonder if they were there to keep something in or keep something out.

"Keep it under the speed limit. We don't need to visit with the local police." Ziki leaned back against the stiff upholstery of the front passenger-side seat, running the mission through his head. He had gotten detailed information, Mossad had deciphered the safehouse documents, names and new instructions came from Tel Aviv.

"Yes, sir," said Erik, his hands resting atop the steering wheel in bored solace, his eyes peering off into the kilometers of empty road that spread out before him. His mind wondered... a road to oblivion, nothing much for kilometers. The men were equally comatose save for Alex. Alex was lost in quiet meditation, carefully weaving together in his mind the closure that this phase of the mission would bring: his family's closure, his closure; on a long enough timeline, the survival rate drops to zero. These old men cozily tucked away behind a mansion of plaster and guarded iron gates would learn that soon enough. They would finally pay a prize.

"Halle—23 Kilometers," said the passing sign, the color of the sign breaking the monotony of the fields and patterned fences enough to draw the eye. It stretched out of the earth like a plant; like somebody had planted a seed for the sign and with enough light and water it grew outwards. Towards them. Beckoning them.

Even amid the darkness of the East German countryside, the lights of the city illuminated the sky... Halle was now the tattered shell of a once prosperous and industrious city; the lights burned bright, yearning in the darkness for those with enough resolve to find it, to reach it… Maybe cleanse it of its past…

"Gentlemen," said Ziki, "I hope that everyone has gotten enough rest…"

"Let me guess," muttered Amit under closed eyelids, interrupting, his hands laid across the chest of his reclining body as if they had been thrown there and landed in that posture, "we're almost to the outskirts of the city and you want to make sure that all of us still remember what our mission details are?"

Silence… "Very good, Amit.

"Nothing more until further notice…Go ahead rest." Yielding sometimes gave the men respect; that was a good thing. With that, Ziki placed the palm of each open hand between the back of his neck and his seat.

Rustic colors continued to rush by. The night seemed to blend them together, making them all look the same: kilometer after kilometer of everything that looked like nothing; blurred pigments on the painter's canvas.

Erik pressed the gas pedal to the floor, the vehicle reacting sharply to this new command, speeding even faster to their destination—but his foot immediately eased off the gas; Ziki's orders—stay within the speed limit.

**He kicked his feet out sharply in front, raising the knee up to his chest before repeating the procedure with his other foot**. He would continue this all the way down the line to the end of the ornately crafted black iron gate, turn smartly on his heel until he was facing the direction that he had just came from, and continue back along the line.

At the midway point, Arnold would do it all over again; the barrel of his rifle rested on his shoulder, his left hand on the butt. The goose-step: a remnant of the glory days of the German people. This was guard duty, and he didn't mind too much. It was better than pulling kitchen duty in the mansion. Arnold Scholzel was a private security guard.

"I'm a soldier," Arnold told himself, and he would look the part and act the part. All the instructors at the academy said that he had potential, and he knew they were right. They must be right. He liked the uniform, the way it impressed the women in the city whenever he got a chance to visit there on leave. The kind words and encouragement from the older men that looked as if they had gone through hell and back, and survived with alcohol on their breath, their eyes rimmed with red, memories on their lips.

Being a soldier was in his blood. His father, his father's father, his father's father, his line probably ran back to the Germanic tribes that used to fight on horseback with swords to the thundering of trumpets against the rampant attacks of barbarian tribes… In his blood. He accepted it.

2330. Time for him to rest and for a fresh man to relieve his post. He walked gingerly to the guard station, a little white box of an office midway between the enormous lengths of the gate. It was tucked a few meters behind where he met the guard marching identically in the opposite direction, his friend Dorre on this night that sucked the heat out of the skin and sent chills from the soles of the feet to the tight circles of flesh on the top of the head.

Beyond the gate lay an enormous mansion built in the fashion of ancient castles that evoked the ethos of a different era, an era of Germany's imperial ambitions. Be that what it may, Arnold Scholzel was proud of his country. His people. Their history. Within the guard station's line of sight, Arnold could see the officer on duty, his friend Dietmar. He barged in the small dilapidated door, making as much noise as possible in order to avoid the barrel of a gun being shoved in his face.

"Is it that late already?" asked Dietmar into his coffee, his eyes mindlessly scanning a late edition of a newspaper in the small yellow light afforded from a small lamp with a filthy shade.

"You know it, Herr Ober. You know, one day it'll be me sitting here in the power position...," with that his voice cracked a little, a chink in his armor, his youth poking through the creased, shined, and clean exterior. His voice did that once in a while. Some of the men at the EM club gave him a hard time over it. He cleared his throat into his gloved hands, regaining his composure before continuing. He took his hat off and flipped it on the small desk right beside Dietmar's elbow, drawing no response. "Ahem. Excuse me. Anyway, yeah, one day I'll be the one sitting here while you're marching around these gates." He smiled. Dietmar smiled back. They had known each other from childhood, and a little good natured competition had been engrained into their personality years ago, a love-hate relationship based on mutual friendship.

"Sure, boss. But they say that it might not be too long before those old men you're guarding are on the move again. They don't stay in one place for ever. Something about heightened security. It's all over the papers how our Fatherland veterans have been disappearing, killed in the most hideous ways imaginable; in their sleep, in front of their families, bullets to their foreheads.

"They say secretly that Israeli hit squads hunt them forever... Stuff like that." Arnold had heard the stories, the rumors. He did feel it odd that he would be guarding a mansion in the middle of an old and bombed out city. The air around there was so bad, during periodic phases all the soldiers had to wear masks. A safety procedure they called it. Arnold felt it had something to do with the older chemical plants that had been destroyed during WWII now spewing smoke again run by the Russians, but he never said anything. Something in those old plants had left buildings still standing covered in layers of soot and stopped the green plants from growing. Nothing grew in a 15-km diameter surrounding the city's old center. People had moved away if they could. It was not safe, but there he was sucking it all up and depositing it in his chest.

"Who are they anyway, the old men? I mean, why would they need armed guards at all hours of the day?"

Dietmar looked up from his paper, a gleam in his eye. "If I told you that, I would have to kill you." They both laughed at this melodramatic line.

"No, really. Who are they?"

"I don't know for sure, but I've heard the old men saying that they're holdovers from the war, you know-Nazis, big ones, important. We shouldn't talk about it. Scientists or something, that's what some say. Others think that they're the ones that escaped...you know?"

"Escaped?  Like escaped from the Americans or the English?"

"Exactly.  Men that any of those would kill to get their hands on if they only got half a chance.  And especially the Israelis, they want them dead.  But they don't get that chance, do they?  No, not with capable men like you and I on the lookout," he gave Arnold a playful slug on the shoulder.  "Isn't that right?"

"Did you see them?"

"Who"

"Ahh, they got some visitors today, I think Arabs."

"So what?  That happens all the time, I saw once from the balcony a big package of money change hands."

"You know it."  The sound of heavy footsteps foretold that the next guards had already taken his place, patrolling the area already worn underfoot from Arnold's previous watch.  He would need to get the hell out of there before too long.  Take a shower.  A shave.  Take Fraulein Brunhilda out in his security-issued vehicle.

"How are you two doing with her?"  asked Dietmar, his mind already back to absorbing the paper's black and white information.  He had heard Arnold rambling on and on about this girl.

"Promise not to tell anybody, but I'm planning on proposing to her the next chance that I get.  Maybe tonight."  The excitement in his voice was tangible.

Excitement.  Would she say yes?  No?  Oh, it didn't matter, he would go now.  Show up at her doorstep still dressed, fresh from duty.  A man in uniform, taller in his boots.  He would say, "Hello, my love."

His hat.  He had forgotten it on Dietmar's desk.  A dumb mistake.  A rookie mistake.  In his haste he had forgotten one of the most important parts of his ensemble.

"How are you going to cut an impressive form in the doorway without your hat, you moron," he muttered to himself, stopping dead in his tracks and turning back toward the guard station, the moon illuminating his path.

He got closer to the guard station and looked up.

Dietmar was gone.

"Dietmar?  Dietmar?" He called out into the night.  He circled around the little guard house, making sure that Dietmar hadn't slipped through.  "Come on, I don't have time for stupid games…  Don't be a jackass.  Now come on, I've got to get out of here.  Come on."  He circled the guard station again.  Nothing.  Dietmar must have let the men on patrol in on his little game.  They were nowhere to be found either.

"Great, just what I needed."  He walked down the length of the gate, the same length that he had been patrolling earlier.

"Dietmar?"  Nothing, nothing except a strange smell.  What was that smell?  He had smelled chemicals before, and was all too familiar with the everyday stink of the city.  But, no, this was something new.  Something strange.  He held his gun at the ready and continued on in the opposite direction, the moon through the gate's pattern casting sinister shadows.  He stalked on silently, sucking his breathe between his teeth with every movement.  His heart beat in his throat, the pulse in his wrist that held his weapon banging frantically away.

The smell intensified. He got to the  eastern-most edge of the fence and stopped.

Dietmar and the two guards sat plopped on the hard earth, their backs together, their wrists bound together with tape that gleamed in the fragments of light. Unconscious, but still alive, still breathing, their breath manifesting itself as visible steam that shot from their mouths and nostrils into the cold air.

"What in the….!?  Dietmar!?" yelled Arnold, freezing in shock, the image in front of him being the last thing that he would have wanted to see. He gripped his weapon tighter.

The hand was around his mouth so quick that it was still open from the scream he had tried to unleash. The smell was all around him, inside him, swirling around his mouth and seeping down his throat. His head grew heavy, his vision a collection of gray pixels that started to fray at the edges. Heavy limbs. Slack tongue. His weapon dropped from his grip. His knees buckled. The tiny spark of consciousness inside him was being blown out quickly.

"That's right," came the voice attached to the strong arms that held the chloroform cocktail over his mouth and squeezed around his torso and lungs, forcing him to breathe deeply, "go to sleep. It's all just a bad dream. Go to sleep."

His lids were heavy, the rest of his body a blizzard of pins and needles, his mind somewhere out in the darkness.

"You forgot your hat," came the voice again. The last image Arnold witnessed before completely fading to darkness was his hat falling, fluttering down towards the ground. And then nothing… Silence.

Relaxing his hands and letting the young guard slip from his grip, the chloroform insert still stuck in his mouth, Yaakov spoke into the transmitter that spiraled around his ear on one end and formed a mouthpiece on the other end, the one closest to his mouth.

"The last guard is down. Repeat. The last is down."

"Good work," came Ziki's reply.

"Make sure, bind him with the other men," ordered Amit. Alex was silent. He had grown unusually withdrawn into himself on this mission, even more so than usual. He freaked Yaakov out, the way he looked at him. His amber eyes brooded silent power. What he must have seen, must have experienced to become not a man, but an object carved of wood was beyond Yaakov. He just tried to avoid him whenever possible, avoid confrontation.

"Affirmative," he whispered into the microphone. He peered down at the young guard. He couldn't have been much older than Yaakov was. Maybe the same age. He almost felt sorry for him. Ziki's orders had been specific. No harm must come to the guards. They were not the ones that they were after. . "But just think what they're guarding." Just roadblocks barring them from the mansion.

He bound the guard's wrists and ankles and dragged him over to where his associates sat in chemical-induced slumber. "Babies don't sleep that well." Yaakov found the chloroform and other 'stuff' kit fascinating. When he needed to use it, he broke the small chemical vial within the package, starting a chemical reaction that produced its most endearing quality: namely, the ability to knock out a 100 kilogram man in less than three seconds. Chemicals. He shook his head. What will they do next?

"Finished with the binding. Proceeding to rendezvous point. Repeat. Proceeding to rendezvous point."

"Clear," came the disembodied reply. Giving the captive men one last glance over his shoulder, Yaakov started towards the rendezvous point.

Alex was busy placing acid compound on the fence. He would have to be precise. The wrong place and the gate wouldn't budge a centimeter. Too much and their surprise was blown. Only what was necessary: a controlled soundless blast.

"How's it coming?" asked Ziki, intrigued at the intensity with which Alex worked.

"With any luck," replied Alex, never for an instant removing his eyes from the conduits he held in his hands, a mustache of sweat on his upper lip, "two minutes, three at most. It will destroy the alarm system as well. Then we're in." A wry smile appeared on his lips as he completed the wiring of the concoction he had on the locks of the wrought iron gate before continuing on to the next one.

"That's what I like to hear," said Ziki. He looked through the gate at the massive lawn it contained, manicured hedges, two fountains that were visible, and a moat capped with a bridge. Flowers filled the bowers that he could just make out under the huge windows that dominated the mansion's exterior. He nudged Erik with his arm.

"Would be impressive if they weren't what they are?" Erik nodded.

"Yeah, probably one of the few kept-up buildings in this whole Godforsaken city. The lap of luxury. And to think, all from money funneled through Odessa. Bastards." He gritted his teeth.

"True. Just hard to believe that so many of these war criminals were able to escape. Makes you wonder whose side everybody is on." The other men nodded their assent. It was well known that the Russians and, to Israel's dismay, the Arabs, had vested interests in using Nazi scientists to work for them. Used them for their own ends and, in the case of the latter, for their own despotic plans.

"Why not?" chimed in Amit. "Why waste the minds that the Nazis cultivated and trained? To me it makes sense. Supply and demand. Why spend time training men to know what these men know when they're already there? Crystal clear."

"Let's see if we can't do something about that," said Alex, putting the last of his gadgets in place. "Gentleman, if you don't mind standing back. There may be some shrapnel, I have arranged the charges so that any pieces that fly off would be going in the opposite direction. This is an acid silent explosion, something new, I hope it works." That was Alex. Professionalism personified.

The group backed up. Alex pressed the button in the middle of his gadget.

Five simultaneous soft hiss sounds and the gate was opened…."Amazing stuff."

"Piece of cake," said Alex, smirking.

The smoke from the 'explosions' was sharp in the nose, adding to the scent that clung to the bottoms of the clouds and streaked out across the ground, propelled by the wind. The group moved in quickly… The Odessa organization was there to secure and protect SS men—World War II war criminals, ex-SS, to hide out in relative wealth and obscurity around the globe, to commend them for the deeds that they had carried out. Nazis. Ex Gestapo and their men. Maybe the Fourth Reich. The money was holed up in neutral banks without predilections of where it came from. Swiss banks. The same banks that Ziki and Mossad used. It wasn't greed that compelled the Swiss to secure the funds—death funds—It was just business.

The Odessa organization was founded by Nazis that had escaped with access to the riches of the Swiss vaults. Their agenda was clear. They would stop at nothing until the establishment of the so-called "Fourth Reich" was completed… Nazism. Funds exited the organization's coffers through 'Obbers,' the purpose being the protection of the remaining Nazi scientists, many living in South America. Scientists trained to develop weapons of mass destruction: "dirty" bombs, nerve agents, strains of diseases unknown in the world and with no known cures, even nuclear warheads.

The stakes were high, and time was running out for Mossad to make sure that these scientists didn't have the chance to relinquish their knowledge before a cataclysm of epic proportions. With each passing breath and passing second, the sworn enemies drew one step closer to their ultimate goal. Abu Nidal and Salameh were a link to Odessa.

The chloroform didn't quite cut it with the large body of another guard. So Alex clubbed him on the side of the head, just above his ear. The guard fell, his legs giving out from beneath him, the top collapsing down upon them like a building made of cards. Blood streamed out of a small violet gash.

"Damn," he said, watching the body drop. Alex didn't want to hurt the man. His beef wasn't with him. It was with those inside the mansion, the ones with the real blood on their hands. This mission had special significance for the group as a whole: a mission of pay back with a bonus; Salameh and maybe Nidal. But for Alex it extended beyond that, to even the score, to a sense of closure finally being pulled over the appalling horrors of Europe out of his mind forever. His family… An eye for an eye.

He bound and gagged the guard, placing him in a pile alongside the dark first story hallway amid Bavarian furniture and a mahogany billiard table. Lacquered end tables adorned with antique vases were peppered around the entry; oil paintings of men long dead and forgotten adorned the walls in every direction. Blatant luxury. A cornucopia of decadence. Taking one last parting glance at the comatose guard over his shoulder, Alex entered another luxuriously decorated room to see the others binding more guards.

"Get him?" asked Ziki, stretching a length of tape around the thick head of a guard with mid-length curly black hair and large hands.

"Yes, Sir." The moon shone in through the large French windows, cutting black shapes that fell onto the floor. Crisscrosses of trees sweeping as the wind made them dance back and forth, raking the glass, causing it to shriek.

"Six," Ziki said to himself quietly as he watched his men round up the rest of the guards and tie them up. Thus far no noise, no sounds. Six, that was the number of Nazi scientists Malkielly had told him were hiding out within the confines of this labyrinthine mansion. Of course, the boss hadn't bothered to mention the number of guards that were patrolling the area outside and inside. This mission had moral and effective value to the continued safety of humanity at large, Ziki wanted to make sure that he would be connected to it.

He pulled back the hammer of his Berretta pistol to ensure himself that his special ammunition was locked and ready to go. This was a signature of Mossad, leaving no doubt in the minds of El Fatah or Odessa of who had been responsible.

The room, its crystal chandeliers hanging from the ceiling, its expensive furniture polished to a mirror-like shine, its large dominating fireplace with gold fixtures, its rich tapestries that hung on the walls and covered the floors. Ziki spat on the ground in disgust.

Too easily. These men lived too easily, slept too well at night, ate food too rich. They should not be living so well, they should not be free to continue uninterrupted. They should not be living their lives with carefree and reckless abandon. No… They should be sweating when they heard a sound in the night, shaking before they opened the doors into their darkened rooms, paranoid and paralyzed with the fear of knowing that they were hunted men. That they were dead men walking. That at any second, in some way, they were being stalked and weeded out, being wiped off the face of the earth just like those they had killed. That their time had come and that they should not die peacefully of old age.

That's what this mission was about. That was why Mossad had assembled '*kidons*' to seek out and eradicate the worst of these Nazis. A bonus—Salameh and Abu Nidal.

Mossad might not be able to get them all, too many. Ziki wanted to have all of them cowering on their knees and begging for the mercy that they had never shown. He would put fear into their hearts. Make them think twice about walking across the street or about going out in the darkness alone, about living and breathing calmly. He wanted to make sure that they didn't sleep soundly in their beds anymore.

**0100. Kurtz Waldheimer stayed up too late and was exhausted;** his back was cramped from sitting hunched over his desk, his fingers cramped half from the arthritis and half from hammering on his typewriter well into the night. He had almost completed a manuscript that outlined a rudimentary understanding of how it is that a rocket fuel unleashes the energy that it does, the same energy that can be harnessed and directed to create propulsion in the form of warheads. He'd already finished the script for the Egyptians on the works of the Bubonic Plague stuff. Now Salameh's Jihad group wanted the stuff as well. Why not?

He re-positioned his bifocals on the ridge of his nose. He sighed. He knew he shouldn't have been wasting so much time explaining everything in this manuscript, as he knew that the words would be manipulated and something would be lost in the translation from German to Arabic in the Middle East, and worst, into Persian, where the publication would be headed just as soon as he was done with it and satisfied. Iran was the big new player. But that wasn't up to Kurtz. He took his orders just the same as any other soldier from Odessa. It made him smile. Writing this manuscript not only made sure that the plethora of ideas that swam in his head would forever be preserved but there was always the very real possibility that he would become praised for it. His real expertise was in biological warfare.

Bubonic plague base germs was easy; getting uranium for the others wasn't his job. His was to just get it all down on paper and provide the program that would spark the imagination and intelligence of these men enough to give them control of the power that his science provided.

Kurtz ran a slender, bony hand through his large mop of silver hair, pushing it towards his forehead before pulling the skin of his sunken and sanguine face downward. He let out a slight breathe before sitting up from his high-backed chair and leaning over to turn off his desktop lamp. He left the small alcove of a study with its shelf after shelf of yellowing books bound in leather, walked down the massive hallway to his room that was dominated in the middle by a large four-poster bed covered in thick blankets of deep lavenders and blues.

The rest of his colleagues had already retired, and the Arab, Salameh and his unnamed friend left immediately after they took the details. They never stayed in one place too long. Kurtz felt a little foolish that he had stayed up as late as he had. It was quiet all throughout the mansion, a refreshing silence unmarred by the rapid talk of everybody going in every direction at once and the loud stomp of the guards ordered to patrol the building at all times.

He took off his shirt and his trousers, folding them neatly and placing them on the bottom shelf of his oak armoire, shutting its ornately carved mirrored doors silently before walking over to the side of his bed and peeling back the layers of covers one by one methodically. He climbed in and reached across his body to turn off the light that sat perched atop a small end table piled with books. He took the gold watch that wrapped around his left wrist and placed it on the table as well, followed by his bifocal glasses. Without those he was lost, and he placed them equally balanced on the thick texture of a large book so that they would not fall off.

Silence. His breaths came and went, his chest rose and fell. He quickly fell into the monotonous patterns that begin at the onset of a deep and well-deserved rest.

A noise. He opened his left eye, scanning the room, looking out the window at the branches of a mighty tree that thrashed about outside in the howling wind. A click. He sat up in his bed and looked towards the door. Still shut. Maybe it was a mouse or something. A rat. After all, they were on the outskirts of the city, pushed up right next to a forest. He tucked himself back into bed and pulled the thick layer of blankets all the way over his head as a means to block out any more noises that might disturb him.

*"Sprechen sie Deutch?*….Do you speak German?" came a booming voice that seemed like it came from everywhere and nowhere at the same time. Kurtz

thought that he was dreaming. He must be. There was no way somebody was in his room.

*"Sprechen sie Deutch?*....Do you speak German?" repeated the deep voice menacingly. He propped himself up on the sagging flesh of his elbows to reach over and turn his bedside lamp back on. The light revealed a man dressed entirely in black standing directly opposite his bed, a pistol in his raised hand, the barrel trained right on Kurtz's forehead.

Shaking, he answered, " *Ya...ya ich spreche Deutch...Ich bin ein Deutcher.* Yes...yes, I speak German. I am German." So great was his shock and horror that he almost choked on the words, spitting them out like a piece of sour food, barely finding the answer to the simple question that the man posed? Kurtz's back was a puddle of cold sweat that he felt seeping out of every pore. The man with the gun continued.

*"Ich sprche Hebreish, sprechen sie Hebreish...*? I speak Hebrew—do you speak Hebrew?" A slight grinning sneer appeared on Alex's lips as he said this, the pistol gripped tightly in his hand. Kurtz's mouth dropped open, his muscles tensed, his hands gripping the blanket in his hands so fiercely that he might have ripped it in two. He knew what was next;, it didn't prevent a whimper from escaping his throat and gliding out his teeth into the silence of the room.

" *Ich spreche nur Hebreish* ....I speak only Hebrew—*Ich bin von Israel.* I am from Israel," Alex's voice boomed. "*Und ich bin hier fur dich farflughte schwein.* And I am here for you, you evil swine.*"*

*"Nein, Juden! Israelinishe!"* Kurtz exclaimed.

Bang.... Bang. Two shots to the forehead, the Mossad signature. This left the message in the form of the bloody husks that a moment ago contained life to whoever was to find the six bodies the next morning... Beware; the pendulum is swinging back in the opposite direction.

The Angel of Death had come in the night, and his quest for justice was not yet satisfied...

# Chapter 41

**Germany-**

*Noch edvas bitte mein her?* What can I get for you, Sir?" asked the bartender as he passed a white rag over the bar. Ziki sat on a stool in the hotel's third-story restaurant …The bartender broke him from his revelry.

"Oh," he said, looking up, " *dopple vodka, danke.* double vodka, Stolichnya. Wide-rimmed glass if you have one. Ice."

" *Yah vohl,* sure thing."

It was his third drink of the night, and he decided that would be it. He pulled a pack of cigarettes from his shirt pocket and picked up a box of the bar's matches from a silver ashtray. He struck a match and lit the cigarette, blowing a stream of smoke across the bar. He tapped his ashes into the ashtray.

The bartender brought him the check: fourteen Deutsche marks. He looked at the number again, and laughed. How ironic. Ziki had kept thinking of the number fourteen the entire time he had sat at the bar drinking. Six was the number in Halle. Eight in Jenna. Fourteen total.

Jenna was not the same ruinous pit of destruction that Halle was. Flowers bloomed. Tap water didn't carry floating rainbows of oil. Children played in the street, tucked away in a corner of the world where nature had had a chance to heal herself and maybe, he thought, it could in turn heal the human spirit…Or could it? Ziki wondered—evil lurked behind the façade. Jenna was the home of a covey of evil men in the mansion overlooking the town.

Ziki looked up from the check at the other patrons around the bar. Slow music strained out from overhead speakers. Pieces of private conversations fluttered in the ears. The outline of a woman approaching the bar caught his eye.

She approached from the side opposite Ziki and sat down, the bartender already upon her to take her order. Her amber hair was done up in a spiral bun that sat like a coiled serpent on the top of her head, wisps of it careening down her temples, swinging gently as she moved. Stylish sun glasses rested on the bridge of her nose, covering lavender eyelids, accentuating the deep red of her lips. In her hand, held against her chest loosely, was a leather portfolio trimmed with gold accents. Her hands were adorned with glittering gold rings. Looking up at the bartender, her face blossomed with a cherubic smile that exposed dazzlingly white teeth. Her laugh was the gentle tinkle of crystal. Ziki watched as the bartender brought her a woman's drink, all sugar and curves. Not like the wide-rimmed utility drinks sitting empty and lazy at his elbow. He watched her across the bar out of the corner of his eye and unconsciously began thinking again of Gavriella and the mission that had just ended.

**Jenna had been like Halle in more ways than one:** a mansion at the fringes of the city decked out in painstaking luxury; guards milling about at the outskirts of the perimeter, all of them young, no match for his men. They were caught off guard, clubbed on the head or chloroformed, then bundled up together in restraints. No complications, not even inside the mansion. The mission had run like clockwork. The Nazi scientists had been the same aged and decrepit former shells of authoritative men that they had found in Halle. They put up no serious resistance. Within that night they had all been executed. Two shots to the forehead to sign the tale of what had happened. A grim Mossad reminder that in time... On a long enough timeline, Ziki reminded himself, the survival rate goes down to zero…

**Back at the bar,** her amber eyes clearly visible through the shield of her glasses, the woman finished her drink, slowly sipping up the remainder of her Manhattan before biting into a ring of pineapple. She dabbed a corner of her lips, her eyes trained on Ziki. He peered up guardedly.

She moved up to the stool beside him. She dropped the portfolio down across her lap and pulled a pen Ziki hadn't noticed from behind her ear, like a journalist about to unleash a barrage of questions. Ziki interceded before she could begin.

"Can I help you?" he asked.

"I don't think so, but maybe I can help you."

"Oh?"

"I couldn't help but notice you looking at me from across the bar. I thought maybe you could use some company."

"What's your name?"

"Gretchen." She smiled. "Gretchen. And you?"

"Hans Breckenbauer. Nice to meet you." He took her hand and shook it firmly. The bartender came back and asked if they would like another round. Ziki declined, but Gretchen ordered another Manhattan.

"So, Hans, what brings you to Berlin?" she asked, taking a sip from a bottle covered in ice crystals. "Business or pleasure?"

"Business. Medical equipment." He reached into his shirt pocket and took out his cigarettes. "Cigarette?" he asked, holding them forward...

"No, thanks. I've got my own." She dipped her arm into the purse that hung at her side and withdrew a metal tin from which she took a long, brown monogrammed cigarette. She lit a match and put it to Ziki's cigarette, then her own, before shaking it out and dropping it in the large ashtray. The blue smoke lingered before finally dying.

"Interesting brand," Ziki commented.

"Sometimes it's good to pamper oneself."

"You only live once," Ziki said. She moved closer and batted her eyelashes, soft light glowing around her face. Ziki thought of what this woman would look like naked, but soon realized he could not hold the image and the conversation simultaneously.

Then he thought of Gavriella.

Just then, as if on cue, a hand reached out and grabbed him on the shoulder. It was Yaakov, the rookie kid.

"We've been looking all over for you. I should have known to look here." He then noticed the woman sitting next to Ziki and flushed a deep red, hoping that he hadn't interrupted anything promising. "Oh," he said. "Excuse me"

"Nonsense," cut in Ziki. "Paul, I'd like you meet Gretchen here. Gretchen, Paul." Yaakov, a bit confused as to why he was being called Paul, reached forward to take Gretchen's outstretched bejeweled hand.

"It's a pleasure," he said.

"Mine as well," she replied.

Ziki got up from his seat.

"How about you two get acquainted? I've got a call to make. My apologies, Gretchen, for having to leave. I'll be back before you even notice I'm gone."

With that he put a twenty-Deutch Mark bill on the bar and left the two without intention of returning. He looked back over his shoulder, and it appeared he had already been forgotten. Ziki didn't care. He had felt sheepish, guilty at having felt her magnetism. He wanted to be loyal…To whom he thought—Henny? Gavriella—or?

He got into the empty elevator and punched the sixth-floor button. He got off and came to the door of his room. Fumbling in his pocket for his room key, he also found the extra key to Yaakov's room. With the distraction of Gretchen he had forgotten to give it to him. He headed back toward the elevator and the bar.

Stepping out of the elevator and making a left turn down the bar's adjoining stairway, Ziki paused.

The same Americans that had been riotously drinking and talking were still there and as loud as ever. But no Yaakov or Gretchen. Their seats were empty, their glasses were still there, the only testament to them having been there.

"Excuse me," said Ziki, getting the bartender's attention. "Did you see a young man with curly hair and a good-looking blonde sitting here? I left just a few minutes ago and now they're not here."

"Yeah, they had another drink after you left and left together. He told me to just bill the room for his drinks and to send up a bottle of champagne and two glasses. My guess is they're in for the night. Sorry you missed 'em. Can I get you anything else?" Ziki shook his head.

"Thanks, it's getting late."

"Okay. Enjoy your stay." Ziki turned and left. Yaakov must be smoother than he had taken him for. Not five minutes had passed and he had picked that girl and somehow convinced her to go to his room. No dinner. Just drinks. Ziki shook his head as he opened the door to his room. He turned the lights on and shut the door with a click.

**In the morning, Ziki and his men met in the hotel lobby as agreed.** Everybody was there except Yaakov.

"Where is that kid?" said Erik. "You didn't get him plastered in that bar last night, did you?"

Ziki shook his head.

"No, he was up there with a woman for about five minutes before going back to his room with her."

"That's all? He didn't say anything to you about meeting down here this morning?" asked Alex. "Are you sure he knew?"

"Yes, I'm sure." Ziki remembered that he still had the key to Yaakov's room, and fished in his pocket for it. "But since I have this," he said, dangling the key from his hand, "I'll just go up there to pay him a visit. Anybody want to come?" Nobody was willing, Ziki walked back to the elevators and punched in Yaakov's floor.

He got off and walked to the room number that was on the key. He opened the door and walked inside.

He could make out the shape of Yaakov under the covers. Two wine glasses and an empty bottle were on the small table on the side of the bed. His clothes lay in a heap on the floor where he had thrown them, in haste.

"Hey, Sleeping Beauty, *boker tov*—get your ass up. Come on; we got to go. Rise and shine." He pulled back the drapes, hoping the sunlight would stir the young Casanova. It didn't. Ziki moved to the side of the bed and clutched the sides of the down blanket in each hand. In one motion, he yanked the covers to expose what lay beneath.

Blood… Dripping from the side of Yaakov's head… Splattered on the blanket. Seeping into the pillow and the sheets beneath. Dried. Moist. Blood everywhere...

"Oh my God," instinctively checking the side of Yaakov's neck for a pulse that he knew he wouldn't find. Two bullet holes in the side of the head. A gruesome and all too familiar sight. Small caliber, probably a small 22 pistol that could be easily concealed. The scene smacked of professionalism. Only now it was on the other side, a horrible death, a good young man. Now all that he was, erased.

Ziki felt his heart rise in his throat. His anguish melded with anger. Looking around the room for any other clues as to what happened, he noticed something on the small table, nestled between the glasses and champagne bottle. An ashtray. Yaakov didn't smoke.

It couldn't be. Ziki fought to keep the notion out of his head, but an inescapable realization hit him like a kick to the solar plexus. He looked in the ashtray at the long, brown, monogrammed cigarette, longer than his middle finger. With ruby colored lipstick on the filtered end.

*Gretchen.*

He drove his fist into the pillow next to Yaakov's. Her pillow. She was gone. With the palm of his hand he shut Yaakov's eyelids and pulled the blanket back over his head.

It could have been him. If he hadn't left the bar last night when he did, it could have been his bullet-riddled body in the bed instead of Yaakov's. He thought it should have been…

Ziki vowed that Gretchen would pay. But who hired this professional hit? That's who needed to pay. Ziki lumbered to the doorway to go tell his men.

**Gretchen Gantz was, it turned out, her real name.** She had ties to Stassi— But why? Nah—this smells like PLO, El Fattah. This was intended for Ziki but Yaakov was dead… Was it retaliation for the safe house in Zurich?

**"Yes, it is a shame that your man got lost,"** Malkielly had said in his grizzly voice over the telephone to Ziki when the overseas operator had put his call through, "but I cannot let you go pay the bill. I know what it's like, believe me. It weighs on my conscience every day." There was a pause on the line…

"I can't let this thing drop."

"Ziki, I order you to come directly back here."

"I'm on my way. Right after a slight detour to..." A sigh came from the other end of the line, rattling the earpiece nestled up close to Ziki's ear.

"I don't know why I put up with this. Why I don't just put you behind a desk."

"I need to do this."

Static and a click and the line was dead. Ziki hung up.

# Chapter 42

**Amalfi, Italy**

He spat on the ground in disgust as his motorcycle clung to the road as if by magnets, carrying him to the edge of the lake and the small cottage surrounded by gardens. Carrots, olives, lettuce both green and red, some purple.

The motor shook, revving and adding to the madness that clutched him. The weapons were secured in the small handlebars and side compartments of the bike, invisible to the observer. He could still smell the perfume she wore in the bar that night, the harsh scent of her expensive cigarettes. Ziki stopped the motorbike fifty meters from the house and leaned it against a tree.

From his perch, he could just make out what appeared to be movement from behind the yellow curtains of the cottage's rectangular front window. A man, dark, possibly her lover, came out the door, stopping in the threshold. That's when Ziki saw her—Gretchen. She gave the olive skinned man a long, deep kiss before wishing him farewell. The man got into his small green sedan, backed out of the driveway lined with stones and sunflowers, and was swiftly on his way.

Ziki moved in. Silently he swept down across the fresh green lawn, stopping at the back door. No deadbolt. Not even locked. She was living a carefree existence, unaware that she who had been the predator had now become prey.

The door open, Ziki moved quickly into the entryway, crouching low, listening closely, making sure that only he and Gretchen were inside the house. Ziki remembered the night at the hotel. Never assume.

She came down the stairs and froze like a deer in headlights. Ziki pulled back the hammer of the gun and aimed high, at her chest. "Freeze in place." She did.

"Don't shoot, it was just a contract, I'll tell you who, just please don't kill me."

"Who hired you?"

"The name was—Ali Hassan Salameh, it was nothing personal, please don't kill me."

"Salameh? I should have known."

She turned around as if to escape back into the safety of her room. But she reached for the umbrella stand, her hand came out with a gun.

She would not make it. He depressed the trigger. The slug hit her in the small of the back, went right through the spine. A scream escaped her lips as her back bent unnaturally, her hands flailing about, grasping the carpeted stairs, the banister. Ziki moved closer in.

"Remember me?" he asked, his eyes piercing. She didn't reply. She only clutched the lower part of her stomach, trying to stop the bleeding from the bullet that had torn all the way through her.

She lay at his feet; she moaned and reached up a bloody hand, as if asking for help.

Ziki was incredulous. "Help? You want help?"

"Please...I beg of you. I...I...I do my job." A trickle of blood escaped from the corner of her mouth. "If I don't...."

Malkielly had once said that he, Ziki was like an angel sent by heaven. Ziki did not understand.

"How could I be an angel? Look at the things I have to do."

Malkielly continued—"When God sends Gabriel or an Angel of vengeance... What kind of angel do you think that be..? Gentle? I don't think so.... Not all angels are gentle! God's work can be brutal. Some angels have to be like that, Ziki."

"Rest in peace," said Ziki with a touch of sorrow in his voice, his throat spewing the words. "What a waste." He closed the eyes on her face before getting up and searching the room for anything he could learn, about Salameh.

Finding little, he slipped out the door into the dusk. Taking his bike from where it still sat against the tree, he started the motor with a roar and was gone, dissolving into the horizon...

**According to tradition** a man has to be buried as soon as possible after he dies, enabling his soul to go to Heaven. He is put to eternal rest on the soil that he gave his life to defend. Ziki and his men were not going to bury Yaakov in Germany. His body was sent to Israel.

European media coverage exposed the raid at the Zurich safe-house, the death of the Nazis in Halle and Jenna, the lone killing of Gretchen in Italy. Ziki's men had stripped themselves of all identification that could trace them to Israel. They had taken Yaakov's dog tags and wallet, and anything else that would identify who he was or where he came from. Pictures—Letters he intended to send to his mother that would never be sent. Anything that would connect him back to Israel or Mossad had been carefully disposed of. To the world at large, he would be a man without a past, without a history.

To his family, though, Ziki knew, he was Yaakov. Ziki promised himself that his family would see him one more time. Closure. His parents...Buried at the

Mount of Olives in Jerusalem with full military honors… As other heroes are.

The four remaining men would sit apart on the train. They would each travel as though alone, drawing as little attention as possible. They would speak the language of whatever country they were in to blend in as natives or tourists. And then Ziki would break the news of Yaakov's death to his mother. He would look her in the eye and tell her that her son was dead. The responsibility for what had happened to Yaakov that night was his…. The burden rested heavy on his shoulders.

# Chapter 43

## MRS. BEN DOR

**He stood silently at her doorstep.** The wait was over.

He wore his military dress uniform. A deplorable task: telling a mother that her only son was dead, and no, he couldn't get into the details of what had happened. Just that Yaakov had died heroically.

He knocked on the door three times, slowly.

No response, he knocked again.

Again, nothing. He stood there for the better part of a minute staring at the door through his dark sunglasses. He had started to turn and leave when he heard the knob of the door. A small gray-haired woman, shrunken but still firm and full of vitality, opened the door, a knitted shawl around her shoulders.

"Can I help you?" she said.

"Mrs. Ben-Dorr?"

"Yes," she said. "What can I do for you?" Her eyes scanned his face, his eyes. He wore the sunglasses for that exact reason, to protect himself from scrutiny—from exposure… It was a cold maneuver, he knew it… It was his only defense.

Emotion welled up within him as he asked her, "You are Yaakov's mother?" His voice, as far as he could tell, betrayed nothing, and he was ashamed for a moment at the relief this brought him.

"Please, come inside. There is a chill out here." She backed away from the door and retreated toward the living room of the small dwelling. Ziki hadn't noticed what the weather was like.

"Sit here," she said, motioning to a small, well-worn sofa beside a pine coffee table scattered with magazines and half-read books. He did as instructed, drawing his legs up to cross them.

*"Toda, giveret Ben-Dor.* Thank you, Mrs. Ben-Dorr."

She studied him. "I would like to know your name."

"Ziki, *Gveret*—ma'am. Commander Ziki Barak." She took the outstretched hand he offered and shook it with a firmness that belied her diminutive size.

"Would you like some coffee, Ziki? You look tired." She rubbed one of her hands in the other, like someone trying to keep warm.

"Coffee would be nice. Thank you…." She smiled faintly, as though holding onto that moment in time, and went around the far corner of the room into the kitchen, where Ziki could hear the clinking of dishes and utensils. He tried once more to collect his thoughts, going over in his mind exactly how he would break the news to her. No matter how many times he rehearsed it to himself, he never found a good way to say it. She was back all too soon.

"It's special coffee. Yaakov's favorite. I always make it when he decides to drop by and pay his mother a visit." She looked down briefly at the rug under her feet. "You'd think he would come by more often, but as I'm sure you know, once they've seen Paris…." Her voice trailed off as she held up her cup to take a sip.

Ziki thought of his own mother. How long had it been since he'd paid her a visit? Written? He made a mental note to do just that the next chance he got. One never knows which chance might be the last.

"Now, I know you didn't come here to drink coffee with an old lady." She looked at her hands, then up at Ziki's face. "Do you have something to tell me?"

Ziki looked across the room. "Yes, ma'am…." But he couldn't say any more.

"Your coffee's getting cold." She motioned toward his cup, as though it were the most important thing in the room. "You haven't touched it."

Ziki fumbled with the cup, bringing it to his lips and taking a long swallow before putting it back down on a wooden coaster on top of the table.

"What is it you're here for, Commander?"

He wanted badly to keep the grim reality of Yaakov's death from becoming a part of her life. He wanted to invite her to an awards ceremony in her son's honor, to tell her that Yaakov was waiting for her in Tel Aviv and that he, Ziki, was to be her personal escort. He wanted to tell her anything but that which he had come to tell her.

He realized, though, that his mere presence here had already told her. Lone officers in dress uniform visiting the families of soldiers were not… They typically came with one purpose, and here again Ziki thought darkly of his role as an angel. Yeah, but what kind? For it was nothing less than death's immutability that he was here to deliver to Yaakov's widowed mother… Was there a word for being widowed by your son?

"Commander Barak," she said, looking at him now with a hint of anger, "please take off your sunglasses." He had never intended to come inside and had forgotten he was still wearing them. He took them off and slipped them into an inside coat pocket, but he did not meet her eyes.

"That's better," she said. "Now, please: What is it you are here to tell—?"

"Gveret Ben-Dor, Ma'am," he cut her off. "Your son died in the line of duty."

There. He had said it. The words had come out rapid-fire and lacked all of the practiced nuance and niceties of his rehearsals.

She sat still, weighing the gravity of what he had just told her. She took a petite sip from her cup and cleared her throat.

"How did it happen?" she asked with quiet calm.

Visions of Gretchen flashed through his mind. Her lipstick. Her scent. Her cigarettes… Her bloody corpse on the stairway of a cottage near the river in Amalfi. Should he tell her the truth about what happened? Could he?

Truth was a relative matter here. There was the unadulterated, unedited truth of Yaakov's youthful blunder at the safe-house in Zurich, of the haunted look in his eyes after he had killed his first man, and the truth of his blood spilled much too early on hotel-room sheets as the life seeped out of him before he had the chance to live his life. Such truth, however true, was too much to divulge to a grieving mother. "I'm sorry ma'am. I can't tell you that."

Tears welled in corners of her eyes, red veins already starting to swell with blood. "I can tell you," he said, "that if it weren't for men like Yaakov, we wouldn't have the freedom we have today… He died a hero."

She nodded. "Was he shot?"

"I can't…"

"Stabbed? Poisoned? Car crash? What was it?" Her voice had begun to rise, hysteria setting in as her suspicions about this young man in front of her came true. "Why can't you tell me what happened? Where is my son?" She stood up at this point, straight, only slightly trembling. Tears streamed down her cheeks, but she did nothing to stop them.

Ziki stayed seated, willing himself to remain emotionless. His voice was flat, his feelings somewhere between drained and suppressed. He hated the charade of this, but he knew, in his clearer moments, that it was the best way. He mustered his strength to detach himself as much as possible to make sure that he didn't break down as well. He had to be the pillar of support for the survivors on these missions. If he was vulnerable, they were more vulnerable. If he couldn't compose himself, there was no way they would be able to. It was bad enough to deliver such news. The least he could do was to be strong.

"All I can tell you, ma'am—Mrs. Ben Dor—is that your son died heroically. That his death, his work, had more significance attached to it than you know."

She squared her shoulders and fairly spat: "Significance! You speak to me of significance? How dare you! That was my only son, the only thing that I had left in this world."

Ziki was on familiar ground here. Frequently the grief turned to anger, anger at him the messenger, and he was better trained at confronting animosity than negotiating with tenderness. "I'm sorry, ma'am," he said, calmly but truthfully. "I wish I could tell you more. It's just that…"

"Ziki?" she said, interrupting, looking him dead in the eye.

"Yes, ma'am?"

"Thank you for coming." She put down her coffee cup, which she had been gripping tightly. "Will you do me a favor?"

"Of course. Anything."

"Please leave." Firm. Cold.

He was at cross purposes, with an unclear mission objective if ever he had had one.

Her voice began to tremble slightly as she held on to the edge of her dignity. "I have my son's funeral to get ready for and I would like privacy."

"I understand." It occurred to him that this might have been the truest thing he had said since announcing Yaakov's death.

"No," she said, "you don't." She softened just a bit. "But thank you."

He got up, looked around to see that he hadn't left anything, and moved to the door, opening it for himself. He paused for a second and looked back.

"I just want you to know that I'm very sorry. I know how much your son meant to you, as you did to him. His country thanks him. And the nation thanks you, Mrs. Ben-Dor." And how much he meant to me, he wanted to add, but composure was paramount. "That's all."

She said nothing, just stood there in the middle of the living room, surrounded by pictures of her son: Yaakov fishing, Yaakov graduating high school.

He shut the door behind him with a click.

## Chapter 44

### The Funeral

**The funeral took place the next day.** Ziki's men gathered on the Mount of Olives in Jerusalem, at the military cemetery that was eternal home to countless fallen.

At the entrance is the Tomb of the Unknown Soldier, a tribute to those fallen in battle that were so badly destroyed that their bodies could not be identified. It bears a sign that states: *"They gave their tomorrows and all they had for your today."* It sent a chill up Ziki's spine, took his breath away every time he read it, and he had read it far too many times.

Ziki and the men stood just beyond the Tomb of the Unknown Soldier, their uniforms crisp, immaculate under the overcast sky. Dark clouds hung in the air above the procession, a grim foreboding of rain. Yaakov's mother and relatives sat up front, dressed in black. Hands holding handkerchiefs rose discreetly to dab at tearful eyes. A tall flagpole stood at the center of the graveyard, visible from all angles, dominating. The large Israeli flag whipped furiously in the wind.

Another funeral was going on in the background, though Ziki paid little attention to it. One funeral was enough. Staring out across the hills filled with headstones and plaques, he felt a grim reminder of just how delicate and fleeting life really was. Precious… Young life.
When would it all end?

A mournful dirge filled the air, along with the laments of the survivors. Birds sang from time to time, their long calls echoing through the expanse of the cemetery, their wings flapping in the humid air.

Yaakov was buried with full military honors, which included a formal tradition that few could shake from their minds, Ziki and his men included.

A company of IDF Special Forces *Tzanhanim,* was in attendance, wearing formal uniforms, filled with solemn vigor in their burgundy berets and dark burgundy boots that shone despite the darkness of the day. They stood lined up on either side of the small, plain coffin and burial mound. The sergeant-at-arms stepped to the head of Yaakov's grave and began, in a barking baritone, to take roll.

"Ziki Barak?"

"Here!" Ziki took a step forward, saluted, and stepped smartly back.

"Alex Cohen?"

"Here!"

"Erik Bar Lev?"

"Amit Marmour?"

"Yaakov Ben-Dorr?"

No answer.

"Yaakov Ben-Dorr?"

....Silence.

"Yaakov Ben-Dorr!" There was a demanding finality this third time, as though it was Yaakov's last chance to rise and join his brethren. Silence crept up spines and made hairs stand up on the backs of necks.

"Fire!" shouted the sergeant, and a deafening crack rent the funereal air as seven rifles discharged in unison.

"Fire!" Seven more for Yaakov.

And again. A 21-gun salute. It was a fitting farewell to a hero.

The remaining men began to lower Yaakov's coffin into the grave, and emotions ran high as the immediacy and permanence of his death sank in. His mother had to be restrained several times, her mournful laments broadening out in every direction as she tried to rush the coffin, to stop the procession, to bring her son back. A military Rabbi began to read the 21st Psalm and said Kadish.

Ziki walked toward the coffin and swallowed hard. He scooped up a handful of the fresh earth beside the grave, looking at the cold brown dirt for just a second before pouring it onto Yaakov's coffin. He picked a flower from a large wreath and let it slip gently from his hand into the hole. "Shalom, Yaakov," he said quietly.

He stepped away.

As he turned to the left, into the cool of the wind, he saw something out of the corner of his eye. He looked up. A desert eagle had lit upon the top of the flagpole. Against the wind, it spread its great wings and let out a piercing cry that split the vastness of the sky and the air....maybe it lifted Yaakov's soul to the heavens.... A cry...

# Chapter 45

**YAFA—MEANS BEAUTIFUL**
**Kirya—just North of Tel Aviv**

**Dark coffee, light French pastry, and a sunset firing the clear sky.** Ziki lounged in the cavernous Mossad cafeteria, the din of the few hundred lunching personnel reverberating from the walls, the sunset heating the air of the atrium reserved for special ops. Dust motes curled in the red air around Moshe Levy, General Chief of Amaan as he exhaled a blue cloud of smoke and lifted his cup close to his lips. He sat across from Ziki, his back to the sun.

Ziki laughed and shook his head. "Same old stuff, my friend: 'Have a pastry while I tell you what hell we're sending you into.' I've always enjoyed our social meetings."

The General clattered his cup onto its saucer without having taken a sip and shrugged from eyebrows to shoulders. "We won't have another chance to speak unofficially before your briefing."

"Unofficially?" Ziki pressed his fingertips to the smooth heat of his cup. "I know what Amaan knows—countries have been running Nazis out of South America with the threat of the international court's powers of extradition—Cairo has offered 23 of them protection and money in exchange for their work. Odessa is involved but their brain heads in Jenna and Hale are no more-*caput*."

"Cocktails," Levy clarified. "Biological, Bubonic plague and chemical weapons—horrific stuff. Well, what am I telling you? You uncovered this whole nightmare in the Ba'albeck raid. Now you have to deal with it."

"I was waiting for it. Our friendly neighbors." Ziki cracked a sarcastic grin. "Just another in line to wipe us off the map."

"Reconnaissance confirms that the facility and lab are in the Egyptian Sahara near the Sudanese border just as you discovered. And—" Levy paused.

"Just let me have it." Ziki swallowed coffee ready for the punch.

"Zhukov wants these scientists."

Ziki sipped coffee. "Your coffee's getting cold." He had willed his features to remain smooth, and not a one of them betrayed the knot of sudden surprise that had his lungs. A Russian hero.  A giant among the world's military men… Damn. General-Marshall Gheorghey Zhukov, in WWII when he took command of a tattered Red Army—starving men with fingers and toes black from frost bite—and turned the Germans back from Stalingrad. It was the Germans' first defeat of the war. Some credited him with winning WWII.

"Do you think he would autograph my ass?" Ziki asked.

Levy's expression remained flat. "He wants this done without KGB or Kremlin involvement. I think he is going behind their back."

"And that's where I come in."

"Yes."

The Russians had claimed Egypt as a surrogate, and the Egyptians got arms and Soviet training.  "There are Ruskies all over Cairo."

"They probably had the pyramids bugged for God's sake."

Ziki met Levy's eye.  "Moshe, have you ever thought about retiring? This stuff is too much…"

Levy ignored Ziki's use of his more private name. "The Russians don't trust the Egyptians."

"Saturdays with your grandkids…"

"Imagine a biological disaster that could take out the cradle of civilization and spread to who knows where."

"And hundreds of American tourists."

"I was thinking closer to home, and yes that stuff could spread anywhere."

"Travel," Ziki suddenly proposed. He could see Levy in a pair of explorer's shorts with one of those beige hats.  His legs chalky white.

"The Russians hate the Nazis even more than we do.  But won't risk an incident—the Arab oil"

General Moshe Levy could look ominous when straightening his slouching back and displaying his very tall frame.  He shot his most withering look at Ziki indicating that Ziki's game of nonchalance was over.  "I need you full throttle on this one."

"Are you going to eat that?" Ziki gestured at Levy's untouched pastry.

"I'm sending you, we need to get this job done."

Ziki took a moment to consider the situation as described.  He rubbed his mouth and chin with a rough palm.  "Nabbing twenty-three men. . .  General. . . It sounds like a black hole—Why not take out the lab and the whole place from the air?  A night strike with unmarked planes.  Plausible deniability—the Egyptians won't admit openly that they harbored Nazis; the Russians would turn a blind eye or the UN would be all over them."  A few greased palms and newspapers would cover the incident as an unexplainable accident.  Explosions and spills hardly worthy of the front page.

"Young and impatient," Levy surmised.

"Some people would consider those strong points."

"We want the Nazis alive.  The Russians, Zhukov wants them alive. Besides, it will take technical experts on the ground to destroy that place so that the stuff doesn't spread. It cannot be done with an air strike. "

"I guess I don't get that week off you promised."

"Commander," Levy's voice remained grave, "Zhukov wants the Nazis and we want a deal with him."

"OK—that's where red flags go up. The Russians already have some of the most deadly bio/chem agents on the globe. They aren't just looking for new combinations for death."

Levy shrugged. "No, the Egyptians did all this without the Soviets' approval. The Russians don't trust them with this horrible stuff; they'll close an eye to what you're about to do. You're asking what's in this for us."

Ziki made a fist beside his coffee cup. "The risk factor to my men—"

"Zhukov is willing to make a trade. We give him the scientists and he guarantees that nothing they produce will ever come back to haunt us and..." Levy paused...

"And what else, General?"

"You will know 'what' on a need-to-know, Commander."

"This stinks to me." Ziki shook his head. A promise. The Russians had the second largest standing army in the world and in that world Zhukov was a God. "I don't know. . .You trust that Russian bear, Moshe? It's too convenient; something else is going on here... What is it that you are not telling me, General?"

"I know. You will know as I said, on a need-to-know basis, Commander... I also know Zhukov personally," Levy answered. "I'd stake my reputation and a thousand men on Zhukov's word."

Ziki sat back and searched Levy's face for any trace of misgiving. But no. Nothing. Not a hint of uncertainty. A tingle spread across Ziki's nape.

Levy pushed his untouched pastry toward Ziki.

"The briefing is at 7:30, Commander. You'll want to be ready for deployment to Egypt after a quick stop in Beirut."

"Beirut?"

As Levy pushed his chair back to rise from it, someone nearby issued a slow and resonant whistle—the sort reserved for construction sites and waitresses who choose to wear their uniforms opened a button too low. Levy instinctively stalled, looking over Ziki's shoulder toward the site of commotion.

The familiar murmur of peripheral conversation dimmed. Ziki shifted in his chair and turned to see what had captured the attention of the room.

"Take a look at that. . ."

A woman.

No. . . An olive skinned siren. . .

She cast a long shadow into the cafeteria, stepping from the sunlit main entrance that swirled with tobacco smoke. In her late twenties or maybe early thirties, she was exotically beautiful, with smooth skin, a slim hard body and a full sensual mouth. She wore black leather, raised-heel boots with laces that wrapped around her calves, stopping just short of a tight black leather skirt. The heels made her seem tall, intimidating. Tight about her torso was a white blouse, the large top button provocatively left open, kindling the imagination of those men who couldn't help themselves with visions of what lay beneath its taut surface. A cascade of shining brown curls luxuriously rolled over the shoulders of her well-tailored black leather jacket. Her eyes were a fierce emerald inside circles of charcoal, saying, 'Don't mess with me' without a word spoken.

Ziki watched with fascination as men lapsed in conversation, seemingly dumbfounded by the rhythmic click of her heels against the granite floor:

. . . Click …click …click. . .

A bundle of dynamite, Ziki thought as his eyes traced the curve of her thigh at her every step, the curve that led from behind the ear, between the collar bones, to her left nipple. Ziki had learned to override the instinctual responses that often ruled the body. He watched her with an outward calm that did not falter. Did not falter even when she scanned the room, caught sight of him, and steered a sudden course to where he sat. Levy remained half-in and half-out of his chair.

It dawned on him that she wore no identification, no visitor's pass, no markers at all to identify her rank or what business she had at Mossad. He tried not to assume that she had stupefied the youthful security guards at their posts—like a witch from some ancient myth. Stupefied—suddenly he understood what the word meant.

She stopped directly across the table from Ziki and planted her feet—a move that read like a challenge. In another situation he might have risen to it. He saw how the line of her eyes softened momentarily and her red lips played out into a smile more forced than sultry. And while Ziki felt quite suddenly hot as he smelled the floral spice that emanated from her, the collar of his shirt tight around his Adam's apple, he did not have the will to hold his facial features in a pretend stillness. She might know how to turn heads in a room and wrap men around her little finger, but when it came to him she was scared.

"Shalom, Ziki Barak," she said, stiffly stretching a hand towards Ziki. "I am Yaffa Yardeni."

"Yardeni? Not related to—"

"Rafi Yardeni's daughter? Are you and your family faring well?" Levy asked Yaffa.

"I have no family left, but I am fine." General Rafi Yardeni had been murdered; terrorists had come in the night and blown up his home on his farm in the upper Galilee soon after his retirement.

"Your father was my friend," Ziki uttered.

"Yes." Her lashes flicked down—a daughter's grief, not an act, Ziki was certain—before she nodded in response. Her eyes shone with purpose once more, however, when she sought Ziki's face. "My father told me that I should come to you if I ever had need of. . . help."

". . . Yes," Ziki answered, then he began to troll his memory—trying to fit those smoky eyes incongruently with the eyes of a younger woman. Perhaps once, a few years back, a balcony picnic, a blue ribbon in her hair, and her giggling at every older man. . ? He took her hand with a slight rise from his seat. "Shalom." But he did not stand—she wanted something and until he knew what it was, he wanted to keep it this way. Her palm was cool.

"My condolences, Miss Yardeni. You will sit down?" It was Levy who played the gentleman, drawing out a chair for her.

"Thank you." She sat, suddenly prim and pert. She crossed her legs and smoothed her skirt over them. The slit at the side slid open again.

This woman was perfectly capable of taking care of herself, Ziki thought. And she knew what she was doing—she knew how to make an entrance and how to play a man against himself—or rather the part of a man that made it difficult for him not to be played by a beautiful woman.

"You are very kind." Again she let her hair fall over her face. Her blouse had fallen slightly open so that the shadowed line of her cleavage hinted at what more she had beneath her blouse.

"Your father was a good man," Ziki said. And he meant it. "And, yes, he was a good friend. The world is a lesser place without him in it."

"Thank you. He spoke well of you." The light of her eyes locked onto his. Did she see the disinterested critic in him, evaluating her every move and line?

"Yes."

Some of her emotion thinned. "In the Galilee, where I was raised, they say that you can tell what a man is thinking by looking in his eyes."

He grinned.

"Is there somewhere we can talk in private?" she asked, glancing with feigned hesitation at Levy.

Levy had the good grace to appear nonplused. "And I was just on my way," Levy said, pushing from the table.

Ziki gestured his introduction. "General Moshe Levy, Miss Yardeni."

"General Levy." Yaffa straightened, noting immediately her faux pas, but then offered him her hand. "My father spoke well of you as well. But I'm afraid my business is with Commander Barak."

"I am going to borrow the Commander for just a minute longer, Miss Yardeny, lets step over there," he motioned Ziki.

**The intelligence is reliable**——all was confirmed by Mossad's own informants in Egypt and rechecked by Aman. The Ofek satellite surveillance system confirmed and pinpointed the activities at the installation at Bir Misahaa, manufacturing both chemical and biological agents with the beginnings of nuclear ambitions, the Iranians have a hand in this, as evidenced by the centrifuges and separating equipment flowing in.

The response is clear: Wait for a moonless night, fly in, kill the scientists, deactivate or commandeer any completed weapons, and destroy and blow away to hell everything else.

Levy had brought up the topic almost casually, but Ziki knew he would lead into offering him command of the attack; otherwise why discuss the matter with him? General Levy was not a man given to gossip. Instead, the conversation took a surprising turn. Levy shook his head left to right, "We can't kill them."

"Like hell we can't," retorted Ziki.

Levy smiled, but clearly was not joking. "The Russians want them. More specifically," he said, leaning towards Ziki and bringing out an edge to his voice to indicate that they no longer spoke as friends but this was army business, "As I've told you Zhukov wants them," he whispered.

"Gheorgy Zhukov? The Zhukov who surrounded the Germans in their first defeat of the war at Stalingrad?"

"The Zhukov who won the war… The man who never lost a battle".

"If Zhukov wants these scientists from us," Ziki groped for the logical conclusion, "it means— What?"

"I've told you Commander, it means they don't trust the Egyptians or the Iranians with germs, poison and nukes."

"I don't blame them. But why don't the Russians just tell the Egyptians to knock off the chemical bullshit? They've got to have them by the balls and on a tight enough leash for something this substantial."

Levy smirked, "The leash works both ways. When it comes down to it, the Soviets could wipe the land of the pharaohs off the map, but who wants that?

The Kremlin always plays a good game of chess, plotting and planning three or four moves ahead. They'd much rather flatter their oil-rich friends than flatten them, and let the Jews take the blame and their new toys away."

Levy looked down at Ziki—literally, as he was much taller—and said, "Your impatience is starting to bug me Commander. Besides we've been over this bit when your 'walking beauty" Yaffa Yardeny showed up. This time wait for the briefing."

"But that's why you love me," Ziki grinned.

Levy, looking more the general than ever, quietly said, "No. We're going to take them alive. You'll find out more in the briefing."

"Yes, well it's easy for you all to say 'take them alive.' You know how many complications this involves? And needless risks to lives of our men."

Levy leaned back and shrugged. "Wait for the briefing".

"The briefing, yes, yes", with sarcasm in his voice, Ziki pressed the issue, realizing he may have been pushing too hard. "All right, all right I'll be there".

"Why do I indulge you, Ziki? I must be a fool" Levy smiled through a grimace as he rubbed his eyes.

Ziki knew it was because he had saved the old man's life more than once, but also knew it need not be spoken. "I've never heard that."

"Anyway, you want to tell me why it's worth the cost to take them alive."

Levy leaned forward again. "The Russians want the Nazis for themselves, and are willing to pay dearly for them."

"No amount of money is worth it"

"It's not money"

"What then?"

"Later at the briefing and on a need to know only"

This made some sense to Ziki, but still didn't seem to adequately explain it. "Don't they have enough German prisoners?"

"You can never have enough Nazi scientists and these are apparently special to them."

"I've got none, and that's enough."

Levy lightened up again. "Well, if you do what you're told at the briefing you'll have 23."

Even after the briefing, the successful capture operation, and the planning for the mission to East Germany, it still didn't all quite add up to Ziki.

Levy nodded his understanding. "7:30, Commander." He tapped the table and his pale-blue eyes shifted to Ziki's, scanning them with an unmistakable question and an unspoken commandment.

Ziki nodded. "7:30." Levy's look meant that Ziki would report the details of his conversation with the devastating daughter of Rafi Yardeni offering an accounting of the security breech: her business with him. Ziki had no such intention. This was his friend's daughter.

Levy took his leave.

**"Somewhere private,"** she said again, looking about her almost furtively. "My father seemed to think—. . . the walls and the tables in this place have ears."

"My office—"

"No, no—There's a café I know—"

"Off site?"

"Please. My father. . . left explicit directions."

Again he saw a flicker of grief. He watched her closely.

"Yaffa," he said slowly. A common name for daughters. In Hebrew "Yaffa" means beautiful. —Beauty in English, Bella in Italian. But "beautiful" didn't quite capture Yaffa Yardeni, nor the confident poise with which she comported herself.

"You will excuse me, but every Yaffa I have ever known has—"

"Turned out to be ugly?" She smirked. "Yeah, I've heard that one already. My friends and I used to laugh that naming a daughter 'Yaffa' is a truly sick joke. As if her parents hope that she will one day live up to her name."

"And how did your father feel about you?"

"Please," she said. "My father told me you were his friend."

Ziki blinked slowly, considering her once more. What did he owe Yardeni? Did he owe him anything?

Hmm . . . there was that time in Romania—complications and it had been Yardeni who had pulled Ziki out by the skin of his teeth. Two of Yardeni's men had almost died saving Ziki's behind and Yardeni had taken it full blast when the Chief of Requisitions finally received the bill. A private jet,—toast. Not to mention those compromising photos of the Ambassador's oldest daughter that were never recovered.

Ziki let his mind linger a little longer on the Ambassador's oldest daughter . . . a pair of red silken under drawers—. . .

Yeah, he owed Yardeni.

Enough to at least listen to his daughter. . .

"Give me an hour," Ziki said. "And I'll meet you at your coffee shop."

**On the top floor of the Mossad HQ,** the air of the strategic and logistic command rooms hummed, constant and electric. It was dim, the only light cast by ominous monitors of scrolling colors and updates, continuously displaying maps and data, with particular detail given to Israel's borders and anyone who so much as sneezed among any of Israel's *"friendly neighbors."* All flights in and out of the country, commercial, cargo, industrial, and military, all major check points and military compounds were monitored, movement to and from mapped and tracked, displayed and tallied.

Computers like hulking soldiers lined room after room, visible through picture windows the size of parking lots, rows and rows of dark brooding machines with giant spools of magnetic data-tape for eyes and teeth that were flashing red and white checkerboards.

It was the home of the little men, Ziki liked to say. As pale as their doctor-like gowns, as gray as their uniforms and caps. Stooped and squinting little men who always had a collection of pens in their pockets. The light of day—hell, a good six months off to lie in the sun and breathe fresh, non-ionized air—would do all of them an immense good. He often wondered if anyone really cared or knew exactly what they did all day, as long as everything worked when someone came in need.

At the security check point a low buzz requested voice identification before he could enter the next chamber. He spoke into the mouthpiece and in a matter of seconds his words were converted into bits of data and immediately matched against samples of his voiceprints. The low buzz repeated at a higher pitch and the bulletproof glass doors in front of him slid open with a hiss. The acrid smell of electricity and magnetic tape wafted over him as he entered.

The future, some said. Rooms like this.

The second set of doors lay several strides down the corridor and required that he stand stock-still for what always felt like an infinity as his facial features were scanned by high resolution surveillance cameras. He could hear the gears and whirring and then the fast click of data comparisons as the computer "recognized" his features. Again, he was approved and allowed entry—whisss, the doors opened.

He stepped into the darkened alcove equipped with devices that would detect a concealed weapon. The security system here, too, allowed him to pass without incident despite the sub-mini-Uzi he wore tucked under his right arm—.

The final check was a tried and true procedure of identification.

"Eli," Ziki hailed the bored security guard, standing at attention beside the final door.

"Commander," the guard responded and waved him through into the marble-floored lobby.

Hallways branched from it into many directions. His steps echoed loud in the empty hallway as he strode toward the door to his office. A simple scan of his thumbprint and a numbered combination opened the door. His office was well lit, the blinds left open from his morning's desk time. The coffee he'd left next to the Tel Aviv Times, Maariv was cold and black.

Ziki quickly logged onto his terminal and typed the access codes to the mainframe. A few more commands and he accessed the databank of the morning's images from security cameras at the main entrance and other key checkpoints throughout the building. No, no—she wasn't there. He flipped quickly through photo after photo.

Okay, he regrouped. Lesser thoroughfares. Side entrances.

No.

No sign of her.

How the hell had she gotten into the building—wait?

There.

There she was—the west stairs. She had come from the VIP parking garage. It seemed the General's daughter had no lack of credentials herself if she parked there.

He fed the computer another series of commands to capture the screens that she appeared within, re-cut the best three to cross reference, and added this input into a search bolstered with her and her father's names.

Yafa Yardeni. She had said she was Rafi Yardeni's daughter and Ziki didn't have reason to doubt that. But what else might he find out? What else should he know?

A beep emitted from the computer.

Ziki jumped back into action—switching on his the printer. Stalling to toss his cold coffee in the trash.

A hum, a buzz, and a lurch. The printer's knob of letters began to slap the paper, ripping a line of print across the page. Paper fed from the printer in a long string, folding over onto itself on the floor. His screen glowed with the scroll of information.

Yaffa Yardeni.

She was a fighter pilot?

She flew Sikorsky and Chinook helicopters of US make—Mc Donald Douglas. Which meant that she had to have been trained in the US to fly the huge top-prop planes. They were cargo carriers—massive flying machines that could carry cranes or even an APC.

She was definitely qualified for Boeing's big twin-bladed CP46s, the 'Jolly Green Giants.'

He also saw that she was trained to use mounted arms, small and medium, guided missile systems and instrumentation, as well as aircraft-mounted heavy machine guns. Hmm… she excelled in that. Impressive.

A hell of a woman. Gorgeous. Skilled. Smart. Powerful.

So what the hell did she want with him?

He read through a few more pages trying to read her mind, see connections, trolling through information that repeated itself, repeated itself, repeated itself, until the name of an area in southern Lebanon leapt out of the dross and stalled his fingers.

Waady Al Cushni.

David Becker.

—That ambush Ziki had heard about a month, two months ago. . .

Ziki turned back to his computer terminal and input David's name. The printer paused and then burst into a renewed stream of text.

David Becker dead.

Yaffa Yardeni's fiancé.

Her father and her fiancé killed in the same month.

**Waady Al Cushni, a mountainous region full of caves**, was an ideal location for El Fattah terrorists to collect themselves. Close to the Israeli border, they could come and go before rousing notice, then hole up out of sight, coaxing the Israeli patrols to try their hand at the traps laid for them in the mouths of their caves.

The region was particularly known for hiding a faction, the Al–Aqcsa Brigade — It was just the end of a killing spree. An Al–Aqcsa group made their way up north, using the West Bank to pass from Israel to the north and finally into Lebanon. When all was said and done, they slipped quietly back across the border and back into their cavernous holes.

A young Captain, David Becker—the picture showed a handsome young man, with windblown hair and wide white smile—got the call to follow them as they escaped. He, his six men, followed orders; catch them, dead or alive. Followed orders right over the Lebanese border, in hot pursuit—. David and his small patrol tracked the terrorists up a trail deep into the mountains of Waady Al Cushni, right to the mouth of caves that they'd heard too much about. Men went in; men did not come out.

Caves strung one after another on the slopes of the mountains for as far as the eye could see. Lush mountainous peppered with trees.

His radio hissed and spat. " Northern Hawk, come in Northern Hawk, over."

"We read you, hawk one, over." The smell of his own breath and sweat clung to the speaker mouth.

"Talk to us, Northern Hawk. What's your situation?"

"We just lost visual—but we're still on 'em. Over."

One of his young men was examining the ground. He stood and waved as if he were on fire, "This way. We're close!"

David and men followed the group now as a hunter stalks prey, from cave to cave.

Before entering a cave, standard army strategy required securing the entrance. A couple hand grenades tossed into the cave before entry or grenades launched with a grenade launcher generally did the trick to avoid surprise. Men could walk in, without the fear of an ambush. Often the thunderous underground explosion took care of anyone waiting inside the caves—eardrums torn, shell shocked, crushed by the cave's collapse. If the first round left anything moving, more grenades did the trick.

David's patrol followed procedure to the letter. They blew several caves and reported their progress on the radio. After each explosion, the mountains and the mountain caves lay quiet as cathedrals. No terrorists.

David squatted on his heels and rested his rifle over his knees.

They were out there and he'd get them.

"Captain!"

Something. Finally, something.

His men could see—a woman in Arab garb.

She was sitting on the rocks outside the dark opening of another cave, a child in her arms, suckling.

"Dammit." David lowered his binoculars.

It didn't feel right. Hadn't she heard the explosions throughout the mountains? Why would she just be sitting there. . . ? Waiting?

He turned his back to her and looked up at the sky, reflecting blue-green. Blue; the deep hue of the Mediterranean. Green; cedars on shore of the water below. In the distance he could see the city of Haifa, ancient Acre.

"Captain?" one of his men queried. They were waiting for orders.

The woman, the baby didn't move. A knot of ice water was slowly dissolving in his gut.

His second in command drew away from him and motioned to two of the men.

"Ze'evi, you got plenty grenades. Get on it. Use that launcher before she spots us."

Hesitation. None of them wanted to move without David's say-so.

David raised his gaze to his second's. A silent message between them and David looked down at the dirt. What choices did they have?

David felt sick to his stomach. He couldn't speak.

"Move. Do it now," his second said muscling men into positions. "That was an order."

Resistance.

Ze'evi was chewing his fingernails.

"What about—?"

Men pawed grenade launchers, but rifles hung limp.

"Send her to hell; she's one of theirs."

"Fire already."

"Give me that thing, you pussy shit. I always knew you'd pussy out."

"Here, already. I'll take care of this." Amram was the biggest man in the unit. He grabbed the launcher out of Ze'evi's hands.

"Amram, stay out of it," David heard himself saying.

"If she's a martyr, I'll send her directly to Paradise—that's where they all want to go, don't they?" Amram lifted the grenade launcher and took aim.

David found himself on his feet, though the iron weight in his stomach threatened to drop him to his knees. He pushed the nose of the launcher toward the ground.

"No grenades."

A sudden silence between men.

In the heat, he could smell their sweat.

A baby at her breast. His throat was burning. "Use the bull horn; tell her to leave the mouth of the cave." She did not move.

**Ziki went quietly past Malkielly's office, he didn't want to have to account to him for Yaffa.** Even though it had been Malkielly who had recruited Ziki from regular Army and had become Ziki's mentor through the tests and the training and the preparations for Ziki's first mission, Malkielly's real name had never been revealed to Ziki. And Ziki knew that if they ever met on the street, off-duty, he was to pretend he had never seen him before, turn on his heel and make himself gone.

Malkielly's office was not like other offices at the Mossad. It was dark, ominous. Even sinister. A big corner office, it might have been brightly lit as most corner offices were, but if it had windows, they were covered by thick shades. Computer monitors hung from every wall—a smaller duplication of the strategic war room. The screens flickered with data drawn directly from the mainframe. They also served as the only light in the room, so that every corner was dark, faces could not always be read, and Malkielly could sit in a corner of his own, unseen when he wished, a shape of shadows but for the glowing cherry on the tip of his Cuban cigar, planning out the moves that had made his name in the Mossad. He was not a man to suffer fools gladly.

His desk was heavily carved, the size of a queen bed, antique, European, Eighteenth Century, with a comfortable and equally massive dark brown leather chair. Another man might have napped in that chair, but Malkielly preferred instead to glower down at whoever sat in the six tufted leather armchairs in front of his desk. Ziki hated to be one of the ones that occasionally had to sit there.

He preferred—they all preferred—to sit at the enormous conference table that was polished to perfection, guarded by fourteen high back leather chairs. Despite the size of this table, despite the Persian carpets, Renaissance paintings in gilded frames, it was the desk that dominated the room.

And the trophies: big game trophies; a mounted lion's head at center behind Malkielly's desk, bordered by a pair of seven-foot tall African elephant tusks, the entire skin, paws and head of a behemoth Siberian Grizzly bear. The joke made in the cafeteria—well out of Malkielly's earshot, or so they hoped—that the bear looked just like the man who'd brought it down.

**Ziki followed the directions Yaffa Yardeni gave him.** Daughter of General Rafi Yardeni, fighter pilot, weapons expert, and exquisitely beautiful—and. . . completely unqualified at giving directions. He exited the Kirya and drove south on the Haifa – Tel-Aviv highway, but took a wrong turn, ended up in the middle of nowhere and got himself even more lost by trying an intuitive short cut to the road past Natania. It was a beautiful, beautiful day, beautiful sun and sky, beautiful little town with little white houses perched on cliffs overlooking the Mediterranean—but the beauty paled as he recalled his last visit to the town center. A bombing had taken out the convention room of the local hotel, a tourist hotel where people had been having dinner.  Some seventy had been wounded and… he was lost.  Lost.

On a hunch he took the road on past Hertzlia, another township by the sea, and drove through Ramat HaSharon, and suddenly he knew exactly where he was. He drove through the North Tel-Aviv suburbs onto Rotchild  Boulevard.  Foreign Consulates had their buildings, manicured flowers.  He was back on track again, through the city down to the seashore to a café off Hilell Street.  He pulled up and parked just across the street from Café Moograbe, where she waited.

Yaffa. .

The café had a terrace overlooking the beach and tables outside as well. Inside it was shady and enough of a breeze  cut the heat of the day. His eyes adjusted to the dimness as the hostess directed him to Yaffa's table—outside, where he was momentarily blinded, but the roaring spots in front of his eyes subsided to reveal her reclining in her chair, as if worshipping the sun.  The wind lifted a few of her hairs.

She'd chosen a table that sat apart from the others.  Outside.  The breeze and the wave noise.  No way could they be tapped.

She had stripped off her white blouse and sat now in a fashionable gauzy camisole, her bronzed shoulders, peppered with slightly darker freckles, bared to the sun.  The skirt seemed shorter than he remembered.  Her legs stretched in front of her, one crossed over the other.

The moment she saw him she slipped back into her vixen posture, lifting a hand to trail a finger across her chest and uncrossing her thighs so that the sunlight reflected from the white panties she wore underneath.  She immediately pushed her skirt down, as if caught having forgotten herself.  Was it to get him to look? He was not certain. He allowed himself to look, as a hungry wolf looks, not as those foolish puppies back at the cafeteria had mooned after her.

She was flawless—no strap marks on her shoulders, not a hint of white where the camisole dipped lowest between the swell of her breasts.  Beautiful breasts; firm, a small hand-full.  They might be sun-tanned beneath that pale camisole.  She could have been to Europe or to some other country in the last few days where she had sun bathed topless.  He heard himself rehearsing his descriptions and appraisals in his head—he tried to be impervious to such charms.

"Were you followed?" she asked, sitting up.

"Hello, to you as well.  May I sit?"

"You think I'm paranoid."

"I think I'd like a Chianti."  He turned and waved for the waitress.  She was a young woman with elbow length blonde hair.  Pretty in a sweet-sixteen sort of way, but her eyes were far too sad.  He wondered absently if she'd known any of the victims in that last bombing.  Another girl her age?  A friend.  Had the force of the explosion broken the windows here?  Rocked the floor?

"I'm not paranoid.  I know your people," Yaffa said.

"And we know you—," he returned perfunctorily, while finding and opening the wine list.  "Trained in the UK and the US.  Security clearances.  Not bad."

He ran his finger down the list of reds, found a good dry Czech, and pointed it out to the waitress. He asked for bread and cheese as well—chef's choice. "But not cheddar, it gives me migraines." The girl nodded and hurried away.

Yaffa's brow had tightened. "OK. I get it. What is the problem?"

"You're playing games," he shrugged.

"Ziki, I need to trust you."

"You don't want a man, you want a lap dog. And there are a dozen or more back at the cafeteria who'll sniff along after you as long as you keep flashing some T and A. You want me, you cut the cheesecake act."

She sat back and there was a high bloom of color on her cheeks. Speechless. . . Ziki refrained from smiling to himself.

"Beefcake," she corrected softly.

He raised an eyebrow.

"The expression, American—is beefcake," she corrected again.

He laughed and looked away from her. "You are your father's daughter."

She gave a slight shrug of acquiescence.

"Were you under my father's command?" Yaffa finally asked.

Ziki craved a sip of the wine he'd just ordered. "No. We did a couple of missions together. You might say we were friends."

"You know what happened?" Her lashes were lowered so he could not see the expression in them.

He nodded. In fact, Ziki had seen a complete report of the incidents, the write-ups, the photos, the profiles, but he didn't say that to her.

Raffi Yardeni had been murdered by the El Fattah's group, they came in from Lebanon—most likely through the refugee camp of Shatilla just above the Be'eka valley. Ziki had seen Yardeni's home once, perhaps that's where he remembered Yaffa from, when they'd stopped off after a long haul. At a Moshav, a communal farm, the Yardenis were central to the community of farmers that they had helped build since the village's formation.

Raffi Yardeni's house was on the outskirts of his Moshav. Yardeni didn't have security any longer. He had always been a man to want privacy. He was home alone when the terrorists came, maybe hunting for him personally, at random, no one was sure.

They'd killed the old dog on the porch and by-passed the security system with a few cut wires. Explosives placed on the foundation of his house—the explosion had killed Yardeni. Ziki had seen the residue analysis. The explosive used was a C4 variant, military grade. Its residue carried the trademarks of Libyan labs, but the recipe for C4 was all over lately, its making wasn't rocket science; any little backwater that had a lab turned it out on a regular basis. A ten-year-old could find it in any market in Lebanon or Libya, Syria as well.

The terrorists—got away clean.

They'd set the explosives with time delayed fuses and wired a detonation device into his telephone.

They called him.

He woke up and picked up the telephone.

Boom!

"I was sorry to hear about your fiancé as well," Ziki said.

Yaffa was looking out at the Mediterranean, her mouth set in a hard straight line. "I want the men who did this dead." She looked straight at him.

"My father told me that you and a few of your men can get anything done anywhere on the globe."

"Your father may have exaggerated."

She sniffed and drew herself up straight but didn't look at him as she began. "I have money—there was a portion of the farm, I didn't sell all of it, and a trust fund. I have one million American dollars. It is yours if you do this thing."

Ziki sat back, suddenly chilled. "What thing, Yaffa? I'm not an assassin for hire." God and Country and patriotism—I am not a killer for hire. "I don't kill innocent people."

"Innocent," she scoffed. The look on her face did not change. "Terrorists… They murdered my father and my fiancé."

"You're dismissing our rules of engagement; this is pre-emptive."

"If they've taken out a General's home while he slept, who else is next?"

"You've got the wrong man. I am not a mercenary."

"Ali Hassan Salameh and that Chemist that always hangs around him might be there as well." She watched Ziki's face when she mentioned Salameh, Ziki's old foe. Ziki's expression did not change but his eyes narrowed just enough to encourage her. "You'll need five or six men. I've worked up a list—select a crew. No one at Mossad must know anything about this."

"Yeah, no kidding."

"That won't be easy after the entrance you made. You have a thing or two to learn about discretion."

"Tell them we're sleeping together."

"What makes you think I haven't already?"

She shook her head slightly. "You're a man of honor. You wouldn't do that."

"What else do you think you know about me?"

"That you'll help me."

He tried to play it off. "Help you?"

"You wouldn't have come if you didn't want to."

He sighed. "Let's get out of here." He was already half out of his chair, pulling out his wallet and slapping far more bills than necessary on the tabletop.

"Where—?" She was on his heels.

"You drive," he said, but he said nothing more as he strode ahead of her to the street.

Her car was sweltering inside—a little sports car, an Alfa Romeo she got in Milan, it convected heat like a toaster. She lowered the windows and a breath of air mercifully filled Ziki's lungs. He sat back against the leather seat. Sweat began under his arms.

"Which way?"

"The motorway," Ziki ordered her as she started the car.

She fell silent, eyeing him sideways in furtive spurts, as she drove.

"You are going to tell me where we are going?"

"Drive North. I'll tell you when to turn off."

She eyed him again, then nodded and did as she was told.

For a long while Ziki watched the city go by outside the window: coffee shops and dress shops and students and people living their lives on the sidewalks of Tel Aviv. When he was ready, he squared his shoulders and looked straight ahead.

"So. Tell me about this job."

"You'll do it?"

"I didn't say that." He lit a cigarette and dangled it out the window. "Take the next exit."

She nodded. "There is an abandoned English fort in the northern Sudan at Jabel Hidada—you know it?"

"No."

"It's south of Sallema Oasis and north of Lakia Ottaba and Lakia Hammerun."

"By the Egyptian border."

"Yeah. It's deserted."

"Unlikely. But possible, go on. . . " He took a long drag on his cigarette and blew out smoke.

"I have it from a good source. There will be a meeting."

Ahhhhhhhhh. Ziki raised an eyebrow. "Who?"

"Jihad Yousef Halil Hamdan. Ismail Mussa Mohammad Il Jubran. Makhmud Midal. Mussa Abu El Kalif. Ibrahim Musa Salim Abiet. And Mustaafa Al Sayidi, and maybe Ali Hasan Salameh."

Ziki knew all those names, especially the last, Salameh. She knew their whereabouts. Was this a vengeance hit? She rattled all those names off the top of her head, she'd memorized them well.

She began to spill faster. "They're making plans for a coordinated effort. One against the Americans and the other in Jerusalem, where they're planning to blow up something big; the hospital is an item on their list. I don't know what the other targets are; in America they are trying to get two dirty A bombs, and there is talk of chemical –biological staff, Anthrax that they already have."

"What's their target in the US?"

"We don't know yet, but I bet that if you question one of them in the Sudan we'll find out. I've heard about your interrogating and brain washing techniques."

Ziki flashed a brow at her and tossed his cigarette to the roadside. "Take a left here. What else?"

"There's a hit on a ship that is already in the works. Iranian money is financing their hits—"

"—And the Iraqis are going to supply the armor, ammunition and Intel information, explosives and other goodies." Ziki shook his head. "Those bastards have all the balls in the world."

"So, you're in. I can count on you?"

Ziki laughed. "Just what is it you want me to do?"

"It's a question of global proportions."

"Bullshit. I heard you say Mustaafa Al Sayidi would be in attendance."

"They're going to kill thousands—"

"But Mustafa Al Sayidi already killed your David, didn't he?"

She whitened and went rigid. "We'd be doing our country a favor… We'd be doing the whole world a favor."

"—But I'm not sure it's worth standing in front of an IDF military tribunal when they find out I've done this under the radar—a dozen crimes."

"You can pull it off then?" There was hope in her eyes.

"The question, lady, is why would I want to?"

She pulled the car over abruptly, raising the din of several horns and the shriek of tires as she cut recklessly through three lanes of traffic to do so. She braked so hard that Ziki's forehead hit the glass of the windshield.

He exclaimed in pain and clasped a palm to his hairline. "*Mamzeret, bat zona.*"

"Why? Why not? Why won't you do it?"

"Aside from the fact that you just made jelly of my frontal lobe?"

"Ziki… My father. . . I came to you because my father…."

"Enough already—I get it. I know what it's like to want to kill so badly that you'd throw it all on the line."

Her hands fell uselessly on her lap. "What can I do to convince you?"

He considered this a moment. "First thing you have to do is reveal your source."

She shook her head. "I can't do that. You know I can't do that."

"I don't know shit. I don't know about getting a team of my men into the Sudan, the Sahara no less, for G'd's sake, I don't do illegal assassinations, and I sure as hell don't know you from any other orphan or widow that walks into Mossad on any other given day."

"What if I can assure you that nothing will happen to your career?"

Ziki laughed. "You think you can get me off the hook if this hits the fan? Your daddy's friends were not that powerful."

"No. But my friends are."

Ziki's crooked grin drooped.

"You're going on a mission in two days. I know all about it."

Ziki sat up. "What are you telling me—?"

"You're the commander on the mission into Egypt near the Sudan border that is to nab some twenty or more German scientists brought in fresh from South America, ex SS Nazis, Odessa stuff, that are now working for the Egyptians, and you are to destroy the biological plant they're in. Germans. Nazis. Developing biological germ warfare and chemical stuff for them."

Ziki squinted. How? "How do you know about a fantasy like that?"

She shrugged her shoulders. "Not through my father's contacts, no."

"That type of information—if it were true—is classified. It's top-level clearance—I haven't even been briefed on it yet."

"You'll find out tonight how close you'll already be. A detour—and we've got those bastards. Just think about it. Al Sayidi. Hamdan. Jubran. Midal. Abu El Kalif and Salameh... All of them in one place."

"Oh my good God, what am I hearing? This stuff floating around, leaking like this. Do you know what happens to people that talk about this kind of stuff? Loose lips go to jail. If Mossad gets wind of this? I should put you in fucking jail. I should tie you up and take you back right now. How the fuck do you have this type of information?"

She did not change her expression. "A friend."

"Who are you fucking at Mossad, that you have this kind of information? Only five or six people have that sort of clearance."

She nodded slowly. "I lost my father to these murderers. He said you were his friend."

Ziki lowered his eyes. "All right."

"You'll do it?"

"You convince me... I suppose the world'll be a better place for it…These are ..."


"Who are you sleeping with? The prime minister or the *Ramatcal*—Chief of Staff?" She pouted her lips. "I knew you'd do it."

"Call me a fucking hero."

"My contact does . . . It is Finkle…he says—"

"Shit," Ziki whispered. It couldn't be. "Please tell me it's not Finkle."

Her brows drew together momentarily. "All right. I'll tell you it's not Melvin Finkle."

"Melvin," Ziki said, his voice seething. She had called him by his first name. "That little rat turd of a worm. What could possibly drive you to sleep with—"

"Some secrets— a price one has to pay."

"No… No. Not him." There was an image in Ziki's head now—it caused a nauseous confusion and pain. Get it out! Get it out of his head!

"Ugh."

"I know." She shifted petulantly.

"Melvin Finkle. . ?" Ziki's mouth dropped open. He didn't want to believe it. "You're sleeping with Melvin Finkle?"

Her gaze dropped. "He took money, too." Some women will do anything. . . it wasn't a question of morals or scruples or reputation—they took the shortest route to their aim.

It made his stomach turn to think of Finkle with her. The greasy little man and the statuesque Yaffa... Cut from stone, they were like an ancient Greek myth—the rape of Leda, the kidnapping of Eros. . . some men… all the luck. Ziki's mouth twisted into a half-grin. Leave it to a worm like Finkle, a cash bribe to take a woman like Yaffa to bed.

Ziki was spot on. "He called the money I gave him his 'retirement fund,'" Yaffa intoned. She began to explain how she transferred money to Finkle's account through a series of accounts and reroutings—Swiss banks. A Mossad greenhorn could crack the series of moves she'd made in a heartbeat. "I wasn't the only one—Finkle's got a little nest egg set aside for when the time is right. I'm betting he'll move to Switzerland."

There was a sourness in Ziki's mouth. Amateur stuff, really–Mossad could track transactions to Swiss accounts with a single phone call. They might already know that Finkle had received funds . . that she'd sent them. What a mess. . . He stared out the car window, searching the sky for some piece of color. Now she was telling him about the sorts of things Finkle had "located" for her—the names and home addresses of various El Fattah terrorists—ones the Mossad watched closely and waited for, the locations of equipment—guns, helicopters. And Ziki's agenda coming up in Egypt. Finkle had hardly needed asking to produce that.

"He doesn't like you, does he?" Yaffa asked Ziki.

"No." Ziki's grin was wry. "I don't need him to like me… I need him to stay the hell away from me."

"Are you worried about implication? Don't worry," she finished, "I've hidden my tracks. My father taught me—. . . "

Ziki felt his spirits dropping in line with her downcast expression and jumped at the sudden self-awareness. Look at me. . . He didn't want to hurt her feelings; she suddenly looked vulnerable. He kept his mouth shut, letting what she'd told him sink in slowly, slowly, letting his mind supply the ink by which to connect the dots.

At the back of his mind was an itch of fear that Mossad would find out he'd been humoring her. What was the charge—accessory? To bribery? Conspiracy? Assassination, he corrected himself. She'd told him about Finkle. . . told him about the money.

He sat thoughtfully, head down and body still.

Think, think. . . there must be a really good reason for him NOT to help her.

Stealing, 'borrowing' equipment from Mossad. . . Entering a foreign country without clearance. . . assassinating several terrorists without authorization. All "crimes."

Damn. . . what a shame that she was so beautiful and that money was so crisp and green, and could she replace Gavriella?

She must have read his mind. She laid a hand on his arm. "Those terrorists' deserve to die… Mossad should have already planned this mission, then we wouldn't have to… They've killed a lot of innocent people."

People she loved.

She tilted her head just so, letting her gaze fall to her hands. "The money is an extra—"

"—I don't want the money. I don't need the money."

"Children and my father. I need to do this thing. They are murderers, they will murder again! Not even to speak of what plans they have for the future… So you're doing me, my father, Israel, and the world a favor to rid the planet of these murderers.

"Will you take the mission?"

"I'm sorry—you must have mistaken me for a fool."

"No," she shook her head. "You haven't decided yet. I can tell. You're looking at me like—you like me—not physically, that's not what I mean—you're disgusted by my thing with Finkle—"

"Is that what they call it these days?"

"Come on, Ziki—I know something about your missions—what's the name of that American you sleep with, ohh yes, Gavriella, to open doors to the US State Department? You'd have screwed Kissinger, too—or let him screw you if Malkielly had ordered you to—"

"You've a hell of a nerve."

"Yeah, you're looking at me like you like me. I can tell. My father was right: underneath all that surface is a good person."

"Did your father know how far you'd go to revenge his death?"

"I'm going after them alone if you're not coming with me. They'll probably kill me—in your book of memories make a small footnote; Yaffa Yardeni, my friend's daughter, put her faith in my hands one day, and I said no! Ahh—well. And then, just put a red rose on my grave if you find the time... There's no one else."

"You think you can work me like that?"

"I can't talk to anybody else. Do you understand, Ziki? There is no one else."

"I'm taking men on that mission—under my wing. I would be endangering—there's a lot at stake."

"I just want a simple funeral. See that they put me next to my father, o.k?"

"Do you actually get away with this stuff?"

She didn't have to answer. He knew—of course she did. Men were suckers. Just look at Samson, the poor bastard lost his hair to Delilah's charms and then his life.

He couldn't really think straight when he was looking at her....

It's the money! He told himself. An awful lot of money. There was that boat he'd been looking at. . . and maybe a villa on the winding road on the Amalfi coast overlooking the Mediterranean in Italy.

This woman had put some kind of spell on him—wake up—wake up—Ziki—wake up—find a prostitute down on Yarkon Street near the pool hall—you know the spot. And you'll feel better once you forget this whole stupid thing.

Killing for hire! A paid assassin... I've never done that. I would never do that. What I do is different. I do what I do for God and Country. . .

"Good luck on your mission in Egypt, Ziki." Ziki nearly growled.

A long moment of silence hung between them. Ziki could hear the clock in the car's dashboard tick off the seconds.

"All right," he finally said. What the hell . . . how did this woman get so far under his skin? "All. . . Right. . . I need a couple of hours to clear my head and think about this."

She leaned forward, surprising him with a kiss, hovering, with her mouth still close to his as she said, softly. "Thank you."

Her blouse had gaped open as she moved, exposing the line of her cleavage, the swell of her soft skin, a peak of a hot pink and a black lace bra. Hovering—and Yaffa knew that Ziki was looking down her blouse, checking out the shadow in there. He could smell her and felt the heat of her skin—she knew that too. She is some piece of work.

She knew how to play it. Some women know how to just open their legs, enough of a hint—just a little bit to give him a glimpse—just enough to make his mouth flood with saliva and his lower regions tingle, waking up. And then shut them, give just a flash. Keep him waiting, keep him wanting.

Yaffa knew. When a man thinks with his... No reason or rationality. She had him. He knew she had him and she knew that he knew, but still—he just couldn't stop the thoughts flashing through his head.

"Let's say I do say yes—" he said suddenly. "I'm not saying yes, but suppose I do. What then? How do you want to do this thing?"

She sat back in her car seat and blinked as if only now considering the enormity of what she proposed.

"You don't have any sort of a plan. . . " he realized.

"I will be paying you to do this sort of thinking for me." She pressed her fingertips to her eyes, collecting herself.

"You're not paying me anything—I haven't agreed—"

"Right. Right," she assented. "Ok, then. We're talking about your raid in Egypt. We're talking about the Sudan. Third-world countries— You'll bring more equipment than you need—for your Egyptian raid. Requisition three big helicopters instead of two."

"Equipment and men is only one thing. My question to you is—who knows what 'they' are going to do once we take things rogue? When they find out that we've crossed borders and did things not on their orders—?"

She nodded. "With a million dollars, you can go anywhere, be anywhere, be anyone. No filth from any backwater will be able to touch you."

Ziki nodded—no. "I don't think you understand. This rogue mission without support of any kind. Ten million dollars can't hide me or you from Mossad."

"You're too much into practicality."

"Practicality?" He laughed. "If you want practicality, why don't you just go after these men—get them one by one. You can try a kill contract with your million dollars...I know a good team of assassins for hire in Africa. But I have to admit, contract killers will not get them easily—." He paused. "We'd be flying in Mossad's face—an act that will attract more attention than a strip joint in Jerusalem's Mea Sha'arim. A contract would be the cheapest, most effective way for you."

"No logistics."

"The devil is in the logistics, sweetheart. I'd just be hanging you out to dry if I didn't make that clear, and you are my friend's daughter."

"All right. Maybe you're right—I want revenge—I want to make a boom that all those other murdering bastards will have echoing in their dreams at night. I want them to know that I found them and I took them out—I want their families and friends to know. Maybe it will slow the rest of them down."

"I can't help but notice that you keep saying 'me' when really you mean 'you.' When push comes to shove, darling—it's my behind that will be out there painted with bright red circles and you'll be home in your pajamas, reading Vogue with a glass of wine."

"You're going to do it."

"Where did you get that? I didn't—"

"You just said you were going to do it. And it's all over your face, Ziki. I can hear it in your voice."

He paused. "I haven't decided."

"You're already talking like you've got a stake in this." She smiled broadly—radiantly. "I can tell—you'll decide to come along. Yeah, you will."

Was she flirting with him? She wiggled herself a little in the car seat and gave Ziki a look that would melt butter. She was a woman.

"I need time. I need to think." He said nothing. He wasn't sure. She was so certain of herself.

"I heard that you hang around with that Davidoff," she said suddenly. "My dad mentioned him. Dad said that he is good on work like this. And he works well with you."

"None better."

"What about Avi, that big one?"

"What you see is what you get with Avi."

She smirked. "Like so many men."

Ziki laughed. "Davidoff," he said softly. "You know . . . he would be good too. . . Why not let me run it by him? See what he thinks."

She tensed. "I don't think that's a good idea."

"I want his opinion."

"I also want to keep this under our hats."

" I don't need your permission, Yaffa girl! Your dad would trust him."

She bit her lower lip. "Will he keep his mouth shut—?"

"Davidoff? Definitely."

"All right then if you say so. Talk to him." She turned her face away—looking out the window at traffic and the sky. He considered her, looking at her askance while turning a corner. "I need to tell you something. . . Just for the record. . . And just so you know." She didn't like the sound of that but she shrugged her reserve off.

"Go ahead." And she steeled herself visibly. Ziki pressed his lips together before beginning. "I am going to leave a secured letter. Secured—not in my desk—I'm going to leave it in the safe in my office. Everything you've told me will be in it. And that's going to be opened if I get killed. And that's also going to get opened if something bad happens to my mission in Egypt because of anything you may have said or done." She objected with a noise.

"No, listen. I'm documenting everything. And if this goes badly—you're going to be cooked. We're whipping up a hell of a lot of security issues." She had not even turned her head to watch him while she listened.

"If you betray me or my Egyptian mission," he continued, "they're going to hunt you down. Just so you know. I'm going to arrange for that. So—whether you go alone or with someone else. Whether I go with you on this mission, or if I don't—I'm going to take care of things in a way that makes sure there's a failsafe. So whether I go with you or not, all we've talked, all we discussed, all that Finkle told you"—he put his finger over her lips—"those lips stay shut—understood?"

She was silent for a long moment.

He appraised her uneasily.

"Ok?" he nudged her for an answer.

"Ok," she said simply.

He released a long breath. "I won't turn in Finkle. I haven't decided yet what to do with him. And he might yet be useful."

She smiled faintly. "I don't give a damn about Finkle. Do what you want with him."

"He's not smart enough to be called a snake and not high enough on the food chain to be called scum—and you should know that, too. Don't trust him. Not for a second."

"I'll keep my eyes on him." She shifted slowly in her seat and turned to Ziki. "Since we're talking about security and covering our rear ends, let me be clear as well. It's not a good thing to start threatening me like that... I am a fighter pilot with the IDF—do you think I got there on my back? Ziki—I have security clearance and they trust me. I can get places that you only have dreams about."

What a woman?

"Point taken," he acquiesced. "But you keep in mind that you've never worked with me before. Finkle only knows half of what he thinks he knows. He owes me his life and his job."

"And your father's friendship—it's good to hear. But, girl, he knew me when I was green—He didn't know half of what Malkielly's sent me into. They've sent me into the mouth of bloody hell and I came back, still alive."

"Ahh. . . I've injured your pride."

"You sound like you're with me then?"

"Maybe." It was a step closer to yes.

"Ok, then, I need some time by myself. We'll meet at café Alhambra. We'll meet there at 5:00 o'clock."

"You want people to think I'm sleeping with you? Bring me chocolates and clean yourself up a little."

"I was trying for scruffy but handsome," Ziki muttered.

"Don't fear the razor in your own hand."

"Tell me where you want me to drop you off."

"No," she answered abruptly with a shake of her head. She looked suddenly tired. Her façade of fire and ice and promises fading like flowers in the sun. "I'll take a taxi. It's better that way."

"All right then, I'll see you at 5:00 o'clock at the café.

He drew the car to the curb and kept his head bent as she tossed the strap of her handbag over her shoulder. She unlatched the door and opened it an inch, but before pushing from her seat, she swung closer and pressed her mouth to his cheek.

He was hot suddenly. The smell of her and her hair and mouth. Her mouth. Soft and insistent. He'd wanted to remind her that he was strong; that he could show her about power. When she took her mouth from his cheek, her eyes were heavy-lidded and smoky.

"Thank you . . . " she whispered.

He smiled with the cold calculation her statement inspired twisting his mouth into the menace of a smile.

"Don't confuse me with your conquests, beautiful. When you come to me, it will be because you can't keep away."

She pushed away from him and out of the car, swinging the door shut and skipping to the curb without a look back. He watched her walk away. Watching the dark leather hug her hips. The wind caught her hair and blew it over her face. Ziki returned immediately to the Kirya.

**In the barracks Davidoff was sleeping off a late night.** Ziki sat on his bunk and bounced indelicately. Davidoff rolled over, drooling on his pillow and cheek. Ziki shook his head. Davidoff looked almost peaceful.

"Get up!" Ziki shouted at him, his voice splitting the quiet of the barracks like a bugle. Davidoff jerked to a sit, drumming his head into the bunk above him. The frame made a long, low clung and Davidoff fell backward with a groan. Ziki winced. That had to hurt.

"Ohh, Ziki. Damn." He flopped back on his bed, swiping the drool from his chin.

"Get up, you lazy ass. It's late."

"Go away—what do you want?"

"Get up," Ziki said. He bounced on the bunk. "We need to talk."

A few minutes later, Davidoff was awake enough to hear the whole Yaffa story—start to finish. Ziki kept most of the best details to himself. He hadn't been able to shake off the ache in his head since leaving Yaffa almost an hour before.

"How much money did you say?" Davidoff was now fully awake.

"One million American dollars."

"A million. . ? As in one and six zeros?"

Ziki took a moment to count the zeros in his head. "Uh—yeah."

"A million dollars? American dollars?"

"No Chinese! Yes, American dollars."

"How much would each man get?"

"$50,000."

"Why do you get $950,000?"

Ziki raised an eyebrow. "Because it's my mission and you're an asshole—and my take isn't $950,000—I have to get at least four other men and we're going to have to pay them, too."

"Right. . . I'm in—You have a plan?"

"I'm working on it."

" Is she good looking?"

"Naaww, with a name like Yaffa, are you kidding? A dog."

"You want to sleep with her, don't you? He. he, what about the American? Gavriella, ahmm, Gavriella."

"Shut up."

"Well, can I come along to the meeting?"

"No—you can't come along to the meeting. You stay out of it. I'll tell you what's going on later."

"I'm going to talk to Avi."

"No… No, you can't talk to Avi—Avi's too… he's too straight. You can't talk to Avi—he'll never go for anything like this. You can't take Avi. Keep Avi out of it—he's to stiff for something like this."

"Avi would never turn on us. Yeah… Maybe… I trust Avi with my life; he's my body guard, we've been all over the world even Africa and yeah, yeah,— But, maybe you're right—he's just too straight."

Ziki laughed. "Who's calling the shots here—you or me?"

"He'll be going in on this thing in Egypt—maybe you should  take him."

"I'll have him reassigned. I'll find us four other men."

"Some of your crazy bastards—maybe your *Golanis*, maybe a couple of *Duvdevanim*?"

"Are you jealous?"

"We're gonna need some real crazies to get this one done."

"Like that actor, Swartzneger said in a movie—'I had to kill some people, but they were all bad.' That's what you're talking—isn't it? Mercenaries."

"You want to call it that—Okay. World class mercenaries. But if you are talking morals? This isn't Sweden we're going to visit—or Canada. We're talking some real bad ass predators, is what we're doing. Murdering sons of bitches—every single one of them. If men like us don't hunt them down, who will?"

"When did you become a philosopher?"

"Asshole."

"So, you're in?"

"Hell. . .  I don't know. The risk—IDF equipment. Assassinations. We could end up…"

"Yes, pretty boy." Ziki tusseled his hair. "Then you'll have your picture in all the papers, and all the girls can send you letters in jail, and the world will be a little safer because we've cleaned some scum off the map."

Davidoff sighed. "I'm in."

"Good. Let me decide if I am and then we'll see where we go from here."

"Wait a minute—you didn't tell me you hadn't decided yet."

Ziki grinned. "Which way does it look that I'm leaning?"

**Ziki located the Selema Oasis and Jabel Hadada in the Sudan's Sahara on maps.** Yaffa was right on the money—the base she'd mentioned that the terrorists were going to use for their meeting was not far from Bir Abu El Husein where the Nazi scientists were toiling without suspecting Ziki's oncoming raid.

In a short while he'd be right where she wanted him.

As she had told him. The woman was something.

Ziki walked slowly to the cafeteria, running the thing through his mind. He had a coffee by himself and ran it through again and once more for good measure. He could ask the two experienced Golanis to go along. They were unmarried, young, had been on many a missions with Ziki—they'd do just fine. He'd seen enough of their off duty hijinks to know he could keep them quiet; they were loyal to him.

He crushed the empty paper cup in his hand and strode from the cafeteria towards one of the records rooms—they kept records of everything. . . and there was something he needed to check. The final lynch pin that would help him know what his answer would be this evening when he met with Yaffa Yardeni.

Ziki approached the security scanner and put his right eye to the cup. A quick flash of laser-scanning that made black and red spots appear on the back of his cornea. Before he could see clearly again, a small green light blipped on at the doorknob. He input the key pad combination, fumbling briefly for the appropriate sequence, then nailing it, and turned the handle. The door popped open and swung inward.

A little guy with thick-rimmed glasses worked that section. Ziki found him and walked to his side. What was his name? He drew a blank and so just smiled at him and slapped him on the back in greeting.

He wished he could remember if he was married, had kids or a dog—something to butter him up with.

It wasn't necessary. The man recognized him and asked Ziki how he could help him today.

"I need some information—from a mission at Khan Yunis, in Gaza a while back. Can you pull the files?"

"No problem. Gotta date?"

"Yeah, tonight. A hot little fighter pilot—"

"For the mission," the man replied without the hint of a smile.

Chagrinned, Ziki shrugged. "Just trying to make light. Can you look it up through my ID number?"

"Sure—whatever's easiest."

Ziki repeated his number with little inflection and looked around the room as the tech clicka-clacketed on the key board, calling up computer files.

"Ahh, yes—yes—Khan Yunis. Here it is." His eyes scanned the record quickly, taking in the details. "Shit. You're lucky you made it back in one piece. A hell of job in one hell of a shithole place."

"You don't have to tell me."

"Makes me glad I have flat feet."

To go with his flat head? He looked at the little guy.

"Who was the officer in charge of the search and rescue? He pulled me and my men out of there—my mom wants to thank him with a coffee cake."

"Ahh. . . here it is. The officer in charge was. . . Yardeni. Special Forces."

"Right. That's it—thank you."

Yaffa's father.

So he did owe the man.

"Thanks," Ziki said as he patted the guy again on the shoulder. He turned back as he started to leave. "You need to get out some. You're as white as a plucked dead chicken."

"Thanks a lot," the tech replied. "Thanks a lot."

As the door was swinging shut he heard the tech swear so that Ziki could hear him.

"Asshole," the tech said.**

**Yaffa was waiting for him at Café Alhambra.** Five o'clock sharp, she was there, punctual. From his car, he saw her check her watch and go in. He saw her take a seat at a table—the farthest table from the bar, closest to the seashore where the noise from the Mediterranean's waves, as she had said, would again drown out their conversation if anyone was listening. Who was he kidding? She'd kissed him once and he'd given it right back—he was going to have to keep on his toes. He didn't get out of the car, but watched her, wondering if she knew he was watching her as she checked her watch again and smoothed her palms over her thighs, pressing down her leather skirt.

She had the same outfit on. She hadn't changed anything; a little tired, but she still looked better than good. He shook himself and set his demeanor to icy. Leather skirts, silk blouses, a little shake when she walked—he bet that's how she got men to do the deeds she wanted them to do. He remembered her sigh, he took in a deep breath to freeze the image—he would be professional... He was in charge here.

She'd had a point. Terrorists, killers—no one, no one who knew what those men were—would miss a single hair from their heads.

He got out of his car and walked confidently to the door of the café.

She stood as he approached her, looking a bit nervous, a bit shy.

But that coy, little girl act—one of the many she had shown in the few hours he had known her—wouldn't unnerve him.

"You've decided that my side trip is worth a look."

"Yeah," he said, as he took a seat.

She sat too, pushing a wayward strand of hair behind her ear. A waitress came up and took their order for dark cappuccinos and chocolates. When the waitress left them, Ziki shifted into a more comfortable position, watching her the whole time. No, it was no act. Yaffa was nervous.

"I'm considering your offer very seriously."

"But you're not totally sold. . ." The disappointment in her face seemed real.

Ziki crossed his ankles and sat back. He drew his pack of cigarettes from his breast pocket and lit one. He offered her one and she took it, leaning forward to accept the light he offered.

"It's a big risk," she said… "It's dangerous. But I thought that is what you do."

"Murder?" She looked away and blew out smoke impatiently. "You don't think it's murder. You know it is not. You're no moralist. Mossad should have placed this one on the front burner. We are just speeding it up for them."

"I'm considering your plan. And the money you've offered. I've talked it over with Davidoff. I've checked out some basics. I think it's doable. I think we could do it. Could," he stressed.

This brought a smile to her face, but she didn't buy his reserve. "I knew you were my man."

"In a manner of speaking." He blew out smoke. "So tell me what you have in mind. How big do you want this blow out to be?"

"Sky high," she answered. "The way I see it—you're going with equipment and men into Egypt to destroy the chem-bio factory and to grab 23 Nazis out of there—most of the way home for us. You're already going to need a couple of CH46—the big ones—or even those new beauties—the CH47 Chinook helicopters."

"Right—that's what I'll need." He nodded slowly. She did know her stuff.

"And you're going to land your men, blow up the place, load up those 'passengers' and transport them back to our 'friendly' airspace, right?"

"Something like that, yes."

"My source tells me that you're going to be right at Bir Abu El Husein—near Bir Kiseiba. We're talking fast movement in one of those Chinooks. You pick up—your flight plan will be to fly one of them just over the Egyptian border. With a detour deeper into the Sahara of the Sudanese border you'll be just a short way from the Selema, in the Jabele Hadada region."

He nodded. "I saw it on the map that way—sure. But I don't think it's going to be the Sunday jaunt that you describe."

"You're worried about flack? Soviet rockets? Sudanese MiG's?"

"Among other things—not to mention the timing. Someone is going to notice that the return trip took a little longer than expected."

"Your men and twenty-three scientists—you only need two helicopters. But you can requisition three. Take an extra CH46 Chinook, a Jolly Green Giant. They fly like Ferraris, cut the air like it's cream, and they can carry half a dozen vehicles and equipment, can't imagine how the Americans came up with those."

"Three helicopters—I won't have the man power to pilot all three."

"Man power, no. Woman power, yes."

"You're coming along?"

"You thought I'd stay home and wait for the phone to ring?"

"All right," he said tersely. "I can requisition three choppers. And I've got your men.  But you're still in Tel Aviv and I'm in Egypt."

"I'm going to steal it."

"Steal it?"  She was five cards short of a full deck.

"Right out from under your nose—in a manner of speaking—You're going to let me steal it, in Egypt."  She mimicked his previous tone to the letter.

"They're going to put us in jail forever."

"You don't have to have anything to do with stealing it.  I'm doing it."

"What? That is stupid, I'm sorry Yaffa."

"Think it through, Ziki.  Egyptians stole the damn thing—their second thought will be that it failed on takeoff and you had to leave it behind—destroying it, of course."  She seemed somehow too certain about the theft.  "I will steal it!"

"Like candy from a sleeping clerk.  I'll send the other choppers and the men on their way, have the third one linger, we'll board it, you'll fly it.  You're smarter than you look."

"We'll destroy it when we're done in the Sudan and then we'll say that in the firefight with the Egyptians at the plant they blew this one up?"

A load of money down the drain:  a few hundred thousand US dollars, maybe a million or more with guns and ammo and special equipment.

"Yeah, that's it.  We'll ditch it and destroy it once we are done."

He shook his head, "I just don't know what you're getting me into here."

"It's not going to break the bank, you know—they loose these even in training sometimes.  The government writes it off—  You get that third extra, and please make sure the they're going to have this equipment on them.  They're going to need air to ground guided rockets, right?"

"Yes—of course."

"I'll need a couple of Gatlin guns on board."

"Standard equipment on the Chinooks," he assured her.

"The only thing that I don't have completely figured is what we do with your pilot."

"You're not going to kill one of my pilots?"

"No, no—we don't have to kill him.  I know what to do."

"We can't come with a helicopter all the way to this place and then hide it, the satellite photos show the terrain flat with no place to hide.  They'll see us."

"Per your mission—you'll land at night, yes?"

"Yes."  He was really starting to dislike the amount of in-depth details that she had learned about the Egyptian raid.

"Ohh, for God's sake," she scoffed.  "What the hell is the matter with you?  You are forgetting that I am a fighter pilot with security clearance almost as high as yours."

"And you're sleeping with  Finkle."

"Could you just drop that?"

"Like a hot rock."

She scowled.  "Arrange for 'our' chopper to land as far as possible from the others.  Within your scope of the doable—yes?"

"Doable."

"Load the Nazis and the men who aren't with us in the other two choppers."

"That's what I just said."

"We take the third one, right?"

"We take it—we take off. Ok." He kept his features impassive. "So that's the plan?"

"That is the beginning of a plan." He sought her gaze and held it. "You know what you're in for if this goes south? The theft of IDF military property—crossing international borders without permission or government sponsorship. There's not a chance in hell anyone will be able to get our asses out of there if this goes bad."

"I'm aware of the danger."

"And you're still sure you want to do this whole thing?"

She returned his gaze with determination. "Do I look unsure?"

"If we don't get killed—all of us—and there is a good chance of that. If the Egyptians don't get us when we cross the border, if the Sudanese don't get us—"

"The Sudanese are nothing. Their air capability is limited."

"Limited? You're aware that they have Soviet MiGs, fighter jets."

"The Sudanese can't track us in the air—they have some Russian Mickey Mouse radar systems, but they can hardly use them—most of their men can't read the instructions—I heard they are in Russian, let alone tell a chopper from a flock of geese." She smiled. "You've had your share of intelligence briefings on their systems and you're familiar with their capabilities—tell me honestly. Is it the fucking Sudanese you're worried about?"

It was the first time she had said "fucking" and it took him off guard. It was so sexy when women used obscenities.

She shrugged. "Don't underestimate me. I'll fly low and be under their radar and I'll be under the Egyptian radar too."

"The Egyptians have the latest in Russian radar technology. I don't take that lightly."

"Do you know the rate of Egyptians who speak Russian? The Egyptians have the Russian technology—but the instructions are also in Russian. To date, they haven't had a Soviet technician to the sub Sahara region of Egypt to brief any of them. I'll fly under their radar and they'll never know that we've passed through."

"I hope you're this cocky when we're being strip searched in some desert prisoners camp."

She leaned her head on her hand, taking the next cigarette he offered. "Do you remember that cartoon on the front page of Maariv, the morning newspaper? The Soviets had just supplied the Egyptians with 600 MiG fighter jets and Mossad worried about the new capability; in this cartoon two Israeli generals are walking on the runway and one says to the other, 'All that modern fire power—new MiGs!' Are you worried?"

Ziki knew the cartoon and the sentiment behind it. "And the other answers, 'Ahh don't worry about it... How are they're going to fly those new planes barefoot." I've been face to face with some of those bare-footers—it doesn't serve any of us to think little of them."

"I'm just saying, Ziki. That's what this is about. I understand their radar systems and I can outmaneuver them, trust me."

"Yeah, and the Sudanese?"

"Sudanese—I already told you, there's no chance they'll track us. You don't have to worry about them."

"I always worry. That's how you stay alive in this business. The Sudanese have MiGs and not all of them are flying 'barefoot'. One MiG, just one and we're dog meat. In helicopters we have no chance—don't tell me with a Gatlin' gun and a couple of rockets on a chopper you're going to fight a MiG?"

"It's been done! But they're not going to spot us."

"You're that good?"

"I'm that good."

"You're going to have to be."

She smiled. "My dad would be pleased with this enterprise."

Ziki sat back once more. "We go through this—bull—scheme of yours and if the Egyptians don't get us and if the Sudanese don't get us and we get where you want us to get—we're talking how many terrorists?"

"I have five names—the principals. There are going to be twenty-four of them altogether. They're meeting at the Salema Oasis. They're going to come from all over the place—Libya, Algiers, Lebanon, Iraq, Iran and Syria—to coordinate their activities for the next few months. We're doing everybody a favor ridding the planet of these bastards—Europe alone should get down on its knees and kiss our behinds. My father and David would tell you the same if they could. But they are dead thanks to those bastards… They are speaking to you through me." It was getting harder to argue with her logic.

"They tell me that they hope that you hear their voices and stop hesitating."

"If they don't get us at Salema , they're not going to come holding their dicks, they're going to be armed to the teeth and they could have additional men with them, we must plan for more than twenty-four. This is not going to be a piece of cake."

"Yeah well, that's why I'm calling you in and don't overlook a small matter of 1,000,000 American dollars."

"We have to get out of there. We'll be making a hell of a lot of noise and we'll have to calculate and deal with fuel range, the CH46 is not exactly a quiet piece of equipment."

"There are some specifics; would you please take some notes."

Now she's having me take notes like a secretary. "Just tell me, remember I'm trained to memorize such things."

"All right, hot shot, here it goes. Get a CH47 or at least a CH46 Chinook with these specs; a glass cockpit that is equipped with a multifunction integrated cockpit management system, automated flight controls; we need model D that has a 2068-gallon fuel capacity that doubles the range, it needs the ANVIS-7 night vision system and individual goggles from Elbit and must be Nimrod  standard night vision compatible. The communication suite must include jam resistant HF and UHF radio systems—get the Rockwell or Raytheon—and equipped with AN/APX-100 identification – friend or foe-IFF interrogator Allied signal. Auto fire control, Sidewinder guided rocket system and A Javelin anti tank rocket system with Predator-Kestrel, one AVIBRAS saturation 70mm. Rocket system, communication helmets, headsets, intercoms and field telephones. Three M134 machine guns, two in the crew door on the starboard side and one mounted on the port side. That's about it:  the rest is standard equipment on a combat chopper like the Chinook."

"Hmm."

"You got all that?" she smirked.

"Yes, yes… I've got it, but just to be double sure you make me a list." Ziki was impressed, she rattled that right out.  He didn't remember it all and she knew it .

"You have to make a plan that gets us out, how we're going to get out of there. To get out, we again have to go through Egypt or we have to get to the Gulf, the Red Sea .  What about that, what are we going to do then?"

"What is the rest of your plan? Do you have one?"

"That's your business, you have to design the rest.  All I planned is how to get in there and how to do this thing, in general, but that's why my father  told  me to call you in, Ziki; now all that's left to be seen is are you worth your stuff, or am I paying you $1,000,000 for nothing  and my daddy was wrong." Ziki was pleased that the rest of the details and planning were left to him; if he was going to screw up he wanted to do it by his own hand, not someone else's plan.

At times she looked professional and hard, but now she had the look of a little girl that needed to be rescued. She sat there looking at Ziki with this hopeful look. Ziki decided that her intentions had noble roots, and right there he decided that it was not about money, not for her and really not for him!

"Okay count me in, I'm in."

She got up, took a step forward around the table put both her hands over his, bent forward and pressed her lips against his cheek.

"Hey, hey all right, enough, where we're going and what we are about to try and do—kisses from girls like you won't do a damn thing to keep us alive and make the bad guys dead."

"Yep, you're right about that.  You can count on it, definitely no more kisses."

"So, Yaffa, what do you want to do about the money?"

"Well you do trust me, don't you?"

"No—Yaffa.  I have only known you for one day, and we've gotten a lot going for one day, don't you think?"

"On a mission like this you're going to have to have some trust in me—we have to trust each other."

"That may be true, but I haven't seen you act under fire yet.  I want to know that the money is placed somewhere.  I have to guarantee my men that I can pay them."

"I've already taken care of that. I'm prepared to deposit $500,000 in an account in your name under a secured number in a Swiss bank. Half of it now and the other half will be set to be automatically deposited two weeks from now.

"Half?"

"Isn't that how they usually do these things in the movies?" she said seriously enough. "The second half is always delivered after the mission is completed. I'll have my bank take care of the transfer to your account—one way or another. Whether I'm dead or not. The instructions are already in."

"Before you knew whether I was in or not?"

"Yep."

"I want it put in a bank that I've used in Liechtenstein."

"Consider it done, just give me the numbers."

"Fine."

"Even though you're putting up a million dollars, there is no question as to who gives orders here, is there?"

"No, you do, all right!"

Ziki was relieved—that would have been a deal breaker. "I would not be willing to go otherwise. We meet on the Muslim Sabbath at the South end on the outskirts of the camp at the exact coordinates I will give you before the end of this day…at Bir Kiseiba in the Sahara in Egypt at 2:00AM."

"Wait a minute, you said 'we will meet'; we're going to meet there?"

"Yeah, we will meet there; you have to make your own way out there."

"Right…Okay, I'll be there."

"That's where I want you."

"Helicopter's going to be there?"

"Count on it; I will place a requisition order for it as soon as we get going from here."

"That's real good. Make it a Chinook if you can."

"Ahh, don't forget to give me that list of things you want on that chopper."

"Hey, I thought you were 'trained to memorize things like that.'"

"That's right, I am," he mumbled, "but make the list."

"Ahmm, okay." She let him get by with it.

"I don't want anybody to know that you exist on this planet; I don't want any contact with you from here on out, is that clear?" She nodded her head.

"I don't want you to be seen with me from this moment on. I don't want you calling me, my phones could be tapped. I don't want you talking to me, I don't want to see you any longer. I want you to be ready and available in the place I'm telling you, at the coordinate on the map at Bir–Kiseiba in the Egyptian south desert. Make your way out there. We meet in person one more time today."

"Right, I understand. I'll be there."

## Chapter 46

### Judas and Zurinsky

**He needed special gear...** More guns and some of the gear on her list, Tow and Milan missiles and secured channels, radio and interception equipment: detection devices that hooked up to external global positioning systems to locate incoming private jets or helicopters. Gear that he could not justify for the Egyptian mission. He knew exactly where to go.

Those were first on his list. They'd need an unmarked, untraceable to Israel six-wheel- drive vehicle to use thereafter to trail the Sahara. Untraceable. Fast. Armored and loaded to the hilt.

One man could pull that off.

**The chop-shop smelled of new oil and old exhaust**. It was cool and vacant, echoing with the clang of the metal door behind Ziki. Most of the men had knocked off for the day. Zurinsky would be in his office, tallying up his scores, making love to his money-books with the black and red pens he kept special in a gold-plated pen dispenser behind the name plate that read "Manager." As if a shop of his sort needed someone to field complaints. The office was thick with cigarette smoke. There was a new smell. Zurinsky's old dog lay in a corner, wheezing heavily. Any other man might've put the mutt down long ago, but not Zurinsky. A thief with a heart of gold, he'd haul the cur's carcass out to sunny grass six, seven, eight times a day to let the old thing do his thing and enjoy some fresh air. Zurinsky wouldn't let his guys park their cars anywhere near the green strip that was the dog's last connection to an independent life.

"Lookin' good, Judas." Ziki crouched and rubbed the dog's ears. The animal lifted its head slowly and drew in the scent of Ziki and the lingering Mossad offices' smell on him. It gave a half-hearted growl and dropped its head to its paws once more.

"Now, you come. It hasn't been a good day for us," Zurinsky said. He stood and clasped Ziki's hand over the grand desk. The surface was a mass of books and papers, receipts and girlie magazines and empty paper cups stained with coffee and tobacco juice. "The police came near 10 AM; I'm closed for three days at least. I tell them I know Mossad, I work for Mossad, I'm a legitimate business man. Do they care?"

"If they'd have called me, I'd have told them to lock you up and throw away the key."

Zurinsky shrugged elaborately, "But then who would replace the muffler on that old thing you drive right now? I heard you three blocks away. If I'd have wanted to avoid you, I'd—"

"You'd still be trying to revive Judas and get him into your car."

"Sit. Sit. Tell me your troubles. What's her name this time?"

Ziki smiled. "Yaffa, believe it or not."

"Yaffa. You know what that means—beautiful."

"Yeah—beautiful. I know."

"She ugly? Most Yaffas I know are ugly as sin."

"Yeah, this one to," he lied.

"Always you with the luck; just put a bag over her head. And what can I do to meet this beauty?"

"You can get me equipment I need by tomorrow night."

Zurinsky's eyes narrowed. "Is there a party? You never invite me."

"You're glad I don't invite you. You'd get your ass shot off and then Judas would have to carry you to outside to pee."

# Chapter 47

### Chinook CH 46

"A Chinook CH46— with these specs: a glass cockpit that is equipped with a multifunction integrated cockpit management system—"

"Your handwriting sucks, Ziki. Is that a 'd' or a question mark?" Davidoff was not nearly as excited as Ziki showed him Yaffa's list of requests.

"—automated flight controls, model D with a 2068-gallon fuel capacity— that will double the chopper's capacity to range. . . and it needs the ANVIS-7 night vision system and individual goggles from Elbit—" Ziki had had her write her wish list before he'd taken his leave at the cafe. He made no promises, but he was certain he could get most of what she'd ask for. He could probably requisition anything he wanted and Zurinsky would get the rest. He might have to crack a joke or two, or pitch a fit about security, but what was a little drama to the guys behind desks? They'd seen most everything he could throw at them in the past—including an autographed pair of panties with red hearts all over them and several illegal imports: cigars, a rare orchid, a pair of prize-winning German Shepard pups, and a lump of stone from Red Square in Moscow.

"—Nimrod standard night vision compatible. The communication suite must include jam resistant HF and UHF radio systems. Get the Rockwell or Raytheon. And make sure it's equipped with AN/APX-100 identification–friend-or-foe-IFF interrogator Allied signal. We'll want that."

Davidoff took one look at the list and pursed his lips as if to whistle. "GPS fire control. Sidewinder guided rocket system and an A-Javelin anti-tank rocket system with Predator-Kestrel? Pretty demanding. I can see why you're into this girl—she knows the difference between a 46 and a 47."

"I'm not into this girl," Ziki replied.

"No?" Davidoff raised an eyebrow and smeared his thumb across Ziki's cheek. "This lipstick on your cheek certainly isn't my shade."

"Get off me—" Ziki shrugged away from him. "You don't want the money, you don't have to come."

"I didn't say I wasn't coming—settle down, I can't let you have all the fun. Just so I say it once—It is not about the money, and you know it. This list is just so. . . . Does she think AVIBRAS saturation 70mm rocket systems, communication helmets and field telephones grow on trees? And listen to this: she wants three M134 machine guns, two to be placed in the crew door on the starboard side and one mounted on the port side. None of this is standard equipment on these choppers. Not the Chinook."

"Yeah. It's long," Ziki said.

"—It's precise," Davidoff corrected. "She knows what she wants right down the number of crescent wrenches in the mobile mechanics' pack she wants us to bring along. I don't know who is going to attach the water filled sand filters she's requested—I suppose she wants us to requisition an inflatable and remote-control chopper tech, too?"

Ziki coughed in disgust at Davidoff's lame joke. "She knows what she wants. That's good for us—fewer surprises down the road."

"I'll say." Davidoff flopped down on his bed scanning the list closely. The back of the paper was covered with ink squiggles—her handwriting scrawled on the back to resemble a laundry list, a doodle pad, a note from a bar. If Ziki lost the list—he'd never remember its contents a minute after she'd handed it over. Prep for a mission—not this illegal adventure across three borders to wipe out a nest of vipers.

"MREs?" Davidoff asked. "You said this was a pit stop on the way home—what are we going to need MREs for?"

"That's how we're going to kill the terrorists—" Ziki said blandly: "Canadian corned beef."

Davidoff frowned and for a long moment Ziki was certain Davidoff thought that the actual plan involved some sort of poisoning attempt.

But then a light dawned in Davidoff's eyes as he realized Ziki was joking.

Davidoff made an exaggerated "yuck" face. "You are aware that Canadian corned beef is on the UN's list of banned interrogation methods?"

"No shit?" Ziki leaned against the lockers. He lit another cigarette and blew out smoke, letting himself relax.

In the quiet recesses of his mind he was having second, third, and twentieth thoughts about the whole thing. Yaffa had seemed so certain—of herself and the mission. He too, had seemed certain . . . when he was with her.

"Give it up, Ziki," Davidoff urged. "MREs? How long will we be 'lost?'"

Ziki shook his head. "I don't know the air time yet between our bio-chem lab and the touch point in the Sudan. Yaffa will tell us when she's got the flight pattern figured out."

"She's got us requesting an awful lot of extra fuel."

Ziki shrugged.

"And this is a hell of a lot of extra to request. You know the supply guys are going to think we're up to something."

"Let them think what they want—no one will know what we're up to and I am getting the stuff on the lower list from Zurinsky. Malkielly has us going off on one of his wild goose chases as usual—we zip our lips and remind them it's classified—need-to-know only."

"What are we gonna tell Avi?"

"Nothing—absolutely nothing. He'll be on another chopper and he won't have a sense that he needs to look back—right?"

Davidoff considered this and loosed a long breath. "So we're talking overnight? Two days—two days? That's a long time to be in enemy air space without—"

"You want to play kids' games—fine."

"Dammit, Ziki—don't bite my head off—I'm just saying—"

"Those hombres at Salema are not going to be just sitting there—"

Ziki knew that Davidoff was right. He was wound too tight. He drew smoke from his cigarette and then sat beside Davidoff on his bunk. "I'm not sure yet how we're going to get out of there," he admitted quietly.

Davidoff nodded. "We have to go through Egypt again. . . Just a day after we've swiped twenty-three of their prize horror scientists and blitzed their little shop of horrors? We'll certainly be popular with the locals."

"If we head out for the Red Sea or the Gulf—"

"The whole north of Africa is going to be on alert."

"That's it," Ziki confirmed. "I can't believe that we won't be followed."

"And we'll be making a hell of a lot of noise—the CH46 is not exactly a quiet piece of equipment," Davidoff agreed.

Ziki felt his buddy also turn glum. "They're going to come and if they do? MiGs armed with more firepower than an American battleship, more fire power than we could handle."

"Think of the money."

"And her short skirts," Davidoff said.

"Ahh, yes. . . " Ziki responded with more appreciation than his rational side wished. "Those, too."

Despite his better inclinations, he called Yaffa and set up a meeting for midnight at a bar near the café where they'd first met. She met him on the beach where he stood in the shadows smoking and drinking an Ouzo, waiting for her. The waves rolled up the beach and rolled the sand and pebbles into a clatter as they withdrew. The tide was low, but the surges of water were still loud enough to cover their conversation—he'd known she was concerned. She had changed into a tank top and loose linen pants. A different look, gorgeous.

"I thought you asked not to call ." She had kept her distance from him and stood stiffly—now as icy as before she had been languid.

Her manner irked him. "I do want anyone watching to think we're lovers—" he said. "Though anyone listening on the line would have thought you're a cold fish."

Her eyes sparked with anger and a tinge of resentment. She folded her arms. "Don't blow this, Ziki Barak—we're too close to pulling it all together."

"What about the requisitions?"

"They are in the works and shouldn't be a problem."

She turned toward the waves and nodded. "Good. Tell your men that I already deposited $500,000 into the secured account as I've told you I would. Half of it now and the other half to be automatically deposited two weeks from now. Does that arrangement suit you?"

"It doesn't."

She turned to face him, her brows drawing downward. "You—"

"—I wanted it put in a bank that I've used in Liechtenstein, I told you that; they're not doing it for the money, but I want to be able to pay the men, here are the numbers."

"Oh." Her shoulders dropped an inch or two. "That's no problem. Consider it done." He couldn't stop his eyes from scoring the outline of her figure— she was vaguely outlined by the light from the bar in the distance. The music blared and the sound of laughter and shouting was carried on the salty air. No, he said to himself, don't even look at her, his heart not allowing him to replace Gavriella.

She folded her arms once more. Defensively, he thought.

"Is there anything else?" she asked him, meeting his gaze with her own.

He let a half smile curl his mouth. "Yes. As a matter of fact." He lit a cigarette, slowly, drawing out the pause between statements. She didn't like it, he knew. The balance of power between them was shifting. The dark was working for him.

She tilted her head as if to say, Well?

He blew smoke toward the ocean. "Once more even though you're putting up a million dollars, I want there to be no question as to who gives orders here."

And suddenly she had found her sea legs once more. "Is that the deal breaker? You won't take orders from a woman?"

A laugh burst from him. "You think this is about your being a woman?"

She spread her hands open. "It is, isn't it? If I were a higher ranked man, would we have needed our meeting tonight? Would I have needed to let you hear all about Finkle? You might be surprised to hear this, Ziki—but I was and am disgusted with that."

"If you were higher ranked, man or woman and Mossad," Ziki returned, a sudden fire in his temples, "I would never have had to call you this evening to deal with the logistics of a mission that's putting my butt in a sling. I'd have it all worked out already—flight plans, a mole at this meeting we're crashing, the requisition order would have been logged two weeks ago, and I certainly wouldn't have had to plant a few kisses, show my breasts and wiggle my ass in a tight skirt to entice someone to follow me. I'd be five steps ahead already and certain not to put my men's lives in jeopardy."

"And you think I'm cold," she scoffed. "The flight plan for our side mission will be waiting on your desk tomorrow morning—until then, good night." She turned away.

He was two steps behind her, angry and confused and wondering why in the hell the storm between them had blown such full force. He caught her arm and tugged her back, turning her to face him. The light caught her face then and he saw how tired she was, how ragged. He suddenly felt like a jackass.

The moment she knew he'd seen this—the true depth of pain and fear that she'd hidden under masks of coquetry and manipulation, feeding the flames of her hatred for the men who'd taken away so much of her world, and planning her final revenge—her face collapsed and her lips turned downward. He felt her knees buckle and caught her by the elbows, drawing her to his chest to keep her from falling to the sand. She convulsed silently, her face in his chest, hands clenching at the lapels of his jacket.

"You can't know," she choked out between the clenches of her throat. "My father was everything to me." She sniffled. "He was not like other men. He was the best of men." Ziki held her close.

"And David," she said. "He was my best friend and I loved him. I loved him, and now I've slept with that worm who could give me a toehold in the Mossad files to avenge his death, and I can't remember—I can't remember what David's voice sounded like. . . I can't remember what he smelled like." She breathed raggedly.

Ziki made the comforting hiss that had stood the soothing test of time. "Shhhh," he murmured. "It's all right." His hand raised to slowly smooth her hair from her face and over her shoulders. He stroked her back.

"It's not all right," she replied. "I'm only holding on with everything I have—but it's not enough. I sold my farm to pay Finkle, but money wasn't enough. And so I let him take me to bed and I let him do to me things that you never want to hear about. And I'm giving you all the money I have left—and it's okay. Because I don't plan to come back. You and your men will be safe, if I have to stand between every murdering bastard in the Sudan to keep them so."

"No," he said. "We won't leave you behind. And we're all in this together."

"I know I should pay you more—and if had more money, I'd give it all to you. I'd give you everything, if you'd just help me get those bastards."

"I'm going to help," he said softly. "I'm here now and I'll be there in Egypt."

She coughed softly and buried her teary face into his shirt. He felt the wetness soak his shirt. He felt her breath hot and unsteady as it warmed the skin beneath his shirt.

"Thank you," she said. "I don't know who else I could have gone to."

Ziki held her close, his cheek pressed to the top of her head, silken hair that smelled of honey. "You came to the right person. I'll have everything ready."

And he shushed her again and rocked her gently as she broke into another convulsive set of sobs. "Thank you," she said softly. "Thank you."

"It's okay. Everything is going to be okay."

## Chapter 48

**Egypt \*\***

**The night air at the bio-chem plant was heavy with the stink of something like fertilizer**—a strong chemical prick in the nose that became a cloying acid in the back of the throat before it brought on the dull pangs of nausea. The men had been choking on their own bile since they'd touched down.

"Damn stink," he heard Davidoff on the com-link.

"Radio silence," Ziki reminded him and there was the sudden crackle of dead air, then the rush of noise that was his men ushering lines of blindfolded and bound "cargo" from their labs and dormitories.

"How did the gas work?" he asked Avi as he walked into the entrance of the central building of the research facility.

"They were sleeping like children," Avi replied, leading Ziki down the partially illuminated hallway.   Signs of a recent, one-sided fight were visible everywhere in the main corridors.

"Bad boys, it looks like; they didn't cooperate, hmm?" Ziki said in response to the number of dead bodies being dragged out of the main hallway.

"Well, some didn't know when to put away their toys.  We've got a good number of guards alive, though.  Holding them down in the basement of the barracks.  Building three." Avi bent down for a moment to pick up a blood-stained Kalashnikov and remove the magazine, which he placed in a pocket before throwing the rifle down a side hallway.

"Keep them there. Unless there's any reason they'll be in—"

"Not so fast," Avi interrupted. As they had been walking, Ziki had assumed the lead and  gotten a few steps ahead of Avi but evidently missed the door to the staircase, which Avi now held open. "Down here"

Ziki smiled and followed.  "As I was saying, keep them where they are unless they're in the way of the specialists."

Avi shook his head. "Where are they anyway?"

"The specialists?"

"Yeah, shouldn't they be with you?"

"A couple are still outside with their Geiger counters seeing how radioactive the whole damn place is. The others are helping interrogate some of the scientists to make sure there aren't any goodies buried in the backyard."

Avi opened the door to the third story below ground and led them into another hallway, this one fully lit. "I hope they don't take too long," he said.

"Me too. This place seems bigger in person. Hopefully they were dumb enough to keep all the chemicals in the same place. If not, we may have to take a risk and destroy the place before we have a chance to—"

They both heard a metal door slam open followed by loud, quick footsteps echoing down the long hallway. They instinctively crouched and looked down both directions of the hallway but saw no one. Ziki whispered, "Which floor are we on? How many of us are down here?"

"Four," said Avi, meaning from the bottom. "Just three, holding the facility Commander for you to view." The footsteps, halting at times, continued.

Ziki switched on his mike and softly said, "This is Desert Eagle One. Whoever's running on floor four, stop in place...now." The footsteps continued.

In his ear, Ziki heard, "This is Sgt. Regev on floor four. Would you like me to send some men out to investigate the noise?"

"Negative. We'll handle it." The footsteps were now coming from behind Ziki and Avi, heading towards the staircase. Avi leaned against the wall as he raised his Galil. Ziki walked slowly forward, keeping himself close to the opposite wall so as not to block Avi's vision. In Arabic he shouted, "Whoever you are, stop, put your weapon down, and lay down." The footsteps halted for a moment, as if trying to figure out the source of the shouting, but then continued. The footsteps were almost upon them. Ziki waited. A moment later, a shirtless, shoeless man raced around the corner and into a 9mm bullet.

Avi lowered his gun and relaxed, slinging it back over his shoulder. But suddenly Ziki came running at him, gas mask on and signaling for him to do the same. Avi quickly put his mask on and barked into his mike, "Gas on floor four. All floors below six are to be sealed-now."

Ziki slowed to a walk as he approached Avi. "Shit," he said through the mask's filter.

"What happened?"

Ziki shook his head in disbelief. "He had three vials in his hand. One broke when he fell. Some kind of white powder."

Avi felt Ziki's wrist to take his pulse. "Are you breathing normally?"

"As much as I can with this mask on."

"How does your head feel? Dry throat? Runny nose?"

"Fine."

Avi, let go of his wrist. "Normal. If it's plague, it could take a while. But what do we do now?"

Ziki looked over at the Egyptian, but with a hole through the top of his chest he was clearly dead. " Get a specialist down here."

Avi blew his nose into his handkerchief. Maybe he caught a cold from someone on the flight—or?

**The operation had gone smoothly**.

102 Golanis, chemical and bio weapons experts, and demolition specialists had boarded three large Chinook helicopters flown from a base just north of Eilat, down the Gulf of Aqaba and across the Red Sea.

On board were the usual Commandkas—six-wheel-drive vehicles, each holding up to eleven men and their equipment. Perched on tripods each armed with an 8,000-round-per-minute, vicious, fire spitting, six- barrel machine gun and modified French-Milan missile launchers, to the rear a fifty-caliber machine gun. They and the three choppers' full armaments, including armed side ports and air-to-ground missile systems, would be adequate by Ziki's calculations to handle the defenses of the facility and the small airport nearby. The helicopters would commandeer the depot and refuel for the long trip home.

What had concerned Ziki most was the danger of exposing his men to the germs, Bubonic Plague, said the report, of a mutated strain that has no antidote. Or worse, that it could spread uncontrolled. They had trained to take precautions, but no one really had known what half-finished, uncontained state some of these agents and microbes might be in when they had kicked in the door. They carried has-mat gear and masks, but so did most of Israel's civilian population. These scientists were surely looking for a way around that obstacle.

Most of the men around him hadn't seemed too preoccupied with this factor, though, partly due to confidence in themselves and partly the mutually supporting bravado that develops in these elite units. The men, when they had spoken, had been more likely to complain about the bumpy ride of the ground-skimming helicopters, the uncomfortable night-vision goggles, or even a suspected unfaithful girl back home before they would express fear about the mission.

"Ziki," Davidoff had half-yelled over the din of the helicopter motor.

"What?"

"I had a profound realization," Davidoff had grinned.

"A what?"

Davidoff continued, "Why did we go to all the trouble of putting officers and enlisted men in unmarked uniforms if the officers all make themselves pretty clearly known with these damn things on our heads?"

"Ah," Ziki had chuckled. "Don't you see that's been accounted for? If we get captured, the Egyptians would never believe someone with as dumb a face as yours could make it past corporal, so the rest of us are in the clear."

The few men who had been able to hear the exchange had laughed heartily. Davidoff's complaints had referred to the small light cameras on the officers' helmets that relayed images back to the mobile HQ, allowing them to see real-time images of the battlefield. For a mission so tightly scripted as this one, with little room for tactical adjustments, the cameras wouldn't be much use. Hopefully neither would the full surgery bay in Helicopter 2.

They had landed a little more than five kilometers away from the facility and assembled quietly into platoons. The Commandkas would carry most of them relatively quickly to the outskirts of the facility, while the various chemical experts would be brought in via the noisy helicopters once the outside of the compound was secured.

The ground had been expansive and offered little cover, making the speed and surprise of their attack essential. Seeing everyone organized and all the equipment operational, Ziki had given the order to the platoon commanders to advance. 1:45am. Communications lines had been disabled by the first wave, done silently and efficiently by the specialist squad. The wireless waves had been jammed for the entire compound. This was of critical importance: with a call in or radio to Cairo the Russian MiGs could show up. The jamming and wire cutting had gone well.

The firefight had been brief and successful. The informant's information and satellite details to the exact location of the guard towers and barracks had been correct. The facility had been swept of enemy presence in a matter of minutes. Ziki's stomach had lurched upwards as Helicopter 1 had made a quick dip for its second landing. The guards at the facility had put up almost no fight; they had been in shock at the rapid ferocity of the enemy from the sky. It almost seemed a pity to have killed so many of them. He'd much rather have killed the scientists and captured the confused and terrified guards.

**The chemical weapons specialist leaned over the vials for a minute.** From their viewpoint a few yards down the hall, Avi stopped coughing. Ziki could see the expert reach into his case every now and then. Ziki looked at his watch; he worried about the time. The specialists were still on schedule destroying some stocks in the upper floors, but if this vial turned out to be a major issue, they would be thrown off schedule... The specialist suddenly rose. He turned around towards Ziki and Avi with one of the unbroken, but now unsealed, vials in his hand. He took off his mask to reveal a large smile underneath.

"This is real dangerous stuff—pure heroin," he said with a laugh.

Avi ripped his mask off with more than little annoyance and uttered into his microphone, "False alarm on floor 4. Cancel the seal."

Ziki uttered to himself but loud enough to be heard, "That idiot got himself killed for a few grams of heroine?"

The specialist shrugged. "It's good news that this garbage is not some ugly stuff, right Commander?"

"Yeah, that's real good, but keep checking for any bad stuff."

"Yes, Sir." Avi motioned forward to Ziki to continue to the Commander's office. Within less ten minutes the specialists had scoured the facility from top to bottom , safely destroying all the weapons except for a few that were either too intriguing to destroy without further examination or too dangerous to destroy easily. These were placed in sealed canisters. Also destroyed were all computer data, schematics, equipment. The scientists had long been hand-cuffed, drugged and piled in one of the helicopters in a manner far too comfortable for what they deserved.

"Commander," the demolitions chief said, "the charges are ready."

Ziki turned to his junior officer, "Report as to status, any losses: is everyone accounted for, Avraham?"

The young man nodded, " None fallen, commander, two flesh wounds and one shoulder shot, none life threatening; 102 men and 23 pieces of cargo."

"That's good"

Ziki turned back to the demolitions man, "Set the timer for 15." They would be set for a 15-minute delay after take off and were strategically placed to collapse the center building, floor by floor, into the lowest basement level, where all the toxins were stored.

"All right, number 1 and number 2 helicopters, head out. We'll get the rest of the equipment on number 3 and meet you guys for drinks on Dizengoff in a few hours."

"Understood, sir," the lead pilot responded. The rotors picked up speed quickly. Most of the men filed on board and strapped themselves in.

Avi lingered. "Why are you staying with the baggage?"

"A captain goes down with the ship, and a mission Commander makes sure everything goes smoothly, even the details," Ziki responded tersely.

Avi still looked puzzled. "What's really going on, Ziki?"

"It's on a need-to-know basis. Better get on your helicopter, Avi." Ziki folded his arms.

Reluctantly, Avi followed the order. He paused a moment, looking Ziki in the eye, then turned and jogged towards the number two helicopter.

A lone company completely annihilates Egypt's chemical and biological warfare weapons program in a single night, without a single fatality on the Israeli side. It usually took him a while to unwind and let go of the combat adrenalin that a mission brought out. But this time, there was no time to unwind; this meticulously planned mission now had to be followed by a borderline insane dash into the Sudan desert, the Sahara, it lingered just to the south.

He reached for a cigarette.

Davidoff crept out of the darkness from behind a crate.

The gun fire was over. They'd taken the guards by surprise, entering the compound stealthily, the helicopters had landed a good distance away.

Ziki crouched in the shadows. As the last men passed him, he followed, turning back to cover them as the others crowded the scientists into place.

"Avraham!" Ziki shouted. "Is your cargo accounted for?"

"Yes, sir—all 23 of them."

He was rehearsing his cover story as he sighted the dark mass of the Chinooks; they were still loading and had not yet left the ground. There seemed to be some confusion: it was dark, the three helicopters were still in place, most of the men were boarding with the scientists on number one, some of the men were boarding the other helicopter. Ziki waved and lowered his mouthpiece. "Lieutenant, get one and two copters moving."

"Yes, Sir."

"On my order."

"Yes, sir—at your order."

"I've got number three, I'll be a few minutes behind you. Do not wait for it, stop for nothing, deliver the 'cargo' at home. Do you understand me lieutenant?"

"Yes, Sir."

He checked his watch—Yaffa should be in place now, if all had gone as planned. He waved the pilots the go ahead, as he dodged into the shadows and skirted the cinder-block wall of the compound toward the third helicopter.

"Go, go now!" he shouted into his COM link as he ran full-tilt to the landing site of the third.

Without a hitch—the first two lifted off and took flight toward the Mediterranean. Avi next to the pilot of the second and Moshe the first—they'd be safely across the border into the great Sinai Desert in minutes with their valuable goods. Within minutes the two hulking transports were elegantly silhouetted against the dim moonlight just below the horizon. Ziki watched them head off with more than a little pride. Success.

And now for mission number "Not on Any Page." Davidoff and Eli and Manny and Gideon each with his own task to help Yaffa prepare for lift off.

Ziki tucked himself into a shadow and fitted his night vision goggles into place—the compound behind him was only just recuperating from the attack. He heard a shout and the crash of metal drums on the ground, a jeep squealing on pavement, and more shouts. But no shots. And no interest in their direction at all.

Yaffa had been right. She'd shown him on the satellite maps where they could land the Chinook in the distance. The others had lifted off and led their eyes in the opposite direction—no one had even noticed they were still there.

Good.

Ziki turned his attention to the chopper. He could see Yafa in the distance. How he knew it was her, he wasn't sure—the way she moved, perhaps; her silhouette was obscured by the flight suit she wore—her hair and face were covered by a black stocking cap, the sort worn by bank robbers, he mused.

Let's hope that we aren't thought of as those. . .

He checked his watch—right on time. It was 4:00 AM—she was punctual. Time to switch to a channel secure even from Mossad for inter-group communication. He flipped on the voice activated walkie-talkies and attached the small microphone to his collar.

There was the sound of heavy air and then Yaffa's voice, soft and clear. Just one word, "Go."

That meant the pilot had been taken care of—. A few drops of chloroform on a cloth, a syringe of sleepy-time, and the guy melted into a cargo container that had been loaded swiftly onto the helicopter with the scientists. He wouldn't wake until they were landed safely in Tel Aviv and he'd been off-loaded with the other 'goods' that hadn't been used. And then what would he be able to tell anyone? He wouldn't have been seen, the pilot would never know who'd gassed him. Could be the Egyptians—who would know? The amnesia drug that was shot into his arm would make sure to do that. But Davidoff recruited the pilot, was now a part of the team. Better still.

Davidoff's voice came softly over his COM link. "It's a go," he whispered, meaning everything was going along as planned.

The other men checked in as well.

"Go," Eli said, indicating that he'd refilled the gas tanks and had the extra fuel ready for the trip.

Gideon said, "Go," to indicate that the Comandka, six-wheel-drive vehicle in the back of the Chinook was also loaded and ready. Guns were in place. Charges were loaded and their packs were lashed in the cargo bay.

And finally, a clank of metal and a static, Manny came on his mike, spitting loudly. Ziki ratcheted his volume to "Off" as his ears rang with the clamor.

"Sorry 'bout that," Manny apologized, "Go." And Ziki knew the sand filters had been installed over the air intake units on the Chinook for the deep Sahara sands.

"All go," echoed Yaffa. The rotors of the Chinook began to wind and slowly spin.

"All set for that court marshal you ordered, Commander."

"Air silence—that's an order," Ziki snapped. He climbed out from the shadows, scanning the compound behind him. The whine of the helicopter was sure to attract some attention, though the whole camp seemed to be in a daze of leaderless confusion—as if they couldn't wrap their heads around what had happened just moments before. Some shouts and the sound of wild machine gun fire. Someone calling in Arabic for others.

Yaffa had the chopper warmed and ready; her face was lighted with purpose as he dashed from his place of lookout to the chopper's side door.

"All go," he repeated, as he rolled into the opening. He came up on his knees as the huge American-made whirly-bird lifted with a shudder into the air. Yaffa lifted it high into the air and dove away from the compound as if she had been born with a joystick in her hand. Ziki climbed into the co-pilot's seat and pulled off his night goggles and helmet. She smiled over at him and gave him the thumbs up. He repeated the gesture, with a nod of confidence that Davidoff's joke had actually deflated.

What had he been thinking? A court marshal and a small damp jail cell that would be his home for a very, very long time. And Malkielly would throw away the key. He was committing more crimes in this one night than he had ever committed in his entire life; he just might have to take Yaffa's $1,000,000 and hope they never found him. But that was ludicrous—an impossibility. Because if they wanted to find him, there was no place to hide. They would find him and they would make him—make them all—pay for the actions in which they were about to engage. His only consolation—if they put Yaffa in a cell next to him—many of his friends might come to visit him just to see what sort of woman would make a sane man lose every shred of sanity… Ohh, Ziki, what have you done? On the beach in Tel Aviv she'd seemed so vulnerable...

"Don't touch anything," she said, turning on the modules for the autopilot system. She made certain the gate was shut in back and asked one of the men to visually check that the ramp was secure, and that the Commandka was locked in place.

"Do you want the side doors shut, Ziki?"

"Leave them open, the night air smells good." She ran the engines, first bow then stern. As they ascended, Ziki noticed on the field adjoining a small two propeller plane, glowing bright on the infra red screen from the heat of its engines. He hadn't noticed it before—somehow the emptiness of the desert had obscured from his vision what was now so obvious. As the helicopter climbed and kept climbing, he returned his attention to the chopper's, instruments. Yaffa was flying high and north, the opposite direction they needed to take.

"Yaffa, what are you doing?"

"I want them to know where we're going, meaning, it will register that way on their Radar . I want the Egyptians to have a track on their Russian radar— which they can't really read but eventually will—in the direction we're now going, north—leave a false trail." She had not said it pertly, to snub his outburst, but as someone who knew and expected but did not resent having to explain her decisions. She seemed meditative.

Abruptly, the helicopter dove down and encircled the base until cruising low, little more than five meters, over the open desert, rising only a meter or so as a small slope in the sand passed beneath them. Ziki flexed his buttocks in his seat and grabbed the safety belts she betrayed a smile.

The helicopter was loud he had to shout. He fell into silence, the hum from the engines and the sun now rising settling him as he looked across the vastness of the Sahara. He spotted the characteristic black tents and wandering sheep of the Bedouin and saw them waving; he waved back. Through the open machine gun ports he could feel the desert heating up fast, the hair on his face and arms raising to make felt the fine grains of sand imbedded in his skin.

He walked to the back of the chopper looking for a spot to stretch out. Davidoff and the rest of the men were already asleep on their packs, their faces relaxed, not imagining, as Ziki did, the dangers of the mission or the trouble that could be awaiting at their return. So long as he assumed he had a response he could stop thinking about it for now.

"Can I go upfront, sit with her now?" Davidoff asked. He must have woken him walking into the cargo bay.

"Stay away from her." Davidoff scoffed at his command. Out of habit he checked the equipment, though it had been checked before, and went back up to the cockpit.

"From here on you take orders, you understand?"

"Yes I understand," Yaffa said, without opposition.

"I don't want you to fly over the compound to see it when we arrive, or scout it out. Pull up and land one kilometer out. There's a gully at two o'clock. Once on the ground we're going to camouflage immediately."

"Yes, understood. But look at these—satellite photos of the terrain and the airstrip, and the buildings in the compound."   The satellite photos were precise he could have read the license plate on a cart, had there been one.

"You only slept with him once?"

Yaffa turned her head as if to say, go to hell. He knew who she slept with—Finkle, security clearance had its own attraction and he had managed to sleep with Yaffa and bartered away this mission for the sex Ziki could only imagine... Should have left him in Syria—maybe I should have just killed him.

They were not far in to the Sudan from the Egyptian border line, the helicopter did not fly in a straight line, instead it circled slowly around the regions of radar Yaffa knew from the charts she'd gotten, occasionally zigzagging, using satellite guided avoid patterns and an onboard jamming device to out-maneuver the Soviet Soliuz radar.

On a typical mission backup would track them via satellites, offering the chance that if things went wrong someone might come in to help.

Yaffa lowered the helicopter into the gully, the dust cloud rising from the ground likely visible for miles, but it could have been a wind storm. Behind him, the men were checking their weapons, Tony Mizrachi and Moshe Regev releasing the magazines from their Galil's, ensuring they were full, and snapping them back into place.

Deplaning, Ziki ordered the men to place camouflage netting over the helicopter. The netting was heavy, and it took some ten minutes to position it over the chopper and fasten it to the ground. From the air the Chinook would be hard to see, but with infrared they could be spotted until the engines cooled.

As soon as dusk came they ate from cans of Canadian beef. Ziki walked towards Yaffa and stood by her, hoping she'd start a conversation.

"So, you're going to kill all these men and then go relax on some beach with a Martini in peace?"

"Are you out of your mind?" He hadn't slept for two days, and she was yet to make such a suggestion.

"Why, did I hit a nerve?"

"You play every card you can to drag me out to the middle of what could be hell on earth, including claiming a debt that I may owe your father, and now you are questioning my morality when this is all your doing?" She stared at him but he couldn't determine what she meant by it.

"This was your show. If the heat is getting to you and is singeing your panties, now is a good time to call it off. Let's pack up and go right back."

"It's not me; I told you I'm going to kill them. The difference is I am going to kill them because they murdered my father and my husband-to-be. You are doing it for a million American dollars."

"When you talked me in to this thing you said that they murdered women and children, right?"

"Right."

"You said that they murdered your father, my friend, without provocation, right?"

"Right."

"And you said that they blew up buses with people on their way to work and a kindergarten with children in Natanya, right?" She didn't answer.

He raised his voice. "Is that right?"

"That's right."

"And all of that is true, and they'll do it all again, correct?"

"Yes."

"Take the night vision goggles and sweep the ridge. Every two minutes switch to infrared to detect any body heat. Set it on the size of a human, not some small animal, alright?"

"Alright." She looked as if to tell him his instructions were obvious, but didn't.

The compound was located near the oasis, and in the cool night they walked through brush that reminded Ziki of the elephant grass in Africa. Climbing out of a gully, the south wind erasing their footprints in the sand as they walked, guns loaded slung over their shoulders.

Out of the gully he stumbled over a plaque with the inscription Ejaba Hudada, Elselma Oasis. From the plaque he shifted his eyes to a view of the sandstone wall around the abandoned British compound and airstrip and its dilapidated buildings beaten raw by the desert sands. The wall looking like old Jerusalem sandstone, and the one large building in the middle of the compound like an old desert fortress with an impressive entrance through huge wrought iron gates. In the heart of the desert, the British would have slept well.

Yaffa leaned against him. He could smell her, a nice smell, like hair shampoo. Finally, waiting, Quaiess, in Arabic, okay, came over the radio. Ziki, Yaffa and Davidof started toward the front gate, their feet making small noises as they stepped on dry grasses.

At the gate, Ziki clenched his fist, signaling the men to wait while he moved in alone. He swept his eyes wide, looking for fresh footprints or tire marks, seeing David crouched at the other side of the compound wall, across the courtyard. Walking into one of the farthest atriums, he found a room that had once been a kitchen stocked with food and water containers, several trays of baklava pita and fruit, a portable cooking stove and propane tanks, as though someone had been sent to prepare a catering party in the middle of the Sahara-weird.

They walked again towards the entrance. A Russian-made jeep stood around the corner of a wall in the courtyard, a 44-gallon drum in back. Ziki and Davidoff went to further scout the compound before the rest of the men took their positions. Davidoff started for the main entrance, Ziki the kitchen—he anticipated that, after the long trip, food would entice whomever had arrived early. He crept toward the atrium and peered through the door, not realizing that it opened both ways. The door swung back and caught his head against the molding, a rifle butt hitting him in the chin as he fell, his head shaking. A huge Sudanese with turban headdress stood over him, bellowing, who are you. Who are you? With a fist like a watermelon he bent down and hit Ziki, not waiting for an answer, only stopping to unsling his Kalashnikov. His rifle at the ready he picked him up by the collar. Ziki reached for his knife and, as the man prepared another hit from the butt of his gun, shoved it between his exposed ribs. The man groaned once, not resonant but shallow. Blood from his nose soaked his shirt, blood on his hand. It had only taken a moment.

Davidoff arrived and dragged him into the desert, out of sight. The rest of the building was now secure, he and Ziki returned to the ridge where the others waited. Ziki ordered one of his men into the kitchen to act as cook wearing the Sudanese's clothes and another to guard the compound's entrance. It was almost time. Ziki wiped the blood from his nose.

Two luxurious helicopters appeared suddenly from the sky. Ziki just waited and watched on the ridge. Within minutes two small jets also landed on the airstrip, Ziki watched as 12 men deplaned, leaving one guard behind at each. These men had probably just finished their morning coffee, were maybe awaiting breakfast at the compound. A few wore western style suits they walked from the hip. Ziki watched as each entered. He'd told Moshe in the kitchen to speak as little Arabic as possible, so they'd not notice his Israeli accent.

Moshe was to wait until all were in and seated around the square table. Tony had punctiliously delivered some food; Moshe conspicuously glanced at the kerosene lamp and lit a match to light it. Reaching into the hurricane glass, he intentionally burnt his thumb, apologizing in Arabic, and tipping the lamp over. Letting it catch before setting it aright, he ran to the kitchen for the blanket they'd left there, pretending to attempt covering the fire that was now spreading in the meeting room, but only making more smoke. Like napkin sopped water it spread across the ceiling, becoming so choking that all begun to leave, coughing, and covering their mouths. Obscured by smoke and confusion, Moshe ran up to the roof. They waited until all had run out, then, the shooting begun.

Like a broken egg the terrorists spread. Ziki could see their faces. He could tell they had seen this before. The ones that were dead lie face in the dirt. A few ran towards the helicopters, shooting wildly at Ziki's men on the roof. Others ran towards the jeep, Yaffa, arrived in the helicopter, strafed first the airplanes on the strip and then the courtyard, the jeep ignited into a ball of fire. The Russian helicopter came airborne; it fired a missile at the roof but missed, and now aimed at Yaffa's Chinook. Yaffa fired two Sidewinder missiles, and their helicopter exploded, its blades spiraling. The second helicopter opened fire from its side port, puncturing the sides of the Chinook but without causing major damage. Putting her chopper on autopilot she and Avi fired out of the two open side ports.

Ziki wanted a couple be left alive so that they could be interrogated—Yaffa wanted none alive. He wanted to know of any ongoing operations, any future plans. Moshe had heard a few words when they first entered, but nothing significant. The second helicopter down, Yaffa landed the Chinook right outside the gate, running to the interior of the compound. Leaning over one of the dying men, she dug a knife into his chest, ignoring Ziki's screaming.

"What are you doing?"

"I didn't come here to kiss them..." He yelled at her again, he told her to stop. She responded, her calm even calmer when compared with his anger. "I didn't hear you over the machine gun fire. What? She yelled back." Ziki shoved her, she fell over. "Do you feel better now that you know we're all assassins?"

"Yes, she said. All these bastards are dead. We can leave now."

They landed the helicopter two kilometers away, installing a delayed charge detonation. They headed east in the comandka, toward the Persian Gulf and Salala near Rus Abu Shagada.

Ziki scouted the old Yemeni port. An old Greek cargo ship docked and loading, was about to be headed up the Gulf towards the Red Sea and the Gulf of Aqaba. They spoke to the Captain, told him they were married, stranded, wishing to go to Jordan, and he told them he was headed toward Akaba, a stone's throw from the Israeli port of Eilat, and that he'd charge $300 American. Yaffa handed him $2,000, to include her 'friends'.

They picked up the rest of the men and dumped all but their concealed Uzis into the sea. All climbed aboard the ship. They ate and slept, one man positioned on deck, one behind the Greek captain, explaining the Uzi beneath his jacket. Ziki fell asleep, as did Yaffa, awaiting home.

**At the Sheridan hotel, near his Tel Aviv apartment, Ziki sipped a few vodka's.** He had climbed in his Alfa Romeo and drove home slowly. He was tired, alone, having told Davidoff and Yaffa that he'd seen enough of both of them, that he didn't want their company for a while, they sat separately on the bus back to Tel Aviv.

In the morning he heard loud knocks on his door—the Shin Bet, wasted no time. With his face still unshaved he dressed quickly and walked to the door. Two men he did not know stood, requesting politely but officiously that he follow them.

Ziki had once said that Malkielli had a pact with both the devil and God. Standing in his office, Ziki didn't salute. Malkielly was sitting across from him in his deep leather chair, looking old, but beyond reach. Ziki noticed a woman's figure in the dark shades of the room, the same corner where he had seen the dark vission long ago, she was smoking a cigarette, wearing a red leather jacket, short.

"Shalom Commander." Malkielly began. "I believe you know Yaffa Yardeny here."

"Yes, we've met."

"You know how much that Chinook helicopter you lost in the Sahara costs with all that it had on board?" Malkielly grimaced.

"It's in the desert, The Egyptians—they blew it up, poof—sorry."

"It's ten years pay. And do you know how much jail time all that has happened is?" He paused.

Ziki looked straight at him. "Okay boss—get it over with. Go ahead, put me in jail?"

"I should, but it won't give us our helicopter and I will loose you Commander. We'll buy another with her money."

"Yaffa here agreed to pay the $980,000 that she was going to pay you for the lost helicopter."

"It's not her money any longer."

Malkielly reclined in his chair and blew a cloud of smoke from his Cuban. "So, I always wondered since I took you out of baby diapers, when you came here

sucking your thumb, if you were available for hire. Now I know that you are."
"No I am not—I am not, this thing needed to be done, the money—well—was an extra. I wanted to do something good with it."
And that you will, yes, something good—you then, since it is 'your money' are going to pay for the helicopter and I suppose an extra $20,000 will cover the Commandka. Luckily, we have access to all the money that she put for you in Lichtenstein. And...
a little bird tells me that you still need that little thing that you hold in your pants because I hear you use it now and then, you could loose that in the long years in jail? So what choice do you make Commander?" Ziki shrugged.
"My, men? Nothing happens to them, right? It was all my fault, they were just following my orders."
"Right, I will presume that."
"You have $1,000,000 in that little account in Lichtenstein."
"How do you know?"
"You'd be surprised what I know."
"We're you testing me? Was the Femme Fatale' in on it? He looked at Yaffa. Was this whole fucking thing a test?"
"No, nobody's testing you everything was real. The only thing you didn't know, and it is my justification for saving your ass now, is that what you've just done would've been your very next mission, you would have gone on following the Egyptian raid."
"Is that so Sir?"
"You had satellite coverage—we knew everything that you were doing, we were tuned onto your communications, though you didn't say much. We had you covered just in case you got into serious trouble. But you seem to have managed— the only trouble you have is with me."
Malkielly smirked. Yaffa stood frozen. She hadn't dared yet to look at him—she'd been staring out the window. "I will not see you again with this type of thing. The next time you pull a stunt like this you can count on the fact that you're either going to die or I'm going to put you in jail for the rest of your life."
"Yes Sir." Ziki looked for the ray of light in the dark corner of the room, it did not appear.
"Consider yourself one lucky man Commander."
"Is there anything else?" Ziki looked at Yaffa...
"Get out of here, get some sleep, never speak of this incident again and see me in the morning. Other than that-no."

## Chapter 49

**Beirut**

*"**Sallam aleicum**, sorry to keep you waiting."* The medium-sized man said in Arabic, as he slid into the seat across from Ziki. Ziki was sitting at a table on the outside veranda of Sa'adat Café, a small restaurant that had a view of the city and the Mediterranean bellow from its high perch in Beirut, waiting to meet a Mossad operative that had his base of operation in Lebanon.

"You have me mistaken for someone else, do I know you" Ziki smiled back.

"I doubt it," he replied, resting his arm on the top of the seat next to him. "What did you order, the *dolmades,* stuffed grape leaves?"

"I don't mean to be rude but—"

"Alright, alright," the man laughed, "they still keep you Tel Aviv boys with a stick up your ass."

Quite unconvincingly, he said, "Maryland is a beautiful state, you ever been there?"

Ziki rolled his eyes. He nodded. "Yes, beautiful. So is Ohio."

"I guess so. Columbus is a big football town. You in the railroad business?"

Ziki shook his head, "You're supposed to say 'railroad line.'"

The man shrugged his shoulders and started speaking in Hebrew. "Hey shalom, you know who I am.? I know who you are. This code bullshit gets dreamed up by some desk clerk, I hate fucking clerks, they are men that are given a little power and they use that to the extreme against all of us." He positioned himself directly in front of Ziki. "It's their way of asserting power against the world where usually they're ordered around by their wives."

Ziki looked shocked. He turned his head away towards the window and away from the restaurant. *"Shu hada ya majnun."* "What the hell are you doing are you crazy?" he responded harshly but under his breath, still in Arabic.

Ziki was not known to be a stickler for rules, but he was surprised by the man's breach of protocol, speaking Hebrew in a country at war with Israel.

The coded greeting confirmed that he was Norman Gantz, an Aman Military Intelligence agent who had met Zhukov a few years prior during some arms dealings with Czechoslovakia. No one briefed Ziki if Israel was buying or selling to the Czechs, but it must have been high-level stuff for Zhukov to be there.

Again in Hebrew, Gantz responded, "What are you worried about?" He motioned to the restaurant around them, "These people know we are Israelis they spotted us the moment we walked in the door, maybe not you Ziki, but me for one, I want them to know and make them give way. They're not going to do anything about it, they are afraid of us and it is good to keep them that way." Ziki turned to respond but Gantz cut him off.

"Think of it this way. We speak in Hebrew and they know we're Israelis and that's about it, or we talk in Arabic and they hear Russian generals, scientists, and all this other nonsense and have a story to tell."

Ziki wasn't happy about it, but Gantz had a point. "Alright, I've heard about this stuff but it is quirky when you actually do it "he said. "Your city, your way."

Gantz smiled, "Beirut is too beautiful a city not to relax in it, if these maniacal sons of bitches don't destroy it. They've already started to blow each other up in the Shuff Mountains over there." Gantz now pointing to the mountains east of the city, "and there's shooting all around the city's outskirts. " He moved his arm pointing at the mountains in the distance. "It's a fucking hot bed with more Palestinians spreading their turf over into the Christian Phalanges territory."

"You're sure its okay for us to openly speak Hebrew?"

"Screw the little bastards, yeah its okay, I told you, they're scared of us so they make like we're not around, we are invisible; but here we are!"

"I suppose that's good it keeps them away from our border."

"Yes it does, and fear of us and what we'll do to them is the only thing that keeps us safe, so little brother look tough and don't let them see you sweat."

"You don't need to worry about me, I don't sweat". Ziki replied with one eyebrow raised and a stern voice. "So they all play here?"

"Oh yeah, you've got all the terrorist groups running around like mad dogs, El-Fattah, Black September, the Tanzim and so called Martyrs Brigade, Islamic Jihad and Islamia, Hezbollah and Hamas, a new one called Iz a Din Al-Kassam, Abu Nidal, just to fucking many to count those are mostly Palestinians, then you have the others, the Druze in the mountains and the Christian Phalanges with the Christian Maronites, they all chase each other and like roving gangs they hate each other and kill each other every chance they get. This place, Beirut and maybe the whole of Lebanon is going to blow sky high, you wait and see they're going to destroy and turn this place into a shit hole—one big slum.

"It's a shame; I grew to almost like this city." Gantz now makes a gesture of disgust with his face and continues. "They all have one thing in common."

"What is it?"

"They all hate us and the Americans with the same passion that they hate each other, maybe more." "Every place they're in, they destroy. Just look at this place, it's the beginning of turning it into ruins, just wait and see."

"I'm sure they'd love to do the same to Tel-Aviv and Haifa, it's your and my job not to let them."

"Yeah you're right, on this we agree"

The waiter came up to the table, "A plate of humus and tabouli salad, oh yeah and a beer," he ordered, in Arabic but said in Hebrew to Ziki, "the lamb shawarma is really good here." The waiter nodded and walked off.

Ziki rolled his eyes with exasperation. "Was that necessary?"

"You're still bugged about this? Listen, this isn't Teheran."

"Yes I think I understand."

"These people share a large, border with us. They not only hate us, they fear us. They understand the relationship, that as long as they don't let to many terrorists cross the border into our country from theirs and piss us off, we will not retaliate against them. "Their mentors the Syrians know this and so do the people."

"Believe me, the only language they understand is force, any concessions they call weakness and weakness in this part of the world gets you killed, never show them your soft under belly."

Ziki looked around and couldn't help feel that Gantz had a point. The restaurant seemed to have quieted down since they began talking, and no one sat within a few tables of the two. The waiter's deferential acceptance of the order in Hebrew was surprising. "We'll see if you're right, I sure hope you are." he said.

The waiter placed a glass on the table and poured a bottle of Anwar, Egyptian beer. *"Shukra."* Gantz said.

"So what can you tell me about Zhukov?" Ziki asked his impatience showing.

Gantz shrugged, "Not much".

"Almost everything you can really know about him, it'll appear that you'll know within seconds of meeting him, but don't be fooled he is a complex man. In my book, a great man."

"A big mouth?" Ziki asked.

"Yes and no," Gantz said, shaking his head, "A big aura. You ever met a man with an aura? Not quite a halo—a bigger-than-life presence."

Ziki nodded. "Once," he said. "Ben-Gurion."

"So you know what I'm talking about. Well Zhukov is, if anything, even more awe-inspiring than Ben-Gurion. And meaner by miles."

Ziki ate his last stuffed grape leaf. "Is he trustworthy?"

"It depends," Gantz said, "Yes and no."

"That sounds like a diplomatic way of saying no."

Gantz shook his head. "He'll want to drink, pretty much all the time, and insist that you do the same. Of course, he'll have more practice and gain an advantage on you this way. He'll also make sudden and bold pronouncements seemingly; one second he'll want to send you all back to Tel Aviv, the next he'll offer you a governorship of Belarus. Don't laugh at them, but he's really just testing you."

"But this I can tell you, if he shakes your hand and gives you his word of honor, you can count on it. He takes pride in that. In his whole life he never broke his word of honor, but remember that you must get that and shake his hand. It's his ritual… Not just a nod. His handshake."

Ziki was skeptical, "That's what Moshe Levy told me. But a man who survives and thrives under the KGB can't be that honest."

Gantz looked directly in the younger man's eyes, "Or maybe honesty and predictability was the only way to survive under them."

"Maybe." Ziki pushed his empty plate to the side of the table. "Anything else you can tell me? I came all this way for this?"

Gantz considered for a second and his demeanor changed. For the first time since he sat down he looked less than relaxed and carefree. In fact, he actually looked around him as if to see if anyone else was listening, and leaned forward to speak more softly. *"Ascultama` bine"* to Ziki's shock, the words came out in Romanian. "Just one last thing," he said.

Ziki leaned forward as well, "How did you know I speak Romanian?"

Gantz waved off the question with his hand. "If you only take one thing out of this meeting, let it be this: Zhukov does not make small deals. You think the man who fought back a 4 million men German army of Nazis really gives a shit about a new contract for a Czech halftrack factory or, in your case, what is it?—a few extra scientists? Oh I'm sorry, I was not suppose to know about this one, uups."

The frustration that had been quietly simmering in Ziki during the whole affair burst out, "You read my mind, but Mal—" But Gantz shut him up quickly.

Still in Romanian, he said, *"Am crezut ca tu te pazesti"* "I thought you were a cautious one. Just keep your head. If you play your cards right with him Zhukov will probably tell you more than anyone in Tel Aviv has." Suddenly changing volume and tone, he grinned.

"So what do you say we get out of this place? See the nightlife of Beirut while there's still is a city here, they do bring in some not bad European hookers that are not too diseased."

Ziki shook his head, "Going straight back across the border and then I've got a plane to catch early in the morning."

Gantz frowned, "Youth is wasted on the young." He couldn't have been more than forty…

## Chapter 50

### ZHUKOV

Stirring his coffee, Ziki gazed down at the peaks of the Alps bursting through the scattered clouds. The American-made Boeing 747 jetliner that bore him cruised north at 500 miles per hour.

A couple thousand years ago in this very spot below, Hannibal had passed in the opposite direction with 37 elephants.

Ziki was going to have to do the best he could with his cargo of twenty-three ex-Nazi scientists, experts in the manufacturing of chemical and biological warfare agents, that were being separately transported aboard a chartered Ilussian, Soviet-made cargo plane, and flying under the command of Davidoff at Ziki's orders toward the same rendezvous destination near East Berlin.

The cloud cover thickened and the Alps slowly passed out of sight. Ziki leaned his chair back slowly, so as not to spill the drink on the tray behind him, and tried to relax. Looking at his surroundings and  checking his appearance—not to mention feeling under his arm the Berretta automatic pistol and double checking that he had with him the international concealed weapons  permit and his  Diplomatic passport—he felt like just another business executive. He thought about what it might be like in that corporate world, if he were on his way to Berlin for a trade show:  drinks on the company's dime and an open expense account for a hooker or two; that was probably the height of excitement in most men's lives. But these people around him, sitting in their comfortable Lufthansa Airline seats and thousands like them, would never come close to understanding the intensity that attended Ziki's mission.

A mission that would lead to and begin on the other side of the "Iron Curtain" in Soviet occupied East Berlin.  No sure horizon of its conclusion as it presented fluid circumstances with unpredictable players and surly characters including dealings and confrontations with one of history's great men of the Twentieth Century, Soviet General—Zhukov.

Only a few weeks before, Ziki and the lanky, square-jawed Moshe Levy had sat in the Mossad cafeteria drinking much better coffee than this airline stuff, discussing the twenty-three German expatriates who had set up their shop of horrors near the Sudanese border.

These ex-Nazis—some of them "legends to the Fuhrer" in chemical and biological weapons research and production, one of them the inventor of the VX gas, two others that evolved the Zyklon B gas and others used for the "Final Solution" in the death camps of Europe—had been recruited from all over the world, as Moshe Levy had told Ziki, by the Egyptians.

They had been safely ensconced in South America, financially supported by the Odessa organization, the one dedicated to the new rise of the Fourth Reich. It supported ex-Nazis in hiding, SS and others on gold bullion and Swiss bank accounts, gotten mostly from stolen money and stashed out of Germany towards the war's end. Now they had been generously compensated by the Libyans and Egyptians for giving up their South American hideouts.

They came for the money and another chance, Ziki thought. But this is not the same as Europe during their Nazi domain; the wheel has turned. These are Israelis toughened by the land they live on; they don't just quietly go to their death praying. The boot is now on the other foot.

In their worst nightmares these Nazis could not imagine being in a worse place than taken prisoner after being caught with their hand in the cookie jar once more, by Special Forces soldiers of the IDF; and they'd heard of the Shin Bet and Aman special branches of Mossad in whose hands their lives were now hanging by a very thin thread…

*"Mehr Kaffee, mein Herr?"* **said the stewardess.** *"Bitte,"* replied Ziki. He didn't really want anymore, but enjoyed the stewardess's frequent attention.

Pretty as she was, his mind soon turned back to the meeting at hand.

How was Zhukov involved? Had he gone too far in purging the Soviet army of political officers? Had the old general acquired substantial power yet again? And how much was he acting without knowledge of the politicians in the Kremlin? He'd probably never figure out the politics nor did he care.

The mission itself was enough to worry about. "There must be more behind all this than I've been told", he thought to himself, but in good time it will come out to me, in the mean time settle yourself down an deal with what's at hand".

**The Nazis, and eight elite Golanis** were guarding them, they were being flown separately in the Russian made Ilussian into the exchange point, a Soviet army camp a few kilometers away from East Berlin.

While Ziki stretched his legs and flirted with the stewardesses of the business-class jetliner seat, they were riding in the utilitarian discomfort of an army transport plane.

So as not to attract too much attention as the Americans and West Germans kept an eye out for Israelis that flew straight into East Berlin Ziki wouldn't fly directly to Berlin, but would divert the track by landing in Frankfurt. Pick up a pre arranged rented Mercedes that would not trace back to him, and drive to the meeting trough 'Checkpoint Charlie', using a different passport than his own.

Then he would attempt to exchange 23 of the world's most talented and unscrupulous chemical weapons scientists for? Ziki rolled his eyes, for something he was not allowed to know yet. He'd hand over the Nazis and get what in return? Documents? Arms? Stockings for Levi's wife? If politicians want to keep secrets from him then they should get their behinds out from behind their desks and do this stuff themselves.

He would report to Tel Aviv before the exchange was completed to ensure the Soviets kept their end of the deal.

Mysteriously Malkielly and Pientz were absent from this whole affair, but Ziki knew that his boss was the one behind all this.

The price of youth, he thought, they don't tell everything all at once because I'm young. But a nation can't afford to ignore the energy of its young men, after all that's who does all the thirty work.

Ziki sipped his coffee and peered out the window. The Alps had given way to splotchy farmland and a network of rivers. Though he knew this part of Germany to be heavily industrialized, from far up the land looked lush and pastoral. Quite unlike the dry and broken terrain of the upper Nile in southern Egypt.

*"Damen und Herrn, Wir haben unseren Abfell angefangen und werden in der halben Stunde landen.* Die Zeit in Frankfurt ist 7 Uhr. Die Temperatur beträgt 11 Grad Celsius."

The stewardess's voice clicked off as abruptly as it had begun.

Ziki brought his seat forward again and slipped his feet back in his loafers. It seemed cold for Frankfurt in October, but he supposed it was appropriate weather for a meeting with the hero of Stalingrad. He had been sure to pack a heavy coat, if only to look more imposing.

The Mein River grew from a thin, dark line beneath him to a swelling, barge-laden waterway. Roads became visible and miniature cars seemed to make their way along them. Smoke and steam from individual buildings wafted into the air. The ground rushed up to meet them and, compared to Ziki's usual flights, he was on the ground in smooth fashion.

Stepping out onto the tarmac, Ziki smelled Frankfurt. The air was tinged with the soot and sulfur of heavy industry, Frankfurt was primarily a banking city, the financial capital of Europe according to some. Ziki found some irony in this; the city's had a long history of violence.

The bellhop at his hotel had a pair of hooks on his left hand but was far too young to have served in the Wehrmacht, even in the latter days when 14-year olds were impressed into service. Ziki smiled and tipped him generously.

Ziki locked the door and bolted it. He closed the blinds and removed his jacket. Finally he was able to remove the shoulder-holstered Beretta and place it on the dresser next to his bed. And though the night was still young, after a small glass of Vodka from the mini-bar, Ziki collapsed into sleep.

**"Sir, are you sure you wouldn't like our special roadside assistance**

**package?** Only 10 Marks per day extra."
Ziki smiled. "It's the brown Mercedes right? I think I'll be fine."
The rental agent shrugged. "Very good sir. Here are your keys. Your car
is in spot J-19. Would you like any help out with your luggage?"
"No thanks," Ziki said and carried his suitcase out of the rental office.
It was sunny, but still relatively cold. He unlocked the brown Mercedes sedan,
placed his suitcase in the trunk, and placed himself in the comfortable leather seat.
The engine turned over and he found himself smoothly transported to the autobahn
within minutes. Germans they do make good machines, he thought to himself.

**A light rain fell as Ziki idled in line at Checkpoint Charlie.** His radio
picked up the Beach Boys singing "In My Room" in German. The sign in front of
him acknowledged that this one link between East and West Berlin was least of all
likely to be used by Germans:
"YOU ARE NOW LEAVING THE AMERICAN SECTOR," it read, then
"ВЫ ВЫЕЗЖАЕТЕ ИЗ АМЕРИКАНСКОЙ ЗОНЫ," and then, in interest of
international amity, "VOUS SORTEZ DU SECTEUR AMERICAIN." No German
translation.
Ziki wheeled his Mercedes around the final turn of the zigzag that led up
to the guard house. The guard knocked on Ziki's window with his gloved hand. Ziki
rolled it down, letting in the misty rain and the Russian guard's bad breath.
"*Ursprungland?*" asked the guard.
"*Kanada.*" Ziki answered. If anyone challenged in English, his accent
could always be explained as some distant Canadian province. The guard nodded.
No real reason to sneak in to East Germany, security was decidedly laxer in this
direction, not like going the other way.
"*Bestimmungsort?*"
He was really headed for the Soviet Army Camp outside Ehrenswald, but
answered, "Beeskow."
"*Zer gut gehen zie durch*"
The guard waved him through. Ziki rolled up the window and pressed the
accelerator. After passing a few well-maintained military buildings and entering
into the heart of East Berlin, the difference between East and West, years under
Soviet occupation and years after the construction of the wall, was striking. Even
along the main thoroughfare of Friederichstraße, everything was drab and run-
down. Much of the city had not yet been rebuilt from the combined devastation of
allied bombing and the thirsty Soviet assault on the city.
The rain didn't help.
The towering Brandenburg gate standing within a stone's throw away from
what was Hitler's bunker complex underground, where the symbolic giant swastika
was perched during the Nazis time, was gone, the Russians dynamited it off.
He soon passed out of the downtown area, through the outlying residential
suburbs, and into the Brandenburg countryside. It was once the heartland of the
Prussian aristocracy, but now it found itself under the wheel of a car from Frankfurt
driven by an Israeli on his way to turn over some of "*Germany's finest*", and

most despicable, minds to the Russians who held East Germany under indefinite occupation behind the Iron Curtain.

Driving along the narrow, but unpopulated road, Ziki wondered if he would have done better to change cars in Berlin and obtain one of the small, boxy vehicles that seemed so prevalent. As the meeting neared, as usual, various doubts crossed his mind.

How expendable were the scientists to Zhukov? What else was in play? Yes, that was the big question—what else was in play? How far could Ziki push Zhukov?

The cargo plane they were on was rigged with explosives, but he could really only effectively hold the scientists themselves hostage in a crisis, he couldn't stare down an entire Soviet division.

**He pulled onto the recently paved side road and soon reached a gate.** He stopped not far in front of the three East German Stasi police who huddled together under the roof at the front of the small guardhouse. Ziki rolled down his window expecting one of the *Polizei* to walk up to him. Instead they just stood by, staring at him, not seeming particularly concerned. After about a minute of this, a Soviet officer raced up to the gate in a jeep type vehicle driven by an enlisted man. He hopped out as the three Stasi opened the smaller, man-sized door through the gate for him.

The officer, bespectacled and not tall, though his driver was a brute, walked up to Ziki's door.

"Identification?"

Ziki showed him his Israeli diplomatic passport. "I'm here to see Mareshal Zhukov."

The Russian's eyes flashed with surprise. He looked directly at Ziki for a few moments and then spoke some words to him quickly and in Russian. Ziki only caught a few words, the officer's excitement made him effectively incomprehensible. Ziki gripped the wheel and looked over at the Stasi guards.

No longer relaxed and passive, they gripped their Kalashnikov sub-machine guns and spread out a few meters from each other pointing them at him.

In German he tried to reassure the officer, "Just ask General Zhukov. I'm expected. He just thought I was coming by plane."

The officer looked suspicious but nodded.

"Just sit here. We'll see how expected you are." He turned and quickly walked back to the gate. Ziki heard him contemptuously tell the guards. "Don't let him go anywhere." He hopped back in his jeep, and almost before he was seated his driver was racing back down the gravel road.

Again Ziki was left alone with the three Germans. They looked careful and attentive now. Ziki reached down into his seat, but the guards raised their guns one coked a round into the chamber with a whirring noise and tensed at this sudden motion. He smiled at them, raising the pack of cigarettes that he had reached for. The two on the right still looked suspicious, but the younger one on the left grinned back. Ziki held the pack out of his window.

*"Americanish,"* he offered. The one in the middle, seemingly the dominant personality though not superior in rank, shook his head. The one on the left was not about to be dissuaded and jogged up to the car.

*"Spasiva—danke,"* he said, taking one of Ziki's Marlboroughs and lighting it himself. Ziki watched the young guard walk back to his comrades with a mixture of amused embarrassment and satisfaction. He then lit one himself, rolled up his window except for a crack at the top, then leaned back to wait and see how long news took to get to the top of the Soviet military command structure. The three guards relaxed some as well, keeping vigilant, but more, it looked, for when their superiors came back than out of concern for Ziki.

He turned the engine off and watched the rain run against the windshield.

Damn it, he thought, they've trained me to deal with pain, hunger, extreme temperatures, interrogation, and VD. But there's never a training course on coping with waiting.

**In the end, they wouldn't let Ziki drive his Mercedes through the gate and make his capitalist entrance.** Seated in the back of the jeep and offered an army raincoat, which he turned down despite the increasing downpour, he mentally prepared himself.

General Mareshal Gheorgy Konstantinovich Zhukov was, like Ziki, initially a regular soldier. When the Germans invaded, Zhukov became, out of necessity, a master of defensive doctrine and originated the Russian "Bear defense," where you dig in and stay in your den until the enemy goes past your lines and wears himself out, then come out and trap him in ambush. This was orchestrated better than foreseen showings at Kiev and Smolensk, followed by the great saving of Leningrad and an outright victory at the gates of Moscow.

Later he was appointed to command the defense of Stalingrad against the last most dangerous German offensive of the war. He effectively stymied the assault on the city and by the 23rd of November had completely encircled Field Marshal von Paulus's 6th Army. The Germans would never again win a major tactical victory on the Eastern Front, and Zhukov's fingerprints would be on every defeat.

This was the first defeat the Germans had in WWII, and many credit Zhukov with turning the tide and beginning the end of the war.

Now he was getting some of the Germans who escaped his grasp.

With surprising efficiency the SS quickly established the Odessa organization to smuggle them out—there were all too many of these—scientists, and others—alive and well. These twenty-three were captured because of their hubris at coming back to design weapons of mass destruction against Israel.

And here Ziki was, giving them yet another chance to live. And who knows, Zhukov or his successor could just as easily decide to sell them back to Egypt, Iran, or who knows?

The jeep raced past a row of odd-looking T-62 tanks—Ziki would later learn they were the new T-64s—on its way to the central compound of two-story buildings. The driver halted the jeep just as abruptly as he started it and Ziki was led towards the door of one of the larger brick buildings. Through the rain he saw the runway a few hundred meters away, but his cargo plane had not yet landed. He looked at his watch—just another hour unless the weather delayed it.

"This way, Commander," the junior officer motioned. Ziki almost laughed thinking about the possibility of the plane crashing in the adverse weather and the whole meeting set up for nothing. If his eight Golanis and pilot weren't on board, he almost would have preferred it. They led him to the official reception room of the camp. Furnished on a budget and clearly designed for the tastes of visiting Russian political officials, it did not quite seem the place for negotiation.

As they entered the room the officer stopped, smiled politely, and said, "Is there anything I can offer you while you wait, comrade?"

Ziki made no motion to sit. "Wait, what wait? I've been waiting half the day out there by the gate. Where's Mareshal Zhukov?"

The officer hedged, "Comrade Generalissimo Zhukov will be pleased to host you when the plane arrives, as was the arrangement."

"The hell with the arrangement," Ziki fumed at the officer almost his own age. "I'm in command of the envoy. You can't just keep me on ice."

"I truly apologize, Sir. I was just told to escort you here and make sure you were comfortable." The officer, Maximov if Ziki was reading his Cyrillic correctly, seemed to genuinely answer.

"Well," Ziki said, approaching him, "here's what you can do to make me comfortable. Go see your superior and tell him the way to make me comfortable is to let me see Mareshal Zhukov immediately."

Maximov nodded and began to leave but hesitated a moment. Ziki assured him, "Don't worry, I won't spit on your polished floor, you can leave me alone." The young man smiled faintly and quickly began to walk out. Just then the roar of an Illussian cargo plane filled their ears and shook the walls.

"Never mind," Ziki said. "Just take me to the plane."

Maximov looked relieved. "This I can do. Follow me."

**Their jeep reached the landing strip just as the cargo plane rolled to a halt.** The rain had stopped, but the mid-day sky was still gray and the ground was damp to the point of being muddy. By this time, a couple hundred Russian soldiers were being lined into place by their officers. In their dress uniforms, these were surely for show, but the four tanks rolling into place on the runway behind the plane and the sharpshooters quietly climbing into place at the guard towers and the occasional roof were not. Whether Zhukov would actually contemplate storming the plane or simply wanted more convincing muscle for negotiation purposes, the General did not mess around.

Without waiting for Maximov, Ziki leapt out of the jeep and walked towards the huge plane. He placed the small speaker in his ear and yelled over the din of the engines into the small receiver, "Joel! This is Ziki, do you copy?" Now they'd see whether the short wave transmitter he'd carried all the way across Germany still worked. He heard nothing, he was within range.

Maximov had walked up behind him, but some commotion further behind both of them drew him quickly away. Ziki did not pay attention to him, still facing the plane and trying to establish radio contact with the young Golani lieutenant who led the eight men guarding the "cargo." He yelled again into the small microphone, "Dolphin one…. This is Red Falcon, respond if you can hear me."..." Over."

"This is Dolphin, understood, Commander," Joel said, squinting in the brilliant red light of the late sunset…

## Chapter 51

**Erenhardt**

**The heavy and heavily decorated Russian General rolled himself out of the back seat of the jeep and approached Ziki.** "I am General Petrovksy," he said in German, contempt dripping from his voice. "You come with me, comrade Maximov," he said to the young officer beside Ziki. "Stay and make sure the plane doesn't go anywhere." Not waiting for either of their responses, he sat back in the jeep and then gestured to the front seat for Ziki.

"We just missed each other, General Petrovsky, in Geneva when you met with the Americans—General Sam Armstrong…Remember the little flair up," he gestured with his hands. "Boom—off the South African coastline?"

"Hmm," he growled.

Ziki nodded and hopped into the seat. Just then he heard Joel in his ear. "Red Falcon this is Joel. We heard you earlier, just a minor malfunction on our end. Can you hear me, over?"

As the driver pressed the accelerator and Ziki lurched back in his seat, he responded quietly in Hebrew, "I read you. They're taking me to Zhukov right now. Just sit tight. Nobody gets on or off the plane without my orders."

Petrovksy had obviously heard Ziki quietly speaking in Hebrew to himself and leaned over to him, laughing. "Are you praying back there?"

Ziki wasn't amused but didn't want to start things on too bad a foot. He ignored it.

Joel responded, "Affirmative, Commander."

Petrovsky snorted a laugh as they pulled up to a larger brick building. "No need for embarrassment; if I were going to meet Mareshal Zhukov for the first time, I too would pray." Ziki held his tongue.

The doors leading to Zhukov's office were dramatically thrown open a few feet in front of Ziki's advance, which was frustratingly slow in order to keep pace with Petrovksy. A pair of soldiers walked in front of them and another behind. As intimidating as this was, it was more the reception that Ziki initially expected. Ziki was more nervous in the role of negotiator than that of field work. Hopefully

Zhukov's style would resemble the former more than the latter, apart from the bloodshed of course. They finally halted at a large, birch door. Petrovsky raised his eyebrows and then walked in. Ziki lingered behind, waiting to be introduced, but heard nothing for a few moments.

From inside the room he heard an annoyed baritone exclaim, "Well, where the hell is he?" Ziki's stomach dropped at his error and he walked in, taking off his wool hat and starting to remove his gloves.

Behind an unnecessarily enormous desk stood—Ziki could hardly picture such a mythic figure sitting—General Gheorgy Konstantinovich Zhukov. His uniform was undecorated, unusual for a Russian. His mammoth desk was mostly empty; Zhukov was likely little bothered by paperwork. Zhukov himself was not a large man, neither tall nor unusually heavy for a man his age, but exuded largeness in a way that few men ever have.

Ziki had no idea how long he stood there gawking before Zhukov turned to Petrovsky and barked in Russian, "What is this? I said bring me the envoy, not his fucking driver." Ziki wanted to interject, but decided to keep the fact of his knowledge of Russian, which was tolerable but not fluent, to himself.

Petrovsky shrank back. "That's who he said he is. At least that's what comrade Maximov told me."

Zhukov looked Ziki in the eye. Condescendingly and in German he asked, "Where is your boss?"

"I'm in charge, General," Ziki responded, somewhat surprised at his own brashness.

Zhukov's eyes flashed. "Oh, you're in charge?" He walked towards Ziki from around the desk as Petrovsky carefully moved to not impede the General's movement. "I'd say you were a little young, but you're more than a little young." Though Zhukov's German was good, he seemed to deliberately blur the pronunciation of "jung" or "young" to where it was hard to distinguish from "Junge" or "boy." Ziki imagined this was not accidental. "But in my age," Zhukov continued, paternally putting his arm around Ziki's shoulders, "I take what they send me. Let's go see what you've brought me."

He started to lead Ziki out the door, and Ziki, swayed by the overwhelming presence of this tremendous historical figure, almost unswervingly followed him. But his good sense got the better of him and he interrupted. "I'm sorry, General, but I think we've got something to negotiate."

Zhukov looked surprised at this rebuff, but almost—maybe it was Ziki's natural optimism—in an intrigued way.

"Negotiate? What do we have to negotiate?" He removed his arm from around Ziki's shoulder but still stood uncomfortably close. A close talker. Ziki hoped he did not have too bad a breath. "You've got the Nazi *dreck* scientists, and I'm more than willing, as agreed, to take them off your hands. You want to start making demands now? Even if you were that dumb, you don't have much to bargain with—we can take them whenever we want."

"We had a deal, General. I don't think you're so old that you'd forget a thing like that." With an incredulous, concerned look at the other side of the room,

Petrovksy shook his head, transmitting to Ziki that he was going too far.

But Zhukov seemed energized by Ziki's chutzpah, "What are you going to do if I just take them?"

"I was told," Ziki replied, "that you were a man of your word."

Zhukov gave a short but loud outburst of laughter and then leaned against the front edge of his desk, motioning to Ziki to sit in one of the smaller chairs nearby. "Well," he said, smiling, "don't believe everything you hear."

"Thank you," Ziki said, sitting down. "I should warn you, General, that I am not unprepared for an attempt to take the scientists. But I do not believe you would do it."

Zhukov raised his eyebrows. "You know why it's hard to read me? I don't make up my mind until the last minute. You can't tell what I'm really going to do because even I don't know. But something tells me you wouldn't let me take them easily." He was still patronizing, but an air of respect seemed to seep into his voice.

"I'm afraid I would not," Ziki responded.

"Petrovksy," he bellowed across the room in Russian to the two-star general who was still standing at attention, "this kid's pretty smart. And balls too. You think we have a place in the NKVD for him?" Ziki noted with some amusement that the NKVD had been termed the MVD now, but the old general persisted in the original name. Petrovsky didn't have a chance to respond. "What do you think?" Zhukov said, turning to Ziki and effortlessly switching to German. "You impress me. Why go back to your pissy little country when you can come work for me?"

"No thank you, General. That's flattering, but I'm happy where I am."

Zhukov did not seem the type to take no for an answer but let the offer go for now. "We'll discuss this later," he said, grabbing Ziki's shoulder again. "Now let's go see those scientists." Ziki again resisted, but Zhukov stopped him before he could speak.

"What are you, scared of me?"

"No, I'm not scared of anybody, General, but I don't know if I like the way this is going."

"Don't worry 'Tovaresh,' Comrade, I told you, I myself don't know yet were it's going."

"My men are safer in that plane than out of it. I saw that you've got more than the ordinary welcome party out there."

Zhukov smiled, "That's the ordinary Russian welcome party. Don't worry about it. Since you're so skittish, let me put it to you this way; would you negotiate for something you've never seen? I just want to see the goods; you can keep them for now." Zhukov did not continue but turned again to Petrovsky. In German he demonstratively asked. "Can the Jew trust me, Petrovksy?"

# Chapter 52

**Israel - Tel-Noff Air Force Base**

"**We found three pretty standard bugs in the cabin and one a little too obviously placed in the pilot's headset.** They're self-powered and still operating so we're going to place them in the back of a cinema downtown. While the flight is en route, they should be screening 'From Russia with Love.' And we definitely found all the homing devices," the Mossad technician reported to Ziki.

Ziki nodded. It was nice to see that Mossad was able to effectively cope with the tricks of a rival agency with probably 100 times its budget. "Anything else?"

"Well," the technician said reaching into the case and pulling out a plastic bag with a device the size of a small eraser in it, "We found this in one of the engines. It's a small, remote-controlled explosive that would take the engine out of commission without blowing the whole wing off. The funny thing is that there's only the one—the other engine is clean—and they know that the Illusian can fly at almost three-quarter speed with only one engine, so it's not sufficient to force a landing."

Ziki looked over the device. "Maybe they just wanted to see if we could find it. Kind of a dry run for future use. Because if we could, then the Americans could just as easily."

The technician looked annoyed. "The Americans wouldn't be so cheap as to be riding around in a borrowed Russian plane."

Ziki sensed he had stepped on the technician's professional pride. "How soon until you'll have the whole thing wired with our explosives?"

The technician shrugged. "It depends on how big an explosion you want. Enough to destroy just the plane or the whole airport around it?"

"How about all of East Germany around it?"

The technician smiled. "I'll see what I can do."

Ziki nodded and walked out of the hangar into the small building adjoining it. He made his way to a large room where the Nazi scientists were all lined up. They were already in their bright pink jumpsuits with large black numbers on the front and back from one to twenty-three. They were daisy-chained together when transported, but were unbound now, standing in front of a long table as Davidoff paced back and forth in front of them. He turned as Ziki entered.

"Come on in, Commander. I was just explaining how our cargo can—if they use their heads—can stay alive long enough to reach the comforts of Siberia." The scientists looked exhausted and scared; their faces registered little else. A few, however, could still not hide their contempt for their captors.

Ziki walked towards them. "Have they taken their 'vitamins?'" he asked Davidoff.

"We were just getting to it," Davidoff grinned. To one of the young soldiers standing behind him he asked, "Gideon, will you bring in their 'pills?'" Turning back towards the scientists and changing his tone, he said officiously. "You will each be given a pill and a cup of water. Take the pill as I call your number so that I can watch you swallow it, and set the empty cup down in front of you."

Gideon and another man walked out with trays in their hands and set down a fairly large pill and cup in front of each Nazi. The pills seemed to be coated in a thick gelatin, and it was likely one or more of the scientists perceived that it was not designed to dissolve inside them. One by one, they obediently downed the pill, though a few had a trouble with its size. All of them followed the orders, except one.

"Number eight!" Davidoff barked, "take your pill." All the eyes in the room were immediately drawn to the defiant Nazi. He did not dare reply, but his face spoke volumes. Davidoff rushed up to him and picked up the pill. "This isn't Germany, number eight. You are in Israel, in our hands, and you are going to take this pill or we will surgically insert it in your ass…with no anesthetic." The mention of surgical insertion brought shocked and frightened expressions to the faces of the other scientists. Those who hadn't picked up on it before realized that this pill was not for their health—Still, Number 8 did not budge. Davidoff suddenly struck the scientist's face with the back of his hand. He called out, "Gideon, come hold number eight's arms."

"That won't be necessary," Ziki quietly said, walking calmly towards them. Davidoff looked puzzled and somewhat annoyed at Ziki's intrusion, but backed off. Ziki looked at the scientist, whose eyes watered from the pain of Davidoff's blow.

"Jonas Kasich," Ziki uttered. The scientist's eyes were wide with surprise. "Did you really think we don't know who you are?" Ziki asked him, "And not just that. Do you really believe we have no idea about your services to the Third Reich? … I'm afraid that is not the case. We know all about your Doctoral thesis at the University of Heidelberg on the danger to mammals when using pesticides with hydro-cyanic compounds. We are also aware of your employment at IG Farben and your subsequent volunteering to the SS and, of course, of all the fine work you did for them. I even seem to remember some information coming to mind recently about your young wife, what's her name? Carmella? Carmelleza? Oh well, San Rafael is not so big a town. Be happy that this pill is not one of your own creations of Zyklon B gas concentrate."

Ziki grabbed the pill from Davidoff. "I'm going to satisfy your curiosity as to what this pill is and why you're going to take it," he said, standing directly in front of Kasich. "This pill is a small bomb that can be detonated by remote control. Not a tracking device, not a vitamin, a bomb. You may think that you are too valuable for us to kill. You are wrong. Every man in this building would personally leap at the opportunity to execute each and every one of you. The Russians want you alive, we don't, and they are making it worth our while not to kill you. So take it, now, or I will shoot you, right now, in the head." Ziki's outstretched hand offered the defiant scientist the pill.

Kasich's hands trembled, but he took the pill from Ziki, placed it in his mouth, and threw back the cup of water. Ziki's expression did not change as he walked out of the room, wiping the hand that briefly touched the Nazi on his arm.

## Chapter 53

**"*Dreck*, Shit, who got this steering wheel muddy?"** Zhukov bellowed, wiping his hand on the leg of his uniform. The great hero of the Soviet Union insisted on himself driving Ziki from the headquarters building back to the landing strip. He started the engine, put the jeep into gear, and accelerated as Ziki pulled his hat more tightly onto his head so it wouldn't fly off.

Ziki spoke into his trans-receiver, "Joel, take the prisoners off the plane and line them alongside it. Keep them bound together and keep them well guarded; be ready to shoot them or anything else, but only on my orders. They are still ours for the moment. I'll be there in a couple minutes."

The speaker in his ear crackled back, "Understood, Commander."

Zhukov couldn't understand the conversation, but likely understood what was transpiring. "What kind of shape are these Nazis in?" he asked.

"Oh," Ziki replied, "pretty good shape. They are drugged a little part of the time, but not abused unless it's necessary."

"That's too bad. They could probably use more abuse. But still," he said, "you Jews have done a good thing capturing them all. I wouldn't mind seeing you go after more of them."

Ziki decided to press him a little. "General, if we're doing such a good thing, why are you supporting all the Arab countries against us?" Zhukov laughed.

"Which ones?"

"Oh, the Egyptians, the Syrians, the Iraqis, the Libyans, Yemen, the Sudan, the PLO, El Fattah, Black September, Islamic Jihad and all the other terrorist groups. Should I go on General?"

"Don't ask me," Zhukov replied, yanking the wheel to the left to intentionally make a sharp turn at speed. "That's all up to the politicians, and you know they," he gestured with his arm, "have oil and you don't."

"There is right and wrong, General and I heard that you are a man of morals."

"There are no morals in politics, my young friend." Ziki felt here some regret on Zhukov's part; at a briefing he'd learned that the General was not happy with the Soviet huge military support of the Arab states.

"It's hard for me to imagine, General, that you don't have anything to do with political decision-making."

"Trust me, son," Zhukov confided, "that's how you get to be an old man in this business; don't fuck with politics and politicians." Somehow, Ziki believed him.

Still at full speed, they raced up to the landing strip and right past the plane, as Zhukov buzzed the line-up of Nazis and Golani throwing muddy rain water off the not so well cared for tarmac. Ziki saw that Joel had wisely left three of his men on the plane, in addition to the pilots. Seeing the Russian jeep race past them did little to calm the nerves of either the prisoners or captors though. Zhukov stomped on the brake a few dozen meters in front of the plane and leapt out with surprising speed for a man his age, leaving the engine running. Ziki rushed, staying close to follow him.

"Hui!" Zhukov exclaimed to no one in particular as he strode towards the Nazis.

"Seeing these sons of bitches brings back bad memories." Of course, there was no way the General could have met these twenty-three, but Ziki wasn't about to interfere with a man who had seen his country's twenty million Russians dead in ugly ways to the German war machine. The man hated them; he didn't try to hide his facial expression.

Zhukov tromped across the muddy ground up to the closest Nazi, stopped for a moment and then spat a big wad in his face. *"Yob' tvoyu ma,'"* he growled at the cowering scientist. He switched back to German. *"Swein hund, Nazi scheis.* You know what I'm doing for you? Saving you from the Israelis. I bet you know what they'd like to do to you...cut it shorter and feed it to..." he said, making a motion with his hand to demonstrate exactly what he meant.

Ziki glanced over at the East German Stasis who lined the airport. Fortunately for them, he thought, they managed to hide any sympathy they might have felt for their fellow countrymen.

The IDF Golanis, however, had their Galils raised and tense faces at the sudden and strange behavior of the high-ranking Russian in their midst.

"Put your guns down," Zhukov roared at them. They didn't move. He turned to Ziki, "Tell them to lower their guns, we've got four T-62 tanks down the runway, and I don't want to end my career on an accidental Jew bullet."

Ziki nodded to Joel, who understood German, who relayed the order to the men who did not. They lowered their guns some, but not their guard.

"These the right mother fuckers, Maximov?" he asked turning away from the Germans and walking towards Ziki who had lingered a couple of meters back... Only now did the scientist wipe his face.

"Well, let me see," Maximov hedged, pulling a series of photos out of his leather case. "That's definitely Stromberg, and, uh, Borba over there. And, well—"

Zhukov cut him off, "Make sure all twenty-three are the right worms on your list, and check finger print records too."

"Yes, Sir," the junior officer replied, fumbling with his bulky pile of photographs.

"Let's go back and talk," Zhukov said, starting to walk back towards the headquarters without his jeep.

Ziki tried to keep with him but stay within earshot of his men. "General, what about the Nazis and my men?"

Zhukov stopped. "What, you think something funny's going to happen while we're away?"

"I don't know, General, this is your place; you tell me."

Zhukov paused to consider for a moment. "Well, since you are so suspicious we'll keep them with us."

They all began to walk, on Zhukov's instructions in Russian and Ziki's in Hebrew, the quarter mile back to the main buildings: Ziki and Zhukov a few dozen meters in front, the twenty-three Germans chained together in a line with five Israeli soldiers beside them, all surrounded by several hundred Russian military and East German Stasis keeping out of earshot but not out of range. Ziki marveled at the giant unwieldy walking party. "Hey General," he called out, "is this what it looked like in Leningrad?" No response from Zhukov.

**Zhukov was silent and Ziki was not going to start the conversation.** Occasionally Maximov would call out in confirmation that one or other of the Nazis was in fact the person he was supposed to be. Zhukov only nodded in assent. Ziki marveled at his quick stride and constant pace. The shackled Nazis were having a difficult time keeping up, but maybe this was Zhukov's intent.

A few minutes into the walk he broke the silence. "Look at those German *pizd'uks*," he said, pointing at the Stasi, not the prisoners. "They try to hide it, but they're looking sympathetically at their comrades; they're all *pizd'uks* fucking Nazis."

"I don't know, General, your communist comrades worked on them for a long time," Ziki replied, "These Stasi look young, and the Nazi days are long ago; all they remember is that their parents lost the war."

Zhukov shook his head. "This is where you are ignorant, my young friend; where do you think all the Nazis have gone to, to the moon?.....No, the mother fuckers are all still here, right fucking here under our noses, and how do you think their fucking Nazi parents raised them? Hmm?...Do you think they raised them to love Jews and Russians?"

"Yeah, maybe you're right, General."

"You bet I'm right, just look at the Stasi: we feed and clothe them and if they could, they'd gauge our eyes out, you because you're a Jew and me because I'm Russian." Ziki began to formulate a response, but thought better again.

They reached the bricked headquarters building, and Zhukov halted to let the ungainly train catch up to him. The damp ground was worn and muddy here in the main square between the administrative buildings. Ziki stopped with him, but kept his distance, wary of the newly quieted general's intentions. He raised his arm to signal to Joel to halt the prisoners a few dozen meters in front of the building.

"All right, Commander," Zhukov declared, "We've got them now, you can go home; *davay...davay...* I'm getting tired of all this *schweinerai;* be on your way."

"Oh General, I thought you a bigger man than this *scheis,* I'm disappointed that I was wrong about you, Gheorgey Zhukov." Indignation and a look of regret appeared on Zhukov's face; for a moment it looked like he wanted the respect of this brash young Israeli Commander.

"So you're not going to keep up your end of the bargain, *Tovaresh* Zhukov?"

"Hmm.....Oh, we will," Zhukov assured him in a tone of voice not convincing anyone. "Just get back on the plane and I'll contact your superiors about the rest of the deal; I'll tell them that you did a good job delivering them to me."

"General, I came here with respect for you but one thing you can be sure of, these prisoners of mine do not stay here unless you and I have a deal and the deal is complete. I believe that when you think about it some more, you'll know this to be so."

Zhukov smiled a wry smile, "What I do know is that you never should have let me take them away from the plane. I've got a gun trained on every one of your men, you included —"

"...Not every one of my men, General; count them. I have two snipers that arrived early, about 1500 meters away, trained on your and General Petrovsky's foreheads, General."

He looked around to see if he could spot anything in the surrounding hills. "You Jews cannot make a 1500-meter shot, even if I believe you that they're there."

"They never miss General."

Zhukov looked surprised at the impertinence but continued. "Not a bad bluff, Commander." Then he hesitated for a moment. "...Do you know what would happen to your pissy little country if your snipers shot me? You don't have to answer that, I'll tell you; there would only be left a smoking field of it all."

"Yeah, maybe General, but that wouldn't help you any, you'd be dead ... We're looking too far ahead don't you think?"

Zhukov looked to be thinking ...... "Any chance of negotiation was lost when you left the cover of the cargo plane and its rigged explosives that I know you have on there. ...So, for everyone's sake, young man, take your men and get back on the plane and consider yourself lucky that I'm letting you go. Many have died for less insolence. I understand it's a disappointment to you—in fact, I'm a little disappointed in how easy this was—but you're young. You'll learn from this, providing you are smart enough to stay alive today."

Ziki fought to control his temper throughout this smug speech of Zhukov's. Returning to perfect restraint, he paused for a moment. Most of his men could not speak German, but they were not dumb and could see what Zhukov was trying to do. Joel retained a look of confidence.

"General," Ziki moved closer to Zhukov, "let me show you something that might solve our little problem here."

Zhukov looked intrigued. "Show me what?"

Ziki smiled deferentially. "It's a surprise."

"I usually like surprises," Zhukov grinned. "Will I like this one?"

"We'll see, General," Ziki smiled back.

Maximov shouted out, "Mareshal, be careful. They may try to—"

Zhukov waved him off. "Stop worrying, Yuri. These Israelis aren't suicidal."

"No not us, General; I hope you and your men feel the same," Ziki assured him. "Just come over here and take a look at this one's mouth." Ziki gestured towards Jonas Kasich, number 8, the Nazi who had at first refused to take his pill. Kasich's eyes widened at the gesture.

"What about his mouth?"

"You'll see, General."

In Hebrew Ziki said to Joel, "*All ha-pkudah shelli, bseder.* When I say..." Joel raised an eyebrow in acknowledgement.

Zhukov followed Ziki over to Kasich. "So what's so interesting about the mouth of this ugly little German? Okay, *efne deinen mundt sweinhunt nazi sheiss, und mach schnell,*" Zhukov barked at Kasich.

The general moved even closer. "You've got to take a close look, General, at what's in there."

Kasich' legs were shackled but the prisoner's hands were free, he somehow got hold on the airplane of a sharp metal bolt, a shank, he waited for Zhukov to get closer. Kasich saw Joel's hand move to the remote control device. Sweat poured down his brow, he opened his mouth. He made a sudden motion with his armed hand towards Zhukov.

"He sure looks uncomfort...—" With a loud thud of an explosion, the German's stomach and chest tore open and spewed  its contents onto Zhukov, splattering onto the muddy ground around them. Zhukov fell over on his behind with the shock.

...All hell broke loose. Petrovsky was now on top of Ziki with a Makarov pistol pressed into his jaw. Each of Ziki's Golani had six or seven AK-47s pointed in their faces but they still held onto their Galil machine guns cocked with a round in the chamber set on the ready for fire, pointing at the Russians. Ziki had both hands raised in the air as another put a pistol to the back of his head. The prisoners instinctively cringed in surprise and fear, though no one seemed to be paying them much attention. And everywhere the unintelligible, confused swearing in Russian filled the air.

Slowly, through the multitude of voices rose a loud and uproarious laughter. The Russian shouting quickly died down as they recognized the source of the mirth.

Zhukov, sitting in the mud and covered in the blood and guts of the dead Nazi, was nearly hysterical with a loud laughter. With surprising control, looking in Ziki's direction though, he let out a great sigh and barked with annoyance.

"Over here, Commander, don't just stand there—help me up." Confused, but again passive, Maximov and Petrovsky lowered their pistols as they stared, perplexed, at their commanding officer.

Ziki then walked over to Zhukov, leaned over, and stretched out his arm. The Russian grabbed Ziki's forearm with surprising strength and pulled himself up.

"Look at this shit," he bellowed, brushing the chunks of flesh and guts off of his uniform. " You could have just told me he had a bomb in him."

"Well," Ziki said, "you might not have believed me, and I thought you might appreciate the surprise."

"You may be right," Zhukov grinned. "Do the rest of them, hmm...?" he gestured towards the scientists, "have stomach problems like this one inside?"

"General," Ziki said, "if you try to take them, I'll blow them all to hell. If you somehow kill all of us here, my men on the plane can set off the charges remotely and if not them then the outside snipers that are out there can do it...... Oh, and in case you're curious, if the plane is destroyed, the charges inside the Nazis go off automatically."

Zhukov smiled warmly, looked at Ziki with admiration; he now put his arm around Ziki's shoulders.

"I like this boy...**Now you're dealing like a Russian!** I think you also saved my life. All right, you've convinced me, I think we'll make a deal." For the first time Zhukov offered his hand to Ziki. Though it was covered in blood and grime, Ziki knew that such an offer was rarely made and always earned. He shook it with a firm handshake immediately.

"And, General, I have your word of honor, right?"

"You have earned it, my young Israeli friend." He looked at Ziki with new respect. "Yes, you have my word of honor."

"*Spasiva,* Generalissimo Zhukov." Ziki backed up one step, stood up straight and in attention, and raised his hand in a brisk salute to the General. Zhukov saluted back.

"Come with me now, Commander."

"Yes Sir, just one moment."

"Captain," he ordered Joel, " release control of our cargo to General Petrovsky."

"When, Commander?" Joel responded.

"Right now and without conditions." Ziki intentionally gave the order in German so that Zhukov would understand.

"Yes, Sir."

Zhukov had on his face a look of quiet admiration for this young Israeli Commander. "Now you are my guest, Commander."

**"Come on," Zhukov said, motioning towards the main building.** "I'm gonna get this shit you put on me cleaned off, and then we'll get on to some eating and drinking Russian style. I'll show you real Russian hospitality. What are you looking at? He barked at Petrovsky, this man saved my life."

Ziki followed the disgusting-looking, but impressed general across the mud and up the brick steps. "Were you really going to...?" he trailed off.

"Of course I wasn't," Zhukov assured him, as if the whole thing had been his idea of a joke. The guard at the door opened it for him, but looked incredulous at the great general's appearance. Ziki winked at him.

"General, I need to get going…"

"I won't hear of it, you are staying right here….*harasho tovaresh Comrade, Ziki.* You are not going to insult me, are you?"

"No, no General, but…."

"No but, I'll cover with your superiors; they know if I get insulted I'm like a Russian bear in Siberia. You don't want to see that, do you?"

"No, no I don't but…."

"I had a visit in Moscow with your General Moshe Levi; I like him but for a tall man he cannot hold his Vodka. Usually you Israelis don't know how to drink. A man must know how to drink, here is yours, Comrade Ziki…..Let's see what you're made of."

Ziki remembered his grandmother's saying, "Drink in—truth out," so there could be a lot of value in hanging around Zhukov for a while; besides there wasn't much choice.

"What kind of a name is Ziki, ha..ha…. *nazdrovia."*

*"Nazdrovia* to you, General, and just so you know, only my friends call me Ziki, it's a nick name."

"Only your friends, hmm? Maybe we will become friends: I'm almost beginning to like you, Commander, even though you almost killed me and spilled shit Nazi guts all over me."

"What about yours? Where did you get Zhukov, what kind of name is that? Ha… "

"It is Russian nobility name."

"No, no, I know that your parents were farmers."

"Yes, and that is Russian nobility." By now they had both had a few vodkas, Ziki trying to hold his own with this bottomless Russian bear. There was no way he could stand with him drink for drink. The Russian must have been drinking since childhood. Ziki wondered if the large potted plant next to him would show signs of being drunk, because that's where as many vodkas as he could get away with— without Zhukov seeing him do it—ended up.

"I have to take a piss; you do know what that is, don't you?—They do piss in Israel, don't they?

"Yeah, they do, General."

*"Harasho,* Okay then that's where I'm going."

After a few minutes of silent waiting with Petrovsky, Maximov, and the other wary-looking Soviet brass and their underlings back in the reception room where busy bees in large numbers had now converted it into a Russian style banquet room, Ziki was again joined by Zhukov.

"I said don't start without me," the general said as he walked in, "but I didn't mean just sit on your asses staring at each other." The other officers automatically parted as he moved through the room, seemingly arbitrarily finding his seat. "Lejtenant," he barked, " have the cooks bring the food in.

"Where are your men? Call them all in. I hope you are not still worried, Comrade Ziki, because if you are that would be an insult to me after I gave you my word of honor and with it I offered my friendship."

"No General, I already took the liberty and asked some of them to come in."

"*Harasho,* good, now we have a Russian feast..... We did good today, you and me, my young friend." He raised another shot of Vodka and poured Ziki one more. "*Nazdrovia,* and I can tell you now; there was and is, a lot more at stake and on the table than the stinking Nazi scientists."

I knew it, Ziki thought to himself, but nodded his head acknowledging Zhukov playing as if he knew all that was behind the scenes. Those bastards in Tel-Aviv sent him into the grizzly bear's den and did not tell him all there was to know.

"*Dah,* caviar and vodka, there is nothing better." The caviar display was spectacular: a bed of chopped eggs and the Beluga caviar was artfully arranged in a hammer and sickle design.

"General—"Ziki began, "talk to me about your meeting with our General Levi in Moscow."

"Good," Zhukov interrupted, sitting down now. "We'll have lots of time to talk about the details. Right now, I need another drink and so do you."

There was no way out of the drinking, and the plant next to Ziki was getting awfully soggy and for sure drunk; just don't let Zhukov catch him pouring it in there, he thought. The other Russians in the room knew that he was pouring as many of his drinks into the plant as he could and some winked at him and didn't say anything. Must be that instinct of man to pull for the underdog; they all knew that Ziki was no drinking match with Zhukov.

The sheer amount and variety of food that was quickly brought in not only put to shame even the most extravagant dinners thrown on Israeli military bases; it likely beat out all but the most momentous high state functions. Thus began for Ziki a gauntlet of sensory indulgence that was unmatched in volume. The eating was heavy, since there seemed to be no real rush on anyone's part to finish; it could be handled and now with some drinks in him Ziki begun to relax and maybe even enjoy the company of his famous host.

Courses were brought in as room on the table was made available and not on any timetable. Ziki quickly realized that he would not be able to keep pace with even the smallest Russians' drinking, and Zhukov, who made a point of refilling Ziki's glass whenever it got empty—or even when it wasn't—was hardly the smallest Russian. The Vodka itself was good and real Russian, who knows what proof; in the amounts the two dozen or so officers and some of their assistants were drinking, this could put a dent in the Red Army's coffers.

After a course or two of God knows what, and as many drinks as would ordinarily cause Ziki to cork the bottle and stumble to bed, Zhukov, who showed absolutely no sign of being affected, despite drinking much more than the others it seemed, called in his next surprise. He motioned to the officer managing the service and whispered something in Russian in the young lieutenant's ear that Ziki could not catch. While this was going on he again made another of many deposits of vodka in the large potted plant on the floor behind his seat.

"Bottoms up, Gavriella," Ziki said.

"What?" asked Zukov, turning back to him.

"Sorry," Ziki replied, shaking his head a bit to keep the cobwebs out, "I didn't mean to say that out loud."

Zhukov laughed heartily at this. "Come on, Commander," my grandson puts away more than this before getting on the tractor in the morning.

"General," Ziki responded, "If a grandson of yours is driving a tractor, I'm Lenin's long lost nephew."

"You cynical capitalist," Zhukov chastised, "You've got to earn your keep in Russia today, there's no favoritism for my offspring. And, besides—oh wait," he stopped, seeing the doors swing open to allow a small band to shuffle in nervously. "You're going to like this, my Israeli Commander young friend."

"Are they going to serenade us, General?" Ziki asked before stuffing a forkful of stuffed cabbage-*galubshi ,*followed by a *piroshky* in his mouth.

"Music is good for digestion, but there's more than just music.  Wait and see."

Ziki was not interested in the talents of a Soviet Army band, but he feigned interest.  The uniformed 10-piece started up an up-beat Volga, volga, but somewhat melancholy, tune.  Ziki nodded his head and smiled for show.  Zhukov slapped his shoulder and then pointed to the doors as if anticipating something even greater. After a few bars, four young men in form-fitting pants came dancing out, in that uniquely Russian knee bending way, from the kitchen doors and proceeded to march up, bouncing up and down as they went, to the center of the room in front of Zhukov and Ziki and even up on some empty tables.  Their dance fit the music, and they were like circus acrobats—their thighs must be like iron to do this stuff, Ziki mused—but it was hardly worth the excitement the old general seemed to exhibit.

As the song finished, Zhukov grinned and boastfully asked Ziki, "Eh, what do you think of that?"

"I don't know General, the food is great…."

"Yes."

"The Vodka is good…"

"Yes comrade Ziki?"

"The caviar is really good…."

"Yes…but what?" Ziki and Zhukov shouted over the music.

"Well General they're a little fagoty, the dancers in tights"

"What did you say?" Zhukov's face redder than just from the vodka. "This is mother Russia that you see. You are one lucky Jew that you are my guest, what in hell do you have in Jerusalem?"

"Well General, not exactly in Jerusalem, Jerusalem is a little to holly for men like us, but in Tel-Aviv we have girls dancing on tables not men in tights."

"You know, your balls are bigger than your brain, but I must admit you have a point there." The General gets up and shouts to Maximov. "Yuri, send into Berlin and have them bring those dancers we had here for General's Zlotsky's divorce party, and some of those girls that helped all of us, you understand me?"

"Yes General, I'll take care of it."

"Bring many."

"Yes sir."

"Bring the good looking ones."

"Yes Sir I will."

You don't have that in your little country. He pointed at the caviar."

"Bah!" Ziki scoffed, his mouth clearly unhinged by the vodka, "I am impressed by the caviar.."

Zhukov roared with laughter. "I like you even better now! I think you deserve some women, but first the caviar." Without waiting to be told in so many words, the servers brought forth a dozen buckets of caviar.

"There must be a lot of broken-hearted mother sturgeon," Ziki observed at the entrance of so many fish eggs.

"What do you mean?" Zhukov asked indignantly, "You don't take the eggs after they've been laid; you cut it right out of them."

Ziki shook his head. "I know, I know, I was joking."

"Joking?" Zhukov asked, scraping his bread across the top of the caviar, "Maximov, tell him how the jokes work around here."

Maximov was across the room, but wisely kept an ear out for his commanding officer's voice at all times, even less than sober ones. "If Mareshal Zhukov doesn't find it funny," he answered, "It's no joke."

Zhukov laughed and slapped Ziki's back as Ziki took the opportunity to not-so-accidentally spill some of his vodka. "That's alright," he said, "You're not Russian, so I give you permission to make bad jokes."

"That's nice General," Ziki smiled back. The mention of cutting caviar out of the fish rubbed Ziki's mind the wrong way. He'd better make sure nobody was cutting anything out of his scientists. "And now," he said, shifting his chair back and then standing, "I'm also going to take a piss."

"What do I care," Zhukov replied, "You need somebody to hold it for you? I'll send one of the girls if you can hold it until they arrive?"

Ziki patted Zhukov's back as he crossed behind him to get to the door, "That's alright. I can manage."

He made his way around a few increasingly unbuttoned and red-faced Russian officers and to the main double doors at the front of the room. He asked one of the door guards for directions and made his way to the special guest lavatory. He passed one of the dancers in the hallway and could scarcely keep himself from laughing. The vodka was clearly taking its toll. The dancer didn't seem to notice, politely doffing his cap and walking by. Passing by a window, Ziki saw that nightfall had come and gone without his noticing it, as the dining room was peculiarly placed without sight of the outside.

And perhaps his expectations were a little high, but the utilitarian restroom was hardly what he expected Gorbachov relieving himself in. It was clean, but not plush. Luckily there was no towel attendant. After checking under all the stall doors for legs, Ziki walked by the three sinks, turning them all on full blast. He splashed some water on his face, trying in vain to counteract the effects of the alcohol his liver was desperately trying to break down. He wiped his face with a towel, and then sat down on the ground under the sink.

"Joel, this is Ziki," he said, speaking quietly into the receiver in his jacket. He took the small speaker from behind his collar and placed it into his ear.

After a few moments, he heard Joel. "This is Joel. I read you, but there seems to be a lot of background noise."

"What's your status?"

"Seems to be fine. They haven't tried anything funny. They brought us some food, it probably isn't what you're eating, but it's not drugged. I had one of the Russian soldiers take a few bites of my food."

"I really don't think they'll try anything, but alert me and the plane if you feel any effects."

"They gave different food to the prisoners. At first, I declined, but it looked pretty bad. There was nothing in it that looked designed to dislodge the explosive devices."

Ziki heard a noise from above, but it was metallic and was probably just some pipes clanking. "Yeah, they'll probably try to give them diarrhea, but it's going to take more than that now that the pills have expanded in them. Anyway, this party doesn't show any sign of stopping, and they keep pouring drinks into me, so I'm probably going to be mentally out of commission for a while. So you're effectively in charge if that happens."

"I understand. No budging, right?"

"Good man. They don't get a single one of those scientists alive until Tel Aviv tells me the deal is done, and I tell you the deal is done, but I think we have a deal with the General. If you've got to take them back to the plane, so be it, I understand."

"Got it."

"Try to get to me with some of those caffeine pills in the aid kit."

"Yes. Hang in there Commander. Out." Ziki removed the speaker from his ear, stood up and turned the faucets off. He started to leave, but realized his bladder really was bursting.

He walked back in to the dining room to find the party if anything even livelier.

"I was just telling the boys," Zhukov bellowed over to him, "The girls are on their way."

"Good to hear, General," Ziki yelled back as he moved across the room. "Where do I stand on the pecking order? As a guest or as the man with the fewest stars on his shoulder in the room?"

"You take first choice," Zhukov deferred as Ziki sat down next to him. "After me, of course!" The room rocked with laughter.

"Yeah, okay but if we get the same one and you go in there first make sure you wash it before you put it in you old bear," laughed Ziki.

Zhukov then put his arm around Ziki and drew him closer, speaking in a much quieter than the earlier banter which had been for the benefit of the entire group.

"Why do you have to contact your friends?" he asked with surprising seriousness, "Don't you trust me?"

Ziki tried to read the general's expression, but couldn't. However, he figured he shouldn't try to hide any more than he already had. "Tell me General, do you really have the toilet bugged or is this just one of your hunches?"

"Never mind how I know, I know. Don't worry about your boys. They'll be very comfortable." He pulled Ziki closer and refilled his glass.

"Well that's good to know, General."

"Here," Zhukov said, pushing the glass into Ziki's already somewhat unsteady hand, "Drink up before the girls get here. Who knows how good looking they'll be?"

Contrary to Ziki's expectations about what the Soviets could drag up in the middle of the night in rural East Germany, the women were great looking. But then, he was probably on, who knows what number vodka by now, and the plant as well. The women came in a wide variety of ages, shapes, and sizes, probably owing to what they could find. Some were clearly hookers, dressed to attract men, but most had on general, tasteful clothes, and a handful even wore something you'd expect at the office. Whatever they're making, Ziki thought, even with the occasional gig for the Russian brass, they could make four or five times as much on the other side.

"What do you think, Commander?" Zhukov asked, "We got German, Polish, Romanian, even Czech I think, right Dagmar?" One of the women smiled and nodded in assent.

"Anything but Romanian," Ziki responded, "That's where my grandmother was from, so it would be a little strange."

"Romanian, eh?" Zhukov asked, with much more meaning than was apparent. "They really did pick the right man for this job."

"I'm not sure what you mean, General."

"Never mind. Who do you like? I'm partial to the blondes myself—call it a weakness from too many American movies." He put his arm around Ziki again, "Hey girls, here's the guest of honor. But watch out, he's a Jew, so you know what that means."

"Help me out, General," Ziki asked, "What does that mean?"

"I don't know. Just scaring the girls, he…he."

"In that case, I'll take the one who looked the least scared," Ziki said, pointing to a brunette on the end.

"Where you from, darling?" Zhukov asked her.

She stepped forward from the crowd, took her cigarette from her mouth, and answered coldly, "Österreich."

Zhukov laughed. "She's definitely the one for you, about the right size, but wait I want to see them dance with us. I'm an old-fashioned man and I hate rushing into things." He took this opportunity to yet again refill Ziki's drink. "So comrade Ziki Barak, is this better than the Red Army male dancers?"

"Much General, but I never told you my full name."

"Mossad is not the only game in town"… "Austria hmm…"

"She's not really from Austria?" Ziki asked, as the girls shuffled to the front of the room as the band began to play again.

"Of course not," Zhukov responded, "She's a German. She thinks if she repeats it enough we'll let her go over to the other side."

"You don't have a sister in Munich, do you?"

"No," said Greta, Ziki's pick who he had not abandoned him even after seeing his awkward dancing. She swung her legs around to the edge of the bed and sitting up, "Why do you ask?"

"No reason," Ziki responded. He rolled over onto his side to face her exposed back. "Don't leave yet but I am sorry, I am involved with someone."

"I know, don't be sorry, we didn't do anything, even when you were drunk you mumbled something about a Gavriella. You kept saying I love you, I love you."

"To you?"

"No, not to me, to this Gavriella whoever she is. A lucky woman—most men would not have refused me."

"And don't worry I am not going to say anything to the Russians that you refused to have sex with me for some woman that is not even here."

"I'm not leaving," she said reaching down into her handbag, "You getting sentimental already? I'm just trying to find a cigarette."

Ziki tiredly motioned over to the chair on which he left his clothes. "Try my jacket over there. There's some American if you want them." She got up and walked over, her body silhouetted against the diffused light passing through the cheap curtain. "My lighter should be in there, too," he said, relaxing onto his back again. "Anyway," he said, as she walked back over to the other side of the bed, "I'm just afraid that when you leave he'll make me start drinking again."

She sat back in bed, propping her back up against the wall with a pillow under it. "He?" she asked.

"Zhukov," Ziki replied, "Are you really Austrian?"

"Will you tell him?" she asked, reaching over to place the cigarette in Ziki's lips long enough for him to take a drag.

"Depends," he said, "Depends on how much he makes me drink."

"I suppose it doesn't matter much," she said, leaning back again.

"He doesn't really believe it."

"The joke is that I'm really Russian."

"I don't get it," Ziki said, turning over to face her again. "You look German, you speak German, and, if you forgive me, you dance like a German." She laughed.

"You'd be surprised," he said.

"Well not with men," she smiled.

She put out her cigarette…

**Ziki was awakened for breakfast at 6am sharp.** A junior officer gently tapped him on the shoulder, provoking the always-bewildering experience of waking up in a totally unfamiliar place. Greta was long gone by then, as was the rest of his pack of Marlboros. He was led onto the veranda where Zhukov, in full uniform, was sitting down to breakfast, except that Ziki soon discovered that "breakfast" for the great general meant eggs and more vodka.

"A little of the hair of the dog that bit you, eh General?" Asked Ziki, sitting in the only empty seat.

"I was bit by no dog," Zhukov responded without looking up.

"What I meant was—"

"I know the phrase," Zhukov smiled, passing the serving tray of eggs and then the bottle to Ziki, "But you have to be bad to vodka for it to bite you. Love it, cherish it, and like a good woman it will treat you right."

"That's very good advice," Ziki smiled, scraping some eggs onto his plate." Any chance of my getting some orange juice?" he asked to no one in particular.

"Ah, American screwdrivers," Zhukov said, "Why not? Dimitri, bring us some orange juice."

"So General," Ziki said carefully, sensing Zhukov to be in a compliant mood, we've had the celebration, let's talk about your end of the deal?"

"Who said the celebration was over? Are you tired of our company, Commander?"

"Not at all," Ziki smiled back, "But my men are probably getting tired of the company of those Nazis."

"They're more than free to get back on the plane and go home. I'm told the plane has been refueled and is cleared for departure whenever you like," Zhukov offered.

"That's very generous," Ziki said. A server handed him a glass of orange juice, which he made a clear show of correcting with a healthy shot of vodka.

"Speaking of generous," Zhukov said, "What about my offer?"

"Your offer?" Ziki asked quizzically. Was he talking about letting the plane go again?

"To come work for me. An apartment in the center of Moscow and a vacation cottage in the mountains... What? Did you think I was joking?" Zhukov asked, shoving some eggs in his mouth, "Maximov, tell him the policy on—"

"I heard the policy on joking," Ziki said, "But I'm happy where I am, General."

"What do they pay you?" Zhukov asked, "If you don't mind my asking."

Ziki took a chance. "More than General Petrovsky," he said.

Petrovsky, who had seemed in something of a coma during much of the conversation, was incensed. "How dare you, you *pizduk Jidan,* Jew!" He thundered over to Ziki, only to be restrained by the firm interposition of Zhukov's forearm.

"That's enough, Grigory," Zhukov said, "Sit down. Who knows? The Commander may be right."

Petrovsky was still enraged, but did not defy his boss. Petulantly he asked, "How does the Jew know how much I am paid?"

"General Petrovksy," said Ziki flatly, "I know that you have a house in the Crimea registered under the name VS Trubin. I know that you arranged for your daughter to be secretly treated for leukemia in a Swiss hospital because of your fears of Russian doctors' incompetence." Petrovsky's already red faced swelled with anger. Still, Ziki continued, "I know about your troops breaking the Baikonur miner's strike back. I know how much you are paid." Petrovsky was almost twitching with rage. "And moreover, General Petrovsky, I know that you are a lifelong anti-Semite, so I have no compunction about shaming you in front of your officers."

Petrovsky bolted up, his arms and legs stiff with anger. "Permission to kill this impudent son of a *pizduk* right now, Comrade Generalisimo Zhukov?"

Zhukov shook his head, "Permission denied. This man saved my life. Calm yourself, my friend. That's an order."

Petrovsky could not be reconciled. "Permission" his mouth frothed with a desperate attempt to restrain himself "to…*promudobl'adsksya pizdopro'evina…*" he grumbled to himself walking away from the table and out towards where some soldiers were drilling.

"Oh," Zhukov sighed, "I think Petrovsky's going to take his rage out on someone, but you" he said, pointing to Ziki, "are to blame for some young man's pain that is about to occur."

Ziki laughed, "I kicked the dog."

Zhukov leaned towards him. "Don't get so cocky. You kicked a dog that would tear you to pieces if I didn't have him on a chain. But," he conceded, "I must admit that I am impressed with your country's intelligence…providing it's all true of course. I think the mining thing made the papers, so that's nothing."

Ziki smiled, "The papers you read, General, but not the ones the Russian public reads."

"Well," he laughed, "what do journalists know? I still haven't changed your mind, eh?"

"No, I'm sorry."

Zhukov shrugged, "Let's go look at some tanks."

Ziki was surprised, "What?"

"The new T-64s. Come on," he said standing, "It's always good for digestion to take a walk after a big breakfast."

"But I haven't finished…my…" Zhukov walked off without him. Ziki stood up and threw down his napkin, all to the amusement of the other dining officers.

**Ziki had no way of knowing.** He would spend the next two days drinking, carousing, and killing time with the general, as his men anxiously waited at the cargo plane. He figured that Zhukov's plan was to wait for the Nazis to pass the bombs through their system, but after a full day when it was clear that the devices were intentionally obstructed, the old general seemed not to mind. Indeed, for one reason or another, Zhukov seemed to be prolonging Ziki's stay out of a subtle kind of affection or exchanging information each man thinking that he is outsmarting the other while drinking and eating.

The wild party of the first night gave way into more sober and relaxed events, with long discussions of military strategy, the role of the soldier in an increasingly political world, and life in general. Ziki was almost sad when it became clear the whole thing was to come to an end.

The two sat alone in Zhukov's office, a half-empty bottle of vodka between them. Zhukov was slumped in an uncomfortable looking wooden chair, while Ziki leaned back in the leather one. "All right," said Zhukov somewhat glumly, "We can end the charade. I appreciate your patience."

Ziki smiled, though he was puzzled and almost concerned at the now very old looking man's dejected air. "What charade?"

"You've been more than kind to play along with this little standoff—me trying to keep you here until my men figure out a way to disarm the devices in those Nazis—and pump you for intelligence information, but, of course, we both know it's all pretty much beside the point, don't we?"

Ziki nodded reassuringly, "I didn't want to spoil the fun earlier, General, but yes it does seem an excessive amount of time and energy for something so miniscule, especially for someone as important as yourself."

Zhukov smiled in a distant way. "I'm not so important anymore. At least not noticeably. To those politician bastards I've been dead for years. But when I'm truly gone it will be as if the Volga itself is gone... They take me too much for granted... Still," he laughed to himself, sitting up in his chair and reaching for his glass, "I've got this deal with you on them."

"They don't know?"

"You know the KGB used to be under military command?" Zhukov dodged. "You can trust military men, we're in for life. Every day you turn around—" he snapped, "And there's another comrade politician in charge. They don't trust the military anymore in Russia. You know you probably know more about your country's foreign policy decisions than I do at mine."

Ziki shrugged.

"Like this whole deal. You know what I'm giving you in return for the scientists, don't you?"

"It was somewhat hard to believe," Ziki bluffed, "I'd like to hear it from you."

Luckily Zhukov had laid off forcing Ziki to drink and was more affected by the vodka at this point. "It's true. You're going to Romania. The whole thing has been set up."

"Romania," Ziki said. Ahh....yes "

"It is hard for me to believe I'd end up back there." Ziki bluffed as if he knew.

"Well," said Zhukov, "I'd prefer if the MiGs were assembled at home, but you have to make political concessions to your allies. The Romania economy wouldn't exist without Red Army contracts."

Not by choice, Ziki thought, but this was too important a conversation to get sidetracked with gentle prods at Communism. "We're talking about the new

MiGs, right?" he asked.

"Of course the new MiGs. What kind of benefit would it be to your country to destroy all the mothballed Arab MiGs?"

Ziki opened his hands in a gesture of deference. "You're right, you're right. Again, I couldn't quite believe the whole thing was true."

Zhukov offered his hand. "You have my word." Ziki quickly seized the hand and shook it firmly again. Zhukov continued. "In return for getting the scientists for us, not to mention the other thing, I assure you that the small *'bugs,'* homing devices, 600 of them that are going to Egypt alone, mind you, will be operational after you insert them in the MiGs headed for Iran, Syria, Iraq, Libya and Egypt."

Ziki's mind raced. They'd stab their own surrogates in the back this strongly for a few lousy scientists? Naww… Allowing Israel to install homing devices in the latest most modern planes on the planet? Those that are going to be delivered to the Iranian and Arab air forces? Allowing the Israeli pilots to hone in on them and maybe, be able to destroy them on the ground before take off like sitting ducks? The scientists must truly be worthless compared to this "other thing." But in God's name what's that? Something big enough to make Zhukov consider permanently alienating their oil-rich friends.

"How will you trust us to keep our end of the deal on the 'other thing'?" Ziki tried to lead.

"The same way we knew they were there in the first place. And you Commander Barak will give me your word of honor as I gave mine."

"We will agree here and now not to attack you directly with our Red Army as your spies have already heard, and you will remove and withdraw from within range of the Soviet Union the nuclear tipped **Jericho** missiles. I will hold you personally responsible for it. You will see to it that your government honors your word. Do you have the authority Commander to make such a commitment?"

Ziki did not yet answer. "I really can't talk about details, but believe me, we know about each and every nuke you've positioned that's being pointed at us by your little country on those Jericho missiles.

I don't want to have to keep one eye open at night on your country. It is bad enough that we have to worry about the Imperialist Capitalist Americans, and NATO and Western Europe—You know the fucking French have nuclear missiles? –To *pizduk* China, and now you pipsqueaks…" He shook his head, "Chinese *khokols*! As if we needed any more threats in our own backyard…Some fucking politician over there in your country gets nervous, your Jericho's are pointed at us—within reach of Moscow, and… Puff."

"Yes, Commander I heard…South Africa, uranium, the Indian Ocean, double thermo nuclear tests—The American's Vela satellite system and… ***"The Samson Option."***

"I respect that, Commander. You may have given me headaches, but I have nothing but respect for you and your uppity little country."

Ziki started to speak, but Zhukov shushed him with a raised hand. "And, yes, we may never see eye to eye, but these two days have been a big treat for me. And trust me, son, praise from Zhukov does not come easily. I will consider you as one of my friends."

Ziki looked into the general's eyes for a moment, trying to formulate an appropriately meaningful response. But Zhukov was not one for sentimentality; he stood up and walked to the door.

**Ziki could not remain passively diplomatic much longer.** "It is an honor General, and I would like to consider you as one of my friends. I hope you forgive me General but I must say this to you." Ziki paused and looked fiercely at Zhukov.

"You think you are the ones surrounded by enemies, General? We are a mere 5 million people in my country and we are faced with the threat of extinction from 13 Arab countries surrounding our borders and their population of 300 million Arabs, and in addition to that, you, one of the two superpowers, think they need your help? Now we hear the threat of direct invasion by the Soviet Red Army?"

Ziki understood what he had really known all along. The MiGs bugging would be offered in exchange for Israel removing its nuclear missiles from within range of the Russians that were poised towards Moscow The Nazis were just the cover red herring for the deal and something perhaps to hold over the Arabs if they found out about the betrayal.

"We heard things General…We heard that you, the Soviet Union would attack us directly with the Red Army in the next war." If we go down, General, this time we're not going to do it quietly—We will take you with us."

Zhukov was quiet for a moment. "You Israelis really are serious about this 'Samson option," aren't you?"

Ziki had his own gut instinct, but could not believe that the top brass thought any other way. "Have you read your Old Testament General?"

Zhukov smiled, "Not in a while. But I seem to remember the gist of it."

Ziki nodded, "Good. Well Samson back then didn't mess around. And neither do we."

Zhukov shrugged. "That's what I thought. You will, of course, keep this to yourself—"

"Of course," Ziki interjected.

"—but your country is not taken entirely seriously by a number of my high-ranking countrymen. Some are even convinced that the underwater testing business with yourselves and South Africa, as well as all the missiles, is all being underwritten and controlled by the Americans. And that the Americans would not allow a retaliatory nuclear strike for something as petty and small as Russians invading Israel. After all, they did the same thing in Vietnam and did not give Ho Chi Minh the opportunity to nuke anybody."

"Something that small?" A determined look covered Ziki's face. "With all due respect, General, let those countrymen of yours know that we mean business, and we don't have to ask the Americans or anyone else for permission."

"Well my young Israeli friend you mentioned the Americans."

"Yes…"

"Don't forget that they, the Americans used their own army, air force and navy along side the South Vietnamese against North Vietnam and did the same thing with their army in Korea against the North."

"Yes, they did, what is your point General?"

"Why would you be so surprised that we, Russia would act as they did against you?"

"Point taken General, and you just might have, but the North Vietnamese and the North Koreans did not have the "*Samson's Option…*"

Zhukov smiled at Ziki's indignant attitude. He continued, ignoring Ziki's nuclear threat. "Do they, or you, think we don't know about everything that Walters is up to? With that PLO deal and the oil interests, "Everything we've got, we had to work and scrap and fight for."

Ziki paused and in a calm cold tone while looking Zhukov in the eyes, spat out.

"The nuclear tipped Jericho missiles can reach Moscow and most of your cities but we are not crazy General, we don't want to die in a war with a Super Power."

"What the hell then were your politicians thinking Commander positioning those within range?"

"Well, General we intercepted the Kremlin and General Petrovsky's counsel to your politicians that you intend to attack us with Red Army troops and the Soviet navy to support the Arabs…Believe me General that if you do that we will use the Jericho's and the countdown for *Samson Option* will be activated… From that there is no turning back."

"I do not doubt it, Commander." Zhukov smiled, "This is the most excited I've seen you. However, my political superiors do not have the advantage of speaking to you in person and instead rely on their perceived behavior of your people. But I believe you and take your word, as you take mine."

Spent from his tirade, Ziki nodded politely. Zhukov paused for a moment and regained his dominant air.

"So I have your word, and that of your government that everything will be pulled back?" Zhukov asked, "The Jericho nuclear tipped missiles near Izmit, and all four, yes we know about them, diesel subs in the Black Sea. All of them will be pulled out of range?"

"You have my word General as I do yours…And my government will honor it, at least as long as I am alive. You will see to it that your Kremlin politicians remove your naval fleet away from our shores and no Red Army invasion threat is in sight… Or in the works?"

"Everything outlined will be followed through," he said.

"Good, we have a deal and you get a bonus with the little buzz... buzz's on the MiG's" said Zhukov, leaning over towards Ziki, putting his hand on the younger man's shoulder. "I respect you, Commander. And now a little insurance from Zhukov-listen carefully. If anything were to happen to me or you cannot reach me there are two names that will honor my promise to you and you to them, remember them well, they are rising stars in history. The first is Michael Gorbachov, he is a politician, but he is my friend and you can trust him to honor my word, the second is young and KGB-Vladimir Putin. You may give me headaches, but I have nothing but respect for you and your uppity little country."

"By the way why are the missiles named Jericho? "

"The walls falling, Jericho."

"One more thing, I have already arranged everything for you in Romania, but I regret to tell you that you have to that job in person, I know it is work that you would ordinarily leave to subordinates; it has to be done by you personally."

"I understand."

"Call your people. Tell them I'm fulfilling my end of the deal... Then get back on the plane." Ziki walked through the door and then hesitated, turning around. Zhukov leaned against the heavy birch door, but frowned, albeit somewhat comically at Ziki's hesitance. He slapped his oversized dress uniform hat on his head, and shut the door.

Ziki never saw Zhukov again. After making as secure a phone call as he could manage, via an encoded line on the plane, he returned to the tarmac only to see his eight Golani men lined up with Maximov behind them. The Russian told Ziki that Zhukov was indisposed with other matters and could not see them off, though he sends his regards. Ziki nodded, understanding, and boarded the refueled cargo plane.

# Chapter 54

### Romania

**Ziki's feet touched down with a thud on the ground.** Carrying his forward momentum, he half-skipped half-jogged a few meters as his parachute collapsed behind him. Unfortunately, the clay-heavy ground was wetter than his desert training landings. His left foot stepped and slid forward, sending his whole body collapsing sideways and dragging forwards at an uncomfortable speed. After finally coming to stop, he lay belly-down on the earth for a moment. Welcome to Romania, he thought, wiping the mud from his face.

He quickly gathered and packed his chute. The sun had just set, but there was still some light—enough, hopefully for Ziki to find his large duffel bag which had dropped somewhere in the wheat field behind him. His chute bag cleverly designed, or mis-designed, to resemble a cheap daypack that a laborer in an Eastern Bloc country might carry. His boots, instead of the high quality jump boots he was used to, were 50s-era Romanian army surplus, heavily worn. He pulled his wool cap out of the pack and tucked it on his head.

He looked the part, now he just hoped his accent held up. A few minutes walk brought Ziki to the fence separating the fallow field in which he landed from the wheat field. Seeing no one, he cavalierly hopped the fence and strode through the waist-high winter wheat. The air was cool and pleasant. Ziki enjoyed for a moment the peaceful solitude.

He walked deeper into the field, running his hand on the top of the wheat stalks. He could tell already it was going to be a pain finding this bag in the high wheat, but somehow he wasn't concerned. Though he was deep undercover, no one, had any reason to be looking for anybody in Romania. On second thought; if Zhukov's office leaked somehow? Who knows? He had hope that if something went amiss, Zhukov—might bail him out. Maybe!

A distant farmhouse puffed dark smoke against the still-illuminated western sky. The smell of *mamaliga* and *carnati* wafted in the air, reminding him instantly of his grandmother's kitchen.

It was too faint to tell exactly what it was. Smell is the sense most closely linked to memory and its trigger of childhood memories was subconscious. He now reached what seemed to him to be the geometric center of the field, the target for which he aimed when dropping the bag. He turned 360 degrees, looking for the patch of crushed wheat that would show the bag's location. He saw nothing; it was getting darker by the minute.

He sighed and started walking northeast; it was the direction the plane was flying when he dropped it. He figured his aim was better than his timing so it must be somewhere along the northeast-southwest axis. He trudged a few yards forward, making a zigzag as he went. As he strolled along, he realized that his whole stay here would be a lot like this search for the bag, long, boring, and lonely. Oh well, he thought, the payoff will be amazing. Suddenly—

*"Stai—cine este acolo? Stay pe loc sau trag* …Stop—or I shoot!" Bellowed a voice, in Romanian.

Ziki froze. He slowly turned his body and head towards the voice. A short, stocky farmer stood about 50 meters to his left with an ancient rifle tipped back on his shoulder. Ziki judged the breech-loader as pre-World War two, but, he figured, accurate enough in the hands of someone with practice.

The farmer walked forward. " *Ce faci acolo pe pamantul meu?* What are you doing walking through my field? *Strada este pe jos.* The road's just down there," he said, gesturing back behind the farmhouse. "*Am de ajuns probleme cu vulturi, iesi de aici,* I get enough trouble with crows, get out of here."

Ziki took off his hat. "*Cu respect Domnule*, I don't mean any disrespect," he said, bowing his head just a little. "*Fiul meu a pierdut ceva pe aicea*—my son ran off and left something of mine in this field. *Am venit sa caut pachetul,* I came down to look for it."

The farmer walked even closer, though he did not raise the gun. *"Fiul tau?* Your son? *Nu locuiesti pe aici.* You don't live around here. *Ce ai pierdtut?* What did you lose?"

"My son and I were traveling through, on our way to Timishoara," Ziki said politely, "We were camped up the road a ways and my son ran off with a bag of mine. ."

"He said he left it out here."

*Yesi de aicia.* Get out of my field," the farmer said, gesturing back towards the road with the butt of his rifle.

" *Va rog frumos.* Please," Ziki pleaded, "I only need-"

"No," The farmer insisted, moving towards Ziki with his left hand spread out as if he was herding a sheep.

Ziki reluctantly complied, shuffling in the direction of the road. Little did this farmer know, with his ancient rifle he was making himself a major obstacle to the security of a nation thousands of miles away. After following him for a few meters, the farmer halted. Ziki turned his head as he walked down to the road, and the farmer waved, shaking his head. Ziki could just as soon have disarmed him, but he figured that attacking a man who was defending his own property was hardly the proper tack in a new country run by the *Jandarmerie*. Instead, he sighed again, he would have to wait for darkness and crawl for the darn thing…

" *Numele….?* Name?" The large foreman asked.

" Zigu Popescu," Ziki replied. *"Sunt trimis in locul  muncitorul bolnav.* I was sent as the replacement for the sick guy."

*"Ah, da"* the foreman said, looking at his clipboard. He then looked over to his left towards the Russian political officer leaning against the wall. The Russian, a thin, gaunt man, nodded his head. *"Harasho.* Alright."

The foreman slapped the clipboard down on his desk, "You can start work tomorrow. You'll find a punch card with your name on it over there. Absolutely no smoking on the factory floor. This is not only a termination offense, but a prosecutable offense. Shifts and breaks are staggered. You will start at 7:30. We'll have a pair of overalls for you when you get here." He abruptly turned away from the small desk near the employee entrance.

Ziki looked around the high-ceilinged factory. Even though the building he stood in was only a small part of the much larger Soviet MiG21- assembly factory complex, it seemed far grander than anything Romania could have built before Soviet occupation, not that the Romanian workers seemed very excited about it.

A large segment of the MiG 21 undercarriage was assembled here, including the big hollow screw into which Ziki would insert the self-powered homing device. The Russian political officer was clearly informed of Ziki's importance but had no idea of exactly what he would be doing; he glared contemptuously and jealously at him as soon as he entered.

Smiling at him, Ziki turned and walked out, pocketing his Romanian identification card, which the foreman had not even bothered to ask for. He returned by foot to the small, one room uncomfortable apartment which Zhukov's men had arranged for him. The building seemed to be owned by the Soviets, and he had no neighbors he ever saw. He wasn't sure what the building was used for, the KGB tended to indulge in former manors and palaces for their local headquarters. But, then, he didn't think that  the KGB had approved of Zhukov's operation.

The next couple of days proved to be a long and boring process. He arrived at work promptly and spoke to no one. Every day he brought in his sack stuffed with homing devices and was questioned by no one. Another of Ziki's men had parachuted in at the same time and did the same thing in another part of the factory, but Ziki was not to have any kind of contact with him unless either ran into trouble. The women at the factory were uniformly drab, and the ones who might have been attractive seemed to have all their charisma drained from them, somewhat similar, he thought, to the romantic country in which they lived and its stultification under communism. He had no contact with anyone in Israel, besides the one phone call he made to a pre-arranged Romanian local number to inform them of his arrival and initial success.

So, when he wasn't working, Ziki could only be found in public when he was out eating, or the night he allowed himself to visit a local *curciuma,* tavern. It was full, though hardly boisterous, most quietly watching a small black and white television play taped soccer matches. Most of the men at the *curciuma's*  were barely distinguishable from the men he worked alongside, and some, were the very same men.

Ziki was sitting in the corner facing away from the television and drinking some surprisingly decent Romanian wine. He was part of the way through a Romanian novel he was trudging through, which he had picked up in a local shop. It was diverting enough, and a good opportunity for Ziki to sharpen and update his language skills.

When the stranger sat down across from him at the table, it was not too much of a surprise, since the bar was especially crowded that night. Soccer, Romania was playing Hungary for some sort of Eastern Bloc bragging rights. Ziki did not overtly look up, he used his peripheral vision. To his confusion, the stranger gazed directly at him, with an uncomfortably confident smirk on his face. Ziki slowly marked his place in the book by bending down the corner of one page and set the book down. He returned the gaze of the stranger; the man was neatly dressed, they were probably his best clothes. Ziki took a sip and nodded at him.

The man smiled even wider. "You don't know who I am, do you?"

Ziki shrugged, "You probably have me confused with someone else."

The man laughed, but Ziki still couldn't place his face. "Well, I know you, friend."

"I don't know you. But since you say you know me, let me buy you a drink."

The man seemed surprised at his generosity. "I could not accept such a thing, from a man who must travel along country roads on foot with his young son."

Ziki immediately placed him—the farmer who wouldn't budge. "Now I know you," he smiled. He was silently overjoyed at the innocuous ending to the mystery. So mundane and slow was the work that, he had gotten bored in the last day and must have let down his guard, not watching for tails. "Aren't you a little far from home?"

The farmer grabbed a passing barmaid by the shoulder as she passed by, "*Zuica te rog.* Arak, please."

Without waiting for an answer to his first question, Ziki decided to keep the farmer on the defensive. "Isn't it a little early in the year for Arak?"

"Like you said, I'm far from home. I don't often come to town, so I can't pretend to be the fancy. I just get what I like."

Ziki nodded at this, "Don't tell me you came to town all the way to see me. You couldn't have found my bag because, if you permit me saying so, I could not let it lie in your field so I retrieved it after darkness fell."

"Oh, I'm aware you did so. I can hardly blame you, seeing that the bag was more than just personal mementos, yes?"

Ziki's stomach dropped, "What do you mean?" The bag was securely fastened with a small lock, and only Ziki held the combination. When he recovered the bag, there was no sign of tampering.

The farmer leaned forward, "You're not Romanian, are you?"

Ziki got defensive, but in a calculated way, "My mother was a Hungarian Jew, if you must know. Aren't the Nazi times over?"

The farmer grinned at Ziki's feint, "That's not what I mean. If you're afraid to discuss it here, let's go for a walk."

Ziki thought for a moment, and then nodded. "Let's," he said, dropping a few Lira bills on the table hoping that he would not have to kill this man.

I am your contact in Romania that is why you landed in my field… All is well…

**The "Six-Day War" that came soon thereafter, it was won by Israel in the first few hours of that war.** Most Arab fighter planes, MiG's, were destroyed while still on the ground. Many were hit dead center…Was it great shooting? Sure, but the little buzz, buzzes, devices did their job.

## Chapter 55

**AFRICA**

**"Spook work," Ziki grumbled.**

"Maybe it's spook work, maybe it's not. I'm not sure myself what it is, but what I do know, Soldier," Malkielly said flatly as he slid a pile of airline tickets across his fittingly monstrous desk, "is that it's yours."

Ziki was a lot of things, but he was no spook. Sneaking into places, bugging meetings and steal foreign documents, turned his stomach and sharpened his tongue. He seesawed between pouting and lashing out in response to Malkielly's blunt words, but, noticing a scowl on the Shin Bet head's face menacing enough to send a bead of sweat down the back of his neck, Ziki settled in the middle on keeping his mouth shut.

He looked around. Nothing new. The room was still dark; white walls, navy carpet, portrait of a young David Ben-Gurion. The oval oak conference table sat twelve, but only six suffered its accompanying narrow, straight-backed chairs today this was his second office, this one in downtown Tel-Aviv. Ziki fidgeted, convinced the expression "pain in the ass" originated right here, in the hard right angles of these chairs.

The nutty odor of unlit cigars—chronic companions of Malkielly's jacket pockets—saturated the air, and Ziki stole a quick glance at his watch to start the timer. How far would he get today before reaching for a smoke?

Halmi Pientz, who headed Mossad and had been there long enough to lose nearly as many young men as he'd like to count, was a bit more compassionate when it came to doling out missions. Just as Malkielly was ready to wave Ziki and his itinerary toward the door, Pientz spoke up. "Do you know why Israel is so interested in Africa, Barak?"

"The same reason everyone else is, I assume," Ziki responded. "Natural resources and I know….oil and uranium. You will start in Kenya."

**Nairobi-Kenya**

**At the Oasis Club in the Sahara Hotel.** It was late into the night, right smack in the middle of Kenya. The bar was not a bad place to be. Ziki had had a few imported Russian vodkas and, from this view, the world looked to be okay. At least for now. In the morning, well, he'd think about that then.

Everybody—everybody that counted in Ziki's business, that is—set up shop in the Oasis. Its bar room was big, yet cozy to sit in. It had that comfortable feeling you get when you're in a familiar place, and Ziki had been there enough times to feel real comfortable.

The tables were small with leather tops mounted on polished brass and ebony wood bases. The big leather armchairs—fottels—gave a man his space.

Maybe in Africa they knew that, just like the wild predators outside, humans are territorial creatures; they like to mark and guard their territory.

On nights like tonight, large tables had to be brought in from the ballroom to accommodate the foreigners whose liquored breaths and cigarettes permeated the air and turned it bluish gray with smoke. A five-piece jazz band played standards on a simple, spot lit stage and, as Ziki entered the club, he stopped to listen. A long-faced Louis Armstrong-type singer was joined by a fabulous woman who belted out blues and jazz American gospel style. Not bad… Not half bad.

Behind—but not too far behind—Ziki, leaning on the brass railing of the bar, stood Avi. He had a drink glass in his tanned olive hand, but you could be sure there was no alcohol in it. Ziki had found liquor a good accompaniment to talk sessions, but the scowl threatening to fuse Avi's unkempt eyebrows with the perfectly sculpted brown waves above his forehead suggested he did not drink on duty.

Two years before, an IDF team had been unloading the last of several cargo helicopters at Ben Gurion airport in Tel-Aviv after a long and brutal mission along the Turkish Straits. Someone found a pack of Marlboro Lights dropped between two ammo chests that generated more drool than the Jayne Mansfield pinup hanging in the cockpit. Everyone dove for the pack but Avi, who had refused, deadpanning, said; "No smoking during working hours."

Never mind that they had lost a man, had half their equipment destroyed, and avoided an RPG to the fuel tank by no more than eighteen centimeters on their way out. Avi's only opinion on tobacco until the remaining ton of cargo was safely locked into storage was, *"No smoking during working hours."* It became his nickname. He had no desire to make or break rules and orders.

Considering Avi's job was to protect him, Ziki couldn't complain. At a hulking six-foot-two, Avi had been trained in the elite Golani Special Forces core of the IDF. He looked like someone to avoid pissing off; even when the nine millimeter Jericho automatic pistol tucked into his belt at the right hip wasn't visible. Avi was in Africa, Ziki assumed, to make sure that only good things happened to him.

It was both insulting and flattering. On the one hand, Mossad must have thought Ziki needed babysitting and could not take care of himself, by himself. But on the other, they must have also considered him important to keep him so well looked after with a constant bodyguard.

Encouraged by the few drinks he had already had, a thought flashed through Ziki's mind; I bet I could take Avi! He is too big to be quick moving. I know I'm faster. He smiled slyly. Avi caught his eye and gave a puzzled look.

Eh, why would he want to try? Avi would, if needed, take a bullet for him. He'd tear anybody apart that would harm a single hair on Ziki's head. Avi was the reason Ziki could sit there, relaxed. After all, not everyone in the room—maybe not even at his table—were friends. Ziki's little country had no shortage of foes.

But in this room—and this room alone—things were different. Perhaps there was an undeclared truce here. Perhaps African witch doctors had "tweaked" the club's atmosphere and the mindsets of all who entered it. In any case, KGB, NKVD, CSIS, MI6, BOSS, CIA, Mossad—the world's most notorious acronyms—convened peacefully at the Oasis and adjoining Carnivore bar.

They sat. Drank. Told lies. And sometimes, truths trickled in between. The trick was being able to separate the two.

Officially, Ziki was there as part of a *"diplomatic mission."* He was hobnobbing with important Africans, making nice with their haphazard governments, keeping tabs on other foreigners doing the same. But Ziki was no diplomat. Africa was a hotbed of fighting, tribal killings, warlords, ethnic unrest. The struggle for power was continuous and a blood thirsty dictator waited at every bend in the road. Ziki's deployment came under special order from the security section of the Knesset. A committee had met and decided the situation down south was too big to ignore and too serious for civilians. As far as Ziki was concerned it was all a preamble to dealing with Uranium rich South Africa and the Afrikaners. It was true; Africa had a lot of potential. And the better half of it was for disaster…

That night, like every night, the Club Room at the Oasis had become so full there was hardly room to stand.

Awujami, a large, soft-spoken Zulu ran the show. As maître d', he had everyone pegged and held them all under a watchful eye. Ziki and his men won his lasting favor when, driving back to the Carnivore one night, they stopped three locals from raping a young girl the men had cornered in an alley.

In Africa, families often held women responsible for their own rapes and shunned them as a result. The girl—Fatima—who turned out to be Awujami's daughter, begged Ziki not to tell her father what had happened. But, aside from a ripped blouse and some scratches, nothing had happened, Awujami and his enforcer Dkembe, who Ziki found out later was a Kenyan assassin for hire, was grateful and very accommodating to Ziki and his Israeli crew from then on.

He made sure they had privacy when needed and let his waiters know when Ziki wanted to make "friends" with other foreigners so they could reserve a prime, central *fottel* for him. Awujami never missed and, because of him, neither did Ziki.

The Oasis took in few locals. Most of them couldn't afford it. Those who could were businessman looking to make a deal and politicians who ate and drank free because the foreigners all fought over which one of them would pay. Was it bribery? Sure. *Bakshish*—the favored word—in Turkish. And considering a few drinks could lead to a foothold in Africa, the Oasis peddled the cheapest *Bakshish* in town.

Various agents and intelligence services from all over the world filled the place like an international bazaar. Ziki's eye was on the KGB and the NKVD, there from the Soviet Union, working at full steam, and treating Africa like a communist empire waiting to happen. Ziki had a few ideas about how they planned to prod it along, but he was looking for specifics; locations, means, tactics, with an eye towards the uranium in South Africa and oil rich Nigeria. Ziki headed a large Israeli contingency. Kenya was a launching point.

They were happy to talk, too; you just had to leave it for late in the night—two, three a.m.—when they were good and drunk.

Those Russians could drink. They downed more vodka than the Americans did whiskey, and timing had to be just right: if they'd had enough for a chat, but not so much that they'd pass out during it, well, Ziki's grandmother always told him; "Remember this; 'Drink in, truth out'."

Ziki had buddied up with a Soviet early on.

**"It is our vodka you drink."** A brutish man with a pock-marked face told Ziki as the maître d' under Awujami's watchful eyes escorted him to his seat.

"Local stuff'll kill you," Ziki responded in Russian, raising his glass, *nazdrovia*, and climbing over stray legs and empty tumblers toward the waiting *fottel*.

"Trust me," the man added, "ours can kill you too." He tilted his glass and downed the rest of his drink in three, accentuated gulps. Coming up for air, he capped off the gesture with a raucous, "Ha!" It drew Ziki's attention to a pock mark on his chin that looked more like half a bowl of scar tissue than a leftover from the man's acne years.

The Russian must have noticed Ziki's lingering eye. He raised a finger to his chin. "Young s.o.b. Old injuries. But you can bet the other bastard now has a hole like this sitting on top of his neck instead of a head." Offering a twisted grin and a stubby hand, he introduced himself.

"Ivan Stoyvich."

Ziki took the hand and gave a polite nod. "Ziki Barak. How's—"

Before he could finish, Stoyvich let go, turning his attention elsewhere. "Hey! Vodka!" he called behind him. His eyes, already hazy from liquor, swung around and consulted briefly with Ziki's glass. "Just bring the bottle!" he added, once again, in the general direction of the bar.

Stoyvich shook his head in disgust. "Jesus Christ—"he started, before pausing to look Ziki up and down.

Ziki had stuck with the Israeli delegation's standard uniform that evening: stiff, oversized black leather car jacket, cotton pants, and tightly laced black leather boots. The pants flowed a few inches below the knee, the jacket a few inches above.

"You're with the Jews, right?" Stoyvich asked, the now familiar grin creeping back across his lips.

Ziki took in the burnt orange rayon concoction of Stoyvich's pants and sport coat. He knew the KGB was never short on funding and wondered why they'd buy their men suits that looked anxious to unravel at the first snag.

Shrugging, he answered Stoyvich's question. "Sure, Ivan, I'm 'with the Jews'. And you're with the circus, yeah?"

The wool, fur, and crushed velvet of Mother Russia wouldn't' fly in the African tropics; the KGB must have raided an American manufacturing warehouse in China to compensate.

"Ha!" Stoyvich delighted, clearly amused by Ziki's dig. "No, the Russians, but close enough. Ha, I like this Jew." Now standing, he turned to face the bar. "And I would like to buy him a fucking vodka!"

Ziki noticed Avi had moved to a spot directly behind and a few feet closer to the Russian. He gave a nod to let him know things were fine.

"Jesus Christ—Jews don't mind 'Jesus Christ,' right?—I spend all day babysitting a hundred Cubans who don't know the holes in the barrels of their guns from the holes in the barrels of their asses and all I want is a decent round of drinks and some decent fucking service!

"So," he said, motioning behind himself, "where's your mask?"

Stoyvich was referring to Avi and a pair of wire-rimmed sunglasses with black fiber glass lenses. Ziki had gotten so used to seeing him wear them that he hadn't even noticed them attached to the man's face even in the dimly-lit club. A dozen IDF men and women—Ziki included—had bought the glasses at a Parisian flea market several months back and now wore them en masse while making their daytime rounds to African politicians' offices, government buildings, and neighborhoods. He chuckled to himself. For a guy who wanted nothing to do with spook work, he sure did his best to look like one.

Ziki patted the top left side of his jacket. "Right here," he told Stoyvich.

"Ah, pockets on the inside." Stoyvich raised and eyebrow. Half his scars shifted upward a quarter inch. "A big coat like that must have quite a few of those."

"Nope. Just the one." The Mini UZI on Ziki's right side sat in a holster strapped to his shoulder and chest. The jacket only helped cover it up.

Stoyvich's jabs and inquiries were pretty tame for a Russian. Especially a drunk one. First impressions told Ziki Stoyvich wasn't a die-hard countryman. He was in this business for its perks; free liquor, free hookers, free weapons, and the occasional opportunity to put a bullet or a blade through another man's midsection. Devotion to Russia and KGB duties were secondary to the power that came with being KGB. This probably meant the tier of information he had access to was median, but the chances he would talk were high, so Ziki decided to stick around and keep the "*drink in*" Ivan Stoyvich for the night.

By 3 a.m. Stoyvich had "accidentally" knocked an East German STASI agent's full glass into the man's lap for the third time.

"Scheiße, my German friend, these hands! I am clumsy like an ox." Stoyvich glanced at the man' doused crotch and clucked. "And in the very same awkward spot each time. I am so sorry. It looks like you will not be able to wear that suit you've been wearing the past seven nights in a row again tomorrow night."

The corners of his eyes turned up, smiling the patronizing grin his still-somber mouth resisted. "It is a good thing I am holding this glass and not my Kalashnikov. That really would have done a number on those pants."

The man flushed with anger, but, eyes bulging simply got up and left the bar. The Russians outnumbered the Germans here by at least ten to one, and that meant those like Stoyvich—those who wanted to—could get away with anything.

"Ah!" Stoyvich groaned, addressing Ziki as the German disappeared, "I never thought that would get old, but yes, it has." He paused… "You know, the fucking Nazis never left Germany, they're all still there. Ha..ha, except maybe the ones our great General Comrade Zhukov keeps like trained monkeys to work for him." Yes, I hear that you Jews are supplying Zhukov with fresh German meat... You do know who Generalissimo Zhukov is? Don't you?"

"I've heard of him."

He paused again and shook his head vigorously. "The air in here. It's making me dizzy. It's…it's this place."

"Hey, you should be happy vertigo's the worst thing this place has given you."

"Yeah, that and a sharp pain in my ass."

Ziki laughed, but Stoyvich was expressionless.

"I need a permit from a different bullshit organization every time I want to take a piss."

Everyone had the same problems in Africa. Local enforcers and a muddled bureaucracy made it very difficult to conduct business in the place. Loyalties and intentions bounced back and forth with the hours and one group's *baksheesh* was good only until another's came along.

"Yeah," Ziki said, "Africa's like a game of chess with no strategy and too many players. Maybe you guys should back out," he joked.

Stoyvich, staring straight ahead, answered seriously. "No. We've come too far, too many Rubles—if you know what I mean. And we've already got Kenyatta halfway in our back pocket. Let me tell you getting clearances to move around this place is a bitch, but …."

His trailing off was less a dramatic gesture than a seeming loss of concentration. His eyes were locked across the room on nothing in particular. Ziki wanted to prod for more information, but didn't want to set off and risk losing the connection to someone who, given the right incentive, was obviously willing to talk on his own. Ziki scanned the leather table top. It was barely visible through the clutter of empty glasses.

Jomo Kenyatta—Kenya's president—was enough to start anyway. Crossing borders and accessing air space wasn't so difficult with the right friends. The Kenyatta government could be very influential in making the Soviets' biggest problems go away, or not.

Or, for that matter, Ziki's.

"As long as Okelo does his job," Stoyvich muttered. "But too many people trust him. You can't be loyal to everyone…."

"Huh? Okelo? Who's Okelo?"

"He's on Zanzibar." Stoyvich's focus returned to Ziki. The sunburn had drained from his face, leaving behind pasty cheeks and dark circles under his eyes. Again, he gave his head a firm shake.

"I need a stretch," he said. "And your friend looks lonely."

Avi. Good old Avi, the  nickname stuck; *'No Smoking During Working Hours.'* He was a little blurry at this point but, as far as Ziki could tell, he hadn't budged more than an inch the past three hours. Ziki wondered how long he could stand there before collapsing.

Ziki grinned and raised his glass to Avi, who offered only the faintest of nods in return. A moment later, his maître d' friend, Awujami, stopped in front of the table.

"Sir," he began in broken Russian, "is everything alright here?"

"Yeah, fine," Ziki replied. "What, my big friend send you over to check up on me."

"He is known for to be…." Awujami fumbled for the right words.

"A lush? A blowhard? A—"

"A very, eh, not friendly man, Sir."

Ziki burst out laughing. Awujami fidgeted, frustrated and a little embarrassed. Ziki caught hold of himself and replied, "Sorry, it's just that Ivan Stoyvich's gotta be one of the ugliest sons of bitches in Africa—"

"No, no, Sir, it's not what I meant. He is angry… He is bad man. You should—"

"I know what you meant. You're a good man looking out for me, Awujami, my friend. I'll be alright."

Ivan returned, empty handed, and Awujami hurried away.

"I am sick of this fucking place and these *pizduk* people!" Stoyvich declared as he clumsily maneuvered himself back into his chair. "Africa… Africans. Their sun that makes you blind, that is the worst. And their people in the streets banging on drums and talking bullshit about snakes and spirits. And it smells like…like…I don't know what it smells like. Chickens and hot cow shit!

"And!" he suddenly bellowed, "the fucking sun! It's like I am being interrogated by the NKVD every time I walk into the daylight!"

Ziki sat back, amused. What spawned this rant? Then he saw. Stoyvich's hands were empty. "Where's your drink?" he asked, already knowing the answer.

"'No more drinks tonight, Sir,' they tell me. Ha! No more fucking drinks! I show them these wads of Rubles in my wallet…."

Ziki smiled to himself. No wonder Awujami had come to warn him. Stoyvich must have thrown a fit at the bar. Russians did not take well to being told they had had too much to drink. And he felt fairly confident Stoyvich didn't take well to being told anything.

The raging Russian now had coins and bills strewn across the table, the latter sopping up the leftovers of glasses he'd knocked over. He capped off the scene by hurling his KGB insignia wallet at the wall two yards in front of them. A loud crack sounded when it hit.

Ziki spun to face the wall, surprised he could hear the wallet's impact over the noise of the…band. When had the band stopped? He looked around. The stage was empty. Most of the tables were empty too.

Avi was now walking towards him, followed by two penguin-suited waiters and three other men who, judging by their getups, knew Stoyvich.

Avi spoke to Ziki in Hebrew. " *Maspik—nigmar ha-erev la Russi,* everyone agrees the Russian is finished for tonight."

"He was fine a minute ago," Ziki said. "Well …. Must've hit him when he stood up."

"Yeah, knocked him right on his ass."

"Huh?"

Avi waved to some upturned chairs near the bar. "Didn't you see him fall into that table over there?"

"Well, I'm not surprised. You had no trouble keeping up with him."

"Alright, but pick up my things first! Look, money everywhere!" Stoyvich was slung over one of his men, giving orders to the others. "Where's my fucking wallet and my identification? My proof," he slurred, "that you all rank below me." Ziki stood, sending a rush of blood to his head. He felt Avi's thick hand on his shoulder. "I got it," he said, making his way to the wall, where he pronounced, "Wallet."

Avi tossed the hunk of brown leather to one of the waiters, who quickly handed it to Stoyvich as the others began the  haul back to his room.

"Just give me a minute," Ziki told Avi once they were gone. "Sit down, will you? You been standing all night."

Instead, Avi walked over to the wall and bent over. "What's this?" he asked, picking up a small metal button.

"Lemme see," Ziki said. It was the clasp with a KGB emblem that held together the flap of Stoyvich's i.d. wallet. "Huh." He shoved the piece into his coat pocket. "I'll give that back to him tomorrow night, it could be useful."


The next day Ziki found out that five years before, Ivan Stoyvich got working for the KGB recruiting spies from the editorial offices of American agencies and whatever else he could get, later he advanced to be an assassin for them.

"Come to the bar. I'm going to let you buy me a vodka."

Ziki smirked. "I only buy drinks for women," he said following behind Ivan Stoyvich. He didn't intend to try to keep up with the Russian tonight, but, as Stoyvich's right wingtip went astray and collided with a fottel leg, Ziki couldn't help but hope one or two might prove…useful to him.

"Ha! Only pays for women? I bet that is true. Okay, then. These will be on Gorbachov." Stoyvich threw down a few shillings and turned back to Ziki. With a grave scowl, he added, "And, Ziki, my sympathies for the loss of your man."

"Thank you," Ziki nodded. "He was a good kid and his was a great loss." The maître d' handed the men two vodka's.

Surprised to see him behind the bar, Ziki asked, "Awujami, someone call in sick tonight?"

"Eh," he responded, his dark eyes rolling upward as he thought, "no, Sir.

Not that I know of."

"I mean," Ziki clarified, "why are you serving drinks?"

Awujami shrugged. "So many people. One person is not enough back here. But do not worry," he added, "a table has been saved for you—for you both—at the front. We have an excellent band tonight. An excellent band."

Stoyvich gave Awujami a sideways glance. Suspicion dripped from his voice. "That table?" he gestured. "Near the band? Maybe we should have our drinks and nice conversation on stage with them. That way we can talk directly into the microphones."

Awujami looked puzzled but said nothing.

Ivan rolled his eyes. "I am not interested in the band. We can find our own table."

"Very good, Sir, *kushtuka*, jerk. Awujami mouthed in Swahili, before moving further down the bar to take another drink order.

"I do not trust him," Stoyvich said, absently sipping at his vodka. "I think he has this place bugged."

Ziki's eyebrows raised in amusement. The slight provocation was enough to rile Stoyvich.

"I'm serious," he protested. "You shouldn't be so friendly with him." "Always slithering around like a helpful little snake. I heard he was a spy for the English until just before Kenya broke off, he has something to do with the Zulu in South Africa, I hear rumors that you boys have your eyes on their Uranium, maybe I will see you there. Helpful little snake," he mumbled again. "In the end the blacks, they only want to help themselves."

"Don't we all?" Ziki joked, trying to steer Stoyvich onto another subject.

It was the right move. The Russian's scars smashed together in a big grin as he jabbed Ziki's arm and agreed, "Don't we all."

Stoyvich led them to a back corner of the Oasis where a tall table and a few bar stools sat empty. The backless wooden contraptions were an eyesore compared to the plush fottels, but Stoyvich seemed happy enough, so Ziki let it go.

"Well," Stoyvich said, holding up his glass, "it seems I have already begun, but still, a final drink to my final night in this crevice of hell."

They toasted and drank.

Coming up for air, Ziki mocked, "Aw, back to Mama Russia tomorrow, huh?"

"Ha! Yes indeed, via Iran, a little business venture, you know." He gave his head a violent shake, and then said nothing.

"Sounds like you'll be sorry to leave Africa."

"I'm not leaving Africa."

"Oh?"

Ziki saw a familiar vacancy overtake the Russian's eyes. His heart beat a little faster as he quickly scanned the room for anyone who might be watching them.

"No. Just moving on to a smaller, hotter, more miserable African hell." Though Stoyvich's words carried emotion, the voice that delivered them was steady and flat.

Ziki swirled the remains of his vodka and tried for nonchalance. "What's this crevice call itself?"

Eyes still locked on nothing, Stoyvich responded, "Nacala. Mozambique, closer to South Africa. I told you, I will see you there?" Ziki did not respond.

"Awujami, I'm sorry we didn't take you up on your offer. Those guys," Ziki gestured toward the stage, "are amazing."

"Yes. Le Grand Kalle is a good man. A good friend. He and his band always perform well for us."

Ziki nodded, then leaning in close enough to whisper, asked "You put something in the Russian's drink, Awujami?"

The maître d' stopped what he was doing and looked up. "Vodka, ice, some lime—"

"You know what I mean… Something that made him talk? And act like that?"

Awujami shrugged, his face giving nothing away as he busied himself behind the bar again. "The drinking brings out many things in people. It is bad for some." He was silent for a moment, then, when Ziki said nothing, stopped and looked up. "It is good for others, I make 'em that way *angu mafiki*, my friend."

Ziki grinned. "I'm grateful, Awujami."

"Yes. So am I to you..."


**Ziki transferred his last few belongings from the hotel room's armoire to his suitcase.** He breathed a sigh of contentment as he shut its heavy chestnut door. Looking around, he pitied the poor bastard—another, a replacement finally—who would take over the room. He loved the Oasis, but one of the many perks of leaving Africa was going to be leaving this room.

On the plane, Ziki leaned back and lit a cigarette. He took a deep drag and held it in for a few seconds before breathing out a thick screen that covered the row's window and what was still visible of the flat brownness of Nairobi.

"So," Avi asked as they began their taxi down the runway, "you don't like Africa?"

Ziki kept his eyes straight ahead. "Let's just say I won't need more than one finger to bid it farewell."

"I have news from home, orders you are not going to like, at the stopover we are changing planes. He handed Ziki a large folder, here are the details, we're going to South Africa.

## Chapter 55

**South Africa**
**Johannesburg**

Johann Botha's tongue ran back and forth along his top teeth; his pen tapped the glossed bubinga of the massive desk before him.

Outside, twenty stories below, the business district of downtown Johannesburg had cleared out. Johann looked at his watch. 9:30. He had told Marita two hours ago he would be home in forty-five minutes. He had also promised her he wouldn't leave her alone with the girls past 9:00 until he hired new overnight security guards to replace the four he had fired the week before. With only one man now patrolling his 5000-acre farm and home, she was going to be angry.

But Johann couldn't dwell on Marita just now. He was anxious about the coming days, his country was in danger, the whole continent, it seemed, wanted to kill the Afrikaners. Irritated with his inability to squelch the anxiety, and still fuming over that morning's disappearance of a 60-carat stone. Despite extensive security precautions in the mining compounds—barbed wire, watch towers, dogs, a blanket of mesh fencing covering the areas to keep materials from being thrown over the fifteen-foot stone walls surrounding them—clever Kaffir hands always found ways to jam uncut jewels down their throats and onto the awaiting black market.

A knock at the door. Johann looked up with a start.

He had been expecting Hendrik, one of the board of the company's salesmen and son of a member of its board.

A short, pink-cheeked, cross-eyed man of thirty, Hendrik's specialty was rambling and grating, two skills that prompted Johann to avoid him when possible. However, his ability to sell—diamonds, stock, and, in this case, South Africa itself—made him a valuable addition to Johann's entourage. Foreign interests always seemed to eat up the little twit's pushy enthusiasm.

Johann ordered his visitor to enter and watched as Hendrik's dirty blond head bobbed its way in, bidding Johann a good evening. They spoke in Afrikaans, the language of white Dutch South Africans.

"Well?" Johann asked.

"Hmm, they arrive Wednesday morning, Sir."

"And the mines?"

"The cabinet thinks we'll be able to draw around a thousand kilograms primed for seventy percent or above on the year."

"Mm. And this will be enough?"

"It should be plenty, Sir."

"Very well. Any word on the stone's whereabouts?"

"No, hmm, unfortunately, no, Sir. It was almost certainly swallowed by a Kaffir whose contract ended just before he moved out of the compound. But forty of them moved out today alone—perhaps this was deliberate—so it will take us a while to investigate each one."

The stone wasn't even the half of it. Even those still in the compounds were getting out of control. To say nothing of the ones still allowed in the city. Johan clutched his head in his hands. The Kaffirs were getting out of control. And the Afrikaners had to put them back in check, it was contagious, snowballing; the whole continent—no the whole world was ganging up against them.

**Even amidst a continent of stark contrasts, Johannesburg was an anomaly.** The growing countries of Kenya and Morocco, the dormant, isolated villages of Ethiopia, and the expanses of Egypt, whose myths and mystic finds link the world to civilization's infancy, all suited Africa. A thriving seemingly European metropolis situated comfortably at its southern tip did not.

Despite his ever-obliging hosts' offers of private safari tours, extravagant dinners, and accommodating female escorts Ziki, as was de rigueur for his initial encounter with a place, opted to go it alone his first day in Johannesburg. He didn't need the locals manipulating first impressions—especially these Afrikaners who would have given much to gain his recommendation for a partnership with Israel.

On that day, downtown Johannesburg was a blanket of haze. The hundred-degree air hovered, thick and stagnant, above city goers' heads, teaming up with a blaring sun to cover and distort the urbane esplanade. Tall buildings housed insurance agencies, consulting firms, brokerages, and banking corporations. Opulent hotels sported marbled façades, while swanky boutiques sold the couture fashion and accessories frosting the bodies of the hotels' guests. Traffic was heavy and loud, and throngs of exhausted Bantu stood chatting and patiently awaiting the buses that would take them miles outside the city to what were probably not, Ziki knew, suburban bourgeois homes. Barely visible from where he stood were the sandy-yellow piles of Johannesburg's gold dumps, immense playgrounds, someone later told him, for Bantu children.

Ziki wandered the streets, looking at local goods, stopping in shops to check out the prices for a shirt, a pair of shoes, a dozen eggs, a milkshake. He used these things to develop a sense of a city's place in the world, and, from what he saw, Johannesburg was definitely in the black. Jaguars, Rolls Royces, and Mercedes packed roads and parking lots, and Afrikaners and English-speaking whites showed opulent elegance in manner and dress despite the brutal heat.

While black Africans were well kempt in slacks, sport coats, skirts and blouses, Ziki knew they did not do their shopping in these parts. The average income of the day for an Afrikaner was many times that of the Bantu for the week.

Taking it all in, Ziki ambled through the city's hub in a daze. The dense air filled with aromas of bread and figs and oranges from outdoor markets. You could make a meal out of their scents alone.

Ziki wandered toward the stalls, with their elaborate arrangements of swirling colors and the manicured white hands rifling through them and scrutinizing each find. A butcher's shop shelved rows of chicken and ostrich eggs and dangled huge slabs of biltong—dried, salted meat—from the slanted ceiling above. Its display case advertised the city's best alligator sirloin and special deals on caterpillars, all breaded and ready for the fryer.

Ziki stopped paying attention to the noise and commotion around. He also stopped paying attention to where he was going and ended up the other half of a minor collision.

"Oh, excuse me. My fault," he said, turning to face a tiny, old black woman. Peering up at him, trembling, she slowly lowered to her knees.

Surprised and embarrassed, Ziki grabbed her hand to pull her up. She tried to avert his eyes, but he could see in them a look that both asked and begged not to know what would happen next. She thought he was an Afrikaner. And she was terrified.

*"Asseblief, dit spyt my,"* she began, hands together in prayer, then caught herself and switched to English. "Please, please, I beg your pardon. Such a—I'm such a clumsy, foolish old woman. Please do not hold it too harshly against me… Please, Sir."

Touched, but disturbed that this menial incident could elicit such fear in a person, Ziki searched for the right words.

"No, ma'am, you did nothing wrong. It was all my fault. See," he pointed to the ground, "two left feet. They get me into all sorts of trouble. I'm very sorry."

Still, she squinted her eyes, panicked. Ziki looked around for backup—someone else to tell her what really happened. He didn't know how else to explain that everything was okay. He tried, instead, giving her a soothing smile and a hug.

From across the street, a white South African, dressed head to toe in whiter linen, looked on. As the two embraced, his brow furrowed and teeth clenched. Making a beeline for the woman, he thrust a badge toward Ziki with one hand and walloped her across her face with the other.

"You filthy Kaffir! Don't touch him!"

She let out a tiny yelp and raised her hands to her face. Blood trickled down her chin. The Afrikaner—apparently a policeman in civilian clothing—cocked his arm for another shot. "Stay down there. All you Kaffirs belong on your knees. Dumb, dirty old hag."

Ziki watched the Afrikaner's square jaw flap in anger. Suddenly, he snapped to and realized the woman must be thinking the two men knew each other—that the whole incident was a cruel setup devised by a couple of bored whites to injure her. Ziki's rage snowballed; he reached for his gun flashed to his side. Calmly, evenly he pointed it at the Afrikaner's belly….

"Touch her again and I'll put a hole through that faggoty white suit."

The Afrikaner turned, eyes widening, drops of sweat appeared on his brow and ran down his face generously flowing, he let out a series of whistles. Immediately, a half dozen uniformed policemen, complete with their own guns, came running.

"Turn over your weapon!"

"You are under arrest!"

"Do it now!"

"Do not force us to open fire!"

Great, Ziki thought. Three hours off the plane and I'm in a face-off at gunpoint. "Fuckin' Africa," he mumbled.

Making eye contact with the nearest armed policeman, he spoke slowly and used his free hand to reach for his inside jacket pocket. His shirt, which had dampened from the heat before, was now dripping with sweat.

"Now hold on. Give me just a second to show you my passport and papers. I'm here a guest of your government." The hand emerged with the forms. "I have diplomatic immunity. Here," he gestured toward the same man. "Just call this number. Your government—see what they say. "

The policeman looked to his cohorts for approval, then gingerly stepped forward. His pudgy pink cheeks and hesitant expression told Ziki the man was even his junior and probably hadn't seen much action aside from roughhousing Bantu. As he reached out, Ziki considered whispering, "Boo!" but Junior's shaky trigger finger kept him quiet.

Growing agitated, the square jaw let out a few gruff words in Afrikaans, the Dutch-derived language of the Afrikaners, and Junior quickly snatched the documents from Ziki's hand and scurried over to a white Land Rover.

Seconds later, he shouted back a few words to Square Jaw, whose eyes widened once again, and the five remaining guns lowered instantly. They rushed apologetically toward Ziki.

"We're very sorry, Sir," Square Jaw gushed. "What an awful misunderstanding. Of course we had no idea. Can we drive you somewhere? Get you anything?"

"Yeah," Ziki replied, "give me your jacket."

Square Jaw paused, a bit confused, then removed the white linen suit coat. Ziki took it to the woman, who still cowered on the ground, and began wiping the dirt and blood from her face and hands. Her terror turned to confusion, then awe.

Not bothering to face them, Ziki said in a low voice, "I want you to call a taxi for this woman and then leave us both the hell alone."

Square Jaw's eagerness to oblige was being tested. "Of course, Sir," came the pinched reply, "Right away."

Waiting for the taxi, Ziki asked the woman's name.

"Fatmah Bijahwy."

"Fatmah Bijahwy, I am Ziki Barak, I am not from here—I am not an Afrikaner, I am from Israel.

" Ahh" she exalted, stunned and not knowing what else to say.

"It's a pleasure to meet you, Fatmah Bijahwy."

She smiled shyly and, as Ziki held out his hand, the cab pulled up. The cab. It must have caught his attention for the split second it would have taken him to stop her, because by the time he saw it coming, it was too late. Instead of extending her own hand, as he had intended, Fatmah bowed forward and kissed his.

"Oh, no, please," Ziki stammered, "I…I didn't mean—. I didn't want you to—. You should never have to—." He was moved by her gratitude, but angered by its implications… He choked back tears. This is how it worked here? Were the Afrikaners such bastards that small acts of decency from white to black merited gestures of worship?

Ziki helped Fatmah into the taxi and paid the driver to take her wherever she wanted to go. He bent down to say goodbye and kissed her on the forehead. "You take care, Fatmah Bijahwy, it is a big world but I will see you again….Take her to Soweto driver."

If Ziki had come into South Africa with bias thoughts, this incident only intensified them. He looked at the hunks of gold and diamonds and upturned noses on the Afrikaners around him and wanted to throw up.

He could never work with these sons of bitches and determined to say as much to his government. The next morning's meeting with Afrikaner representatives would be a formality. Ziki couldn't wait to advise the Knesset to tell these people to go to hell.

**The Afrikaners sent a car and a cross-eyed escort for the Israeli delegation early Thursday morning.**

"Hmm, good morning, Sirs," he singsonged, ushering the men through an open door. "I am Hendrik Hindon. Hmm, I trust you had a comfortable and restful sleep. The Excelsior is most accommodating, hmm. Coincidentally, it dates back to…"

Davidoff leaned over and whispered, "What is he buzzing or something?" As Hendrik "hmm"ed a string of useless details about "Johannesburg's premier lodging establishment."

Ziki tuned him out, wondering how a Bantu gold miner's hourly wage would look in comparison to this useless white professional ass kisser's. The diamond-faced watch on Hendrik's left wrist was probably worth more than many of them would see in their lives.

"…and you can certainly feel right at home in our magnificent Rand Club. Almost as old as Johannesburg itself, hmm…"

They were now sitting in the back of a Rolls Royce limousine, creeping through the city's morning rush hour. Just as he saw them boarding buses the evening before, Ziki watched countless black men and women getting off the rickety tin cans now. Their clothing was drab and dusty. Shirt sleeves were too long, pant legs too short, jackets too small. Through the bus windows, he could see them boisterous, laughing, but as they reached the sidewalks, they became more subdued, saying their goodbyes and walking away quickly. A dozen police officers hovered at or near the bus stops. They stopped random people in the crowd and spoke with them briefly.

Most of the men and women produced a piece of paper from their purse or jacket pocket; Ziki saw South African secret policeman grab the arms of the few who didn't and shove them back towards the buses.

Hendrik noticed Ziki staring out the window. "It's amazing what we've done here, hmm?"

"Huh?" Ziki asked, shifting his focus back toward the group.

Hendrik gave him a wet, smarmy grin.

"Yeah. It is. Amazing."

Hendrik led them through the massive carved wood doors and into the Rand Club. Founded shortly after the discovery of Johannesburg's diamond mines, it was a stomping ground for the so called, elite's elite.

Rich wood paneling, what looked like solid gold chandeliers, and an art collection worthy of museum walls greeted guests in the main foyer. The sitting room was covered in dark velvet and leather, and filled with waiters begging to bring guests drinks, smokes, and hors d'oeuvres. Soft flecks of light bounced off the diamond-crusted candy dishes, which rejected their typical fare in favor of neat rows of Cuban cigars.

The Israeli party joined several Afrikaners in the sitting room and went through polite introductions. Then, aside from Hendrik, who tried to make small talk about the great bounty and magnificence of Southern Africa, the men sat silently in plush tufted leather armchairs, smoking and looking at each other with polite suspicion. They waited for the last Afrikaner, the team leader, to arrive.

John Vorster, South Africa's Minister of Justice sat directly across from Ziki, stiff in a beige tweed suit and immaculate brown patent alligator shoes that must have cost a fortune. Ziki thought about complimenting them to break the tension, but they were so hideously ugly that his lips couldn't produce anything but dense bursts of cigar smoke and the occasional "pop" after a heavy drag. Cigars were not his thing, but they seemed to go with this place.

The buttery texture of the chair, the Cuban in his right hand, and the straight Russian vodka in his left had him feeling a-okay with the skepticism and silence.

There was plenty of time for menacing looks and suggestions for where the Afrikaners could shove their visions of alliance with Israel later. Why ruin the present moment of peace?

Ziki took it all in. Surreal, he thought. Europe recreated in the heart of wild Africa. His gaze moved to Vorster's right. There sat the triplets—uniformed South African military brass. Erect, blank-faced, obviously there for show.

Ziki whispered Hebrew in Avi's ear. "Look at all these medals they gave themselves."

He held back a quiet laugh. These three boosted their team's numbers, filled out its line. Ziki arrived with five men. The South Africans wouldn't have settled for anything less than a six-on-six match up.

"**Now, I know you are well aware**, Sirs, that South Africa houses over ninety percent of the world's diamond mines. But did you know that we also reap the benefits of lots of gold, silver, and copper mines as well? Hmm, every woman's dream come true...and every husband's worst nightmare! Heh, heh, heh!"

Strike that. Six-five matchup; Hendrik barely made Waterboy.

"Yes, hmm...and the one other item in our mines that we know attracted your attention to our beautiful country...."

"What's that?" Ziki asked, interested in the response, but irritated at having to give him an excuse to yammer on.

"Uranium, Sir, lots of uranium. We know that you gentlemen have been shopping for it all over the world, and we hear that no one wants to sell it to you. Hmm, isn't that right?"

So. Hendrik wasn't the complete dolt he made himself out to be.

Ziki tried for nonchalance. "We have what we need." But he couldn't help exchanging a few quick looks with his entourage, gestures that did not escape the Afrikaners.

The thing was, a few years ago, Israel made a decision.

Invasion, war, and death had all happened before and anyone who could think straight wouldn't think for a minute they wouldn't happen again.

Five million Israelis—three hundred million Arabs at war with them? Not to ignore the fact that the Soviets were fed up with their cohorts, the Arabs losing all the wars thus far and most of the Russian supplied armaments.

General Zhukov died; he kept his word while he was alive—but now? Gorbachov? Putin? Maybe? The Kremlin may decide that on the next war, they, the Soviets would invade Israel with their own Red Army…...

Nuclear weaponry and the means to deliver them was speeded up …A secretive place in the Negev desert called Dimona… And advanced Jericho missiles.

Hendrik wound up to begin again, but stopped short. "Ah! Sir," he addressed Vorster, gesturing with his head, "he has arrived."

An usher lead one of the strangest looking men he had ever seen toward them. At 6'2"or 6'3", he sported a bushel of sculpted silvery hair. Small, beady eyes shone, but were no more than flecks lost amidst dense layers of deeply-tanned skin that Ziki bet had been described as 'leathery' in the man's twenties. Now—most likely his mid-forties—'rawhide' was a better word for it. Must be the African sun, Ziki thought.

His upper body was massive; a long torso and bulky pair of arms sprouted from a robust balloon of a chest that looked like it could swallow his comparatively tiny head.

Even more surprising were the two, frail, matchstick legs that supported it all. Even with his baggy trousers covering them, the unequal distribution of mass on his frame was disturbingly clear. Physically, he looked…well, he looked like a fowl being fattened up for a feast.

As the man reached the table, everyone stood and a giant hand, laden with a thick, gold ring, stretched toward Joe Stein, one of the few middle-aged Israelis in their party. Ziki was so amused by the exaggerated arrogance the man showed in assuming Stein headed the Israeli party that he didn't even think to be offended. The thought did occur to him, however, after Vorster pointed out the mistake and introduced Ziki as Commander Barak, head of the Israeli contingency.

The man let out a thunderous belly laugh that eventually turned arrogantly apologetic.

"I'm sorry, Commander," he said, extending his hand once again, "it is just surprising that someone so…young…would be sent to handle dealings of such… importance."

"We are both, an old and young country," Ziki replied. "I didn't know that age made you smarter, Mr…." Ziki's voice trailed off. He had missed the initial introduction and though he knew the name from briefings back home…was it Bolla? Votta? He turned to Davidoff…"*Ma hashem shelo—? What is his name?* "

"Please, it is good. I am Johann Botha. Call me Johann."

Johann wore an off-white linen suit, similar to that of the South African plainclothes policemen but with an expensive tailor's cut. The previous day's sour taste returned to Ziki's mouth.

"Have you enjoyed your stay here? I trust you got along alright yesterday? I heard you turned down our offers of hospitality."

"I'm always more comfortable adjusting to a new place on my own. Your city is …interesting."

"It is. We have gone to great lengths for our successes. And we are trying very hard to ensure that they continue."

The men went on like this for a while, tiptoeing around the issues at hand with icy civility, until Botha, with no warning, decided he was ready to deal. He asked Ziki.

"Do you like Israel, Commander?"

"What kind of question is that? Of course I do."

"Of course. And why do you like Israel?"

"There are many reasons."

"'Oh—so many reasons,' he says. Come, Commander, I talk to you like a grown man." Ziki ignored the comment. "Why do you like Israel? Because it's what you know. It is where you are from…. Because it's your home…. Johannesburg, South Africa; they are my home. I'm not a newcomer to them and I'm not an immigrant. I was born here. My wife and children were born here. My parents, their parents, and their parents—all born here, in Africa. I did not steal this land from anyone and I do not belong anywhere else but on it."

Johann Botha was a man of the past—a myth-filled past of constant sacrifice, hardship, and death that colored every part of his life and the lives of the men in the room with him. One of the other men entered the talk;

Let me tell you about Herr Botha, young man." Without waiting for approvals, he began;

Three hundred years before, enticed from their native Holland with thousands of others, Johann's ancestors had braved the terrible dangers of the sea to settle on Africa's southernmost point, the Cape of Good Hope... He went on. The Afrikaner National Party took power and made Apartheid the law of the land.

A firm Christian conviction that God ordained the "*separation of the races*", and an unyielding commitment to the preservation of Afrikaner power and purity—Johann displayed these openly. The man's face was red with excitement; he looked around the room and paused.

There was a momentary, uncomfortable silence as Ziki gave Davidoff a puzzled sideways glance. Tension and arguments and erratic behavior often made appearances at important meetings, but they usually didn't kick them off like this.

Botha continued from there. "You know, gentlemen, this is not a conquered territory or a new homeland. I am a native of this country, do you understand? I was born here just like them, the Kaffirs...

I have nowhere else to go. But they want all white men out of here. They want to take our land and drive us from the only country we know. So who is to say? Maybe they are the bigots. Have you ever thought of it that way, Commander?"

"But," Ziki cut in, "can you blame their anger? You don't treat them much better than slaves. They're uneducated, poor, killed at will—"

Botha threw his arms up, looked furiously at Ziki and stood as if to leave. "Ah, there's not point in talking to him. He's a naïve child and a communist!"

Ziki sat calmly, and, voice cold, said...

"Mr. Botha, you invited us here. You want something from me. Me! You seem to have forgotten that it is I who will say yes or no to you—to your country. My recommendation to my government will be the deal maker or breaker. I see that you are old, but to attack me like this.... You are obviously not wiser with age."

Botha grinned. Something caught the light. Ziki squinted, trying to get a closer look. Could the crazy Afrikaner have something buried within the thick, stiff folds of his face?

"Ah," Botha said, "so talk of communism gets a reaction. Come on... Sit down please. We'll discuss this like we're both grown men now... I'll tell you a story from the *Talmud*. You're familiar with it—Jewish law, thousands of years old?"

Ziki nodded, noticing that Botha's deep, heavily accented English unraveled considerably slower than that of most South Africans he had encountered. It seemed deliberate... Patronizing. He ignored it. A quote from the *Talmud* surprised him. Perhaps there was more to the Afrikaners than met the eye.

Botha began, "A man comes from a barn with a blood-soaked knife in his hand. Inside the barn lies a man dead from a stab wound. According to the Talmud does that make the man holding the knife guilty of murder?"

He paused for effect, but not long enough for an answer... "Of course not. He is innocent until all circumstances and explanations become clear, until proven guilty. Your Talmud says: "One must hear all sides of the story." Another, longer pause. "All sides, my young friend... Then, and only then, can such a grave accusation be made."

"You and your party are descendants of this ancient wisdom, Commander, and all I, and mine ask is that you hear us out and keep an open mind."

"Now," Botha said, "some Schlibovitz—Romanian vodka... You'll like. And tell me, what do you think of the hotel we have provided for you? Nice, yes?" A slimy grin—and, again, that glint—began the Schlibovitz and small talk. The Afrikaners loved to mix business with pleasure.

Several rounds and an antelope steak dinner later, Johann picked up the issues at hand as abruptly as he'd dropped them before.

"What is it that these poor Kaffirs want, Commander? What do you think we should give them?"

"I don't know," Ziki said, looking at Botha through the bottom of his upturned glass. He hadn't been prepared to resume negotiations just yet... "How about a fair shot?"

"Level playing ground?"

"Sure. A chance to succeed...Equality."

"Equality? Is that what you think this is about?" Botha sneered.

In retrospect, Ziki saw he'd stumbled into a trap. Botha had been waiting for a chance to let loose.

"You think the Kaffirs are pouring all of their hatred and resentment into equality? Ha! It's a pathetic illusion, equality. An ideology of the naïve and stupid. And the Kaffirs aren't just naïve and stupid; they're ignorant. Uneducated, untrained, living in shacks with no electricity, no running water... We didn't take these things from them; how could we take what was never there to begin with?" He circled his arm and bottomed his drink.

"Look at the rest of Africa. Poverty, famine war—it's impossible to keep track of who's fighting who and what they're fighting for. They look at our world, what we've accomplished, and of course they want equal rights, equal pay, and equal opportunity."

"They also want our land, our mines, our cities, our industries—the South Africa we built and the prosperity we brought. They want it all; they want to oust us, take it from us, and divide it—equally, of course—amongst themselves, that is Communism Commander... What would you do in our place? Allow centuries of work and toil to be minced up and doled out and sent, right back to the third world? Not in this life, Commander. We've worked too long and achieved too much to step back and let it happen!"

"They are communists; they rock themselves to sleep at night with visions of all that is ours now soon belonging to all off them. Only we say, 'Over our dead bodies!' And we, gentlemen, are not ready to die. Are we, my friends? Heh, heh, heh."

It was perfect. The handful of Schlibovitz's Johann downed before delivering the speech gave it the aura that this man believed all that he said. Well, it was something to think about. Catching Avi's eye, Ziki wanted to shrug, but the third and fourth Schlibovitz now working their way through his system had other ideas. Instead, he chortled loudly into his napkin.

The beady eyes across from him unclouded, snapped to. "Heimlich, Commander?" Botha growled.

Oops. Ziki looked up. "I'm sorry?"

"You appear to be choking. I thought you might require the Heimlich Maneuver." Not surprisingly, Botha had little tolerance for laughter and amusement when they were had at his expense.

"I'm fine."

"That's reassuring. Hendrik," he said, eyes still on Ziki, "you must remind me to ask that the staff cut the Commander's antelope steak for him from now on. To ensure the pieces are bite-size. We wouldn't want any more close calls, now would we?"

Hendrik, eager as ever, moved to answer the rhetorical question, but before he could open his mouth, Ziki decided he had had enough.

Voice steady, he began, "After one hour on your streets, Sir, I saw your Afrikaner policeman broadside a helpless old woman because she was black. Three more pointed their weapons at me because I tried to help her..."

"You pass laws to all but ban 'Kafirs'—or whatever this ridiculous name you degrade them with is—from 'white land', and then, when they do walk your streets, you make sure every step is taken with fear. You call them ignorant one day, establish a shoddy school system for them the next. Demand a full day's work; pay them an hour's wages."

"Don't forget our history, Johann Botha; my people have been the underdog for a long time."

Botha interrupted, "That's not what I hear these days. They tell me that Israel has one of the world's strongest and most advanced armies. Isn't that, after all, why we're talking? Hm?"

Ziki's eyes turned cold and steely. "You know what, Johann? Let's talk business. I don't know why I'm talking to you old man. You want my help? You want me on your side? Then you better come up with something a helluva lot better than a liter of fancy Schlibovitz and a fifteen-second outburst about equality."

Johann's face curdled. He looked as if he'd just eaten a bad clam. "You don't believe me?" he challenged. "Fine, we'll go to them. To Nonoto. And we'll see if they don't shout at you, attack you, and try to take everything you have. We'll go tomorrow and then you can tell me how harsh and cruel our laws and security police are."

Ziki was ready for some rest and anxious to be rid of Johann's shriveled head for a while. He agreed to reconvene in the morning.

"Then it seems we have no further business at the moment. If you need anything, Hendrik will take care of you." A pause. Botha sniffed and pushed back his chair. As he stood, his chest bloated and, from the tendons now protruding from either side of his neck, Ziki could tell everything from teeth to sphincter was tightly clenched after Ziki's last comments.

"Good day, gentlemen."

He took a few stiff steps forward, giving Ziki another glimpse of the strange, spindly legs. Then, swagger returning, he continued through the door.

Once he was gone, Ziki leaned toward Avi and whispered. "Well, he looks like a turkey and walks like a turkey…."

Avi grunted, gave Ziki a look, and said. "That went well…"

**Three black Range Rovers pulled up to the Excelsior's front door early the next morning.** Ziki and his men were getting a tour of the city's factories, military encampments, and a diamond mine twenty kilometers northwest of its limits.

The factories were modern, efficient, European. The diamond mine turned out to be a massive compound. The mine itself was unimpressive. A lot of heavy equipment. A lot of armed guards.

"A lot of dirt," Avi said flatly.

"Hmm, yes," Hendrik piped up, nudging Avi's shoulder, "that's where the diamonds are hiding!"

Before Avi could react, Ziki spoke up. "Gentlemen, I think we're all agreed South Africa's has a lot of diamonds. Show me something I didn't already know was here."

Heading out from the city, they drove their guests through swanky Johannesburg suburbs and well-manicured golf courses that were conveniently "on the way." Ziki had made sure he got in one of the cars Hendrik didn't, so he was spared the constant, grating narration of yesterday's car ride. Heh, heh, Davidoff hadn't been so lucky.


**A mass of smoke engulfed the settlement ahead.** Around them, the sun bounced off reddish-brown earth and mixed with gray wafts that had wandered outside the village. They cut through thick, stagnant air, and the singed smell of rot it held seeped inside the cars, sending several men into coughing fits.

"One of the dumb shits probably tripped and fell into the fire," an Afrikaner soldier, hand over his mouth, mumbled.

The driver, through showy gasps, added, "Yeah, or a lost tourist wandered through looking for the rest of his safari friends. They usually just stone them to death, but if the hunting's been bad…"

The Afrikaners yukked it up while Botha grunted approvingly.

Ziki rolled his eyes. "Dry heaves and cannibal tales, huh? So you boys never been shot at?" He shook his head. "Or in any real combat for that matter. Well, I can see why you'd need our help."

"Turn here!" Botha burst out, half grabbing the wheel. Then, facing Ziki, "We make jokes, yes. But they come from the truth. Maybe you would like to see for yourself." Back to the driver, "Pull over."

The convoy eased up alongside a cluster of dying bushes.

"Pretend," Botha said to Ziki, "that you trust me. I'm not going to hurt you." He extended his hand. "Just for a moment, give me your gun."

Ziki was unmoved. "I don't think so."

"Okay," Botha continued, "leave your gun down here. Or," he said climbing out of the car, "leave it back there with your men. Then go into that neighborhood alone for fifteen minutes. Take a look for yourself, ask them for a tour. I don't think you'll come back alive."

Ziki followed him outside and motioned for Avi and Davidoff to join them. "Why would they hurt me? I'm not one of you. I don't look like one of you. For all they know, I could be there to help them."

Botha's dark face softened, turned fatherly, but his tone mocked. "Such youthful ignorance. 'But they might think I'm their friend!' 'Don't you understand? You'll never get a chance to tell them who or what you are. They look at your face, they see white. White, means white man. They want white man dead."

"You and these," he hissed, gesturing wildly, "waltz in, fresh out of your swaddling clothes, and think you can teach us a lesson about the people we've been dealing with for decades."

"Well, if you think you can do it, please, Commander, go right ahead." Botha smirked, looking toward the rest of his men, who were trickling out to see what was going on, then added, "I'll bet five hundred American dollars the Israeli, big shot won't go in there." Finally, eye to eye with Ziki. "He hasn't got the balls."

"You're on!" one of the triplets blurted out. This was the most action he'd seen. Vorster, slightly more subdued, offered.

"I'm in for five hundred dollars. He'll go in alright. I've been to Israel and they're all crazy sons of bitches there."

"Avi," Ziki called, handing over his weapon, "take my gun. I'm going for a walk."

Addressing his group in Hebrew. If anything went wrong, they were to come in. Fire a few rounds into the air.

"Ziki, come on," Davidoff objected. "It's 900 degrees out here, Avi's sweatin' his balls off." Davidoff curled his lip. "And it fucking smells like the dead dog that rotted in my grandma's basement for a week before she remembered she had a dog. Come on, we didn't come here for this. They're the ones supposed to be proving shit to us."

Davidoff was right. They weren't the ones who needed to prove anything. But Ziki had realized right after Hendrik's snaky comment at the club that it wasn't going to be as easy to write off the Afrikaners as he had first thought.

It was true; the Israelis were having trouble finding someone to sell them weapons-grade uranium. And nuclear defense—or at least the ability to threaten nuclear defense—was fast becoming a necessity with the Soviets looming again.

If uranium was part of the deal the Afrikaners were anxious to make, Ziki had to pay attention.

**Nanoto**

**The village was splotched with rickety slum houses and a few decrepit trees.** Everything was dry and brittle looking. Even the ground appeared ready to crack and crumble at too heavy a step. No electrical wires ran this far from the city and the half dozen women carrying pails on their heads suggested water supplies came from a public pump somewhere outside the village, not from indoor plumbing. Ziki, now a couple hundred meters inside the settlement, was glancing around for the source of the stench and smoke, when a group of black teenagers surrounded him.

They moved in, shouting, picking at his clothes, searching for the wallet he was glad he had thought to leave with Avi. He tried introducing himself, telling them where he was from, telling them where he wasn't from, that he was not Afrikaner.

The shouting became louder. They swore at him in English, Afrikaans and Swahili spitting up bits and pieces of languages. Ziki felt dirt and small rocks bouncing off the back of his neck, his knees, and his chest. The mob's hostility grew. So did the size of their ammo.

Avi, yanked a South African policeman from one of the Rovers' wheels and wasn't far away. Barreling towards Ziki he plowed through the crowd raised his UZI and fired a few rounds out the backseat windows into the air. Avi pulled the pin from a concussion grenade, released tear gas and at the same time hurled a smoke grenade, giving Ziki a chance to duck away from the line of fire.

The villagers scattered.

Avi gave Ziki a dopey grin and said, "Didn't we do real good boss? Had a little trouble remembering which part was the pin and which was the grenade, but we came in real fast when it looked like trouble, just like you told us to." His pant then fell to a smirk.

Ziki barely heard the dig. He was too relieved to be heading out of there. No doubt, had his men not come for him, the mob would have killed him.

"Well," Ziki's Rover driver said as the four men rejoined the group, "he had balls going in there—did the kefirs rip'em off before letting him out?"

Ziki responded with a slap to the back of his head. The group returned to Johannesburg in silence.

**Back at the Rand Club.** Botha traded the triplets in for Jan van der Mewe, head of Johanesburg's Security Police, and asked to meet again in the private conference room upstairs.

Ziki motioned for Davidoff and Avi to follow them, but left the other three to pass off the time in the main lounge.

"So you've seen."

Ziki's voice filled with contempt. "You set me up!"

"Incredulous," Botha clucked. "Ha! He waves his fist at me. He says, 'You set me up.' How could I do this? You saw how they reacted, what they tried to do to you. They're like animals, Commander. There is no setting up, no striking a deal with animals."

Van der Mewe spoke up. He was stocky and red-faced, early forties, with short, receding blond hair. His thin, oddly dark mustache bounced up and down when his upper lip moved and his English was much rougher, more broken than Vorster's and Botha's. "This was no one incident, my gentlemen. It is the same in any kefir town around Johannesburg and Cape Town. And they are moving, you know. I mean they are starting to come out—"

Vorster cut in, "Gentlemen, we understand that they are angry and that they hate us and that they are envious we have done and built things they cannot."

Vorster thought for a moment, then began again. "Do you know what the annual return to foreign investors was before Sharpeville, gentlemen? Twenty-seven percent, a steady, constant, for many years, twenty seven percent. Unfathomable for a country that wasn't dependant on Europe or America.

"And then, afterward…a field of dead Kaffirs and the tides are turned. Suddenly, my country became…distasteful. Investors took their money and disappeared. Were left to defend actions and policies that have been around for decades to countries full of people who got rich because of them, including America. Outsiders," he scoffed, "are so quick to support people and things they know nothing about."

Vorster stopped and stared at the bits of setting sun poking through cracks in the heavy burgundy curtains sealing the massive bay window in front of him. Ziki considered him the surprise. Still, in person, Ziki found him the most tolerable of the men. He cleared his throat, bringing Vorster back from his daze. "So enlighten me then, Mr. Vorster. Tell me why black South Africa, The African National Congress, the ANC, does not deserve for me to recommend Israel's support to my government?"

"Do blacks and whites share employment opportunities? Are their wages the same? No, not by a long shot. But are blacks' opportunities and wages still better here than they are in Angola or Rhodesia or with a tribe in the middle of the jungle? They must think so, or why wouldn't they leave? Why wouldn't they go out and build their own industries and infrastructure and systems of education? No one is stopping them from leaving."

Vorster shrugged. "They want to kill us for what is ours? Fine. We'll fight back. That's how it's always been. But now." He glanced down sighed, then, eyes up, said, "Now is where your interests lie because now it's different. Now they have help."

"From Moscow, direct from the Kremlin." None of this was happening by chance; it all had a detailed plan and all the pegs had to fit into the right holes. Entangled with these small armies and their new, communist dogmas was the African Liberations Movement from the West African coast, central, and South Africa. Cargo planes and ships full of weapons are pouring in to them. Soviet Special Forces, instructors…"

"We have a gift for you Commander. A free gift, a gesture of good faith."

" And what is that?"

"Information. An assassin from the KGB named Ivan Stoyvich has been given a contract to kill you, he has a team of killers some include local Zulu's, a man named Dkembe is one of them. Some mention of an association with General Zhukov came up. Moscow wants to get rid of you nosing around Africa, especially South Africa. Nanoto may have been a set up, but not by us."

**The ANC, warring tribes.** Anyone angry and hungry enough to scratch commy backs in exchange for machinery and training had access to anti-tank weapons, land mines, hand grenades, helicopters, ground-to-ground short range missiles, you name it. Special Forces drilled them on the basic how's, when's, and where's to use the stuff, then moved on to some of the finer points of guerilla warfare. C4 explosives with detonating timers left in crowded urban areas, slow bleeding by random killings, a slow war of attrition building up to bigger things.

Once the Africans had the means and the methods down, the trade was simple: kill, anyone in the way—all were to become sources of terror and fear. Success was making people afraid to leave their homes. And then making them afraid to stay inside.

Israel, unhappy with the idea that communism fed by more terrorists into the Middle East  could consume an entire continent with an unlimited supply of manpower only a short distance from its own borders, put itself in the Russians' way.

The Russians sat back and watched as Communism spread like a disease. The elite of the NKVD, a secret division of the KGB, even started recruiting African hopefuls to train in Moscow at the Vladimir Lenin School for Terrorism. They would become NKVD equivalents, drilled by the world's best instructors in military activities.

The Africans jumped at the chance to head north, as brainwashing and temptation—good meals and money—made the Soviets' propositions an attractive one. These people were poor, their families, starving. They had nothing to lose.

Africa became the tree producing poisoned fruit.

The foundation many Middle East terrorist leaders and training camps was wide open here: The Taliban in Afghanistan, Hezbollah in Lebanon, PLO and PFLP in Tunisia and Algeria, and Islamic Jihad in Egypt, Hamas, and Al Aqsa Brigade in Gaza. Nukes being developed in thirty six locations in Iran. A springboard for all Israel's neighbors.

General Pientz, took charge of African development for Israel. If their, the Russian's cause became too costly, too time-consuming, too large a pain in the ass, it wouldn't be too hard for them to drop it, right?  Simple concept.

Ziki didn't know if getting rid of them was even possible. But, mind-boggling as it was, it would be up to him to find out.

With shiny new equipment and combat training, hordes of black Africans were primed to turn the tables and lash out at the White Afrikaners. These days, the

Afrikaners weren't just worried about attacks from within, but invasions from above, next door, maybe even overseas. Add Moscow and Castro to a billion Chinese and, well, their faith in their ability to protect diamond mines and deluxe homes got shot down the can.

**"There are a lot of people out there who want what we have, Commander."** Botha said.

"Yeah," Van der Merwe added. Ziki and Davidoff exchanged looks, almost smiling. "Sounds familiar," they said.

"Ah! You're beginning to see, aren't you? That South Africa and Israel. We have these obstacles, right? Subjects of much international debate. 'Oh!' they say, 'the war, the bloodshed, the poor, defenseless people these Afrikaners oppress!'" By now, Botha had traded in his condescension and forced composure for the eagerly bobbing head and strange facial contortions of a poorly drawn cartoon character. Once again, Ziki noticed bits of light bouncing off...his mouth? Something inside his mouth?

Botha continued, "But these people, these 'underdogs', as you call them, are the ones who want to take all that we know! And to kill us in the process!"

Ziki, solemn once again, now spoke. He didn't like the "common bond" talk did not sit well with him. He didn't know all there was to know about the Afrikaners situation and he knew they sure as hell didn't know a whole lot about Israel's.

"I think, Mr. Botha," he finished, "You have no idea what you are talking about, we were there, in Israel, or Judea as you called it five thousand years ago... Five thousand years ago. We were always there, my family can trace back ten generations, we are not the invaders, and your comparison makes me sick....We are leaving."

**Johann found Ziki's annoyance amusing,** he knew that this was his last chance to strike a deal, so he simply shrugged in concession and said, "Maybe you are right."

After Ziki had nearly been stoned to death in Nonoto, had heard of Dkembe and of Stoyvich's plans, Johann knew Ziki had softened. The young Commander still tried to see things in black and white. Segregation, inequality, bigotry—these things did not yet have gray areas in his mind.

"Listen," Johann said, then stopped. He took a slow sip of Port, put his glass down, ran his tongue over his teeth. "I'm just going to talk straight now, okay? You—and by 'you' I mean Israel—". Another sip. Another run of the tongue. "You are hated by a very large number of people. But you—a tiny blip of a nation, strong and scrappy, and all these millions of Arabs are devoting their lives to destroying you and the Russians...you know all this, Commander. But do you also know how in the hell you manage to stave off and defeat them? Because I, for one, do not. And I—we—South Africa—are very anxious to find out."

Johann's eyebrows shot up as he cocked his head to the side, indicating it was Ziki's turn to speak.

Ziki took a slow sip of vodka, put his glass down, ran his tongue over his lips, and said nothing.

Botha went on, "Commander, you have seen today that the kefirs do not want your help. And, more importantly, that they don't need your help. They have plenty of it coming from the Russians and China and—"

"Alright, Johann," Ziki interrupted, "so my views about them have changed. That doesn't mean my views about you have too."

Johann grunted approvingly. "Ah, good boy. He knows the enemy's enemy isn't necessarily a friend—"

Ziki continued, talking over him. "And I'm just not sure white South Africa has anything Israel needs."

Bluffing, Johann thought. Hoped. Slowly, deliberately lifting his right hand, he said, "I don't think you've thought about it enough."

The three Israelis reached for their guns as Johann moved his hand beyond his breast pocket to his mouth, which fell open as he reached inside.

"What the—" Ziki said, stopping short when Johann's lip collapsed beneath his gum and his top row of teeth clanked to the table.

Johann watched Ziki turn, confused, to his muscle man, who was too busy gawking at the teeth to look up. Ziki's gaze shifted downward.

Satisfied with its effect, Johann rumbled." Fifty carats, gentlemen," and tapped on a diamond molar. He saw Ziki failed to look unimpressed and was now certain the Israelis' ears were open as wide as their eyes.

Johann slid the denture across the table. There were many rumors about the "Rand Lord's" jeweled mouth, but not many knew the truth behind it. Of those, even fewer had seen the stone up close. Johann told his guests its story.

"Why'd you turn it into a tooth?"—Davidoff—asked.

"Your commander is not the only one to have ventured into Nonoto on a dare. Only when I was young and stupid enough to do it, we did not have the fancy hearing devices you used today. I was on my own from beginning to end.

"Yes, they crowded me and threw things at me. Then one took a swing. Then another. They beat me to the ground and I was yelling at them to get their hands off of me. One of them saw inside my mouth. I had gold fillings. Solid gold. I don't know how they knew this; maybe they didn't.

"Some of them held me down and some of them held my mouth open and some of them got their knives. They only got three teeth out before I bit off a finger." Johann wrinkled his face in disgust.

"After that they knocked me out. I woke up in some woods. I was bloody. One leg was broken. I had no teeth. I could not believe the warthogs or the hyenas had not gotten me.

"I called out and crawled, a group—tourists on a safari—found me. Ha! Those fillings might have been worth a few thousand Rand. When I recovered, I got these," he said, pointing to the table. "Three million American dollars are there. I said to myself, 'Now they'll have something worth stealing.'"

Now, Johann said jovially, "If you're not averse to fondling my teeth,

Commander, you may inspect the perfect diamond for yourself."

A gummy smile followed by chuckles from van der Merwe and Vorster.

Ziki shrugged. "I'll take your word for it, Johann. Now what's this whole performance got to do with me?"

"I am on the board of directors for a company that controls ninety percent of the world's diamond mines. Israel has a long history of diamond cutting craftsmanship… Here is our offer to you:

Our first offer is ninety percent of our raw product, sent to Israel to be cut and sold. That's eighty percent of all diamonds in the world filtering through your country."

"Okay," Ziki replied, "that's the first offer. What's the second?"

Johann continued, "Your Arab friends have oil, you do not. "We have Nigeria in our back pocket. Oil, Commander, lots of uninterrupted oil."

Diamonds—a nice perk, but not a necessity. Oil—a necessity, but still not worth jumping in the sack with these guys over. "Now—your attention Commander, real attention."

"Weapons grade uranium, Commander, all you need."

The magic word.

"We know you're being threatened by the Russians and that they are developing nuclear warheads in Iran, by a government that is very hostile to you. We have it… We'll get it to you." Botha slid the row of teeth back inside his mouth. "South Africa will produce all you need. According to our calculations, potential for enrichment of that crop is seventy percent at minimum. We can arrange it so that Israel receives the raw material to produce all the HEU it needs."

"I think you can agree," he finished, smug, "that this is quite the nice package for the mere tactical support and friendship we seek in return. And one more thing; deep Indian Ocean access of our coast to test thermo nuclear bombs. Where else on this planet does your country have a better offer Commander? "

Ziki felt like diving across the table and choking him. Avi was probably good to go; ever since the diamond disappeared from sight, the big man had stopped salivating and snapped back.

Ziki had hated Botha from the start and now he hated that this terrible man was offering Israel the key to a security it had never before felt.

The men stood to leave and Botha took Ziki's hand. With a syrupy smile, he whispered, "*Mazal u Bracha,* my new partner and friend." The words ricocheted from his flickering molar.

Ziki hesitated and then not wanting to hear himself he mumbled. *Mazal u Bracha,* in Hebrew. Jewish tradition had it that diamond deals were sealed with a handshake and those words.

How many sides to a coin? In South Africa, there were at least six. But Ziki's government only cared about three. And right here, right now, he had to look at the hell-eating grin on the misshapen figure looming before him and decide; heads or tails. The Afrikaners or the African National Congress, the Bantu.

Fatmah Bijawy crept into his head. So did the Russians, Stoyvich, the Chinese, the baker's dozen of Arab countries and the Soviets looking to wipe his country off the map.

"Yes," Ziki said, "it's a deal. And, Johann, *"ani mekave she tahcnok all ha yaalom ha zeh shell 50 karatim, mamzer shamen ben zona"*. "I hope you choke on your 50-carat tooth, you shriveled son of a bitch."

Botha's chest inflated with pride. "Thank you, Commander, you will not be sorry, you'll see this is a great enterprise."

"I'm already sorry, but we have a deal"

The Israeli team gathered their things and headed back to the Excelsior. Early the next morning, they boarded the jet back to Israel where Ziki would meet with a team from the Knesset and advise them to create an alliance with the Afrikaners of South Africa.

Ziki drank coffee and sat in silence most of the flight, but just as they entered Israeli air space, Avi leaned over and said, "Hey, you're stopping in Europe, it is to meet Gavriella isn't it?"

"None of your business."

"What'd Botha whisper to you while we were leaving?"

*'Mazal u Bracha'."*

"No shit! What'd you say?"

"I said, 'I hope you choke on your 50-carat tooth, you shriveled son of a bitch."

"Well it looks like we're going to dance with the Devil, doesn't it?"

"Yes it does."

"Wars make strange bedfellows..."

## Chapter 56

**Salzburg, Austria**

**Ziki pushed up her nightshirt**—the same white Oxford he'd worn himself the night before—and stroked her left leg's smooth golden flow of skin.

"Stop." She shooed his hand away. "I'm reading."

"You can read while I touch." He crept further up her thigh.

"Well, I'm cold." She yanked the shirt back to its starting position. The dull onslaught of the Safe-House in Zurich and Salameh was already creeping up too many parts of her; she didn't need Ziki's lust adding to the confusion.

In response to his admonishment, Ziki took the scolding hand and ran it across his cheek. He paused after the second round trip to examine its two missing fingerprints.

"I did this to you," he told her.

Gavriella, stretched on her side and propped up on an elbow, was making a failed effort to compare *La Gazzetta di Mantova*'s and *The New York Times*' reports on Monday evening's Presidential address and picking at a chipped nail. She was only half listening to Ziki's confessional, but hoped the dismissive "What?" she returned communicated the "leave me alone," she meant.

"I am responsible for this scar."

She sat up and dangled a leg over the bed, enjoying that the mattress was so padded her toes still hovered a foot above the floor. It had been a solid ten hours since she—assisted by the salted cleavage of one of *Bar della Pace*'s elegant marble busts—had taken her last shot of tequila, but the room still resisted her attempt to focus on it.

"Ziki, Baby, don't be such a sap. You didn't do this." She gave her eyes a few hard blinks. "I ultimately stabbed the man who did this."

"I know."

"Remember Zurich? I tried to help you, I got him. I may have saved your life. He was the one that shoved me into that basement." She turned to face him. "With the knife he used to do it."

Ziki stared at the sheets, nodding in agreement. "I know. I know you did.

But I'm the one who—I sent you out there to join them for us."

"No, Ziki," she sighed, "you asked me if I wanted to go and I said yes." The dull pain of a headache worked its way up the back of her head but, as she moved to stand and retrieve the pillbox from her purse, Ziki pulled her back.

A hint of desperation inflected his voice. "But, Gabby, I made you think these things and I made you risk…these things."

Gavriella rolled back down and narrowed her eyes. "Risk what?" Now the word came off as one delivered by someone who was paying very close attention to something she did not want to hear. "Risk my life? Would I risk my life for you, Ziki? Well. You didn't send me anywhere and you didn't make me do anything. I chose, Ziki. I chose to go and to give you what you wanted for a cause I came to believe in…Your cause, I was wrong, very wrong before … I—"

"No, Gabby, listen to me…He looked down at the floor… I need you to know the truth. I made you believe what I wanted you to believe. I put that stuff in your head… I brainwashed you and made you fall in love with me, and then I sent you to him, to Salameh, the PLO… they could have.…" He flinched and looked away.

"I knew what they would do to you, Gabby. If they found out…"

Gavriella felt her hands begin to quiver, but was otherwise steady. She scooted backwards until her shoulders dug into the gilded rococo carvings winding through the bed's headboard. It wasn't far enough. She looked at the crystalline sphere minding the door. At the drawer to the gold leaf console table that held its brass key. At the drawn cranberry drapes covering the window. What floor was she on? Was the *parterre* of daisies or the brick path below her? She closed her eyes. A minute; she just needed a minute away from him. Away from a, hung with remorse Ziki… "Gavriella."

His hand gripped hers again; this time the sensation catapulted her to a gravelly field between the mountains of Lebanon's Ba'albek…

Everywhere the ground was dry and brittle. Except in front of her. There, moist and nourished, the earth glowed brownish-red… Nausea—induced by flashback?—returned her to the room they're in and the Louis XV bed.

She flicked her eyes open—"Listen, Ziki," –she snatched back her hand. "I don't know how this thing played out in your head, but if you were thinking I'd reaffirm your choices or rub away your guilt you better think up again. You want to second guess your decision to make a career out of blowing away terrorists that's just fine. But don't make this about you and me. Don't talk to me like I'm some eager child you duped into being your—your…" Gabby flicked her hand and gave an angry grunt, unsure if she was more outraged at what Ziki was saying or that she couldn't think of a word for it.

She continued, stiffened her back upright and raised her chin high in the air. "I am not one of your Israeli-operated spooks, you know. I am top-tier CIA…She raised her chin up high in the air." Her lips trembled.

Ziki touched her forehead and traced down the sides of her face…She shuddered.

Trying to keep her dignity after what she'd heard. "I am an American operative…I did what I did of my own free will."

He reached her neck and smoothed his thumbs across her throat. His touch infecting it, her voice shook.

"Our countries just so happen to have mutual goals and…"

"Gabby," he breathed. "I am sorry. Just believe that I am sorry they hurt you." The pressure behind her eyes made his blurry, but she believed them. Green eyes. Trusted…they were sincere. She thought of telling him the truth—the worst part of this mess. That the only thing he had ever successfully made her do was love him. The believing, the trusting, the Syrian training camp—mere by-products of the falling in love with him that she had done all by herself.

Gavriella blinked the blur away from his face and nodded her acceptance of his oath.

"I-I might do anything for you Zik…"

## Chapter 57

**Gaza Strip.**

**He twisted open a bottle of Revenge.** Wafts of formaldehyde squeezed themselves through its tiny neck and entwined with those of the blood and must still alive on the woman's body. He surveyed a limp hand, noticed it was too dark. Too rugged.

His eyes moved back to the hovering brush in time to watch a fat drop of red fall from its tip and blend imperceptibly into the damp eating through the woman's side. How had this polish never seemed so ugly before?

He squatted down and, balancing on the balls of his feet, drew in the woman's right hand.

Her nails were short, cuticles overgrown. A gnarled and discolored mess wrapped around her middle finger, three hairlines blood streaks running reddish brown beneath its surface. His heart hurried its pace. Would the polish cover this? He didn't have a file. He scratched at the ridges for a few seconds. Or a sandblaster. Too quickly, he picked up the wand and plunked a glob of Revenge in the middle of the deepest ridge.

The glob took a moment to waver before it streamed diagonally into a crevice where the mangled nail met skin. Shit, he thought, quickly wiping off the brush so he could use its clean bristles to distribute his impulse.

Together, the two smeared Revenge back and forth across the woman's nails and over both his and her fingertips. When he finished, he stood back. It looked awful. Like the woman had tried to dig her fingers into her side to stop the bleeding.

He sighed and dipped the brush again.

**Salzburg, Austria.**

**Gabby angled her hand inward and fanned out her fingers on the deeply stained end table.** She sat sideways, perched on a peach bergere with thick gold threads crisscrossing through its upholstered cushioning and strangely lone armrest, mimicking the chair's regal right angles with her own. Ziki lounged on the equally-peach spread of the bed across from her, sucking on vodka coated ice cubes, wondering why Salzburg hotel rooms were all so girly, and watching.

Gabby's brush fanned and swiped from moon to tip; one; two; three times on each nail. A perfect wet arc of Revenge stayed in its wake. Ziki blew an ice cube—*clink*—back into its glass, then tipped the glass up in search of a new cube, freshly saturated. Gabby dipped the wand again, letting it hover over the bottle's open mouth as drops of red pooled and fell off. Ziki admired her method.

"Why don't you just wipe it off on the rim? Gabby, you're driving me nuts just letting hang there. Drip…drip…drip—like Chinese water torture."

She stopped, put the wand back in the bottle, and shifted her attention. "Well. I like to wait the extra three seconds per dip because using the sides of the bottle to discard the excess thrusts the remaining polish into the brush's bristles, which, in turn, leave tiny indentations in the applied polish during their initial strokes which in turn requires an immediate second coating which in turn increases the chance for smudging and air bubbles in the polish by a factor of six which, were the odds were indeed to favor smudges and bubbles, would necessitate the complete removal of the polish followed by the drastic measures crucial to ridding the finger of the red stains that develop as a result of prematurely removing nail polish. Did you get all that detail?"

"Furthermore," breath, "Ziki." She gently recovered the cap and let it dangle above the tiny hole. "If you have a problem with my application methods, you can go suck and blow ice cubes in your own room."

*Drip.*

*Clink…*

## Gaza Strip

**He returned the wand to the bottle and slammed them both into the dirt.** "Fuuuck!" He glanced around. Had anyone heard him? It probably didn't matter. A simple "fuck" wouldn't mean much to the world outside his van right now.

"I can't do this…Disgusting—he kept on." He rolled back to his heels and whipped around to face a stack of duffle bags. Grabbing the bottle of acetone that sat next of one, he poured a third of it onto a dusty rag and reassumed his position in front of the hand, hanging limply, fingernails, fingers, and palms covered in sloppy splotches of Revenge.

Beginning with her cracked knuckles, he scrubbed hard. Half of the polish transferred to the rag; the other half grew and spread, staining her hand. He reopened the acetone and, sloshing some of it straight onto the trouble spots, used his own nails to scratch away the rest.

Progress was slow. His fingers hadn't felt so clumsy since they'd tried to mince the six gloves of garlic his mother's Kabob recipe called for. It was years before. He had just returned from army training and was showing off the agility with which he could put together an UZI.

When he had finished, she had pointed the blunt end of a knife at him and, unimpressed, said, "Good for you. You can shoot a fancy gun. Now you can chop my fancy *shum,* garlic."

The second little finger at last complete, he sat back on the sweat-stained floor and examined his smudged red palms in disgust. "Like fucking war paint," he mumbled.

The remaining acetone sloshed into his hands, which he rubbed until the bright nail polish faded and fused with their newly-raw pink tone. Fingers burning, he opened one of the supply chests and dug around for the blowtorch he had hidden there earlier. As he grasped its stumpy neck, his watch passed into view. Less than five minutes to finish, bag the woman, and get her on to Tel Aviv.

He pulled a pair of goggles over his eyes and flicked the torch a few times to test it. Satisfied, he walked back to the table thinking that burning the woman's face off damn well better be easier than painting her nails…

**Salzburg, Austria.**

**Gavriella flicked the brush across her right thumbnail for the third time and** fluttered her right hand to complete the first half of her application process. Ziki, having chosen not to return to his own room, contemplated her tactics; Always paint right hand first. Polish to be applied from pinky to thumb. Each finger receives three, sweeping brush strokes.

"So," he wondered aloud, "what am I watching here? A well-executed technical procedure or a meditative ritual?"

"Well," she began, not breaking her focus, "these are certainly some advanced and precise techniques. And I guess the process does have a calming effect." She stopped to finish the second and third swipes of her left ring finger before continuing. "But I'd classify it as more of a science—I figured out what I needed to do to get the desired effect then I did it. And kept doing it. I'm pretty sure I have everything I do on a regular basis down to a science—it's what makes things doable."

Unable to help himself, Ziki gave a grave nod. "Of course," he agreed. "How else could you bear Kissinger?"

Gabby didn't miss a beat. "Oh no, there's no science to that." She considered her words. "Well, then again, I don't know…maybe…." Her voice was straightforward, but her eyes, now locked with Ziki's, expressed its intent to instigate. "Do you think pure, unabashed animal lust has a scientific basis, Zik?"

The force of his response blew a wisp of hair across her face.

He took a moment to calm down. "Ahh, that's clever Gabby, that's clever." Gave his eyes a dramatic rub. "I can't remember that last time I laughed so hard." Clutched his side. "I think I pulled a muscle in my gut." Looked at her innocently and said, "I think I really hurt it, Gabby."

Gavriella scowled, gently returned her polish wand to the bottle, gingerly pinched a section of gold fringe lining between the pads of her painted thumb and forefinger, and hurled it and the satin pillow attached to it at Ziki's jugular.

"Fuck you, Ziki!" she yelled from behind the wave of loose hair the motion sent to join the wisp already in the middle of her face.

Ziki grabbed the pillow and tucked it behind his neck, admiring the way her dark strands picked up bits of light as she casually blew at them and shook her head and twisted her neck trying to return them to their proper place. His chuckles— not so forced this time—wound up again.

"Alright, yeah, it's hilarious. But come on, Zik, my nails are wet. Can't you laugh and get it out of my face at the same time? I haven't put the third stroke on my right index finger yet, and if the first two dry before I do...."

Ziki brushed away her hair, put his hand, and then his lips, over her mouth...

## Chapter 58

**The Mossad - Tel-Aviv.**

"**Commander.**" Malkielly, chewing on his usual cigar, exuding his usual gruff of self-importance, looked up briefly from a mess of papers.

Ziki recalled the combination of awe that used to run through him every time he came within fifty feet of Malkielly. Over time, one by one, all those emotions had faded. Now the man himself angered Ziki as much as the smell of stale ash that had embedded itself in the ancient relics and gilded statues lavished around the General's office.

Staring at the wall, Ziki tried to keep his voice detached. "The body's downstairs."

"In the lab?"

Ziki flinched. "In the morgue."

"So you took care of it."

"You gave me an order, I did as I was told."

"You killed her yourself."

Behind his back, Ziki's squeezed his hands into tight fists and released them, partly to release some of the rigid tension from every other muscle in his body, partly in preparation for knocking off Malkielly's lower jaw. "I did not."

"But you watched." Malkielly's sagging face, which had remained pointed down, disinterested, throughout the conversation, now tried to tilt up imperceptibly take a quick survey of the strayed young man before it. What was his physical state? Did he look tired? How was he handling the interrogation—the brutal questions delivered as flippant declarations? What did his answers, his posture, his blinking suggest? Had he learned his lesson? Did he know whose side who was on now?

Malkielly's attempt at discretion was a failed one. Ziki saw and understood it all. Didn't he realize his protégé had followed this procedure himself many times before? That he had learned it from him?

"I did not watch."

The thing about Mossad interrogation tactics was that recognizing and understanding them in no way made the receiver immune to their effects.

"Then," Malkielly leaned forward, dislodging his cigar, "how can you be sure it was done?"

The poor bastard was already so rattled and exhausted and scared by the time the questions began, all the person delivering them had to do was perfect the techniques. Ziki stood his ground.

"Because I dragged her body halfway across Gaza and to here!"

An easy feat when one practiced them on a daily basis.

"Mmm," Malkielly's lips pursed into a tight smirk, "you did. So we will go see then. This…labor of love."

**…The morgue was cold and white.** Lab coats decorated with identities and clearance tags hovered above cadavers and below powerful fluorescent lights. Ziki shuddered and squinted through the familiar harsh brightness.

Malkielly had already alerted a mousy young woman with shy green eyes and dusty brown hair of his business and was following her to a numbered steel chamber. According to her coat, she was Esti Gilboa, #406753, intelligence level 4, security clearance 7.

Intelligence level 4 was fairly high for a Mossad employee who did not work either on the building's top floor or its bottom two floors, or in the field. Ziki assumed her intelligence meant, more or less, that Esti Gilboa was allowed to pay attention when she rooted through the mouths and spliced open the stomachs of acquired targets in search of "helpful" information they may have hidden there in the face of death.

Security clearance 7, on the other hand, was the second lowest. It meant that, were she to come across a vital piece of information, she would have to call in someone else to deliver it to those who could use it.

Esti, like most people had no idea who Malkielly was. After all, the head of Mossad, and even Shin Bet itself, did not officially exist. The ID tag on the impeccably dressed, dignified presence behind her read "Jacob Datz", and his intelligence and security levels claimed 2 and 3 respectively. Once the visitors had gone, Esti and her lab friends would speculate in hushed tones over scalpels and draining blood who he was and what he did, but, via the numbers on his left lapel, all they would ever know for sure was that his authority outranked theirs.

Ziki, for his part, had not even checked the false identity he was assuming this time. As Esti stopped to peck at a keypad, he glanced down at his tags: Hans Breckenbauer; 4; 6. Well below Jacob Datz. Did they really lower it? Ziki rolled his eyes and looked up as chamber #601 buzzed to life.

A concrete slab fitted onto a conveyer belt rolled out before them and, on Malkielly's command, Esti Gilboa left the two men alone.

Malkielly pulled back the thin cotton covering and, without pause, stared at the face of the woman beneath it. "How did this happen?"

Ziki had crafted and gone over the details hundreds of times. "The target was walking towards the passenger side of a gray Peugeot."

He worried that the debriefing would sound too rehearsed, but he hoped Malkielly would take his fake report for the emotional numbness a man feels after his orders forced him to blow up and kill the woman he loves.

"At approximately two meters, she seemed to notice something on the ground in front of her and bent down to look at it. Eight seconds later, a clicking sound came from the car. The target remained bent over, but looked up. The car exploded."

"And then?"

"As you know, an unanticipated violent outbreak occurred earlier that day in Gaza—at approximately 1100 hours."

A motley and mostly disorganized El Fattah "cell"—eight men in all—had run through Gaza City opening fire on anyone who looked to be Western including some Red Cross women. Our men stationed there were mostly rookies on patrol. That's what they did. The disturbance escalated and my men responded, we were in nearby Khan Yunis, I knew that Gavriella Ramon was with them. She was shot on my orders…

"Once we regained control of the area," Ziki continued, "I sent my men to assess the damage and assist the injured. Vehicles were in high demand. I took the body and made my way on foot to the security zone near Nahl Oz. There, I commandeered a van, shoved the body in the back and drove straight back to Tel Aviv, here..."

Ziki paused to absorb the satisfaction oozing from the wilted folds above Malkielly's eyes.

Ziki held back…Swalowed the words. *"But before all that,"* he wanted to say, *"This dead woman at the Morgue, the one with the painted red nails, is a stray woman's cadaver I picked up in Gaza... Gavriella…? I hope she lives a good life. So fuck you boss."*

"Good." Malkielly stepped back from the body and smoothed the arms of his gabardine suit as if brushing off bits of pathetic deadness the body may have spread during his inspection of it. "Then we're finished here." One last flick. "And now that this matter is off your mind, Commander, I expect that there will no longer be anything to interfere with your focus and duties. No more distractions, until the next one. Right?"

The presumption hung in the air between them; Ziki left it there, having no desire to tell the man what he wanted to hear and no energy to deal with the repercussions of telling him what he did not.

"Ziki," Malkielly finally sighed, his expression softening, "it took you only six hours to convince her of our cause. And you weren't even sleeping with her then that I know of."

He signaled to Esti Gilboa that they were finished with the body and led Ziki to the door. "Don't forget she betrayed us at Khan Yunis, and don't forget the three men you lost there…How long do you think she could have lain at Salameh's side and lived under his protection before his passion and his mania began to become again hers?"

## Chapter 59

**Goodbye**

She picked up his slippers. "I'm keeping these so you'll have something to remember me by."

Ziki smiled.

"What?" she said coyly, "I know you'll never forget who took your slippers."

Ziki sighed, "Gavriella—"

"Oh, pthhhhhh." She mimicked his exasperation. "So you like them a big damn lot. They're only slippers. Just indulge me. One last time, okay? I—"

"Take the slippers for G'd's sake! I don't care."

They stood in a suite near Piazza Navona that someone with a Midas touch for milky tones had had a field day in. Luckily clothes—mostly hers, scattered everywhere—added several coats of color to the muted wall tones. It also gave the impression that the two people in the room would not be sending one of them on a permanent trip to Australia in just under four hours.

"How could you think, after all this that I'd forget about you? Ever?"

Ziki took a moment to exhale the sudden sadness that had overtaken his voice. This was her charade and he knew it well... He could have shouted at her.

"Are you at all scared right now, Gavriella Ramon?"

"I make it a point not to experience fear."

"What if we were to blindfold you and tie you down—"

"Then it would be dark and cramped."

"—and have Malkielly give you a makeshift appendectomy."

"Okay, let me clarify my statement. I make it a point not to experience fear when the possibility remains that I will emerge from the experience alive."

"Yes. Do you know why that is?"

"No. Do you?"

"We have our theories. But we'd like to hear your best guess. Please, Ms. Ramon."

"Fine, how about this: I don't actually mind whimpering and carrying on when I'm in the moment, it's the 'after the fact' that makes my skin crawl.

After my brother was blown to bits, my parents sent me to counseling. So this man, half bald, half curly, looked like an Airedale—tells me I have 'an innate aversion to the effects of 'Emotional Residue'. I can purge my sadness and fear with the best, but when the best leave and I'm all alone, it's just…too empty… I shut down.

"After two sessions, I came up with a quick fix… No more sadness… No more fear. Just put a wall up and skirt the issue. Whatever comes—maybe its destiny?"

"Gavriella," he continued, tossing the shabby twosome of suede over leather into a nearby pile of heels. "Gabby… I will never forget you… Look at me... I breathe your name…"

Ziki filled her empty hands with his own as the city's dim blue dawn fell across her eyes. They danced, crystalline in its light.

A week from today, he would have filed a courtesy report of her death with the CIA. They would send someone to her mother. Though faceless, he could see her shoulders cave, her body crumble. She would wail and cry, "No!" but would not doubt the truth. She knew the nature of her daughter's entanglements.

Her father, retired now, would call rank and demand to see the file. He would want the details, telling himself he had seen it all before and this would bring him closure. Perhaps the CIA would sympathize with him, one of their own. They would let him look. He would wish he hadn't and never tell her mother.

Gavriella tried to hide it behind a fresh manicure, but Ziki could see her mouth twitching with giggles.

Confused and a little hurt by this seeming mocking of his sincerity, Ziki yelped, "What's so funny?" To the tune of a caged puppy appealing to his captor.

Sensing her offense, Gavriella straightened her face and gave a maternal sigh. "Oh nothing, Zik… I'm just a little punch drunk heading into all this. And," she considered her words for a moment, "I'm just so grateful for you. And," she approached and embraced him, "for the romance and passion you—and only you—can put behind a four-letter adverb."

More giggles, hot with her breath, rippled past his ear.

He stiffened and feigned irritation "I believe," he said, "that 'sex' has three letters. Is that all you are interested in?"

The exchange was cute—merited a few chuckles, maybe a friendly bump of the shoulders as acknowledgment for one another's knack for clever banter. But standing face-to-face, static for now in a cream-colored sea of love and grief… The unspoken sentiment was that this would be their last chance to laugh together.

So they did. Erupted into hearty, sidesplitting howls that peaked and ebbed in unison and left them flushed and breathless.

Laughed until they turned shades of pink and red autumn's palette would envy. Toppled onto their unmade bed in peels of delight until, at last, their laughter faded into the solemn sense of the inevitable that they had been fighting since Zurich.

They stood again. Gavriella bowed her head and tilted it away from him as a few stray waves of hair rushed from the soft bundle tucked behind her ears to hide what was still visible of her profile. Ziki turned and paced the six-step round trip between where he stood and the door.

When their silence broke, Gavriella hesitantly said. "I know I shouldn't ask this, but you have to do something for me." A pale blue envelope, small, the kind that might carry a party invitation or news that—"It's a boy!" emerged from her pocket and slid into his hands. His face turned pale. No, it's not what you think, she said.

"This is my parents' address," she continued, now daring to look somewhere just below his eyes, "in Ohio."

Parts of her—the splotchy cheeks, swelled and textured like rising dough, the eyes brimming mascara... Her green eyes that could have been the remains of a bonfire—the parts of her that already knew what he would say—pleaded with him to ignore the severity of her request. To pretend that she had not just crossed a line that had been drawn long before their story began.

But emotions ran hot. And she stopped and waited, staring somewhere not at him and he watched her for too long, took too long to absorb the scene. Resentment surged, bled into his sorrow and love and guilt, overpowered them all. He snapped before he could ignore or forget.

"Gavriella, don't ruin this." He rumbled.

"I know, I—"

"Do you want them to come after you? Kill you themselves this time? Because I guarantee you they will. A bullet," he dug a finger into the scowl between his eyes, "right here... they, never give up."

"Here is your new identity, study it well. You are Nancy O'keefe from now on. You are a half owner of the Staccato Club and Bar at the top of William street in the Kings Cross section of Sydney. Your partners are Mickey Engle and Abe Saffron. It's all in there. Study it well."

"But Ziki they've—"

"And then they'll come for me. And then," he shook the envelope with the balance of the rage his lungs couldn't process, "they'll go to this address. To your parents'. In Ohio.

"God, Gavriella, how much more of myself...?"

She stood hunched and rocking at the hips, nodding. Tears streamed silently. One blink and her stare became vacant. She made no further appeals.

Ziki started toward her, but quickly recoiled. Something had changed. Her body was drained of all passion and resolve. Even the desperation seemed to have dissipated and disappeared, leaving only a vacant white shell. If he touched it, or even brushed it, she might wither.

An image of the day before—Mimosa leaves, beautiful but lifeless, crunching beneath their feet on the gravel pathways winding through the untamed trees in Villa Borghese—flashed before him. They had walked for hours, there in the park and along Via Veneto, pausing in the lazy shade of manicured gardens and ducking into cobble stoned piazzas to admire fresh olive breads and old women selling old cheese. Noticing all, Gavriella had said, the daily forgettables.

They had forced themselves to ignore the movement of the sun and ran their favorite flavor of gelato—nocciola—through a combined eleven-language repertoire. It turned out that no one could say "hazelnut" as beautifully as the Italians.

At sunset, Ziki traded a few thousand lira for a jolly vendor named Angelo's last bottle of Chianti and Gavriella seduced a gawky young waiter out of two balloon glasses for its drinking. She made the toast: "To not winning the game, but to faring a helluva lot better than most who play it."

And she was right. Their abilities to sadden the very people they loved were unparalleled.

But now, looking at the woman before him, Ziki panicked. Had they—had done too well? Planned her death too perfectly.

"I'm sorry Gabby," he finally choked. "I wish I could do anything for you. I've tried to... I just—we're not like everyone else."

He tried to make his words soothing, but knew the honesty driving them offered no comfort. "The life I have to go back to will not let me keep compromising the security of my country. You know you can never try to contact me."

When, he thought, did the truth become such a lame excuse?

"John. They blame themselves for my brother John." Her voice was small, her position and movement unchanged. "They tried to keep me at home first. And then, when I left, in Washington. My father called Kissinger, but I—I knew him better."

She was quiet again and Ziki, for once, had nothing more to say.

Ten minutes later—forty minutes?—he had no idea, the clock in their suite clanged through the five o'clock hour, alerting him of the two hours he had left to know her.

The sound lifted her chin. Maybe it said something similar to her. She lurched forward, but stopped before reaching him. Ziki watched as she smoothed her hair and pulled the sleeve of her suit between her fingers and palm. Lifting it to her face, she cleared away the streaked mascara, half-dried tears, and remnants of a running nose. Holding out her arm, she gave a weak smile. "Cover Girl."

He returned the smile. "At least it's black."

Her face knotted and, now fully regaining her complete lack of composure, she smoothed her hand over his forehead and down the back of his neck, squeezing hard.

After starting four times, tears rolling down her cheeks, choking, and giving up, she finally managed... "Now, Ziki, I know this is hard. But it is one of the easiest things you and I, have ever had to do... Isn't it? Would you please stop all that childish blubbering?"

She rested her forehead on his scruffy cheeks. "You're starting to make me afraid."

Ziki pulled her closer. Her arms, his neck, his arms, her waist—they entwined, inhaled each other, intent on holding tight until the clock's next performance...

## Chapter 60

**Mehrabad –The Irananian wilderness**

**Shifting sands swirled on the dunes outside Mehrabad.** The Russian technicians and their German assistants sat silently near the instrument panels. Two Mullas from Teheran and their guards were calmly sipping hot tea.

The rest of the men sat on splintered benches sunken into a dirt floor. The room was windowless and damp; if the smell of must and perspiration weren't enough to gag you, the local concoctions served here would finish the job. At least it was deep underground; it kept out the wicked heat of the afternoon sun.
On the surface black Bedouin tents were pitched disguising the gathering bellow, guarded by some twenty Revolutionary Guards and one Russian in civilian clothes.

The helicopter landed suddenly without warning and one of the most dangerous men in the world strode into the large black tent, then walked towards the elevator that led to the underground compound. He wore a *kafia* headdress in the Moslem turban style of the Mullahs in Teheran and a *galabiya,* a long black robe. The President of the oil-rich country, appointed by Khomeini himself said nothing. The desert showed a maze of oil rigs as far as the eye could see, flames burning atop each rig spewing an orange glow.

Allah had blessed Iran with untold wealth, and he, the President, was entrusted with Allah's work. The Imam himself had told him that destiny has chosen him to free the Moslem lands of infidels, create an Islamic empire across North Africa to the Mediterranean.

On that glorious day, he would march into Jerusalem. The Jews and the Christian Crusaders will be consumed by a fierce fire. It starts here, bellow this simple Bedouin tent, their cities and their people will be vaporized.
He spread his prayer rug, faced towards Mecca, and prayed, then rose from his knees and entered the elevator; it descended to the lower enclave.

**Iamael stood behind the fingean serving tea to** Ziki's friend Awujami the Zulu——Aiman Zawahiri had brought Iamel, Salameh introduced them to each other before his end in Beirut.

Iamael now traveled with Zawahiri. Stoyvich had brought Awujami and Dkembe from Africa. The Syrian general sat quietly in the far corner, watching.

Three containers filled to the brink with Semtex explosives, staked on top of each other were doing an unconvincing balancing act—Awujami was watching those before him with nonspecific fascination. Groups like this had come through his door before at the Sahara, and though he knew they were up to no good, the thick wads of Swiss Francs they offered in return for his help and services were enough to make "no good" good enough for him.

This meeting must have been more important than the rest because Stoyvich's payment for it had doubled.

"I even tossed a few extra bottles when he wasn't looking, Stoyvich said."

"If the Iranian sees alcohol we're all dead."

"Alcohol's the only way a sane man can stay that way in a shithole like this blurted Stoyvich.

"So what now?"

"We wait for their President' Stoyvich said.

"Plan doesn't change. That Israeli, Ziki Barak, we'll just have to kill him sooner. Well, you Dkembe will have to kill him sooner. He is one man that could screw this whole thing up."

"Take care of your mistakes yourself." Awujami said.

"I thought I'd be doing you two a favor, give you a chance to make some real money and a little bit of action outside the whores' downtown Nairobi. Huh? A shame to kill him, I almost liked that Jew."

The Russian had shown Dkembe the money, raised a finger to his lips, and then flashed two Makarov pistols inside his coat. Dkembe had gotten the picture and nodded vigorously. Guns had little effect on him, but the money…he was still catching his breath. Awujami was silent and was watching.

Big decisions were being made here. He listened hard for names and repeated words he might remember and have translated later.

"Why not push it off to one of the animals in your KGB menagerie, the German said?"

"Don't waste my time with stupid questions I tried that In Baghdad. Stoyvich spoke, this gets traced backed to me and we're both dead, I don't need Mossad on my tail. Just take the money and let the African do it."

Awujami had heard many rumors about the fate of Ziki and his country.

The Iranians had made the best offers, but—and this was another reason Awujami was curious about today's guests—the Russians were now working with the Iranians.

"We have to get rid of this Israeli-Ziki Barak." Awujami heard again; he stepped over, without a word-he met Iamael's eyes as he whispered, "get word of this location to Ziki." Iamael nodded.

All Dkembe and Awujami knew was that before the foreigners arrived they and their family might have had meat twice a year. Now they had it every day, but Awujami stayed loyal to Ziki.

**The German scientist moved closer to the instrument panel.**

"The countdown is ready to commence, Sir." The Iranian President nodded, then gave the go ahead.

An ominous roar thundered as the ground trembled. The huge Shahab missile ascended as the desert opened the underground vault to its secret. The rocket gained altitude, then overcame gravity and streaked into the upper atmosphere, and then it returned to its desert target.

The Russian announced the touchdown just thirty kilometers away. A flash of the nuclear test showed on the horizon and on the monitors.

"Do you think the "Big Satan" is watching?"

"Who?"

"You know, the Americans."

"Ahh, after this—he's not so big anymore."

The Iranian spoke for the first time, he looked at Aiman Zawahiri and then the Syrian, ignoring the Russian. "Do you think that a man can change destiny? "

"I believe that a man has to wait until destiny is revealed, Zawahiri answered."

"Today the world will know that a superpower has risen in the Middle East."

"Sleep well America."

# AFTERWORD

Zhukov kept his word, while he was alive the Soviets did not attempt to invade Israel. Ziki kept his word as well, Israel withdrew the nuclear tipped Jericho missiles.

Gavriella Ramon has a new identity and is one half owner of a club and bar in some part of the world.

Iamael stayed 'with' the PLO's El Fattah and still loyal to Ziki, he sometimes travels with Al Qaieda's Aiman Zawahiri.

South Africa got rid of Apartheid… Africa is still Africa.

The ODESSA organization is thinned but still in existence, plotting the Fourth Reich.

The "Wrath of G-d" campaign was launched by Mossad.

Melvin Finkle, well, he had an accident. A Ford pickup truck ran him over.

Arafat is dead; perhaps he is with his 72 virgins.


## Mig 21

The Americans were waiting in the air, circling by the southern Turkish border with a wing of Phantoms. No Turkish airplanes were in sight. As Munir's MiG approached the Iraq-Turkish border the squadron escorted him, fueled the plane in mid air, and led it over the Mediterranean where it was intercepted by six Israeli jets. The Phantoms returned to their base.

Josef and his family of forty were moved through the mountainous terrain of Northern Iraq through Kurdish territory. Through dirt trails, they reached Al Amadiya where they were met by Ziki's team of Duvdevanim dressed in Turkish garb and taken to Israel.

The MiG was safely delivered. Josef and his relatives were given refuge and he was given the promised one million American Dollars. They were settled in homes throughout Israel.

$\mathbf{M}$unir Redfa, the pilot, not wanting to live in Israel, asked to leave. He was moved to Chile. Shortly thereafter a KGB and Iraqi Secret Police team found him and shot him outside a grocery market.

$\mathbf{T}$he Russian MiG was minutely dissected. Israel invited the Americans to see the MiG. It allowed the West to compensate and finally out design this jet fighter phenomena.

**HUNT FOR SALAMEH, ABU NIDAL AND THE EMERGING NEW ONES**

$\mathbf{A}$ll this could have been finished in the refugee camp at Khan Yunis, years earlier had Gavriella not warned Salameh of Ziki's oncoming raid.

$\mathbf{A}$bu Nidal  split ranks from El Fattah and created his own terrorist organization, he survived until recently when he 'committed suicide' In Baghdad, with five shots to his throat.
Yehia Ayash was a student of "The Engineer" and took that title; he was also dubbed "Abdul" interchangeably

$\mathbf{M}$unich Olympics—the murder of eleven Israeli athletes at the hands of Palestinian terrorists.  Images of the incident were emblazoned across television screen around the world.  While the world talked and did nothing, Mossad met and made decisions.
After dumping the body of one of the hostages onto the street   near the Olympic Village apartments, the terrorists released a list of demands.
The demands included the release from prison of 234 Arab and German prisoners held in Israel and West Germany, including two leaders of the infamous German-based Baader-Meinhof Gang.

Rejecting offers from Israel to send a team of hostage rescue commandos, the German Police instead deployed five officers to the airfield equipped with sniper rifles, one for each of the terrorists.  The plan was to wait until the terrorists were a "safe" distance from the hostages, then to open fire simultaneously, killing all the terrorists before they could harm the hostages.
The German's plan began to unravel.  When the terrorists arrived with their hostages, the Germans knew that there were eight terrorists, not the five they had planned for.  With only five snipers there was no way for the sharpshooters to shoot all the terrorists at the same time.
Still  the order was given to open sniper fire.  One of the terrorists lobbed a grenade into the helicopter where it exploded.  When the smoke finally cleared, the full scope of the failure-to-rescue operation was clear.
All nine of the remaining hostages were dead

Remarkably, Ziki later found out from informers in the East German "Stasi" that none of the men selected had sniper training or experience in engaging live targets. The shooters also lacked vital equipment such as night vision devices. German soldiers who were to hide in the airplane and open fire at any sign of trouble decided that the mission was too dangerous and left the scene without telling. Later Mossad investigations would reveal that agents attached to the East German Olympic team were deployed to the airport to observe the operation and 'learn." Mossad learned that these agents communicated the movements of the German police to the terrorists, betraying the security plan.

Israeli retaliation was swift and massive. Three days later, an air strike was launched involving some 75 aircraft. Fighter-bombers struck terrorist targets in Lebanon and Syria, Israeli fighters shot down Syrian planes that were protecting them over the Golan Heights.
Israel felt that even more had to be done.
Mossad decided that a message had to be sent not only to those who participated in the Munich massacre, but also to those who had planned or are planning terrorist attacks against Israel in the future. "Committee X" authorized the assassination of individuals involved-directly or indirectly-in the Munich attack. There would be no captures, no arrests

The goal was to kill those they could find, and in so doing, deter and intimidate those they could not.

In order to carry out this task, Mossad activated its assassination unit, known as Kidon-Hebrew for "bayonet". Kidon teams have been responsible for high profile terrorists assassinations.
At the time of the Munich attack, the Kidon were housed with Mossad's Metsada department, known today as Komemiut. Each Kidon was composed of nine man teams.

Mossad covertly supported the hit teams, both operationally and financially in Swiss banks. In this way, they were able to operate with autonomy, completely outside the Israel government structure. The only mutual point of contact between all the personnel was X. They would provide a list of target names and all other information necessary to achieving the group's goal of hunting down and killing terrorists.

Malkielly and Pientz (*code names*) allowed these men great latitude in their operations, removing ranks structure and encouraging them to be creative. Mossad didn't just want all the targets eliminated, it wanted the terrorists to feel that there was nowhere--absolutely nowhere--that they could go and feel safe from Israeli reprisal. Malkielly wanted them to experience the same terror they had inflicted, and would settle for nothing less.

There was one rule about which there would be no doubt; targets would only be acted against after the team attained one hundred percent identification. If this could not be achieved no matter how much time or energy had been devoted to a target, the hit was to be called off. It would not permit any "collateral damage."

There were thirty-five plus targets for whom death warrants in absentia had been issued by a secretive panel of three judges. The terrorists were divided amongst the teams. On the list of one such team were eleven terrorists known to have played a role in the Munich massacre.

Operating from a covert location in Geneva, this team set out to track down their eleven targets. These included the following:

**Ali Hassan Salameh**—Developed and executed the Munich operation
**Kamal Adwan**—Chief of sabotage operations for Al Fattah
**Hussein Abad Al-Chir**—PLO contact with KGB in Cyprus
**Dr. Basil Paoud Al-Kubaisi**—Responsible for logistics inside the (PFLP)
**Abu Daoud**—The Black September Organization
**Dr. Wadi Haddad** – Commander. Mahmoud Hamshari –PLO and technical coordinator of Munich
**Kamal Nassir**—PLO
**Abu Yussuf** –High rank PLO
**Wael Zwaiter**—Cousin to Yassir Arafat, Al Fattah

The first selected from the list was **Wael Zwaiter**. Once the decision was made to move against Zwaiter a support team took up observation posts within visual range of the hit team.
They fired two shots into the terrorist's head. He died instantly.

Special attention was given to instilling fear into the terrorists they were stalking. It was becoming clear through the first killing that Israel was more than capable of conducting assassinations far from the streets of Beirut Lebanon. The decision was made to make the terrorists feel that they were not safe; even in the safety of their own homes or borrowed ones, wherever they were.

**Mahmoud Hamshari** was selected as the second target. For this action, a third party was directed to phone him at home, posing as an Italian journalist.
A silent signal to a detonator ignited the explosive charge placed in the telephone. Hamshari, like Zwaiter before him, died quickly and violently.

Four more terrorists, **Dr. Basil al-Kubasi, Adad al-Shir, Zaid Muchassi, and Mohammed Boudia** met similar fates, and were dead within the next few months at the hands of Kidon.

Muchassi, not on the original list, was included when he assumed the position of PLO contact with the KGB in Cyprus.

Having successfully eliminated five of their eleven assigned targets the teams were ordered to return to Israel. Upon their arrival, the team was notified that three original members of the list **Kemel Adwan, Mohamer Youssef Al-Najjar, and Kamal Nasser**-had been removed from the list for unspecified reasons. Mossad still wanted them dead. The three along with known terrorists, were expected to be present at a meeting in Beirut.

**S**imultaneously Israel launched Operation "**Spring of Youth.**" This involved the participation of about forty elite commandos from Sayeret Matkal, Sayeret T'zanahim, 5-13 and Zvulon, (the Israeli equivalent of the U.S. Navy SEALS) and Unit 707. The commandos covertly came ashore across a Beirut beach and were delivered to their targets by Mossad drivers. Some of these personnel were assigned specifically to go after **Adwan, Al-Najjar and Nasser**. These terrorists were killed when their apartments were raided during the assault. By the time Operation "Spring of Youth" was over, one hundred and two terrorists gathered in Lebanon were killed.

After a full year of searching, Israeli hit squads were able to locate an individual they were
convinced was **Ali Hassan Salameh**. He has become PLO commander of Force 17. **Yassir Arafat's** elite personal security squad.

Acting on gained intelligence, a small team was dispatched to Lillehammer, Norway, to investigate the lead that Salameh had been seen in the city. The surveillance team watched the individual as he entered a local public swimming pool. The man appeared physically identical to Salameh, so much so that the surveillance team called in the group's action Kidon team; they registered under assumed names at the Oppland Tourist Hotel.

The man soon left the pool, with a pregnant woman not previously identified and attended a film at a nearby theater. When the movie ended, the assumed Salameh and his female friend took a bus to a stop a short distance from his apartment. As they approached the building, two Kidon personnel exited their automobile, pulled out their 22-caliber pistols, and opened fire. Their target dropped to the ground, dying in a pool of blood. Tragically, the man targeted by the Kidon was not Salameh, but a double who looked remarkably like him, a Moroccan born waiter. Harari had made a tragic mistake.

Later a Kidon team deployed to Switzerland after receiving word that Salameh scheduled to meet other PLO leaders in a church on 12 January. False intelligence—again no Salameh.

Intelligence placed the terrorist at a house in Tarifa, on the western most point of Gibraltar's coast. Salameh slipped out before they got there.

The "**Wrath of G-d**" campaign did come to an end.
Mossad finally caught up with their elusive target, **Ali Hassan Salameh** on the streets of Beirut. Going to a meeting with Gavriella Ramon, arranged by a phone call from her, he passed a vehicle while walking down a street. The car had been placed there—it contained a high explosive charge, to be remotely detonated. The blast and two bullets to the head ended the long campaign to kill him. This time it was Salameh.

Iran is developing thermo nuclear warheads in thirty six deep underground locations. Arafat, Abu Nidal and Salameh are no more, but others have taken their place. Osama Bin Ladin and Aiman Zawahiri, Salameh's mentor, are weakened and wounded but still in business...

Ziki Barak? Well—he is around somewhere...

Some day it will end...